# THE HOUND OF THE BORDERS

*Peter Tonkin titles available from*
*Severn House Large Print*

One Head Too Many
The Point of Death
Thunder Bay

# THE HOUND
# OF THE BORDERS

## Peter Tonkin

**Severn House Large Print**
London & New York

This first large print edition published in Great Britain 2006 by
SEVERN HOUSE LARGE PRINT BOOKS LTD of
9-15 High Street, Sutton, Surrey, SM1 1DF.
First world regular print edition published 2003 by
Severn House Publishers, London and New York.
This first large print edition published in the USA 2006 by
SEVERN HOUSE PUBLISHERS INC., of
595 Madison Avenue, New York, NY 10022.

British Library Cataloguing in Publication Data

Tonkin, Peter
   The hound of the Borders. - Large print ed.  -
      (The master of defence ; 3)
   1.   Musgrave, Tom  (Fictitious character) - Fiction
   2.   Animals, Mythical - Scotland - Fiction
   3.   Great Britain - History - Elizabeth, 1558 – 1603 - Fiction
   4.   Detective and mystery stories
   5.   Large type books
   I.   Title
   823.9'14 [F]

   ISBN-10:  0-7278-7491-8

Printed and bound in Great Britain by
MPG Books Ltd, Bodmin, Cornwall.

*For Cham, Guy and Mark,*
*as always*

Black Dog monsters have been reported all over Europe, North and South America, but their origins seem to be in the British Isles. One is reported as early as 1127 in the *Anglo-Saxon Chronicle*...

In the North of England, the (phantom) Black Dog is known as Trash, Skryker or The Barguest...

*True Monster Stories*

# One

## Eve

*London, 24 December 1594*

As soon as he heard the screams, Tom Musgrave started to run towards them. At his second step his sword hissed out, its blade glimmering like quicksilver. By his fourth step he knew it was the Queen herself who must be screaming. As he ran towards the shocking sound, his mind leaped onward, questing like a well-trained hound along the thorny, twisting paths of logic. But if quick Logic bounded ahead, cool Reason nipped at his heels like a cur, always a step behind.

Tom tore across the backstage area of the temporary stage that the Lord Chamberlain's personal company of actors had erected at the end of the Great Hall in White Hall Palace at the direction of Henry Carey, Lord Hunsdon and Lord Chamberlain, whose Men they were, against the celebration of Christmas on the morrow with the first performance of Will Shakespeare's new play. The hall was closed by Lord Henry's direct

7

order to let them rehearse. In all the kingdom, few enough would dare disobey Lord Henry – and of those few, only one was a woman.

The Queen herself, then, reasoned Tom, the Master of Logic, as he ran; but what devil had tempted Her Majesty to peek into the forbidden hall, and what in God's name had she seen to affright her so?

At the very point of the question, Tom tore past the heavy curtains that decorated the stage front and hurled himself down on to the floor of the hall; and there indeed, just inside the great door, with her hand to her mouth, her face utterly white and her eyes wide, stood Queen Elizabeth – Gloriana herself. Blade in the variable ward, lowest of the basic defensive positions, he skidded towards her, watching her eyes widen still further.

With Tom's great logical mind too far ahead and his good sense too far behind to see what a mire of danger he was sinking into here, his Good Angel took a hand. Before he could take another step towards the startled Queen he lost his footing and crashed to his knees, sliding to a stop before her even as the door behind her was torn open and a tall, slim courtier hurled himself to her aid, also reacting to her screaming; also drawn and *en garde*. But whereas Tom was supported only by the Chamberlain's Men – and most of them dressed as fairies – the newcomer was backed up by several familiar, unfriendly faces. And by Her Majesty's personal guards.

8

Tom recognized the newcomer, in spite of the fact that, like the Queen's, his face was masked in the thick white powder so fashionable at court, and his heart sank. Then, as his wild slide slowed, so he turned a little and became able to see what Her Majesty could see. On the stage past which Tom had just run, in the midst of an enchanted forest, sat young Sly, dressed as the Queen of the Fairies. Behind Sly stood Will himself, costumed as the Fairy King, agape with horror; and, saw Tom, the Master of Logic, all too late to moderate his dangerous reaction, the cause of Her Majesty's affright knelt between them. It was Will Kempe, the Clown, the greatest and most famous of the players – Kempe in the revealing rags of Bottom the Weaver, bearing on his shoulders the great ass's head so carefully and realistically fashioned for the magical translation scene.

The icy point of the familiar courtier's rapier resting on the pit of his throat turned Tom's head back, and he tore his gaze away from the stage to look up along the gleaming length of finest Ferrara steel into the steady dark eyes of his greatest enemy.

'Drawn in the Queen's presence,' said Robert Devereux, the Earl of Essex, quietly.

'That means death. Even for a Master of Defence,' added his nearest, sneering companion, as white-faced as Essex, whom Tom recognized as one de Vaux. Like his master, de Vaux was clearly enjoying the situation hugely.

But Her Majesty was recovered now. 'Tush, My Lord,' she said briskly to Essex. 'The man was running to our aid. These latter years we are not so well supplied with gallants that we can afford to despatch such valiant protectors in such a cavalier fashion. And this is the famous Master of Defence you say?' she demanded more generally.

'Thomas Musgrave, Your Majesty.' Tom was well placed to make his own introduction, needing to do and say almost nothing more, bowing on his knees as he was.

It was then that the door swung wider still and friends joined foes around the person of the Queen. 'What, My Lord of Essex!' came the blessedly familiar voice of Lord Henry, the Lord Chamberlain. 'Drawn in the royal presence. Do you put so little value on your head, sir?'

'Robin was protecting our royal person, My Lord. We give him leave. And Master Musgrave, come to that. They may stand drawn in the royal presence if occasion demands it. There cannot be two such game cocks in all our kingdom as swift with their steel or as loyal with their hearts.'

'Protecting you against what, Your Majesty?' asked Lord Henry softly.

'Against an actor in an ass's head, Henry – and good Will Kempe at that, if we are any judge in the matter. We have not been so frighted since we were a girl. By a monster jumping out of the woods! Yourself, like as

10

not, or one of Master Shelton our guardian's children.' Her Majesty recalled that long-lost girl in a peal of laughter that might have graced the throat of any child. 'By an ass's head forsooth! *Walsingham!*'

'Your Majesty?' came the distant voice of Thomas Walsingham, Tom Musgrave's closest friend at court.

'Are the Shelton girls at court within your train?'

'They are, Your Majesty.'

Tom could have told the Queen the truth of that matter, for Kate, the younger of the Shelton sisters, younger daughter to one of the children who might have played with the youthful Queen, was his mistress; as Audrey, the elder, was Walsingham's.

'Good,' said the Queen, sweeping out of the hall again, with all of the court in tow, 'then we can expect much amusingly lewd speculation as to whether the ass's head might be matched by other, more private, parts – and of equal proportion.' Laughter began to recede – laughter no longer so innocently girlish in its nature.

'Course they are,' said Will Kempe, rising as the door closed. 'What else d'ye think gave Will the idea in the first place? "Give me the head of an ass, Will," said I, "for you know I am hung like a donkey in truth..."'

As the Chamberlain's Men joined Kempe in their own peal of laughter, Tom pulled himself erect. He stood a little shakily, and it required two attempts, separated by a deep breath, to slide the long Solingen blade of his sword home again, feeling the sensitive side of his thumb rub against the reassuring roughness of the running-wolf trademark etched into the steel. He would never know whether it was the proximity of majesty, disaster or death that affected him so.

Yet, he thought, grimly turning back towards the rudely interrupted rehearsal of *A Midsummer Night's Dream*, given his intimate acquaintance with death and disaster of all sorts, it was the closeness of Her Majesty that seemed most likely to have shaken him so badly.

Or, he came to suspect later, perhaps it was a premonition of what was coming next.

Although Will's new play was set in a magical forest beside ancient Athens, the actors wore the cast-off finery handed down to them from great houses – not least that of the Lord Chamberlain himself. Their costumes were contemporary, therefore, if slightly old-fashioned; and the swordplay between the lovers Demetrius and Lysander was a dangerously comic exhibition match in the new Italian style of which Tom was the undisputed master.

Tom was putting a final polish to this dazzling piece of comic byplay when Thomas Walsingham returned and called up the length of the great Hall, 'Tom. There's a messenger newly arrived from the North. He's with Lord Henry now.'

'Indeed, sir,' answered Tom. He stepped back and sheathed his sword once more. 'Why do you condescend to bring this news to my notice?'

'Because,' said Thomas Walsingham shortly, 'the message is for you.'

The little reception room was on the east side of the palace and its window looked along the river towards the distant span of the bridge where Tom's last adventure had come to its bloody end six months since. Lord Henry stood beside the casement, the glorious colour of his court costume sucking life even from the thin grey light of a midwinter's afternoon – he alone of all the men and women Tom had seen at court this afternoon disdained the rage for powdering his face with arsenic powder – but Tom had eyes for neither the emotive view nor for his dazzling patron. The familiar figure of the messenger turned towards him and he, like the screaming Queen, was put in mind of the most frightful moments of his childhood.

'Hobbie?' he said, uncertainly, striding forward. Then the wrinkled, leathery face creased into the ghost of a grin and uncertainty fell away. 'Hobbie,' he said with simple certainty and enfolded the wiry old frame to his bosom. Halbert Noble, called 'Hobbie' through all the wild Borders, had taught him everything he had known of weaponry and survival until he had entered the Master's School of Maestro Capo Fero at Siena some half dozen years since. Save for the matter of

13

fighting with foil and rapier in the Italian style, even Capo Fero had been hard put to better Hobbie's tutelage; and, as his common name implied, he knew the border country as well as one of the sure-footed tireless ponies of the place. Hobbie horses, they were called; creatures that could go, with a rider, into places a man on foot hardly dared venture. There was no track on moss, moor or fell he could not follow, no mark of bird or beast in all the North that Hobbie could not recognize.

'I've come with hard news,' said Hobbie forthrightly as soon as Tom released him. 'Heavy tidings.'

'Are they for me?'

'Aye.'

'Then if they are mine, give them to me. Straight, man.'

Hobbie Noble's eyes met Tom's, seemingly level for all that one man was wiry and bowed with age while the other stood youthfully tall. 'It's your brother, the Blacksmith of Bewcastle,' he said, adding the unnecessary phrase of his title as a measure of great respect; for Tom had only one brother, John, two years his elder, and Hobbie Noble wasted nothing – certainly not words. 'He's dead.'

Tom licked his lips. The news had shocked him though he had been half-expecting some such words since Thomas Walsingham had called him out of the hall. 'Was it an accident?' he asked. Smithing was by no means a safe trade, even for men as massive and expert as his brother and father had been.

Hobbie's head shook in that atom of communication which characterized that man.

'A raid?' – which was how his own mother had died, cut down by the red McGregors come reiving across the debatable land when Tom himself was scarce weaned; not killed but crippled then, doomed to linger for sixteen more years before winning her blessed relief. But Hobbie shook his head again.

'Then what?' demanded Tom.

Hobbie's eyes slid away. Tom looked, frowning across at the resplendent Lord Henry, who was, amongst other things, the Lord of the North, Her Majesty's eyes on the Northern English Borders as they marched by southernmost Scotland.

'Your uncle, who still signs himself the Lord of the Waste, I note, has written of the inquest he has held into the circumstances,' said Lord Henry. 'He reports that your brother's body was found in the lower branches of the Great Oak that stands at the head of the Black Lyne. It is a dangerous river in a wild place, as I recall. You know it?'

'And the tree, My Lord. It has stood there hard by Arthur's Seat since the beginning of time. It must reach nigh on two hundred feet to the crown. The lowest branches must stand twelve feet above ground.'

'Nigh on fifteen feet,' agreed Hobbie.

'Even so. Your brother was discovered dead on the lower branches, kneeling, looking downwards, frozen like marble.'

'Frozen?' echoed Tom. 'He died of the cold?'

'No. The Lord of the Waste reports that there is no doubt that he died of fear – of sheer, stark terror.'

Tom laughed out loud at that. 'There's nothing in all the world would frighten John to death!' he said. 'What makes them think such a ridiculous thing?'

A fifth figure leaned forward at that, a slight, dark-clad, gold-haired stripling lost in the shadows behind Lord Henry until this moment.

'Something beyond the world,' said a steady, cool voice. 'Something came from another, hotter place altogether. Tell him, Hobbie.'

'All around the trunk, the Great Oak was clawed,' said Hobbie reluctantly. 'From the grass, to near the branches themselves. The bark torn off and the live wood splintered, bleeding. Clawed like a great bear can claw a dog at the baiting. But clawed, as you said, for two full fathoms. For twelve sheer feet. And clawed clear to the heartwood beneath the blacksmith's body.'

'By a bear?' said Tom, simply dazed. 'Did you say a bear?'

'No, lad. This was never the work of a bear.'

'Then what? Hobbie, what was it?'

'It was a hound, Tom. They were the marks of a monstrous hound.'

The stripling youth stood up and closed

16

with Tom then, and with another huge jolt of surprise he recognized her. No youth come south at Hobbie's heels, but his own sister-in-law Eve – Eve Graham as was, when they had dallied on the heather fifteen summers since, before she had fallen in love with the slow, shy charm of his big brother, and begun the relationship that had driven Tom himself so far away from home. Eve Musgrave now, his brother John's new-made widow.

Eve's still grey eyes held his gaze as fathomless as the Kielder water. 'Don't you see, Tom?' she whispered. 'It was a hound, but a hound such as no man can look on and survive. It was the Barguest, Tom. We know it now for certain, and rumour says he wasn't the first to die. But he was the first we have found. And so it is certain now. The Barguest is out on the Borders and it has taken your brother's soul.'

# Two

## The Lord of the North

Ten minutes later Eve and Hobbie had gone about some undisclosed business, taking Thomas Walsingham as their guide and leaving Tom beard to beard with Lord Henry. Tom was still stunned by the awful news, but the effect of the shock on his unusual mind was to make his faculties even sharper, his logical acuity even greater. Around the awful void at the heart of his mind where his understanding of the world grappled with monster dogs the size of horses capable of reaching twelve feet up a tree and stealing away the soul of his brother, there was packed a glittering vortex of dazzling, blessedly distracting detail.

Even in the absence of the other three the little chamber still felt crowded to Tom. Lord Henry was a big, powerful, virile man, the echo of his father – the limb of his half-sister, begotten by King Henry on Anne Boleyn's sister, so they said, while his unfortunate queen was awaiting execution. He had lately mounted a mistress nearly forty years his

18

junior, the lovely and multi-talented Amelia Lanyer.

However, it was not Henry Carey's personal power that seemed to fill the room so much as his political power as Lord Chamberlain, Lord Hunsdon and Lord of the North. The North had been his stamping ground since before the lovely mistress Amelia had been born. Tom's first childhood experience of war had been the carnage Lord Henry had left all too near his home, keeping the northern Marches safe for his queen as Howard and Drake and the others had been hardily guarding the South.

The shock of Hobbie's news, and Eve's dreadful suspicions, set the Master of Logic to working busily in Tom's head, and his amazing power of reason was focused upon Lord Henry while the wise old courtier thought the matter through and framed his plans for Tom. Clearly there had been more in his uncle's letter than the simple report of the blacksmith's death, though that would have been enough to worry both men on several levels.

This had been a bitter winter, alternately sodden and frozen in London; but snowless as yet. Such news as had come south in the approach to Yuletide had told of similar – if infinitely icier – conditions to the north. The Borders were frozen solid, but open still. The dangerous pathways so popular with reivers and invaders had been layered with ice but none of them blocked with drifts yet this year.

For a country still surrounded by enemies to the south, with King Philip by all accounts busy about another armada to replace the last and finish its work, it was nevertheless well to keep an eye on the dangers to the north. King James in Edinburgh had troubles enough of his own, with his marriage to Anne of Denmark scarce five years old, and the witch trials arising from his near-fatal courtship still distracting him, so that the Borders over which he had little control at the best of times remained a potent source of worry to the Queen and her Council.

In such a situation, the mysterious death of the blacksmith responsible for arming one of the most important garrisons in the western Marches must assume a terrible political significance; and if, as Eve had said, this was but the first proof of a rumoured plague of such deaths, then the overall effect was hard to calculate.

Even taking John's death alone and discounting rumour altogether, things might well look bad. In such a situation, at such a time of year, the death of such a man in such a terrible manner must have an impact of almost incalculable weight. For who along the icy wastes by Hadrian's Wall stood to gain most from letting loose the Barguest in the Borders and keeping all the Yuletide revellers from Carlisle, east to Berwick and south to New Castle all locked up fast at home, too fearful to venture out into the hound-haunted dark?

The apparently personal little tragedy that had struck at the Musgraves might well be the signal for anything from a border raid designed to steal a few head of winter cattle to a full invasion designed to set flame to the Catholic tinder from Berwick to Nottingham, Scotland to Sherwood.

'You will want me to go north, My Lord,' said Tom.

'With all speed. To the Lord of the Waste, *self-styled.*'

'To the Captain of Bewcastle, at least,' soothed Tom, giving the uncle after whom he was named the title to which he was due. 'And with all haste, as you say – and as has been arranged, I have no doubt, by Hobbie Noble and my newly widowed sister – to discover the true fate of my brother, beyond the first report of my uncle's inquest. That is knowledge which will set many a heart at ease. Not least your own. And Her Majesty's.'

There came a little silence. Rain blew up-river like a fistful of gravel cast against the glass of the casement. 'If you can prove there was no hellish work in it – that it was never the Barguest...' said Lord Henry. 'Such a creature cannot exist,' he added after a moment.

'It is a creature I have feared since child-hood, for I learned of it at my mother's knee.'

'But such a thing cannot be real, can it?'

'King James in Scotland is still at work to track down all the witches who held magical black masses to christen cats in graveyards

21

then sailed out on the wild sea in sieves and summoned the devil to drown him when he went a'courting in Denmark – and, indeed, the political enemies at his court, and some others, who employed the witch women to do these things to him. If witches can be employed to summon devils to such work, perhaps they can be employed to call up hell-hounds too – or do it just for evil's sake. Or perhaps, once in a while Satan's gates stand wide and things slip out we wot not of.'

'You believe in this thing – this Barguest?'

'I believe I have seen it – or something like it – when I was a child. But that is not the same as saying I believe it is out on the Borders now. Nor that it was the Barguest that killed my brother.'

Tom leaned forward over the table, frowning with concentration, suddenly burning with urgency and energy. 'That is a tale for another time, My Lord. Now tell me exactly what you want me to do in the North.'

Thomas Walsingham interrupted the very last of this conference when he returned with Eve and Hobbie. The three of them waited for a moment as Lord Henry gave his final instructions to Tom. Then he put his seal – and that of the Queen's Council – on the last of the documents the Lord Chamberlain's secretary had prepared so rapidly in the interim, which the Master of Defence was to carry up to the Bewcastle Waste.

So that when Tom stood at last and turned, he spoke with the voice of the Lord of the

North. 'Is everything ready?' he demanded. 'Ready,' affirmed Hobbie.

'We go back the way you came, along the Great North Road,' said Tom, all decisiveness, as though the spirit of the preoccupied Lord Henry had truly inhabited his youthful body. 'Meet me at Bishopsgate within the hour, with horses and passes as arranged. A hard ride will get us to Ware by darkfall; and then our journey will truly begin, I think.'

He turned, bowed to Lord Henry and was gone.

A wherry dropped Tom at Blackfriars steps some quarter-hour later and he hurried briskly up towards his lodgings and School of Fencing above Master Robert Aske the Haberdasher's shop. Here his two closest friends awaited him, all unaware of his dreadful news and the urgent business it had engendered.

Close friends they might be, but both of them had proposed to leave him alone during the next twelve days. Kate Shelton was to be at court, in Sir Thomas Walsingham's train, dancing attendance on the Queen, hoping to follow in a family tradition and become a lady-in-waiting. What with the hot bloods like de Vaux painting their faces with arsenic to go ruffling and swashbuckling in the trains of the wilder courtiers, like Essex, Southampton and their circles, the Queen got through ladies-in-waiting at an alarming rate – even when Sir Walter Raleigh was away. Kate would have no liberty to continue her passionate affair with Tom until after Twelfth Night.

No more would Ugo Stell, invited for the festivities to Bleeke House, residence of the Van Der Leydens, father and two daughters, hoping to get through their first Yuletide in a foreign country – they were, like Ugo, Dutch – and their first Christmas without Frau Van Der Leyden so tragically murdered six months since during the terrible affair of the heads upon London Bridge itself.

Now a swift leave-taking of sweet Kate was all the shocked and grieving Tom could afford; and Kate, like her sister Audrey, knew well enough what the demands of the political and secret worlds could be, for both of them had worked as spies for Audrey's affianced lover Thomas Walsingham and his adoptive father the late Sir Francis, unrivalled director of the Queen's Secret Service for more than twenty years.

Kate, womanlike, went straight to the heart of the matter. 'This woman, this Eve that has run, in her grief and loss, straight into your manly arms – what is she to you?'

'An ex-lover of my callowest years. Not even that, for she was her own woman even then and would never yield to me. She came to me fresh from setting another pair of brothers the one against the other, as I recall, and came near to doing the same with John and me. She is my sister and nothing more, therefore, except, perhaps, a bitter memory come with

24

hard news of a terrible tragedy.'

'Of a hell-hound the size of a stallion that tears oak trees into shreds.'

'A monster that I must go and face, Kate, though it break my heart.'

' 'Tis likely there will be more than the monster to face,' she said, 'and more hearts broken than your own. However, let us see what Ugo can supply in the matter of facing monsters...'

Ugo himself, his panniers packed long since and wanting nothing but a convenient moment to ride down to Bleeke House, was happy to take his impatient friend into his workroom. There, as he sorted through his weaponry, he could talk things through at careful length, balancing with his phlegmatic Dutch thoroughness the fiery impatience of Mistress Kate and her all-too-vivid concerns, in the face of Tom's stunned quiet.

'A hound as big as a horse, you say? With claws to rip the heartwood of an oak? Wood as hard as copper, if not bronze. Only a weapon as big as a dunderbus would kill such a creature – always supposing the beast were made of flesh and blood and liable to death in the first place. Do you believe in such a creature, Tom?'

He took Tom's silence as assent and continued with hardly a pause, laying out upon his workbench a range of dags, pistols and handguns as he spoke. 'Even the most powerful of hand weapons would hardly hurt a creature of that size, unless you could direct the shot straight into some vital part or organ. As with your rapiers, Tom, it is not the size of the wound but the precision of its placing that does the damage.'

'On the other hand,' insisted Kate, 'there are times when size matters. A monstrous creature such as this must take monstrous killing. Have you nothing here that can make a huge wound though the gun itself be small?'

'A dunderbus fit for milady's purse?' mused Ugo. 'No. Such a weapon will tax future generations. It is beyond my own talent at present.'

'What is this?' asked Tom, picking up a strange-looking device that lay half-hidden at the back of the workbench.

'A failure. A kind of bastard, ill-born. You see that it has four barrels? Although they are short, they are strong. Each will carry a full load and a shot such as the other pistols. I had hoped that I would be able to rotate the whole so that each barrel would click into place up here by the pan and fire individually of the others; but no matter what I do, all the barrels discharge at once. I have even tried a new type of pan and lock – you see the flint here and the striker here so that a spark may fall on the powder instead of a match? All to no avail. It has near broke my wrist more times than I can tell!'

'But,' said Tom, cradling the bastard pistol in his long, strong fingers, 'were a man wishing to fire four shots at once, then this might indeed do some damage. Four shots delivered at the same time near enough to the same spot, vital or not – this would be like to blast a hole the size of my fist, even in something almost as big as a horse.'

'Are you mad? Only someone fit for Bedlam would trust his life to an engine whose one recommendation is that it refuses to work to its creator's original design. Here, take this matched pair instead.'

Tom had little time for argument and so he took them – and a goodly supply of the powder, shot and accoutrements that went with them. Then, as Ugo went down to arrange the loan of Master Aske's horse from here to Bishopsgate, he went through into his own quarters. Unwilling to waste time on changing into better clothes for the travelling, he simply added more layers – mostly of wool and leather – until his girth had swollen like the belly of an old tavern knight. His waist remained lean, however, and, disdaining the new fashion for swashes across his shoulders, he had no difficulty in strapping at each hip one of the matched pair of Solingen swords that were the richest source of his living and the surest protectors of his life.

As he dressed, at his direction, in the face of his unwonted sorrow and depression, Kate lowered herself to the station of the merest housemaid. She packed his panniers, and slid in amongst the lawn and linen the pistols Ugo had given him. That done, she lovingly crossed, across the base of his spine, the two daggers that matched the swords, and settled

27

the weighty leather sack of his purse beside the Ferrara silver basket of his right-hand blade. Over his shoulder at last went the heavy leather satchel in which the orders and observations of the Lord of the North were packed. As he settled this against his short ribs, Tom felt an extra shape, and extra weight within it. Frowning, he pulled the flap back a little, and glanced up, to catch the eyes of his loving but frightened mistress. For there, poking out of the parchments and the seals stood the familiar, ugly butt of the four-barrelled bastard pistol. He caught her to him and kissed her, moved more than he could express.

'Take care,' she admonished him, her voice breaking.

'I will,' he promised – lying though he did not know it – 'though I go to chase a tale of froth and fairies. A winter's tale indeed, told me by my dam and grandam.'

'Even so,' she said, prophetically enough. 'Those can be the most dangerous tales of all.'

He clapped Ugo on the shoulder, again in silence. He swung the heaviest of his cloaks around his shoulders and pulled the widest and most waterproof of his hats on to his head, swung up on to Master Aske's strong mare and was gone into the steely, sleety afternoon.

# Three

## The Bishops' Gate

Bishopsgate was nearly deserted. In the mid-part of the afternoon of Christmas Eve there were few people making their way into London – and fewer still making their way out. Those coming from any distance to visit the city at this particular season were mostly here and within doors. Those simply coming from nearby to stock up at the markets against the festivities were still at Billingsgate, Smith's Field or on the Cheap; and those still at work were working – for the short days brought fewer hours, not fewer demands.

On the other hand, thought Tom grimly, no one in their right mind was likely to be venturing far away from the city if they could help it – quite the reverse, given the terrible state of the last harvest. Half the country was seemingly on the edge of starvation. The desperate poor were thronging to the city rather than watch each other being famished to death. Going north, particularly, where things were said to be hardest all round, would obviously fit a man for the first big building along the road they were due to travel: Bedlam.

Hobbie and Eve were easy to find in the near-deserted tavern beside St Botolph's Church immediately without the great stone gate. In the little square made by the inn front and the opening of the Hound's Ditch, which ran eastward along the outside of the Wall, Tom made swift arrangements to return Master Aske's mare, then entered the low building to join his travelling companions. He did this quietly, guardedly, made careful in both senses of the word by his sorrow and his suspicions that Eve at least – as ever – was by no means dealing plainly with him here.

Eve's good sense in travelling dressed as a boy was borne upon Tom at once. It was very much in the character he remembered. Like many another border woman, she was quick and able to take the initiative – the equal of any man in many matters, in fact, if not yet in the eyes of Church or Court; but still, he hardly needed to remind himself, although Eve was his sister, she was still a stranger – had never been anything else, in fact, even when she lay laughing in his arms upon Kielder Heights. He had not looked into those sad, still, disturbingly familiar eyes since he had taken the wits of which he was so proud northward from Carlisle Grammar School to the University at Glasgow, leaving his smitten brother wrapped happily in her toils; and that was more than twelve years since.

Now Eve sat at ease beside Hobbie, the pair of them fortifying themselves against the long hard journey with strong bread and weak ale. The last morsels of the bread still steamed with the hot breath of the pottage in which it had been soaked, and Tom was tempted by his wiser spirit to invest like them in something warm and substantial to cling to the inside of his ribs as his good cloak clung on the outside.

Swift as ever to take the initiative, therefore, Tom called over to the innkeeper, 'Another brewis here and small beer.'

Then he settled himself across the table from the pair of them and his cool gaze wandered from Eve's steady regard to Hobbie's guarded visage.

'She made me bring her,' said Hobbie with only half a laugh. 'Or rather, she made the Lord of the Waste to order me.'

'She has good reason, no doubt,' replied Tom. 'Have you not, my lady?'

Her mouth twisted at that. 'More than you know, you turncoat scapegrace. More than you can guess at, I'll be bound.' Her voice was dismissive, bitter. Had there been even more bad blood between them than he remembered?

'I doubt that,' he answered angrily, surprised by the anger, shocked that his grief should come out so. 'For though I have been absent in body this long while, I have been there in mind and spirit; and it cannot be that things are so different now that I cannot

31

fathom out your dangers and your desperations.'

'Well then?' she challenged, again with more anger than he had expected. Her rage and grief struck him deeply, for he felt that they were in part directed at him. Had he been in the Borders instead of at Court, her anger seemed to say, then his brother would have been alive today. This outraged woman would not have been a widow. The Barguest might have been kennelled still in whatever cavern of hell normally housed it.

Her rage compounded his still further, for he felt the truth of what he supposed she thought; and that rage spurred on the Master of Logic, so that the Master added to his own fine wits some of the information Lord Henry had shared in his fears for the North and he made of the whole a mirror to hold up against her memories, thoughts and motivations that reflected the whole as though he had been some faery creature sitting in her secretest heart the while.

'The whole of the Borders will have been wild with speculation throughout this bitter, bitter Advent if what you said is true. It is the Barguest's season, and if there was talk of dead men stark with fear...' He paused and looked at the pair of them. 'But you'll likely have paid less mind to it than John did. For John had seen the thing – with me, when he was a lad; and God knows, he was still scared of it when I left. A fear, I trust, he left behind at last.'

Eve's head nodded, once. 'Until it caught up with him,' she whispered.

Tom proceeded from the general to the particular. 'They'll have carried him home on a wicket – Hobbie, like as not, and the rest that found him. None will have dared to tell you of the Barguest at first and you'll have been shaken and stunned with grief. But the look on his face will have led you to question and your questions will have gotten an answer – from Hobbie himself, like as not.'

The pair of them exchanged glances, Eve's wind-reddened cheek beginning to pale still further. Tom's brewis arrived, rough bread sopping in a wooden bowl of thin pottage with a horn spoon to eat it with. His small beer was flat and thin – little more than water, save that it was not like to poison him.

'He died in the night so they brought him home in the morning and you'll have had the story by nightfall. Black night and stormy and the Barguest out and terribly close to home. But you'll have gone in the darkness – alone, if I'm any judge – up to Bewcastle fort, to the Lord of the Waste. Not to ask his advice – not that – but to demand his protection mayhap. But he could not offer it or you would never have left your husband cold to run south.'

'I buried him before I left him,' said Eve, as though she was angry with both the brothers.

Tom savoured his brewis, and chewed on a string of mutton, deep in thought, seeming not to hear her. 'Protection not even Thomas Musgrave, Captain of Bewcastle,

Her Majesty's right hand on the Marches, can give. But he has Hobbie here, ready to ride south, for these are matters to be reported to the Chamberlain and the Council. It is the reiving season and the Blacksmith of Bewcastle dead. Could even Carlisle be at risk? With the Barguest out on the Borders, anything must seem possible. So – my uncle cannot protect you but he sends you south to Lord Henry instead. What can the Lord of the North offer that the Captain of Bewcastle cannot? Something more subtle than the protection of twenty men-at-arms on horse and foot that he has at his immediate command; or than the two hundred he can summon within the hour could offer. Something that neither the Musgraves nor the Grahams, nor both combined, can guarantee; and they, combined, could protect you even against the Armstrongs and the MacGregors, like as not.

'Not protection from the violence of war, then,' pursued Tom almost in a whisper. 'Therefore it must be protection from some violence of love.'

Eve was white now, save for the black rings under her grey eyes and the red wound of her mouth – as white as a lady, powdered for court.

'Perhaps,' continued Tom ruthlessly, recklessly, 'there is a lover close at hand who you fear will overcome you at once, someone who has been battering at your peace already, while yet my brother lived. But that seems less than likely, for my brother was a loving,

34

proud and short-tempered man with the hardest fist in the Border. No man could have loved Eve Musgrave while the Blacksmith of Bewcastle lived and 'scaped with his brains safely between his ears. Therefore this is like to be a more general fear.

'But, beautiful and sought-after though you are, once were, and will be again, Eve, you are not a proud woman concerned with her looks and her conquests. If you fear that you are set to become the hind amongst a pack of hounds on a love hunt, then there is something more than your own fair person at stake; and that can only mean property or land.

'I know our family's worth to the nearest groat. So it is not property. Therefore it is land.

'What land do you own, in your own title now as a childless widow, that puts your peace of mind to such terrible test that you must throw yourself under the protection of the Council for it?'

She stared at him, her eyes wide, as though stunned – as though he had punched her.

'The Black Lyne,' she said, dully. Her voice echoed with wonder, almost with horror, at how clearly the Master of Logic could strip her reasoning bare, like a woodsman stripping the bark of a willow wand.

'The Black Lyne?' he echoed, stunned himself. The three words opened new vistas of darkness and danger. 'The river or its valley?'

'Water and valley both; east side and west,

from Arthur's Seat to Brackenhill. It came to my mother from her mother. It came from my mother to me. John kept our ownership of it secret between himself and the Lord of the Waste. Or we thought it was secret. But now...'

Tom looked over to Hobbie. ' 'Tis the back door to the west march,' he said, simply awed. 'After Liddesdale it is the surest way from Scotland over the border. Whoever holds the Black Lyne can skirt the Bewcastle Waste, bite his thumb at the Captain of Bewcastle, and fall on Carlisle at his leisure.'

'And whoever holds Carlisle,' rumbled Hobbie, 'holds the key to the north, mayhap to the kingdom. You could anchor an armada safely on the Solway under its protection and land an army there.'

'Whoever wins my hand,' said Eve, 'owns the Black Lyne; and should he not wish to use it himself, why he can rent it out, exact the blackmail, let the Armstrongs and the Kerrs come riding south – and bigger men with larger armies than even they, perhaps.'

Just the way she said it made it impossible for Tom to tell whether the word was 'riding' or 'raiding'. Then he remembered that in the Borders, they meant the same thing in any case.

The three of them sat silently for a moment, studying distant vistas of terrible possibility, all of which turned upon what the terrible spectre of a monstrous black dog seemed to have done to his brother.

36

Hobbie stirred again. 'Ye reet?' and, on Tom's nod, went to pay the reckoning.

The stables were low and dark, but surprisingly solid and secure – not at all what one might have expected behind such a dilapidated inn; but then, looking around, Tom was struck by the quality of the horseflesh they contained. This was where Lord Henry's messengers set out hot-foot to take his orders to the North; and Lord Henry's messengers did not ride broken-down nags.

The creature that the tavern's ostler brought to replace Master Aske's mare could hardly have been more different from the strong but stately family horse used to carry the haberdasher and his wife together. It was a long-legged, fiery black gelding, all thew and temper, one of three near identical, set aside for the use of the Chamberlain's messengers riding the long road north.

'This is something like,' enthused Hobbie, and Tom caught the ghost of a smile crinkling the edge of his sister's eye – a girl who had been taught to ride astride with her brothers almost as soon as she could walk. They bred no fine ladies with precious, courtly airs amongst the Grahams, thought Tom, with an indulgence left over from wilder times, and some relief that his disquisition seemed to have lightened her burdens a little.

As Lord Henry's man and a northener, nephew to the Captain of Bewcastle, Lord of the Waste, Tom had some general knowledge of the system that sent messages flying from the Borders to the Council on a weekly – sometimes twice-weekly – basis; but this was the first time that he had found himself caught up in the overpowering mechanics of it, for all that he had discussed with Lord Henry the details of his proposed journey northward. He was quick of study, however, and soon learned the ropes that seemed so familiar to Hobbie and even Eve. With no further thought, he tightened his saddlebags and panniers, settled the gloves of Spanish leather that matched his thigh boots and leaped lithely into the saddle once more.

# Four

## Ware Riot

So, as the inclement afternoon began to gather lingeringly towards dusk, three black figures, almost indistinguishable from each other astride three black horses, thundered up the Roman road past the opening to Hog Lane, past Finsbury Fields where the flag on the theatre, for once, was not hoist, and away towards the distant village of Islington.

The road was well maintained this close to the city and the horses seemed to know every flinty stone within its hard-earth, ice-bound surface. Silent, each deep-wrapped in their own thoughts – and with much, God knew, to think about – the riders gave their horses their heads and galloped flat out. Talk would have been impossible, even had any of them been foolish enough to break their concentration. For the horse hooves drummed on the icy ground, the great sides heaved and breath bellowed out and in. The wind, stirring from the north, beat at their faces, eyes and ears like thunder, only slightly diminished by the swathes of cloak gathered up around shoulders up to noses and cheek-bones. As they galloped, so every steely piece of tack, every leathery belt, flap, bag and rein made a wild, discordant music, all creaking, banging, jingling and jarring to the rhythmic drumming of the hooves.

An hour's hard riding brought them to Enfield, where they showed their passes at the next waiting inn and, hardly stopping for breath, exchanged their horses for two chest-nuts and a rangy roan that heaved smoothly under Tom and that seemed to know the road as well as the black had done, even though the light was fading faster now. As they rode through villages and hamlets, the bells for evensong began to chime. Away to their right, a freezing mist began to gather over the valley of the Lea and the wind that whipped at their faces armed itself with sharper barbs of frost. Lights began to flicker in the gathering dark, bright gleams issuing star-like from the distance, for the most part from the same direction as the echoing bells: Bull's Cross on their left, on the rise beneath the charcoal sky; Waltham Cross on their right, glittering through the gathering mist as though the warmth of gold could freeze. Then the great straight thrust of the roadway through silence and darkness up past Hoddes Town towards Puck's Ridge.

The horses had never been meant to carry them that far. As they crossed the outer reach of Hertford Heath, so the grey-smoking river swung round across their way and the road beneath the galloping hooves began to fall towards the bridge at Ware. They crossed the river as the town clock struck six and night seemed to fall on the stroke of it. Up the High Street they came, the sound of their urgent horses desecrating the sound of a choir at worship, until Hobbie, half a length in the lead, swung his chestnut beneath an arch under the thrust of an overhanging upper chamber, and the other two, following, found themselves crowding into what little was left of an old inn yard beside a big black travelling coach with four great horses harnessed in its traces, blanketed against the cold and waiting quietly to go.

Stiffly now, they all swung down and Hobbie crossed to the inn door and hammered upon it.

'There's like to be little answer from the innkeeper,' said Tom, 'with evensong not yet done.' Even so, he kept glancing over his shoulder at the coach, with its sconces at each corner holding four big torches ready to take fire, its heavy leather blinds tied tight down over the gaping windows, and the dried mud clinging to its solid, businesslike sides – a little more than a day or so old, that mud, he thought.

'You're half in the right at least,' said Eve. 'We are expected and will be answered shortly – though not by the innkeeper, to be sure.'

The door opened as she spoke and two tall men surveyed them. One was cloaked and

41

booted, ready for travelling – ready, like as not, thought Tom, looking at the great padded gauntlets on his ham-like fists, to take the reins of the waiting coach and guide it back whence it had come, to the North; and, like Hobbie Noble, he had one of those still, fierce faces that spoke most eloquently of the hard lands between York and Berwick.

He and Hobbie exchanged a nod that bespoke acquaintance and Tom realized at once that the coach was waiting for them. All they had to do was get their passes checked and they could proceed; but there lay the rub.

Beside the coachman stood a stout country bumpkin, all soft southern roundness in cheek and belly, clutching a constable's staff. 'Papers!' snapped the constable officiously.

From the frown with which the papers were taken, it was clear that the good Parish Constable of Ware by no means approved of folks that travelled on the eve of one of the holiest of days, keeping him from worship as they did so – especially as he saw all too clearly that the journey was not likely to be completed before the holy day itself began in six hours' time, or began to dawn in twelve. Not all the passes and warrants from the Chamberlain, the Council nor the Queen herself – for all she could style herself, like her father, Defender of the Faith – could convince him there was an urgency here that surpassed even the importance of evensong on this most holy festival; but it was his duty to check the identity of every traveller who moved through

42

his parish, and to check their passes and permits. Upon his order, common vagrants could be jailed, pilloried or whipped. At his reference the local justice could brand, lop or chop. It was his duty and his responsibility, though it was clear that he could hardly read.

He took the whole bundle of passes and permits and sat at the nearest table, straining under the meagre light. Tom caught Hobbie and the saturnine driver exchanging a look, rolling their eyes to heaven at the slow tracing of his diligent finger from line to line and the laboured fish-like gasping of lip as he silently spelt out the words. Then the driver glanced back to another, shadowed portion of the dim, half-lit unwelcoming parlour and Tom saw another man there – a second driver, with his padded gloves; another settled, northern countenance.

Tom crossed towards Eve, thinking that if they were to be cooped up in a coach for the next few hours, then now might be the time to mend some fences with her. ' 'Tis as well I'm not here to be counted at the command of Caesar Augustus and you're not heavy with child,' he observed with dry blasphemy, 'or this would be a sorely familiar situation.'

'Indeed,' she said shortly and, disappointed that the sally had not extended the good work that his description of her true plight seemed to have begun, he wondered for an instant whether she had picked up a Puritan streak she had never shown in her wild youth. Not from brother John, he thought; and the gloom

43

of sadness and loss descended upon him, compounded by the sudden delay, the faltering in the momentum of his quest. As it did so, she walked away from him, past the second driver and out through a side door into the yard.

'Eve,' he called quietly after her, fearing to raise his voice in case the constable have something else to add to his slow outrage; but there came no answer as she disappeared into the freezing shadows. How she must be suffering, he thought. His own memories of John were sunny and warm.

Except for the time they had seen the Barguest, of course.

In the silence after her departure, Tom suddenly became aware that the service in the nearby church must be over. The choral sounds of regimented worship had ceased and the more general shuffling of a departing congregation was suddenly lost beneath a valedictory peal of bells. A moment later the first of the parishioners arrived. A glance at the broad face, as red and meaty as a boiled pig's head, told him this was the innkeeper returned. Behind the tun-sized girth of his belly there crowded a scrawny wife and a brood of brats all like plucked chickens wrapped in sad cypress – not an ounce of flesh amongst them, except for that which padded their well-lined father; but, fat or thin, they all shared the same pinched and disapproving look and, observed Tom wryly, they all bore suspicious similarity to the constable.

'They still here then, master Constable?' demanded the innkeeper, much aggrieved.

'Still here,' answered the constable, looking up, losing his place and returning to the top of the pass he was reading now.

'It is not right,' observed the innkeeper, 'travelling on such a holy day. 'Tis blasphemy pure and simple. No good will come of it, as the vicar said in his sermon, and more evil's like to fall on our poor heads as a result. The crops are lost already and starvation looming for all of us in the iron heart of this icy time.'

' 'Tis the order of the Council,' soothed the constable, 'and there's a good few bishops and such upon the Council.'

The innkeeper's belligerent superstitions seemed to have caught the mood of the desperate townsfolk, for Tom could see, beyond his scrawny family, some rather more substantial and no less truculent neighbours beginning to crowd across the Great North Road. He caught Hobbie's eye and then those of the driver and his mate. The three men began to sidle towards the carriage and, looking across at the vehicle, Tom was surprised to see that the blankets were off the horses' backs and a slim boyish figure was framed in the open doorway, ready and waiting to go.

Tom stepped back, therefore, and briefly rested his right fist apparently casually on the table between the pile of documents which the constable had finished reading and the last pass, which still claimed his sluggard attention. 'Unless that is the watch that you have summoned by some exercise in magic,' he said quietly, glancing meaningfully out through the inn door, 'then you have an illegal congregation gathering, master Constable. 'Ware riot, sir. 'Ware riot.'

The constable looked up at that, and saw that, as Tom had warned, some thirty strapping farmers dressed in their Sabbath best were crowding across the High Street, as though spectacularly unaware that the season of goodwill was hard upon them. As he did so, three things happened in swift succession.

Tom reached down and gathered his papers together, sweeping them out of the startled constable's grasp. Just at the same moment, the driver lit the first flaming torch on the right-front corner of the coach and it exploded into a dazzling shower of flames; and a pair of horsemen thundered up the High Street at full gallop, hurtling into the black-clad crowd in the shadows, smashing them ruthlessly aside with the power of their pounding steeds, and were gone again into the darkness before the first of their victims could tumble, broken and screaming, on to the icy ground. Tom caught a flash of their impact on the crowd: a black stallion rearing; a head split by a sharp-spurred, stirrup-armed boot; the bulge of a saddlebag behind with an ornate device upon it; shocked men and women hurled brutally aside.

Then the constable really did have a riot on his hands. The farmers went from congregation to mob in a twinkling, as though some philosopher's stone had transmuted their essential being. Into the inn they came boiling, outraged and looking for a fight – after the blood of the only strangers left within their grasp.

Stuffing the papers into his satchel, Tom swung out of the little parlour side door that had let Eve out to ready the horses, but he knew he would be lucky indeed to reach the carriage unchecked. In the brightness of the second blazing torch, the driver and his mate could see as much and the pair of them leaped down while Hobbie steadied the frightened horses and Eve called curses from the carriage itself, her spirit returning through rage where gentleness and wit had failed to stir it. Then the mob was upon them all.

Tom had neither time, room nor inclination to reach for his swords. Even the daggers would only have added to the bloodshed, and therefore the delay. Clutching the precious satchel tight under his right arm, feeling the weight of the four-barrelled bastard pistol ironically heavy against his heart, he pushed forward, swinging his left fist manfully at the first face in his way. A stool flew past his shoulder, and smashed into the next face he was targeting. Quick as a flash he caught it and swung it upwards as a makeshift club, the threat of it enough to make his next two foemen fall back. The driver and his mate arrived on either side of him then, and the three bundled forward all abreast. As they pushed through the mob, there was much elbowing and jostling but, thought Tom grimly, a bruise or two was a small price to pay to get out of the place.

'Hobbie, leave the horses!' Tom bellowed, and his old friend obeyed at once, swinging back to take the driver's place at Tom's right shoulder even as Eve replaced the second man at his left. Then the three travellers were in the solid vehicle and the drivers, aloft, were whipping up the horses.

The hooves of the rearing, plunging leaders cleared away those last few men still on the High Street – for at the very least they had seen the damage that the sudden riders had done to their friends still lying at the roadside in varying states of disrepair. It was as well that some of these, at the outskirts of the riot, had pulled the wounded clear, otherwise there would have been a good deal of death dished out; for once the carriage was moving, neither the sharp-shod hooves nor the heavy, steel-hooped wheels would have stopped for anyone.

Seemingly lent wings by their terror, the four horses plunged up the hill, scarcely under the driver's control, and the coach behind them bounced and swayed, throwing its occupants hither and yon as though they had been dice in the hands of an energetic gamesman. In the darkness they bounced off one another, exchanging a good few more bruises before they could settle on the big broad seats. Only as the vehicle attained the straight run of Ermine Street itself, and the steady rise up to Puck's Ridge, did some semblance of calm return.

'What in God's name happened there?' gasped Eve.

'I think the constable slowed us on purpose,' Tom answered slowly. 'I think we must have an enemy somewhere capable of acting more swiftly even than we – someone who has sent messages to Ware and riders to the North, riders ordered to overtake us at any cost and perhaps to wait in ambush for us; certainly to organize some mischief for us later.'

Eve laughed aloud at that. 'You cannot know this!' she spat. 'You're simply making it up.'

'Perhaps,' said Tom. 'But even if I am doing so, would we not be wise to act as though my guesses were gospel truth?'

'Lad's got a point,' said Hobbie dryly.

'But whoever they were and whyever they came,' continued Tom more reasonably, 'they came and hoped to go in secret, for they rode with muffled hooves. In spite of the season and the terrible danger, they rode with muffled shoes. How else could they have come over the bridge and in amongst the townsfolk so sudden and unexpectedly? No. From this moment onwards, we must behave in everything we do as though we face a great and ruthless enemy.'

Tom lapsed into silence then, as though the exercise of so much logic after such an affray

49

at the latter end of such a long and exciting day had tired even him. The coach rattled and heaved as the four strong horses hauled it up past Collier's End. The blind over the open window, knocked loose in the escape, flapped open and torchlight flooded into the box of shadow within. Tom was sitting strangely on the wide, padded seat, his cloak thrown back, his right glove held between his teeth and his right hand moving inside his jerkin.

'Tom, what is it?' asked Eve, her voice suddenly strident with worry.

'Tom?' called Hobbie, catching her sudden tone.

'God's my life, I've been stabbed,' said Tom. He pulled his hand out of his shirt and in the unsteady, golden light, it seemed almost as dark as if he had resumed his Spanish-leather glove.

Tom looked at it for an instant with frowning concentration while the other two sat riven where they were; and then he keeled over on to his side.

# Five

## The Nightmare Journey

No doubt, thought Tom, looking back on it all from near the end of the affair, it was the swaying of the coach that had made him dream that he was flying at first. It was, probably, the massive howling of the gathering nor'easterly gale that had made his dream of the Barguest later; and it was, no doubt, the distant voices of the Christmas bells that had made him dream of death in the end. But when he discussed matters with Eve and Hobbie, it seemed that much of what he had dreamed was true, if others of his logical assumptions were a good deal less so.

The pain in his side and the words of his rough nurses wove in and out of his dreams seemingly at will. While they did this, the black-cloaked, huge-fisted, ruggedly inexhaustible drivers hurled them all through the night at breakneck speed, and the coach charged onwards at nearly ten of the Queen's new statute miles in every hour, north to New Castle.

Tom dreamed he was an eagle – an angel

51

seemed so unlikely – skimming over the wild lands of his childhood home, a home drawing near again in all sorts of ways as he tossed restlessly upon the coach's seat in the grip of his nightmare vision. Below him, all clear-etched by a low sun in a cloudless sky, lay the rough rock waves of the Marches from the Cheviot Hills to Teviot Dale. Two waves of moor land moss they seemed to him, frozen waves of rock running from north-east to south-west, spanning less than fifty miles in all, with a trough of a valley between them. The Teviots stood in the north, contained mostly in Scotland, coming down from Berwick towards Dumfries; and south of them ran the Cheviots, from Bamburgh towards Carlisle. Between them was fixed the border, which wandered invisibly but vitally from moss to fell to wilderness, from sea to sea. Two rocky, mountainous walls designed by God to keep the Scots and the English apart, more effective even than Hadrian's wall skirting the southern slopes of the Che-viots away to the south on Tom the dream-eagle's left.

'Tom?' asked Eve's voice. 'What're ye doing, Tom?'

'I'm flying,' answered Tom. 'Flying away home.'

'Lie still,' commanded Eve more roughly. 'I'll not lose two men within the week. Hobbie, hold him down.'

But not even Hobbie could hold down the dream-eagle Tom had become as he skimmed away back to his home. The walls of rock had been worn away over the years. Due north and due south ran the river valleys, pathways leading easily through the forbidding highlands, allowing constant raiding and reiving from one land and law into the other – Coquetdale, Redesdale and Tynedale through the Cheviots into England; the valleys of the Jed, the Yarrow and the Elvan out of Scotland.

As he flew from east to west, into the glimmer of the setting sun, Tom seemed to settle into lower air, skimming between Kielder Heights and Hermitage Hall, England beneath his left wing and Scotland under his right, with the border under his belly as he flew; the border under his belly and the Bewcastle Waste close beneath his heart.

'Tom', whispered Eve, 'this will hurt. I've to close up your side, where the dagger...'

Still through the rough walls of wild wasteland, like daggers through ill-fitting armour, even through the stout breastplate of the Waste itself, stabbed the dark river valleys, wooded with cover, steep-sided, secret, shadowed and convenient to mischief, two of them running in parallel and the most deadly dangerous of all: the river-dales of the Lidd and the Lyne coming down to the Esk river and the Solway Firth, on either side of the border; between them the debatable land, neither English nor Scottish but a lordless, lawless morass of constant war, tomb of political dreams and graveyard of armies. Up and down their dangerous valleys marched warriors beyond counting, times out of number.

'There, Tom. That'll do,' said Eve. 'You'll rest easier now.'

And so he did; without disturbing his dream or his thoughts. Now Eve Graham Musgrave, it seemed, widow of his brother and his sister within the church, had the northern tributary, the Black Lyne, of a sudden, under her hand and within her dower.

No wonder the canny Captain of Bewcastle had sent her to seek the advice and the protection of the Lord Chancellor. For only a man like Henry Carey, Lord Hunsdon and Lord of the North could hold this coil, this cockpit, together.

Outside his dream, he sensed the coach stop. The driver got down and showed the passes. The door opened briefly to let in the light and the thunderous howl of the gale that came bellowing in off the North Sea over the fens to Stamford, where they had been stopped by the watch and waited to change horses. But inside his dream he was flipped out of flight, air and time. In a heartbeat Tom had lost the bewildering vista of the Borders and the silver Solway stretching towards the sun. Instead he was caged within a woody coolness. There was a leafy, deep-green, fragrant stillness all around him. And, if he had never experienced the breathless reality of flight except in his imagination, then he knew the truth of this. For it was not imagination at all. It was reality rehearsed – memory made more vivid by the dream; terror made more poignant because he knew what was going to happen next.

'My Lord's woodsmen will never catch us now. Not even Hobbie will find us here, Tom,' said John then, his voice louder, deeper, than Tom remembered it.

He turned, and John stood at his shoulder, tall and slim with his dark shock of hair – gangling and bony still, yet to fill out and square up; twelve years old to Tom's ten; both of them breathless with excitement at their adventure with Hobbie, doing a little poaching here in Inglewood Forest.

' 'Tis the best of ambushes,' Tom acknowledged. 'The heart of a yew in the midst of a forest, surrounded by trees not like to have been disturbed since the Romans needed wood for the Wall.'

'Since Noah needed wood for the Ark,' fantasized John. 'Near at the dawn of the world.'

'If the Flood ever reached here,' dared Tom, blasphemously clever even then; and about to learn a lesson from his unwise words. 'And I'll lay odds it never did! Why, there could be creatures in these woods, John, that lived before the Flood. Think of it: things hid like us in the black heart of this timeless place, never seeing the full light of day. Undiscovered. Unsuspected. Things condemned of God but never...'

He stopped then, for he was frightening himself and his wild suggestion seemed suddenly quite plausible, for the forest was huge and dark. It had about it that very air of infinite age, as though it had in truth stood here untouched since the dawn of Time, and theirs were actually the first human feet to disturb its ancient loam.

And the instant Tom stopped speaking, the hound howled.

It was a huge sound, haunting and over-powering; and all too close at hand. Both boys screamed at the sound and ran to clasp each other. Their screams were echoed by another fierce howl, a howl that tailed off into the guttural baying of a hunting animal.

They stayed tremulously embraced for the merest instant and then they were in full flight; but whither should they run? Whatever was out there seemed huge, seemed all too close by; seemed to be after them. The ancient yew tree within which they were hiding had reached out a massive tent of pendulous branches, each one taking new root where it touched. These branches made a tight-woven palisade near thirty feet across at whose heart stood the original growth. This was more a matted sheaf of thigh-thick stems than one great trunk, but it made easy climbing. The boys went up it side by side like squirrels – and not a moment too soon.

A huge head smashed through the outer wall at the very weakness they had widened to come in here themselves. Tom, still climbing wildly, had leisure for only the briefest glance over his shoulder at the great black face of the thing – a head, he later swore, that must have been near as tall as he was himself; a drooling, slobbering red mouth wide enough to have swallowed him down at one fell gulp, could he have fitted past the fangs as long as wild boar's tusks. In through the hole beneath its jowls it thrust one huge black paw as wide as John's broad shoulders, armed with curling claws as long as his fingers, as grey as flint and sharp as daggers – claws that curled down into soft loam and tore at soft flesh; claws that had never been worn down by hard rock or strong foe. For Tom could imagine nothing ever standing against this monster. It would hunt wolves, gulp boars, chew bulls and shatter bears with one flick of its paw.

The thing pulled back, then howled again, throwing the massive black invisibility of itself against the creaking branches of the ancient tree, tearing them out of the forest floor, roots and all, as it ripped its way in, while Tom, screaming still, looked up for John.

And found him immediately above. John grown to manhood in a dream-instant; frozen in a scream, wide eyes bulging and staring, wild hair standing upright in the icy blast; lips blackened with the shout of horror that had burst his heart, and tongue thrust out like a slate gravestone, stark dead of terror, staring down at Tom from an inch away.

Tom screamed and fell backwards on to soft, warm ground; and the great hound bounded over him, grown like the boys to full size in the interim, reaching up twelve feet sheer with those terrible claws fit to tear out the heart of a mighty oak tree as it stood like a massive sentinel and looked from Arthur's Seat down the valley that the dead man's wife owned – down the dale of the Black Lyne into the defenceless heart of the Borders.

Down which, of a sudden, Tom saw them carry the body – flat on a wicket under a blanket out of respect; down off the high fells, away from the tree towards the little stone kirk at Blackpool Gate. As they brought the laden wicket down, so the bells began to chime, a wild peal of joy.

'No,' cried Tom. 'That's not right!'

'Hush now,' soothed Eve. 'What is it, Tom?'

And she was there at once in the dream, standing tall at the open door to the church with her black water running over her black land at her little white feet. She smiled, as full of joy as the bells.

Tom looked across at the men with the hurdle, and all of them were Hobbie. All of them were smiling as they walked across the water – water that came off the fell-side black as tar with the blood of the peat higher up; black and gold with the heartsblood of the oak tree, bleeding great golden angels where the Barguest had ripped it open; black and gold and red with the blood of the men that had died to get it and hold it and ride up and down it. Men who were piled up the fell-side so that their blood made the river flood at

Eve's feet, the red running wildly into the kirk at Blackpool Gate. There in the kirk, in the blood with the dead he had made while Tom, in another childhood, had watched, stood Robert Devereux, the Earl of Essex himself; and the Barguest stood at his side, as big as a horse, with his shoulder at its shoulder.

'No!' shouted Tom.

'Tom!' shouted Eve.

Both seemed to be speaking in the last of the dream but the dream was fading now – fading into the heady joy of peal after peal of bells.

But the dark vision lingered, there by the Black Pool, by the kirk by the Gate, with Eve, Essex and the Barguest itself and Tom and the corpse on the wicket held by six smiling Hobbies – lingered long enough for Tom to take the dream-edge of the dream-blanket and jerk it back off the screaming face, to see the wide bulging eyes and the wide black lips and the big black tombstone tongue. But the face no longer belonged to John.

It belonged to Tom himself.

'Where am I?' Tom asked, as reality swept over him in a blaze of light and a peal of bells like the high waterfalls at the Devil's Beef Tub.

'New Castle,' said Hobbie, as terse and succinct as ever.

Tom sat up without thinking, such was his shock at the news. Some sense of movement had informed the visions of the night but nothing could ever have prepared him for the news that the coach had continued its incredible progress hour after hour all through the near eighteen hours of the night. They had come very nearly two hundred of the Queen's new miles since they had escaped from the riot at Ware.

It was as well, he realized at once, that Hobbie and Eve were both well schooled in simple surgery. His side was easy, its stiffness as much to do with tight bandaging as anything else. Further careful movement, however, revealed the familiar pulling sensation that told of several stitches. 'A long, shallow gash?' he hazarded. 'A good bleeding to sharpen my senses and restore my humours and little more.'

Hobbie looked back at him from his position immediately outside the coach's doorway. His eyes were narrow and guarded; but that, thought Tom, might have been because the Good Lord had seen fit to let the folk of New Castle celebrate his birthday beneath a clear, frosty and dazzlingly sunny heaven.

'Restore your humours but ruin your linen,' supplied Eve's voice from beyond him suddenly. 'Heaven help the Lord of the Waste's washerwoman when she sees the mess you're in. But you're in the right of it. It was a long shallow wound in the soft flesh above your hip. You've cause to thank all that easy living in London, mind. Were you leaner, you'd likely be dead.'

60

'In no fit condition to ride the Wall, at least,' said Tom easily; 'but I should be able to do it now, thanks to your tending.'

'If we take it slow,' warned Hobbie, 'and if we ever get to start.'

Feeling the still-damp clothing beginning to set and crisp scratchily against his ribs, Tom slid off the seat and stepped out of the coach. Light-headed still, he let the overwhelming day swirl and settle before he let go of the coach itself. He looked around, mind whirling into action.

At first it seemed to him that Hobbie and Eve had been teasing him and they had not left London at all, for the coach was standing beside a bridge upon which stood houses and shops all brightly decked and glittering under the sun. But no: this bridge was smaller than London Bridge, for all that it seemed to bear a village on its back like its bigger cousin in the South. Seven spans served to step across the Tyne, and there were no great water-wheels at either end to pump water or grind corn; there was no great stone gateway festooned with poles and severed heads. And, of course, there was the dream-like memory of the night with its stops and starts; its pauses to check papers and change horses counting through the hours as he had dreamed.

Even as this thought occurred to Tom, so the pair of drivers returned. 'We're clear,' growled the big driver to Hobbie. 'We're to take five horses and go on. They didn't like it, mind – not on Christmas Day. They're all

*Christians* down here.'

Tom knew then – knew that the two drivers were to come with them, to guard them along the Wall, likely as not, and keep them from kidnap or the blackmail. And he knew who these two were – their names and clans, if not their individual titles yet – for it was a well-known story, often told a visitor to the wild haunts of bandit-reiver heartland of Liddesdale, looking to find a kirk on the Sabbath and finding only castles, forts and peel towers, had asked, despairingly, 'Are there no Christians in Liddesdale?' Only to receive the answer, 'Na, we's all Elliots and Armstrongs here...'

# Six

## Riding the Wall

They left the carriage at the south side of the bridge and crossed it on foot. Through the deserted roadway between the bridge houses over the River Tyne, the two guides led the little party to a quiet inn upon the north bank, hard by St Nicholas' Church, which seemed to lean back upon the Wall they were destined to follow west.

The whole of New Castle seemed deserted at the moment – or outside St Nicholas' Church and the others close by it did. For, as in Ware the night before, only those with special – crucial – business would be out of church at this time in this day, while the Christmas services were on, thought Tom, shivering a little with understandable concern that the imperative of this ghastly business might well be putting his soul as well as his life in some dark and deadly danger.

The inn was called The Wall's End. Here Tom and Eve were led into a small private room that had clearly been prepared for them some time earlier. Here Tom and his sister-in-

63

law were further accoutred, while Hobbie and the two guides brought out arms and armour that clearly belonged to themselves. There were jacks for all, the quilting in the heavy leather coats well designed to keep them warm as the metal sections sewn on the outside were designed to keep them safe – full jacks at that, with skirts to guard their lower backs, not the shorter, lighter jackets that were coming into fashion. Both Tom and Eve joined the other three in setting aside the back- and breastplates that were also on offer. They were due to travel fast and light; and, in all conscience, it would be a black heart indeed that would attack poor travellers on this of all days.

By the door, however, lay five steel bonnets in the modern burgonet design, five long lances, a couple of Jedburgh axes with their peculiar, curving blades. On the wall above these jutted a shelf on which lay three un-strung bows with quivers full of arrows, a couple of crossbows with quarrels to match and a solid-looking arquebus, flask of powder and bag of wadding and shot. Tom was really beginning to feel at home.

The door opened and a solid man entered, grey-bearded, thick-haired and wild of eye-brow. His deep-set eyes fell on Eve first and he frowned but held his peace. Then he looked across at the others. 'Hobbie,' he said, with a nod. 'Sim. Archie. Food?'

'If ye've any handy and to spare, Clem,' said Hobbie. 'We'll naw be up on the Waste afore evensong. The lass is strang enough, I doubt, but the lad here lost a deal of blood in the night.'

'There's an eel pie in the baker's oven.'

'If ye can spare a crumb of that, I know the Lord Chamberlain in London himself would be grateful.'

'I'd rather the Lord of the Waste were grateful; and certain Armstrongs and Elliots I could call to mind – in the matter of cattle particularly.'

'I'll speak for the Armstrongs,' said the man called Sim.

'And I for the Elliots,' said Archie.

'And I for the Lord of the Waste,' said Hobbie.

'And I'll still speak for the Queen herself, for the Lord of the North and for Her Majesty's Council in White Hall Palace,' said Tom, easily.

The innkeeper's eyes switched to Hobbie, his bushy eyebrows raised.

'Aye,' said Hobbie. 'He can that. D'ye no mind Long Tom Musgrave, brother to the Blacksmith of Bewcastle? He's a big man at the Queen's court these days.'

'I do,' said the innkeeper, shortly. 'Ye're welcome in my house, Master Musgrave.'

'And welcome, I hope,' said Tom in reply, 'to a flagon of your good New Castle ale to go with the crumb of your fine eel pie; but not before I ask a question of you, Master Clem.'

'And what wid that be, Master Musgrave?'

'Two men riding hard on horseback overtook us in the night. Is there any word of them here as yet?'

'None that I know of, Master. And I would know if they came or if they went.'

'Good enough. And thanks for your honesty. Now as to the other matter...'

And so it was done. With allowances being made for the importance of the Queen's business – and Her Majesty having the right to dictate in the matter, being Defender of the Faith – food and drink were served and consumed, work done and reckonings paid all at the holiest hour of the holiest of days; and weapons taken and ponies readied and mounted. So that by the time the good people of New Castle came streaming out of the South Door of St Nicholas' Church, the five weary wayfarers were gone westwards along the North Wall – the Wall built by the order of the Roman Emperor Hadrian seventeen hundred years before, that led from here to Bowness, west of Carlisle, on the south shore of the Solway Firth.

Tom had ridden the Wall as a child. Some folk never stirred more than a mile or two from their own front door through all of their lives, but Tom had always been a restless soul. The adventures in Inglewood Forest had made John seek to stay close to home, but they had done the opposite to Tom. Where John had remained on the Waste for the rest of his time on earth, Tom had come away with Hobbie, exploring the Scottish Marches as far as Edinburgh and the English Marches up to Berwick, Carlisle, New Castle and all before he was sixteen summers old – needfully so, for he had become a scholar at Carlisle Grammar School before his twelfth birthday and had trotted there and back each day thereafter. Then for a short while before his studies took him north to Glasgow, his exploration had moved to another level and had taken him less far afield. Those had been the days of dalliance with Eve Graham and a host of other beauties, from Carlisle Cross by the Solway in England to Hermitage Castle at the head of Liddesdale in Scotland.

Tom assumed leadership of the little band as of right, but he was the kind of captain content to let his command display their own strengths. He kept a clear eye on the disposition of the group, but was silently satisfied that Sim Armstrong took the lead with Hobbie close behind him and that Archie Elliot brought up the rear, allowing Tom himself to keep a closer watch upon Eve.

Once they were clear of New Castle, they used the break in the Wall, at Heddon, to cross to the sheltered south side after the first hour's riding; and they began to make good time over the flat country as it gathered gently up towards Harlow Hill. Their indefatigable little mounts jingled forward over the frost-crisp grass at a steady trot, consuming perhaps half a dozen miles in an hour, sending plumes of steam behind them, thinning away in the wind that whipped over the Wall. The distance travelled was quite easy to judge, for every thousand paces on the wall there was a small fort; and the Queen's new statute miles were based on the Roman thousand-pace miles. Soon they settled into the rhythm that Tom remembered from his youth – one fort passed every count of six hundred.

Unlike the ride up the Great North Road, there was light and space here, and, apart from the keening of the wind in the timeless stones and the distant clamour of the marsh birds down on the Tyne, it was quiet. Tom soon urged his pony up alongside Eve's so that they could talk.

'I've been wondering,' she said at once, her breath smoking up over her steel bonnet as though her throat were afire.

'About?' he asked, sending his own cloud of breath into the crackling cold of the air.

'About who stabbed you.'

'And I've been wondering why they stabbed me. But I admit to some surprise. Surely you must be wondering more urgently about John.'

'What wonder is there? The Barguest took him.'

'You believe in the Barguest?'

'You do not? Now *I* am surprised. John did. The whole of the Borders does. Those that doubted when there were only rumours on the wing are hard-certain now. Because of John. And you were right. He always believed in the thing himself. He said that you and he had seen it – once, in your childhood, away in

68

the depths of Inglewood Forest. You were lucky to escape it, he said.'

Tom rode on, silently, framing his thoughts and his words. 'We saw something,' he admitted after a while. 'But I would be loth to swear that we saw a hound of hell lately unleashed by Satan himself.'

'You saw it again in your dreams last night. You screamed and raved.'

'There's the rub,' he said. 'In my dream I saw a dream-monster. I mind it well enough from my childhood and I can call to my inward eye a picture of it as easy as looking at you. But it is still a thing of fantasy. I see what the child saw in memory and in dream; and I am no longer that child. So perhaps the man would see something different now. Does not the Bible say, "When I was a child I understood as a child – but now I am a man I must put away childish things"?'

'Then what killed my John?' Eve asked, forthrightly, 'if not the Barguest?'

'What indeed? Or who? And why?'

'The same questions you asked about that wound in your side.'

'And no coincidence, my lady. Is it not likely that when a man comes to search out the truth of his brother's death and is greeted by a dagger thrust, there may be some link between the two? That it is rather more likely there may be a link than that it is simply a coincidence of accidents? In short, that whoever slid the dagger into my side wanted to stop me looking into John's death? And that in turn makes me question the matter of hell-hounds more closely too. For if Satan sent the Barguest after John, why should Satan not do as much for me? And if a cold blade is sent instead of a monstrous dog, then it is less likely that hell is involved at all – especially as the steel went awry and left me to be nursed back to fitness in a trice. For the Devil needs no daggers.'

'And makes precious few mistakes,' admitted Eve. 'I see where logic leads you.'

Eve was quieter after that, and Tom took the initiative, as was natural with him. As they trotted down the last of the hill into the wide valley of Tynedale towards the bridge at still-distant Low Brunton, where the Wall stepped over the North Tyne, he took her through and through the events surrounding the death of his brother as far as she knew them. She was able to give him chapter and verse of what had happened after the body had been found; but unexpectedly, unsettlingly, she was less able to tell him what had happened to John immediately before. It seemed that at this season, unlike most others, their various duties were apt to keep them apart.

Three hours after they had left New Castle, they crossed the North Tyne river and began the long, steepening climb towards Stanegate. The Wall stood on their right hands, cresting the great Whin Sill whose cliffs fell increasingly precipitously as the land the five rode gathered up, extending the Wall's barrier on the north. South of them, down the increasing slope across which they were trotting with such deceptive ease following the ancient track of the Romans' Military Way, lay a great bank running parallel to the Wall itself. Beyond that, Tynedale settled in the blue-glimmering distance into the broad valley where the South Tyne wandered, curling up towards them as they rode onwards, beginning to smoke with frost mist as the sun began to settle lower, shining directly into their weeping eyes as the fourth hour of their riding became a fifth.

Tom saw Sim Armstrong turn to Hobbie and Hobbie turned to Tom, waving and calling, 'Spur on. Spur on apace!'

Tom turned to Eve and saw from her curt nod that she had heard. Tom drove his heels into his pony's flanks and the game little mount picked up the pace willingly enough. They pulled in together as their ponies cantered up the slope, and Tom, coming up on Hobbie's shoulder, saw what he and Sim could see. Through a break in the Wall called the Busy Gap, a vista northward opened over Houghton Common and the mountainous heights immediately beyond; and on the skyline there, at the one point for ten miles and more that might command a view of anyone riding the Wall down here, there sat a horseman, etched black against a sky as blue as the Virgin's robes in a stained-glass window.

'We are looked for,' said Tom to Hobbie, reining to a stand, with the others gathering

71

around him, their ponies stamping and steaming in the chilly air.

'Watched and followed. As we were at Ware.'

'D'ye think we're hunted?' wondered Sim Armstrong grimly.

Even as Sim asked the question, so the horseman seemed to settle in his saddle – turning, Tom decided; and from the midst of his black outline came a gleam of dazzling light.

'Hunted,' confirmed Tom; 'and if we can see the signal, then he's calling someone close at hand.'

'We should run for it,' said Archie Elliot at once, 'helter-skelter and each for himself. We should make Greenhead and mebbe Thirlwall Castle within the hour.'

'Haydon Bridge and Langley Castle in half that time, if we run due south,' said Sim. 'We're just coming up on the road south to Haydon.'

They would clearly both be gone; but they turned to Hobbie for a ruling. And Hobbie turned to Tom.

Tom was still looking north, watching the lone rider vanish beneath the skyline, heading away north into Scotland or coming south to join the men he had just alerted – it was impossible to say.

'Wait,' said Tom. 'Let us take thought before we take flight – for a moment at least,' he added, sensing the restlessness of the two guides as their ponies pawed the frozen turf.

'Let us say that we are hunted then. The horseman has signalled to a band of men nearby and they are coming to find us now. It would need to be a large band, would it not, to overpower five hardy and well-armed fighters such as we are. Also, it would need to be a well-chosen group, made up of men with strong bonds with each other and few wider ties. For look at us – an Armstrong and an Elliot, close kin to half of Liddesdale; a Graham, related to most of Cumberland; a noble, whose family lives all along the Lyne Rivers, Black and White – and who is owed a life debt by Jock o' the Side for getting him out of New Castle gaol – and by a goodly number of other Armstrongs to boot; and a Musgrave, close kin to the Lord of the Waste, who can by his patents, speak for the Queen and Council – though I know well enough how faint their voices will sound up here.

'So, unless we are hunted by Kerrs from Teviotdale or by Johnstones from Annandale or, God save us, by MacGregors or worse, then we are in as strong a position to talk as to fight.

'On the other hand, all of you know well – as well as the man who let us spot him before he signalled – that if we do take flight, then we must needs spread out – perhaps even split up. We will be easy to pick off and hard put to make any defence either with weapons or words. If the men who hunt us are reivers, then we will be easy to take in pairs or alone and will be caught for the blackmail or slavery in Scotland. If they be men confederated with the riders who overtook us at Ware, then we will be easier to take for questioning or worse – easy enough for us all to vanish like five puffs of smoke into any of the dungeons between this and Hermitage Hall.'

He mentioned Hermitage again calculatedly, for he wished to make his point most strongly to Archie and Sim, and both of them would know well enough about the haunted, Satanic castle that stood glowering at the head of Liddesdale, a place of infinite evil, to be talked of in whispers, owned by devil-worshippers and worse – at least one of whom had been boiled alive almost within living memory. And that, well *within* living memory, had been the haunt of Mary, Queen of Scots, and her doomed Bothwell, who had been, for a time, the captain of the place.

Of course, Tom wanted a message driven home to all here. For he reckoned it a fair wager that one of the other four watching him now owned the dagger that had been slipped into his side at Ware.

# Seven

## Fort and Farmstead

They went west away from the Busy Gap,
therefore, in a tight group with Tom at their
head, riding like the wind; and they were wise
to follow him, for it was clear to all there that,
with his reasons spoken or unspoken, here
was a mind that could marshal such strengths
as lay in their dangerous position; and that if
any could get them safely through, it was the
Lord of the Waste's nephew, who had clearly
inherited much of the old man's genius for
war.

Tom had not revealed the whole of his
thinking, in any case. For he was relying on
the childhood memories that he had called
into question with Eve. It was the same boy
who had seen and feared the massive hound
in Inglewood – and remembered it now as the
Barguest – who remembered a huge safe
fortress a little more than a mile on up the
Wall, with a two-floored bastle farmhouse
solidly built against the south wall.

Just as it was with hounds, so might it be
with ruins. He remembered the fort and

farmhouse as being a solid refuge, easy to defend, commanding the sort of salient easily raked by fire from longbow and crossbow, armed still with heavy oaken doors that might be proof against burning and walled and floored with heavy stone to two levels with a stairway almost impossible to climb leading up to the second floor, where farmers lived above their stock; a narrow, easily defended staircase overlooked in any case by an overhanging battlement from the strong slate roof. The fort had been strong enough for Hadrian's men and the bastle farmhouse would serve the five of them, if they could get safely into it. Or it would do so if it all still stood as the child in him remembered it.

Side by side Hobbie rode with him, looking along the Wall and trusting their ponies to keep their feet. 'Who farms at Housesteads now?' called Tom.

'Hugh Nixon,' came the answer.

'If he's there, would he give us shelter?'

'Depends who's coming after us. He's an Armstrong. Pays his blackmail to Jock o' the Side; and he watches the Busy Gap for him too, like as not. He'd stand with Sim and with me for the sake of the family. Unless he's a better reason not to. But he'll be down in Haltwhistle today, I'd wager. 'Tis the nearest kirk – and the nearest tavern, if ye take ma meanin'.'

'Family?'

'None as I know of.'

'Then we have our shelter, if we can reach

it before whoever hunts us comes snapping at our heels.'

'Aye. I thought as much. It's a good enough plan – and fall back into the fort itself if we cannot get up into the farmhouse? Hold out there for as long as we can?'

'And that may not be too long a time. If the men that hunt us know where we are, then, like as not, the Lord of the Waste will know it too; and know that we are hunted.'

'Ye were always a canny lad – nigh on witch-craft some days.'

They came over the crest of the hill-slope above Busy Gap as Hobbie spoke, and there before them the Wall settled down into a west-sloping valley, though beyond its broad grey eminence immediately to the north there still fell a considerable cliff. On the side of the valley, reaching southward at an angle from the Wall itself, stood the ruined Roman fort; and against the outer wall of the fortification, in the strongest possible defensive spot, stood the solid little farmhouse for which Hugh Nixon paid his rent to some local landlord living down in Carlisle, like as not, and his blackmail to Jock o' the Side Armstrong living up in Liddesdale – and spied for him on the comings and goings through the busiest gap in the Wall.

Tom's thoughts were interrupted at once by Hobbie's urgent call of, 'There!'

Away at the foot of the slope in the hazy distance a solid group of riders was spurring up out of the frost mist over the lowlands called Beggar's Bog. No sooner had Hobbie called out than the gathering wind stopped whimpering through the Wall beside them and backed, so that the thunder of hooves on the iron-hard ground was carried up to them.

With no further word, the little group spurred on. It would be a close-run matter, for the distances looked about the same, but at least they were riding downhill. The lay-out of the fort would help them too, for the hunters would have to skirt three sides of the fortification while Tom's little command were heading straight for the foot of the steps leading up to the stout oak door.

Down to these steps they came, even as their enemies reached the far side of the ruin and began to come round the outer walls towards them. Here there was a big door that stood open, for Hugh Nixon had no stock in the byre at present. Tom leaped down and ran up the steps while the others helped Hobbie get their horses in.

At the top of the steps stood a solid door, closed tight. Tom, trained in the black arts by two London lock-picks, threw himself to his knees and pushed his dagger into the massive mechanism of the lock. He was feeling for the tumblers that would pull back the bolt when Eve reached over his shoulder and turned the handle. The big portal swung open with a scream that would have appalled the devil himself. 'He pays his blackmail to Jock o' the Side,' she said. 'No one's likely to take anything in here.

'Unless he has some secret fortune hidden away,' she continued as the pair of them stepped into the little room and were joined by Sim and Archie, 'then there'll be nothing worth risking the wrath of the Armstrongs over.'

'Sim, close the door,' said Tom and the big reiver dropped a solid balk of wood into two brackets across the door as Tom pulled up a trap in the floor – the only part of the floor not made of stone – and signalled Archie to pull up the weapons that Hobbie was unloading from the horses and passing up out of the byre below.

Then he joined Eve at the narrow window that looked due south, just as a dozen riders pulled up at the foot of the wall. For a moment words would have been wasted amid the snorting and the stamping of the steaming horses; but then a kind of quiet settled.

Tom had to break it, of course, for he did not want the riders to realize just what a range of weaponry was coming up through the trapdoor with Hobbie: 'My name is Tom Musgrave, kin to the Blacksmith of Bewcastle and the Lord of the Waste, messenger to the Lord of the North and the Queen and her Council. Is it me that you seek, gentlemen?'

In the continued silence that answered his announcement, he gave the birth, lineage and alliances of the other four as well, for he had not been speaking in jest when he had said how wide their web of family and influence might spread across the border; and if anything went wrong, there was the birth of a fair few feuds in prospect here. 'Think well what you are about, gentlemen,' he warned, 'for the shedding of our blood will beget the shedding of yours – and blood to be shed for generations to come.'

In a lower voice he said to the others as they joined him at last, 'Do you know any of these men?' – only to be answered by shakes of the head. Hardly surprising, for they all rode heavily cloaked – against the cold if nothing else. It was impossible to see either face or any significant detail of person or clothing – and Tom had been trying to the top of his bent since he arrived at the window.

Tom's eyes narrowed now, his brain still racing. The men gave the impression of having paused, nonplussed. They did not seem to be waiting as part of any plan or for any purpose, nor in expectation of any new arrival – though, he calculated, it might just be possible they were waiting for the man who had given the signal.

Now might be the time to test their resolve, however, he thought, as even Eve joined the other three stringing the longbows and winding up the crossbows. Before they made up their minds to action, he could test the riders' mettle, test their own armaments and start his own blood feud all at once.

'Pass the arquebus,' he ordered quietly, and his nose wrinkled at once with the stench of the match being lit even as he felt it pressed into his hand. He laid it on the sill of the narrow window and took aim at the foremost of the riders, even as that worthy swung round to direct some gruff orders to the others. The match came into the pan and the powder exploded at once, mercifully expelling most of the thunderous noise and resultant smoke with the shot.

The leader of the riders was blasted back out of his saddle and sent rolling across his horse's hindquarters into the face of the horse in his rear. That horse reared, unseating its rider in turn, and all the other ten plunged and curveted, shocked by the noise and the action.

'Did ye see that?' asked Hobbie.

'Aye,' said Tom, regressing through ten years of courtly education. 'Tartan under the cloak. They're Kerrs.'

'Kerrs right enough,' said Hobbie; and he pronounced the name 'Cur', which showed his opinion of the clan.

'Have you killed him?' demanded Eve.

'With this?' laughed Tom. 'Only if he's mad enough to rely on plaid instead of plating.' He struck the metal plates on his own chest even as the fallen man amid the scattering horses rolled over and began to pick himself up.

'Now, Master Kerr,' he called, pronouncing the name 'Car' as the Kerrs preferred. 'We have longbows and crossbows enough up here to put holes in your jacks, breastplates and hides enough. We have provender, water and a lively expectation of help at hand. Will you depart, will you parley or will you die?

The choice is yours, and is only offered out of respect for the holy season.'

'You are grown into a braggart, I see,' said Eve quietly at his shoulder. He put out his hand and she put a crossbow into it.

'Hobbie, who is the man amongst the Kerrs most likely to be at the head of such a band? Do you know?'

'I know few enough of the rogues,' growled Hobbie, 'but I would say Little Dand is your man.'

'So, then, Little Dand Kerr,' continued Tom, 'I see you have recovered your wind and your wits well enough to stand. But I warn you that you stand beneath the point of my quarrel with my finger on the trigger of my crossbow here. And I still await your decision and your reply.'

He dropped his voice again. 'Sim, Archie, keep an eye on the rest of the rogues. They'll be getting into positions if they mean to fight. Hobbie, you go up and overlook the steps and doors. You prefer the longbow, I recall.'

'Aye,' came Hobbie's distant voice, from high behind Tom as though the little reiver were halfway to heaven after all. A sigh of icy wind seemed to whistle through the place and he was gone behind the battlement on the roof.

No sooner was he up there than a voice called over the restless keening of the wind: 'Ye're in the right of it, Master Musgrave. My name is Little Dand and I lead the Kerrs who stand around ye. But 'tis not my breast that

82

stands beneath yer quarrel. So, here's the start of the bad blood between us.'

'Rider coming in!' called Archie.

Tom had already seen him, thundering in from the right hand, low over his pony's withers, reaching down to grab the man standing helplessly in the line of fire and swing him up behind him. It was a daring act, arrogant and masterful. Tom saw instinctively that he could not allow it to succeed, for it was finely calculated to give heart to the nonplussed Kerrs and demoralize his own small band.

The alternatives were immediately obvious to him: kill the man, kill Little Dand or kill the horse. It would be an act of charity to kill the beast, a beautiful but soulless section of creation, if by doing so he could preserve the lives and souls of the men involved. Just at the moment the two men took hold of each other he fired.

But at that very same moment Eve, standing close behind him, unused, perhaps, to the tension such critical moments can bring, stirred and struck the crossbow's stock, so that Tom's aim was knocked awry.

Such was the tension in Tom's long body, however, that his aim was moved only infinitesimally; but enough to make all the difference. The heavy metal of the solid-steel quarrel sped with shocking speed and power towards a point just behind the horse's withers. Here Little Dand had grasped at once the reins and the solid pommel of the saddle with his left hand, as he reached downwards with his right. The quarrel hit hand, rein and pommel, just as Dand took his friend and was jerked right back in the saddle. The impact of the missile splintered the saddle, sundered the reins and shattered the hand all at once. The stump of the arm jerked up, all anchor and purchase gone in a twinkling. Little Dand Kerr was whipped backwards over the rump of his horse to tumble atop the man he had risked all to rescue, screaming with a mixture of shock, agony and frustration. The horse stumbled, regained its footing and ran on, leaving a heaving pile of entangled humanity in its wake, still solidly in the field of fire as Tom, silently, white with shock himself, reached back to his stunned sister for the last loaded crossbow.

'Sim?' he yelled.

'All still.'

'Archie?'

'The same.'

'Hobbie?'

'They're on their knees from what I can see. Saying a prayer, like as not, for protection against the dark arts. That shot was pure witchcraft.'

'Blind luck, helped by my sister's elbow. If there's a witch involved, then it is she,' said Tom, still stunned.

'No!' cried Sim. 'They're up. Now what's toward?'

'Hobbie? Can you see?' called Tom.

'Naw, but I can hear. There's horses coming along the wall. Coming up from Haltwhistle, I'd say.'

'The Lord of the Waste – or his men, like as not.'

'Whoever it is it's put the fear of God into the Kerrs. The whole pack of them are scurrying away back down towards Beggar's Bog.'

'That just leaves Little Dand and his companion,' said Tom, squinting down at the two of them there.

'Ye'd be best to finish the job and kill them now,' advised Hobbie grimly. 'It's bad blood indeed when a man is crippled. He'll be stirring up the Kerrs to come against you and yours until the thing is settled anyways. Settle it now and save yourself some grief.'

The slight figure Tom had struck with the ball from his arquebus and that Dand had tried to rescue had taken off its cloak to wrap it around the ruined hand. Little more than a lad, he stood tall and strong, with black hair seeming to soak up even the light of the setting sun. Tom looked at Eve and saw her frozen, horrified face, wide eyes resting on him still full of what she had done – and made him do.

'I cannot,' said Tom.

'I can,' grated Hobbie. 'Both of them in half a minute, for I have the longbow here...'

'*No!*' cried Eve. 'Hobbie! Think of the day!'

And so, when the Lord of the Waste arrived with his score of mounted men-at-arms reinforced by volunteers from Haltwhistle – Hugh Nixon himself amongst them – he found the little band in no need of his protection after all.

Tom tersely explained what had happened, and Hobbie advised Hugh to pass the message up to Jock o' the Side that the Kerrs had come and gone through the Busy Gap at the orders of men unknown about evil in spite of the goodness of the day – had come down led by Little Dand Kerr, but had gone back led by One-Hand Dand, which nickname would follow him through the Borders for what little time the Good Lord continued to allow him life.

# Eight

## The Castle on the Waste

As darkness fell, the twenty-five riders that made up the Lord of the Waste's party turned on to the Roman road above Gilsland village that led like a bowshot across the Waste to the castle of Bewcastle five miles distant. They had changed horses in Gilsland at the expense of Tom's uncle, who had been made expansive by relief and joy at the rescue, and the new ponies were fresh. They would be home in an hour. Even so, in the village itself they had bought flambards and these they lit as the last of the light bled away low on their right, and rode within two roaring, unsteady columns of golden light.

Tom would have known the uncle after whom he was named anywhere. Sir Thomas Musgrave, Captain of Bewcastle, was a tall, straight man approaching his fiftieth year with as much virile vigour as Lord Henry Carey, the Lord of the North, to whom he reported so regularly. His head wore a cap of steel grey, curling hair that seemed to make his steel bonnet unnecessary. He wore his beard in the full, square-cut fashion of an earlier time. His nose was an eagle's beak, broken out of line. His lips and eyes were narrow, the latter guarded and calculating, even when, as now, twinkling with expansive good humour. He was a kind of mirror to Tom, showing the younger man how he would look in twenty-five years or so, if he survived the intervening time.

But if Tom remembered his uncle almost perfectly, he found he had all but forgotten his domain. He had forgotten how much of a waste the Waste of Bewcastle really was. The last glimmers of day before the flambards were lit exposed in its blood-red light a heave of desolation fit to flatten the cheeriest soul; a frost-bound desert moorland stretching up before them and away on either hand, wrinkled more than valleyed, with sparse woods where the land folded down; full of hummocks and hollows, the latter gathering mist to their grassy bottoms, low pools of mist set writhing and roiling by the bitterly incessant wind – mist that warned of water in the deadly traps of quick marsh there, bottomless bog-holes designed by the devil himself to suck the unwary to hell; and here and there above them as the blackness closed in, those gleaming little fires, lethal will o' the wisps, that had tempted many a benighted traveller to stumble blindly to his death.

Yet the desolation was not without its signs of humanity. The road along which their ponies trotted, though grassed over centuries since, was still a road easily discernible across the wild heave of the moorland, telling of the hand of ancient man; and beside it, moving out and away in fathomless patterns across the Waste were standing stones, great burial mounds, the half-open wrecks of ancient huts and habitations. And – who knew? – of pagan temples, where unrecorded blasphemies had been committed to the worship of long-for-gotten deities before the one true God had been revealed to the long-dead inhabitants of the place.

But, thought Tom grimly, that Holy revelation had led the natives – among whose later generations he must himself be counted – to build castles, not kirks. In years to come, he suspected, when he and his were dust, there would be ten ruined forts to be counted here for every ruined church.

As darkness fell, the wind came up more fiercely than ever, setting the flambards' flames to battering and roaring, and howling in the distant crags and caverns like the Barguest out and hunting – the Barguest with its pack of spectral hounds, all in full cry together and at once. The sound – the Barguest itself – seemed the very soul of the place. It had been easy enough down in London, and even on the road north, to talk to Eve about his unreliable memories of childhood, for he simply now refused to admit such a thing could exist, even though he remembered seeing it with his own eyes. He was, in much of his thinking, a rational humanist, given that he was a man of his times – given, therefore, his solid Protestant faith. He saw nothing in his Bible, and heard nothing in the commentaries that expounded it to him every Sabbath and each holy day, about great ghostly dogs; but up here – up here on the Waste where it was said to be hunting and the devil did, in all conscience, seem very near indeed ... things might well be different up here on the Waste.

Tom had to begin something of a reassessment of his gloomy thoughts as soon as they arrived at Bewcastle itself. The grim old fortress had been softened by a sprawl of outbuildings extending from the outer walls, whose occupants would retire within the castle itself as soon as danger threatened, no doubt. Even so, the presence of the byres, workshops, stores and dwellings bespoke a time of restful peace in the recent past at least, for they would make useful cover and dangerous kindling for any serious besieger of the fort; and the look of them, from the distance, lamps and torches lending the brightness of a golden necklace, bestowed an almost festive air to the craggy old walls.

Within the walls themselves, the first thing Tom saw and heard as he trotted with the others under the great portcullis of the gate, squarely in the corner opposite the main building of the keep, beside the stabling and the castle smithy, was the chapel. As the portcullis grated down behind them, shutting them in and the fears of the holy but haunted night outside, so he heard the bell begin to ring, summoning them all to prayer. At the door to the chapel they were greeted by the Lady Ellen whom Tom remembered from childhood, a round, apple-cheeked woman, with a warm heart and boundless good intentions that sometimes overstretched her ability to fulfil them. She gave him a hug that threatened to tear his side open and a smacking kiss that caused the priest to turn and frown – and thus Tom recognized yet another old friend. Father Little had educated him from his first catechism until Carlisle Grammar School had seduced him far away.

It was into the chill, bare garrison chapel that they repaired as soon after dismounting as nature would allow, to celebrate an evensong extended and illuminated by a service of thanksgiving for their delivery from the Kerrs and safe arrival now. As Tom stood shoulder to shoulder with the little garrison and their guests, listening to the short sermon expounding on the Christmas text set down for the day, he was struck by the manner in which even here his uncle's old-fashioned tastes almost thoughtlessly dictated what went on. The service was from the old Prayer Book, with much less accommodation to Catholic sensibilities than the new one. The priest was a solid, down-to-earth lowland Scot, as Tom knew well, a man walking warily – sensibly – in the footsteps of Calvin and his Scottish acolyte John Knox. But little hellfire and damnation was called down, and when the congregation – and he called them his congregation – was called forward to the Eucharist, Tom saw that the priest was of that number who allowed the consecrated bread and the wine to touch the lips of everyone at worship; even of Eve and the other women, led by the Lady Ellen, not Sir Thomas's wife (the old man was single and childless), but a widowed sister who kept house for him. Lady Ellen was likely to be the busiest person in Bewcastle during the next twelve days, thought Tom, with a glow of affection. The priest was content to let them take their place where they stood in the order of communicants – not saving them for last as lesser souls, as some did.

By the end of the service, exhaustion and starvation were at war within Tom's sagging body, fighting it out to see which would claim him first. Exhaustion was not an option, though, for as they came out of the chapel into the central square of the ancient fortification, the Captain of Bewcastle clapped him on the shoulder.

'Matters of the spirit being satisfied, lad, let us turn to matters of the flesh, eh?' boomed Sir Thomas Musgrave. 'Even in these sad times. My Lady Ellen, is all prepared?'

'It is, Sir Thomas, as ever,' sang back the fair Ellen.

Three sides of the hall had been laid out for the Christmas feast. The top table sat raised on a dais and the two lesser tables stretched down the hall from the ends of that one, with trenchers, chairs and benches arranged down the outer sides only, leaving in the centre a broad area where servants could pass and entertainments be offered. Sir Thomas himself arranged those few who did not already know the order of their degrees at the table – Tom on his right hand, as honoured guest, and Eve, to her evident surprise and confusion, on Tom's right.

In the brief interim between the service and the supper, when the travellers had been shown their accommodation and allowed leisure for quick ablutions, Tom had taken a moment to rearrange his clothing, assess the damage to his linen done by the blood of his wound and readjust the bandages that held it stiff but safe. Of course, his aunt Ellen came to see how he did and to make sure he stood well aware that the offices of the fort – basic though they must seem after London and the Court – were all at his service. He warned her about the state of his linen but assured her that the wound itself was trifling. Then, fit for the court in all but his lack of face powder, he descended with her on his arm.

He did so to discover that Eve had changed out of her travelling clothes into the plain dress of green, blue and lavender squares in which she sat beside him now, which Tom recognized as the Graham tartan. Beyond his silent sister stood an empty place, in memory of his dead brother, and beyond that sat Hobbie.

Tom tore his eyes away from the vacant seat

and looked around the hall. Here at the muted Christmas celebration he would expect to find the men closest to his uncle, and their wives. Order of precedence – as important here as at Her Majesty's Court – would dictate that, apart from honoured guests, relatives and their widows, the men seated closest to Sir Thomas would be the men who held most power from him. On any other occasion, in any other circumstance, he might have expected a reception line where, at his uncle's side, he would have made the formal acquaintance of these men; but things had fallen out differently tonight. Even the Lady Ellen was seated on the far side of his uncle, so any enquiries he had for her must needs be shouted across him. Tom must needs make use of Eve, therefore, in the times when Sir Thomas was not honouring him with his attention, and find out who else held what power within the keep and upon the Waste of Bewcastle.

The two that sat closest, beyond Lady Ellen on Sir Thomas's left hand, were a short, square man with a wrinkled, jowly bulldog's face, and a tall, square-jawed soldier, captain under Sir Thomas of the band that had saved them from the Kerrs.

The bulldog had not come with the rescuers, so his role in the castle was not military. Financial or organizational, then. Eve identified him as William Fenwick, the laird's factor, by which Tom understood at once that this was his uncle's agent, who ran his farms, dealt with his tenants, collected his rents and balanced his books – who took care of the business that Sir Thomas had no leisure or inclination to do for himself.

Fenwick the Factor was clearly a man of importance here, but he did not take up as much of Tom's attention as the other man – the soldier. Whenever Tom looked up, it seemed that the soldier was watching him with a brooding, almost threatening intensity. He wore a doublet of military cut – almost a jacket – and a sword. Most of the men at the table sat down still armed, a breach of etiquette that would never have been allowed in London at a formal occasion such as this; but this man's sword was unusual. It was a basket-hilted broadsword, thick of back and sharp of blade with a curve like a Jedburgh axe. Tom had heard swords like this called claymores, though the name was also applied to the big two-handed highland battle-sword; and from the look of things, this was a potent man-killer, no matter what you called it. 'That's Geordie Burn,' Eve told him later, 'captain of horse.' But no sooner had she given him the information than Tom made the more intimate acquaintance of Captain Burn, and of his claymore.

The feast itself began with a loyal toast, drunk to Her Majesty in good French wine, followed by another to the guests and a third to the season, and the feasting began when the porpoise was brought to the high table for Sir Thomas to carve. The porpoise seemed to have been baked in the bread oven recently vacated of the black bread trenchers sliced on the wooden ones before them. Sir Thomas took a fat slice of the choicest section behind the creature's head, and passed some, with due ceremony and courtesy, to Lady Ellen first, then to Tom and Eve. Then, as the fish, in increasing stages of dismemberment, worked its way down the table, those first served fell to eating. The porpoise was followed by a spiced pottage of oats and codfish. Again, the course began at the head of the table and worked its way slowly down. In old-fashioned ceremony, which seemed to suit very well with the way Sir Thomas ordered everything, the pottage was succeeded increasingly rapidly with baked herring, stewed lampreys and a huge eel pie. At this season there could be none of the sallets of fresh herbs Tom had learned to love in his Italian tutelage, and on this particular day Sir Thomas had ordered there be no flesh served; but the boiled bream and gurnards were at last succeeded with some winter-stored apples and wrinkled warden pears.

As each of the courses was removed from the bottom of the tables, so a toast was drunk, and Tom was soon very glad of the presence on table of flagons of good clean spring water with which the borderers mixed their wine – unlike Londoners, who would dare do no such thing with the foul liquid pumped out of the Thames.

As stomachs filled and the pace of consumption slowed, so conversation flowed. And when that too began to ebb, Sir Thomas called for entertainment. The first part of the entertainment was Sir Thomas's minstrel. Accompanying himself on the harp, this elderly worthy gave them 'The Ballad of Christmas Morning', then, less seasonably, 'The Ballad of Judas' Bargain'. After his songs, he juggled to great acclaim with some half-dozen naked daggers and completed his performance by executing a series of hand-stands on the points of ancient but sharp-looking swords. Next, one of the castle children, tutored by the priest of the kirk who accompanied him on a simple pipe, sang a pretty carol, of a dangerously Romish charac-ter, the youthful Protestant churches being as yet ill served in musical matters. A small con-sort of viols arrived and two pairs of soldiers got up and danced a reel. Two more got up and fell to wrestling, and it was something of a shock to Tom when he recognized them as his drivers and bodyguards Sim Armstrong and Archie Elliot. Pipers played. The last of the food was cleared. To the strains of the pipe, usquebaugh was brought, a rare treat here, and consumed both neat and – by Tom at least, and blessedly – diluted with yet more spring water.

After the whisky there was more wrestling, and another dance. This was done by two bare-footed men who leaped nimbly around swords laid at various dangerous angles upon the floor. The whole thing looked as risky as the minstrel's handstand and Tom was surprised that the floor was not littered with fingers and toes when it was done.

Then, after the sword dance, Captain Burn stood up. 'With your permission, Sir Thomas,' he said, and turned to Tom, frowning slightly. 'Master Musgrave. Your fame, sir, has come before you back to the place of your birth. You are a Master of the Ancient Masters in the Art and Science of Defence, much spoken of, I understand, at Court and upon the public stages of London itself. I wonder, sir, if you would edify us all, by demonstrating your mastery. Here. Now. Upon myself and my own blade.'

Of course, Tom could have pleaded the journey – the wound. He was exhausted, stiff and sore. In London he might have done so; but he was far from London now – as far as he had been in his youth as a volunteer in the Lowlands, at the battle of Nijmagen where his road to fame had begun. This was a garrison at the lonely heart of a dangerous place – none more so in all the kingdom, save a ship or two off the Spanish coast. This was a place where courteous pleasantries must needs take second place to the imperative of knowing your men – knowing who will stand with you and who will not, who will guard your life and who will lose it. If he was to be tested, he thought, then let it be sooner rather than later. Let it be now, in fact.

'Well, I am for you, Captain Burn, with all my heart,' he said and rose. 'With the licence of the Lord of the Waste and the Lady Ellen, of course.'

Sir Thomas nodded, smiling slightly with his narrow lips if not quite with his narrow eyes. Lady Ellen's eyes were anything but narrow, and her face was a picture of motherly concern.

Tom walked slowly round the right side of the table as Burn came round the left. As he moved, Tom unloosed his doublet so that as he came on to the piste between the tables, when all eyes were on him he could pull it off and lay it aside. A hiss of shock whispered round the table as the expectant audience saw the great red-brown stain on his shirt where his blood had dried. The Lady Ellen screamed – though that, mused Tom with an inward smile, could well have been the thought of the washing.

'You have been wounded, sir,' observed Burn.

'A scratch, Captain. Part of last night's adventurings. Sewn closed by the lady Eve and by Hobbie Noble there. Think no more of it.' As he spoke, he eased his back and shoulders, stretching the long-stiff muscles there, and made a pass or two as though he held a sword to see how his legs would react. They held up commendably and he began to think he might still do himself some credit. Escaping without being crippled would be a good start, he thought. 'Your blade is not protected, Captain, and neither is my own. Would you prefer to rely on skill? Or take assurance with a jacket, perhaps.'

'Oh, a pass or two at play, sir. Surely we may rely upon our skill?'

'As you wish.' Tom took off his sword belt as he spoke and slid the long Solingen blade out of its scabbard with a lingering hiss to echo the sound that had gone round the room at the sight of his bloodstained clothes. He wound his hand into the intricacies of the Ferrara silver basket of the hilt and wrapped fingers and thumb into their allotted hooks and handles. With his back casually to his opponent, he performed a series of more testing passes, frowning with concentration as he assessed what his saddle-sore buttocks and thighs could stand and what his side was like to allow him to do before it tore open again. Faster and faster he moved, easing and warming his muscles, only distantly aware of the hypnotic power his flashing point seemed to be having on his audience, particularly at the high table.

When at last Tom turned, he found Captain Burn ready and waiting for him, a little stiffly, in the high ward, as befitted such an elderly, heavy weapon. Tom moved to his own guard, and chose the hanging ward, with his point deceptively low. As soon as he was in position, he said to his opponent, 'Are you ready, Captain?'

A nod in reply, as slight as Hobbie Noble's jerk of the head; and following the action, the claymore came down in a blow that would have made old George Silver proud. But the fighting technique was as out of date as the sword and the English fencing master whose *Paradoxes of Defence* was the bible for an earlier generation. Tom turned the edge of the heavy weapon aside with the surprisingly resilient length of his own sword and stepped back – rather than stepping in to run his opponent through in the *coup de main* that would have ended the matter had this been a fight to the death.

Captain Burn recovered and resumed his guard, seemingly unaware how close to death he had passed. Frowning, he assumed the same dangerous high ward as before. Tom this time settled into the slightly more force-ful open ward. His eyes focused on the point of the claymore as he waited the one beat Burn would take before launching his second attack. It came, cunningly flashing out to the right and swinging in to Tom's head as it came; but Tom's head was long gone. The instant the blade point stirred, Tom threw himself forward. He had the measure of the man and of his weapon technique now. As he moved, so his left hand reached out blindly but unerringly.

So that when Captain Burn completed his blow he found that his sword hilt was held by Tom's firm grip and the needle point of his opponent's rapier stood within a hair's breadth of his right eye, so close that when he blinked he felt it with his lashes. He dis-engaged and stepped back, shocked, unable to overlook how close he had come to losing much more than an exhibition bout. His mouth opened, but if he said anything the words were lost beneath the applause of the audience.

'But this would never serve in battle, Captain,' said Tom quietly as the clapping died. 'My blade is all very well for a show on the stage or the piste – for an exhibition or a duel. Were we to front each other on the battlefield, however, then yours would have the edge.'

What the embarrassed captain would have said to that Tom was never to find out, for as Burn drew breath to answer, a servant burst into the hall. 'There's fifty Kerrs at the gate, My Lord, and they want the man that crippled Dand.'

This time, when the Lady Ellen screamed, Tom knew it was nothing to do with the washing.

# Nine

## The Price of a Hand

During the feasting and the entertainments
the wind had strengthened and the temperature had plunged even further. The sky was
speckled with fiery brightness overhead and
the moon was westering behind them, almost
full and incredibly bright in the crystal clarity
of the wind-scoured air; but something huge
and threatening was stamping out the stars in
the northern sky, over the lands whence the
Kerrs had come.

They sat in a great black mass outside the
Bewcastle gate now. Because of the massive
moon it was possible to see areas of brightness – steel bonnets agleam and cold eyes
glittering just beneath; pale faces with down-
turned mouths. Above them a great cloud of
smoke and steam gathered palely, as though
they had brought some of that threatening
cloud cover south with them.

Tom stood atop the great gate with Sir
Thomas by his side. Both had come – with
the others – straight from the hall, and were
dressed for feasting not fighting. Tom and Sir

Thomas stood up here apparently alone in the bright moonlight, but on Sir Thomas's other side a stream of quiet men came and whispered and went, and in the keep behind them, everything was silently astir. Much of the action, Tom noticed, seemed to centre around the rear of the silent smithy and he surmised there must be a secret passageway of some sort there.

Tom still wore only his bloodstained shirt, carried only his naked blade, and the cold cut through him like the blade itself, seeming to strike at his bones and his vitals; but the tension of the situation, the sudden, over-whelming danger he had brought on Bew-castle almost the very instant he arrived did more to snatch his breath away than the ice-laden wind.

'Who speaks for the Kerrs?' bellowed Sir Thomas.

' 'Tis I, as ye well know, Sir Thomas: Hugh of Stob,' came a cold, calculating, elderly voice from the anonymous heart of the mass of horsemen, 'and I call for the man that took young Dand's hand.'

Tom would have stepped forward at that, but his uncle's hand held him hard back. 'Ye make it sound like a wedding, Hugh,' said Sir Thomas easily, not at all disturbed by the stirring of outrage that went through the squadron of warlike reivers below.

'And if ye make light of the matter, Sir Thomas, then ye'll find that yer wit's not the only thing will catch light this night.'

'You mistake my purpose, Hugh. I meant that, were the affair to be seen as a wedding of sorts, then it might be amenable to a marriage settlement, of sorts.'

'A settlement, ye say?' A hint of avarice affirmed both the age and the Scottishness of the man in Tom's eyes; and just at that moment someone came close up behind Tom himself with his great travelling cloak, so that he stepped back into the shadows and became one with them as he wrapped the heavy woollen warmth around himself.

'Everyone pays the blackmail to someone, Hugh,' continued Sir Thomas. 'Some men pay it to prevent such matters arising, and some men might pay it in reparation for damage done; but call it a settlement for the sake of fair words this holy night.'

'A settlement. And how much of a settlement had ye in mind?'

'He's your lad, Hugh. 'Tis your hand, therefore. Name your price and we'll get down to business. Or is young Dand there with you? He may name his own price if he is.'

'He's not here,' came a new voice, young and clear; 'but I'll speak for him. He lost his hand saving me at Housesteads.'

'That's for you to decide, Hugh. I'll settle with you or with the lad, but when I settle, I settle for all and there's an end to the matter.'

Sir Thomas stepped back at that and dropped his voice. 'That'll give them something to think over, but it'll not keep them occupied for long. We must stay here to keep

105

the pretence alive, but your jack will be up soon with a breastplate and backplate to boot. I'd hoped young Eve would stay to help you slip into the gear quietly, but she and Hobbie have disappeared. D'ye use those pretty pricks of yours in battle or would ye rather a man's sword like Geordie Burn's? I'd stay clear of Geordie if it comes to close work, mind: he'll not have forgiven you for besting him at those passes just now.'

There was time for no more speech, for Hugh of Stob was calling up again: 'He'll no be able to farm again, mind.'

'He never farmed in his life, Hugh. He reived and he whored and that was the sum of it. He can still hold a sword and he can still clasp a wench. It was his hand he lost, not his prick.'

'But a hand's a hand for all that. And there's the saddle to be thought of...'

'He's making time, sir,' breathed Tom. 'He has spies out, engineers coming among your outbuildings with petards like as not.'

'Aye,' breathed the Captain of Bewcastle, every inch the fighting commander. 'That, or he's sent elsewhere for more men.'

'Or both,' answered Tom, every inch his kin.

'We've saddles aplenty here, Hugh – the equal of Dand's, I've no doubt. Why, he can even take the great saddle I keep for my great black stallion when I go to the hunt with my hounds. Take it and welcome, though it would spoil my plans for the morrow; but I see you hesitate, for the saddle's not the issue.

106

It's the matter of the hand, man, and the settlement for that.'

Tom felt a stirring at his back and slipped the cloak off his shoulders, then surrendered his rapier to shrug on a quilted, steel-covered jack like the one he had worn along the wall. Backplate was pressed in place as he fastened it, then breastplate slipped on and belted tight as his rapier was retrieved before a freezing bonnet was placed on his head, the thick leather lining as cold and hard as if it had been steel itself.

'One way or another we're out of time, sir,' he said to Sir Thomas.

'A moment more, lad,' said Sir Thomas, glancing back over his shoulder. 'We need a moment more...'

Tom took his cloak, wrapping it over his armour as he pulled off the bonnet and stepped forward in front of his uncle, apparently dressed for the cold, not for battle. 'I'm the man you seek, Hugh of Stob: Tom Musgrave, Master of Defence.' He thrust himself into full view and saw the ghost of his shadow before him, knowing he was framed against the moon. 'I took One-Hand Dand's hand because he sought to take my life. He was lucky I let him live, for he was set against me and he knew as well as you all do that I am a messenger for the Queen and the Council, carrying letters from the Lord of the North. Be careful what you stir up here, for you will follow the fate of Kerr of Ferniehurst, who marched with the rebel Dacre when I was

107

nobbut a lad, and find your own Hell Beck at his hands. You sound like an ageing man, Hugh of Stob. You saw, I doubt not, what the Lord of the North left of Dacre's rebel army after the battle at Hell Beck; and I'll lay you were lucky indeed not to be amongst those left to rot there or strung up later by himself and Lord Scrope. Think on this, Hugh of Stob – and the rest of you. Is one Kerr hand worth a hundred Kerr necks?' He pronounced the name as Hobbie had done – 'Cur' like a worthless dog.

The Kerrs gave a great shout of outrage at this and all surged forward, every eye among them fastened on the turncoat Musgrave, who had started out one of their own but changed into an arrogant southern courtier now.

And that sat perfectly with the Captain of Bewcastle's plan, for, echoing the shout of rage with a great whoop of attack, the Bewcastle garrison's horsemen came thundering up the little valley that led round from the secret Gully Hole exit on the south side of the castle and debauched on to the flat area outside the main gate. With Geordie Burn himself in the lead, and the shrug of a little hillside behind them to shadow their numbers, the twenty horsemen hit the fifty Kerrs like a thunderbolt. The power of the charging Bewcastle horses shocked the sedentary Kerrs terribly. Tom had bewitched all their eyes so that the wild charge came as a complete surprise. The reiver ranks broke and the black phalanx of the Scottish horse shattered into a morass of melees down the slopes away to the south and east of the ancient keep.

The portcullis of the main gate screamed up at once and Sir Thomas led the foot soldiers out with Tom at his side. In the moonlight it was impossible to tell friend from foe – particularly for the men on foot. Sir Thomas showed the way, however, for every time he threw himself towards a fighting knot of men he called 'The Gravel', and one or other of the combatants answered 'The Waste!', and the hardy old soldier struck at once at the man who did not answer.

'The Grave!' called Tom, charging past Sir Thomas at the nearest group of riders. 'The Waste!' answered the nearest, and Tom thrust his rapier unerringly through thigh, saddle-bag and horse of the next man beyond. The effect was so swift and spectacular that he lost his weapon at once – and near lost the hand that held it, like Dand Kerr had done. The pony collapsed, stone dead upon the spot, trapping the rider's good leg while the other jerked spasmodically, emitting a throbbing spring of blood. The dying man clamped his hands over his wound and let fall a ten-foot spear as he did so. Tom grabbed this and drove the butt end of it against the fallen man's forehead, stunning him as he jerked his rapier free once more; but then he slipped his sword into the belt of his breastplate and held on to the spear as being better suited to attacking horsemen – and easier to replace if lost in the fray.

Then his better angel prompted him to check on the state of his late foe. As he bent to do this, a blade whispered past his head and smashed into the armour on his shoulder where breastplate and backplate met. He turned, and for an instant could have sworn he was looking up into the face of the man he had just helped – Captain Geordie Burn; but then the battle eddied like a river in spate and the two were swept apart. 'The Grave!' he called again, and was off into the thick of it once more.

So things proceeded for an uncounted time. Call and counter-call led Tom from one little melee to another, and he stabbed upwards with increasing confidence and accuracy, unseating horseman after horseman. But the battle was by no means going all one way: the little garrison were heavily outnumbered and the Kerrs had not ridden in alone – as both Tom and Sir Thomas had known all too well. Nor were they stupid or slow-witted men. At last exhausted, Tom called out, 'The Grave!'

'The Waste!' came a hoarse voice from across a little space. Tom turned towards it, eyes busy looking for enemies he might help his companion overcome; but instead he saw with horror that the outbuildings behind the horseman were alight. His attention distracted and his own wits slowed by fatigue, Tom was slow to see what was happening. The horseman who had answered him swung round into the charge and came full at him.

Like Tom, he was armed with a lance, but this one was thirteen feet long and was couched four feet up from the ground and pointing unerringly at his breast.

It was at that moment that Tom remembered riding with Hobbie as a young man, learning from the old master how to spear salmon in the Black Lyne river – spearing quick wild salmon in the brown water, from horseback, with a spear exactly like this one; and he knew that he was dead, but he also knew what he must do to die with honour. The butt of his own spear slammed to the ground and his right foot stamped down upon it. Out stretched his left arm, angling the spearpoint down so that its solid, steel-tipped length pointed directly at the pit of the galloping pony's throat. He raised the Jedburgh axe, turned his body a little to offer a surface that a spear might glance off, gritted his teeth and stood ready for the shock.

# Ten

## Hobbie Noble and the Barguest

Tom was ready for a shock from the front – and was within an instant of receiving it – when he was hit from the back instead – hit from the back and ridden down. The muscular chest of a pony knocked him aside and he spun away to slide across the icy ground as the two horsemen met like thunder above him. The moon shone on the face of the newcomer who had ridden him down and saved him: it was Geordie Burn.

'Back to the castle,' yelled Geordie. 'The Captain is calling for ye.'

Tom picked himself up and ran back through the gate, which was no great distance away. It was lucky the gate was so close at hand, for the ground beside it was littered with dead and dying, men and ponies. The last of the moonlight and the growing brightness of the flaming buildings showed the grim guards beneath the portcullis who he was; otherwise, like many of the bodies littering the flags, he would have been blown back out by the guns they held trained on him.

112

As he entered the courtyard, so his uncle turned to greet him. At the same time, the dog-faced factor Fenwick – a useful man in a battle after all – said, 'That's all in now, Captain, save for Geordie Burn and the others that you know of.'

'Lower the portcullis,' ordered Sir Thomas. 'We'll send out spies through the Gully Hole at once. I want men to find our wounded, guide Geordie and the others back, and discover what in hell's name has happened to Hobbie Noble and the girl and my black stallion.'

'Hobbie's a law unto himself, as ye know, Captain,' said Fenwick; 'and the girl's a Graham. Did ye not see the plaid she wore tonight? Mebbe the Nobles and the Grahams owe the Kerrs some settlement of their own that can be paid with the price of a little treachery and a good horse.'

'If they meant mischief, they'd have led the Kerr spies in through your Gully Hole already,' said Tom breathlessly. 'And there'd be more than your outbuildings afire.'

' 'Tis a secret way,' said Fenwick frostily.

'Have ye any secrets Hobbie doesn't know the truth of?' asked Tom, all innocent surprise.

'The boy's right,' said Sir Thomas. 'If Hobbie was with the Kerrs, then their horse would be among us as we speak – instead of assembling outside the gate again.'

'To continue our discussions about Dand's hand,' said Tom: 'you should let them have

113

me. I'm worth preserving for the blackmail alone.'

'A gallant offer and well meant I am sure; but ye must see that I cannot let them have my kin, nor the Queen's messenger: the names of the Lords of the Waste and the North would never stand the shock. My standing and reputation on the Borders and in the Court would be dead on the instant, and even were I to settle the matter of Dand's hand as I mentioned, there would be no end to the Kerrs, Armstrongs, Johnstones and such who would suddenly find grievances also needing settlement.

'But let us see what's toward, shall we? And draw our next plan of action accordingly.'

There were only five Kerr horsemen now, and they sat well back from the gate where arquebus, gun, crossbow and longbow were likely to do them little damage, out of the light of the blazing buildings around the outer wall of the fort; but Tom and Sir Thomas both knew they had never killed or wounded forty-five – probably no more than half a dozen in all, given the way melees usually came out. So there were forty more of them – with the spies who had fired the outbuildings – all out there in the stormy darkness; and up to mischief, no doubt.

Of Geordie Burn and the last of the garrison horse there was no sign.

'Hell Beck is it, Master Musgrave?' called Hugh of Stob, his voice shaking with rage. 'Ye's'll have me remember Hell Beck? Well,

114

sir, if I might take the liberty, I'd ask you to think on Lord Buccleuch's work in the Middle March with the Kerrs of Stob and Ferniehurst and Cessford at his side. Remember Redesdale and Tynedayle and Coquetdale, sir, and where was your Lord of the North then?'

'Yet to be born, my wee mannie,' bellowed Sir Thomas, 'for 'tis more than seventy years since; and if ye mind the raids Buccleuch did on Redesdale, Hugh, then ye're an older man than I thought ye. As well tell us to remember Bannockburn; and I'll call down the battles of Berwick and Solway Moss and the slaughter done at both, if it's a lesson in history ye want. I'll call down Flodden Field!'

'No lesson in history, Thomas Musgrave,' spat back Hugh Kerr. 'Not from the likes of you. But I'll give you a lesson you've needed this twenty year and more. A lesson in tactics and terror!'

As Hugh Kerr spoke these last words, so he jerked his horse's head in a prearranged signal. The little group split up and scattered now that the negotiations were done, and the five horsemen sped along well-planned lines, each to a prearranged destination.

But, just at the very minute Hugh of Stob moved, as though released by the very same signal, something huge and terrifying came over the western skyline and stood framed against the setting moon on the ridge above the valley that led from the Gully Hole.

It was the size of a horse, and a proper horse

at that – higher by far and heavier than the hobbie horses here: black – coal black – from massive muzzle to sweeping tail; a huge, hulking monstrosity, all massive misshapen head, mouth agape and belching fire; eyes ablaze as red as hell and bright enough to send beams out over the snarling wrinkles of its slobbering muzzle. It raised its head against the moon and such a howl came from it as never was heard on the Borders. As tall as a tall man to the shoulder with its head nearly a yard higher still, it reared and howled and capered on the skyline while round about it gathered a pack of smaller, man-sized hounds, all of them glowing and gleaming with a hellish, baleful light.

Tom stood, thunderstruck, watching the worst of his nightmares take life before his eyes; and he was by no means alone in that.

Then, still screaming and howling, the whole wild pack of them turned and came down the valley into the heart of the attacking Kerrs. A secret squadron of Kerrs that had been following Geordie Burn's surprise attack back towards the Gully Hole came screaming out again, wild with terror; and all the others, creeping on their own pre-plan-ned missions, saw the horror overtaking their clansmen, kith and kin.

Even Hugh Kerr of Stob, their oldest and wisest – and most fearsome – froze upon his horse and sat struck with horror like Lot's wife turned to salt. Like some victim of the Gorgon, he stayed until his horse reared in simple terror at the ghastly horror rushing down on him, burning through the shadows with its huge, howling muzzle seemingly all alight.

'The Barguest!' screamed Hugh of Stob. 'Gods save us, it is the Barguest!' and at his words the whole clan of them took flight.

Wisely so, for their plans were in ruins and their valour broken; and down behind the howling horror came more of the garrison horsemen, led by Geordie Burn still, re-grouped, rearmed, and taking no prisoners. As the wild hunt streamed past the gate, so the portcullis went up again and the rest of the garrison ran out on foot to send the fleeing Kerrs upon their way with shower after shower of arrows, quarrels, shot and curses.

Tom ran out with the rest, his head ablaze and his mind in a whirl. The others slowed at the edge of the light, but Tom plunged on into the darkness after the monstrous dog and its wild pack of hounds. For it was the very creature he had come here to hunt – the thing that had killed his brother John, that could set the Borders alight more swiftly even than godless Kerrs come marauding and reiving and out for revenge on Christmas night itself.

As he ran, he reasoned – he could not help himself. For what sort of a hell-hound was it that one night terrorized an innocent man to death, and a few nights later frightened off an army set to kidnap and ransom his brother –

perhaps even slaughter his uncle? And why had Hobbie and Eve both vanished at the moment they were needed the most? Where were the hounds with which its Lord would hunt the Waste on the morrow? And where oh where was the great black stallion Sir Thomas kept for the hunting?

Tom slowed to a walk, winded and exhausted. The light from the burning outhouses sent a long, unsteady shadow, just visibly, down a slope of frozen moorland in front of him, visible only because it was frozen white and his eyes were adjusting to the starlight; and there they were, in the valley bottom, surprisingly close at hand. He knew it was them because of the dogs, and because of the shape of the great black horse, and because he could hear Hobbie laughing.

'Hobbie!' he called, and the laughter stopped.

'Is it yourself, lad?'

'Who else?' came Eve's cool voice. 'I told you. It's as well we were dealing with old Hugh Kerr of Stob instead of young Thomas Musgrave of London town. There now, boy, you were wonderful,' she crooned to Sir Thomas's great black hunter. 'The mask is off and you're all right, see?'

Something shapeless fell to the ground, giving off in the restless air a smell of candle wax and sulphur. Tom understood almost all of it then, and what he still wondered about could wait until morning, he thought.

'Some hay and some rest and you'll all be

ready for the Lord's great hunt in the morning,' she said.

'He'll still go hunting, even with Bewcastle as it is?'

'Some clearing up, but no rebuilding – we'll all live within the walls until the matter's settled once and for all,' said Hobbie. 'For it won't end here. There's Kerrs must pay for disturbing Bewcastle; and there'll be a good few more widows made on both sides by this night's work. Blood and vengeance: the law of the Borders.'

'Blood and vengeance and pride. And yes, he'll hunt,' said Eve. 'He's the Lord of the Waste. It is Yule. He'll hawk and he'll hunt and he'll scour the moss, for there'll be wounded Kerrs out there, if they make it through this bitter night alive; and the stags he's been saving – if the live Kerrs overlook them – and foxes and hares. All for the hunting by the Lord and his guests on the day after Christmas Day. It's what's expected and he'd never open himself to shame and scorn by doing any less.' Was there bitterness there? It was difficult to tell in her cool, measured tones.

'Naw,' said Hobbie, exultantly. 'There'll naw be any Kerrs to hunt. With horse or without they'll be back in their bothies in Stob before daybreak! And under their beds and shaking wi' fear – those that has beds, at the least. Did ye not see them run, little Eve? I swear one or two took wings and flew they were so overcome with sheer stark mitherin' terror!' He clapped Tom on the shoulder and slid a fatherly arm round Eve as she led the big black stallion back towards the guttering fires of Bewcastle; and the hounds trotted cheerfully at their heels. 'There'll be ballads about this night, mark my words,' continued Hobbie gleefully: 'how a girl and a horse and a cunning old reiver put the whole of the Kerrs to flight. The Lord of the Waste'll get his minstrel to write it, like as not, and we'll sing it at supper on Twelfth Night after the mummers' play. We'll call it "Hobbie Noble and the Barguest" and they'll sing it for years to come!'

Hobbie threw back his head and laughed; and, as they crested the rise and walked into the light, he threw back his head and howled at the top of his lungs, repeating the terrible sound he had made for his make-believe monster.

Out in the darkness, quite close at hand, something answered him.

# Eleven

## The Master of the Hunt

The portcullis would have remained safely down in any case, after the last fires amongst the ruined outhouses had been extinguished. The Captain of the Castle would have talked to his men, hale and wounded, congratulating them on this night's work and warning them to remain on their guard. The women of the castle, led by the Lady Ellen, Eve amongst them, would have succoured the wounded and laid out the dead, two from the garrison and four unrecovered by the fleeing Kerrs. The full garrison would have had to sleep doubled-up on a war footing, with straw palliasses blanketed with plaid replacing tables in the hall. Bewcastle's priest, Father Little, would have celebrated midnight mass in any case.

But all these things were lent an extra flavour by the ghostly echo that had answered Hobbie's last great Barguest howl. That echo, and much that had caused and surrounded it, gave added flavour to the festivities that began early on the morrow, too – especially to the Lord of the Waste's great Christmas hunt.

Tom, as honoured guest, retained the little chamber assigned to him alone, though in a flash of insight he realized it was probably the quarters of Geordie Burn, consigned to the main hall now with his men. As he prepared for bed, deciding wearily to leave his disturbance of his aunt's washerwoman until the morning, he saw that the bandages at his side were damp and glistening. Weary as he was, therefore, he went back down to that area of the kitchens that had been set aside as a hospital.

Even though the chamber in which Tom was housed seemed quite isolated, and finding his way back to the main areas seemed to necessitate his passing a surprising number of open doors and manned guard points, he really never doubted he would find his way to the kitchens. Even could he not follow his nose, he could follow his ears, for he had thought he would find the place by following the screams: he remembered battlefield hospitals too well from his youth. But the whole area was quiet when he got there, women softly passing from one man to another with warm drinks, which seemed to be calming even the severely wounded and offering a kind of oblivion.

Aware of his own standing and importance here though he was, and well schooled in the exercise of precedence and consequence by simple observation of such luminaries as the Earl of Essex at court, Tom was nevertheless

122

content to wait in line. Although all he needed to do was catch the Lady Ellen's eye – or Eve's, come to that – and he would be tended first of all, nevertheless he stood and waited. There were men here with heads open to the bone, arms cut and broken, with stab wounds, spear gashes, hoof-clubbings and the like. His own wound, treated but torn open by the wild activity of the last few hours, seemed hardly worth worrying the women so busily nursing.

Yet as he turned to go and do the best he could for himself, two things conspired to stop him. Eve looked up from the man she was tending and softly called to him: 'Tom, have you ever seen a wound like this?'

The wounded man was Archie Elliot, the second driver from the coach, companion on the ride along the Wall, and champion wrestler of the evening. He had been one of the footsoldiers running out into the melee after Geordie Burn's great charge, evidently, although Tom had seen little of him during the battle itself. He lay face-down now, his shoulders and back uncovered, as Eve completed a neat job of simple stitching on him. 'Have you seen wounds such as these?' she repeated, pulling a cloth out of a bowl of steaming water liberally afloat with dried herbs, and mopping the drying blood from the swollen flesh.

Tom looked more closely. It seemed at first glance that Archie had been cut by three strokes of the same sword, for three wounds ran in parallel across his back and shoulders. Tom tried to imagine how accurately and how swiftly a single blade would have to have been wielded to cause such an effect. A master such as himself would have been hard put to reproduce it on a subject standing still. How it had been done in the heat of battle to a wildly fighting soldier, he could not begin to guess.

'Have you asked him how it was done?' he enquired quietly.

'Before he fainted. He has no idea, save that he was hit hard and thrown down.'

'Hit once, or hit and hit again?'

Eve shrugged, in the French manner. She signalled to a couple of lightly wounded to carry him away. 'Now, what about you?' she asked.

He showed her his wound, self-consciously among so much more mortal damage, but she frowned. 'This may need re-stitching,' she said, her voice severe. 'It needs washing and re-bandaging. And I have an unguent here will ease the inflammation.' She called softly to one of her helpers – and Tom realized with a little start that the other women were all deferring to the Lady Ellen first, as a matter of course, and then to Eve. Then, like any cadet after his first battle, he fell to prodding the cut in his side, surprised by how well it seemed to be healing, how neatly it had been sutured – before his activities had torn the stitches – and by how carefully it had been filled with powders and unguents to speed its recovery.

Or he did this until Eve slapped his fingers away like a mother correcting a child, and handed him something instead. He took a little horn cup.

'Drink this,' she said as she fell to working on his side again. 'It will help you sleep in case the pain disturbs you in the night.'

He sniffed it and looked at her with his eyebrow slightly raised.

'A weak infusion of mandragora,' she said. ' 'Twill rebalance your humours and by easing the fiery elements assist rest and recovery, for it is governed by Mercury.'

He did as she bade him and was lucky to make it back to his little chamber without dozing off on the cold stone stair; though he himself thought that he would have slept like the dead without the bitter little potion, and woken just as refreshed and energetic to greet the bright, brokenly clouded morning.

In fact it was the hounds, not the daylight, that woke Tom. Their well-tuned baying seemed at strange variance with the wild howling they had made last night as they charged down the valley behind Sir Thomas's great black stallion so cunningly disguised. Now it was clear that the pack had been chosen for their mouths, the treble barking setting a pleasant line over the tenor and bass baying. Tom thought wistfully for a moment of his friend Will Shakespeare. For while Tom himself had been in that vicious little battle

125

yesternight, Will himself, or Dick Burbage, in the person of Theseus the Prince of Athens, would have been standing before the Queen and all her court, boasting of the well-tuned voices of his hounds of Thessaly. The words of the play, beautiful though they were, seemed worlds away from the fierce reality outside in the freezing morning – as the dream of midsummer was far away from the reality of Christmas; and, indeed, as Blackfriars was from Bewcastle.

Thus philosophical, Tom heaved himself out of bed, wrapping his cloak – warmed by serving as a blanket – about his shoulders at once. There was a bowl of water by his bed, fortunately fashioned of pewter. He had to punch the surface of the liquid twice before the ice would break. His toilet, therefore, like his dressing, was necessarily brief. Only the razor-sharp Solingen steel of his daggers would have allowed him to make as good a fist of scraping the beard off his jaw as he did. Not for the first time, he thanked God for the prevailing fashion that dictated a point of beard over the cleft in his square chin and a curl of moustaches on his tender upper lip.

As Tom clattered down the stone stair from his quarters, Uncle Thomas met him and offered him the services of his personal barber.

'Perhaps on the morrow,' answered Tom cheerfully. 'It is your washerwoman I need today...'

'Fear not,' he answered. 'It was the Lady

126

Ellen's last word before she went to bed last night and it will be among the first of her thoughts this morning, I am sure.'

The main hall was astir, and Lady Ellen's other concerns were clearly legion. Last night's bedding was being packed away and preparations were in train for the busy social occasion that was the Lord of the Waste's Christmas hunt. Noting in his mind the way in which there seemed to be three levels of authority within his uncle, one to suit each title, Tom passed out of hail of his family relative, Uncle Thomas, through the domain of his social and courtly uncle, the Lord of the Waste, and out into the command of his warlike, battle-commander uncle, the Captain of Bewcastle. Here, in the castle yard between the keep and the gate, he met Geordie Burn returning from his first patrol of the day.

'All quiet?'

Captain Burn glanced down at him and Tom felt last night's enmity still smouldering there; but Burn was content to be civil for the time being. 'Quiet on the Waste,' he said. 'Not a Kerr or a Barguest in sight – as far as a swift sweep can descry.'

'Good,' called Hobbie Noble, stepping out of the long kennel that stood along the wall beside the stable. 'Then the hunting will proceed unchecked. I can finish preparing my hounds. And you, Captain Burn, if you would be so good, may release a couple of your riders to swell the ranks of my men. For I am

Master of the Lord's Hunt and this day of all days that puts me in the highest standing.'

Burn's usually severe face broke into a swift grin. 'After last night, Hobbie, if your standing was any higher, you'd be talking to St Peter at Heaven's Gate.'

'Good,' Tom echoed Hobbie. 'Then I too may be about my business.' Tom called for a pony from the garrison stock, saddled it himself while the groom that brought it look-ed to the rest of the tack and called across to Captain Burn, who was performing the exact opposite of the offices on his own steaming mount. 'The road to the right leads straight to the town still?'

'It does,' confirmed Captain Burn, his smile long vanished.

'And the smithy ten minutes down?'

'Halfway to the town, as it ever was,' confirmed Hobbie.

'Good. I have a visit overdue.'

'You'll need to be quick,' warned Hobbie. 'The Lord of the Waste may forgive your absence at the early meal – may even wink at your face missing from early services; but if you miss the first reception or the Hunt Mass, then you will be struck off the list of his relations. Even though you be the last of them left, lad.'

'You waste your time in any event. Mistress Eve remained in the castle through the night,' said Burn, possessively.

'It is not my sister I mean to visit,' said Tom, swinging into the saddle as he spoke. 'It is

128

my brother.'

In spite of the advice of both Burn and Hobbie, Tom swung easily to the left as soon as he got outside the castle gate. He rode thoughtfully up the slope above Kirk Beck that flowed down to Bewcastle town, then he swung away up towards the Waste itself, his eyes busy on the ground. Only when he had gained a little ridge and could look away across the main section of the Waste itself towards the Scottish border did he pause and sit, still deep in thought. He could see both the forbidding, frozen emptiness of it and the slow gathering of the black cloud above it, but his eyes remained fixed on the vastness as though he could see things otherwise invisible up there. Only after a few long moments did he turn and begin to direct his pony's steps across the fell behind the fort and down towards the town itself.

As he rode down the hillside, he suddenly began to address his thoughts to the sure-footed little chestnut, as though it had been the man with whom it shared its name.

'Ye see, my little hobbie horse, the first part of my own especial hunt must be the Barguest itself. Does it exist or does it not? If it does exist, then how and why did it kill John? If it does not exist, then who killed John, how and why? And who then pulled the Barguest into his murder, how and why?'

The horse gave a soft whinny, as though it was content to mull over these musings with the Master of Logic on its back; but in fact it wasn't. Like all of the animals in Bewcastle fort, it was on edge, high-strung with the excitement engendered by Hobbie Noble, his hounds and his preparations for the other, more physical hunt.

'Have the adventures of the last two nights moved us any further forward?' the Master of Logic continued quietly. 'Silent horsemen following us means that this is not some little local matter – that there are powers here involved; more than just the Lord of the North growing nervous at a lack of snow in the reiving time and a trusted servant's servant dead. Someone else at court is involved – someone who is not close to the Lord of the North, or, therefore, to the Council; but someone with power and influence that can reach even to this godforsaken place. And whoever is not with us must be against us.

'But that is speculation which lies beyond calculation at present. We have other, sharper matters near at hand – a dagger in my side for one, that makes murder more likely, as was explained to Eve; and that explanation calculatedly offered. For is she not the most likely culprit in the matter of John's murder, having the most opportunity, being married to the victim, the most of gain, in the reclamation of her inheritance, the valley of the Black Lyne? And, clearly, having the ability, for she is a strong and intrepid woman and a fearsome herbalist. And the support, should she have chosen to call upon it, for either Geordie Burn or Hobbie Noble would clearly dance all the way down to hell for her. But she says they were not together on the day John died – that he was about his business and she was about hers. Here is a matter to be examined further. And here is a second: why would she call in the Barguest and all this wide, dangerous interest, when she might have done the thing privately and secretly with none the wiser?'

The little horse whinnied then, and Tom looked up to see that there, by the road in front of them stood the smithy where John and Eve had made their home – where Tom's father and mother in their turn had made their home, and where John and Tom themselves had grown through boyhood. The square grey house with the smithy built into the hillside behind stood halfway between the castle and the town. For John, like his father, had been the castle's battle-smith in time of restlessness and the town's blacksmith in times of calm.

Tom would have stopped there, but mindful of Hobbie's words – and of his more urgent mission – he decided to return later, and so rode on down the hill, drawing nearer to the gurgling brook of Kirk Beck, which would become the White Lyne when it attained riverhood further downstream, and over the bridge that was the heart of Bewcastle town. As he rode, he continued to examine the reasons for his sister's guilt, but silently now. Of all the investigation so far, this was the area that he did not wish to discuss at length with the man he was going to visit.

Then he began to speak again, moving on to another topic that might be painful also. 'And Hobbie. What of Hobbie last night? At a stroke he proved he might at will bring the Barguest to life. This was no doubt a skill he would have kept close secret had the Kerrs not called it to light. But it is a cause for concern, is it not? And he could have been as swift with the dagger as Eve the night before. Only I cannot see that they could be confederated together in the matter of the stabbing or I should be stark, not stitched – dead, not deliberating.

'And there's another thing, for I have tested Eve herself now. She could have completed her killing work last night, had the dagger been hers and the stitches the result of Hobbie's presence in the coach. Indeed, she could have despatched me earlier still, I believe, with her unguents and her physics, without waiting for mandragora last night.

'And I have tested Hobbie, too, in case the situation was the opposite within the coach. For if he had stabbed me at Ware and dared not finish his work in front of Eve, then he could have despatched me in the dark last night and blamed the battle or the Barguest as he chose; but, again, he did nothing of the sort.

'Or it could have been an Armstrong dagger in the hands of Sim; or an Elliot dagger in the fist of Archie. Or a dagger of one of the rioters in Ware, confederated to the horsemen with muffled hooves, as were the Kerrs, like as not, or One-Hand Dand at the least, as is someone in Bewcastle fort as well. Someone like Geordie Burn, perhaps, who would have killed me in the melee last night but saved me instead. His motives need untangling, as do all of their motives, I fear – but carefully, like a nest of vipers...'

The kirk after which the beck was named, like the kirk at Blackpool Gate, stood a little back from the stream, and the churchyard that belonged to it stood up the hill behind it. Tom, therefore, was able to tether his pony at the churchyard gate under the sloping hillside and go in without disturbing the services in the kirk itself – services slipped in by a busy Father Crawford Little between the imperious demands of a less than heavenly Lord.

'They've not been able to lay you deep, then, Johnny,' Tom said, looking down along the length of the new-made grave. There was no marker as yet, but it was the only new grave in the yard. Sunlight swept across the place like blades stabbing between the clouds and, as it came and went, it cast the shadow of a great cross over the new-turned earth. The bitter wind came sobbing out of the north, bringing tears to Tom's eyes and making them seem to be freezing upon his cheeks.

'Of course, with the earth like iron, it's a wonder they managed to lay you in its bosom at all. A shallow grave's no bad thing, Johnny, for I may have to summon you up and out of it long before Judgement Day. But let us proceed a little more with logic before we resort to picks or shovels.'

'And to bishops, come to that,' said a familiar voice behind him. 'You'll need the word of a bishop to touch that grave.'

Tom turned to see Father Little standing by the great ancient cross upon which the Musgrave boys had played like Barbary apes in times past.

'I have an order of the Council,' he answered easily, 'signed by at least one archbishop. I am, in effect, the Queen's Crowner here, should I exercise the full extent of my power. That will do in this case, I think.'

'You are grown to high estate then, my Tommy – a great man at court.'

'No, Father. It is the matter, not the man, that is deemed to be great.'

The old priest smiled, his open face crinkling and his blue eyes twinkling. It was not a merry smile, as might be suited to the season, but a smile that took account of the way the world went when one brother stood at the grave of another, talking over the matter of his murder; and yet it was a smile, and it warmed Tom's heart.

'But I interrupted,' said Father Little, softly.

'An exercise in logic, Father,' said Tom, equally softly. 'A chopping through of the matter here in the manner you first taught me, that I carry on in my generation merely like a dwarf on the shoulder of a giant.'

Father Little laughed at that. 'Did I teach

you the wisdom of the ancients that you quote them back at me? I had thought I taught you only the catechisms of your own true faith – and the commandments, so that you might be sure to break them all at some time or another, I fear.'

Tom looked down at John's raw grave. 'You told me that it was a saying of Bernard of Chartres,' he said; 'but, good Father, how many commandments have been broken here?' Then he continued speaking before the priest could answer him. 'The sixth – that's for certain: *Thou shalt not kill*; the seventh, like as not...'

'Adultery. Your favourite, as I recall...'

'Or if not the seventh, the tenth – the coveting, if not the taking, of thy neighbour's wife. The eighth, stealing...'

'Stealing is the Borders' sin. And so, before you add it, is the ninth.'

'But here especially, Father. There has been a deal of false witness here; and much that has been sworn to – and sworn to on oath – is nevertheless false, so the name of the Lord has been taken in vain. The Sabbath, indeed Christmas Day, has been neither honoured nor kept holy. And there is an image abroad, is there not? – An image of a creature that is under the earth. If the creature itself is a demon, then the image is a sin – and people coming very near to worshipping it, this Barguest, real or manufactured.'

'So, all that stands unbroken is the honouring of fathers. On earth and in heaven,' said

Father Little sadly.

'But the chain of logic is not yet complete; indeed I have hardly begun to forge it,' said Tom grimly. 'There are sins here yet to be uncovered, Father. And, like as not, more deaths to come.'

# Twelve

## The Laird of Hermitage

It so befell, and by apparent coincidence, that Father Little had the liberty to accompany Tom back to Bewcastle fort – and the need to go thither at once, or he would be late for the Hunting Mass. Of necessity, therefore, they travelled together, and both in turn astride Tom's pony, for priests in the Borders went on two feet, no matter how urgent their mission, while bishops, archbishops and cardinals went on four. It was a mildly subversive variation on the riddle of the Sphinx that Father Little had taught to Tom, along with so much else, before releasing him to the grammar school in his youth.

It took a good deal of heated negotiation to decide they should take turn about. Then, while they went up the hill with some urgency towards the smithy and the fort, now one walking now the other at the bridle like the veriest groom, they continued to talk.

'You have never taken against your sister Eve,' said Father Little at once. 'You cannot believe her guilty.'

'I have not and do not; but I can see how a man might have reason to,' answered Tom forthrightly, then spent the next few minutes explaining his reason to his new confidant.

'But she loved your brother more than life itself,' answered Father Little, sweeping away logic with all the practice of a priest whose faith is founded in belief before reason. 'Did ye not see the flowers on John's grave?'

'Aye. Christmas roses.'

'Hard to come by. Brought and laid there at great cost of effort, pocket and spirit. A sign of miraculous love, Tom.'

'Father, d'ye not know Eve for a wise woman? I've no doubt she has gardens of herbs and physics behind the smithy though I've scarce had leisure to look. She has packed this wound in my side with secret physics. She put me to sleep last night with mandragora, much beloved of witches. And you point out her sign of love to me...'

'The Christmas roses, aye...'

'...also known as black hellebore – more deadly even than mandrake roots and crocuses and daffodil corms, the juice of poppies and half the toadstools in the darkest woods.'

'You speak with authority, lad.'

'With some. I made the acquaintance of Gerard the Herbalist some six months since over the matter of some poisonings.'

'With hellebore?'

'With belladonna, aconite and such. I'll lay odds we would find nightshade, monk's hood and wolf's bane beside what's left of the

138

Christmas roses in the smithy's physic garden, as surely as we would find rosemary and sage in the herb garden.'

'If they are there, lad, it is because they can help as well as heal. You have yourself said that the infusion of mandragora she gave to you last night helped your wound.'

'It did. It helped my slumbers at the least. And had I been constipated 'twould certainly have helped with that. I am purged, blood-let and balanced in humours; I am a new man altogether.'

'When it could just as easily have torn your soul from your body and destined you for poor John's side – made you new-born with a vengeance,' countered Father Little severely.

This conversation served to carry them as far as the smithy and, had they not both been too well aware that the Lord of the Waste would be impatient for his mass and his hunting, they might have lingered a little, to test the truth of Tom's words; but on they trotted, Tom up and Father Little panting at the pony's head. 'If not Eve, then who next?' puffed the priest.

And Tom took him through his thoughts about Hobbie Noble and Captain Burn.

'Geordie Burn is a proud and stubborn man, short of temper and long of memory,' the priest allowed. 'He has reasons more than most to feel threatened and ill-at-ease when he stands with the Captain of Bewcastle. But I see no marks of evil ingrained within him. He would serve you ill, I've no doubt, for you bested him at the swordplay last night and, he fears, you may best him again with Eve, of whom he hopes great things now she is free to give her heart once more. He has waited in John's shadow this ten years and more. I believe she is the reason he remains when he has so many good reasons to go.'

'Waited? No more than that?'

'Eve would allow no more, even had he proposed it. She loved John; and Geordie feared him a little, as he fears you. So he was with John as he is with you, but that he had no immediate cause to kill him.'

'Except for the hope of Eve's hand.'

'Now where is your logic, Tom? To kill John would be to lose her for ever. Would she marry the man that had killed the husband she loved – though she loved the murderer still?'

'Ho! Now there is a question fit for the Borders! Or for some twisted tale in the telling of Kit Marlowe, Tom Kyd, or their like. Not even Will Shakespeare could untangle such a knot as that one!'

'But your answer, Tom. Ye see that Eve could never love him then?'

'Aye. I see it.'

'Good. But remember, you do not sit in that blessedly safe seat. Geordie might think he has reason to kill you – especially if Eve's eyes turn more kindly towards you; and it was to yourself, remember, that she ran the instant John was underground.'

'Not to me – to the Lord of the North. And

she didn't run; she came south with Hobbie at my uncle's direction.'

'Indeed. So you may believe. And there are two more powders for this potion of suspicion you have abrewing.'

'Hobbie, yes, as I have said, though I have known the man longer than I have known yourself, Father. But my uncle...'

'Your uncle is a desperate man, Tom – a desperate man in a desperate situation.'

'What do you mean by that?'

'Did I teach you nothing, my son? Use your eyes. But if I were to ask any man to explain the deeper, darker matters to you, then here comes that very man now.'

As Father Little spoke, so a band of horsemen topped the ridge above and ahead of them, and went cantering down towards Bewcastle fort with banners fluttering, all gaudy gold, deep blood-red overlain with lavender and green tartan, white-squared, breathtakingly colourful against the frost-dark sky and the frost-white ground.

'And who is that?' asked Tom with a frown.

'That is the Laird of Hermitage, your uncle's opposite on the Scottish side, the Warden of Liddesdale – Black Robert Douglas himself,' said Father Little; and, as though he had said *That is the Lord of Hell, Lucifer, Satan himself*, he needed to add no more.

No sooner had Father Little spat out the answer, than, as though the Black Douglas were indeed a devil to be summoned from hell by the calling of his name, he turned, saw

141

the pair below, held up his hand and wheeled. His whole company followed him around out of their straight path to Bewcastle fort to come cantering down the hill.

Father Little continued speaking very rapidly, dropping his voice as the horses approached until his last words, a fierce, hissing whisper, were lost beneath the stamping and the whinnying and the Black Douglas's cheery greeting. 'Tom, beware this man. For all his gentle Scottish speech and courtly manners, he is deadly dangerous. Were I to choose any man nearby likely to be responsible for all of this, it would be he. He is lord over the Armstrongs, who obey him out of simple terror. He can call to his banner the scum of the Scottish Marches, the Elliots, the Grahams and even the Kerrs. From his eyrie at Hermitage he looks over the Scotts and the Johnstones, the Maxwells and, some say, even the MacGregors. If there is no God in Liddesdale, then it is because this man drove him out! If anyone could steal away Eve Graham, now she is widowed and free, with or without her consent, it is he; and if he should decide to do so, then never look to see her in this life again. If anyone has the heart or the power to snatch the Waste away from your uncle, or the North away from Lord Henry Carey, it is he! And as for the Barguest, he...'

'Halloa! Father Little! Afoot while another rides. Not while Robert Douglas has horse, sir! We treat our churchmen better than that

142

in Scotland. Come, Father, up on my black hunter now, and let us all trot over to the Lord of the Waste's abode.

'And you, sirrah, who ride while the good father puffs at your bridle, you must be the master come up lately from Her Majesty's Court, to the wonder of all men from here to Berwick. Master Musgrave, is it not?'

'It is, sir. Lord Robert Douglas, the Laird of Hermitage, I believe.' Nothing abashed, Tom swung easily down and faced the Black Douglas, offering the courtliest of his bows – widening the sweep of his arm to take in all assembled there, for the instant Lord Robert stepped down from his hunter, so all of his company swung down from theirs. Except, Tom noted, for two. Guests, then, he surmised at once, hoping his bow had hidden his look, for he recognized at least one of the men at once.

Not from the Douglas it hadn't. 'Ah, Master Musgrave,' Lord Robert continued smoothly. 'I see you observe my guests. Allow me to perform the briefest of introductions: Senor Sagres and Master de Vaux, both lately of London.' The two men bowed in their saddles, then both, reluctantly, followed the lead dictated by their host and his men, swinging down to stand at their horses' heads.

Very lately, thought Tom as he straightened. De Vaux had been standing behind the Earl of Essex's shoulder when his lordly blade had rested on Tom's throat and the Queen's

143

screams still echoed at the rehearsal of *A Midsummer Night's Dream* two days since at White Hall. And his saddlebag had an unusual pattern upon it – familiar from that flash of clear sight he had gained of the riders kicking the farmers aside at Ware.

Then he turned back and fronted the Black Douglas. They were big men, Tom and Lord Robert, able to look each other in the eye, able to look down on the others around them. The Laird of Hermitage earned his nickname from the long hair that he wore gathered at the nape of his neck, from the beard he wore barbered to the finest point, and the moustaches that curled down to join it on his chin, all of which were so black that they seemed to take a tinge of blue from the dancing glitter of his eyes. His brows, raised in amused quizzicality now, rose to points then swept up across his temples almost to the tops of his ears. His lashes were thick and dark, like those of an Italian girl.

In his looks and in his vanity, in his consequence and dangerous affability, he reminded Tom of that other Robert of his acquaintance, so recently called to mind, the deadliest of his enemies – friend to de Vaux and no doubt to Senor Sagres too, for there were always Spaniards in his train – Robert Devereux, the Earl of Essex. The Earl of Essex was just such a man as might have the power, the will and the wish to bribe a constable at Ware while he despatched his men to stir up the Kerrs and warn the Black Douglas against him.

'Put up the father, Tam,' ordered Black Robert, his eyes never leaving Tom's as he spoke. Tom glanced over to his companion and exercised his mastery in self-control once more as another piece of the puzzle fell into place so unexpectedly. The man called Tam, moving to obey his master's command, clearly the Captain of Horse to the Laird of Hermitage, was the image of Geordie Burn. Two brothers, then, each holding the same post, on opposite sides in a brewing conflict – who must come face to face and steel to steel, and soon. The same two brothers, like as not, as had fallen out over Eve all those years ago.

Eyes wide and innocent, Tom turned back to Lord Robert and smiled. Behind the smile and the innocent eyes, even as he listened to Lord Robert's conversation, Tom's mind whirled in speculation – speculation as to how all this tangle of confused loyalties and dark motives could have called up the Barguest to kill his brother – and why.

Father Little's protests were cut short and replaced by the sound of the saddle creaking; then Black Robert himself took the bridle and the rest of them all walked up towards Bewcastle fort together as the priest, alone, rode.

'I hope you will be amongst the number to whom I may repay this visit soon,' the Laird of Hermitage continued to Tom as they walked. 'It is a tradition that has grown up during the days of your lamented absence

145

from the Borders, so you may not know of it, but in the season after the Lord of the Waste has his hunt, the Warden of Liddesdale has his hawking. The game does not compare with the fine red harts that your uncle offers for sporting and feasting, of course, but I have hawks, buzzards and even eagles with which we can pass a merry afternoon, and a range of birds from herons to capercaillie that we may kill and feast upon. In return we request only the detail in the matter of Dand Kerr's hand. What a story that must be! Hermitage keep is only rarely graced by courtiers and adventurers such as yourself, Master Musgrave, though we are fortunate that Master de Vaux and Senor Sagres have graced us.

'Ah now, Tam, look where the story carried by those fleeing Kerrs we captured this morning is not true. The outbuildings are burned down indeed. There must have been a sharp fight here last night. I had hesitated to believe them, Master Musgrave, for the Kerrs are notorious liars and these ones told us that the Barguest itself came down and ran them off. But now I see that it is at least partly as they said.

'I assure you, sir, and I will assure the Lord of the Waste, that you shall find them hanging at Hermitage gate when you grace us with a visit – them and any other Kerrs I discover nearby.'

Lord Robert got his chance to assure the Lord of the Waste on the matter of hanging

Kerrs almost at once, for the band of walkers with their thoroughly embarrassed rider went through the main gate to be greeted by a reception line. Drawn up in due order, it was headed by the Lord of the Waste himself, the Lady Ellen at his side. The first formal section of the day began at once as the Lord of the Waste and the Lady conducted the Laird of Hermitage along the line of precedence, making formal introductions. Lord Robert in turn introduced his party and all with apparent amity, disturbed only by the threatening looks exchanged by Tam and Geordie Burn. Tom noted also that, while in the Bewcastle garrison there were a good number of women, the visitors from Hermitage were more like a war band, being made up exclusively of men.

The introductions led across the courtyard and into the little kirk, which could hardly in all its history have held such a magnificent company. Here they all stood shoulder to shoulder, lords and lairds, Scotsmen and Sassenachs, soldiers and reivers, courtiers and commoners, men and women. They bowed their heads when they should have knelt, for there was simply no room to bend the knee. Standing, therefore, together, they spoke the words of commandment, creed, confession; they echoed the blessing and the breaking of the body and bread, the shedding and the mixing of blood and wine. All of them stepped forward to the Communion, the order of precedence breaking down so that there seemed to be no particular order in the celebration. Sir Thomas and the Lady Ellen went first and Lord Robert and his guests came later, soon before Fenwick the Factor and Archie, then Tom who stood beside him. Finally, Geordie and Eve brought up the rear. They tasted the bread and sipped the wine. This was never designed to be a full-sung celebration, so the only music came from the well-tuned hounds outside; and that was apt enough, for, holy worship or not, it tempted them all to hurry through.

Out in the courtyard there had been a bustle during the service. The mass had been for the hunters only. When the Lord of the Waste led them all out into the restless morning, therefore, all the horses were saddled, the hounds leashed but ready. As they mounted – even the women going astride for the going would be hard and hectic – so the Lady Ellen disappeared. The hunt was not for her. Her other responsibilities were fully met, however, for on the instant she reappeared with the castle's entire kitchen staff bearing great platters of steaming food and bumpers of smoking punch.

In spite of his boast that Eve's medicines had made him a new man. Tom partook of little. He could hardly get the taste of the communion wine out of his mouth and the residue seemed to make his lips and tongue tingle irritatingly. A draught of punch and a baked chicken wing simply added to a mild sense of discomfort within him, though they eased his mouth and throat. And he thought no more about it.

The hunt breakfast was a feast of baked chicken, boiled eggs, filled pastries and sliced haggis. The punch was a fragrant mixture of herbs, spices, wine and sugar. It was taken in the saddle and the bones thrown past the hounds to the castle's domestic dogs. Wild with excitement and hunger, straining so that Hobbie and his men could hardly hold them, the hounds led the way out of the castle gate with the riders in careful precedence behind. The musicians from the Christmas festivities swapped lutes and pipes for horns and, as the hunt began to climb the hill to the crest above the Waste, they echoed the music of the hounds. At the crest of the ridge, with the waste rolling away before them, Sir Thomas gave the signal and the horns sounded the commencement. The hounds were unleashed and every heel there spurred into the heaving flank of an expectant horse. In a charge every bit as wild as the charge Geordie had led on the heels of the Barguest against the Kerrs last night, they were off across the Waste.

# Thirteen

## The Kill

Tom was sick of this inaction. He had not yet reached that part of his exercise of logic where he had assembled all the facts and could begin to test them through observation of suspects or manipulation of their actions. He was still caught up in the tangle of events and could see but little of the pattern as yet. His gift for suspicion was being exercised to its limit, but his genius for logic had too little to work upon unless he got down to some serious action: *doing* must take precedence over reasoning. Finding out the truth of the matters that had been described to him must be done at once, before he try any more conclusions.

Tom had been on the Borders for less than a day, admittedly, but he was used to taking decisive action. He still felt that he had been sluggish in the pursuance of his task. His slowness of action, of course, was partly due to exhaustion and weakness from the blood-letting, and perhaps from Eve's treatment of it; but it also had its foundation in the fact

150

that he was being watched wherever he went. It was also because he was being delicately but carefully enmeshed in toils of social expectation whose effect – and, perhaps, whose design – was to tie his hands and hamper his work here. At every turn came circumstances that tempted him to look away from the simple act of his brother's murder itself and into the causes and consequences that might or might not surround it.

The hunt came as blessed relief to this queasy sense of inactivity. It gave him the opportunity to take a little freedom through the simple exercise of some calculated rudeness and careful intransigence – freedom that started now, even though the morning's nagging sickness lingered.

The other horses streamed away after the hounds, heading up on to High Waste and away over Hazel Gill and Calf Sike towards the forested sections of Hart Horn, where the Lord of the Waste had kept his carefully nurtured herds of hunting deer since long before Tom was a lad learning his logic as well as his catechism at Father Little's knee. Everyone, including Tom, knew where they were going; everyone except Tom galloped away to the south-east, therefore.

Tom waited for an instant to make as sure as possible that he was being neither watched nor followed, thoughtlessly wiping the back of his hand over his burning lips. Then he jerked his pony's head to the left and galloped off at a calculated angle designed to take him, at first imperceptibly, north. He was cantering across country he knew as well as he knew the direction of the hunt. He was headed over White Preston and then along the ridge past Whiteside End, Crew Cragg and Watch Rigg, the five miles to Arthur's Seat, some twenty minutes' riding time away.

Tom's destination was the birthplace of the Black Lyne river, its spring in the little coppice dominated by the great oak where his brother had been found dead almost a week ago, the huge tree that they said was clawed to the heartwood to a height of two full fathoms from the ground. The Lord of the Waste, Eve and Hobbie had all said it, but Tom needed to see the thing for himself. Second only to John's body, which must be dug out of its grave to tell him more, that tree must be as full of secrets as all the rest together.

Yet as Tom galloped more freely and urgently along the skyline between White Preston and Preston End, he was unsettlingly aware that he was also compounding the mounting risks he seemed to be running lately. The idea of the danger into which he was so wilfully thrusting himself suddenly made him feel actually, physically, sick.

Simply starting on this journey had earned him a knife in the side, he thought – perhaps provoked by de Vaux and Sagres at the behest either of the Earl of Essex or the Black Douglas; possibly delivered by one or other of his closest childhood friends; or by an Elliot or an Armstrong, either or both in the pay of the Laird of Hermitage as well as in the employ of the Council.

Then, getting as far as the Wall had called down a troop of Kerrs, again probably directed by de Vaux or Sagres – therefore in the employ of the Black Douglas, who was, like as not, confederated with Essex in any case. Escaping them had called forth half the clan and near destroyed Bewcastle itself. In the melee there, death had come its closest yet. Next, this very morning, perhaps by coincidence, visiting his brother's grave had called up Father Little with his distractingly far-flung suspicions, and then called down the Black Douglas himself with Essex's friends as his less than welcome guests. What, Tom wondered queasily, would be the consequence in this deadly game of coming to the ancient oak that stood at the very heart of the matter?

Suddenly the chicken wing and punch, which had been sitting so ill on his stomach after the hunt breakfast, gave another unwelcome stirring, and he leaned over clear of his trotting mount and was copiously sick down the cliff at Crew Cragg. Then, lighter in spirit as well as in body, he spurred up the crest towards Watch Rigg.

Tom paused for a moment on Watch Rigg, for, as its name implied, the little hill summit gave a wide view of the surrounding countryside. Especially against the white heaves of the frosted moorland with which he was

153

surrounded, it was obvious that he was not being followed, unless he had pursuers hidden in the black depths of the wooded river valleys with which the place was surrounded – into one of which, after all, Tom himself was heading.

Due north he continued, into the very teeth of the wind, which had swung round further in the night and was bringing the clouds now, lower and lower, like the Black Douglas straight out of Scotland over the border that lay all too close at hand. Yet, when he paused at last on the shoulder of the cragside above the rounded hollow of Arthur's Seat, a rift in those same dark clouds allowed a brief beam of sunlight as bright as midsummer to rest on the coppice below him, so that the great bare oak where his brother had died seemed a thing of gold and fire. Light-headed with shock and anticipation, at being at the tragic place at last and ready to learn – and avenge – its secrets, Tom spurred down the hillside.

As he rode, he pulled his eyes from the hypnotic horror of the ruined tree and looked at the ground itself. There was nothing soft about the place. Thin earth covered stony ridges, the one as hard as the other in the grip of the unrelenting frost. He could have marched an army over here and left almost no mark, he thought. He reined his pony to a standstill, dismounted and walked back along the track of his own progress. The thin grass and moss lay beaten down by wind and rain uncounted months since and frosted over now so hard that he could find no evidence that his steel-hoofed pony had ever crossed this ground. Thoughtfully, he climbed back into the saddle and trotted on down.

The oak stood exactly as he remembered it. It rose to its majestic height well clear of the little wood further down the hill where the floor of Arthur's Seat folded into the beginning of a valley, deep-throated and steep-sided seemingly before there was even a rivulet to occupy it. Such was the thinness of the earth over the rocks even down here where the soil was at its thickest, the roots rose out of the thin grass like huge serpents frozen in the midst of some writhing battle; and it was a wonder of this particular tree, as Tom recalled from childhood, that when the leaves and acorns came down at the fall of the year, so they were swept away by the torrents of autumn rain that gave birth to the Black Lyne itself. You would find more oak leaves and acorns at Blackpool Gate, so the saying went, than you would ever discover on Arthur's Seat. The fodder for pigs was the best in the county down there.

Above the wild, weird, writhing roots stood the trunk of the tree, so wide it had taken Tom as a boy the better part of five minutes to walk around it, as he remembered. Tom the man had longer legs, but it still took him the better part of a hundred paces. Up above the trunk, truly fifteen feet above, nearly twice as high as Tom could reach, the huge branches sprang out, the least of them as thick as his thigh and most of them as thick as his body.

Between the roots and the branches the tree stood horribly naked, and in place of the bark that he remembered being thick, grey and crusted, there was only the pale gold of the sap-teared wood. That wood had reason to weep its thick amber tears, for it was exactly as Eve had described and he had seen in his fevered vision on the coach: the pale wood had been clawed, torn and splintered. Claw marks gouged in series, overlapping, crossing, hacking, chopping, until the tree's flanks, which should have stood as smooth as any woman's, resembled instead the hide of the bristling hedgehog. Twice as high as Tom himself the wild, bewildering madness reached – higher by far than he could touch on tiptoe; higher than he could reach standing in his stirrups; higher even than that by a yard and more; so high that even the lower branches seemed to be in danger of that savage, satanic clawing. But they were not, for they remained untouched. Indeed, for a good yard beneath the lowest of them there hung a sorry series of shreds and tatters as though the great tree's bark were reduced to a beggar's rags, and what had been stripped away lay strewn in a great untidy circle all around.

The sunlight was gone now and the low clouds threatened a thin, sleety rain. The wind trapped beneath them seemed forced by the wild contours of the place to come sighing like a dirge down to the tree. This creaked and groaned in agony, stirring even to its foundations as its naked twigs and branches set up the most doleful range of sobs, screams and howls.

Tom knelt down beneath the worst-torn section of the trunk. High above here there stood a pair of branches that forked out from the trunk itself like the double tip of a snake's tongue. Here, evidently, John's body had been found, kneeling with one hand and one knee on each of the branches. The ground beneath was clawed, Tom found, after he had cleared the shreds of bark away – clawed almost as badly as the trunk was clawed; and that gave Tom cause to frown thoughtfully, for the ground up on the slope had given no sign at all of the passage of an iron-shod pony bearing a heavy man. This ground was no softer, and yet it bore the claw prints of the creature that had torn the tree. The roots and the thin-grassed soil between them both carried the marks of the claws. Out in a circle around the tree, further and further apart, the marks tore up the ground as though the monstrous hound had been trying to bury something – or to dig something up, perhaps.

Tom followed them, seeking for single tracks, until he found enough to examine individually. Lost in thought, he lay full length on the frozen moss. He brought his face as close to the ground as the steaming of his breath on the white grass would allow.

There were no pad marks. The hound might have come straight from hell, but it was by no means brimstone hot, therefore. Yet it must have had well-spread pads and great weight in itself to drive the four clear claw marks into the thin soil. Tom pulled out his dagger and drove it down beside the marks, and could hardly get the Solingen steel to penetrate the ground. Were these the forepaws or the hind? Tom looked further back, but there were no more marks upslope. He looked further forward, but the mess of claw marks began too soon – he could not find the pattern that would betray the size of the thing.

Yet, he mused, returning to the tree, sinking into deep reflection beneath the ghostly wailing of its agonies within the howling wind, he knew the size of the Barguest to within an ell. With its hind legs resting where his own feet rested, it was big enough to reach up with its forepaws to a point fully twice as high as he stood.

Thank God, he whispered, that John had been up in those branches a safe yard higher still. Then he stopped all thoughts for a moment and tried to clear his mind, for he realized with a sick lurch that he was starting to believe in the Barguest after all.

Then, out of the thin air of his blank mind, the most obvious of thoughts occurred to him: how in God's name had John climbed up there in the first place?

'How did he do it?' came a cold, quiet voice from immediately behind Tom.

Tom whirled, too startled to maintain his facade of imperturbability.

'How did your brother get himself up fifteen feet into the air? Perhaps the Angel Gabriel gave him a helping hand – what do you think?' Lord Robert Douglas enquired.

Tom's mind echoed Lord Robert's first question: how in all the world had he, de Vaux and Sagres come so silently down on him? Then Tam Burn's horse gave a quiet snicker from behind the tree and Tom realized that a combination of the wind in the tree, his own preoccupation and the captain's tracking skills would easily have been enough for the task.

'Or,' Lord Robert continued silkily, 'perhaps his fear of the beast that hunted him lent him wings before it frightened him to death.'

'I doubt, My Lord,' said Tom, as steadily as he could – 'I doubt that he died of fear.'

Lord Robert smiled. 'Do not doubt too surely,' he said. 'People do die of fear. I have seen it happen.' He leaned forward suddenly, so that his lean and handsome face filled all of Tom's vision. 'I have *made* it happen.'

Tom licked his lips. 'I do not doubt *that*, My Lord.'

The Black Douglas sat up straight in his saddle then, with a bark of laughter that put Tom in mind of the Barguest with a vengeance. 'But let us not talk of such dark matters,' he said lightly. 'Let us talk of much more pleasant things. Let us discuss, in short, exactly how you would like to die, Master Musgrave. And, perhaps, how *soon*.'

Tom's eyes flicked from Lord Robert's hypnotic gaze to the stony faces of the three that sat beside him. He opened his mouth.

And a hunting horn sounded. It sounded the view. The sound of it was brassy and thin, strident, raucous, echoing – the sweetest sound that Tom had ever heard. Over the shoulder of hillside above Arthur's Seat came the great hart the Lord of the Waste was hunting, a red deer stag full fourteen points of antler, a prince of its species and fit for such sport. The hounds were close upon its heels with Hobbie close on theirs and his horns close behind him calling to the hunt; but they were no great way behind either, for, as Lord Robert Douglas tore his eyes from the skyline every bit as surprised as Tom had been, so the wild mob of horsemen came galloping over the rise and pounded down upon them.

The stag, seeing men and horses before it as well as behind, threw itself sideways and ran to the north; but the northern arm of Arthur's Seat was steep, as befitted the last ridge before the border itself, and slowed the tired beast still further. Down it came relentlessly, back to the illusory shelter of that little coppice at the head of the Black Lyne; and the well-trained hounds, as keen as they were well matched in voice, saw how its path must go and ran straight down the hillside just before Hobbie, closing to cut it off.

By the time the whole hunt came past the little group by the oak, there was nothing left for Tom to do but swing into the saddle and join in. By the time he reached the rest of them, the stag was at bay with the hounds snapping at it. Tom looked for Eve and, when he could not see her, he crossed to Sim Armstrong, as a familiar face that might answer a question or two.

'A good run?'

'Aye. Though we lost the beast once or twice. And there's a good few of the hunt lost still, I'd calculate. Did ye not see for yourself?'

Tom smiled and shook his head, thinking that Sim's news was to the good. His absence might not have been remarked at all. His standing in his uncle's eyes might remain safely high for a while longer yet.

But where was Eve? Tom glanced around, seeking her familiar shape amongst the last few riders as they cantered down the hillside – seeking, for the moment at least, in vain; but he could not imagine her far parted from Hobbie or from the hunt itself, especially now that they had reached the climax: the kill.

The beast was trapped by the thickness of the undergrowth and the precipitous sides of the little river valley behind it. The hounds were keen and ready to tear into the hart at Hobbie's word, but tradition dictated that Sir Thomas himself should make the decision.

The hart and the hunt, like the Waste itself, were his, after all.

'Call them back, Hobbie,' he ordered as he rode up. 'Now,' he continued breathlessly as the master of the hunt obeyed, 'my crossbow. And you may sound the kill.'

# Fourteen

## After the Kill

The great red hart seemed to leap to meet its death as the black steel quarrel flew from Sir Thomas Musgrave's crossbow and pierced it unerringly through the breast and heart at once. Then, having leaped up, it crashed back into the undergrowth and lay still at once. All the men and women there clapped and cheered the clean, accomplished kill – even, noted Tom, the Black Douglas, whose lean cheeks seemed flushed with sport and excitement.

Hobbie's men, having leashed the dogs, rushed forward again and pulled the dead stag into position so that they could lash its hind legs together. They threw the rope up over the branch of the nearest tree so that it could serve as a gallows and they pulled the dead beast high enough so that its antlers just whispered across the frozen grasses of its deathbed. Sir Thomas stepped down and, taking a knife, he turned to Lord Robert. 'Will ye do the honours, Lord Robert?' he asked, and the Black Douglas, all affability again, stepped down and cut the deer's throat

163

with all the delicacy of a master surgeon at work. Then he handed the knife back to his host with the most courtly of courteous bows.

The very instant that the stag's thick blood began to flow, Hobbie was there with a great metal ewer. The horns were sounded again and again as the blood drained swiftly into the smoking bowl. Then the Lord of the Waste stepped forward once more and, with Hobbie deftly helping him, he stripped the carcase of its hide. So delicately was this done that neither man soiled even the finest parts of his linen with blood at all, and so swiftly that the breathless hunters had little time to do more than pass around the stirrup cups of golden usquebaugh and congratulate each other on another successful day's sport before the head, hide and hooves were off and the next part of the ritual began.

Bread was thrown into the bowl of blood while Hobbie, no longer the gentleman hunter, rolled back his sleeves past the elbow, then deftly opened the deer's belly and slid the intestines, liver and lights on to the ground. The blood was added to this steaming mess and the whole lot was covered with the deer's head and hide. Then, at the master's sign, the strident horns sounded again and again while the antlered head was lifted clear and the dogs were unleashed to feed.

The whole howling pack of them, sounding very much more like the hell-hounds they had figured last night, rushed forward to their grim feast; but even as they did so, a terrible screaming began. The sound was louder than the howling of the dogs – almost as loud as the howling of the oak's branches, but this sound was undeniably human. It was issuing from the undergrowth that had held the stag at bay.

Tom and Hobbie, who was nearest beside him, dived into the bushes at the sound and all but tumbled over the cliff concealed behind them. Here they found, at bay just as the stag had been, the youngest of the Kerrs. Tom recognized at once the arrogant, black-haired youth who had been caught beneath his own crossbow at Housesteads fort and farmhouse, who had cost Dand Kerr his hand and who had spoken up so bravely for him at the castle gate last night.

By no means so brave today, the youngster was near to tears with terror, rage and frustration when they dragged him out into the light. Silent now, if struggling still, he shot a fulminating glance at the dogs whose terrible sounds had frightened him and tricked him into giving himself away. They, however, were too preoccupied with their own vast meal to spare him even a glance in return. Not so the other hunters here. The garrison men sprang down at once and went into the undergrowth, searching in case the boy had any companions.

The Lord of the Waste leaned forward and looked down at the writhing lad from the height of his saddle – and the height of his position as the law in this land. 'How came ye here, lad?' he demanded, gently enough, thought Tom, for a man that might apply any form of punishment, torture or execution with no questions asked.

'I rode,' came the grudging reply, elicited, Tom noted, by a quick turn of the wrist that Hobbie was holding.

'Ye were lucky to make it this far in the dark without breaking your neck – or your pony's. Where's your hobbie horse?'

'In the burn. With a broken neck,' the youngster admitted grimly.

'And how did that happen?'

'We saw...' the youth began, but then thought better of the confession clearly. 'We stumbled in the darkness.'

'We?' The Lord of the Waste was on to the word at once.

'Selkie and I. Selkie was my hobbie horse.'

The Lord of the Waste was not convinced, though the lad looked young enough to be giving names to his horses yet. 'Are ye sure ye rode alone?'

'I did.'

'And ye're still alone now?'

'I am,' came the stout reply; and Sim Armstrong, returning from the undergrowth, nodded in confirmation.

'Then we'll be taking you back to Bewcastle with us and holding you till I talk to Hugh of Stob. And mayhap One-Hand Dand himself,' decided the Lord of the Waste. 'There was killing and wanton destruction of property last night, and someone has to pay.'

'Oh let me take the lad,' said Robert Douglas suddenly. 'I've a couple of his relations up at Hermitage. I could bring the family briefly together.'

That suggestion seemed to lend the slight captive the strength of Hercules. One arm tore out of Hobbie's hand and the other nearly broke Tom's grip. Quick-thinking as ever, he held tight for an instant more, then released his grip as the arm tore back again. The captive stumbled, thrown off balance by the unexpected freedom and Tom, swapping one defensive art for another, knocked him cold with a single blow.

Tom stood over the fallen body, panting slightly. His gaze swept over the two men in command here. 'Sir Thomas,' he said. 'If I could beg you to consider for a moment more before you answer Lord Robert's request. The lad has seen something – seen it by his own admission, and seen it here; and this place lies beneath the tree where they found my brother. What he knows may help me in my quest for the truth. Take him to Bewcastle, I beg you, where I may question him.'

Sir Thomas looked at Lord Robert and Lord Robert shrugged. 'It makes no matter to me,' he said with apparent affability. 'Let Master Musgrave ask his questions.'

'Very well,' said Sir Thomas. 'You may take the lad.'

'And,' added Lord Robert, 'as the hunt is done and the day is darkening, I think we will

167

also take our leave. Ah now I know, Sir Thomas, that you have a feast in the making and the hart here to be roasted and eaten, but if I may do so without incurring your wrath, or that of the good Lady Ellen, I will decline. This place is nearer my door than yours and our parting would be convenient now.'

They split into the groups that had composed the Christmas hunt – the Black Douglas's men and guests, the Captain of Bewcastle's men and their guests, and Hobbie and his huntsmen, who still had business here.

That done, the hunt all turned and rode away.

Hobbie and Tom were left with the hart, the hounds, the unconscious Kerr and half a dozen helpers. Up went the deer's carcase on to Hobbie's saddle-bow, for it was his privilege and duty to carry it back. Up went the hide, carefully wrapped under the head, on to his senior helper's horse. The hounds were leashed and secured to the pommels of the other helpers' horses; and, last, the youth was lifted by Hobbie and Tom himself and lain like the stag over Tom's saddle.

'Lad be damned,' said Tom quietly. 'It's a lass we have here. Do all the ladies of the borders dress as boys to go roistering over the place? It was never so when I was a youth.'

'More's the pity,' said Hobbie, mounting beside him. 'But ye're right. 'Tis a new fashion. If ye want to know more, then here's the lass will enlighten ye.'

168

For over the ridge came Eve herself, her horse at full gallop. She met them halfway up the slope and simply looking at her told Tom that something terrible was in train.

'There's a terrible plague struck the hunt and the fort,' she gasped. 'Archie Elliot that wrestled so well is dead. Geordie Burn is close to death. There's others sick all over the place and I...'

She slid from her saddle and tumbled to the ground, twitching, with a little thread of foam leaking out of the corner of her mouth. Tom swung down beside her and caught her up at once.

'We'd best get her back,' said Hobbie. 'I'll take the Kerr lass at my saddle-bow and you take Eve. The hart'll go over the extra horse and we'll ride him in gently. There'll not be any urgent need of him this day, if what she said is true. But hurry, man. Hurry! Whatever's abroad, Eve has it and the least delay may cost her dear!'

# Fifteen

## Plague and Poison

Even after the canter up over Crew Crag and Arthur's Seat, Tom's pony was still fresh. It had been at fighting pitch, after all, and ready to join in the hunt and gallop until its legs gave out. It gave of its best now with great heart, running back along the way it had come as though it was in truth pursuing the greatest of harts, the double load notwithstanding.

As much by judgement as by luck, intuitively associating his own illness with Eve's news – and his vomiting with his continued health – Tom heaved his fair, fainting burden over on to her belly, and after a while the low swinging motion of her head and the bouncing of the pony's downhill gallop set her to puking weakly. As he galloped, he speculated.

Eve had said plague: *There's a terrible plague struck the hunt and the fort...* But she could not mean the word literally. Tom had seen the plague and knew its symptoms. There were none evident here. She used the word in its figurative sense, therefore. This was not the

Black Plague but some sweeping, overwhelming sickness, swift of onset and fatal of outcome. Strength and heartiness were no great bastions against it, for Archie Elliot and Geordie Burn had been rude, healthy and of soldierly fitness. Both had been robust this morning, therefore the onset must have come since the hunt breakfast. And thinking of the hunt breakfast, of course, put him in mind of his own sickness again.

Accidental poisoning was by no means unusual. In London, particularly, he was often mildly surprised that it was not far more common than it seemed to be. But even up here, away from all that filth, humanity and vermin, in the midst of chilly spaciousness, clean water and careful, prudent lifestyle, it could never be ruled out.

Any of the foodstuffs in the kitchen, most of which would have been preserved for some time, could have become tainted: ill-preserved apples or pears; ill-smoked pork, hanging since the winter slaughter several weeks since; fish, perhaps becoming sick-making on their journey from the river or the sea; oats or barley going damp and musty in the store – or infested in the field before harvesting. The local sheep – gathered in winter folds at the moment but still providing mutton to the rich that could afford them – could become tainted through tainted feed. Even the chickens that ran around the kitchen door until they were forcefully invited in could become dangerous through bad food, careless

171

cleaning, faulty preparation. Was it not for wholesomeness as well as taste that the prudent housewife stuffed them with that natural poison-killer, sage? – as had Lady Ellen for the Hunt Breakfast, remembered Tom.

Of all the possible culprits in this case, the chickens were at once the least likely, for they were the only elements of the hunt breakfast that had been slaughtered freshly – last night or this morning, in fact. On the other hand, they were also the most likely, for, as chicken was all he had eaten, Tom thought the guilt must lie there if anywhere; and, unlike the rest of the food on offer, the chickens would have been handled and roasted individually – allowing one to do the damage to a limited number of people – as seemed to be the case here.

If not the food itself, continued Tom grimly, then tainted utensils, perhaps. But again, not likely, for he had actually been impressed with Lady Ellen's housewifery thus far and she had an abundance of clean water nearby, and a good staff with which to work. Even using the kitchen as a hospital last night had not seriously upset the domestic arrangements, as far as Tom could see. Tainted utensils would logically have spread any sickness further – unless, of course, it was widespread and the hearty huntsmen who had killed the hart were now, like Archie, Eve and Geordie, dead or sick unto death.

Yet, he persisted as he rode wildly down the

slope above Kirk Beck, if one of the chickens were the cause of the problem, again, it had passed between fewest hands. It had come under the least number of knives and through the merest bucket or bowl in any case. It had simply been killed, plucked, cleaned, stuffed with dry sage, baked in the oven, sectioned and handed round. Where could any sickness spring from in such a simple ritual as that?

The punch, then – a possible contender, certainly. A capable housewoman like his aunt would be trying to use up the last and worst of the castle's wine supply – without letting Sir Thomas or any of his guests know, he thought. The water added to it and boiled would be twice potable – clean from the well and purified through boiling. The herbs and spices might be tainted, ill-chosen, or...

And that was where logic had taken Tom as he rode under the stone gateway and into the castle itself. If he had expected chaos, he was pleasantly surprised. This was a front-line fort, used to crisis piled upon disaster. True, there was no sign of the festive feast, the ritual roasting of the skinned hart. That, of course, would have to wait – as would Lord Robert's invitation to go hawking at Hermitage. In the meantime everyone had a job to do and went quietly about it, while those whose job was to heal the afflicted went skilfully about that business too.

Tom threw the reins to the stable lad who had been waiting since the keen-eyed sentry called down. He swung down off his horse

173

and pulled Eve into his arms. The same sentry had warned the castle of his burden and the Lady Ellen came fluttering out of the keep as he turned.

'Follow me, my dear,' she said at once. Only when they were inside the building and alone for an instant did she enquire, 'Dead?'

In truth, thought Tom, it was hard enough to tell. 'Fainting. She has puked, an act that helped me, for I believe I have been tainted too.'

'If it helped you, then let us pray it will have helped her. And it must have helped you if you are right, for otherwise we would be carrying you like we had to carry the others, living and dead. Not the kitchen,' she continued sharply, for Tom had turned that way. 'Wounds are one thing. This is quite another and I want it nowhere near our food.'

This brought Tom back to his own train of thought and so, as he carried Eve in Lady Ellen's footsteps towards the back of the keep, he asked, 'What do you think it is, Lady Ellen?'

'I think it is poison,' she said forthrightly.

'I agree,' said Tom.

'What do you know of poisons?' she enquired sharply.

'Little enough,' he admitted. 'I have talked with Gerard the Herbalist over some such matters, but I am far from wisdom myself. I had simply applied logic, for I believe some part of the hunt breakfast unsettled me and I only had a bite of chicken and a sip of punch.'

The Lady Ellen fell silent at that. She led the increasingly breathless Tom through into a small, warm room not unlike the chapel, right at the back of the keep. It was lit by several lamps, for it had no windows and its one other exit, a door with a pointed lintel in the old Gothic style, was tight shut against the cold; but there was a chimney to the outside against a second wall, and beneath it blazed a good fire well stocked with logs and winter peat. Here lay Geordie Burn, white and feverous, but sweating profusely. He lay in a little truckle bed, plaids and skins piled up on him. A three-legged stool stood by him and upon it stood a little horn cup not unlike the one that had held the mandragora Tom had drunk the night before. There was another bed convenient for Eve's still form.

'You were expecting more patients?' asked Tom as he laid her down.

'This was Archie Elliot's,' said Lady Ellen severely, 'but he rests in the chapel now. We'll need to get Father Little to bury him in proper form when he gets back from Blackpool Gate.'

'Why has he gone there?' asked Tom.

'To say a service in the kirk. He's a busy man this season. Let me look at you a moment.'

'But Eve—'

'I cannot give her the tending she needs with you here. I need to see you're well enough to get away from here and let me work.' As she spoke, Lady Ellen was

175

examining Tom's face and eyes. She looked into his mouth and smelt his breath.

As she did this, Tom himself looked around and was struck at once by the way the little room was filled with little pots and jars, how the rafters above the pointed door were hung with drying plants and herbs; by the little cauldron convenient to the fire.

'You'll live,' said Lady Ellen. 'Take a sip from that cup and then you may go.' She indicated the cup by Geordie's bed.

'What is it?' he asked. 'Not more mandragora.'

'It is infusion of all-heal. It's eased Geordie's breathing so it may settle you as well. If ye want to know more, go ask your friend Gerard.'

Thus dismissed, Tom went back the way he had come, his lips pursed in thought. Apparently at random, he wandered unhindered out across the courtyard and through the main gate. Round the burned-out ruins below the walls he went, looking for that unusually shaped door. The thing was of wood and, though heavily barred and bolted, from the inside at least it had shown no sign of fire damage. Yet if he had understood the layout of the castle correctly, it must lead to the outside. Where was there, therefore, an area beside the castle wall untouched by the Kerrs? Where and why?

It was a little graveyard. Edged with a low dry-stone wall and marked with one or two mouldering monuments, it stood green and undisturbed among the charred wreckage of the little stores and outhouses. At the uphill end, there was a little gate and Tom came in through this – necessarily so, for immediately inside the wall all around there grew a strong yew hedge to shoulder height. But it was not so much the wonder of a place so undisturbed that called Tom in, nor the sense of eerie calm and sense of timelessness here; it was the fact that at the castle end, where the soil was richest and deepest, over the bones of the very dead had been planted a garden – not just any garden: the very garden he had told Father Little he would find behind the smithy. He might have known it by the winter form of any of the herbs and plants he had discussed with Gerard himself, but he knew it at once, and with absolute certainty, by the little clump of Christmas roses with all the blossoms gone.

Then, wondering how much difference to his calculations might be made by the fact that it was the Lady Ellen and not Eve herself that was the wise woman here, he wandered back into the castle.

His next object would no doubt await his attention too, for it was Archie Elliot. In that apparently wayward and unfocused mood that Ugo Stell or Talbot Law, his friends in London, would have recognized all too well, he strolled across the courtyard. Hobbie raised a hand from the stables where he was unloading the deer and their insensible captive alike, but was surprised to receive no reply. Sir Thomas, glancing down from the in-facing window of his little study, caught his eye but again received no sign of recognition. Yet when that vacant eye fell upon the tiniest thing that seemed strange or out of place, it fastened on it as though riveted.

The courtyard had been swept since the departure of the hunt – necessarily so, given the predilections of excited horses, well fed and watered and brought to their highest point in the areas of urine and manure. The manure had mostly been added to the pile beside the stables, convenient to the midden chute that led out through the wall beside the Gully Hole, to the only other area near the wall not torched by the Kerrs the previous night. Straw had been scattered over the flags and probably swept up again after the rest of the hunt had returned. Yet over there, beside the door Tom was approaching, between the well-worn, well-swept flags, there lay a little black scrap, spurned by the brooms, obviously, and pushed back towards the doorstep instead of over towards the manure heap. Why it attracted Tom's eye only Tom could tell – perhaps because it looked so strangely out of place; perhaps there was even some spark of recognition too deep ever to be registered. Or perhaps it was his Better Angel once again. Tom stooped and picked it up, wondering at first what on earth it could be. It was a little tube of black leather, stitched to a point but open at an end. It was of a size to slip over a finger. Tom almost slipped it over

178

his own finger – but refrained at the last moment and put it into his pouch instead. For he had recognized it. He knew what it was, at least. It was the finger of a glove – cut off and cast aside; the finger of a black, Spanish leather glove.

It was just at that moment that Hobbie Noble's hand closed on his shoulder and recalled Tom to himself.

'Come, Tom,' said Hobbie. 'No more of this waking dream. We've work to do and a Kerr to practise it on.'

# Sixteen

## Selkie

'We have dungeons of course,' said Sir Thomas, looking at the young woman. 'Were you the lad you appear to be, then I would lock you there.'

'Were I a lad,' spat their prisoner, 'then no doubt I'd be in the Black Douglas's dungeons by now.'

'You're lucky not to be there in any case,' said Tom equably. 'I know little of the Laird of Hermitage, but I cannot suppose you would be enjoying the experience.'

'I'm not enjoying this one,' she hissed back.

'At least it involves no direct discomfort, yet,' said Tom. 'And mind also that you're likely to survive it. Lord Robert says that when we visit Hermitage next there'll be at least a brace of Kerrs hanging by the door to greet us.'

'Come,' said Sir Thomas shortly. 'You know the reputation of the man as well as I do, lass. He's famous through the Borders. If you were in Hermitage instead of here with us, d'you think you'd be sitting in Lord Robert's private chamber with a glass of sack to steady you and Lady Ellen to look to your bruising as soon as she is free – whether Lord Robert is truly associated with your clan or they with him?'

'And d'ye think if I was safe home in Stob with Hugh and Dand I'd be worried over either of ye?'

'I do,' said Tom forthrightly. 'I know nothing about Hugh of Stob, but I know that Dand and the others of his band – including you – were called down to Housesteads on the urging of a man that's guest with Lord Robert and that ye were called down there to put a stop to me. For all your saying, hissing and snarling, you answered the Black Douglas's call swiftly enough, did ye not? So at home or abroad and with Dand if not with Hugh, you are worried about the thoughts of the Laird of Hermitage – and if not you yourself, then those whose orders you obey.'

'Ha!' she spat. 'D'ye think I obey...'

'Of course not. If you obeyed anyone – parent, priest or the elders of your clan – then you'd never be roistering around the Borders dressed as a lad and getting into worlds of trouble. If it were not for you, then none of this coil would be wrapped around us. Dand would still have his hand.'

'It was you that took it!'

'It was you that he was helping when it was taken; you that was trapped out on the moss and likely to die there and then.'

'D'ye think I don't know that?' she shouted

in return. 'That's why I came out last night and braved the Barguest!'

'Ha!' This time the derisory laugh belonged to Hobbie. 'Did ye not know it was a trick, girl? A horse done up with a false head?'

'No! Not that one, the other one!' Her voice trailed away and she frowned back in silence at the three awestruck gazes resting on her pale, determined countenance.

The sound of that second howling echoed in Tom's memory, certainly, and he saw that it echoed also in the minds of the other two.

'You cannot have seen it,' he said. 'Child, it would have killed you on the spot as it is said to have killed my brother, through simple terror.'

'I did not see it, no,' she answered. 'But I heard it.'

Hobbie laughed aloud at that. He laughed with relief, thought Tom, that an explanation might be offered after all; for they were all, it was clear, afraid of the phantom dog.

The girl thought that he was laughing at her. 'I heard it hunting me,' she snarled, stung into more truth yet. 'Only the strength of my little Selkie kept him off. I went away north along the ridges past Crew Crag, but it hunted me to Arthur's Seat and I could ask no more of Selkie. So we went under the great oak and into the undergrowth there, for there is a cavern there...' She tailed off and they watched her in silence, for once again her tongue had worked faster than her mind and betrayed her.

After a moment she looked up at them defiantly. 'There is a cavern above the spring there, in the little cliff below the bushes and I thought to be safe and mayhap a little warmer there. And so I was, by the luck of the Good Lord; but Selkie fell and I lost her. And *it* ... it came on down after me. I could hear it outside the cave mouth howling...'

The place was obvious enough, under the clawed oak tree and behind the bloody pit left by the disposal of the stag. Still Tom said, 'Here?' and the girl Janet nodded. Because they were all confederated upon a larger, more disturbing quest, she had lowered her guard to the extent of her name and her word that she would attempt no escape. Though there remained in Hobbie's mind, as he made no secret, a question as to the worth of a woman's word. Still, he kept his concerns fairly quiet, secure in the certainty that if she broke it, she wouldn't get far before he caught her and taught her the lesson so clearly lacking in her upbringing so far.

Tom looked down, wondering whether he should call for the rope he had thought to bring with him this time; but then his manly pride asserted itself. Janet Kerr had made it down here without a rope last night, he thought – in the dark and in the grip of a good deal of well-warranted terror. The undergrowth at the lip of the cliff was torn away and, now that he was looking for them, he could see twin sets of marks – of Selkie the

pony falling to her doom and of her mistress
– scrambling down and up; down last night
out of the reach of the Barguest, and up this
morning and into the teeth of the hounds. No
wonder the child had screamed.

Well, then, he thought, let us see what we
shall see, deciding against further questioning
when his own good eyes could tell him all he
wanted to know at the moment. Holding on
to a strong-looking branch that leaned out
over the little abyss, splintered at the bottom
as evidence of Selkie's passing if not the
Barguest's, he swung down.

At once Tom found himself hanging, one-
handed, over a drop of ten feet or so. Fortunately, near seven feet of this was covered
by his own stretched body and so it was a fall
of only one yard more before his feet hit the
slippery slope below. He skidded a little, but
then stood firm and turned to look around.
The bank rose immediately behind him with
a narrow crack showing just enough disturbance to mark it as the cave mouth. There
were bushes around it that would have
hidden it perfectly in the summer and he
wondered that he did not know the place
himself, for it was a very heaven for children
down here, he thought. Or it had been before
the Barguest came abroad.

That thought made him shiver. He had seen
the thing in childhood, and yet he had
questioned his own memory. The thing had
clawed the tree above – and yet he had convinced himself there must be some other

184

explanation. He had heard it last night and supposed it an echo of some kind, and now this girl had seen it

Yet, his rational mind persisted, even if the beast existed, was that proof that it had killed his brother? And the word of a girl, terrified and on the run ... What was it Will had made Theseus say in his new play of the midsummer dream, about being out in the woods?: 'Or in the night, imagining some fear, | How easy is a bush supposed a bear...'

Even as these thoughts attempted to distract him – like Father Little yesterday morning before Lord Robert had arrived – he was busily at work. Here, clearly, poor Selkie had fallen, only to slither deeper down the vale with legs broken for certain and neck, too, most likely. He would follow that broad pathway later, for he had a more immediate focus now. Here had the girl leaped free of the horse and, in a panic, run inwards into the cavern; and here, something had followed. But what, precisely? The Barguest, if she was to be believed; and it had been here twelve hours since, its huge pads scratching where his good boots scuffed.

Where were the marks down here like the ones that its claws had made above? Where were the sharper-than-a-knife incisions into the ground where it walked? There were none. But something had been here, for the bushes by the cavern mouth were torn; some of the branches seemed to have been chewed. What looked like drool was frozen among the icicles, thicker and yellower than they; and everything around the narrow entrance certainly smelled of dog – dog and loam and mould and ... something else? What else? Something metallic perhaps? His mind closed down in concentrated thought...

So that when Hobbie dropped like a petard exploding right beside him, he jumped and slid away from the place again. But Hobbie, ever practical, just reached down and pulled him back, and that he did one-handed, for Hobbie had brought a torch with him.

'Sir Thomas,' he called up, 'do ye wish to see the place? It's slippery but safe enough. No Kerrs in waiting to kidnap any of us after all. Shall we bring the lassie down?'

'I'll guard her here for the present,' came the answer.

'Wise enough,' said Hobbie; 'there's no telling what else may be down here even if there's no more Kerrs. Shall we in, Long Tom?'

Thus warned to mind his head on the roof at least, Tom nodded, and the pair of them squeezed in. The little cavern opened out and upward into the cliff immediately behind the deceptive little door. They stepped over a low sill into a great crackling nest of leaves and branches, thick and springy enough to provide a warm, safe bed.

'The child's right,' Hobbie said in wonder. 'This is a sizeable place. It's as well the entrance is so narrow,' he continued, 'or we'd be like to waken a winter bear! That would

186

remind the pair of us how to hop, skip and jump, eh, Tom? Or is there magic in those great long swords of yours that would bring even a bear to its knees?'

'Are there bears still?' asked Tom, paying Hobbie scant attention as he searched the place with narrow eyes.

'So they say. In the deep woods still – the wild woods that still lie even at the hearts of Inglewood Forest and some of the others up here. Bears like the ones they bring to be baited from Russia into Berwick and New Castle with the grains from Gdansk; and big black boar such as they still hunt in High Germany; and a wild grey wolf or two, left from the days of Robin Hood, like as not. Ye can hear them howling on full-moon nights, I'm told, in the last deep thickets as the iron-masters and the metalworkers clear the forests for charcoal for their furnaces and the shipwrights come in deeper and deeper, looking for heart of oak and straight, tall pines for the fleet to answer the next armada when it comes. Or maybe the wolves are all as dead as Robin himself and it's the Barguest they've heard instead.'

Tom was still paying scant attention, though it was unusual to hear Hobbie wax so sad and lyrical. The walls of the little cavern were consuming his lively attention. They were strangely banded with ridges, and the ridges seemed to glitter in the light. Following the gleaming glitter down, he stirred the thick-piled bottom of the cave.

'Looking for smuggled goods – such as the Kerrs would leave convenient in a secret place like this?' asked Hobbie more brightly.

'I don't know what I'm looking for,' said Tom. ' 'Tis likely a distraction to be looking for anything at all. And yet ... Hobbie, do you know what sort of rock this is?' Tom straightened with a piece of rock the size of a crab apple in his hand. It glittered dully, a greeny golden colour.

'Nay, lad. I know about reiving, not metalworking.'

Tom nodded and slipped it in his pouch.

'Mind,' continued Hobbie without thinking. 'If ye want to get an idea, then ask John the Blacksmith...' He stopped, frowning. Tom nodded.

'And failing my brother John? Who should I ask then?'

'I know of no one else to ask about the rock. But you could ask your sister Eve, who John would have asked if he did not know the answer.'

'Later perhaps, when she is stronger, if I feel the toy has import.' Tom tapped his pouch dismissively. 'But to the matter in hand. Is that opening proof against something of the size and power of the creature that clawed the tree, d'ye suppose?'

'Not if it was hunting. It'd be in here like a terrier after a rat.'

'But if the lass is right, then it was hunting. It had chased her for nigh on five miles.'

'She's mistaken, then. 'Tis not a likely tale

in any case.'

'Yet you heard the hound echo your own wild call.'

'I heard an echo, aye.'

'Then, my master huntsman, let us grant her a grain of truth. And let us exercise some logic. We heard the cry, therefore there was something that cried. The girl heard it too and heard it follow her. Therefore it followed. She glimpsed it and she heard it over five long miles. Therefore it hunted. It brought her to bay here and could have dug her out if it wanted. But it did not. It left her and it went away. Therefore, old friend...?'

'Therefore it's all a lie. Therefore she was not hunted. Therefore 'tis all moonshine, man.'

'Therefore it was not the rider that the great hound hunted. Therefore it was...'

'The horse!'

'Indeed. Let us look to poor Selkie, who may indeed have saved her wild young mistress's life.'

As they slithered down the icy slope after the unfortunate horse, Hobbie said, his voice low, ' 'Twould needs be a monstrous hound indeed to hunt a hobbie horse.'

'Thus are we come full circle, are we not? 'Twould need to be a monstrous hound to do that to the great oak, and to kill John through pure fear. 'Twould need to be a monster such as you released against the Kerrs last night.'

Hobbie, slightly in the lead, pulled back the last of the bushes and froze. 'Why Tom,' he said, his voice unsteady, 'I think it may well be.'

There in front of them lay the place where Selkie had fallen. It was a little clearing, made wider by the thrashing of the unfortunate animal's body. Everything was stained with blood – the exact opposite of the ritual cleanliness of Sir Thomas's hunt this morning. That was all. The little clearing had been turned into a very shambles and then left empty.

Tom and Hobbie looked at each other, lost in wonder. For whatever had hunted Janet Kerr's pony had brought it to bay here and slaughtered it; and then it had proved big enough and strong enough to carry poor Selkie's body away.

# Seventeen

## Spate

All four of them went after it.

The three men would have fain left the girl but none of them wanted to stay with her – and Janet needed restraining as well as guarding, thought Tom with his usual insight, for her warlike blood was up. She wanted as much as any of them to go after the creature that had so terrified her in the night. She wished to be in at the death of the monster that had slaughtered and stolen her poor beloved Selkie, though she knew the experience of finding the pony would test her to the limit, let alone the experience of finding whatever had carried it off. The knowledge deepened the respect he felt for the girl into something different.

They tethered the four restless ponies beside the clawed oak. Tom unloaded rope, spears, Jedburgh axes and the pistols he had still kept in his panniers. The four-barrelled bastard pistol Ugo Stell had warned him against remained, regrettably, in the satchel containing his papers in Sir Thomas's study, but under the flap of his saddle instead was the very arquebus that had nearly despatched young Janet Kerr, in the time before Tom had known her or liked her. He exchanged this for his swords. Hobbie and Sir Thomas both had crossbows like the ones that had claimed Dand's hand and killed a full-grown four-teen-point red deer stag with one shot. Tom smiled grimly at the arsenal they thus revealed. No one rode unarmed in the Borders, he thought – except for captives, like Janet herself. She went unarmed, though mutinously, for she was clearly accustomed to getting her own way, beyond reasonable expectation.

Tom took the lead with Hobbie, falling into old ways with unsettling swiftness. The whispered exchange of monosyllabic signals, the silence of sign and countersign were things born of poaching expeditions away south in Inglewood, away down the years; but they all came back in a flash, he thought. To be fair, though, they needed few enough of these, he knew, for they were crossing a part of Sir Thomas's territory that no one even bothered to patrol; and if the land belonged to anyone other than the English knight who was tracking carefully through it, then it belonged to the woman currently being tended by the Lady Ellen.

Tom soon saw that they needed few of their tracking skills either, for the Barguest and its victim had left a considerable pathway through the rough foliage and the low coarse bracken and winter-thin fern with which it was interspersed. They followed this pathway, therefore, which was to Tom as wide as the primrose path to the everlasting bonfire, down the gloomy little valley towards the head of the Black Lyne river itself.

Every now and then Tom's eyes glanced up from his feet to the higher spheres above. The heavens, increasingly distant above them, were covered with restless, roiling clouds and, although the wind which set the sky all adance was kept off their faces by the high walls astride them, nevertheless it still caressed them at unexpected moments with icy little tongues of air. It still brought strange, unsettling threads of scent, smell and stench that set Tom's hair, for one, to prickling uncomfortably; and all the while in the tree tops near and far, it whimpered and howled.

As they followed the pathway so clearly marked by the drag-marks of a heavy body sluggishly bleeding from a range of gashes, so Tom found himself being distracted by the simple ease of the tracking. Any one of them could have followed poor Selkie's final passage without exercising any real skill at all. The only thing that kept even part of his busy mind on such an easy task was the fear that he would round some bush or boulder and walk into the Barguest's supper – a situation, in his opinion, likely to result in them all joining the feast themselves: as an extra course.

Yet Tom found that the way the little spring bubbled up out of the frost-bearded moss from under two great boulders, bleeding so thinly out of the earth, and battling at once to break free of the ice that sought to bind it, made him frown with distant wonder. Its very pathetic gasping seemed to be the breathing of a new-born babe – a dwarf child all but lost in the heart of this valley fit for giants. An apparently unconnected thought drifted into his mind, of the way that the acorns from the damaged oak behind them at the head of this great valley were most often found away downstream around Blackpool Gate – a thought placed there, perhaps, by the first drops of rain that attained sufficient size to batter through the branches, twigs and winter-sere leaves all so tightly packed above him. He realized with a start that it must have been raining for quite some time. And raining hard at that.

Immediately, rain was everywhere, draining over the frozen slopes across their path along the Barguest's track down into the little rivulet on their right. The water of the stream was dark in colour, as though the sudden myriad of tiny tributaries slithering under their feet were washing Selkie's blood down into it. Abruptly Tom was finding that the silent signals between Hobbie and he were more useful. It would have required a considerable shout to rise above the hissing and the howling with which they were sur-rounded. A new urgency entered their movements, even as the noise – to Tom at least – urged caution. For, apart from the track they were following with such ease and speed, everything around them was retreating behind impenetrable shadow and overwhelming sound.

The little river valley too, he noted with a frown, made speed more inevitable, for the slope down which they were tripping steepened beneath their feet. The whole valley seemed to tilt downwards at a greater angle while the narrow floor dropped more precipitously than the walls themselves, making the place seem deeper and darker still. The valley walls had not spread out to any great extent, but the river had widened and had carved a broader, fertile little plain. The trees between which the Barguest had lugged its increasingly tattered prize were taller, thicker, more full of branches, the undergrowth more hardy and virile.

They came to a cliff over which the river jumped in a waterfall ten feet high; and Tom, then Hobbie, stopped – signalling to the others to stop as well. For the trail ended there, at the edge of the cliff.

Tom and Hobbie stood shoulder to shoulder. 'The beast's dropped Selkie over and she's fallen into the pool down there,' said Tom.

'Aye,' concurred Hobbie. 'But then has the thing gone down after her – or has it simply gone?'

'Or is it still waiting here, in shelter somewhere?' Tom looked around with narrowed eyes, thinking, *How dark it has become!*

'We need to look and be sure before we proceed,' decided Hobbie. 'It's one thing to be hunting the thing...'

'And quite another to be hunted by it,' agreed Tom. 'Well, we'd better split up and make a search – in pairs, I think.'

Tom took Janet. If there was reasoning in the choice, it was slight and soon forgotten but, as is often the case, it made a deal of difference. It was bitter cold. They were wet but not yet soaked to the skin, for their cloaks were thick, made of oiled wool, and near watertight. Beneath them both wore jacks and the metal saw off any moisture making it through the cloaks without even disturbing the well-tanned, quilted leather, which was again effectively waterproof. Both wore high boots over thick, oiled-wool tights. Both wore steel bonnets that would rust before they leaked, strapped tight beneath their chins nevertheless. Even in the downpour, therefore, their first instinct – and that so strong and with such good reason that they never thought of giving up and going home to the warm and the dry – was to proceed.

Tom gave Janet a spear and took the other for himself. He laid his arquebus against a tree, for its matchlock would be useless in the rain, and Hobbie gave him one of the two crossbows. He gave one of his Solingen daggers to Janet, and having the short weapon to go with the long one settled the woman's tight-strung nerves, as Tom had planned that it should. With the arquebus useless, Tom reckoned he could no longer rely on the pistols either, but he kept them, dry, tucked in his belt, safely against the back of his shirt – and the flint and powder he needed to set them off, all, again, in a waterproof oiled-leather pouch under his jack against the breast of his blessedly still-dry shirt.

So they made a few simple plans in sign and snatched phrases, then parted company. Tom waved Hobbie and Sir Thomas out to the right, where they would search up the valley slope of the bank that they had been following so far. Then he and Janet, in their high boots, splashed across the shallow, six-foot width of waterfall's head and struck out upon the left bank.

Tom noticed that things were subtly different here and, if anything, worse. There was no track to follow now, and Tom found all his skills in woodcraft suddenly being tested to the limit. Fortunately, Janet seemed to be as adept as he and they formed a team as he and Hobbie had done, using the same simple code of signals. They stayed close together of necessity, for there was too much noise for them to hear anything less than a shout at more than two fathoms' distance and the afternoon had darkened down as soon as the clouds had thickened and the sunlight had left the little valley. More than once Tom looked up to find himself alone with Janet one step too deep in the shadows for him to see her at all.

They had other reasons to stay close together, too, thought Tom grimly. The bank they were exploring led across a very little level area to a steep, forbidding slope. The narrow, overgrown winter-dead woodland had a haunted atmosphere. It was the sort of place where it was all too easy to see enemies behind every tree trunk and become convinced that there were movements in the restless patterns of sound immediately behind your back.

Although the Black Lyne's first waterfall filled only the centre section of the little cliff, the ridge of solid rock reached out in a precipice that jutted right across the valley. Quashing his rebellious nervousness, Tom led off to follow this first, reasoning that it would be easiest to spot whether the Barguest had found a path on downstream along this line. As they worked, however, he found himself easing back from the edge of the cliff itself, for his feet were forever being swept towards it by the gathering runnels of water flowing in crazy motion down the valley side in front of him and down the valley slope from his right to his left, as though the very ground were haunted here, and trying to drag him down.

Had he not been focused so fiercely on the twin distractions of Janet and the monster they were hunting, his agile mind might have warned him that these were signs of considerable danger gathering; and that it was a

198

real, physical danger, not a spiritual or spectral one.

Instead, having followed the cliff edge to the valley wall and found it too difficult for man or beast to climb, they struck back in a semi-circle as agreed at the outset; they were hoping to check for caves. There were none. So, in spite of their careful woodcraft and near-waterproof clothing, it was a disappointed and bedraggled pair of monster-hunters that returned to the top of the waterfall an hour later.

Tom knew that it was exactly the right place, for he could just see his arquebus, still leaning uselessly against the tree; but of Hobbie and Sir Thomas there was no sign at all. It seemed to be near night, so thick had the shadows become, and Tom had decided to return to their horses with all possible speed, when the crisis was upon them.

There was no warning. Such sound as the thing might have made was lost in the sound of the storm around them. If the ground quaked, why they were on the bank of a river at the head of a waterfall – of course the ground quaked. They could not even see it coming, for it was black water among dark shadows beneath thick-set trees. And so it took them: a wall of water chest high, blessedly lightly armed with branches; a wall of water with a full spate of the river behind it, strong enough to throw them over the waterfall that grew on the instant from a fathom wide to five fathoms wide.

# Eighteen

## Gate

Because they were standing side by side, Tom just had the chance to drop his spear and grab hold of Janet before they went over. Because they were standing on the bank of the original stream, they were swept inwards as well as downwards into the deep pool at the waterfall's foot. Because of a great deal of quick-thinking and a good deal of luck, they went locked together and feet first.

They plunged down to the very bottom of the first pool and here their luck still held, as fortune favours the brave. The hard rock of the sill had been worn smooth over the centuries by a collection of rocks and boulders, also by the waterfall's ceaseless action. Down the back of this giant ladle they slid, therefore, and into the bowl of its spoon. Here they plumbed the depths before they were lifted up, over the forward sill of the riverbed and into the next slide into the next pool and the next and the next downstream. Water foamed around them, alternately inundating them almost to the point of drowning, then hurling them high above the surface so that they had a chance to catch their breath, so that they did not drown after all.

Tom held on to Janet with all his considerable strength and found that she was returning the compliment with all of hers. On their sides they stayed in feverish embrace. The clothing that had been designed to keep them dry now conspired to keep them safe. The steel bonnets, particularly, guarded their heads and faces against rocks – sharp as well as smooth – while the steel-covered jacks protected their backs and sides. Long legs fared less well, but both pairs of boots were stout and shrugged off splinters of branch and stone that would otherwise have stabbed them to the bone; and they managed to do this in spite of the fact that they soon filled, first with water and then with pebbles.

Finally, they were fortunate in Selkie. As Tom and Hobbie had surmised at the outset of this, the body of the little horse had been lying at the bottom of the first pool. There had been just enough light and reason in the whirling madness of that first wild plunge for Tom to see her and work out what she was. As they slid down the back of the spoon-shaped pool to the boulder-dancing depths, so the body of the pony seemed to spring against the sky above them. The sky was dull and the water thick, the situation hardly conducive to reasoned observation, but the outline of a horse's head was unmistakable and the rest elementary.

Tom and Janet struck bottom amid the dancing pebbles and very nearly lost their grip on one another; but then the pony, seeming to show the way in the grip of the rushing water, leaped over the rocky sill of the pool and on away down to the next. So they followed in her wake, protected by her bulk, through pool after pool and along runnel after runnel, down to the point where the valley widened abruptly and the spate washed suddenly into a last great pool where it began to lose its force. The lighter matter in the flood, the tree branches, leaves and acorns, swept a little further still. The heavier matter, such as bodies and boulders, stopped its journeying here. This was the deep dark pool at Black Pool Gate, where the river ran beside the little half-ruined kirk.

Battered, breathless, Tom pulled Janet up the pebble-strewn river bank. He was numb with cold and shock. All he could think of was the need to get the girl out of the river, the wind and the rain. So cold was his face that the torrents pouring out of the icy heavens seemed warm against his cheeks, and he was an old soldier, wise enough in the ways of death to suspect that this was a very bad sign.

The storm proved Tom's friend in more ways than this, for the near-darkness of the evening was suddenly rent by a huge flicker of lightning. The brightness was dazzling, almost golden, and there for only the briefest of instants; but it outlined not just the edge of the Waste high above but also the black edifice of the little kirk immediately in front.

As he dragged Janet Kerr towards the place, Tom sought to kick his mind and memory into some kind of motion. He knew that if he slipped into the deep lake of sleepy lethargy that beckoned at the heart of it, then the pair of them were like to die. He knew to within an ell where he was. Who was there lived nearby? And where? Headgate, Todholes, Nook and Knowe were the nearest farmsteads. They all lay at some distance – though a determined man might walk to them, even through this; but half of them had lain untenanted through his childhood; and things had grown worse since then.

The kirk had fallen into some disuse, too, though Tom remembered someone saying that Father Little had been working to re-establish the little congregation there; and had even come over here this morning after the hunt. He would never have waited, however. There would be no one in the little kirk now – no one near enough to help them at all, in fact; no one nearer than God himself.

Even so, thought Tom grimly, aware that the shivering that possessed his frame was rapidly becoming an uncontrollable shuddering, this was their only chance: shelter first; then dryness; then the heavenly prospect – heavenly in distance as well as beauty – of warmth.

First he had to open the churchyard gate. In fact Tom found this first step quite easy, for as he pulled himself up off the pebbles at the churchyard wall, so he leaned against the crazy wicket and it collapsed back off its ancient leather hinges, inviting him past at once. Had he not still been wearing his steel bonnet, his face would have suffered when he fell forward; but the shock of the fall roused him further and gave him the wit to discard the heavy helmets from both his own head and Janet's before he dragged her onwards.

Half-up on his knees and left hand, with the right hand clasped round Janet's wrist, Tom laboured up the pebble path towards the old church door. The kirk at Blackpool Gate was small; so was the churchyard, and the path was miraculously short. It seemed that Janet's heels were scarcely in through the gate before Tom was pulling himself up the first of the two steps into the ancient porch. The storm was coming from the north and the church faced south, so that the porch gave blessed relief at once. Blessed also was the fact that the big old Norman door, solid enough to have withstood siege as well as time, was unlocked. Tom pushed against it and it creaked open.

He pulled Janet through the doorway and into a little chamber, littered with rubble and wet with rain, that stood at the foot of the half-ruined bell tower. The state of the place was worse than Tom remembered it from childhood and it was certainly much more of a ruin than the church he had called into his fever-dream in the coach coming north; but the rubble had been cleared to one side and a path led through to the weatherproof little chapel beyond. The Good Lord had smiled upon them so far, thought Tom, and he hoped most fervently that he would continue to do so – and indulgently. For now that they were out of the storm itself, they needed warmth. Tom had to find in this place enough matter to burn as a fire and something to set it alight.

As soon as they were out of the rain – out of the room beneath the open tower – Tom left Janet lying on the cold flags of the little nave and pulled himself to his feet against the wall. He discarded his sopping cloak and immediately felt almost that he was floating spirit-like, so heavy had the sodden wool become. The jack came next, and another great weight was gone. Would that he could just add some natural warmth, he thought grimly, to this fire-like, airy lightness he seemed suddenly to have about him. Would that he could stop this juddering in his near-frozen limbs. He would fain have removed his boots too, for they were so full of stones and water that they were almost impossible to walk in; but he wisely calculated that the simple effort of getting them off would use up the last of his strength, and that must still be put to better use.

Tom staggered back out into the room beneath the open tower. If there was the rubble of stones here, he calculated, then there would also be the rubble of wood. If the stones had been piled out of the path, why the wood might be neatly stacked as well. So it proved. Over in a corner, as much by feel as by sight in the near-pitch of the darkness, he found great balks standing – a well-chosen corner too, selected by a man with an eye to re-using such matter and conserving God's gifts to men. If stone didn't perish with the action of water, wood most certainly did. The balks were stored in the one dry area of the room, therefore; and, at the cost of a stab-wound or two, Tom discovered splinters and kindling beneath.

Tom marked where the makings of the fire of salvation were and left them there. He was wet himself and feared he would flood their natural elements with his current icy state. Furthermore, though he had the makings, he still lacked the vital spark. Festooned with powder and shot though he was, it was all, like himself, inundated. He had flint and stone about him too, but his tinder was as wet as the rest of him. He must dry his hands, therefore, and explore a little further still; and time was running out. His body was still feeling some relief at being out of the jaws of the storm, but the body of the church itself was still icy-cold and the last of the heat was coming out of his juddering frame at a terrible rate – so much so, that a distracting element of self-doubt, a disturbing fear of death began to lurk at the outer edges of his mind; and yet he fought on against the inner demons and the outer.

At the far end of the place there was a little altar. Father Little's care had placed a little white altar cloth upon the plain wood of the simple table. Tom noted its pale glimmer in the thick darkness of the place leavened a little beneath the high plain glass of the northward-facing window. He touched it, felt its dryness and left it alone as yet. Once dry, his hands would remain so only for an instant or two with the rest of his clothing down to the fine lace of his shirt cuffs still sopping. He needed one more thing – had great hope of finding it. For there were two great candles there, the white columns of their pure wax bodies seeming to glimmer. If Father Little had left candles in the place, then he might well have left the means of lighting them.

And so he had. There, on the altar itself, a black square in the last of the light, lay a little tinder box. Tom picked up a candle and used the stand that held it to move the tinder box aside. Then he took the altar cloth in shaking fingers and brutally scrubbed life into the quaking flesh of his hands and forearms as he dried the water out. Last of all, in a moment of blessed clarity, he swept the thing over his face and forehead, pulling back the dripping mop of his hair.

The instant Tom felt dry, he put the cloth aside and arranged the candles and the little box of wooden spills that sat beside them convenient to his shaking hands. Then he opened the tinder box. He had been using devices such as this since childhood – and in the dark at that. Why were his fingers so clumsy now? Why could he not hold the flint at the right angle? Why not raise a spark

207

against the striker? His breath hissed in and out between his tight-clénched teeth as he struck and struck again. Wetness of cold sweat as well as running water was oozing past his wrists now. He dared one more strike, and raised a spark.

With all the concentration of a drowning man as he fastens his fist around a straw, Tom bent forward and controlled the jumping muscles of his belly so that a slow, steady breath of air fanned the tiny spark in the heart of the tinder until it flamed. With shaking hand, he reached for a spill and slid the end of it into the little smouldering ball, blowing as steadily as he could until the flame spread from the one to the other.

Slowly Tom straightened, unconsciously hunching over the tiny spark of life, protecting it from wind and rain while it ran unsteadily up the shaft of wood, and carried it across the tiny distance to the candle wick.

Even when both candles were well alight, Tom could not relax. He stumbled down the echoing, weirdly dancing chamber of the nave, past Janet, who lay as still as a fallen monument in her spreading puddle of water and out into the room beneath the tower. Like a leper, he skinned his insensible knuckles against the wood as he shifted the bigger balks aside and carried the makings of a fire into the nave. There were no pews – not even a private area for the great and the good. Had the tower not been half-ruined, there would have been nothing in the sparsely furnished place to burn except for the altar, and the priest's chair that also served as pulpit. Then, likely, they would both have died before the bitter night was out.

The tower had fallen, though, and Father Little had piled the smashed wood in a dry corner, and so Tom built his fire in the very heart of God's little house and, with candle flames and a spill or two he set it all alight – set it so and kept it so, all through the long, cold night; but that was by no means all he did.

Once the fire was safely alight, Tom looked to Janet. He stripped her of her cloak before he moved her and placed her cloak with his over the priest's chair, which he pulled as close to the flames as he dared. Then, thinking more clearly as he began to warm a little, and having desecrated the altar cloth in any case, he pulled the solid table over and set up a simple rack between that and the chair using wood from the room outside. That rack conveniently went between the door and the fire, cutting down further on the draughts, especially after he hung her jack beside his upon it. Belts were next – with such daggers and guns as the Black Lyne had left to them – and shirts, though this left them both naked to the waist. The desecration of the altar cloth was compounded as he tried to rub some life and warmth – and dryness – into the marble of her shoulders and back. He did not touch her front, for three reasons: two were soft and white, pink-tipped and tempting even in his icy condition. The third was exactly between them and it was an ugly black: the great round bruise. That mark showed her fortitude, for it must have been a source of potent agony from the moment his shot had struck her to the moment she had fainted of the cold in the rushing river.

The fire was blazing merrily now, the ancient timbers spitting and crackling as the tall flames consumed them. It gave off brightness as well as warmth, allowing Tom's wandering eyes to see the walls and roof of the place. The roof was high and pointed. Just as it kept the rain out, so it kept the smoke in, and already the highest point was beginning to fill with fumes – but, Tom thought, even eventual damnation for this sacrilege was preferable to instant death now. Below the sharp slope of the roof, the walls were rough – roughened, in fact. In the days before King Henry and the split away from Rome there had apparently been beautiful paintings of saints and Bible scenes there. They were gone now, and simple Bible texts etched in black against the rough white were all that remained. Idly, Tom wondered what had happened to the golden candelabra and great gold cross that were said to have decorated the place in the legends of his youth, long forgotten until this moment – until the necessity had arisen, in this place of all places and at this particular time, of distracting his lower spirits from the fact that he was alone with a near-naked woman.

Even this close to the fire the flags of the floor still struck icily through their sopping clothes. When he was sure he could bring no more life into her upper body working as he was, therefore, he lifted her and sat her on the steaming cloaks in the priest's chair. Then he fell to easing off her boots, allowing the warmth of the fire to bring further life into his lower back and buttocks as he worked. Her boots were not quite as long as his, but they were equally full of water and pebbles, both of which slopped out of them as soon as they came free. He emptied each with almost drunken care and stood them as close to the fire as he dared.

'So, this is ravishment, is it? It's a sight more gentle than my mother warned me. And a sight less hot to boot.'

Tom sat back on his heels and looked up at her. In the firelight she seemed a thing made all of gold — above the waist, at least, and below her raven hair. He opened his mouth to rebut the accusation. Then he recognized the tone of her voice. He glanced up further. Her eyes were resting on him like the eyes of a night-hunting cat, as huge as though she had been drizzling belladonna into them. He looked up further still. On the wall above her head it said: THOU SHALT NOT COMMIT ADULTERY; and for some reason that struck him as exquisitely funny.

'Janet Kerr,' he said, his voice atremble with strange hilarity, 'you are safe from me this night. What with the river reminding me of

211

the closeness of death and the place reminding me of the nearness of heaven and, most especially, these boots reminding me of the torments of hell, I fear I would never dare to transgress.'

She sat for a moment, looking down at him. Then she smiled and said, 'Let us remove your boots at least, and see what might follow then, in the matter of heaven at least.'

The morning sun came late and dull. It found them enmeshed in a tangle of cloaks and clothing – and of each other's limbs. Nothing was dry, but everything was warm and, such had been the length of their attempts to visit heaven and their repeated little brushes with exquisite death, the fire was still ablaze. Tom woke first, stirred as ever by his stomach. He opened his eyes groggily, for he had not been asleep for all that long; and the first thing he saw was a pile of pebbles from his boot. In the absence of pillows such as soft southerners were growing used to, they had used blocks of wood, but even so his face was close down to the floor. The pebbles seemed quite a little mountain to him, therefore; and, in the brightness of the fire as it struck across his shoulder, they seemed to be gleaming a little. Still held by the rags of last night's sensual dream, he reached out and felt the gleaming pebbles with an idle finger. They were warm. He stirred them. They were smooth – almost as smooth as Janet wrapped against him. He picked one up. It was heavy. It was very heavy indeed.

Slowly, carefully, gently as though in a dream, Tom sat up. The cold whipped at his shoulders at once but he paid it no mind at all. Even shadowed from the fire, with nothing but the dull cobweb-grey of the morning, the pebble seemed to glitter; and it slid down into his palm with almost sensuous slowness, like quicksilver. But it wasn't silver at all. What in God's creation was it?

Janet stirred against him, coming awake. Gently, even in his dazzled state of mind, he extricated himself from her and began to sort through the gleaming pile. Still almost asleep, as though sleepwalking indeed, Janet pulled herself away from him and stood. She caught up some covering and padded away towards the door. Cold struck again and bore upon him most urgently that they had best get dressed and moving at once; but the gleaming pile distracted him – so that Janet had to scream twice, and at the top of her lungs, before he ran out to see what had frightened her.

Even when he reached her side she had to gesture twice again before he looked up and saw: halfway up the tower was a little balcony, floored with wood and edged with a rough banister. Here stood Father Little staring down at them – staring down and screaming, eyes and mouth spread wide, tongue rigid and protruding; screaming with stark terror.

But screaming silently, for he was clearly dead.

# Nineteen

## Post Mortes

They had not buried John Musgrave in a coffin but in a winding sheet. So it was that Tom could begin to make observations about the true state of his brother even as he oversaw the manner in which his body was eased out of the shallow grave. A coffin would have been unusual, for John was not an important man, but in any case, thought Tom, given the state of the ground it would have been impractical, and given the state of the corpse it would have been impossible.

It was after noon on the third day, the dawn of which had brought Janet's discovery of Father Little's corpse. In the interim, Tom had discovered the father's little pony tethered securely in the churchyard behind the kirk and had used that to make contact with one of the groups of men the battered Lord of the Waste had sent out to search for his still-missing guests in the dawn. He had accepted Lady Ellen's assurance that the kitchen at Bewcastle fort had been cleaned and scoured in case the sickness visiting them

214

now had arisen from some failure there. He had fed, dressed – in a clean, neatly mended shirt for a wonder – and left Janet mutinously in Lady Ellen's charge.

Then he had returned to oversee the removal of the old priest's body from the rough wooden balcony where it stood. Doing this had allowed the Master of Logic in Tom to make certain observations and deductions that he was keen to prove now. For, although Eve and Geordie were beginning to show some recovery, and he himself, although touched by the sickness, had hardly been hurt by it, he had three corpses to compare, and every reason to believe that they had been killed in the same way.

Although he had spent yesterday, the feast of St Stephen patron saint to horses, proving to his own satisfaction that something very like the Barguest must exist, nevertheless he was also certain in his own mind that it had not after all killed these men. For he could say with some certainty that Father Little had not died of fear, and with great certainty that Archie Elliot had not, for everyone said the man had just fallen off his horse of a sudden, calling and convulsing.

Yet if the Barguest had not killed Archie, Father Little and, therefore, John, then something else had – or, more likely, some*one* else. Some person, or some secret confederation of people, was a more likely proposition as the origin of these deaths than, say, a repetition of simple accidents; or they seemed so in Tom's

215

mind. This was because of the attempts on his own life, because of the generality of the sickness within Bewcastle fort, and because he could conceive of nothing that his brother John and Father Little could have shared, other than the company of the same, limitedly local people.

Certainly, thought Tom, checking his logic by assessing it from another angle, the Barguest had left no sign of being in the kirk at Blackpool Gate, though Satan himself might have stood close once or twice in the night, in the persons of the demons of lust. Nothing had clawed the stones or the rubble or the balks of timber beneath Father Little's balcony. Yet something had clawed the great oak – and again, if not the Barguest, then something else, or someone else. Finally, therefore, that person or confederacy had struck time and again, covering their tracks for reasons of their own; but now they must be found and stopped and made to pay. For with the Father's death, all ten of the commandments had been broken now.

Yesterday's torrential rain had ceased. This morning had been brighter but ice-bound once more. Now the freezing afternoon threatened snow. The water of yesterday's flood seemed hardly to have penetrated the earthen clods of John's grave. Perhaps just enough to mould the rough cloth of the winding sheet more tightly about the body and give it a crisp patina of ice. Even to make it almost transparent in places – over the face, particularly. And here the outline of the cloth showed John's face still frozen in his dying scream, but there was no great staining of mud; nor, to Tom's relief, was there any great icy puddle out of which the body might have to be chipped like a precious stone in an open mine.

That had been a particular worry to Tom, who was still castigating himself over the length of time it had taken him to come to this necessary point in his investigation. The God of the Borders was not a forgiving God, and Tom was quite sure that laggardness was almost as much of a sin as the manner in which he had passed last night.

Then again, no: there could be few things worse than the list of desecrations he had committed, finishing with carnal knowledge of a Kerr in the chancel of a kirk.

Tom gave himself a mental shake and called his straying wits, blessed with enough self-knowledge to understand that his thoughts were wandering because of the horror of the work at hand. This, though, was the horror he had been sent into the North to face. Therefore Tom jumped into the icily dry and solid bottom of the grave as soon as he was able. Even as he did so, he was struck by how wide the hole was – something that had not been obvious with all the rough clumps of earth piled neatly on top of it; and he saw at once why this was so. John's body, lying reverently on its back, eyes fixed on heaven, was still spread wide at hand and knee. It was still frozen in the attitude in which they must have found it, kneeling with one knee on one of the two spread branches and the other on the other one. He had remained frozen in that attitude for more than a week now – frozen literally since his burial, perhaps, for all the world nearby had been in the grip of frost and ice for at least a month now; but frozen in other terms than being gripped by ice.

For, thought Tom, taking hold of the marble-solid arm within the winding sheet, Father Little's arm had felt no softer; and, although Tom might allow the kirk at Blackpool Gate to have been icy-cold in all areas except one, it was obvious that the good father had died on his feet, and remained frozen on his feet most unnaturally. Every dead man that Tom had seen had fallen at the point of death, if not before; but not Father Little. He had locked into some kind of seizure, had set like a rock as he died, as though he had seen not the Barguest but the Gorgon itself.

As Hobbie had said while they fought to free the good old man from the balcony, they could have carried him to one of the empty chapels in his church and stood him up as the statue of a saint.

As Tom climbed into the cart beside the solid body of his brother, he was aware that he would have to be quick about the rest of his investigation. It was all very well for the Lord of the Waste to oversee John's post-mortem swiftly and quietly, slipping him into

218

the ground with a minimum of fuss before sending Eve and Hobbie south; but with Father Little now added to the death-list, it would only be a question of time – and little enough of that – before the Bishop of Carlisle became involved. Then, no doubt, the Archbishop of York and all the rest.

Bewcastle fort was an unseasonably gloomy place. Three tragedies within little more than a week, a serious attack by the Kerrs, and the Barguest abroad made everyone tense and jumpy; but all of that was nothing compared to entertaining these three corpses in the chapel – one of them recently exhumed at that.

Having dead men about the place was nothing unusual here. There were other dead men in the chapel now: the dead from the skirmish with the Kerrs. They were laid out reverently, awaiting burial as was due and natural – natural if unfortunately delayed now, given the circumstances. But there was nothing natural about the three corpses Tom needed to examine; and, so the rumour would no doubt go, Tom suspected wisely, there was nothing natural about the things he was proposing to do to them. In fact, all he really needed to do was to use his eyes and his intellect, to call upon the expertise he had to hand, if he found a problem beyond his own experience. To complete a theory – or call upon the Master of Logic to do so; to test it if he could; to prove it true so far as he was able. And to act.

As chance would have it, the recently dead from the attack by the Kerrs would also in their way be of use to him, thought Tom, for they were normally, almost naturally, deceased. There would, Tom suspected, be differences between them and the three he was examining most closely – or two of them at least, certainly – and these would begin with the rigidity of their limbs.

These thoughts filled Tom's head as he hesitated in the doorway of the little chapel and looked in at the six corpses lying there, the unnaturally dead nearest the altar, the naturally dead at the back. This was nothing to do with superstition. It was how Tom had ordered things. His experiences of the night had taught him – amongst much else – that the brightest part of any church is likely to be beneath the window and therefore above the altar.

Tom's orders, disseminated via Sir Thomas and the lady Eve, had been obeyed in other things as well – also adding to the sense of outrage in the fort. Father Little lay exactly as he had been found, except that he was lying down, placed here with no reverent preparation such as was fitting in the face of the Lord – fitting especially in such a holy and popular man, so respected, indeed well-beloved in the place. Tom was all too well aware of the cold and angry stares that were being directed at his back; so that when a hand fell on his right shoulder, he actually jumped.

'Fear not, Tom,' whispered Eve's ghostly voice; 'it is merely myself. And in the flesh, for a wonder.'

'You're lucky it's not her ghost, I think,' continued the Lady Ellen more robustly on his left side. 'But we are come to help.'

'To listen at least,' said Eve wryly, 'if I know my Tom.'

Having the pair of them there gave Tom the strength to proceed; but Eve was right, at the outset at least: they had little to do but to listen and to confirm his observations.

'Let us look at this man first,' he began slowly. 'Killed in battle and prepared for burial but not yet in his winding sheet. His name?'

'Walter Milburn,' said Lady Ellen.

'Very well. What might we expect to see about the man? Even with poor Walter thus attired in his best, we have his face and hands available to us, and we may observe without disturbing him too much. His face is livid, you will agree. His eyes, though closed, are black-ringed and protuberant. You can see that more clearly if I lift the pennies here. His cheeks are sunken. We can see, even though his jaw has been bound, for his jaw is slack and prone to fall open ... There! We can see that his beard is of two days' growth or so.'

'He was clean-shaved as we laid him out,' said the Lady Ellen.

'A hairy man like Esau, then, for that's merely a day since. He has been dead a day and a night.'

'Even so,' agreed Lady Ellen, sadly.

'It is a mystery of nature, My Lady. I have seen it in the unburied dead of battle. I am told that even the nails continue their growth, but that would be impossible to prove here, I fear, in so short a time as this. But let us look at his hand: it is also cold and livid like his face. It is weighty, certainly, but not stiff. See, I can move the fingers with hardly any force applied, and bend the hand back at the wrist – straighten the arm at the elbow, indeed, and rotate it at the shoulder; and I have no doubt that I could do as much for his legs, were that needful. Thus much for our eyes and our fingers. What of our noses next? Is there not about the man a smell of anything untoward?'

'Of the lye soap with which we washed him, when we had him laid out by the fire in the kitchen,' said Lady Ellen, 'and little more than that.'

'I agree, save that I had no knowledge of the soap. Certainly no stench as might be expected from bodily effusions...'

'When we lay them out we stop their passages,' said Eve suddenly, 'or else they leak and stink, as you observe.'

'Even so? My own experience in the matter, sadly, consists of throwing dead friends into pits on battlefields; and, I have to observe, they leak.'

'Then why, pray,' asked Eve tartly, 'are ye come hither to lecture us?'

'Because if that is the extent of my experience with *natural* death,' said Tom lightly, 'my experience with *unnatural* death is far wider.'

As he said this, Tom led them over to the first of the three corpses by the altar. 'We see at once a difference with poor Archie, do we not? He has been prepared for burial but not yet fully dressed, for he was a visitor here and died in the one set of clothes he possessed.'

'Which are being cleaned and mended as we speak,' said Lady Ellen.

'With the last of your shirts,' added Eve with the ghost of a laugh.

'And he is dead for exactly a day. But from the outset we can observe the differences: the man's face is full, almost flushed; his eyes bulge, true, but there is no sign of dark rings here; his lips are set and near as ruby as your own, Lady Ellen; his jaw is bound but needlessly so, for see, his teeth are clenched – quite rigidly, even in death. The cloth is damp here, however, below the corner of his mouth; and he is clean. Has he been cleaned? I see he has – which is why we await his clothes. His hands are folded, but again quite rigid – but in a strange position...'

'He clutched there at his left pap as he died,' said Lady Ellen.

'That left pap where heart doth hop,' quoted Tom thoughtlessly, his mind miles away – and equally far from Will Kempe's speech as he played Pyramus in *The Dream*; but he echoed the words nevertheless.

He rolled the rigid Archie on to his side so that he could examine the wounds on his back again. They were still there, of course, just as he remembered them; but this time he had leisure – and strong motive, indeed – for a closer look. There across the darkly furred back of the dead warrior lay the three parallel wounds, stitched at their deepest parts, livid and crusted. 'I still do not see how this could be done.'

'You're holding the only man that could have told you,' said Eve tartly.

'Not the only one, no. There is still the man that gave him the wounds; but he is likely to be hidden away in Stob with the Kerrs.'

'Unless you can think of a way,' said Eve, 'to seduce the truth out of your fair captive Janet.'

'Well, as to that...' said Tom – and stopped, shocked by how near he had come to confessing all that had transpired in the kirk at Blackpool Gate.

'And as to that?' asked Eve, suddenly suspicious.

'Why, that is an inspirational idea. I stand ashamed I did not think of it myself. She was there. She might well have seen; though what there was to see I cannot think...'

Tom's voice tailed off as he looked even more closely at the livid back presented to him. 'Lady Ellen,' he said more quietly, 'if laying out involves shaving the face...'

'Unless it is bearded, of course...'

'Aye, I see that; but if it involves shaving the cheeks, it does not – does it? – involve shaving any other parts?'

'Such as where?' demanded Eve intrigued.

'Such as the back,' answered Tom. 'Look here...' Sure enough, there, on the hair of Archie Elliot's back, visible now that the thick black fur was slick and wet, there was a line exactly parallel to the other three wounds where the hair on his brawny back had been shaved away.

Janet was dressed in a plaid that Tom scarcely recognized. To be fair, it was not the plaid that took his notice but the transformation the woman's clothing made in the girl. Their eyes met once and hers registered his re-action, then fell. She would not look at Eve or the Lady Ellen. Nor, indeed, would her wide eyes meet Tom's again, over the breadth of Archie Elliot's back. 'I saw nothing,' she said. 'I know nothing.'

'And if you did know something, then you would not tell in any case,' said Tom, sounding more severe than he meant to. 'But even your silence can be made to speak, if we will it so, my lady.'

'Did you just threaten to torture her?' asked Eve, agog, when the girl was gone again.

In fact Tom had meant something deeper and more devious than that, but he shrugged. If Eve thought he was willing to torture the girl, then any suspicions aroused by his care-less tongue earlier were likely to be abeyed if not allayed. It did not at that moment occur to him to think what Janet herself might suppose.

That was hardly surprising, for he was turning to the next part of his task, the one that both he and Eve were going to find the most difficult – if not quite the most unpleasant.

'We found it hard to dress poor Archie,' he said as he moved, using inconsequential conversation to cover pain and stress, as he often did. 'How have we dressed that child so well?'

'It is an old dress of my own,' said the Lady Ellen. 'I've not worn it since my husband died.'

'A lovely thing,' said Tom. And he might have been talking of the clothes – or of the girl who wore them.

The men who had carried John's body in here from the cart had taken the winding sheet off it and covered it like the others with a plain blanket. Tom folded this back now and found himself staring into his brother's eyes; and John was still screaming. As silently as he had seemed to do in Tom's all-too-vivid dream, John's face remained frozen in that wide-eyed, wide-mouthed rictus that looked like the most utter, most abject terror; but still of good colour. Still, seemingly, dead so recently that his screams might be echoing somewhere yet; but wilder of hair, thicker of beard than Tom had ever seen him.

Tom folded the blanket back further still. John's hands seemed to reach up towards him. 'Dead a week and more, yet still set like marble,' said Tom quietly. He turned to Lady Ellen, who watched him over Eve's silently heaving shoulder. 'Have you ever seen the like?'

'Never,' she said.

'Eve?'

'Never, Tom,' she answered, though he had to strain to hear, and he noted she did not need to turn and look.

'Could it be the cold? I have heard of sheep found up on these very hillsides, gone missing in winter, then dug out of snowdrifts in spring still fresh enough for the dogs to eat.'

'Aye, and for humans too, these last few years,' said Lady Ellen, sadly.

'So it could be the cold that preserves him. But then again...'

Tom turned to the last of his corpses and lifted the blanket from Father Little. Apart from the shapes into which the bodies were frozen, they were identical. Eyes and mouth wide, tongues out, strings from jaws to shoulders stretched taut. Cheeks flushed, noted Tom; flesh full. Except that he was dead of terror, Father Little had never looked so well – except that, at the very corner of his mouth, disturbed no doubt by the process of bringing him here, a finger of foam, slow and slick as the trail of a slug, was winding back across his cheek. Frowning as he did so, Tom folded the blanket back again and the same hands reached out, frozen, clutching at the air as though it were a banister rail.

Frowning still, Tom turned back to John's hands. What had they been clutching when he died? After a few moments he turned back again. It was impossible to tell.

'Now, I need you to summon up your

courage here, Eve. You prepared John for his laying out and burial?'

'Of course,' she answered dully. 'Immediately after Sir Thomas's inquest. Who else would do it?'

'And that was soon after they carried him down from Arthur's Seat – from the oak where they found him itself?'

'Hobbie and the others brought him. Sir Thomas held his inquest at once and he was buried within the day. Aye.'

Tom pulled the blanket back off Father Little. 'Like this?'

'As you see him. That was all.'

'But you washed him and you dressed him?'

'As well as I could, for he was as you see him now, set like marble even then.'

'But,' said Tom, with fearsome concentration, 'answer this, Eve. Did you have to wash him before you stopped his vents? Wash his body, his face?'

'No. I hardly needed change his clothes, and that was lucky as you see...' She gestured to the arms and legs that might have made it all but impossible for one woman alone to dress and undress the corpse; but Tom had turned away in something like triumph, and was covering the bodies again.

'What?' said Lady Ellen. 'Tom, what is it you have learned? What can you tell us?'

'This, My Lady: that these three men died as near as I can tell in the same manner and of the same cause – though the force of it was lesser in Archie's case. They did not die of the

228

Barguest and they did not die of mortal fear; and I can tell you more. I can tell you that, although I can say to within an inch where Archie Elliot died, I cannot say where Father Little or poor John died.

'The one thing I am certain of is this. Wherever it was my brother died, he did not die in the great oak up at Arthur's Seat, whether it was clawed by the Barguest or not.'

# Twenty

## St Thomas's Eve

Tom watched the Lady Ellen supporting Eve away across the courtyard, then he turned back into the little chapel. He might have finished talking, but he had not finished looking and he didn't want to lose the light. Swiftly, silently, he pulled back the coverings over John and Father Little. He hesitated as though torn – but really he knew what his priorities must be.

He started with John. Beginning at his brother's throat he loosened the neatly bowed bindings of his shirt and pulled it wide as far as the first button of the dark jerkin. Then he began to unbutton the horn buttons that held the stout leather closed, pulling that and the lawn of the shirt wider together as he worked. Soon he had exposed his brother's torso as far to the sides as his armpits and as far down as the corrugated ridges of his belly.

Here Tom paused in his manual labour and leaned forward. Like his own upper body, John's was only slightly hairy, though less sinewy and more massively developed, as befitted a blacksmith. The skin, in common with many Borderers, was quite fair and almost feminine in its delicate smoothness beyond the lightly forested breast and belly. The armpits were an amalgam. Fine hair sprouted modestly and fair skin stood on either side; and this was particularly important to Tom's investigation because that fair skin and – when he rolled his brother over as he had rolled Archie Elliot, pulling the shirt out of his belt – the fair skin on his back were very faintly marked.

The marks were so faint that he only saw them because he was looking for them – so faint that the shocked Eve would easily have overlooked them as she washed him ready for burial. Certainly she had never mentioned seeing them. Tom looked further, now that the pale expanse of his brother's back was bared. He had half-expected to find the same parallel scars that disfigured Archie; but no – not even a close shave. Frowning, Tom turned to examine the shirt more closely in case that had been cut; but again, no.

Because of the closeness made necessary by the rigidity of John's body, Tom found the lawn of his brother's best shirt almost wrapped around his face; and so, just for an instant, he caught an odour he was not expecting at all. Surprised, he paused, his mind seeming to tick like one of the new Dutch watches Ugo had shown him a month ago at Van Der Leyden's house; but he could make nothing of the matter as yet, and so he left it

231

to one side – and would have forgotten it altogether, except that, when he went to rearrange his brother's clothing and fit him for heaven once more, he noted that the tail of the shirt he was tucking back beneath the belt was very slightly brown.

After John was restored to proper order, Tom crossed to Father Little. He had used a quiet moment in the kitchen earlier to purloin a couple of little pots. Into these, with the point of his dagger, he scraped specimens of the foam that surrounded the dead priest's mouth and then, crossing to Archie, of the dampness that soiled the kerchief binding his jaw. When they were both full, he stoppered them and cleaned his dagger with equal meticulousness. Then he covered the bodies once again.

He turned, ready to exit the icy little chapel; but then he turned again for one last time. He uncovered his brother's hands. They were huge, the massive fingers flat-ended and horn-nailed from years of work in the smithy. The growth of nails within the week had clawed them a little, but Tom could still see that the best efforts of Eve's cleaning had left some blackness beneath them. The point of his knife traced the blackness until little scrapings of soot came out. Tom took these on the ball of his thumb and rolled them with his index finger, squinting at them in the last of the light, sniffing like a gardener judging a rose, easing out the point of his tongue tip to taste and spit before he re-covered the body.

'I cannot tell what you tried to grip when your final moment fell upon you, brother,' he said gently as he worked. 'Nor where they were when the quietus came. But I can guess what your hands were doing a little time before that.' Then he turned and went in search of Lady Ellen.

Lady Ellen was in the kitchen overseeing the evening meal. Although it was usually reserved for a feast, the unusual times meant that they would be eating yesterday's hunt venison. Half of a haunch was roasting on a spit and the rest of it was being chopped, ground and seasoned fit for pies and pastries. The remainder was being wrapped for preservation.

'That won't last long,' said Tom to Lady Ellen as soon as he saw her, 'unless you're putting it out in the cold, like John.'

'It won't have to,' she answered brusquely. 'It's going up to Hermitage with Sir Thomas, when Lord Robert calls us to the hawking.'

'I've come about Father Little.'

'Ready to be laid out, is he? That may have to wait until morning, bless the man; though the weight of the guilt's on your soul not mine.'

'As you say, Lady Ellen. But I called upon you to wait for good reason, I promise; and a part of it shows in this at least: whoever prepares the body must take the most especial care. Even the water that washes him might pass on something dangerous.'

Lady Ellen's eyes were wide suddenly. 'Do

you tell me it's a contagion? Like the plague?'
A plague in an enclosed society such as this
would be the worst thing imaginable – like a
contagion spreading in a ship at sea.

'No. I do not mean it spreads through air
and vapours like the plague, but that it is a
clinging thing that might pass from hand to
hand; so take care. And, again, Archie did not
give vent to any waste before you finished
cleaning him? Especially in the matter of
foam on the lips.'

'He did; but we cleaned him with care and
are cleaning his clothes, as you know. But the
other ... Are ye sure, Tom?'

' 'Tis my next task to find out. By what
Gerard called *experiment*.'

Tom hesitated again on the way to his
experiment. He hesitated, not because he was
doubtful of the importance of his task, but
because he felt himself surrounded by half-
truths and tangled motives. He had arrived
here believing that he knew these people; but
now he found he had done so with the eyes
and understanding of a child.

Now, like the remembered Barguest he had
discussed with Eve, everything seemed very
different to the man. There were new
elements in the mix, new characters and
complications. There were tensions that the
child who had gone away to Carlisle and
Glasgow could never have understood; and,
of course, the young man had only just been
beginning to comprehend the terrible goads
of lust for power, money and sex – and that

from books and study – when he had been called away by his fate. The demons of violence, self-delusion, lies and murder he had conned all too well; but he had grown to his painful knowledge only upon the battle-fields, schools, stews and courts of Europe and the South. And even there, the desperations of privation, starvation and utter ruin were only just beginning to bite. In all the deadly tangle he saw stretching away around him now, he simply did not know whom to trust.

But he went to Hobbie anyway.

'Mice?' said Hobbie. 'If ye want mice, then ask a cat!'

'I need them alive.'

'Still ... Och, come along with me.' They went deeper into the stables and Hobbie kicked a bale of hay that lay in the centre of the byre there. ' 'Tis half the size it was when we put it by,' he said, 'but it's still got the same number of creatures hiding in it. They come out at the calling much easier now. Watch out!' He kicked the bale again and, sure enough, half a dozen thin mice ran desperately out of it. The two men were no-where near as quick as cats, but they captured one each. The cats got the rest.

They carried their squirming captives through into the tack room, where there was a little table. They held the little creatures firmly by their tails as Tom got the tiny pots out of his pouch. As his fingers sought the stoppered vessels, they rubbed against the gold-coloured rock from the cave that Janet had hidden in and the golden pebble itself. More elements to be weighed carefully before they were added to the calculation, thought Tom; but it was the stuff he had scraped from Father Little and Archie Elliot that he wished to test now. Out came the pots; out came the stoppers. Tom placed the little clay containers beneath the noses of the starving mice. They would not touch a morsel.

As Tom and Hobbie sat, nonplussed, the summons to dinner rang through Bewcastle. Both men were as sharp-set as the mice and it required a good deal of Tom's self-control to hold the pair of them. He looked around a little desperately. There, on the far side of the little room hung a pair of panniers like his own. They were stout, leather-sided and strong enough to hold a mouse through dinner. In an instant they were on the table and a mouse with its pot was in each side.

'Wash your hands with care before you eat, Hobbie,' warned Tom.

At dinner they sat in the same places as they had at the festive meal that had greeted Tom's first arrival – except that Janet Kerr was elevated to the place left vacant by John. Thus Eve and she sat shoulder to shoulder, competing for Tom's attention. Eve did this because, still too ill to make much of the venison, she was keen to understand what Tom's investigation had discovered thus far – and, seemingly, to help its furtherance. Janet had other motives and, had Tom been inclined to succumb to youthful beauty beautifully, if modestly, presented in Lady Ellen's tartan plaid, he could hardly have resisted her; but his mind, of necessity, was on other things. Later he might console himself with the thought that it was the importance of his mission, and not any phlegmatic coldness after the fiery heat of love, that kept him aloof from her looks and deaf to her conversation. There was much, on the other hand, that Tom needed to discuss with Eve, no matter whether or not she was strong enough to bear it. With his rough-cut slice of venison haunch upon his trencher, therefore, and its juices running thickly off the solid, black, near-unleavened bread, he turned to her.

'They brought him down St Thomas's Morn,' he said. 'So he died St Thomas's Eve. Where were you then?'

'I had returned home and sat by the smithy, minding the house and waiting for him. There is always much to do in that season, for Sir Thomas always calls us to the fort here in the Yule itself. The whole of his festivity turns around the hunt on the feast of Stephen and he likes the blacksmith to be there for that – in case his guests' horses cast their shoes ... you can see it well enough.'

'I see. And John would be at home himself?'

'Not usually. He was a proud man. He would never wish you to know...'

'If he is watching us now,' prompted Tom, 'then he will not be too proud to hear

237

the truth.'

'He would be out on the good. St Thomas's is the day he'd go agooding. There's little enough wheat or barley grown up here these days, but folk have fallen into the way of sometimes giving a little gift instead of it – if a man has worked hard for them and well.'

'So,' said Tom, his voice constricted suddenly at the thought of it. 'On St Thomas's Eve and St Thomas's Day, John went begging round the men that he had worked for in the year – *gooding*, as it's called. Instead of grain to be boiled with a little sweet milk for Christmas creed or frummety – a kind of porage, as I remember – they gave him other charity. They would give him – what? – an egg here and a chicken there?' He leaned towards her fiercely suddenly, as though the fault were hers. 'Were ye beggars after all, Eve? And ye never told me of it?'

'He was a proud man, Tom. He would never have come to you. And, in any case, he said it was his right. He had earned it; he was owed it. Therefore he took it, little enough though it was.'

'And his uncle here, the Lord of the Waste?'

'Sir Thomas was the soul of generosity whenever we came to him; and we came, of course, every Yuletide – whether we were needed or not.'

'As soon as the gooding was done.'

'As you say.'

'And your secret dowry? The Black Lyne: the river and both sides of the valley? Was that not an item ready for the market when the hard times came?'

'He would have none of it, Tom. I would have sold it a thousand times, but he would have none of it.'

'As you say: a proud man, then. And this St Thomas's Eve?'

'I was at home, preparing. Yes.'

'Dear God, Eve, 'Tis like pulling teeth. I'm no barber-surgeon. Let me reason past your reticence. If you were at home, then John was not. Agooding all the day?'

'So I thought, yes.'

'But not in fact?'

'He had no clients up at Arthur's Seat, Tom. There was no good to be gotten there.'

'But that is the cunning of the Barguest, Eve. Making him seem to have died under its claws cuts us off from anything before that. Where he was and what he was doing on Thomas's Eve seems unimportant in the face of that. All that is important is that he was hunted and killed by this monster; but I tell you he was not – neither up the Black Lyne nor out over Arthur's Seat. John did not die there, Eve. He had not been there. He died somewhere else and his frozen corpse was taken there later.

'So now the question of St Thomas's Eve does become important after all. Where could he have been, scarce seven days since? Not *any* St Thomas's Eve, but *this* St Thomas's Eve? If not with you in the smithy, then where?'

Hobbie leaned round the frustrated Janet on hearing Tom's question – asked far louder than the inquisitor would have liked, had he been thinking clearly. 'Why, Tom, there's no mystery about that. You need only have asked me and I'd have said. 'Tis no secret and I thought you knew: the day before he died, the blacksmith went up to the Hermitage in Liddesdale, to see Lord Robert Douglas.'

# Twenty-one

## Black Robert's Invitation

'Yes!' said Hobbie quite fiercely. 'Arthur's Seat is on the way back from Liddesdale; and Liddesdale's where he went, for I saw him myself that morning all dressed in his Sabbath best as we found him. So he went to the Seat on his way back down. Or mayhap even on his way there, though it's unlikely that the Barguest hunts on a sunny afternoon, even one as cold as that. Arthur's Seat's likely where I'd go myself if I was being hunted by the Barguest!'

'But he wasn't being hunted,' repeated Tom angrily, 'and he didn't go there. He was taken there when he was dead already.'

'Dead how? Taken by who?'

'That's what I'm hoping to test at the next stage, and perhaps offer some proof. After the supper.'

'Proof?' demanded Sir Thomas suddenly, turning from his factor Fenwick. 'Proof of what?'

'How they were all killed,' said Tom forthrightly.

241

Sir Thomas looked at him for an instant, his face haggard and set. The adventures on the Black Lyne yesterday seemed to have aged him, thought Tom. Certainly they had done nothing to improve his temper. 'Ye think ye're making good progress with that, do ye?' Sir Thomas continued.

'I believe so, yes,' answered Thomas gently, and a lot more guardedly, suddenly aware of how little he had shared with his uncle so far.

'Well ye'd best get your arguments clean and clear with all the despatch ye may,' grated Sir Thomas. 'This place has been attacked by Kerrs at the very least. I've not heard back from Hugh of Stob nor One-Hand Dand over the head of our visitor there; but I've had men killed, property burned, men of my family and my command threatened as they've gone about their legitimate business for me, and my reputation damaged. There's reparation to be made.

'I may have stayed my hand a little because of the season, and given your mission and your loss; but the Bishop will be up over Father Little's death and that will stir up both Church and Court alike. You may be on the quest over your brother's death, but you've no commission to stand crowner to the rest. We've our own law up here and that must take action. Time is running out. I'll be sending down to Carlisle for the garrison soon, whether I hear more or not; and we'll be scouring out bandits and Barguests from here to Annandale if needs be...'

242

No doubt he would have added more besides had a servant not come scuttling into the hall at that very moment. 'There's riders at the gate, Captain Musgrave,' he said.

Such was the coil that the last such announcement had brought with it that this one was a call to arms at once; but the watchman's nervousness had also overstretched his nerves. The riders at the gate turned out to be a leader and two followers.

'It is Sir Nicholas de Vaux,' called up the leader in a courtly, southern accent. 'Do I speak to the Lord of the Waste?'

'Ye do,' called down Sir Thomas.

'Then I bid you good even, My Lord. I beg to inform you that I bring the Laird of Hermitage's compliments, and an invitation to all here...'

Sir Nicholas de Vaux gave extra life and some badly needed gaiety to the dinner in the hall. In spite of the fact that he had ridden from Hermitage, he was dressed for court and powdered as white as the fashion demanded. The darkest suspicions must needs be put aside: he was a guest and an honoured one, welcomed by the Lord of the Waste himself. He must be treated well – treated well but watched like a hawk. He was invited to the high table at once and occupied the Lady Ellen's seat upon Sir Thomas's left while she went to ensure that the meat with which they would entertain their late guest was still of the finest quality – which he obligingly, effusively, said it was; and that compliment, of course, cheered Sir Thomas himself. Tom, suddenly aware of her absence, looked around for Eve, but she had gone to Geordie Burn; and that was apt enough, for in the face of the powdered interloper he suddenly discovered in his own bosom the same truculent mistrust as Geordie must have felt for him.

If de Vaux felt any embarrassment at separating the lord from his factor Fenwick, he did not show it, being content apparently to sit and radiate goodwill and cheerful bonhomie like the god of amity come to life. Unlike Tom, who had never really lost the plain blunt border roughness, de Vaux was a practised courtier whose manners were as burnished as his golden rings. It was hardly surprising that Tom's dislike and mistrust of him, founded on the knowledge that he was one of the Earl of Essex's faction, grew. For, no matter how flattering the man might be as a messenger and bearer of an invitation to go hunting at Hermitage on the morrow – a mysterious message in that they had been promised hawking – nevertheless, thought Tom, what an elegant spy he must make. What an effective engineer to come armed with a petard of deceit to undermine still further the defences of Bewcastle and those still left alive within it.

The practised courtier remained cheerfully evasive, however, easily able to shrug off Tom's most probing questions with courteous, inoffensive and impenetrable answers.

Yes, he was of the Earl of Essex's faction. Indeed he had come north from one Lord Robert to another – from Essex to Douglas – with gifts and greetings, little more. And his silent companion the Spanish Don: a foreigner and a man impossible to know – of what interests and expertise he could not begin to fathom; nor of what interest to the Earl or the Laird, come to that.

With growing frustration, and finding himself in Geordie's position, feeling like a sulky child in the face of de Vaux's brittle cheerfulness, Tom almost unthinkingly resorted to Geordie's first tactic, if not his actual words.

'I see you favour the rapier, sir. Would you care to edify the Lord of the Waste and the Lady Ellen with a pass or two at play with me?'

'With you, Master Musgrave? With the famous Master of Defence? I fear I am not worthy, sir. I should show myself as little more than a figure of fun, like that foolish actor Kempe that frighted the Queen so terribly. Has Master Musgrave told you of the incident, Lady Ellen? Too modest, perhaps. Well, I was there and I can reveal how Master Musgrave and the Earl of Essex both together won the patent of standing with naked weapon in the royal presence by protecting Her Majesty ... *from an ass!*'

Finding himself unexpectedly foolish in de Vaux's barbed but witty account, Tom had little choice but to sit and brood as Ellen and even Janet had their heads turned by their stylish, sparkling guest. Then, before he knew it, Tom found that he had been challenged in his turn.

'A Master of Defence must needs be fleet of foot,' gushed de Vaux. 'I stand certain Master Musgrave must be at the very point of fashion in the thing. I will assay the lady Janet and he must take the Lady Ellen. Will you not, sir?'

'In what? Take the Lady Ellen whither? Forgive me, I...'

'In the *volte* – it is still quite the rage. I saw Her Majesty herself perform it at Penshurst...'

Tom gaped like the veriest hayseed, scarcely able to credit de Vaux's stupidity – or daring. The volte was the most scandalous of dances, requiring the male to grasp his partner around the waist – or on any convenient hand-hold lower – as he threw her up into the air. De Vaux might look with pleasurable expectation on tickling young Janet's fancy in such a way – and she, all aglow, was lost in innocent anticipation too – but the thought of such an assault on Lady Ellen's modesty was beyond what Tom dared. As he would never have done in any other circumstances, he pleaded the wound in his side as an excuse and made an ignominious escape out of the hall.

'It must be poison,' he said to Hobbie, finding that he did indeed need someone with whom to share his suspicions. The Master of Logic needed to see and hear his ideas being

246

bandied by a confidant as surely as the Master of Defence could only practise to his utmost upon the blade of an opponent. 'I would judge it must be the same poison for Archie and Father Little. On the other hand, Father Little and John share other, subtly different signs. Let us say, however, that there was one poison, which killed John, Archie and Father Little and even touched myself, Eve and Captain Burn.'

Hobbie looked down at the stiff corpses of the mice. Distantly, from the hall, music was struck up. 'The same poison used at least twice, then, and at times and places far apart at that,' he said. Then he paused. 'Unless of course it is a poison tied to Eve herself.'

'Why do you say that?'

'Because Eve was at each of the places at both times, was she not? John went out agooding upon St Thomas's Eve, but was called to Hermitage by Lord Robert. Who's to say he did not come home and partake of the poison in the smithy? He went out agooding again and was taken by the poison and died.'

'Halfway up a clawed tree in the middle of nowhere,' inserted Tom.

'As maybe. And clean enough at that, for it was I who lowered him into the cart with my own hand. But then she washed him and laid him out, did she not? Why, then it could have passed to Eve exactly as we have passed it to these mice; and she, before the force of it took her, passed it to you, who sickened, and to those who died – as, no doubt, the cats would sicken or die if we fed these mice to them. Why could it not have gone like that? Apart from the conundrum of the tree.'

'If you mean that Eve passed the poison on like an infection, then I agree, it could be done, for so I have warned Lady Ellen; but if you do mean that, then we must ask, *Why now?* Why did she not pass it on to me in the coach – while she was tending my wound? Or in any of the taverns or ordinaries we frequented on the way, in London or New Castle?'

'She could never have passed it to you in the coach,' said Hobbie thoughtlessly. 'She was too busy filling your wound with unguents, potions and powders for that...' Then Hobbie stopped speaking, as though he realized of a sudden that he had broken an important confidence.

Tom paused, his mind racing. Then, in the face of Hobbie's continued silence, he answered his own question: 'She would have chosen to do it now only if she knew the truth of it ... if she were passing it on apurpose. And even then, why wait?'

'Your head is as swelled as that courtier de Vaux,' answered Hobbie shortly. 'Does it never occur to you that, even if she did pass it on apurpose, she might not be aiming for you – that she might have plans and stratagems that do not concern you at all? You've been a soldier, man: have you never seen one man struck down by a shot aimed at another?'

248

'Then why was I poisoned? By accident?'

'Why were any – except the man she meant to kill? If it was she, and she meant to kill.'

'Why would Eve wish to kill Archie Elliot? Why would she wish to kill Father Little?'

'Or Geordie Burn, who she now nurses? Why would anyone?'

'Learn that, Hobbie, and I think there would be few questions left to ask and no more answers needed, like as not.'

'If you say so, master.'

'But this is all moonshine, is it not? For there are several things that make the whole hypothesis unlikely if not impossible. In the first place, John could not have died at the forge because Eve could never have cleared his person and raiment of the foulness of death, could never have washed his clothing, dried it, re-dressed him and carried him to the oak; never have swung him up into the branches and left him there for you to find, having left no trace but the Barguest's claw marks.'

'Not alone she couldn't,' said Hobbie; 'but then no one could have.'

'Secondly, what reason could she have? They were poor, but she says they were happy. He was proud and intractable, but she loved him. There may have been temptations, but she was proof against them. Why would she kill him and put up this charade, therefore?'

'Again, why would anyone? Singly or confederated, why?'

'Thirdly, why indeed? What good does the resurrection of the Barguest bring to whoever has brought the beast back from the midwinter tales our grandams told us to frighten us to sleep? It did not kill John. *Quod erat demonstrandum.*'

'What?'

'As has been demonstrated. What good can they pretend?'

'Well, however he did die, he *looked* as though he had died of fright,' observed Hobbie.

'Indeed,' said Tom, dropping the scholarly mode. 'And if you were suddenly saddled with a corpse that looked as though it had died of stark terror, upon what else might you blame the fear? What else is there on the border here that might stop a strong man's heart with terror?'

'Apart from Black Robert Douglas, the Laird of Hermitage, ye mean?'

'We'll talk to Lord Robert on the morrow. Let us leave him aside until then, and think, perhaps, a step further. For John's corpse and the fear on its face has been used, has it not? It could have been hidden. Dropped in a boghole up on the Waste and never seen again. What has the rebirth of the Barguest gained for somebody?'

'Well,' said Hobbie without further thought, 'it has stopped all visiting and wassailing. The season is more like Lent than Christmas since John's body was brought down. Even visiting church to hear mass has ceased after darkness. Apart from that mad southern gentleman who doubtless knows no better, only the Kerrs dare venture out after dark – and only then in large companies. Everyone else bolts their doors at sunset and shivers or prays in their bed all the night. 'Twill be the ruin of the kirk at Blackpool Gate that Father Little had such hopes for. No one will ever go there now.'

Tom fell silent then, thinking of his own visit to the kirk at Blackpool Gate, quite distracted from the matter at hand. The strains of music from the great hall echoed as they had done since soon after his departure – and the clapping and stamping told of energetic dancing too. He continued to disregard it all, so fearsome was his concentration on the dark matter in hand. He must find Janet later and take matters further with her; but in the meantime, there was the matter of the heavy golden pebble he had discovered in his boot there – and, indeed, of the golden-coloured rock he had pulled from the cave Janet had used to hide from the Barguest the night it had taken Selkie.

He opened his mouth to bring his discussion with Hobbie on to a new level, when they were interrupted. 'Ah, Tom, here you are,' said the Lady Ellen. She was flushed, breathless and aglow. She might even have been elevated in the volte, from the look of her. 'They said in the servants' hall you had come out here with Hobbie, but I could scarce...' She fanned herself with her hand, then continued. 'Nevertheless, I have come to tell you your sleeping quarters have been moved.' The pink in her cheeks deepened to denote embarrassment. 'I offer my apologies for the inconvenience, but there is no help for it. Sir Nicholas de Vaux is honoured guest and you, though honoured, are Musgrave, and family. Sir Thomas therefore says that Sir Nicholas must have the chamber you occupied so lately, and you may move down into my little herbal – the room you saw me treating Eve and Geordie Burn in. Apart from Geordie, it is private; and he's in the deepest of slumbers. We'd another bed in there to nurse Eve, but she is well enough to move in with me. You will be warm and dry.'

In the face of her obvious embarrassment Tom could not be anything other than magnanimous; and, as she said, he was family. ' 'Twill be my pleasure to obey the Lord of the Waste,' he said with a bow that might have graced de Vaux, 'and infinitely warmer and drier than my sleeping place of last night to boot. Doubly welcome, therefore.'

'That's strange,' said Lady Ellen, tartly; 'young Janet says ye were warm and snug enough, the pair of ye, last night.'

That was the end of any conversation Tom could sensibly have with Hobbie, whose eyes were suddenly wide and aglow with a dangerous combination of speculation and amusement.

Tom left the stables with no further thought except that he should cross the yard quickly, mount the stair silently and move his belongings from his late room before the music stopped; but the cat prevented him.

The cat was unremarkable – no different from any of the castle's cats except that it was stiff and dead. It lay at the foot of the little flight of steps that mounted to the main door. It lay with its face in a puddle of milky liquid that had obviously been cast down from a window in the hall immediately above. It lay in a puddle of torchlight also cast down from the window, so it was easy to see in spite of the fact that it was of one colour with the shadows. Tom knelt beside it and stirred it with his fingertips. It was warm and stiff, as though someone had contrived the experiment he had discussed with Hobbie just now and fed it with one of the poisoned mice.

Tom had reached thus far in his thought when the window above him opened again and someone's shadow fell on him. 'Gardy...' sang out a servant's voice.

'Hold!' cried Tom, and the man obeyed. Springing erect, Tom looked up a few feet into the eyes of a young servant who held a washing ewer. 'What is in that?' demanded Tom.

'Why, water, sir.'

'What water, man?'

'Water from where Lord Thomas's guest washed his face when he was hot with dancing.'

'As he did some moments since?'

'As he did indeed, sir. And I threw it down

253

as I throw this now.'

'Very well,' said Tom, and stood well back. Then he crossed to the well, filled up the biggest bucket and washed the whole milky mess away – the corpse of the cat along with it – down into the mud of the Gully Hole. Lost in thought, he returned to the empty stables and there, under the light he rinsed out one of the dangerous pots and shook into it the contents of the glove finger he had found on the ground close by. A grain or two of fine white powder – which turned to seeming milk in the water. This too went down the Gully Hole, to the obvious suspicion of the soldier taking up his night-time guard there.

Much later than planned and deep in thought, therefore, Tom skipped past the door into the hall and scurried silently up the stairs. He could have made much more noise than he did and still have passed unnoticed, for the consort of viols had been joined by a lute and a pipe. As he passed, 'Lang Flat Foot of Garioch' passed energetically if not very accurately into 'The Dead Days'. Distracted by the dark aptness of the music and by an unexpected mental vision of Janet hurled high in the volte by de Vaux, he ran on heedlessly. Round the final corner he sped and into the little passage outside his late room. Only to freeze.

All unaware, he had caught up with the man who had supplanted him. De Vaux swung the door wide and entered Tom's room unaware that Tom was behind him, deep in

254

conversation with the man who had sat beside him at dinner. Over their shoulders, Tom could just see the tell-tale saddlebag lying across the bed in place of his own; and, on the settle beneath the window, a pewter bowl of fresh water where his precious letter pouch had lain.

He breathed a silent sigh of relief and would have turned away again – except that Fenwick stayed him with his first word: 'Janet,' said the factor. 'A pretty filly. Hot to the hand. With all the wildness ye'd expect in a Kerr, and something more.'

'Indeed,' laughed de Vaux. 'She dances as though she were all fire. I believe I've come near to burning my fingers. If a man had the mind to her, she'd answer well enough – in place of a hot brick to heat the sheets.'

'Well, time will tell, no doubt, sir. And I may risk my own fingers in that particular furnace, if time or opportunity should arise; but in the meantime, the Lord of the Waste bids me tell ye...'

The door closed.

Tom was against it in an instant, his ear pressed to the wood.

'...the girl...?' said de Vaux, a seeming snarl in his voice.

''Twas worth the risk ... for Elliot, after Burn ... with the club. 'Twould reveal all...' Fenwick's voice came and went, sounding low but forceful. 'And she'll be...'

'...not at the supper nor the dance...' insisted de Vaux.

'...Burn,' explained Fenwick.

'...take your word. But even so...'

'...be there on the morrow...' insisted Fenwick.

'And in the meantime, the smithy...' De Vaux's voice came suddenly straight towards the door. His foot trod down on the boards immediately within. The handle turned.

Tom, thinking at fever speed, took the handle on the outer side and turned it further, pushing the door apparently by accident into de Vaux himself. 'Oh,' he said, foolishly, as the pair of them came face to face. 'I thought you were dancing still.'

'Obviously not.'

'I came for my chattels.'

'Gone – to wheresoever you are destined to go.'

Fenwick came up behind de Vaux's shoulder, his bulldog face folded into a frown. 'Lady Ellen went to find you, sirrah,' he huffed.

Tom had been standing still, locked eye to eye with de Vaux, but his hands had been busy enough. Now he held up one black leather glove. 'I seek the pair to this,' he said. ' 'Twill have fallen by the bed, as like as not.' And in he stepped, avoiding de Vaux as though he had been a clumsy opponent on the piste.

'There,' he said at once and stooped, seeming to catch up a second glove from the floor. He held it for them both to see. 'Oh,' he said, seemingly foolish once again. For as he had

256

stripped the thing so swiftly off his hand, so he had curled his finger and one finger of the glove itself now lay inside out within the palm, and the glove, seemingly, was lacking a finger altogether.

Tom looked up, and just for an instant he thought he saw something in Fenwick's bloodshot, baggy eyes.

'Now that you're in here, Master Musgrave,' said de Vaux, his voice like poisoned honey, 'I must tell you I bear a message for you as well. It is from my friend and master and it is this: *Interfere in any of my business again and I will see you die for it.*'

'That will be a message from Lord Robert, will it?' asked Tom at his most urbane. 'Douglas or Essex, 'tis all one; but I have an answer either way. I serve the Queen and Council. My business is theirs. And should either friend or master interfere, 'tis not my head will answer it.'

'The voice of the Queen and Council are but far faint echoes here, Musgrave, and you know it,' sneered de Vaux at that.

But Tom leaned forward until de Vaux stood back. 'Their tongue may seem to be distant,' he whispered, 'but their *teeth* are very near...'

The herbal room was dark and still the half of an hour later – silent, apart from the rustle of the settling fire, whose embers cast only the deepest dull red glow, as though this were some dungeon in the foundations of hell itself; but it was snug and warm and there were lamps available to taper ends that brought Tom a little light. A little physical light, at least; mentally things remained murky still, despite all he had reasoned, seen and heard tonight. His panniers, swords and clothes lay neatly arranged on the little table where Lady Ellen made her medicines, potions and possets. Remembering Eve's words, Tom thoughtlessly caught up the last of his washed and mended shirts. Under the bright lamplight he could see that the bloodstain was gone, and that the holes that the dagger had left were neatly darned. The cloth itself had a strong, warm smell where it had been dried over the kitchen fire, and he smiled to see a tiny slip in Lady Ellen's perfect housewifery: the shirt tail was just a little discoloured where it had been hung too near the fire.

There came a scratching at the door. 'Aye?' he answered quietly, folding the shirt with a soldier's easy expertise. As he turned from returning it to the pile on the table, there was Eve in the doorway.

'You've come to see Geordie,' said Tom, still whispering as though the man might awake. 'Come in, come in.'

She sat, perforce, on Tom's bed as she tended Geordie. Tom watched, silently to begin with, as she performed a simple routine to check on his vital signs and comfort the last thing at night. Her hands were brusque, almost impersonal, as though she wished every gesture to establish that the man she was tending was nothing more than a patient in her eyes.

'So,' said Tom, at last, able to contain the Master of Logic no longer; able to resist the chance to talk to her utterly alone no more. 'John went off agooding in his Sabbath best as he always did on St Thomas's Eve, and that was the last you saw of him 'till Hobbie brought him home.'

'That's the truth of it.'

'And the messenger from Hermitage who called him to Lord Robert – he came to you first?'

'No: he must have met John upon the way; but there's no great matter there. I was not at home through the whole day – I was called up here to help Lady Ellen; and there was nothing new there, for Lady Ellen often needs my help, especially at this season. You can see it, perhaps, as part of the price of our Yuletide entertainment, year on year; and John would have gone up to Hermitage in any case. Black Robert owed him a gooding the same as many nearby.'

'He'd worked for Lord Robert Douglas? In what regard?' Tom's voice remained lightly enquiring, though he was actually surprised. He had taken against Lord Robert, firstly through Father Little's words and then through the Black Douglas's own threats beneath the clawed oak, and finally through his messenger de Vaux and the message he had sent.

Eve shook her head as though angry –

259

upset, perhaps, that she could not enthuse about some special skill, some unique ability that marked out her dead beloved. 'Smithing,' she spat. 'What else do blacksmiths do?'

A simple question, on the face of it, but one that echoed, resonated. What else did blacksmiths do?

'Is the smithy locked?' he asked suddenly.

'Locked?'

'I came upon a house left open in the wall, you'll remember – but only because the owner paid his blackmail to Jock o' the Side. I doubt either John or you would pay the blackmail. Or that you would need to, living this close to the Lord of the Waste's protection. So, is the smithy open? 'Tis well past the time I should have taken a look at it.'

# Twenty-two

## The Black Smithy

As silently as they could, they saddled two ponies and led them to the Gully Hole. The sentry there let them through, and gave them a flaming flambard to boot. As Eve explained in a whisper while they trotted down the first of the hill below the castle, all the sentries knew her and John – and their comings and goings, even at night.

The sky was black, so the flambard was welcome. Right from the start, however, its rugged flames were under common assault from the brutal wind. Still in the north, and responsible for the blinding cloud cover, the gale was howling fit to burst and gusting icily, at the very edge of bringing snow. Too cold, opined Eve; snow would come when the frost eased. Then the chill would really close in.

The darkness was so total that only the sure feet of the ponies knew the way down from the castle. Had it not been for this, Tom would have had to walk at his pony's head, using the wildly guttering flambard to actually see the path. As far as Tom was

261

concerned, they were riding with their tiny star of light at the black heart of the universe. The howling, sobbing of the wind could have come from amongst the icy, untuned spheres, straight from the frozen heart of hell. There was nothing at all to take the eye except the flambard in his hand, and that near blinded him with brightness every time he looked at it. Yet such was the fathomless ocean of dark upon whose bosom they were tossed, his eyes seemed sometimes to play tricks on him, bringing tiny glitters of brightness to the very corners of his eyes, there and gone like fireflies in southern climes, as beguiling as the wills o' the wisp that tempted benighted travellers to their doom in the bottomless bogs.

Concentration was difficult, clear thought out of the question – and conversation a rank impossibility. It seemed to Tom that they had little enough to say for the nonce in any case. Tom himself could not conceive what work John would have done for Lord Robert up at Hermitage, for Lord Robert must have a smith of his own. What could John do that the smith of Hermitage could not?

Tom wasted a few moments on speculation – and the speculation was not ill-founded after all, for he had been brought up in a smithy and he knew well enough the range of work that a blacksmith might be asked to undertake; but what for the Laird of Hermitage that he could not – dared not – ask his own smith to do? Another question for the morrow, perhaps, but in the meantime, Tom was confident that his brother's smithy would tell its own tale, had he the light and the eyes to see.

The door was locked and double-locked, a fact Tom had not noticed while passing the place with Father Little at his side so seeming-long ago in the final moments before Lord Robert, the Black Douglas, had entered the picture. He noticed now, however, as he held the flambard so that Eve could put her keys into each of the locks. 'That's new,' he said. ' 'Twas never so before I left.'

'You've been gone a long time,' she snapped and pushed the door wide.

He stepped in first with the flambard and was cast back into far memory in an instant. He had last seen this room at sixteen years, near half a life ago; but it seemed to him he knew every detail of eye, ear and nostril as though he had been here only yesterday. So overwhelming was the feeling that he forgot all his caveats to Eve and Hobbie about seeing childhood things with new eyes now that he was a man.

The place had been designed and built as a smithy and the focal point was the fire. In this, the domestic section, the door at which they lingered led into a living area floored with hard earth and furnished with one rude table and a scattering of chairs. Beyond, against the rear wall, stood the open grate under the bell-shaped chimney. The back of the grate, he knew, rose only a little up beyond the skirt of the brickwork bell of the breast. Beyond it, on the other side of the wall, out in the smithy itself, the great fire, with its bellows and open grate, would whoosh like the flames of hell itself up into the same great chimney, day and night, year on year. He had never seen it dark, he realized – never in all his life. Above, and reached by a ladder in the corner, the sleeping room had space for the smith and his wife and their family; and, as was common here – and not just with smithies – the whole was roofed with slates that would not burn rather than thatch that would.

Around the walls stood chests and dressers exactly as he remembered; an ancient wooden sideboard with a great metal ewer and a pail for water up from the river hard by. Out at the back, beyond the smithy and up on the hillside were the sink and the usual offices.

As he stood and gawped like a hempseed looking for the first time at St Paul's or London Bridge, Eve brought a taper and used the flame of the flambard to ignite a couple of lamps. When that was done, she turned to him.

'Well?' she demanded. 'What is it that ye need to see? Be quick or we'll be taken for ghosts. Or lovers.'

'The smithy,' he answered at once, and walked past the dead fire to the door that led on through. Eve let him pass through; for, again, the door was locked.

264

The sight, the very smell, of the cavernous smithy carried him back through time like a sparrow lost in the blast of a gale. Yet he could not waste precious moments on distant years. Roughly he dragged himself back to the immediate past – and the prints that it might leave upon the present: to St Thomas's Eve, little more than a week since, in fact, and what John might have been doing here before he went agooding to collect his Christmas dues.

The smithy was as Tom remembered it, except that it was cold. The great fire gaped full of charcoal, wood and black sea-coal brought laboriously up from the coast. The bellows lay beside it, one pair on either hand, like dead birds awaiting stuffing. The anvil stood before it and the hammers, tongs and chisels hung serried on the wall to the right, for John, like his father before him, had always been a neat worker.

Along the wall on the left-hand side stood the work benches, cupboarded beneath, where the fine work might be done when the work of blacksmith and farrier began to overlap and John was called upon to do more than simply shoe the horses. There, indeed, above them hung the tack, the reins, harness and blinkers in various states of repair; and, beyond again, another area where John's expertise with metals overlapped with others. For here lay bits and pieces of weaponry: jacks only half-covered with metal plates; armour bent and battered; bonnets broken and bruised – to the terrible damage, Tom had no doubt, of the heads that once had worn them. Here stood the great grindstone, and swords in various sizes, styles and states of repair; daggers, knives, axes – common axes for felling trees and Jedburgh axes for felling men.

At the end of all these workbench cupboards stood the big double doors, the equal of any in barn, byre or stable, where the horses were led in for shoeing, and various stock for marking or mending in various ways. These doors were locked, bolted and barred. The bolts in particular, fashioned no doubt by John himself, were new.

There, between the trailing tack, the battered armour, the half-sharpened weapons and the padlocked doors, was a little area of unexpected refinement. Tom's eyes narrowed and his brow creased, for this area, too, was new. Here the massive hammers, tongs and chisels were replaced by balances and crucibles. There were solid metal moulds, a range of fine equipment, all neatly packed away. In place of the anvil, a mortar and pestle, designed to grind down ... what?

'What was John at work on here?' Tom asked at once.

Eve shrugged. 'The new passion for shooting – and with crossbow as well as guns. There's a fletcher in Brackenhill, but he's old and works with longbows only. Not that his arrowheads are up to much these days either. He'll not fashion good steel quarrels. So my

John does. Did. Then, you brought an arque-bus and a matched pair of pistols yourself, besides whatever that monstrosity is in with Lord Henry's letters...'

Tom frowned at her, still not quite follow-ing.

'Carlisle is a good long way away, and that's the nearest gunsmith, down in Botchergate. John would mend, for he could not make. He was in a lively way of supplying quarrels for the crossbows and shot for those that will not make their own...'

'Hum,' said Tom. He knew a gunsmith well: Ugo Stell, his closest friend; and there was something on this bench that did not quite fit with what Tom remembered from Ugo's bench in Blackfriars. 'Hmm,' he said, as though satisfied. Perhaps the difference lay, as Eve suggested, in the fact that John was not a gunsmith, merely a mender of guns that others made; or that he fashioned quarrels as well as shot. Even so...

'Had he any particular customers?' Tom asked, crossing to the bench and lowering the flambard to bring the brightness closer.

'None,' answered Eve, again dismissively.

Tom touched the icy instruments as though they might tell his sensitive fingers what his mind could not yet frame or fathom; but it was his eyes not his fingers that gave the game away, and his memory, not of Ugo's work-shop at all, but of Master Panne the Gold-smith's that he had visited on London Bridge six months before. Yes: that was it. These were

267

not just the instruments of the gunsmith and the blacksmith – but of the metalsmith as well.

Above them, on the wall, stood a new cupboard Tom did not recognize. It opened under his absent-minded grasp and, sure enough, there stood several guns: an arquebus, clearly in need of a new matchlock; a new Dutch dunderbus, bell-mouthed and dangerous-looking, the screwheads holding its side-plates firm all gleaming and recently tightened; and a pistol, almost the match of his own beautiful pair, exquisitely chased in silver and gold. The gold chasing had clearly seen better days. It was dull, and the foil was beginning to peel off. One side was in far better repair: John had clearly been part-way through replacing that as well. Thoughtlessly, Tom brought the flambard lower. Eve hissed with fright.

'What?' he asked, without turning.

'He has black powder over there. He grinds it himself.'

Tom did not raise the flame. Instead he pushed his finger into the bottom of the mortar and stirred the powder there; and his frown deepened. For he knew black powder well. He had helped Ugo Stell prepare it. He knew its form and formulation at every stage of its composition from rocks of ore and blocks of charcoal to the finest, most explosive grains; and no black powder he had ever made or seen had tiny flecks of gleaming metal within it – metal like the gleaming grains that lay in the mortar here. Without thought or calculation, Tom unloosed the top of his purse and pulled out the two rocks it contained. Lowering the light still further, oblivious to Eve's strangled gasp, he put them down beside it and poured the glittering contents out. He saw at once that the gilded pebble fate had washed out of the Black Lyne into his boot was far too bright to bear comparison; but the other, on the other hand – the rock he had found in Janet's cave up beside the oak – that rock was identical in colouring. Indeed, he thought, still far removed, almost in a world of his own, if he was to grind up this very rock, he might well get dust of identical colour, indistinguishable from this...

'Where did you get that?' asked Eve again, hitting his shoulder and making the flambard flicker.

Tom jumped awake again and the howling, stormy night crashed in on him like the waters of the flooding river. He realized Eve had been almost screaming at him and she was doing so again: 'Where did you get that rock?'

'This?' he pointed to the bright pebble.

'No! Not that! The other...' But before he could answer, a massive crash came against the door beside them. Whatever had hit the wood struck with sufficient force to pull John's new bolts free of their sockets – pull sections free of their planks.

Tom passed the flambard to Eve at once

and reached up into the cabinet full of his brother's latest work. A second great blow pulled hinges loose and ruined the seeming strength of the new bolts. So that at the third blow the door sagged, from floor to roof, and fell back, half-opened.

Tom pushed Eve back and stood before her as the brunt wind threatened to tear the flames of the flambard out and scatter the fire into the little house. Then the wind hesitated. The flame sprang up. Out of the darkness appeared a part of the darkness; a tall man on a tall horse, both as black as the night. A black-gauntleted hand pulled a black cloak back to reveal a pallid face framed with red hair at whose heart burned feverish eyes.

Eve gasped again – a very different sound from the one she had made when she was considering mere explosions. 'Ye know me, woman,' said the man, and Tom felt her nodding silently.

The wind came, stirring the black cloak so that Tom knew their visitor too, and his expression gave the game away. For though the horseman needed a gauntlet on his good right hand, he needed none for the bandaged stump of his left.

'And you know me, sirrah. And I know you, Master Musgrave,' hissed One-Hand Dand Kerr.

# Twenty-three

## Liddesdale

Tom swung the dunderbus up until the wide bell of its deadly mouth pointed at One-Hand Dand. 'I know you, Dand Kerr,' he said easily, 'and I stand sure you have half of Stob and probably of Liddesdale at your back; but I warn you: if you make a move or say a word beyond my liking, your head at the very least of it will join your hand in hell.'

Dand eased himself in his saddle, the stirrups and girths creaking. 'And after me,' he answered, 'it'll be yourself sent hot to hell, Master Musgrave, and then the lady Eve, the Lord of the Waste and the rest; but I've a choice to offer ye before we fall to fighting here.' The shallow eyes wandered apparently thoughtlessly away, past Tom himself and on to Eve.

'And that is?' pursued Tom, well aware of how little time he had in hand.

'Come to Hermitage,' said another voice, a new voice, cold and strange from the darkness – strange and yet oddly familiar.

There was a second of silence.

'Hell or Hermitage,' said Tom. 'That's not much of a—'

The blow took him smack across the back of the head at ear-tip level. It felt as though he had been hit with a Jedburgh axe, so piercing was the pain; but the feeling lasted less than the flicker of lightning that seemed to outline Dand. Then all was darkness, into which he pitched as though falling.

'Don't kill him,' came an urgent, echoing voice that soared away up into the air as he fell. 'It is he who keeps the Barguest alive.'

His forehead hit the hard earth floor and bounced. It seemed that the crown of his head must have broken off like the top of a roasted egg. The darkness was joined by a whirling, rushing roaring that sucked him down to its depths. All sensation vanished.

Except, from an almost infinite distance, a sudden and terrible pain in his hand. It was there and gone in the merest atomy of time, but it speared his unconsciousness for just long enough to release a terrible, fearful revelation. Dand and the Kerrs had taken Eve; and Geordie Burn was confederated with them, carrying her away to Black Robert's lair. For the second voice had been Geordie's – there was never any doubt of that.

The pain in his hand woke him first, though the pain in his head was likely to have done so soon. 'Agh!' he shouted. Then he whispered, '*Eve!*' Of course, there was no reply. His whirling, stunned and sickened senses informed him he was face down on the floor. He stirred, automatically, tensing to push himself up – and regretted it at once, such was the agony in his right hand. It felt as though he had plunged it in a crucible of boiling metal. He remained where he was for a while, bathed in icy sweat and gasping fit to burst. Then he opened his eyes. It was full day. Dull, wet light was streaming in through the wreck of the smithy door across the hard-earth floor. The dry-mud surface was broken slightly by the sharply indented crescents of hoofprints; and so, saw Tom as he blinked owlishly, was the black leather stretched across the back of his throbbing right hand.

Ready for the stab of agony this time, teeth gritted and nostrils flared, he pushed himself up again. He made it on to all fours, then tore himself erect, lifting the agony of his broken hand off the ground as though the black Spanish glove had contained a great weight. He clutched it to his breast and cradled it in the crook of his left arm, forcing his mind to clear with almost superhuman swiftness. Only the circumstances gave him the strength; and the most potent element of the situation was the fact that they had taken Eve to Hermitage. Years as a soldier, student duel-list, Master of Defence and courtier in some of the darker and more dangerous theatres of Europe had given him all too clear an idea of what Black Robert might be doing to her; and, the daylight told him, all too much time had been awasting since Dand and Geordie had carried her away.

He staggered to his feet, therefore, still moving as though his crushed hand were the same weight as the anvil that stood at the cold fire just behind him. He glared around the wreckage of the smithy, registering how the dunderbus and most of the guns were gone – how the mortar and pestle, with its powder – black or not – were gone; how any piece of weaponry, saddlery or equipment of even the faintest use was gone; except for his own guns and swords, which still hung miraculously safe about him. Mockingly left on the assumption that he could no longer use them, of course. Other than these it was all, like Eve, long gone. It was time to be gone himself.

Back through the wind-swinging doors that Eve had unlocked last night he stumbled, only to find that the light-fingered Kerrs could not resist hobbie horses any more than gold, guns, weapons and helpless women; but he knew from a wide range of sources, as well as from years of childhood experience, that Bewcastle fort was only half an hour's walk up the hill from here.

It was a hard walk, one of the most difficult of his entire life, but he shambled on regardless of the weighty agony in his hand and the stabbing pains in his head until he had achieved his object and the great gate of Bewcastle fort seemed to swim in the air before him.

Tom staggered under the portcullis into the open square of the fort, his teeth still so tightly gritted that he could not even call for help. So it was fortunate that the Lady Ellen saw him weaving across the yard amongst the stable grooms who were sweeping aside the straw left over from the departure of the Lord of the Waste's party as they answered the Laird of Hermitage's invitation to a hunt that day.

'Dear goodness,' she said, rushing up to him. 'What's amiss? The whole of the fort is abuzz with speculation about whither you spirited Eve away to last night. Young Janet is almost out of her mind with rage and frustration. And now you return alone and like this.'

' 'Tis a lengthy story,' he warned. Then he asked, 'How long ago did Sir Thomas and the others depart?'

'Not long. Let me see to your hand while you tell me what's transpired.'

'I will, but we must be quick. It is imperative I overtake them before they get to Liddesdale. When did Geordie Burn leave?'

'He woke a little stronger this morning and so he left with them; but he'd fain have come after the pair of you if the Lord of the Waste had allowed.'

'That he would never do: the honour of the Waste stands on the shoulders of the lord's command; but I must after them as swiftly as I can, and now I bethink me, I had best take along the lady Janet into the bargain...'

'You may take her and welcome, for she is certainly no lady, not after the way she danced the volte last night! But I fear you will have to consult her at the least, for she will doubtless have her own mind in the matter and you are in no condition to enforce your will upon her should she prove intractable.'

Tom sent for her nevertheless, and as the Lady Ellen had worked upon him, so he worked upon her.

'To Hermitage!' exclaimed Janet, her tone more calculating than horrified.

'You must come. You know you have unfinished business there,' he tempted, like the devil in the old plays.

'Perhaps. But what do you know of that?' she countered.

'More than you suppose. I will protect you,' he promised manfully.

She gave a bark of laughter at that. 'From the look of you, you will stand in need of *my* protection when Black Robert gets his hands on you.'

'In that assumption also you are deceived, Janet,' he countered with quiet confidence. 'But let us both own Black Robert our enemy for the moment, and let us stand confederated against him and each of us help the other as we beard him in his den. Was it rape, such as your mother warned you of when we talked in the Blackpool kirk?'

'Rape as ever was. A pretty lass among the Kerrs taken by force on an afternoon's hunting near twenty years since. I'm the result.

276

The vessel of my mother's rage and sorrow and of all my family's shame. I am bad blood and bad cess and Black Robert's bastard. And I doubt he even knows I exist for all he's seen me often enough of late.'

The Lady Ellen's eyebrows rose irresistibly towards her hairline as she worked and pretended, unconvincingly, to be too preoccupied to listen to this sad bitterness.

'And we seek the lady Eve,' continued Janet with a jealous frown; but it was a short-lived expression: Tom had already won her.

'We seek so much more than that, Janet,' he concluded.

Janet sighed and nodded. She was his. So he sent her to change back into the clothes of the seeming boy he had almost killed at Housesteads. Lady Ellen finished her work while she did so, and the pair of them moved on.

Tom took the first pony he could find. He reserved for Janet the little steed that had carried him through the hunt, and was glad to do so. It was a beast he knew well and respected. He soon found that his own was the match of it, however. He could rely on both of them to run their hearts out catching up with the others. He believed that, no matter in what state his wounds or Lady Ellen's tending had left him, he could rely on his own plucky little animal to carry him up with the procession of guests as they headed for Hermitage. He could rely on Janet's to do the same, though he could only guide his mount clumsily enough with the reins in his left hand.

As Janet had changed her clothing and found a light jack to match his own as well as a stout travelling cloak, Lady Ellen had completed her ministrations. His right hand was wrapped in bandages thick enough to make his arm seem almost like a club. Like the wounds to the back and front of his head it had been rinsed and spread with unguents. Unlike them it had also been bandaged, but as lightly as Lady Ellen would allow – too heavily for Tom to resume his glove or grip his sword, but lightly enough for him to move the fingers a little still, as long as he could stand the pain. It should have been in a sling, but his vanity forbade that it should be so and he rode with it at his hip, resting on the pommel of the sword it could no longer hold. Janet rode at his right hand; if he drew a sword, it would be with his left.

Tom and Janet set their ponies' heads a little north of west and they cantered easily over hill and dale, south of Blackpool Gate, crossing the River Lyne at Oakshaw ford and following the steep little valley straight on up past Sleetbeck on to the saddle between Chamot Hill and Wakey. The pair of them came a little south past Beyond the Moss and caught up with Sir Thomas's party on the border itself at Penton as they prepared to cross Liddel Water and swing north into Liddesdale and Scotland. While they rode, they talked: of Janet's birth and background;

of her upbringing amongst the Kerrs, by Hugh of Stob himself, and his wife, and Janet's mother, while she was still alive.

They caught up with Hobbie and the huntsmen as they splashed across the ford, tight-packed and laden with the hindquarter of the hart. There was no way past them and up along the festive column towards Sir Thomas and de Vaux at its head; and, were there no way pass the column now, no more would there be for a good few miles still. For on the west side of the valley, over the river, which grew wider and shallower as it prepared to join the River Esk, the steep hillsides gathered swiftly into cliffs. The roadway all too soon became a pathway, and that narrow thoroughfare swooped off up the valley side into a steep and precipitous little ledge just wide enough for a sure-footed hobbie horse to follow.

With the wild rock reaching upwards on the left hand and the bewildering cliffs falling downwards on the right into a roaring wilderness of russet foam, there was no place to hurry, let alone to overtake. Tom and Janet perforce remained with the quizzical Hobbie, therefore, as Sir Thomas, unreachable, the merest bowshot up ahead, pierced the Laird of Hermitage's stronghold of Liddesdale all unaware of the situation into which he was riding.

'Tom!' called Hobbie. 'Where ye been? And why in God's name have ye brought the lass with ye?'

' 'Tis a long story. Is Geordie Burn with Sir Thomas?'

'Aye: at his left hand up ahead, with Fenwick the Factor and Sir Nicholas de Vaux. Or more likely in line behind him now, for they're up on the narrow path already, I see. The Lady Ellen's cures have strengthened Geordie beyond measure. He's none too hearty, mind, but hale enough for this. Now 'tis your turn to answer me.'

'If I can. What?'

'Where's Eve that ye stole off with like some thief in the night?'

'Eve's up ahead, and I pray she's awaiting us.'

'Up ahead? *Where* up ahead?'

'At Hermitage. One-Hand Dand carried her off last night and the last I heard they were headed thither.'

'Carried her off? And ye're alive to tell of it? Tom, ye're not the man I thought ye!'

'I was near enough dead when they left with her. When you've leisure, you can feel the blood that's set my hair like marble and marvel at the colours – and shape – of my hand.'

'Aye, now I have the leisure to look, I see ye've a great bruise like the eye of a Cyclops right in the midst of your forehead; and that explains young Janet here: a bargaining counter. She'll not be worth much put up against Eve herself, mind.'

'The bruise is least of my hurts, I assure you; and Janet may be worth more than she seems, for she's Black Robert's only daughter.'

Hobbie mulled that over for a while before he asked, 'Who hit ye? Dand?'

'The only one of them I am sure did *not* hit me was Dand; but 'twas he who walked his horse across my hand as I lay fainting on the floor.'

'Ye should have let me kill him – aye, and her, while we had the chance.'

'I know. It is always our good deeds that come back to do us most harm.' His laughing words were called out loudly, to cover Janet's angry retort.

Hobbie grunted with a half-laugh himself and had the grace to look shamed under the girl's indignant gaze. 'True enough; but Dand was for taking Eve to Hermitage, ye say?'

'If not Dand, then one that rode with him – rode with him and stood above him, for Dand answered to his commands.'

'And who was this that gave orders to the Kerrs?'

'I'd have said it was Geordie Burn.'

'But he was ill in bed all night, with many an eye to swear to it.'

'Then it was Tam himself, that fell out with Geordie for love of her all those years ago. Tam has got her at last – but not for himself, of course: he's taken her to Black Robert.'

Their conversation had to end there because the ground beneath their ponies' hooves rose up abruptly and they were suddenly on the narrow path. It was many years

281

since Tom had ridden this route. Then he had been an able, scrawny horseman in full control of his large and steady steed. Now the position was very different. He was a large and heavy body on a little pony, his left hand only clumsily in control of the reins, the pair of them in the grip of a wild north wind that bounced off the wall beside them like the old king's tennis balls, and threatened to topple them into the abyss.

Tom was the rearmost of the procession. The position gave him a little blessed relief from the dangerous wind and pricked his pride into the bargain. All the others – Hobbie laden with a quarter of a deer, Janet with her plaid cloak flapping in the wind – seemed to be trotting forward without a second thought. So he settled himself in the saddle, gripped his right-hand sword pommel until the pain in his hand became too much to bear, and followed the Lord of the Waste into the dangerous valley of Liddesdale and the lair of the laird himself.

# Twenty-four

## Hermitage

The valley side circled round below Hermitage. As they approached the dark old castle, the pathway widened and faded into the slope, becoming a pathway, then a rough roadway, leading up towards the forbidding place; but as soon as it did so, the roadway became contained within defensive walls, so that even now Tom could find no way past the riders ahead to get his message to Sir Thomas.

Tom had no choice, therefore, but to use his eyes instead of his heels and scour the castle itself for further clues that he might use in the coming confrontation with its dark and dangerous captain. To Tom's eyes, Hermitage seemed to have an evil and sinister aspect, fit indeed to be the lair of Black Robert Douglas. The walls were absolute, reaching nigh on fifty feet sheer, grey stone standing on the frost-grey crag outlined against the winter-grey sky without any softening or decoration. Even the smoke that rose from its invisible chimneys was thick and grey and at one with the place and its setting. It was what it was designed for: a perfect blending of form and function, thought Tom – a place of impenetrable defence, a source of absolute leadership, a threat of unrelenting terror. For terror alone would keep the Armstrongs, whose bothies filled the valley below, from the throat of the men who garrisoned Hermitage Castle. A previous captain had been boiled alive in the castle yard before the keep, and the current captain was not about to share his fate.

On the other hand, the man who had built the castle in the first place had been in league with the devil, and that was a dark part of its history that Robert Douglas was, apparently, happier to share. If any man had raised the Barguest from its kennel in the deeps of hell through the exercise of black, forbidden arts, then it was he.

'Witchcraft?' said Hobbie in answer to Tom's enquiry. 'Oh aye. That's what they say. But what grounds they have I cannot tell ye...'

'It is the lights,' said Janet, suddenly, 'and the sounds in the night. Deep sounds that make the whole head of the valley shake. They do not come from the castle, but they spread out down the dale...'

'You had this from Dand, I assume?'

'And Hugh. When the Kerrs do business with Black Robert, they keep their longest pikes to hand.'

' "Who sups with the Devil needs a long spoon," ' confirmed Tom, his eyes looking

284

upwards towards the great gateway that stood astride the road immediately in front of them.

There were two Kerrs hanging at the main gate to Hermitage as Black Robert had promised. If they disturbed Janet, then she showed no sign of it as she rode between and below their swinging feet. Everyone, in fact, trotted into the castle without hesitation or, apparently, any second thought at all – except, that is, for Tom.

Tom reigned up below the slowly revolving corpses and stood in his stirrups, looking up and frowning with thought. They were hung too high for anyone to see their faces clearly, but it seemed to him that their bulging eyes and gaping mouths bespoke terror as eloquently as did John's or Father Little's; and that put him in mind of executions he had seen in his new home of London, where there was a gallows on every major crossroad, with a whipping post, a cage and a set of stocks to match them. For now he thought of it, the faces of all the dead men he had seen of late might well have shared with many a felon in the South that terrible look of someone slowly choking to death, aswing and kicking helplessly in a hempen noose.

Except, of course, for the facts that there had been no reddening of bulging, bloodshot eyes and no thick, bloody tears; no tearing of tongue and lips by wildly gasping jaws; no emptying of bodily wastes. Most especially, there had been no thick black cicatrice around the neck, such as marked an official execution done according to the law. Just how many of these tell-tale signs adorned the corpses hanging at Black Robert's gates Tom could not quite make out. He would have given much to look more closely at that pair of Kerrs who hung like a brace of pheasants ripening for the table.

'As I promised, Master Musgrave,' came Lord Robert's icy voice, as gentle as a devil's sliding through the wind.

'Give ye good den, Lord Robert,' said Tom, swinging a little clumsily down off his horse and recovering into a courtly bow. 'Did the lady Eve arrive safely last night?'

Lord Robert had turned away, however, and was taking his place at the head of his reception line, every bit as formal as the Lord of the Waste had been before his Christmas Hunt. Now at last Tom found himself beside Sir Thomas. He had precedence as honoured guest, as Queen's messenger – or the Lord of the North's at any rate – and as the old man's nearest living relative; but the position at his uncle's side was of no use now, for the man against whom he wanted to warn Sir Thomas was at his other hand, unctuously introducing him to the garrison and their guests in turn – men whom he knew already; but with more detail in the description.

As Lord Robert introduced his uncle, Tom had time for a glance over his shoulder to see Janet indistinguishably join the mass of the Bewcastle garrison at Hobbie Noble's shoulder. Then he allowed himself a swift look around the sparse, functional interior of Hermitage Castle. They stood assembled in a flag-floored yard with what looked like a well at its heart. Here, as in Bewcastle, there were stables and smithies and storehouses leaning against the inner side of the outer wall; but over all loomed the keep. Huge and threatening it loomed on them, rising without any feature at all for three sheer storeys before a balcony thrust out with a great door behind it – a main door fit to welcome kings – three storeys too high for them to reach without wings. Everything below that was impenetrable and unassailable, a killing ground for any unwary invaders caught within the portcullis with nowhere else to go.

Suddenly the dark keep's black captain was talking to Tom himself: 'Of course you must know Sir Nicholas de Vaux, the noted courtier and friend of the Earls of Essex and Southampton. You are aware, I am sure, of his great houses, Camborne House, London, and St Erth under Redruth...'

'Sir Nicholas.' Tom bowed just enough for courtesy: a duellist at the piste.

'Sir Thomas. Master Musgrave...' De Vaux nodded.

'And Senor Juan Placido Flores de Sagres, lately returned from his most Pacific Majesty Philip's dominions in New Spain.'

'I'm surprised that Drake and Raleigh let you through,' said Tom pleasantly, bowing and smiling. Then he continued after a moment of silence in which even Lord Robert

287

was shocked speechless by his crass incivility. 'Ah, a thousand pardons, senor. I see you do not speak English...' The latter words were spoken in his inelegant, if serviceable, Spanish.

'There seems to be no end to Master Musgrave's accomplishments,' Lord Robert inserted smoothly in Latin. 'Let us hope we do not come against an end to them today; but we speak in English here, sir, as Senor Sagres understands, in notion if not the words themselves. There are too many ignorant ears that grow dangerously suspicious of anything they do not understand.' He stepped sideways again, taking Sir Thomas and Tom with him almost irresistibly. 'And this is my factor, Mr Beattie,' he continued in English, as though the foreign syllables, living and dead, had never tripped so smoothly off his tongue.

There was no Hunt Mass. Instead, they were all remounted at once when the introductions had been done. In their saddles, as in Bewcastle, they partook of a brief hunt breakfast – mostly of baked and roasted birds.

'Our hawking went well yesterday,' said Lord Robert, 'and you reap the benefit of it doubly. Not only does it furnish breakfasts now, it also presents us with vital intelligence as to our quarry for today...'

With every eye upon him, Lord Robert rose in his saddle, easily commanding the moment, so that even the restless, excited horses fell quiet under his spell. 'For weeks we had been hearing rumours that something big and dangerous had come avisiting into the darkest of our thickets down the dale; but rumour was all we had and Armstrongs, though brave and resourceful, are not always absolutely reliable in matters such as telling the truth. In any case, for some time since the whole of the Borders has been alive with whispers of the Barguest – which is what the Armstrongs seem convinced our mysterious visitor must be – and the Barguest, as we all here know, is a thing of fable, a toy for a winter's tale – a thing for women to frighten children with; nothing such as would invade the wise credulity of men such as ourselves.

'But yesterday at hawking, down by the mouth of the dale itself, my guests and I found unmistakable signs of the beast. It is there; and I have invited us all here, the best of the Borders, north and south, the flower of Scotland and England, to hunt it.'

A whisper, a rustle, a stirring of breath, of movement of hoof and tack, went round the place as the storm wind battered across the battlements high above. Lord Robert held up his hand and even the wind was silent.

'And, to make the hunting worth more than mere glory, we have a prize into the bargain.' He held up his hand higher in a signal and the great upper door of the keep slammed open. Out on to the balcony three storeys above stepped a pale, fair woman, all alone and apparently moving at her own will under

289

no duress at all.

'To the man who kills the Barguest will go the hand of the woman it widowed. Eve Graham Musgrave has sworn that she will marry the man who avenges her against the beast that killed her husband, and I have sworn to protect her. Under my protection and in my own poor keep at her own request she stays, therefore, until one brave man can prove he has won the quest and may take her and all that is hers at her word.'

As his wild words echoed around the grim old keep, Lord Robert tore the head of his hunter to the right and galloped straight out of the gate. Tom saw at once that the Heritage garrison, also all astride, had prepared for the moment by positioning themselves in a circle around their all-unsuspecting guests. When Lord Robert led, and they followed, so did the Bewcastle contingent, perforce, driven out on to the valley side by the friendly cavalry charge behind them.

To be fair, thought Tom, as he went out with the rest of them, many of the Bewcastle men were following without a second thought. It was only Sir Thomas, Tom and mayhap Geordie Burn who saw something terribly amiss here. For the rest, the case seemed clear and perfectly understandable – perhaps even reasonable. For the laws of the Borders were strict and unvarying, as they needed to be in that constant war zone. Otherwise life in this morass of constantly changing allegiances and ever-shifting family bonds would have been simply impossible. When a man gave his word, he upheld it – thus Sir Thomas and his guests rode under the safe protection of men that would kill them unhesitatingly under different circumstances; and when a woman was widowed violently, she might be expected to go to any lengths avenging the man she had lost. Many a border widow had promised herself, her house and home to the man that avenged her husband, and this was different only in that Eve Musgrave wished to be avenged upon a monster. So she needed a monstrous bargain to fulfil her plans. She certainly had a monstrous friend in Lord Robert to hold the square for her, a friend who apparently had every intention of taking the prize for himself, if he could, so swiftly was he leading the wild hunt down into the valley-foot.

Here the thickest brakes of the most timeless woodland might be found, stands of oak and yew as massive and ancient as the heart of Inglewood, dense enough and dark enough to hide monsters without number over centuries beyond counting. And yet, ran on Tom's busy thoughts as he pounded with the rest of them down the dangerous slope, it was a wilderness under threat, as Hobbie had said. For all along the edges of the forest he was approaching in his scarcely controlled gallop were tall, banked fires issuing slow, thick smoke, burning in steady series, not to give heat – even in this frost-bound season – but to give charcoal. As they turned south on the last clear slopes above the thickest of the trees that stood along the river plain itself, he saw great avenues reaching inwards and downwards, dense with working men. It was as Hobbie had sadly said, he thought. The whole of the dale was like the forests further south, like the circles of Dante's Inferno, where helpless men toiled, lost and hopeless; where the shipmasters and the metalmasters, steelmasters and all the rest, were tearing the heart out of forests that had stood untouched since the dawning of time.

Hobbie was riding on one side of him and Janet on the other. 'Did you know it was like this here?' he demanded of them both, bellowing over the thunder of their gallop.

'Harvests have been bad,' yelled Hobbie. 'They're starving here as well as elsewhere. There's been murrain in the flocks. The raiding took most of the cattle last year. They're starving, so they'll turn their hands to anything.'

'And when the men are starving, the master goes hungry,' added Janet. 'Black Robert'll be suffering lean times. You must know others at court...'

Truth to tell, Tom knew almost no one at court who wasn't desperate for money. Essex would do almost anything to add to the one steady income he got from his monopoly over the sweet wine trade. Why else was Raleigh off searching the Indies? Why else did Drake constantly attack the armadas from New Spain? Only men whose income did not rely upon farming their lands stood firm – men like young Lord Outremer, whose life he had saved six months since, whose massive fortune was earned from the spice trades; men like his friend and landlord Robert Aske the Haberdasher, building his fortune on feathers, lace and silk, buckles, buttons and ribbons shipped in from far abroad; like Ugo, earning his gold through making and selling guns. Only men like these and Nicholas de Vaux were assured, which was why de Vaux stood so close to both Essex and Southampton, whose positions and pastimes consumed gold like furnaces consumed fuel, thought Tom grimly; only men like de Vaux, who could get their riches not from the land itself, but from beneath it, where riches themselves seemed to grow.

# Twenty-five

## The Grave

'The Grave,' called Tom quietly, into the almost impenetrable undergrowth through which he was silently insinuating himself.

'The Waste,' came Hobbie's voice in reply, distantly on his right.

'We need to go over towards him,' said Janet nervously. The gloom of the place, the increasing sense of isolation and the burgeoning fear of what they were just about to meet were combining to shred her nerves at last.

'Perhaps,' said Tom. 'But there are more games afoot here than the one he is playing. *Hola!*' he called, more softly than he had called to Hobbie.

'*Hola!*' came a nervous reply on his left. The Spaniard was still close at hand, he thought; and that was to the good.

Lord Robert had brought their wild charge down the valley and over the shallows of the lowest ford on the Liddel to a halt at the edge of the deepest woodland on the eastern bank, on the very borders of the debatable land itself. Here a circle of silent, suspicious Armstrongs had stood like ill-controlled animals

294

waiting to take their horses. All through this excursion, Tom had been watching Senor Sagres. The man was plainly out of place here – indeed, had seemed out of place in all the companies he had shared with Tom so far. He was no courtier – even in the Spanish Court, with whose forms and manners Tom had a nodding acquaintance, he would have been out of place. He was a solid, sinewy man. His arms and legs were muscular, but his shoulders and hands were massive, almost the match of John the Blacksmith's. Tom had observed those hands through the Master of Logic's eyes. They were broad, spread like the feet of a shoeless peasant. They were callused. The nails were almost as thick as John's had been, and as ingrained with dirt, as were the knuckles. The hands alone told Tom the man's likely occupation; but he was keen to make assurance double-sure.

Sagres was silent but watchful – clearly no buffoon, in spite of his lack of manners and English. His Latin was as workmanlike as the rest of him – conned because he needed to use it rather than enjoyed as a thing of beauty, a proof of his decorated mind. His clothes were no cleaner than his hands – cleaner than those of the Kerrs, of course (except for Janet's), and cleaner by far than the Armstrongs', but lacking that fastidiousness which had allowed Sir Thomas to skin a deer without soiling the lace of his cuffs; failing to meet even the slightly less perfect expectations Tom remembered in the Alhambra, where heat and dust made English Court perfection out of the question. Sagres was no courtier, and that was plain enough.

Nor was he a soldier. He seemed never to wear even a sword other than at the dictates of fashion. He was slow to accept weapons and seemed uneasy in the handling of them. The only men similar to Sagres who habitually moved in circles shared by Lord Robert Douglas and the Earl of Essex were spies, sorcerers or poisoners – or all three dangerous professionals distilled into one; but even this elegant train of logic failed to satisfy the Master of Logic who drew it out. Closer inspection was required, therefore, and testing of his one alternative theory.

Amongst the hunting weapons on offer were Jedburgh axes and crossbows – even the odd arquebus had been pressed on them; but in the face of it all, Tom had preferred the only weapon he could control to his own satisfaction with a left hand and the club of his bandaged right: a huge, long-shafted spear. It had a great iron blade shaped like a sycamore leaf a yard in length, bedded on a vicious cross-piece, all atop an ash shaft as thick as a quarterstaff, more than a fathom long.

Janet, unremarkable still in her lad's clothing and light jack, took a crossbow without raising an eyebrow and followed at Tom's heels like an apprentice with her master.

Sagres had taken the one dunderbus on offer, seemingly unaware in his increasingly nervous state, that this was the least practical, least reliable and least handy weapon here – or, in fact, that Tom was watching him with more and more lively interest. Tom had seen, though the Spaniard had not, the looks exchanged by the others – even his companions in the Hermitage garrison – and knew that everyone would be giving the senor the widest possible berth. Which, as far as Tom was concerned, was all to the good – particularly as it seemed to support the elegance of his reasoning so far. Why bring a Spanish spy or sorcerer here and then avoid him? Either the one or the other was likely to impart information about the situation, or the future, of crucial importance; and even were the man a poisoner, it might well behove someone amongst his employers to keep a careful watch upon him. But no: simple terror of the massive dunderbus seemed to have spread almost as wide as its shot would scatter – if Sagres could get the matchlock to fire in the first place.

'Do we need to follow so close upon his Spanish heels?' hissed Janet, sharing the general – and by no means unreasonable – nervousness.

'I do; you do not,' answered Tom shortly, and so saying, he eased himself through a tight-packed spiny brake into a little clearing where Senor Sagres stood, looking lost and very worried indeed.

'*Hola,* Senor Sagres,' said Tom easily in rough, slangy Spanish. 'Is all OK?'

'*Hola,*' answered Sagres guardedly. 'Is OK.' He wrestled for a moment with himself, and Tom took leisure to observe the man's natural reticence and vivid awareness that he was talking to his employer's foe here both wrestling with the simple desire to speak his mother tongue once more – even with an enemy. Wisely, Tom held his peace, paced silently across the little clearing and began to ease himself into the thickening undergrowth on the other side. Distantly, Hobbie called, 'The Grave? The Grave...'

Blessedly, Janet also had the sense to stay in the undergrowth.

'Senor...' The word grated out of Sagres as though got by a torturer.

'*Si?*' answered Tom airily, apparently innocently.

'This creature that we hunt ... what manner of creature is it?'

'It is a huge hound of legendary size and power. It kills with a look. It carries away horses. It can reach up for twelve feet. It is the Barguest.'

'But surely you jest! Lord Robert cannot believe such a thing exists. None of you can. It is a thing of childhood stories. Like the Seven Cities of Gold and the Fountain of Eternal Youth.'

'Indeed it may be,' said Tom equably; 'but I am here because it killed my brother and I have sworn to kill it in my turn.' Sagres went silent at that, so Tom continued smoothly, 'Had not Lord Robert already told me that you are lately returned from New Spain, then I would have known it from your mention of the Cities of Gold and the Fountain of Youth. Are you, perhaps, some bold adventurer who has sailed in search of such wonders?'

Sagres gave a rough bark of coarse laughter. 'No. I am a plain, honest working man. Much good has it done me!'

'But sir! Surely in the golden glories of New Spain there is work only for soldiers and priests – and accountants, of course, to tally the tuns of gold for the King of Spain's armadas?'

'Not I, sir! You have listed almost all professions except for my own. Where do you suppose all the gold comes from? Does it grow upon trees? Does it flow in the rivers? Does it fall from the sky?'

Thus, for Tom, almost all of it fell into place at last.

Before he could spring into action, however, there came the most awful cacophony of sound. Lord Robert was clearly using the Armstrongs as beaters to scare the dangerous game they sought out of its lair towards them, he reasoned. Judging by the noise, the Armstrongs were close in front of them indeed. If their quarry was between Sagres and the beaters, then they had better prepare for action immediately. He glanced away from Sagres and discovered that Janet had materialized at his side like a ghost – pale enough to be one, indeed, her linen cheeks made even whiter in contrast with her raven locks. What

299

a figure she would cut at court, he thought, irrelevantly, with her cheeks powdered dead white after the current fashion and her black hair bound up in ringlets.

When Tom looked back at the nervous Spaniard, he found that quietly determined individual was taking action where Tom, as yet, had not. He was pushing determinedly through the undergrowth on his left, where the valley side was beginning to gather into a considerable slope, eastern echo of the high-tracked precipice along which they had entered the place. With a speaking glance at Janet, Tom followed the frightened man.

The sounds made by the nearby beaters abruptly changed their timbre. The fearsome shouting suddenly contained more than a note of panic – a whole chorus of panic indeed. Manly bass bellows became boyish treble screams and even counter-tenor shrieks; and below them, like the ground in a raucous song, came a basso profundo snarling. They had stirred the beast they sought, and something huge was crashing invisibly but all too audibly through the undergrowth near at hand.

Sagres broke through into a clearing and took to his heels across it, with Tom and Janet hard behind him, Tom at least only just in control of the fearsome weapon he was carrying. Across the clearing they went, and into a pathway that opened unexpectedly in the press of saplings opposite. Tom realized at once that Sagres was not simply running – he knew where he was going and was racing thither, certain that it would offer refuge against whatever monster the Armstrongs had started in the timeless woods. The path they were following led up the steepening valley side where the woods began to thin. The higher it rose, the more marked it became as other little tracks joined it at unexpected moments, like streams adding to the might of a river, until it became obvious to Tom that here was a road that lay at the heart of lively industry – lively and recent, for the tracks over which they were careering at full tilt had crushed away the frost so that they were running over black mud.

As they came up out of the trees, Sagres seemed to regain his courage and his reason. He began to slow, obviously aware that he was leading the one man destined to remain ignorant – in Lord Robert's plans at least – towards some kind of answer. As the Spaniard turned, bringing up the dunderbus, so Tom, just behind him, brought down the great spear he carried; and he felt the stirring as Janet brought up her deadly crossbow. But, before they could come to blows, events overtook them.

Events overtook them, not in the shape of the Barguest after all, but in the shape of a huge black boar. Its massive back and Herculean shoulders were bristling. Its face was all covered in blood from broad, flesh-pink snout to burning, heart-red eyes – a thick rouge of redness that was smeared across its teeth and huge, curling tusks and was clearly not its own. It charged out of the undergrowth at them, screaming like an Irish banshee.

Sagres swung the dunderbus away from Tom and pulled the trigger. The smouldering match snapped down into the pan, but the pan was empty, the charge of powder long since scattered to the winds. Nothing further happened, and Sagres shook it as though it were a recalcitrant child. Janet's crossbow cracked and whipped. A black iron quarrel slammed into the huge boar's black shoulder and turned it so that it did not trample them after all; but having run past them, it turned and came screaming back again.

The three of them were long gone by the time the monster slowed and turned on the slippery, frost-slick slope. With Sagres in the lead they were at full tilt up the path towards a fold in the valley side a hundred yards or so ahead. The Spaniard had cast his dunderbus away, but Tom still kept his spear in case it came to close work and Janet, cool as a man in this strange sort of battle, was fighting to load her crossbow as she ran, hoping to prevent matters coming to so close a conclusion. Sure of his way, Sagres looked back, his face as white as salt, and gave a gasp of fear. 'It comes,' he shouted. This was no news to Tom, whose ears had told him so much already.

The vertical fold in the rock was just ahead of them, becoming clearly visible only because they were coming so close to it. Like the other cave mouth, a few miles south of here at the head of the Black Lyne, it had once been covered with undergrowth and, but for the pathway that spoke of so much bustling activity, would have been invisible altogether.

As Sagres dived right round a tall, rocky pillar, Tom followed and turned at once, levelling the spear, even as Janet stood at his shoulder, crossbow raised. The boar came charging heedlessly round the little corner, its head lowered, showing all of its terrible armoury and revealing no real weaknesses at all. Another black quarrel joined the first in the solid meat of its shoulder and Tom's spear blade glanced off its solid forehead, opening a terrible wound the boar simply disregarded as the stout shaft shattered.

Had they not been able to tumble backwards on Sagres's heels through a narrow, rock-lipped opening above a high stone sill immediately behind their dancing heels, they would both have died at once; but they could and they did, and so they did not die yet. Instead, they found themselves lying, shaken and winded, on the wide rock floor of a cavern much larger than its little cousin on the Black Lyne, and heard the boar doing its best to tear away the skin of the mountainside, which was all that lay between them.

'This way,' called Sagres, clearly all too certain that the boar was more than equal to the task and would soon be in here after

303

them. He ran deeper into the hillside, down a tunnel – a tunnel which, Tom saw as he picked himself up, was filled with dim, uncertain torchlight. It was exactly as the Master of Logic in his mind had reasoned.

And if the Master of Logic had been correct about this, then he might well be right about the rest of it. 'Take the utmost care,' he said to Janet as she sprang erect at his side. 'There is deadly danger here.'

The mad boar's iron-hard forehead hit the sill outside and the whole cavern mouth shook and rained rubble. Tom and Janet were off down the tunnel after Sagres, so swiftly, in spite of Tom's wise warning, that they left their weapons lying on the floor. The sides of the passage were high, wide and square-cut. Every few yards there stood a three-sided frame of wood designed to strengthen the walls and support the roof. The light gathered, coming from dead ahead, revealing more details of the construction of the mine and also of its reason: the walls glittered with bands of gilded brightness just like the rock Tom had picked up in Janet's cave.

The passage was carefully dug, well constructed and long. Although the floor seemed to be sloping downwards only slightly, there was a gathering sensation of great weight pressing down upon them as though they were in some infinitely deep place and rushing deeper still. It took Tom only an instant to realize that this was because, although the shaft was only slightly angled, the hillsides above it were reaching up into the high, wild fells over which they had ridden to get here this morning.

The pace of their wild retreat began to slow, for the air in here was still and none too fragrant. It brought a savour of sweat and bodily waste to Tom's nose and the most unexpected, disconcerting odour of garlic that took him straight back to his student days at the academy of fencing run by Maestro Capo Ferro in Siena. To the back of his throat, however, it brought a disconcertingly metallic savour. To his lungs it brought little nourishment.

Out of the tunnel mouth the three of them staggered, into a larger chamber where a dazzling array of torches hissed and crackled. Here stood several men whose faces were at first impossible to distinguish, not least because they all had their backs to them, looking down into some kind of pit; but even when they turned, things became little better, for they all wore kerchiefs over their mouths and noses. The pit into which they were looking was edged with a little rail, and as they turned, one of them leaned back nonchalantly against this, the black sweep of his eyebrows rising. Beside him, a smaller man started forward, his bulldog's forehead frowning. Another little piece of the puzzle fell into place for Tom.

'Give ye good den once more, Lord Robert,' he said. 'Tam, de Vaux; Master Fenwick...'

305

'I expected you sooner, Master Musgrave,' said Lord Robert smoothly.

'Your daughter slowed me,' countered Tom, 'and I was waiting for Hobbie in any case. It must have taken him longer than planned to kill the pig and come after us. Though I believe you were expecting the pig as little as I was to suspect Hobbie's treachery.'

Black Robert Douglas gave a bark of laughter, but his eyes registered shock, even in the flickering shadows of the place. Shocked and glowing, they lifted to Janet's face. 'Well I'll be damned,' he said. 'You're right, and I never even realized. You supposed she was confederated with me? You are mistaken in that at least. A youthful indiscretion with one of the Kerr girls, I assume; come back to haunt me now. But not for long. Senor Sagres, I am sorry to see that you have been unwise enough to lead my enemy into the very heart of my secret plans. You will have to join them, I'm afraid.'

As Lord Robert was speaking English, Sagres stood gaping slightly, clearly having no idea what was going on. Tom helpfully translated into Spanish: 'They're going to kill us all. You too.'

Sagres started with shock and opened his mouth to expostulate, but the quarrel of a crossbow was shoved unceremoniously into his back and Hobbie Noble, to whom Lord Robert's words had been addressed, stepped down into the room, pushing all three of them forward.

'Hobbie was right,' said Lord Robert, his sangfroid well recovered. 'Your acuity is close to witchcraft, Master of Logic. It is even as the Earl of Essex warned me. I salute you, though only as a parting gesture. Bring them here.'

'There's no need for the rest of you to stay covered either,' said Tom as he walked slowly towards the wooden barrier. 'Factor Fenwick, I assume you were seduced away from your master Sir Thomas by the promise of wealth from this mine. You are a man ruled by money; the riches promised here must have made that almost inevitable.'

Sir Thomas's factor Fenwick tore the mask off his face at that. 'He knows!' he snarled. 'Lord Robert, he must be made to tell us all he knows, or I may be taken when I return, and then our plans may go for nothing! And remember, the lady Eve is by no means a certain way. Better by far that I continue with Sir Thomas's ruination that you may inherit the Waste through me.'

Black Robert smiled. 'His only hope,' he said, 'is that he calculates that if he throws us such scraps as he has discovered, we will hold off killing him while we wait for the rest of the matter; and that while we wait, we might let slip more of our plans – as you have just done, Master Fenwick – then we will somehow mistake, and he may manage to escape. Do you expect to talk to us, Master Musgrave?'

'No, Lord Robert, I expect to die,' said

307

Tom.

'In this also, you reason soundly, then. Behold your death.'

Black Robert reached back and upward, taking a torch from the wall. As he did so, Tom said, 'I have seen it, Lord Robert – in the faces of my brother, of my friend Father Little, and of the Kerrs hanging at your gate. You have the Barguest in that pit.'

Fenwick laughed an ugly laugh at that and Black Robert stood with the torch held high. 'If you believe that, then you are not the man I have taken you for! But I think that, even now, you fence with me, using wit and words instead of swords.'

'What killed my brother John lies in that pit and you have called it the Barguest – you and the Kerrs your confederates, Hobbie, Fenwick and the turncoats that work with you. What lies in there makes men die seemingly of fear and you have done the rest by rumour and secret strategy!'

'Close on witchcraft indeed. We should burn you, Master Musgrave. But as you see, we cannot.'

They were by the low fence now with the dark pit at their feet and as he spoke, Black Robert dropped his torch. Down it tumbled, flaring, end over end, into a circular well some twenty feet deep, about the same measure across. The sides of the place were lined with one wooden gallery halfway down. There were rough steps leading up here and down to the floor where the torch lay guttering. The gallery was lined with half a dozen men, all looking upwards, all screaming silently, with their eyes and mouths stretched wide, all frozen in place, apparently dead of sheer, naked fear – men, calculated Tom, such as the brace that hung at Hermitage Gate.

The three on the edge of that terrible grave had only an instant to see what awaited them before the torch choked into darkness and Lord Robert said, 'Throw them in.'

# Twenty-six

## The Waste

'*NO!*' screamed Sagres, and needed no translation, the word being the same in both Spanish and English. He threw himself to one side, as though to run away, though the act was clearly futile, as Hobbie was surrounded by half a dozen Armstrongs whose arms indeed lived up to their name. He careered into Tom and Janet. 'You must not breathe down there,' he said in rapid Spanish, his lips against Tom's ear, as he did so. 'It is death to breathe down there!'

Tom, of course, had worked that out for himself long since, and was at least one step further on. For everyone here had died erect, like Father Little, clutching the rails and fighting for breath, freezing solid where they stood, apparently stricken by terror; but John had died on his hands and knees, and Tom could not imagine his brother crouching like that because he was beaten, broken and going down to death without a struggle.

A melee began at once with everyone except Black Robert and Fenwick getting

310

involved in the scuffle. Tam Burn joined Hobbie and his men in subduing the three condemned to die.

Then, most unexpectedly, coming near to confounding even the Master of Logic, another voice, made rough and breathless by the struggle – tantalizingly impossible to identify – whispered in an undertone almost impossible to hear, 'Don't breathe!' and the words were in English this time.

The minute the rough hands closed on his arms and it was clear they were all bound downwards, Tom squeezed his eyes tight shut. He did not need eyes as he was dragged with Sagres and Janet, grimly struggling along the wooden fencing, to the gateway of the pit, but he would need them clear in the darkness at the foot of the pit all too soon. Bearing in mind the advice offered twice, he was trying to control his breathing, all his concentration on sucking the dank but life-giving air into his lungs until his chest was straining full, like a swimmer preparing to dive deep.

At the last, he opened his eyes for an instant so that he could see what lay below him, then the rough hands pushed him and he jumped.

He landed on the balcony halfway down, where Father Little had died and where all the dead Kerrs stood. He let his legs give and he rolled, careful to keep his lungs as full of air as possible. As he paused there for an instant, all of his being focused downwards, he heard Black Robert call the almost

311

inevitable order, 'Not the girl. We'll take her back to Hermitage.' Then he leaped on down again on to the floor of the pit, falling into John's dying stance, down on his hands and knees, looking around with his dark-adjusted eyes to see what John might have been looking for if this was indeed the place his brother had died. Vaguely, he heard Sagres come tumbling down behind him. Then everything except immediate experience was blanked out of his mind.

For Tom saw what his brother John must have seen.

The torch Black Robert had thrown down before them lay on its side, its flames choked to death as surely as any Kerr up on the scaffold – except that, on the side nearest Tom, there was an ember glowing red, still alive, just. As he put his hand towards the spark of hope and fire, Tom felt a little breeze blowing steadily across the back of his fingers. Somewhere, over there behind him, was a tunnel where the air was clean enough to keep the fire alight – cleaner than here, at least; perhaps even clean enough to breathe.

He grabbed the torch and moved it gently around, his eyes on that faint red spark. As soon as it gathered a little more brightness in the breath of that hopeful draught, he began to crawl across the floor, following it. As soon as he moved he could feel Sagres at his side, silently following his lead and crawling for dear life.

The ember guided them like the star that

led the three wise men to the crib of the infant Christ – across the floor of that hellish place, to the southernmost wall. Here the sheer and seemingly solid rock face was pocked by a low tunnel mouth, all but impossible to see in the Stygian gloom of the place. His hand made unerring by the guiding light, Tom pushed the torch forward and the ember started into life – just enough to show the low lintel of the rock above. As he pushed it in and followed it, Tom felt his lungs give their first warning twist of pain as they demanded that he breathe, even though it still meant death to do so.

In that moment he heard a distant voice, echoing mockingly from an ironically heavenly height: 'Like brother, like brother. That is the last I saw of the blacksmith before we dragged his frozen corpse out onto the Waste, as we shall drag you out on the morrow and put you all up in the tree where they found him. Then even the Kerrs will be too scared of the terrible Barguest to venture out in the night!'

The last distant phrase dripped with distracting irony, but it was as nothing compared with Lord Robert's mention of the Waste. Even that, however, sat unconsidered at the back of Tom's mind. For all of his conscious concentration remained upon the point of light at the tip of the torch. He held the thing perforce in his left hand, for his right hand would have dropped it, bruised and swathed as it was; but on the other hand (a distractingly amusing figure in Tom's increasingly whirling mind) he was forced to put his weight on the broken hand instead. Only the fact that he must at all costs contain his breath stopped him from shouting aloud with pain each time he did so. Such was his iron self-control that he remained breathless and silent for minute after minute as he scrabbled forwards through the massive, constricting, freezing, labyrinthine darkness fathoms deep below the Waste. The only other thing that gave him the hope and desperate strength to carry on was the speed with which the little tunnel he was following began to slope back up towards the surface.

After the first couple of minutes, the darkness of the twisting tunnel sides became irrelevant in any case, for the edges of his vision began to flicker and close down. The slope of the ground beneath him also became irrelevant, for he lost all sense of position and direction – as drowning men are sometimes said to swim downwards towards their final end, lost even to the conflicting attractions of earth and sky.

Only the unreal glimmer of the one spark still alive in the near-dead torch broke the narrowing beam of blackness along which Tom was twisting like an arthritic serpent; and, as his sight was beginning to dim, so his hearing was beginning to fail as well. The desperate scrabbling of the man who followed at his heels soon was swallowed in a pulsing, thunderous roar as his starved heart demanded sustenance from his lungs that they stoutly still refused to give. The heart began to overheat, robbed of the cooling draughts of air the throat habitually provided. The hot humours began to swirl in his brain, making him light-headed and bringing curtains of pulsing red over the glowing tip of the torch, while the heavy phlegm of earthy, liquid melancholy sank sadly to his legs and feet, making them almost impossible to move, so heavy did they become.

The red curtains of uncontrolled fiery humour swirling before his eyes became so thick that he almost missed the moment that the spark sprang from ember into flame; but when that one flicker began to spread, as yellow as a field of daffodils in spring, across the wintry stubble of the blackened torch, he realized that the faithful flambard at least had found air enough to breathe. Yet still, almost dead of suffocation, still he did not dare to let his pent breath out. Onward in a kind of frenzy he pushed his shaking body, watching the yellow flames spread like wildfire, yet still refusing to breathe as the fourth minute began to pass and the passageway began, un-noticed, to widen and lighten around him.

In the end, a blast of icy air came battering into Tom's fixed and frozen face. The torch, just below his left shoulder, exploded into volcanic life, singeing his cheek, near singeing his moustache and shocking him into a gasp of surprise. And so it was he found that he could breathe.

'Breathe!' he shouted over his shoulder, in English, so far was he from controlling his thoughts and actions – only to be surprised by utter silence. Not even a croak issued from his frozen throat. His voice, like his breath over the last four minutes and more, was stopped. Twisting on his side and pressing his back against the wall, he thrust the torch back past his feet to bring the message home to the man behind him; but when he looked back into its brightness, to his horror he found himself alone. The tunnel was just wide enough now to allow him to turn, and so he did as fast as he was able, shuffling back down into the deadly darkness, pushing his torch ahead of him, following the cheery brightness of its flame back into the gathering horror below. Sagres had been hard on his heels when his hearing went and he found him first, just at the point where the torch began to gutter, twenty long and agonizing seconds later. He lay face down and apparently dead where the narrow tunnel began to open out. He half-turned and put his beard at risk of singeing like the King of Spain's as he threw the torch away into the good air further on. Then he laced his good left hand into the solid leather of the Spaniard's doublet and heaved.

'Are we alive, then?' asked Sagres in Spanish some time later. They lay side by side immediately outside an utterly unremarkable hole on a frozen hill-slope, gasping like a

316

couple of fish thrown up by a high tide.

'I can hardly tell,' said Tom in the same language, squinting up into the dazzling daylight, 'but we are breathing, and that seems to be a start. Perhaps full life will return if we wait.'

'The air upon this mountainside is already performing that miracle for me,' said the Spaniard dreamily. 'After a childhood in the heat of La Carihuela and a manhood in the deserts and jungles of New Spain, to think that I should thank Our Lady on bended knee for the icy air of this accursed, frozen place!'

'Is it gold they are mining, then?' Tom demanded after a moment. 'Or copper? Or tin?'

Sagres sat up and gaped at him.

'You are an expert in gold mining from New Spain,' Tom persisted, also pulling himself up off the frosted grass. 'De Vaux owns half the tin in Cornwall and most of the mines north of Redruth; but all I have ever heard tell of in these parts is copper, and it must be a metal of some kind or the Armstrongs would never need all that charcoal for smelting what they and the Kerrs bring out of the mine.'

Sagres crossed himself – and not just because his prayer to the Virgin was done. 'Witchcraft,' he muttered.

'Logic,' countered Tom.

'Lord Robert thought at first he must have discovered copper, as you say,' agreed Sagres

317

reluctantly; 'but then indeed he hoped for gold. In the end he got neither, as things transpired; but they have discovered something that might be worth more than both, so they hope.'

'And what is that, pray tell?'

'It is arsenic.'

'Arsenic!'

'Yellow arsenic. It looks like copper – like gold, indeed, in some lights; but if you put it in a furnace carefully, you may reduce it to the purest of white powders, and that is what they have done. There is a fashion, Senor de Vaux and Lord Robert the devil tell me, to wear such powder upon their faces at court. It is popular but fabulously expensive, for most of it must be imported, I believe, from the north of Germany. They find it in the silver mines there.'

'And whoever owns a monopoly on an English supply might find his fortune well and truly made,' whispered Tom, in English.

'That's the answer. The answer to almost all of it, as I knew it simply had to be!' Tom said, after a moment of thoughtful silence, reverting to Spanish as he sprang erect. 'Sagres, d'ye not see where we are?'

He turned the Spaniard round and they stood shoulder to shoulder, looking away south across the gathering slope that folded down into the valley of the Black Lyne.

'I see,' said the Spaniard slowly. 'I know the shafts run northward to Hermitage Castle itself, but there is nothing of worth within them. All the good ore is down here.' He paused, looking across at the vibrant Englishman, then asked a little nervously, 'What is it that you mean to do, Maestro Musgrave?'

'I mean, Senor, to avenge my brother, rescue my sister and perhaps young Janet too. Then I shall put paid to a nest of turncoats and traitors; and, finally, I shall bury the Barguest into the bargain,' he said.

'But how?' whispered Sagres, simply awed by the scale of the prospect. 'How under God can you hope to do so much?'

'Why, Senor,' he answered with grim exultation, 'I can do it because I am dead. I can do it because the pair of us, like my brave brother John, have been taken by the Barguest already and lie dead and buried beneath the Waste! Or, lest ye think me mad when I need you to help me, let me be more plain and square with you: I can do it because Black Robert and his murderous confederates *believe* we are dead and buried. He believes there is no one now living who can interfere with his plans, but he is terribly wrong in that. For I, the Master of Logic, know every detail of what he has done, is doing, and plans to do, so that when I begin to act against him, he will fall helpless into my hands – and mayhap even bring his friend the Earl of Essex with him.'

# Twenty-seven

## The Dark Designs

The pair of them were waiting in Sir Thomas's study when he returned from the hunt that night, with Geordie Burn pale but determined at his side. He gaped to see them together at all, let alone so footsore and filthy. He frowned to see that his ledgers and private papers lay open on the table, some pages marked with rude and muddy fingerprints; but such was his surprise that he forbore to comment and heard his nephew out. Then his astonishment simply grew and grew as Tom tersely briefed him on what he had discovered and the actions they all must now take as a matter of the extremest urgency.

He began with the spy. 'Sir Thomas, can you confirm to me that Hobbie is your spy in Lord Robert's camp, though he pretends to be a traitor to you and yours?'

Sir Thomas hesitated, then he turned to Geordie. 'See to your command, Captain Burn. We will be back in Liddesdale before moonrise, if I am any judge – and ye can continue your quest for the Barguest and your lady's hand then.'

As Geordie left, the Lord of the Waste turned, looking elderly and weary. 'A good man and a good soldier, but there's little place for bravery and honour in this black coil. 'Tis better he remains in ignorance and dreams that Eve might ever come to him, as he has done for half his life.

'Now, as to Hobbie Noble: it is a dreadful, ungodly thing to demand of any man, but on the Borders there is little choice. I am astounded that you have seen so much so quickly in the matter – you are every bit as uncanny as the Lord Hunsdon inferred in his letters, and as well versed in the black arts of espionage. I see I must be open with you and pray that you are correct and that Lord Robert's Spaniard there speaks no English.

'I began to place Hobbie Noble so that he could move in dangerous circles when I helped him release Jock o' the Side Armstrong from gaol a few years since. I have used him sparingly but he has reported fully. Only now have I been forced to risk him in the very heart of the lion's den, for as ye see from my ledgers, my income is shrinking daily, and ruin stares me in the face despite the best efforts of my factor – or I supposed I was getting Master Fenwick's best efforts until Hobbie suggested the man had been seduced away by Black Robert as he seeks my ruin; but 'tis all moon-shadow and will-o'-the-wisp, nothing a man can lay a hand to. Even now, Hobbie seeks truth enough to go to law; but the case must needs be un-answerable and the groundwork set in sure foundation or Fenwick and his true masters will stand across the Scottish border and laugh at our English courts. On the other hand, my other true servant, your brother the blacksmith had come to me with ores he had been sent – from Hermitage no less – to see if he could tell what they might be; but nothing came of that, for he was dead soon after we talked.'

'And ye saw no coincidence in that? I see from your face you did; and I suspect you were not alone in that. A wise move to risk Hobbie, therefore, for there is everything to play for here; but he in turn has risked all his careful placing to whisper a warning to me and I am fearful Lord Robert would not let such a slip pass without notice – and, I doubt not, some action. Has Hobbie returned with you?'

'I have not seen him since the boar broke loose this afternoon.'

'Let us pre-empt them all and counter their dark designs with immediate action. I will explain what I have discovered to you as we proceed. You should know that I have not been sitting idly awaiting your return, but have usurped your seal and authority to summon reinforcements from Carlisle, for we must return to Liddesdale and Hermitage tonight if Eve, and mayhap Janet, are to survive.'

'Well, well,' said Sir Thomas grimly. 'We will

fill the interim with your explanation and then I will judge who's bound for Carlisle gaol.'

'Let us begin with John's death and the lady Eve,' said Tom decisively. 'Whatever she told you at your inquest into the matter, the facts are these: Eve knew John believed in the Barguest – and that he shared his superstition with half the Borders – though he believed he had seen it and the rest of them had not. Eve did not believe the Barguest killed John, however, in spite of the apparent evidence furnished by his terrified face and his discovery in the clawed tree at Arthur's Seat. Her reasoning was simple and based on her own experience, shared with the Lady Ellen: John was clean. Women who have laid men out for burial know that such a thing could not be. Death is a dirty business. Dying of fear releases all the body's foulness in a flood.'

Tom was not sitting idly as he talked. His hands were busy loading guns and sorting weapons on the little table in Sir Thomas's study. Sagres, silent and understanding nothing of what was being said, nevertheless followed suit, so that they would all be ready to leave the very instant reinforcements arrived from Carlisle.

'John was not foul,' continued Tom grimly. 'In fact, his clothes were recently washed and fire-dried; but that had been done in haste, for his shirt tail had been singed, as was my own when Lady Ellen caused a blood-fouled shirt to be cleaned and dried. More than one man must have been involved in the doing of it, for not even Eve herself could remove the clothes from John's frozen body after Hobbie had brought him down to her.

'No simple death of terror in the face of a fearsome monster, therefore. Instead, in Eve's eyes and my own, a complex and sinister conspiracy of murder and concealment of murder by many men over several hours at the least – a terrible, calculated and brutal act, compounded and completed with the raising of John's washed, dressed, still-frozen corpse into the branches of the tree. It was done as you yourself raised up the stag for skinning on St Stephen's Day; I am certain of that, for the faintest of rope marks were left on his back and at his armpits, and the clawing of the trunk beneath completed their fearsome act. And it was an act: an illusion. Like the ass's head in my friend Shakespeare's new play of the midsummer dream.

'Father Little's clothing also had been cleaned and dried before he was returned to the scaffold in the church tower at Blackpool Gate – for the same dark reason and with the same desired effect.'

'But why? If, as you say, it aroused suspicion instead of allaying it, then why?' Sir Thomas now was restless, pacing the study and looking down into the castle yard. Clearly, thought Tom, his uncle was beginning to see what he had seen, and understand a little of Black Robert's dark design – keen, he hoped, for the men to arrive from Carlisle so that they could go off up Liddesdale and into the dangerous dungeons of Hermitage again.

'Because Lord Robert, who lies behind the twisted heart of this whole murderous matter, was willing to run a small risk in order to cover a huge truth,' Tom explained. Then he demanded, 'What was it that was washed off the dead men's clothing?'

'The foulness of their terrible deaths,' hazarded Sir Thomas.

'No.' Tom paused for a minim beat, as though this were a duel with swords and in form. Then he began to explain slowly, for this was near the very marrow of the matter: 'What had at all costs to be cleaned away was the mud from Lord Robert's mine. That is the secret heart of the business here – Lord Robert's mine, which I will describe in more detail later; but in the meantime, Sagres and I have been there and are lucky indeed to have returned alive. Look at us; we are filthy, soiled with mud and stained with the tell-tale green of the ore. So were John and Father Little. Above everything else, Lord Robert wishes to conceal the fact that he is mining. That is why everyone he cannot trust to keep his secret has to die. That is why he must have decided to rid himself of John even though my brother could not tell him what his strange gold-coloured ore could be. That is why he brought the Barguest back to life in the first place.'

'To hide a mine?'

'Indeed. To hide his mine and conceal the

fact that he had the Kerrs scouring the countryside looking for other ways into it. Gangs of Kerrs come and go nightly through the Busy Gap past the bastle farm at Housesteads, where we first met Janet and Dand – and came close to killing the both of them. They range abroad every night, scouring the Waste, while the weather holds icy but snowless. They leave no tracks on the frozen ground, but will do so when the snow comes and so will perforce leave off their murderous excursions if the matter has not been settled by then. Scores of Kerrs come and go, armed with clubs that have steel hooks driven into them – clawed clubs that can scratch a tree to the heartwood like the claws of a giant dog, up to twelve feet from the earth, if they stand in their stirrups and reach up to the fullest stretch. For while they scour the Waste, so they perpetuate the story that the Barguest is abroad.

'I had thought, at first, that it was all like my friend Will Shakespeare's play of the midsummer dream, where men dress up as monsters and bushes may be mistaken for bears; but there is more to the matter than that – much more – and all of it bloodiest and most devilish evil.'

'You have seen these clubs?' Sir Thomas's eyes were narrow, his face pale with horror at the lies Lord Robert was perpetuating. He was almost ready, thought Tom – almost ready to ride.

'I have seen what they can do,' Tom

326

continued smoothly. 'For one of the Kerrs used just such a club on Archie Elliot's back on Christmas night – the night I thought Geordie Burn had tried to kill me, when really it was his brother Tam, Lord Robert's captain from Hermitage, riding in secret with Hugh of Stob. The claw-club left three lines parallel in Archie's flesh and the razor mark of a fourth in the hair beside them. Word of that terrible error was carried up to Hermitage, I would judge by your factor Fenwick; but whoever passed the warning, Archie was murdered the next day by the poison I have just mentioned, and which came close to killing several others of us too.'

'What poison? How?'

'By this, I would judge, and in this.' Tom pulled out of his pouch the apple-sized piece of earth he had found in Janet's cave, which he had seen ground up in John's smithy, and which he now knew to be yellow arsenic ore. Beside it he laid the severed glove finger he had found. 'It was done at the Hunt Mass, and by Fenwick again. I am certain of that this time, for I tested the man last night and saw the guilt within his eyes. And I tested the poison, too, on two dead mice, while de Vaux unknowingly further tested it on a cat.

'He filled the glove finger with the poison powder and slipped it into his mouth. It is of Spanish leather, like my own, and waterproof, but polished only on the outside and not watertight enough to contain a liquid safely. He used powdered arsenic, therefore –

this white powder that Senor Sagres assures me is derived from the other here, and with which all at court powder their faces according to the fashion. He stood beside Archie at communion, and when he seemingly sipped from the holy cup, he emptied the poison in. Archie took the largest dose and died. Eve, Geordie and myself were poisoned too and Father Little, who emptied the cup himself, was poisoned last of all. We were none of us his target – only Archie.

'But, as Hobbie said in our discussion of the matter, we were hurt incidentally to the main object of the crime. When word got out to Hermitage that Eve was amongst the poisoned, de Vaux himself was despatched to contact and castigate the blundering Fenwick and find out the truth of her health.'

It was at this point in Tom's explanation that the men from Carlisle arrived; and Sir Thomas, seeing this, was in no mood at all to linger further. The Governor had sent thirty, and the Bewcastle contingent made the number up to fifty. They were all well armed and armoured in their jacks, plates and steel bonnets – sharp but steady, and ready for bloody work. Within moments they were all formed up and cantering purposefully out of the gate again, Geordie at the shoulder of the captain from Carlisle, but Tom, Sir Thomas and Sagres at the head.

'Unlike us,' continued Tom as they rode up towards the Waste with Sir Thomas leaning over dangerously, the better to hear him over

328

the muted thunder of the troop behind, 'Father Little must have suspected something when the poison began to grip him. He was certain that Lord Robert was up to evil, as he told me on the day Lord Robert and I first met, and must have ridden not to Blackpool Gate but right up to Hermitage to confront him, sick as he was; but the end of all his bravery simply served to put him, like John, in the pit of death that stands at the heart of Black Robert's mine. Like John, he died there, and I can only pray his death was swift and painless, for he was already half-dead with Fenwick's poison from the desecrated chalice.

'Then, like John's had been, Father Little's frozen corpse was removed, cleaned and put on show as another victim of the Barguest – and that gently and secretly, for it was done while Janet and I slept in the kirk below.'

'I had shared some of my suspicions with the good father,' admitted Sir Thomas grimly. 'Unlike you, I am old enough to remember how the confessional can lighten the heaviest-charged of souls. But if they saw you alone in the kirk as they brought the father's body there, why did they not take you or kill you?'

'By this time, my own investigations were the cause of an unexpected effect. They were spreading word of the Barguest ever wider – and convincing even hard-headed men that the beast must actually be real. Suddenly and unexpectedly – and temporarily – therefore, I became useful to Lord Robert, which is why

I am alive to tell this black tale now.'

Tom stopped talking for a while as they thundered up over the Waste, sending the frost-mist swirling away under the last of the light to where the will-o'-the-wisps glimmered over the frozen bog-holes there.

'But what in heaven's name is the motivation for all this madness and death? A mine full of poison somewhere up ahead in Liddesdale?' Sir Thomas demanded, his voice aquiver with outrage.

'Not just in Liddesdale, no. That is the nub of the problem, you see,' answered Tom, with a broad gesture of his broken hand comprehending all the dangerous beauty around them. 'The Waste and all the fells between here and Hermitage are a honeycomb of caverns and tunnels, into which Lord Robert is driving his shafts to mine out his arsenic; but his main shaft starts on the east side of the Liddel valley far to the south of Hermitage. It runs east and south from there, reaching right down to the head of the Black Lyne itself, only a mile or so ahead of where we are riding now. Do you not see what this must mean?'

Sir Thomas folded his forehead into a thoughtful frown, but his nephew had not the patience to allow considered rumination. 'It means that all Black Robert Douglas's new-found wealth lies under English soil! If you cannot reach north across the border to catch at him for plotting dark ruin against you, no more can he reach south across it to mend his own fast-breaking fortunes. The arsenic that will mend the fortunes of Lord Robert and the Essex faction in the Court cannot belong to a Scottish laird, for it all lies south of the border – in our good Queen's realm! It belongs to whoever holds title to the Waste at English law; whoever owns the Black Lyne.

'Lord Robert created the Barguest to frighten all of you off the Waste, and, with John's body in the great oak, out of the Lyne valley as well, while the Kerrs found out the extent of the problem and he worked out his solution – as he has done now.'

'What solution?'

'He knows that the entrances he seeks on English soil are in the valley of the Lyne. He holds the woman that owns the land he covets. He will not let her go. He will keep her and hold the title to the Black Lyne. He sees himself victorious and unopposed now, for he believes that I am dead and he supposes I am the only man outside his control who has begun to suspect the truth. He has only to force Eve into a form of marriage, then he can swiftly widow himself into untold riches. It is his easiest, most certain way.'

# Twenty-eight

## Liddesdale Ablaze

As Tom reached that point in his reasoning, so the war band left English soil to enter Liddesdale and Scotland. As they did so, like a blessing from on high, a steady, strengthening south-westerly wind sprang up behind to blow them on their way. Over the ford at the valley mouth they went, then up on to the path that led across the precipice itself, in through the sheer-sided throat of the place. Here reason must perforce give place to further preparation. As they followed the track up across the curves of the undulating valley side, so Tom and his uncle agreed their plans for action and passed their orders back. When there was no more to be done, Tom returned to his tale of horror and double-dealing.

Tom and Sir Thomas crushed side by side on the narrow way so that the Master of Logic could continue with his explanation to the Lord of the Waste. 'Let us return to the beginning. Eve was nearly certain that John was murdered, then, and likely murdered for the land they owned, because there seemed no other cause great enough to create such a terrible consequence; but in her heart also she feared the work that he was doing – in secret I should judge – on the strange ores that had been brought down from Hermitage to him. Eve is a woman who will not trust what she does not understand. John no doubt felt lowered by this grubbing with metallic, smelly dirt and would not discuss the matter with her. She brought enough of her fear to you, however, on the night after his death so that you held swift inquest and then despatched her with Hobbie to the Council, to the Lord of the North and, ultimately, to me.

'In the meantime, however, she had sufficient leisure to turn to the method of John's murder, leaving aside the reason for it. She reasoned thus: if he was not killed with terror by the Barguest, then she must at once consider poison. Knowing nothing of secret mines and deathly airs, she thought of herbal lore. Mayhap she consulted Lady Ellen, but she had no real need to do so, for she heals with the same mastery as Ellen and that bespeaks equal knowledge.

'There are poisons – poisons close to hand – that might have killed anyone in the way John seemed to have been killed – certainly with much the same effect. Even Fenwick's white arsenic left a corpse in Archie Elliot bewilderingly similar to that of both John and Father Little: the rictus, the straining muscles, the look of tortured agony that might be mistaken for terror. She had a wide variety of possibilities but only limited time for investigation, however, for no sooner were the inquest and the funeral done than you warned her to prepare for the journey south with Hobbie; but the possibility was ever in her mind.

'Then the fear arose that whoever had poisoned John would be as quick to poison the man looking into his death. The elder brother being murdered, therefore, the younger brother might well stand in mortal danger in his turn. The younger brother: to wit, myself. But poisons have antidotes. Indeed, it is a common proof that if a man is to taste the antidote before he takes the poison, then the poison may not touch him at all. So it was that Eve herself stabbed a dagger into my side at Ware.'

'What are you saying?' Sir Thomas came near to steering his hunter off the cliff edge in surprise. 'It was Eve herself that wounded you?'

'Aye. Then, as she tended to my hurt,' shouted Tom to reassure him, suddenly aware of how the wind was strengthening at their backs, 'so she put into the wound, and my medicines, all the antidotes to the poisons she feared might be used on me. The treatment gave me a fevered, dream-filled night as we sped northward in the coach; but it was all to good effect, for I have been poisoned and I have survived!'

At this moment they rode out on to an

outward curve of the path where the whole thin road seemed to hang in very air. Here they came across the first of the great horrors of the night. It was a gallows, recently built into the jutting cliff under which they rode, which reached across their narrow track so that the body hanging from it must needs obstruct their way. A hooded man dangled from it, faceless, but with a body that twitched and writhed in faint but lively agony, aswinging in the wind. The hanging man had been hooded with a bag then bound on to the gallows in such a manner that he could hardly breathe, for there was a rope tight across his throat. Yet there was another rope that held his arms behind him and ran upward as well, taking just enough of his weight so that he should choke but never faint and not quite die until thirst or famine clung him; and, given the quantity of rain of late, it was likely to be a lingering wait before he gained his peace.

Tom and Sir Thomas came up against this unfortunate creature first, for they were in the lead. Had Sir Thomas been alone, he would likely have pushed past with his men. The Master of Logic was given pause and slowed them both, however. At the very least, thought Tom, his enemy's enemy, here displayed, might make a lively friend, as Sagres had done. So he looked up at the jerking body and tried to figure what the face would look like behind the hood; but the form itself was swift to tell its own story.

'HOBBIE!' called Tom, urging his horse forward until Hobbie's pendant feet could rest upon the withers and Tom could reach up in an unconscious echo of the men that had clawed the oak beneath the corpse of his murdered brother. Standing in his stirrups on a steady, patient horse, he reached up with the longest of his sharp-sided daggers and cut his old friend free. Sir Thomas had ridden onward. The rest of the command perforce remained behind.

Hobbie slid down on to Tom's horse, swung wildly out over the sheer drop, then swung in again to bang his hooded head against the sheer wall beside him. 'That you, Tom?' he whispered.

'Aye,' affirmed Tom. 'It is.'

'Should never have warned ye to hold your breath. That devil Lord Robert heard me...'

'But then I wouldn't have been here to cut you down; and he would have found you out sometime.'

'True enough,' croaked Hobbie.

A little more dagger work released Hobbie's hands and allowed the removal of the bag and all the ropes.

'Who did this to you?'

'Need ye ask?'

'Not Lord Robert himself? No. Fenwick, more likely, as proof of loyalty after the flapping of his big, loose mouth...'

'Ye're in the right. And Tam Burn joined in for the pleasure while that whoreson de Vaux looked on and laughed. 'Twas de Vaux

336

suggested the running knots and the slow strangulation – bad cess to him.'

'Is he strong enough to come with us?' bellowed Sir Thomas over the gusty roaring of the wind, rendered impatient rather than sympathetic by this new proof of Black Robert's devilish perfidy.

'Needs must,' sang back Tom. 'There's no one here to take him home.'

'Besides,' choked Hobbie painfully, 'there's the matter of revenge now. So I'll come along with you until we meet the several men I've to settle with.'

For the next few minutes, as they shared Tom's horse, Hobbie and he brought each other up to date with their thoughts and plans. Then Sir Thomas's patience ran out and he demanded the explanations include him.

'Tom's right,' said Hobbie. 'Eve stabbed him then swore me to silence as she tended him with all her cunning. Her object was to make the treatment of a slight hurt at Ware into an armour of fitness against any other poisons that might be fed to him.'

'On the way north she tested my belief in the Barguest too,' continued Tom, 'and found I believed in it as little as she did herself; but she would not confide all of her fears to me – or, perhaps, it was not so much a reluctance to tell me what she feared as a wariness to do so in front of Hobbie, whom she has good reason not to trust.'

'Has she?' demanded Hobbie and Sir

Thomas in unison. 'What good reason is that?' completed Sir Thomas, while Hobbie choked on a cough.

Tom answered his uncle directly: 'The fact that you have not told her that Hobbie is your spy in Lord Robert's ranks. Or *was*, rather. She sees only the double game he was playing, not the single purpose behind it.'

'A fair point,' allowed Sir Thomas, and Hobbie nodded too – once, painfully.

'But in any case, she had good reason not to share all her doubts and suspicions with me, for I was here expressly to find out the truth of the matter, and that truth, she feared, might reveal some ignoble dealing between John and Lord Robert to echo what she feared of Hobbie. For had not John secret contacts with Hermitage over the matter of the ores? Was he not on his way there for his gooding when he disappeared and died? Better by far to watch what I uncovered and to see then how well it fitted with what she believed.

'But that is all irrelevant now, for Black Robert has taken her.' He held up his hand at Sir Thomas's expostulation. 'I know, you believe what Lord Robert said this morning: that she has gone to Hermitage so that he will bring her the Barguest; that she has given her word and he has given his. But he took her by force, and I believe she has demanded the Barguest as a last, desperate ploy – not out of a desire for revenge for John's death, but as a way to slow events. She does not believe the

338

thing exists, therefore she does not believe anyone can bring it to her. Therefore she is safe until we can work out a way to rescue her; but Lord Robert holds one final ace, and if ever a man was born to play it, that man is himself.

'Black Robert knows that the Barguest is real. Janet certainly knows this, because it took her horse, poor Selkie. News of that will have come to him recently, but I am certain Black Robert already had some knowledge of the thing. Perhaps he has even seen it in the wild woods of Liddesdale, as John and I saw it a little further south, when we were young. So if the monster is real and he knows where it lives, Lord Robert can now have Eve and the Black Lyne whenever he wants, all legal and in the full light of day, after all. For Eve has trapped herself: he has only to bring her the Barguest and she must bow to him as she has sworn; and he will take her, body and soul, with all she stands possessed of. Then he will kill her when he tires of her, and all his fortune will be made.

'That was designed to be today's business: to rid himself of all his problems at a stroke; to kill me, in the same way as he killed Father Little and brother John; to keep my body back for display tomorrow; to hang up Hobbie as a suspected spy and leave him as a warning to anyone approaching Hermitage; to kill the Barguest, which he is certain haunts the wild woods of Liddesdale; to win Eve and to lay legal hold of the Black Lyne.

'Things have not worked out that way, however. For the first time since John discovered what was afoot in Liddesdale when he went agooding unannounced on St Thomas's Day and met his end and began all this, Lord Robert's plans have gone awry. He will have them back on their destined road by the morrow, I have no doubt; but tonight belongs to us, and we have the chance, now and only now, to upset these evil schemes of his and bring this all to a happy ending.'

The light was almost gone now and they had not brought torches with them that would only advertise their presence further to the Armstrongs and their master. Torches would never have survived the wind, in any case.

As he spoke, however, so something buzzed between himself and Sir Thomas to spatter and spark off the rock beside his head, and a shot echoed through the gusty shadows. The first shot was followed at once by a second, and the man behind Geordie Burn was hurled off his horse, his bonnet shattered. 'Sir Thomas, we must go down!' bellowed Tom, and the good old soldier swung his horse towards the edge of the slope at once. Even as the rest turned to follow suit, Hobbie leaped off Tom's horse and ran to the suddenly vacated spare mount. Then, fifty-four of them, abreast, set their horses straight down the slope and went sliding into the depths of Liddesdale.

This was what Tom and Sir Thomas had

planned and, except for the acquisition of an extra companion, they had covered every eventuality. Sir Thomas took the fifty riders and went straight into the attack. It was a feature of the place that it was deep, dark and thickly forested, full of *ambuscadoes* where Armstrongs could hide and snipe, particularly at this time of day. The main attack was designed to use the terrain and their own activities most effectively against them, however. Sir Thomas's men went at once for the charcoal fires. Each of these stood ten feet high, a palisade of inward-leaning logs at whose heart was a slow fire, choked of air where the wood was rendered not to ash but to charcoal; but the fires, when toppled with line and long spear and scattered across the ground, exploded into great balls of flame like the fire invented by Archimedes for the Greeks. So intense was the burning of the charcoal when the air of the strong southerly gale breathed new life into it, that it set even the frozen trees of the forest around it alight. There were scores of charcoal fires ranged at the outskirts of the forest between this and Black Robert's haunted lair. The southerly gale funnelled up the valley and blew the wildfire northwards before it, straight towards Hermitage itself. Thus Tom and his uncle's bold plans at once robbed the Armstrongs of shadow and shelter and Lord Robert of his means to roast his arsenic – as well putting his woods and his stronghold at risk. The attack was unexpected, fearsome

341

and effective beyond measure. In seeming minutes Liddesdale was ablaze, a river of fire running true to its element and surging uphill along the valley where the River Liddle ran ever down.

# Twenty-nine

## The Barguest

Down, indeed, went Tom and his companions, but down and away from Sir Thomas.
Led by Sagres, they ran into an upper cave
mouth leading into the older sections of the
mine. Far to the north of the present work-
ings and the pit of death, they followed the
glimmer of the torch Sagres had brought
from Bewcastle along old, deserted passages
that led across the head of Liddesdale and
through the slopes immediately below Hermitage itself. Tom had known these tunnels
must be here, for had not Janet talked of the
haunted sounds issuing from the fort's foundations and echoing through the hillsides?
Sagres had suspected them and indeed had
explored the castle end of some that led out
of the dungeons. As well as that, he had noted
every tunnel entrance along the valley – those
of the old mines as well as those of the new.
He was a useful guide, therefore, though Tom
was glad he had thought to instruct him to
add torch and tinder box to his weaponry.

The four of them ran out into a dungeon

under Hermitage hardly realizing they had done so. The chamber they so suddenly stood in was little more than a cavern chopped out of the hillside whose ice-bound walls were supplemented with roughly dressed stone sections higher up. There was a mess of boulders and scaffolding on the floor, little better tidied than the foot of the church tower at Blackpool Gate. Rough steps were carved in the far wall, visible only as glitters of icy light in the flicker of Sagres's torch, and they led up to a little open-sided balcony, where a rotting door gaped.

'This explains why Black Robert's so desperate for gold,' said Tom as his long sword hissed out into the steady grip of his good left hand. Then, with Sagres still holding the torch aloft, they were off. The door took them to a higher level of dungeons, slightly better walled but no warmer and in little better repair. They were, blessedly, deserted, for no one secured within them would ever have lasted long. Chains and fetters hung from the walls, rust-red and rotting in the torchlight. Only in the torture chamber was there evidence of anything recently used and new.

Through the silence of the deserted place the little band ran on. Tom was not alone in finding the mouldering, icy silence disturbing, he observed, though he alone had been expecting something of the kind. The other faces in the torchlight wore the same expression of half-fearful bemusement that he knew

344

was expressed on his own as he tested his logic once again. He thought back to the band of guests that Lord Robert had brought to his uncle's hunt. It had been that band that had caused this plan, for they had all been men – hardly a social group, though Lord Robert had meant it to be, as a cover for his darker plans at the very least. Had there been women worthy of note in the place, he would have brought them too. Therefore there were none: servants and captives; otherwise men – a front-line command on a war footing. Like Bewcastle on Christmas night – except that the Douglas was prepared for battle, so he had emptied his rotting shell of a castle of everyone except his warriors and the least number of servants needed to see to them. Most of the servants, indeed, were likely to be Armstrongs and able to double as foot-soldiers too.

Now Liddesdale was under attack – down in the valley, currently, with no obvious danger to Hermitage, as had been planned as well. Therefore it was hardly surprising that the garrison was up and out. So logic dictated that the place would be near-deserted – which was why he had been prepared to come with Sagres alone to find Eve and Janet, but was glad to have Hobbie, if not the sickly Geordie.

Sagres led them up to a closed door and then, at Tom's order, he fell back again lest the light of his torch should show through the grille to which Tom pressed his eager face. He found himself looking across the castle's little courtyard towards the keep. They were in the lower sections of the gatehouse, therefore, and there must be men here if nowhere else. The portcullis was either up or down – whichever one, it would needs be moved when Lord Robert rode back again. 'Silently,' he breathed, and they tiptoed away from the door across the tiny chamber towards a second, narrow, inner portal. Tom put his ear to this and heard beyond it the quiet conversation of two guards tensely on watch. He looked speakingly at Hobbie, the door handle and his swathed right hand. Hobbie nodded stiffly and replaced him with his shoulder to the wood. A beat of time and the reiver kicked the door wide. All four of them boiled into the little guard chamber. The work was swift, silent and bloody.

Their weapons thus supplemented and their expedition still secure, the four returned to the door that looked out into the castle yard. They had to compromise their secrecy now, for they could only go out or back. Out they went, therefore, at Tom's back, across the broad way behind the closed portcullis and into the guardroom at the other side, which doubled as the winch room. The inner door that only opened into the safety of the castle yard was unlocked, of course, and the three guards sitting watching the fast-approaching fires were never prepared for danger so close behind. Two minutes later, Tom came back out, thoughtlessly wiping his blade on his bandage. 'Black Robert may knock until hell freezes over,' he said, 'but he's not coming in here again unless I let him.'

Even as the smoke-tainted wind whipped in through the bars of the portcullis and stole the words from his lips, so a scream came echoing out of the keep. The voice belonged to Janet, and Tom could think of only one thing other than the Barguest that could have wrung such a sound from her. At full tilt he ran towards the keep, only to find his steps faltering. There seemed no way into the place other than across that strange balcony three storeys above their heads, where Eve had stood to promise herself to the man that killed the Barguest; but once again Sagres proved his worth, for he led them across to an apparently unimportant little doorway that seemed to pierce the outer wall. This led to a short passage and a long flight of stairs. Up these they rushed, led by Janet's screams that flowed like Ariadne's thread through the compact labyrinth of the place. The keep was massive in construction but small enough in space. This was a border fort, not a great castle like Carlisle. It was not long before they burst into an upper chamber and found the girl tied tightly to a bed, screaming fouler and fouler invective at the man who had stripped her clothes to near rags and was preparing to ravish her. With his breeches round his ankles and his shirt tail up, there was only one part of the man's rear clearly on view. So when

347

Hobbie croaked, 'I'd know that face any-where,' Fenwick the Factor rounded on him in understandable rage.

When he saw who stood in the doorway, however, his rage was swift to wilt. 'He's yours, Hobbie,' said Tom.

'Up with yer breeks first,' said Hobbie broadly, his broken voice trembling with rage. 'Then oot wi' yer sword. Then on wi' ma revenge!'

Tom brushed past the gobbling man and reached down to restore some dignity to Janet; but as he did so, she tore her right hand free of its binding and snatched one of his new-primed pistols from his belt. In spite of the rough handling, there was still enough powder in the pan for a shot; and, although she was badly positioned and partially unsighted, the shot went true enough.

Tom reeled back, his face full of powder smoke, his eyes dazzled by the muzzle flash and his ears near deafened by the sound. 'Janet,' he cried. 'Ye're mad!'

'She is that,' mourned Hobbie. 'She'll have roused anyone left in the castle with that. And she's robbed me of ma revenge.'

'I had call for some revenges of my own,' snarled Janet.

'True enough, but mine took precedence. He only came close to raping you, but the little bastard did hang me...'

'Well, hang him too,' spat Janet.

'I can't. Ye blew his bloody head off.'

Tom's eyes cleared enough to see the truth

of this, and to see that Sagres had put down his torch to restore some decency to the outraged girl. He had priorities of his own, however. As he untied Janet's left hand, unhandily with his own left hand, he in turn spat, 'Geordie, keep close lookout. Janet, where's Black Robert hidden Eve?'

'He took her with him,' answered Janet, slapping Sagres's hands away.

'What?' demanded Tom, simply stunned by the turn of events.

'The Master of Logic did not foresee this?' asked Geordie dryly, glancing over from his post by the door. Then he glanced back and fired a shot himself. 'Kitchen wenches,' he said tersely over some fading screams.

'No,' said Tom shortly in answer to his question, 'I did not guess Black Robert would take Eve out with him. We must out and after them. Quickly!' And, once again they were off at a run, with Janet half-dressed behind, more worried about getting Fenwick's sword than with restoring her decency.

Sagres led them through the empty castle to the stables where the horses belonging to the dead gatekeepers stood. By good fortune, they also found a couple of spare jacks, a bonnet and a breastplate there. Janet was thus rendered safe and secure – above the waist at least – needfully so, for there was never any doubt that she was going to ride with them. Hobbie and Geordie opened the portcullis just enough for them to lead the horses out. Tom regretted leaving it like that

– he had enjoyed the thought of Black Robert locked out of his own fort – but there was really no alternative, if they were all going to stay together.

Tom led them down the slope towards the valley head. What had begun as a wild charge began to moderate at once, for Tom was suddenly much struck by the way in which the fires in the forest were gathering into an inferno that seemed to be rushing up to meet them. The whole of the southward slope and the horizon behind it seemed to be walled with fire. Clouds of smoke came and went, apparently illumined from within – monstrous cousins to the will-o'-the-wisps on the Waste. Outlined against the fearsome and gathering brightness, small squadrons of riders sped across the slope in the distance, the sound of their battling and passage utterly lost in the stormy rumble of the fire in the forest. The flashes of clear sight of these rushing knots of men would have bewildered all but the coolest mind; but the Master of Logic knew well enough what he would see when he had found his goal: a tall figure on a tall horse leading a slighter one on a hobbie. Other than Black Robert and Sir Thomas, they all rode hobbie horses; those two alone had hunters. Sir Thomas would not be leading anyone, but Black Robert would have Eve in tow. To whom else dare he surrender her? Wherever dare he leave her? As he had brought her, he must hold her. She was all that was left of his hope. She was also likely to prove his doom.

'There!' bellowed Tom as he saw the tell-tale pair. Gesturing towards the sharp black figures with the pale club of his bandaged hand, he was off at the gallop again. The others fell in behind and followed – which was as well: Lord Robert and Eve were by no means riding alone. Amongst the half-dozen figures following behind them, Tom reasoned, Tam Burn and Nicholas de Vaux would be close by their leader, but he knew none of the others until one of them turned in the saddle, raising an arm, and Tom saw that it ended in a stump instead of a hand. 'On!' he shouted, leaning forward and kicking his hobbie horse's sides.

Such were the vagaries of perspective brought about by the flickering light that the chase – like the need for it – came close to surprising Tom. The figures came and went as his little band pursued them, passing through weird clouds of smoke. They were there for instants and then gone, leaving only their ghosts to linger strangely in his eyes. There was no sense of them going or coming – just of them being where he saw them, outlined black against the yellow fire. Had he been granted the liberty of guessing how things were proceeding, he would likely have said Lord Robert was fleeing and he was giving chase; but he would have been wrong.

Lord Robert's men came thundering out of the smoke running flat out for Hermitage and Tom's little command ran straight into them,

351

as Geordie's charge had crashed against the Kerrs on Christmas night. There was no warning at all to either troop and their horses simply smashed into one another, head to head, like two fleets of ships colliding under full sail. Lord Robert jerked his hunter's head aside and Tom's horse crashed straight into its solid shoulder. He was hurled forward and near unseated. He had a glimpse of Lord Robert's face made devilish with surprise and rage, then Eve's horse hit the far side of the hunter and she, her hands tied, was thrown to the ground at once. Tom followed the impetus of the collision and swung himself down even as Lord Robert did the same. The air filled with such crashing and shouting that even the gathering bellow of the fire seemed drowned for an instant. Tom tore out his sword, careless of where the rest of the Hermitage men might be, relying on his Bewcastle command to take care of them and watch his back as he went after Eve.

As it had been with the Queen at the start of this, so was it now at the end. A moment more of reasoning would have warned him to be wary of coming between Eve and Geordie at the last, but he had no moment to spare. If he had an enemy more than he had reckoned behind him, he had a better friend there too. 'Tom!' screamed Janet in a voice even more fearful than that which had greeted Fenwick's rapine. He swung round, daring to take his eyes off Lord Robert because the laird was busy pulling Eve on to her feet. He swung round and leaped back as Geordie came charging wildly past him, claymore swinging wildly not a hair's breadth from his head. Beyond the wild figure he saw de Vaux wrenching his horse's head round, screaming something at the four men riding with him – and Tom was certain the word was not 'Attack!' Hobbie and Sagres were close behind him, both spurring wildly.

Janet's cry also made her father turn and Lord Robert saw both his nemesis and his attacker in an instant. He let go of Eve and turned, his hand striking down to his belt and up again with snake-like speed. Thus Geordie ran full-tilt into the point-blank range of Lord Robert's Dutch dag. The powerful little handgun exploded with all the reliability and accuracy for which the weapons were famed. The claymore hurtled forward, end over end, missing Eve as nearly as it had missed Tom. Geordie flew backwards and crashed on to the ground, as still as death already. Tom wrenched out his rapier and continued the charge that had hardly paused during the despatching of Geordie Burn.

The shoulder of a horse hit him and spun him sideways across the slippery grass. In the confusion of the melee he thought that Janet must have ridden him down. But no: it was Tam Burn, Geordie's twin. He leaped out of the saddle, brandishing a claymore, indistinguishable from the dead man on the ground, save that he was up and screaming. 'My blood,' he screamed, 'my brother and my blood.'

'Ye should have done the work for yourself, then,' yelled back Black Robert, his visage simply satanic with rage. He hurled the empty dag into Tam's screaming face and ripped out his own long rapier, but had no immediate use for it. One-Hand Dand burst out of the smoke at his master's shoulder, the last of the troop to stay faithful and still astride. His claymore was the weight of Tam's and it came down from ten feet high with all the Kerr's fearsome power behind it. The blade took Tam on the top of his bonnet and did not stop falling until it had severed the chin strap far below. Dand wrenched it free at once and immediately turned on Tom. He steered his mount on to its new course with his knees, raising his smoking sword once more. Then he hurtled sideways as Janet calmly shot him through the one part of the jack that had no armour, slamming through his breast from one armpit to the other and killing him so swiftly he never knew who had done the deed.

Black Robert had Eve on her feet again, and was reaching for the reins of his hunter, made unhandy by the sword he still held, when suddenly Tom was there. He ducked under the stallion's rearing chin and rested the point of his rapier on Lord Robert's heart. 'It was you who invented the Barguest, Lord Robert,' he said coolly, in a clear, carrying voice. 'Perhaps the lady will accept your corpse in its place – especially as it was you

354

who killed our John and put his body up in the tree.'

The Laird of Hermitage's eyes flicked around the immediate battlefield, but with the senses of an old soldier Tom knew well enough that there was no help for him there. The Burn twins were dead – and burning indeed, he guessed, or there was no hellfire. De Vaux was gone, with the rest of the four mounted Armstrongs to guard him and Hobbie with Sagres in pursuit. Hobbie, robbed of two revenges, would not be happy to lose a third. Janet was up and Dand was down; and that left just the pair of them to fight it out over Eve.

The rapier, Tom knew too well, was often of limited use on the battlefield, and the rules of defence – let alone its niceties – even more dangerously out of place; but this situation was unique. Narrow-eyed and silent, he fell into his guard, therefore, and mutely invited Lord Robert to answer in the form. Perhaps because of Lord Robert's speed and character, Tom assumed the guard called *serpentio* with his hilt hand – the left – close in and his long blade pointing steadily forward.

Lord Robert still held Eve in his left hand and his reins were wrapped around his own hilt in his right. Ever with an eye to the main chance, he began the fight by jerking the horse's head hard down so that its solid jaw – and the metal buckles and rings of the tack – all slammed into the crown of Tom's own head, setting his bonnet to ringing.

355

Tom lunged in answer, but Lord Robert was spinning away, and knocked Tom's blade aside inelegantly but effectively. Eve fell back, but calculatingly, her eyes flicking like the flames from the forest from Lord Robert to Tom to Janet and back. Both the women were as busy watching each other as the men and the fight; and it was a fight not a duel, as this was a battlefield not a *piste*. Tom assumed the 'serpent' guard again, his eyes flicking from Lord Robert's point to his person and back, readying his defence but planning his attack: to the face beneath the bonnet or the throat above the jack, if he could get past the iron gorget there; to the laces of the jack where the leather was not so well protected by the metal plates, or lower, to the groin or thigh where the great blood vessels lay carrying hot life – and quick death.

Lord Robert struck from the 'falcon', swooping down. The attack was not well conceived, for Tom's bonnet had a peak that protected his face from such assaults. He accepted the blade, however, and at once got the measure of his foe as an unexpected dagger swung in, aimed at the very weakness in his jack where Janet had shot Dand dead; but, as with the sword stroke, he stabbed down from on high, and that gave Tom his strategy – the pattern of moves that his Master Capo Ferro had said would come at moments like these, falling into place like complete sections of a chess match, seemingly governed by their own inevitabilities.

Tom stepped forward with his left foot, driving his sword up along Lord Robert's as he angled his body from his solid, steady right heel, and letting the dagger slam down on to the metal plates on his breast. They were designed to stop such blows. They had stopped an arquebus shot; they would turn a dagger point, he thought. They did.

Only the desperate strength in Lord Robert's own right wrist saved his eye – but at the price of a cheek laid open to the bone. He stepped back, but Tom followed relentlessly, leading still with his left – an ability that seemed to disconcert his foe. This time he assumed the lowest of guards and saw Lord Robert frown for the instant he had available as he realized how open was his body to an attack from down there. His bonnet peak would direct an upthrust into his head. All the iron plates on his jack, hanging down like fish scales, would direct an upthrust under and into his chest. Even the metal gorget that protected his throat would simply guide a blade up through his jowls and into his brain. He mimicked Tom, trying for an even lower guard, crouching with his dagger near his knees, almost attaining the 'iron door'.

Tom stepped forward once again and feinted the fearful upward thrust. Up went Black Robert just that instant too quickly, defending instead of attacking, using both sword and dagger to protect his vulnerable body from his belly upwards. Grunting with the effort of turning the feint back into a real attack, Tom completed his low lunge and sent his point through the inner side of Lord Robert's right knee. He felt the blade slide past Lord Robert's kneecap and into the joint itself. He felt the great tendons that held the joint together behind the leg and he twisted his wrist with all his strength at the very instant his feet slipped and he tumbled forward, overreached.

Lord Robert Douglas screamed. Tom hit the ice-hard ground, and shouted aloud himself. His left wrist twisted until it cracked and popped, brought near to breaking, for the hand remained enmeshed in his rapier's hilt. His right hand slammed down jarringly and felt as though Dand had stepped his horse upon it once again. The sounds made by the two men frightened the high-strung hunter. It was already deeply offended by having its aristocratic chin used, like the ass's jawbone in the Bible, as a weapon. It jerked away from its erstwhile master and galloped up over the hillside above, gone out of the firelight in a twinkling, like a shadow. The hobbie horses followed for a little, then stopped. Only Janet's remained.

Black Robert turned, just maintaining his balance on his left leg as he looked down at the utter ruin of his right. All the tendons across the back of his leg were cut. He was hamstrung – a cripple doomed to halt and limp for the rest of his life. Tom hauled back his left fist with all his might and the blade slid out. The sword was useless, for his hand flopped like dead fish tail, almost as powerless as his right. Lord Robert howled, far beyond reason, quite bedlam-mad with rage and, no doubt, the agony of every muscle from right hip to right knee tearing loose of its moorings and twisting into balls of cramp. Such was the simple horror of the expression on his face that neither Tom nor the women watching could move for an instant; and in that instant Lord Robert pulled out his second dag. He was as far beyond speech as he was beyond sanity, but he continued to snarl and whimper as he took the fearsome little weapon in both his hands and levelled it at Tom. Tom jerked up his right hand, pointing it at his towering enemy as though it would somehow protect him, and the moment seemed to freeze.

And into that frozen moment, out of the billowing hellfire of smoke, galloped the Barguest.

To Tom, who saw it from his prone position, the hound seemed monstrously huge, bigger by far than it had looked to the child in Inglewood – bigger even than it had become in his fevered dream aboard the coach. It stood taller than Janet's startled hobbie horse and was more than two fathoms long before its tail came near to adding a third. Its head was the size of a pony's but broader, squarer – red-eyed and fearsome; and that head reached above Lord Robert's shoulder to look him straight in the face as the great brute bounded towards him.

The hound, like Lord Robert, was screaming – using much the same sort of sounds. Its eyes were blood-red and running with the smoke that belched from its choking mouth and nose. Its jowls dripped red, drooling between its palisade of knife-sharp fangs with fire-sparks reflecting the flames themselves, and its coat was all aglitter with red and yellow sparks, terribly asmoulder, horribly near to catching fire. As it bounded towards them, so it left a ghostly, ghastly trail of smoke behind it. The pain and the terror had clearly sent it mad, so that it attacked the first creature that seemed to stand in the way of its wild and fearful flight.

When the Barguest reared up over Lord Robert, it topped him by almost a yard, it seemed to Tom. So huge was its chest that he seemed to shrink against it as the beast crashed down on him. The Laird of Hermitage flew backwards, like Geordie had done, propelled by the terrible impact. He skidded across the icy moss as the monster slid down on him to savage him. It ripped through the upflung arm, rendering it as useless as his spastically kicking leg, and snapped its gigantic fangs across his throat. Only his metal gorget kept the huge teeth from his flesh for a moment – just long enough for him to fire his trusty dag. But the shot that slammed through the monster's chest and exploded out of its back only seemed to enrage it more. The great jaws closed in a snarling scream of fury. The huge head jerked up and back. Lord Robert seemed to take flight as though his soul was ripped in the moment straight up out of his chest. His iron gorget came crushed and twisted in the dripping fangs. Lord Robert's throat came with it. His soulless frame crashed back on to the frozen ground, and in place of his breath, his life's blood smoked briefly on the air around the monster's head.

Then the Barguest turned, drooling Lord Robert's blood, and leaped at Eve. Tom closed the tortured agony of his right hand into a fist then and the entire end of the bandage blew off in a massive cloud of smoke and flame. The little four-barrelled bastard pistol that Kate had stolen from Ugo Stell a seeming lifetime ago, and that Tom himself had wound in the bandages two hours since, did the work for which it had been designed – by Tom and Kate, if not by its maker. The monstrous Barguest slammed sideways, thrown right over Lord Robert's body by the impact of the four close-clustered shots. It rolled over and let out a great, rumbling sigh. Then it died beside the man who had brought it to a kind of life and whom it had killed in return.

It seemed to Tom that he lay on the freezing grass for a great length of time, with Eve on one hand and Janet on the other; and neither of the hands in question would work. Sir Thomas came and looked down on him. On Lord Robert and the Barguest. 'Well, I'll be damned,' he said.

'As will we all,' said Tom dreamily, 'some sooner than others.'

'Boy's run mad,' said Sir Thomas, but there was an ocean of awed respect and no little affection in the gruff words.

'He'll be fine,' said Eve. 'We must get a litter and bring him back to Bewcastle. I have medicines there.'

'I know,' said Sir Thomas shortly. 'I'll see to it. And I'd best be quick about it. The warm wind has brought the snow at last...'

Some time later, as he was bumping uncomfortably down Liddesdale towards the high, narrow path that led out above the smoking ruins of the Barguest's lair, it seemed to Tom that someone rode beside the wagon he was lying in and spoke to him in Spanish. 'I lost them up on the Waste,' said Sagres. 'The Armstrongs left de Vaux and ran for the Busy Gap. He rode away alone with Hobbie hard on his heels. He'll be fortunate indeed to get through a blizzard such as this alive whether Hobbie catches him or not. How my bones ache for *La Carihuela!*'

After Sagres was gone, Eve returned and Tom felt in his purse, having one last mission to fulfil. He pulled out the heavy, sensuous, golden pebble he had carried in secret since that morning at Blackpool Gate while he wondered what to do with it. He pressed it into Eve's cool fingers now, and felt them seem to take fire from the golden warmth of the thing itself. 'Forget the mines of copper

362

and arsenic,' he whispered. 'Forget what lies buried beneath the Waste. There is gold in the River Lyne...' Then his soul, as light as one of the snowflakes, went drifting silently away.

As Tom drifted off to sleep, the silent snow began to fall in earnest. It softened the bleak, stark lines of the empty, masterless fort of Hermitage, tenanted only by the headless corpse of a factor in a bedchamber and five dead men in the gatehouses. It fell over the twisted corpse of Lord Robert and over the huge hound by his side. It fell, hissing, on to the smouldering ruins of the timeless Forest of Liddesdale, which had been the monster's final home. It fell with gathering force across the empty gapes of the deserted mineshafts along the hillsides by the border where frozen Kerrs stood unremarked in the black pit of death. It fell across the reiving, riding and raiding gaps that led from Scotland to England and back again, closing them tight and safe till the spring, down to the Wall and beyond. It fell across Blackpool Gate, drifting down the open tower of the kirk. It fell over Bewcastle fort. And it fell like silent feather-down across the Waste itself, covering sill, crag, moss and moor, filling up all the deadly bog-holes; and covering, beside the largest and most dangerous of these, the shoulders of Hobbie Noble himself, who lingered, leaning on his great long spear, looking down into the heart of a will-o'-the-wisp at his feet.

After a while, the reiver stirred and shook himself. ' 'Tis time I retired,' said he. 'Perhaps

I should get Sir Thomas to arrange for me to be hanged before all the world at Carlisle castle, much as I was hanged in Liddesdale, able to walk away in secret afterwards.' He lifted his head to look at the patient horse that stood nearby awaiting him – the horse after which he was named. 'What a ballad that would make, eh?' he said. ' "The Ballad of Hobbie Noble". Why, they'll be singing it for years!'

So saying, he turned and whistled for his steed and it trotted down to him from the road. In the moment that he waited, he wiped the thick-crusted mud from the handle of his spear until the wood shone pale and clean; and behind him as he moved, beneath the black swirl of his cloak tail, the will-o'-the-wisp seemed to gutter and die. The mist lifted and the deadly pit of quick mire was, for an instant, revealed beneath – as was, at its heart and just for that moment, the dead hand of Sir Nicholas de Vaux, thumb and four ringed fingers reaching up helplessly, hopelessly; frozen to a claw already, just above the surface of the bottomless mire; an arm's length exactly above where the rest of his body was held, and likely to be held for ever, in the icy, iron grip of Hobbie's final vengeance.

# Author's Note

Yes, Hobbie got his ballads, though neither was the one about the Barguest. In fact, he is the only character in Sir Walter Scott's *Minstrelsy of the Scottish Border* with two ballads to himself.

To be fair, the book did not begin with Hobbie at all. *The Hound of the Borders* began with *The Hound of the Baskervilles*. With my English set 9.3 (thanks, guys) I was researching how Conan Doyle came to write his masterpiece when I discovered that the Hound itself was based on historical legends of several spectral monster dogs told to Doyle by his friend Fletcher Robinson. Amongst the most terrifying of these genuine folk tales was that of the Barguest, said to haunt the Borders, where Tom was born and raised. The coincidence was too good to be ignored; but I wanted to introduce the beast itself and make it real. I turned, therefore, to Brian Vesey-Fitzgerald's *The Domestic Dog*. This recounts Tacitus's report that when Romans first invaded Britain, using large mastiffs as war dogs, they were shocked to discover that the British already had a native breed of gigantic mastiffs that stood nearly four feet to the shoulder. These have since died out, of course, but when did they do so, and where might the last of them have lingered?

The book was actually written on the coast below Exmoor (many thanks to Joanna, Belinda and James for use of the computer and the games room at ridiculous hours, day and night) and more than one early reader has detected more than a whiff of *Lorna Doone*. Its Borders setting was carefully researched, however, as well as being based upon personal memory. Thanks to the librarians at Combe Martin and Barnstaple for all their help with books about the far end of the country, as well as to those in Tunbridge Wells for all the rest. I lived in Carlisle for several years when I was younger, coincidentally in a house in Norfolk Road, reputedly exactly opposite George MacDonald Fraser's, of whom more in a moment. My memories of the town and neighbouring countryside up to the (new) Kielder Forest and Water remain vivid – not least from the hours my father and I spent fishing up there.

For the physical detail I augmented memory with the Ordnance Survey's Landranger series of maps, using most of those numbered between 79 and 89. For everything else I turned to several of my favourite writers. Melvyn Bragg and Arthur Mee gave fascinating details of Lakeland's northern reaches and history – as did the National Trust of their property at Housesteads, which included Hugh Nixon's bastle farmhouse that overlooks the Busy Gap. John Lyly and Daniel Defoe gave much earlier records of

366

their travels there just before and after my period. Sir Walter Scott, reputedly the first man to take a wheeled vehicle through the jaws of Liddesdale some 200 years after the events recounted here, supplied the ballads in his collection as well as unstinting inspiration since I first began to read.

But most of all, George MacDonald Fraser supplied a wealth of inspirational historical detail in his wonderful and definitive book on the border reivers *The Steel Bonnets*. He supplied some of the names – but fewer than it appears. I grew up in Ulster amongst these very people, transplanted from the Borders into Ulster by James I, hoping to solve two problems at once. I grew up, therefore, surrounded by Hursts, Littles, Bells and Johnstons (my mother's family and relatives, whose crest is a winged spur, for they were famous horse thieves and proud of it!), Armstrongs, Kerrs and all the rest. No Grahams, though – the name was proscribed by James, and Ulster is consequently sprinkled with Mahargs instead.

A range of more domestic details was supplied by Alison Sim's *The Tudor Housewife*, Antonia Fraser's *The Weaker Vessel*, Mildred Taylor's *The English Yeoman in the Tudor and Stuart Age* and Ralph Whitelock's *A Calendar of Country Customs*.

The herbal lore was culled from Gerard himself and from Culpeper, both now in print. The facts about arsenic and its potential as a poison (as well as as an ore and

367

an early component of bronze) from *Comprehensive Inorganic Chemistry*, ed. Sneed 38; Brastead (Sisler and Pray), vol. 5. The details of arsenical poisoning came also from the Internet (various locations) and the effects of various inert and poisonous gases associated with mining (including carbon monoxide and arsenic gas) came from a range of histories of mining, the most useful of which was by Time Life books.

The Internet also supplied a disturbing wealth of detail about the post-mortem behaviour of bodies – particularly those suffering from rigor mortis; how this could be affected by cause of death (reactions to various poisons) and temperature (especially freezing). But to those with Internet access I would far rather recommend the fascinating pages on the Borders, the clans and the ballads; and I leave you with just the slightest taste of one of them:

From *'The Ballad of Hobbie Noble'*

Now Hobbie was an English man
And born into Bewcastle dale;
But his misdeeds they were so great
They banished him to Liddesdale...

The rest, as they say, is history – or, rather, *minstrelsy...*

Peter Tonkin
Combe Martin and Tunbridge Wells

# Attila the Hun

*Barbarian Terror
and the Fall of the Roman Empire*

*Ruling the Later Roman Empire*

*The Roman Empire:*
*A Very Short Introduction*

# Attila the Hun

*Barbarian Terror*
*and the Fall of the Roman Empire*

## CHRISTOPHER KELLY

THE BODLEY HEAD
LONDON

Published by The Bodley Head 2008

2 4 6 8 10 9 7 5 3 1

Copyright © Christopher Kelly 2008

Christopher Kelly has asserted his right under the Copyright, Designs
and Patents Act 1988 to be identified as the author of this work

First published in Great Britain in 2008 by
The Bodley Head
Random House, 20 Vauxhall Bridge Road,
London SW1V 2SA

www.rbooks.co.uk

Addresses for companies within The Random House Group Limited can be found at:
www.randomhouse.co.uk/offices.htm

The Random House Group Limited Reg. No. 954009

A CIP catalogue record for this book
is available from the British Library

ISBN 9780224076760

The Random House Group Limited supports The Forest Stewardship
Council (FSC), the leading international forest certification organisation. All our titles that are printed
on Greenpeace approved FSC certified paper carry the FSC logo. Our paper procurement policy can be
found at www.rbooks.co.uk/environment

Typeset by Palimpsest Book Production Ltd,
Grangemouth, Stirlingshire

Printed and bound in Great Britain by
Clays Ltd, St Ives plc

# Contents

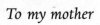
*To my mother*

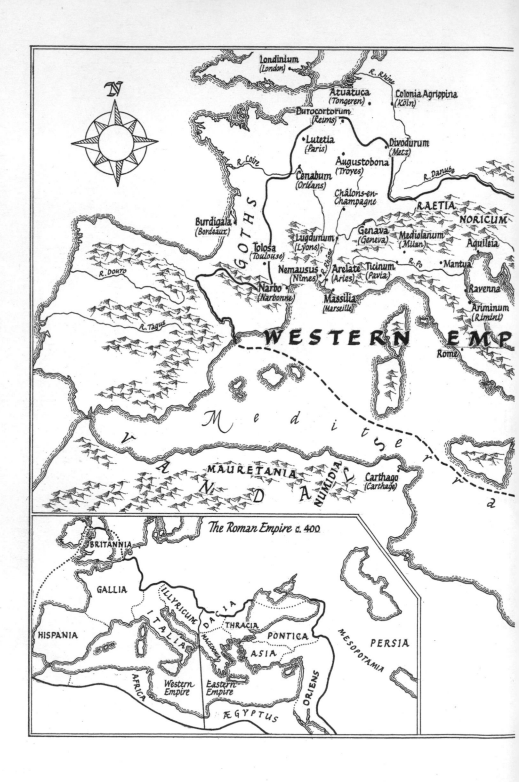

The Roman Empire c. 400

# The Mediterranean World c. 450

—— Extent of the Eastern/Western Roman Empires

PANNONIA

VALERIA

R. Sava

R. Danube

Aquincum
(Budapest)

Singidunum
(Belgrade)

PANNONIA

R. Dniester

Durostorum
(Silistra)

Black Sea

DALMATIA

MOESIA

Margum

Ratiaria

Morva

MOESIA

Tomi
(Constanta)

I RE

Naissus
(Niš)

Serdica
(Sofia)

Philippopolis
(Plovdiv)

Marcianopolis

THRACE

Thessalonica
(Thessaloniki)

Panium

Constantinople
(Istanbul)

Nicaea
(Iznik)

Ancyra
(Ankara)

ARMENIA

ASIA MINOR

CAPPADOCIA

GREECE

Athenae
(Athens)

Ephesus

Antioch
(Antakya)

SYRIA

EASTERN EMPIRE

n

e

a

n

Damascus
(Dimashq)

ARABIA

S

e

a

Alexandria

LIBYA

EGYPT

R. Nile

Red Sea

| 0 | 100 | 200 | 300 miles |
| 0 | 100 | 200 | 300 | 400 | 500 km |

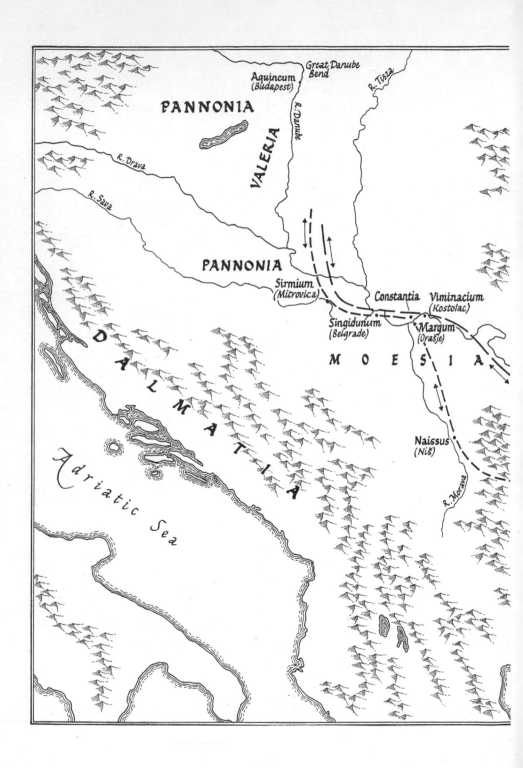

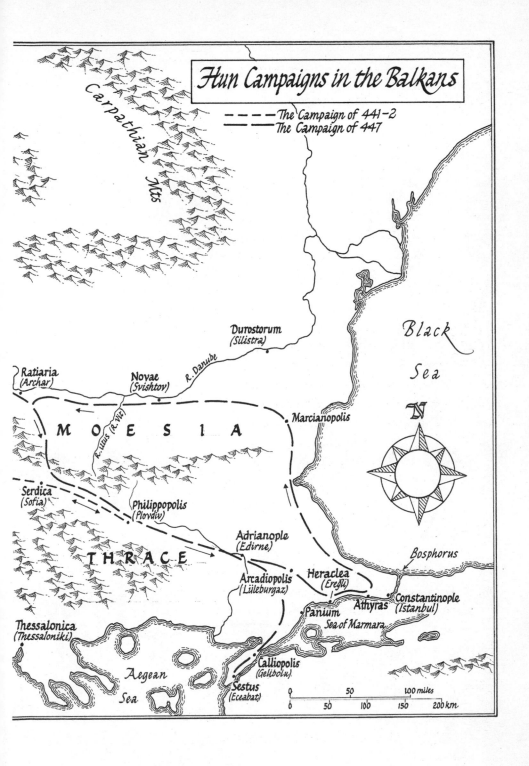

Hun Campaigns in the Balkans

- - - - - The Campaign of 441-2
────── The Campaign of 447

Carpathian Mts

Black Sea

Durostorum
(Silistra)

Ratiaria
(Archar)

Novae
(Svishtov)

R. Danube

Marcianopolis

M O E S I A

R. Utus (R. Vit)

N

Serdica
(Sofia)

Philippopolis
(Plovdiv)

Adrianople
(Edirne)

Bosphorus

T H R A C E

Arcadiopolis
(Lüleburgaz)

Heraclea
(Eregli)

Athyras

Constantinople
(Istanbul)

Panium

Thessalonica
(Thessaloniki)

Sea of Marmara

Aegean
Sea

Calliopolis
(Gelibolu)

Sestus
(Eceabat)

50        100 miles

0    50    100   150   200 km

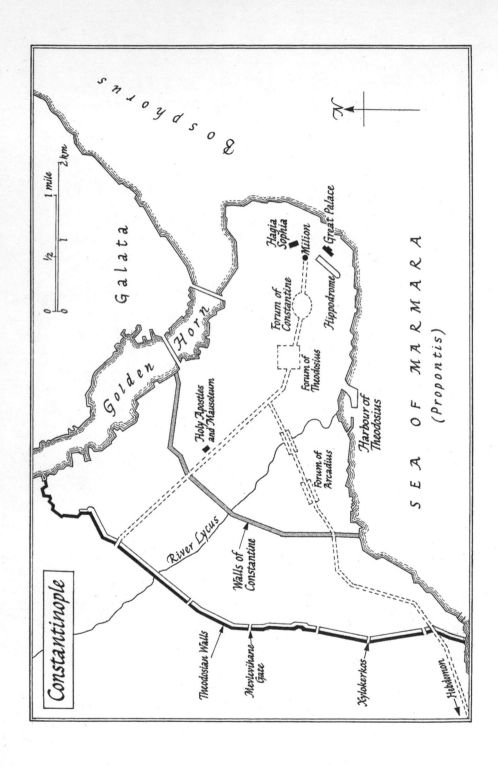

# Acknowledgements

Warm thanks are due to a small – but fiercely loyal – band. For their thoughts, enthusiasm and help I am particularly grateful to Julian Alexander, Richard Flower, Jörg Hensgen, Stuart Hill, Bettany Hughes, Jan and Tony Leaver, Rosamond McKitterick, Lily Richards and Will Sulkin.

Now what's going to happen to us without barbarians?
In truth, those people were a sort of solution.
      Constantine Cavafy, 'Waiting for the Barbarians' (1898)

# The Strava *of* Attila *the* Hun

Carefully concealed in the long grass that covered the plain, the Roman spies watched with growing fear and amazement. In the centre of a cluster of tents pitched between wagons stood a splendid silken pavilion. Its open sides allowed a clear view of the body of Attila the Hun. He was short with a broad chest and a large head. Those who had seen him while alive reported that his eyes were small, his beard sparse and flecked with grey, his nose was flattish and his complexion dark. This was the powerful physique of a man who had died suddenly in his prime, a battle-hardened warrior used to fighting and to travelling for hours on horseback. This was the brilliant commander who had transformed a disorderly band of smash-and-grab nomads into a disciplined force that in the first half of the fifth century AD had marched a thousand miles across Europe from the shores of the Black Sea in Romania to the fertile fields of Champagne in France. Attila the Hun was one of the most frightening enemies ever faced by the Romans. In lightning raids his army destroyed dozens of prosperous and wealthy cities that had remained secure for centuries and even threatened Rome – the Eternal City – itself.

The Huns honoured Attila in death as in life. His body, draped in rare oriental silks, glittered with magnificent jewellery, costly gifts from Roman emperors hoping to buy off an enemy whom they had repeatedly failed to defeat. On his shoulder gleamed a great golden brooch set with a single slice of onyx the size of a man's palm. Like the dark waters of the Danube glinting in the sharp summer sun, the deep-purple stone flashed with the fire of burning brands held high by the horsemen riding wildly round the tent. The faces of these young men were disfigured and smeared with blood. According to the Roman historian Priscus of Panium, they had cut their long hair and slashed their cheeks 'so that the greatest of all warriors should be mourned not with tears or the wailing of women, but with the blood of men'.

Then followed a day of grief, feasting and funeral games: a combination of celebration and lamentation that had a long history in the ancient world. Priscus may have been reminded of the games, movingly described by Homer, that the Greek hero Achilles held for his fallen companion Patroclus before the walls of Troy. Twelve centuries after Homer, the Huns raced horses to salute the achievements of their dead leader. That night, far beyond the frontiers of the Roman empire, Attila was buried. His body was encased in three coffins: the innermost covered in gold, a second in silver and a third in iron. The gold and silver symbolised the plunder that Attila had seized, while the harsh-grey iron recalled his victories in war. The tomb was filled with the weapons of enemies defeated in battle, precious jewels and other treasures. The servants responsible for preparing the burial were killed so that they could not reveal its location. These too were honourable deaths, part of the *strava*, the Hunnic for funeral – and thanks to Priscus' account the only word of Hunnic to have survived.

What most impressed the Romans secretly watching these ceremonies was the dirge solemnly intoned by the horsemen who galloped around Attila's tent. It was a slow, deep, rhythmical chant commemorating a great leader who had established an empire for his own people and hastened the collapse of Roman rule in western Europe. No Roman could hear these words without remembering the terror that Attila had inspired. No Hun could ask for a more fitting epitaph.

> Attila the king,
> Chief of the Huns,
> Born of his father Mundiuch,
> Lord of the bravest tribes.
> He who captured cities,
> He who brought fear to the Romans and their empire.
> Their prayers moved him;
> He accepted payments each year to save the rest from plunder.
> Attila accomplished all this through his great good fortune.
> He fell not by an enemy's blow,

Nor by the treachery of his own followers.
But he died peacefully,
Happy in his joy,
Without pain,
His people safe.
Who can call this death?
When none considers that it demands vengeance?

# PART I

# BEFORE ATTILA

# I

## First Contact

No one in the Roman empire had ever heard of the Huns. It was not until the 370s, a generation before the birth of Attila, that they first fought their way into history. Then reports reached Roman troops guarding the Danube frontier of the sudden appearance of a savage people north of the Black Sea. It was not known how far they had travelled (the possibilities, ranging from Mongolia to Kazakhstan, will be explored in Chapter 3). The newcomers were led by fierce warriors on horseback; their families followed slowly in covered wagons. Moving west across the steppes of Asia, they brought terror and disruption to the edges of Europe.

Around the Black Sea – in modern Ukraine and Romania – the Huns encountered the Goths: first the Greuthungi (the collective label Roman observers applied to those who controlled the territory between the Don and Dniester Rivers) and then the Tervingi (between the Dniester and the Danube). In 375 the Tervingi leader Athanaric marched north to reinforce a group of Greuthungi pushed back by the Huns' advance. The campaign was unsuccessful. Athanaric's camp on the banks of the Dniester was attacked in the night by Huns who had forded the river by moonlight. The Tervingi troops scattered, and the Huns swept onward, in the words of one Roman historian, 'like an avalanche from the mountain tops, carrying away or destroying everything in their path'.

Athanaric's failure to halt the Huns was only to be expected. Six years earlier he had negotiated the end of a war with the Roman emperor Valens. Although they had avoided a major battle, three years of intermittent conflict had wrecked the Tervingi's farms and villages. Their slow recovery weakened Athanaric's authority and a number of high-ranking Tervingi now openly contested his right to rule. Fritigern was the most ambitious; rebuffed in his first challenge in the early 370s, he had taken refuge inside the Roman empire. His second attempt to seize power was financed by Valens. In bankrolling Fritigern the emperor hoped to engineer Athanaric's downfall and his replacement by a more cooperative regime. Roman interference in Tervingi internal affairs could not have come at a worse time. Fritigern's opposition undermined the Goths' attempts to defend their territory. He had no intention of joining Athanaric and continuing the fight, preferring to retreat rather than face the Huns. In spring 376 Fritigern and his ally Alavivus ordered their followers to head straight for the Danube. Pressing hard against the Roman frontier, 80,000 Tervingi insisted that they had nowhere to go but into the empire. In the dramatic vision of one Roman contemporary: 'a great crowd . . . standing on the opposite riverbank stretched out their hands with cries and lamentations, begging to be allowed to cross'.

Valens granted their request. To refuse was too dangerous: the Danube defences were not strong enough to hold back such large numbers, nor could reinforcements be brought up quickly. The bulk of the Roman army was 600 miles away in Syria preparing for an expedition against the Persians further east in Armenia. For the moment, it made no sense to resist the Tervingi and risk the collapse of a key section of the northern frontier. There were advantages too in accepting their offer to settle on land south of the Danube. Here the Tervingi could act as a buffer against any future threats (from the Huns or other Goths) and their young men could be drafted into the Roman army or employed as mercenaries. Fritigern and Alavivus were also aware that Valens was unwilling to offer resettlement to all asylum-seekers. A group of Greuthungi, also fleeing from the chaos caused by the Huns, was denied permission to enter the empire. They were left to fend for themselves as best they could.

For several days and nights the Tervingi were ferried across the Danube at one of its narrowest points, near the garrison town of Durostorum, sixty miles west of the Black Sea. This was a dangerous operation made more difficult by the fast-flowing river, swollen by spring rains. Many Tervingi, frustrated by the slow progress and distrustful of Roman military supervision, ventured across in canoes made from hollowed-out logs; the most desperate decided to swim. Some were drowned when overcrowded rafts capsized. Darkness brought only greater confusion: the shouts of terrified families separated in the crush to board the boats, the wash of dead bodies against the banks and the harsh orders barked by unsympathetic soldiers. The situation was beyond the Roman commander on the frontier. Without warning, Lupicinus was faced with 80,000 refugees crammed together in a makeshift camp. The overflowing latrine trenches threatened an outbreak of disease; the stench drifted into nearby Durostorum. Half-starved Goths crowded round the grain wagons whose infrequent deliveries were made under heavy guard. Some paid huge sums for food on the black market. Others were only able to buy dog meat by selling their children as slaves. The going rate was said to be one child for each dog. Many of those loyal to Fritigern and Alavivus must have wondered whether they should have followed them into the Roman empire; perhaps it would have been better to have stayed behind to support Athanaric and fight the Huns.

In early 377, seven months after the Danube crossing, the internment camp was in danger of slipping out of Roman control. Lupicinus ordered the Tervingi to be moved fifty miles south to Marcianople, a substantial walled town recently strengthened as the base for Valens' three-year campaign against these same Goths. Lupicinus also decided to deal with Fritigern and Alavivus. He invited them to dinner, but permitted only their bodyguard to enter Marcianople. The unrest in the crowd of Tervingi surging angrily against the barred gates of the city was aggravated by hunger and doubts about the safety of their leaders. Their fears were well founded: Fritigern and Alavivus had walked straight into a Roman trap. During dinner Lupicinus had Alavivus and his escort killed, but Fritigern escaped. Lupicinus was later to claim that he had released him once he had promised to calm the Tervingi now rioting outside the walls. That was probably a lie, a calculated attempt by a second-rate officer to justify a botched operation that should have eliminated both its targets.

Letting Fritigern get away was not Lupicinus' only blunder. The large number of Roman soldiers escorting the Tervingi on their forced march to Marcianople had been drawn from garrisons along the Danube. In their absence, a large number of Greuthungi crossed the frontier unopposed. These were the same Goths who earlier had been denied permission to enter the empire. In a serious breach of border security another 80,000 men, women and children made it safely into

Roman territory. The Greuthungi immediately moved south to join the Tervingi outside Marcianople. The combined force wiped out the troops sent by Lupicinus to put down the rebellion that followed Alavivus' murder and Fritigern's escape. With this defeat went any hope that the Goths might be settled peacefully. The Romans were now at war, and with a hostile force that had already entered the empire. Initial attempts to restrict the Goths to territory close to the Danube met with little success. In a bold and imaginative move, Fritigern reinforced his army by inviting a contingent of Huns to join the Goths as mercenaries. There could be no starker indication of the Roman failure to manage the crisis. In the fight for survival, some of the Tervingi's most feared enemies had now become their allies.

In crossing the Danube, the Goths and their Hun reinforcements confronted an empire that had changed significantly in the 400 years since the first Roman emperor Augustus. The consequences of that transformation were most marked at the beginning of the fourth century. Following the conversion of Constantine – the first emperor to embrace Christianity – the Church benefited from state support and lavish funding. Christianity was now an imperial concern. Pious emperors claimed a close and privileged relationship with Christ. In art both were shown dressed in royal purple robes. It is unsurprising that Valens insisted the Tervingi convert to Christianity before they were permitted to enter the empire. This proviso reflected not only the emperor's strong personal convictions, but also a genuine belief that the Goths would be more easily integrated if they followed the new faith of the Romans.

Constantine's religious revolution was matched by a radical political reformation. In the two centuries after Augustus, the security of the empire had been guaranteed by an elaborate network of walls, ditches and forts. Hadrian's Wall in England is only the most westerly fragment of a defensive system that stretched along the Rhine and Danube as far as the Black Sea. This extensive cordon was an effective solution to the problem of policing the frontiers. That said, the concentration of military assets along the edges of the empire depended on the absence of civil war and any major external threat that might require the rapid transfer of troops from one frontier to another. From the middle of the third century such stability could no longer be guaranteed. The causes of the increased pressure along the northern frontier are difficult to trace. It may reflect social changes amongst those peoples living beyond the Rhine-Danube – the direct result of nearly three centuries of contact with the militarised frontier provinces of the empire. Or it may have been simple opportunism as the Roman need to counter an increasingly aggressive Persia drained manpower and resources to the eastern front. In the 270s, a century before the Tervingi fled the Huns, weakened Danube defences allowed Gothic war bands to raid cities in the Balkans. In the same decade the Persians pushed as far west as Antioch in Syria and captured a Roman emperor in battle. Only civil war between rival claimants to the Persian throne prevented the collapse of the eastern frontier.

The Roman empire survived, but at the cost of its unity. The pressing demands of border security exposed the problems of coordinating and deploying military resources across the Mediterranean world. The empire's greatest tyranny was distance. Hadrian's Wall and Antioch were 2,400 miles apart. Against modern expectations, communication times were painfully slow. It could take anywhere between 25 and 135 days after an emperor's death in Italy for officials in Egypt to start dating documents in his successor's name. Seaborne news travelled fastest in the early spring and summer, and slowest in the winter when navigation was often hazardous and sometimes impossible. Given these constraints, an emperor on campaign against Persia was simply too far away – or too dependent on the loyalty of others – to ensure effective control of Spain or Britain. Despite attempts by some emperors to prevent the fracturing of their authority, by the mid-fourth century the empire was split between the East (the Balkans, Turkey, the Middle East and Egypt) and the West (Italy, France, Spain, Britain and North Africa). On some issues the two Roman emperors continued to cooperate. Laws in both halves of the empire were issued jointly in their names. There remained a strong dynastic connection. In the 370s Valens ruled the East, and his nephew Gratian the West. Even so, across the next century the two Roman empires drifted apart, a process of separation forcibly accelerated by the military and economic costs of dealing with the Goths and the Huns.

Strikingly too, in this new Christian world Rome was no longer the capital of the Roman empire, not even of the West. From the

mid-fourth century the western imperial court was resident in Milan
and then Ravenna in north-eastern Italy. Rome was redundant, a crum-
bling museum to the glories of an imperial past. Its public spaces were
crowded with temples, statues and triumphal arches celebrating the
achievements of centuries of generals and emperors who had not
fought under the banner of Christ. The East was ruled from a purpose-
built city on the Bosphorus – now modern Istanbul. This new, model
capital was named after its founder: Constantinople, 'the city of
Constantine'. (Whatever Constantine had learned from his conversion
to Christianity, it certainly wasn't modesty.) On its landward side the
city was protected by a massive wall; at its centre was a large oval
forum surrounded by an imposing colonnade. A broad avenue, flanked
by marble porticoes, connected the forum to the Great Palace, whose
halls, courtyards and gardens were fortified, walled and secluded –
like the Forbidden City or the Kremlin, monuments to the grandeur
of imperial power. Adjacent to the Great Palace, Constantine built a
hippodrome on a scale that stood comparison with the Circus
Maximus, the famous chariot-racing track in Rome. At 1,400 feet long
and 400 wide, it could seat 50,000 spectators. Above all, Constantinople
was designed to impress. For one admiring provincial it was 'the all-
golden city'. The midday sun, catching the walls and terraces of some
of the finest buildings in the empire, flashed like fire from roofs
sheathed in polished bronze. Viewed across the glinting waters of the
Bosphorus, the city – as if heated in a crucible – seemed to rise out
of a sea of liquid metal. The golden dome of the imperial Mausoleum
glowed bright on the summit of its highest hill. Even at night
Constantinople shimmered; it was one of the few cities in the Roman
empire to have street lighting.

The foundation of Constantinople at the beginning of the fourth
century altered the political geography of the Mediterranean world.
Near the Great Palace stood the Milion, a marble pillar marking the
starting point of the major roads that ran out of the capital and
connected it with the provinces beyond. The parallel with Rome was
deliberate. In 20 BC Augustus had placed the so-called Golden Milestone
in the middle of the Roman Forum to symbolise the city's position
at the centre of an imperial world. Then all roads had led to Rome.
By the beginning of the fifth century, Constantinople was the undisputed focus of empire. Straddling seven hills and secure behind its

walls, this dazzling imperial capital more than fulfilled Constantine's proud boast to have established a 'New Rome'. Even Augustus, who once claimed to have transformed (old) Rome from a city of brick into a city of marble, might have been impressed.

The revolt of the Tervingi – now reinforced by Greuthungi and Huns – directly threatened this new imperial world. Constantinople was only 200 miles from the Danube frontier. Valens had no option but to ensure the safety of the city. Forced to cancel his plans for a campaign in Armenia, he agreed a truce with the Persian king. In April 378 he began the 600-mile march from his headquarters at Antioch. Without mechanised transport, large armies with long baggage trains move slowly; on average the Roman army covered fifteen miles a day.

The six-week journey to the imperial capital was marred by a disturbing incident. As the soldiers left Antioch they came across a man lying in the road; from the deep welts covering his body it looked like he had been whipped from head to foot. He was motionless and said nothing, but stared wide-eyed at all who came near. The emperor was informed, but not even Valens could command him to speak. This was troubling; according to the historian Zosimus the man 'could not be considered alive because he did not move, yet he was not completely dead because the eyes seemed bright'. Then the body suddenly disappeared. Those who claimed to understand such portents had only ominous explanations to offer: 'skilled interpreters concluded that this foretold the condition of the state and that the empire would continue to be beaten and whipped like a dying man'.

In Constantinople Valens' mood worsened. Appearing in the imperial box in the hippodrome, he was jeered by a crowd angry at the time it had taken to deploy adequate forces for the empire's defence – it was now well over a year since the Tervingi had crossed the Danube. For an emperor to be insulted in public was a breach of ceremonial decorum; presiding over a morning's chariot racing, Valens expected to be welcomed by loud applause and the carefully rehearsed praises of the spectators. Instead, he was greeted with catcalls: 'Give us the weapons and we'll do the fighting ourselves.' Insulted, the emperor left his capital after only twelve days. Some claimed that he had threatened, after dealing with the Goths, to demolish Constantinople and plough the ruins into the ground.

Valens had good reason to be confident of success. He had received confirmation that his nephew, the western Roman emperor Gratian, was marching to join him. Withdrawing to a country estate not far from the capital, he waited for the reinforcements to arrive. By the end of July he had held his position for three weeks but Gratian's progress was delayed by the need to secure the Rhine frontier. He had no intention of jeopardising the defence of the West by helping his uncle fight a war in the East. At the beginning of August the Goths began to advance and Valens responded by moving his forces one hundred miles north-east to the fortified city of Adrianople. This was an aggressive manoeuvre; Valens was concerned about the vulnerability of the army's supply lines and – despite his ill-tempered threats – the safety of Constantinople. Most of all, he was tired of waiting for Gratian. When military intelligence reported the number of enemy soldiers at around 10,000, the emperor angrily dismissed those who questioned the estimate. On these figures, he could easily defeat the Goths on his own. Why then should he delay and share the glory with his teenage nephew?

Valens' offensive alarmed Fritigern. He may have been concerned about his chances of winning a pitched battle against an imperial army at full strength, or he may have been playing for time, waiting for the Greuthungi cavalry, then operating independently, to return. Envoys sent to Valens offered peace in exchange for permanent settlement within the empire. A confidential letter stressed Fritigern's eagerness to become the emperor's ally, but warned that many Goths would not accept a truce without a show of force. On no account, he insisted, should Roman troops stand down until an agreement had been reached. Valens dismissed the embassy as worthless and Fritigern's offer of friendship as false, but he followed his advice. The following morning, 9 August 378, 30,000 Roman soldiers left Adrianople. Around noon the enemy camp was sighted and the army took up position: infantry units in the centre and cavalry on each wing. Fritigern delayed, still hoping for the arrival of the Greuthungi. Another embassy promising peace was rejected, but later that afternoon Valens finally agreed to talks and the exchange of hostages. The emperor's willingness to negotiate reflected a concern for the deteriorating condition of his men. They were fatigued from standing for several hours in the sun and irritated by the smoke from brush fires deliberately started by the

Goths. By mid-afternoon it must also have been clear that the number of enemy troops was far greater than expected. Roman scouts had only seen part of the army. Once the Gothic war bands had assembled, Valens faced a force roughly the same size as his own. It must now have seemed sensible to have waited for Gratian.

But there was to be no second chance. During the exchange of hostages one of the front-line Roman units broke ranks, probably an accident on the hot, smoke-obscured battlefield. Once the fighting started neither side could be held back. The Roman advance was disrupted by the sudden arrival of the Greuthungi horsemen, who attacked and dispersed the cavalry covering the army's left flank. The unprotected infantry was quickly surrounded. As the Goths pressed forward, the Roman line was compressed. Amidst the heat and dust, many died crushed by their comrades. Hampered by piles of corpses, the exhausted troops were unable to regroup. They were butchered as they slipped on the blood-soaked ground. Only nightfall put a stop to the slaughter.

The Battle of Adrianople was the worst defeat suffered by the Romans for 700 years: out of 30,000 troops, 20,000 were killed. In the chilling phrase of the imperial court orator Themistius, in one summer afternoon 'an entire army vanished like a shadow'. The impact on Roman policymaking cannot be underestimated. Most importantly, the defeat exposed the importance of the Danube frontier to the empire's security. Valens had been critically slow to react to the disruption caused by the emerging menace of the Huns west of the Black Sea. His support of Fritigern hindered Athanaric's attempts to restore order. The crossing of the Tervingi was poorly managed: their internment and policing were left to barely competent officers. It took over a year to shut down the planned campaign against Persia and redeploy the army; in the meantime, the Tervingi had been joined by both Greuthungi and Huns. The decision to fight at Adrianople without waiting for reinforcements from the West was one of the poorest judgements made by any emperor in the history of the Roman empire. The scale of the defeat was a direct result of Valens' petulant rush to seize victory on his own.

During the battle Valens was struck by an arrow. Wounded, he retreated with his bodyguard and sheltered on the upper floor of a nearby farm building. A band of Goths, not knowing that the emperor was inside, set the building on fire. Despite desperate attempts, Valens was unable to escape. He died a chokingly painful death, suffocated in the blaze. It seemed a final humiliation that his charred corpse was never recovered. The splendid tomb that Valens had prepared for himself in the imperial capital remained empty. He would never rest in peace in the Mausoleum that glittered on the highest hill in Constantinople.

# 2

# A Backward Steppe

The Huns did not write a single word of their history. They can only be viewed through the distorting lens of Roman accounts. Writing in the early 390s, fifteen years after Valens' death, the Roman historian Ammianus Marcellinus offered his readers a vivid description of the Huns' customs and society. Twenty years earlier they had emerged from the steppes of central Asia and pushed west of the Black Sea, initiating a complex chain of events that eventually lead to the Roman defeat at Adrianople. Of course no one could blame the Huns directly for this disaster, but Ammianus' contemporaries remained fascinated by a people so barbarous that they had terrorised the Goths and forced the Tervingi to seek asylum in the Roman empire.

The Huns exceed any definition of savagery. They have compact, sturdy limbs and thick necks. They are so hideously ugly and distorted that they could be mistaken for two-legged beasts or for those images crudely hewn from tree stumps that can be seen on the parapets of bridges. Although the Huns have the shape – albeit repellent – of human beings, they are so wild in their way of life that they have no need of fire or pleasant-tasting foods, but eat the roots of uncultivated plants and the half-raw flesh of all sorts of animals. This they place between their thighs and the backs of their horses and so warm it a little.

Huns are never sheltered by buildings, but like their burial places they avoid them as they play no part in the business of everyday life. Not even a hut thatched with reeds can be found among them. Rather the Huns roam freely in the mountains and woods, learning from their earliest childhood to endure freezing cold, hunger and thirst. They wear garments made of linen or stitched together from the pelts of mice found in the wild; they have the same clothes for indoors and out. They cover their heads with round caps and protect their hairy legs with goatskins. Once they have put on a tunic (that is drab coloured), it is not changed or even taken off until it has been reduced to tatters by a long process of decay and falls apart bit by bit.

Huns are not well adapted to battle on foot, but are almost glued to their horses, that are certainly hardy, but also ugly. From their horses by night and day they buy, sell, eat and drink. Slumped over their horses' narrow necks they relax into a deep sleep. No one in their own country ever ploughs. Like refugees – all without permanent settlements, homes, law or a fixed way of life – they are always on the move with their wagons in which they live. In wagons their wives weave for them the horrid clothes that they wear. There too wives sleep with husbands, give birth and look after their children right up until they become adults. No one amongst them, when asked, can tell you where he comes from since he was conceived in one place, born far from there and brought up even further away.

The Huns are not subject to the direction of a king, but are satisfied with the improvised leadership of their chief men, and batter their way through anything in their path. In agreeing truces they are faithless and fickle, swaying from side to side in every breeze as new possibilities present themselves, subordinating everything to their impulsive desires. Like unthinking animals, they are completely ignorant of the difference between right and wrong. They burn with an unquenchable lust for gold, and are so capricious and quick to anger that often without any provocation they quarrel with their allies more than once on the same day, and then just as easily make up without anyone winning them round. Fired with an overwhelming desire for seizing the property of others, these swift-moving and ungovernable people make their destructive way amidst the pillage and slaughter of those who live around them.

Ammianus Marcellinus' description is the only surviving account of the Huns before Attila. It underlies most modern explanations of their customs and society. But there is a problem: despite its apparently compelling detail, this version cannot be taken at face value. In fact, Ammianus is unlikely ever to have seen a Hun. He was not an anthropologist; his information was not based on eyewitness research in the field. Rather, in putting together this picture of the Huns, Ammianus was playing a clever literary game. He intended his readers to recognise a set of ideas and images, some stretching back to the very beginning of classical history-writing.

Many of Ammianus' references were obvious. They reflected a widely held belief in Rome's divinely sanctioned mission to establish order through the imposition of empire. For patriots, it was the obligation to ensure the spread of civilisation that justified bloody wars of conquest. This was Rome's imperial burden.

> Roman, remember through your empire to rule
> Earth's peoples – for your arts are to be these:
> To pacify, to impose the rule of law,
> To spare the vanquished and war down the proud.

These are some of the most quoted lines from the great Roman poet Virgil. They capture an attitude that four centuries later Ammianus' readers would still have applauded. Those who had not been fortunate enough to be subjected to the benefits of Roman rule were, by definition, barbarians. According to this world view, the empire was surrounded by lesser breeds without the law: beyond its frontiers lived ignorant savages lacking morality, good government and self-discipline. Barbarians were recognisable by their ugly faces and outlandish clothes – no civilised person ever wore trousers. These images of inferiority were commonplace. Coins commemorating Roman military success showed barbarians being dragged by their long hair or trampled by a triumphant emperor on horseback. The subjugation of barbarians was always to be celebrated. Scratched across the squares of a gaming board from Trier, not far from the Rhine frontier, is the simple slogan VIRTVS IMPERI, HOSTES VINCTI, LVDANT ROMANI: 'Strength of the empire; enemies bound; let the Romans play!'

The crushing defeat at Adrianople confirmed rather than challenged these prejudices. The Goths had always been thought of as barbarians. In 369, at the end of an inconclusive three-year war, Valens and Athanaric had negotiated a peace settlement formally ratified at a meeting on a boat moored in the middle of the Danube. This carefully worked-out agreement between Romans and Goths was transformed by the orator Themistius into a collision between civilised order and barbarian chaos. He invited his audience to picture both banks of the river: 'one glittering with the ordered ranks of Roman soldiers who looked on calmly and with pride at what was being done, the other crowded with a confused rabble . . . I have not heard the barbarian war cry, but I have heard their laments, their wailing and their entreaties – utterances better suited to prisoners of war than peacemakers.' In an equally uncompromising image Ammianus compared the Tervingi's crossing of the Danube to a volcanic eruption. This was an explosive moment when the barbarian world threatened to flow unchecked across the frontier. Hostile armies covered the land 'like ashes from Mount Etna'. Defeat two years later shook many Romans' confidence in the ability of the empire to defend itself, but not their conviction in the rightness of their cause. Neither their conversion to Christianity nor their victory at Adrianople made the Goths any less barbarous.

For Ammianus, the Huns were also indisputably part of the barbarian opposition to Rome. The stereotype is unmistakable. In appearance, the Huns are half-human ('They are so hideously ugly and distorted that they could be mistaken for two-legged beasts'). Their clothes are filthy, tattered and strange ('They cover their heads with round caps and protect their hairy legs with goatskins'). They are deceitful and dishonest ('Like unthinking animals, they are completely ignorant of the difference between right and wrong'). They have no proper system of government ('The Huns are not subject to the direction of a king'). Incapable of honouring alliances, they are driven only by a lust for wealth and an insatiable appetite for plunder ('Fired with an overwhelming desire for seizing the property of others, these swift-moving and ungovernable people make their destructive way amidst the pillage and slaughter of those who live around them').

On this view, there can be no doubt that the Huns are barbarians, but Ammianus goes much further. Those knowledgeable enough to appreciate references to earlier authors would have noted parallels with the Greek historian Herodotus writing in the fifth century BC, 800 years before Ammianus. Herodotus' *Histories* included detailed accounts of the customs of the Egyptians and the Persians. In his opinion, they could both be thought of as civilised (at least in some respects), although certainly not as civilised as Greeks. The Scythians who lived north of the Black Sea offered a sharper contrast.

In many ways, they were a disquieting inversion of the Greeks: they lived in wagons rather than cities; they herded cattle and sheep rather than cultivating the land; they fought as archers on horseback rather than on foot with sword and shield. There were also unmistakable signs of savagery: head-hunting Scythian warriors made drinking cups out the skulls of their enemies; grief-stricken mourners marked the death of a king by strangling his servants and burying them alongside the royal corpse under a great mound of earth.

For Herodotus, these were some of the characteristic traits of nomads – the modern English word simply takes over the classical Greek term *nomades*. Beyond the Scythians in the featureless expanse of the steppes were men who in their appearance were nearer to beasts and in their habits were scarcely human. Here lived the Androphagi (literally, the 'Man-eaters'), who feast on human flesh. Here might be found the Agathyrsi, who pass their women indiscriminately from man to man, and the Neuri, who turn into werewolves for a few days each year. On the steppes lived another strange race 'who are all said to be bald from birth (both men and women) and snub-nosed and with long beards' and who eat only a kind of fruit cake. Herodotus' views on *nomades* – a mixture of the fanciful, the weird and the imaginary – neatly capture a wider set of attitudes and habits that both Greeks and Romans regularly attributed to peoples living on the edges of the known world. On the steppes civilisation was turned upside down: the further away from the Mediterranean, the stranger the inhabitants, the more inexplicable their customs, the more chaotic their societies and the more unprocessed their food.

Such perceptions of the world beyond civilisation had long been part of classical culture. In the eighth century BC, 300 years before Herodotus, they were important themes in the *Odyssey*, Homer's epic poem that narrated the ten-year-long struggle of Odysseus and his companions to return home after the Trojan War. Blown off course by a storm, their ships finally found harbour in a country far from Greece. But this was no island paradise: Odysseus and some of the crew were captured and imprisoned by the Cyclops Polyphemus. Every morning and evening this one-eyed giant seized two of the men, smashed their heads on the ground and ate them – raw, of course. Escape was only possible after Polyphemus, falling into a drunken sleep, was blinded by Odysseus who drove a sharpened stake into the Cyclops' eye.

Homer's story is not only about the cunning of Odysseus; it is also about a confrontation between civilisation and barbarity. Polyphemus and the Cyclopes are *nomades*. Homer and Herodotus use precisely the same word. The Cyclopes inhabited a land without cities, agriculture or government. They tended their sheep, lived in caves and ate their food uncooked. Odysseus and his comrades could not hope to communicate with their captor; they could neither recount their own unfortunate history nor negotiate their release. Violence was the only language Polyphemus understood. In this biting morality tale of the brutal clash between anarchy and order, the Cyclopes are unsurprisingly one-eyed. Like other nomads inhabiting the edges of the known world, they are blind to the benefits of civilisation.

It is within this rich context, which set the civilised against the nomadic, that Ammianus' account of the Huns must be read. It is not a straightforward description of their habits or society, but one deeply indebted to long-standing classical prejudices and well-worn literary stereotypes. Certainly the educated would have caught the echoes of Homer and Herodotus. They could also be expected to be sensitive to a version of the Huns that went beyond traditional images of the hostile barbarian. What made the Huns so threatening was their utter rejection of the benefits of settled society. For Ammianus, they were a primitive menace to be feared by all those who peaceably ploughed their fields, valued the rule of law, lived permanently in settled communities and cooked their food. Even amongst barbarians, the Huns were the ultimate outsiders.

Ammianus' account of the Huns had its own clear agenda, its own literary spin. That said, it should not immediately be discarded as worthless, especially in the absence of any other contemporary report. Some of the information may have had a reliable foundation, even if distorted to fit conventional ideas of *nomades* or exaggerated in the terrified telling by Goths eager to explain away their failure to withstand this new enemy. It might, for example, be possible to salvage something from Ammianus' description of the Huns as 'so hideously ugly and distorted that they could be mistaken for two-legged beasts or for those images crudely hewn from tree stumps that can be seen on the parapets of bridges'. This disgust may reflect a genuine Roman reaction to the Huns' strange appearance. In common with other steppe peoples, the Huns artificially flattened the front of their skulls. It is not known how widespread the practice of cranial deformation was, but some newborn babies had their heads tightly bound with strips of cloth. These bandages held in place a flat stone or piece of wood that pressed hard against the infant's forehead. The results were striking: the root of the nose was squashed and widened, while the forehead itself was exaggerated and greatly elongated.

Some of Ammianus' bizarre remarks also make better sense in the light of what is known of other steppe nomads. His claim that the Huns do not ever change their clothes 'until they have been reduced to tatters by a long process of decay and fall apart bit by bit' has a parallel in the thirteenth-century injunction (traditionally ascribed to Genghis Khan) requiring Mongols to wear their clothes without washing them until they were worn out. Something too may be made of Ammianus' assertion that the Huns placed half-raw animal flesh 'between their thighs and the backs of their horses and so warm it a little'. Modern scholars have speculated that raw meat may have been used as a poultice to relieve saddle sores on the backs of horses. But Ammianus may be right in insisting that it was for the riders. Hans Schiltberger, a fourteenth-century mercenary and adventurer from Bavaria, claimed to have observed that amongst the Tartars, nomadic neighbours of the Mongols who captured Kiev in 1240, horsemen preparing to travel long distances placed raw meat under their saddles. 'I have also seen that when the Tartars are on a long journey they take a piece of raw meat, cut it into slices, place it under the saddle, ride on it and eat it when they are hungry. They salt it first and claim that it will not spoil because it is dried by the warmth of the horse and becomes tender under the saddle from riding, after the moisture has gone out of it.' Tenderised raw meat seems to have been something of a steppe signature dish. A distant descendant still survives in restaurants (although its preparation requires neither horse nor saddle) as steak tartare.

On other points of detail, Ammianus is certainly wrong. His view of the Huns as living in wagons, where 'wives sleep with husbands, give birth and look after their children right up until they become adults', ignores the everyday use of tents. His claim that the Huns have 'no need of fire or pleasant-tasting foods' passes in silence over their copper cauldrons. One example, found in 1869 at

Törtel-Czakóhalom in western Hungary, stands just under three feet high and weighs ninety pounds (see plates, picture 4). These large vessels are most likely to have been used for cooking. Rock drawings near Minusinsk on the southern edge of Siberia show how one nomadic community in the first century AD set up cauldrons on campfires outside each family's tent (see plates, picture 6). Like the people of Minusinsk, the Huns also preferred their meat stewed.

What is most important in Ammianus' account is his observation that Hun society was fundamentally pastoralist, without agriculture and without permanent settlements. In its essentials, life on the semi-arid steppes that stretch across Asia from Mongolia to the Black Sea has changed little in 1,600 years. It is still a fragile existence, vulnerable to shifts in rainfall, sharp variations in the productivity of the grassland and sudden outbreaks of disease. Prosperity and, in hard times, survival depend on sheep and horses rather than cattle. The Huns were shepherds on horseback, not cowboys. Every year, they drove their flocks across the open plains from winter quarters to summer pasture. For the Huns, in common with other nomadic societies, the ownership of land was of little consequence; what mattered was the right to move across it.

Groups of Huns travelled slowly. Heavy wooden wagons carried their possessions and tents, predictably made of sheepskin or felt from sheep's wool. A monotonous diet of mutton, horse meat, milk and sheep's cheese was supplemented by foraging, hunting and fishing. Successful exploitation of the steppe required collective organisation and the wide dispersal of population to prevent overgrazing. A large area of pasture was needed to support a small number of people. The basic social unit was the extended family. If they could afford it, some Huns took more than one wife and, in turn, up to twenty families may have formed a larger group. Comparisons with modern nomads in central Asia suggest that clans of between 500 and 1,000 members make good economic sense. It would certainly not be right to think of a great mass of Huns moving together across the steppes. In ecological terms that would have been unsustainable.

Above all, nomads rely on horses. To Roman eyes the Huns' horses, like their riders, were squat and ugly. According to Ammianus' fourth-century contemporary, the Roman vet Flavius Vegetius, the Huns' horses had hooked heads, protruding eyes, narrow nostrils, shaggy manes hanging down below the knees, overlarge ribs, wide-spreading hooves, bushy tails and thin angular bodies. These were not stall-fed chargers requiring shelter, special winter feed and warm stabling; rather they were hardy, range-fed animals that could be put out to pasture all year round. Vegetius particularly admired these steppe-bred horses for their patience, perseverance and ability to endure cold and hunger. 'The thinness of these horses is pleasing, and even in their ugliness there is a kind of beauty.' For the Huns, horsemanship was a key survival skill. It allowed them not only to manage their live-stock but also to harass their more settled neighbours. On horseback, a small mobile force could choose the time and place for battle, ambush the enemy and quickly vanish into the steppes. As their attacks on the Goths west of the Black Sea frighteningly demonstrated, the Huns were best at smash-and-grab raids. They appeared as if from nowhere and melted away leaving only destruction behind them. It was impos-sible to establish an effective early-warning system. In modern warfare satellite and aerial reconnaissance have greatly reduced the impact of speed and surprise. In the ancient world only a cloud of dust on the horizon signalled the approach of a raiding party.

The Huns combined rapid mobility with deadly firepower. Hun warriors were able to shoot arrows repeatedly and accurately from horseback. They used a composite short bow about five feet long, its wooden core backed by sinews and bellied with horn; bone strips stiff-ened both the grip and the extremities (the 'ears'). That combination of materials, the back resistant to stretch, the belly to compression, made for a powerful weapon. Modern studies of composite bows from pharaonic Egypt show them to be effective at ranges of up to 200 yards. The same principles of construction, in this case using light-coloured yew sapwood and darker heartwood, were fundamental to the success of the early-fifteenth-century English longbow used to devastating effect against the French army at Agincourt. Hun bows were precious items and it is not surprising that they were considered too valuable to be buried as grave goods. With very few exceptions, only broken bows and discarded bone stiffeners have been found.

The combination of horse and short bow with unexpected raids and equally swift retreat helps to explain why the Huns were so feared. These were not standard Roman or Gothic tactics. Ammianus' descrip-tion of the Huns in battle may draw on reports of those who had

seen them in action against the Goths in the 370s. Above all, the Huns
relied on the disorienting effect of flights of arrows. A destructive
volley was quickly followed by hand-to-hand fighting and the throwing
of 'strips of plaited cloth'. The skilful use of the lasso – a military
novelty Ammianus carefully describes for his readers – was another
example of the Huns' ability to counter heavily armed infantrymen
with a series of rapidly executed and unconventional manoeuvres. 'At
first they fight from a distance with arrows . . . then they advance
rapidly over the intervening ground and engage at close quarters with
swords, regardless of their own lives. While enemy troops are
protecting themselves against injuries from sword thrusts, the Huns
throw strips of plaited cloth over them and ensnare their opponents'
limbs, depriving them of the ability to ride or walk.'

To be successful, these tactics demanded both well-disciplined
warriors and an effective chain of command. While Ammianus is insistent that the Huns were not 'subject to the direction of any king', he
does grudgingly allow 'they were content with the improvised leadership of their chief men'. Ammianus is vague when it comes to who
these 'chief men' were, but it seems he envisaged some kind of council
in time of war, uniting a few clans rather than a whole people. As
always, Ammianus must be read with care. While he offers some credible information on the Huns' organisation in the field, his main point
is to contrast this temporary imposition of control with their normally
anarchic way of life. Again, the comparison is overdrawn. The Huns,
even when not at war, were more orderly in their arrangements than
Ammianus was willing to concede. At its most basic, survival on the
steppes depended on the close control of grazing rights and established
routes to summer pastures. The westward migration towards the Black
Sea must also have been the result of some kind of collective decision.

Most importantly, as Ammianus himself notes, the Huns possessed
bows, wagons and swords. In other words, they had regular access to
the products of settled communities with expertise in carpentry and
metalworking. The skills required for the manufacture of bows are
even more specialised. According to the fourteenth-century Egyptian
expert Taibugha, one of the greatest Islamic authorities on archery:

The manufacture of a bow calls for patience, since it cannot properly
be completed in less than a full year. Autumn must be devoted to the

carving and preparation of the wooden core and to the sawing and fitting of the horn. Winter is the season for binding and reflexing, and in the beginning of the spring the sinew is applied. Next, in summer, the bow, as yet unfinished, is strung and rounded to the curvature required. It is then veneered and painted.

A competent craftsman could make more than one bow a year: as Taibugha's description indicates, the process itself is intensive but not time-consuming. The different conditions in each of the four seasons are used to obtain the optimum conditions for working the various components and for glue-setting. What matters most are the facilities to prepare the raw materials and to store the unfinished bows in the various stages of construction. This combination of highly specialised labour, heavy up-front investment in materials and a long lead-time in manufacture was only practicable in a settled community. The composite short bow cannot easily be made by a steppe nomad on the move.

It is not known for certain how the Huns secured a steady supply of swords, cauldrons, bows and wagons. They may have incorporated smiths, carpenters, wheelwrights and bowyers into their clans. These men might have offered their services willingly or, captured on raids, have been forced to work as skilled slaves. Even so, this would have been only a stopgap, allowing for repairs and emergencies. It is likely that the main source of handicrafts and manufactured goods was trade between the Huns and those living on the more fertile edges of the steppe. For nomads, regular contact with farms and villages is essential. In good years, when there is surplus of livestock to dispose of, it is difficult to sell to other nomads – who have precisely the same surplus at exactly the same time. In poor years, purchasing food stored in granaries can be the only way to avoid starvation. On the steppes, nomads, farmers and craftsmen were bound tightly together in a web of mutual dependence. Only through carefully managed long-term relationships could sheep and horses be converted into grain, wagons, cauldrons and bows. It was never in the Huns' interests to wipe out agricultural communities through repeated raiding.

All things considered, it is difficult to believe that the Huns conformed as closely as Ammianus or his readers might have imagined to the

conventional image of the nomad. They were no bestial horde, ugly
and misshapen, forever shunning shelter, fixed to their horses even
while asleep, a semi-human people without fire, laws or morality. The
Huns were better organised, more economically advanced and less
isolated than Ammianus' selective and overdrawn account suggests. It
is more accurate to think of them as a loose confederation of highly
mobile, well-armed clans without any permanent settlements of their
own, but reliant on regular contact with farmers and expert craftsmen.
Of course, even if more sophisticated than sometimes portrayed, Hun
society still lacked the political and cultural complexities of an urban
civilisation. The Huns were disturbingly different from those living in
the towns that ringed the Mediterranean (in the philosopher Plato's
phrase) 'like frogs around a pond'. On this point, Ammianus was undeniably correct: a vast distance still separated the harsh wilderness of
the steppe from the more comfortable world of the Roman empire.

# 3

# *The Yellow Peril*

On one matter concerning the Huns Ammianus Marcellinus demonstrated admirable restraint: he refused to speculate on their origin. For Ammianus, the Huns belonged somewhere far away from civilisation 'dwelling in the frozen wastes that stretch beyond the Maeotic Sea' (somewhere to the east of the Crimea and the Sea of Azov). Like other nomads the Huns were somewhere 'out there' on the steppes, beyond the limits of the settled world. Modern scholarship has tried to be more precise, but as yet the Huns' homeland cannot conclusively be identified.

One of the difficulties in locating the Huns is the nature of the archaeological evidence. Material remains such as grave goods can only reveal so much about identity, lifestyle and personal habits. And obviously nomads do not leave as many things behind as those living in settled societies. To complicate matters, the very mobility of nomads means that customs, artefacts and decorative styles circulate across huge distances, and many objects that survive are the products of permanent communities acquired through trade. Amongst European cultures, practices such as cranial deformation or items such as bone fittings for composite bows are usually reliable indications of the intrusive presence of outsiders. Not so east of the Black Sea. These seemingly distinctive features are shared by a wide range of peoples from the Crimea to Korea. From an archaeological point of view, one group of steppe nomads looks much like another. There is nothing exclusively 'Hun' about flattened skulls or bone stiffeners.

One theory about the origin of the Huns is certainly open to question: that they are the descendants of the Hsiung-Nu – or in its new-style spelling, the Xiongnu. The Xiongnu were Mongolian nomads who established an extensive empire in the late third century BC. It was to protect China's borders that the emperor Quin

Shi Huang built the first Great Wall, an earth rampart that ran north of the more famous stone wall built nearly 2,000 years later. Tension between the Xiongnu and the Han emperors, who controlled China for four centuries from 206, culminated in a series of conflicts in the first century BC. In AD 48 the Xiongnu empire was split: the southern Xiongnu in Inner Mongolia were incorporated into the Chinese state; the northern Xiongnu in Outer Mongolia were shattered by further Han victories in the 80s and by the Xianbei, a nomadic people pushing down from the north.

At some point, perhaps following the break-up of their empire by the Han or under pressure from the Xianbei, remnants of the Xiongnu were thought to have moved west preserving something of their original identity until – as 'Huns' – they spilled over into Europe. This view was most vigorously advanced in German scholarship before the First World War. Arguments were based on scarce linguistic material and on attempts to make sense out of the frequently contradictory Chinese accounts of the Xiongnu. What was missing from these discussions was any consideration of the archaeological evidence. At the time, neither Hun nor Xiongnu material had been systematically excavated or published. There was also a darker side to the debate. For some writers connecting the Xiongnu and the Huns was part of a wider project of understanding the history of Europe as a fight to preserve civilisation against an ever-present oriental threat. The Huns were a warning from history. With their Chinese credentials established, the disruption caused by their westward migration could be presented as part of an inevitable cycle of conflict between East and West.

Understanding of the Xiongnu changed significantly in the 1930s with the publication of bronze artefacts from the Ordos Desert in Inner Mongolia, west of the Great Wall. These demonstrated striking differences between the art of the Xiongnu and the Huns. Not one object found in eastern Europe dating from the fourth and fifth centuries AD is decorated with the beautiful stylised animals and mythical creatures – horses, goats, fighting tigers, griffins, dragons – that are characteristic of Xiongnu design. At present there is no reason to reject the robust conclusion reached sixty years ago by Otto Maenchen-Helfen, the most authoritative writer of the twentieth century on Hun culture:

The Ordos bronzes were made by or for the Hsiung-nu. We could
check all items in the inventory of the Ordos bronzes, and we would
not be able to point out a single object which could be paralleled by
one found in the territory once occupied by the Huns . . . There are
the well-known motifs of the animal style . . . not a single one from
that rich repertoire of motifs has ever been found on a Hunnish object.

Recently it has been argued that Hun copper cauldrons might be an
important exception. What matters here, as cauldron enthusiasts will
know, are the handles. Twenty cauldrons, nine complete, have been
found between the Danube and the Don. The majority, like the impressive fifth-century example from Törtel-Czakóhalom in Hungary, have
distinctive 'flat-mushroom' handles: that is, square-shaped handles
standing high above the rim and decorated with three or four large
knobs that look like squashed mushrooms (see plates, picture 4). On
the steppes, amidst a wide variety of differently shaped and decorated
handles, two flat-mushroom cauldrons have been found, one at the
southern end of the Urals and a second south of the Aral Sea. One
further example has survived far away in Xiongnu territory near the
city of Ürümqui in north-western China (see plates, picture 5). The
label in the Uighur Museum in Ürümqui, where the cauldron is now
on display, gives a date between the fifth and the third centuries BC,
nearly a thousand years before the Hun flat-mushroom cauldrons found
in Europe and 3,000 miles to the east. Links have also been suggested
between flat-mushroom cauldrons and those illustrated on the first-
century AD rock drawings near Minusinsk in southern Siberia (see
plates, picture 6) and, in turn, with even earlier Xiongnu examples.
    It may be that a convincing set of transformations connect the early
Xiongnu cauldrons, with their circular handles and simple knobs, to the
rounded, mushroom-shaped knobs at Minusinsk and, finally, with
the flat-mushroom handles of the Hun cauldrons in eastern Europe.
The question is whether these changes in style are evidence of migration: that is, that this pattern of development – as some have argued
– can best be explained by the Xiongnu moving west across the steppes.
There is no good reason to think so. The connections between the
various types of increasingly complex handles might be the result of
trade, perhaps involving a number of intermediate stages. It may be
that the innovation of rounded, mushroom-shaped knobs belongs to

an entrepreneurial craftsman at Minusinsk eager to increase his share of the local cauldron market by developing new styles. Or it may be that, amongst the wide variety of cauldrons shown on the rock drawings, those with mushroom-shaped knobs are imports, proudly displayed outside their tents by consumers eager to show that they could afford more than the local product with its dull, out-of-date designs and embarrassingly simple knobs.

Trade too is a better explanation of the presence of the flat-mushroom cauldron at Ürümqui. The early date is questionable: its only authority turns out to be the label in the Uighur Museum. In fact, the cauldron is undated and its find-spot unknown. It was discovered by a local herdsman in 1976, kept in his house and donated to the museum on his death in the late 1980s. Rather than showing the indisputable Xiongnu origins of flat-mushroom handles, the cauldron is most likely an import and might reasonably be associated with the finds of flat-mushroom cauldrons from much further west near the Urals and the Aral Sea. If so, far from being a remarkably early Xiongnu example of the Hun style, the Ürümqui cauldron could have been made much later somewhere on the western steppes and exported back east to China. It would then be evidence not of westward migration, but of eastward trade.

The most recent archaeological evidence from Mongolia further widens the gap between the Huns and the Xiongnu. Russian archaeologists working in the Trans-Baikal region on the Russian–Mongolian border have excavated a number of sites dating from the height of the Xiongnu empire during the second and first centuries BC. At Ivolga, near the modern city of Ulan-Ude, there is clear evidence of the beginnings of an urban civilisation: ramparts enclosed a large, well-planned settlement with dwellings arranged neatly in rows. Its inhabitants were engaged in agriculture, cattle-breeding and metalworking. These prosperous Xiongnu farmers living in their fortified town do not look like Huns. The finds from the burial ground at Ivolga were meticulously published by the Russian Academy of Sciences in St Petersburg in 1996. Although expanding the range and variety of artefacts known to Otto Maenchen-Helfen, they confirm his conclusions: there are still no convincing parallels between Xiongnu decorative styles and any objects in Europe associated with the Huns.

There is, however, one apparently significant parallel between the Huns and the Xiongnu that should give pause for thought. Recent excavations in the Tsaaram Valley (roughly midway between Ulan-Ude and Ulaanbaatar) have explored the imposing burial mounds of the Xiongnu elite. At Tsaaram Complex 7, the largest so far discovered, a raised platform eighty-five feet square, three feet high and covered with clay marked the main grave. The central mound was flanked by 'satellite graves': ten wooden coffins carefully arranged in two rows; all the deceased were males, with the oldest to the north and the youngest (in one row a child of no more than six) to the south. The injuries visible on the skeletons indicate that these ten individuals had all met violent deaths. In the view of the Russian archaeologists, these 'sacrifice burials' were bodyguards or servants killed to honour the Xiongnu noble in the central mound.

At first sight, there are striking parallels between the burial at Tsaaram 7 and the *strava* of Attila the Hun. According to the historian Priscus of Panium, after a day of feasting and horse racing, Attila was buried along with precious objects and the weapons of those he had conquered. Finally, 'so that these great riches would be kept safe from human curiosity', the servants responsible for preparing the grave were killed. 'So sudden death shrouded both the one who was buried and those who buried him.' It is that last detail which seems to hold out the possibility of some link between the funeral rites for Attila and the satellite graves surrounding the tombs of Xiongnu nobles. But matters are not so simple: on the evidence from Priscus and Tsaaram 7, three problems confront any attempt to establish a convincing connection between the Xiongnu and the Huns.

The first difficulty is literary. Priscus' account of the *strava* is not a straightforward report. Like Ammianus, Priscus wished to present himself as a reliable historian as well as parade his extensive knowledge of classical literature. In the description of the ceremonies before the burial, educated readers would have noted the parallels with Homer's *Iliad* and the funeral games for Patroclus. In the same way, the slaughter of the servants to hide the location of the tomb drew on long-standing stereotypes of the cruel tyrant who murders or mutilates his loyal attendants to prevent them disclosing state secrets or the location of hidden treasure. The killing of faithful retainers at the graveside of a powerful leader was also a reminder that the Huns were *nomades*. Those who knew their Herodotus would remember that the semi-civilised Scythians buried their dead kings alongside the bodies of their strangled servants. Of course – and many modern readers may now throw up their hands in despair – Priscus' description could be based on an accurate eyewitness account as well as shaped by his references to classical texts. But especially in matters of detail (funeral games, slaughtered servants, style of burial) it is not always possible to separate hard fact from clever literary fiction.

The second problem with connecting the *strava* of Attila and Tsaaram 7 is archaeological. No Hun burials so far discovered in Europe show evidence of either satellite graves or human sacrifice; nor do any approach the magnificence of the mounds at Tsaaram. There remain some difficulties too with the interpretation of Tsaaram 7. The Russian archaeologists' suggestion that the satellite graves are of servants or bodyguards does not explain the presence of young children. Nor is it clear whether the exclusively male burials are typical of Xiongnu funerary practice. At Derestuy, 150 miles to the west of Ulan-Ude, the same archaeologists found similar burial mounds, but in the satellite graves the skeletons (also showing signs of violent death) were all of women, children and infants. Given this evidence, there remains a suspicion that Tsaaram 7 has been interpreted in the light of Attila's *strava* rather than in its own right.

The final problem is one of logic. Let us imagine that in the future a Hun burial site in Europe is excavated with satellite graves revealing evidence of slaughtered servants, and that by then it is also clear that this is standard Xiongnu practice. Such a discovery would be an important confirmation of Priscus' description of the *strava* of Attila. But it still would not be conclusive proof of a link between the Huns and the Xiongnu. In the end it is a question of the weight of evidence: against an apparent similarity in one aspect of these funeral rites must be set significant differences in art, artefacts and settlement patterns. To establish a convincing link, a Hun burial site would, for example, have to contain items that actually looked like those of the Xiongnu – perhaps some stylised animals, or a pair of fighting tigers, or a beautifully decorated dragon or two. Even then it may be impossible to tell from the archaeological record whether this similarity was the result of migration or the wide dissemination of customs, styles and objects through trade. Some scholars have tried to explain away the differences between the Huns and the Xiongnu by arguing that a great deal was forgotten or lost on the 3,500-mile trek from Mongolia to

Europe. But that is to grasp at straws: on this highly selective basis it should be possible to connect *any* two peoples. It so happens that both the Dutch and the Ming made high-quality blue-and-white porcelain, but that does not prove Chinese migration to the Netherlands.

If, in the end, a connection with Mongolia and the Xiongnu seems highly unlikely, where did the Huns come from? In default of other hard evidence, the best – although still unsatisfactory – solution would be to locate them further west of Mongolia, somewhere between the eastern edge of the Altai Mountains and the Caspian Sea, roughly in modern Kazakhstan. Kazakhstan is a huge country, the ninth largest in the world, at just over a million square miles four times the size of Texas or France. It borders China to the east, Russia to the north and has a western coastline on the Caspian Sea. At its centre is the most extensive dry steppe region on earth, covering 300,000 square miles. The climate is similar to that of the Canadian Prairies, with July temperatures in the seventies and January temperatures no higher than ten and regularly dropping to zero. With its low rainfall the Kazakh steppe is mostly treeless grassland punctuated with large areas of sand. Across this flat expanse, the wind blows strong and cold, sometimes hard enough to knock people over.

Perhaps the homeland of the Huns lies somewhere in this monotonous vastness? For the present, it is regrettably impossible to suggest anything more precise. This may seem a disappointing conclusion, and not much improvement on Ammianus' vague claim that the Huns were originally to be found somewhere 'beyond the Maeotic Sea'. But to relocate the Huns to the Kazakh steppe represents a solid and significant advance on the unconvincing speculation of the last 150 years. It places them firmly within the broad context of pastoral nomadism, while recognising that the lack of any convincing connection with the Xiongnu makes it unlikely that their homeland was ever as far east as Mongolia. Most importantly, moving the Huns away from 'the mysterious Orient' liberates them from a set of modern prejudices. Without a convincing link with China and the Xiongnu, they can no longer be claimed as the first frightening wave of a 'yellow peril' threatening to engulf Western civilisation.

# 4

# Romans and Barbarians

No one knew why the Huns left their homeland on the steppes. Perhaps it was the result of a series of poor summers or severe winters, some natural disaster, diseased flocks, pressure from other nomad competitors or some critical combination of factors. Whatever the causes, the effects (explored in Chapter 1) were clear. After disrupting, in Ammianus' words, 'obscure peoples whose names and customs are unknown', the Huns threatened the Alans, who occupied territory between the Don River and the Caspian Sea. Some Alans joined with the Huns and together they attacked the Goths. In turn, the Gothic resistance led by Athanaric collapsed and a splinter group of Tervingi under Fritigern and Alavivus sought asylum within the Roman empire. The failure of the frontier command to treat these refugees humanely was a key factor in their growing hostility. The conflict that followed also involved a contingent of Huns invited by Fritigern to join his army as mercenaries. In Ammianus' harsh assessment, 'the barbarians like savage beasts that have broken free from their cages' spread 'the foul chaos of robbery and murder, slaughter and fire' as they moved south through the Balkans. This was the bloody prelude to the Roman defeat at Adrianople and the death of an emperor.

No Roman historian mentions the Huns on the battlefield. They may have ridden with the Greuthungi against the Roman cavalry, or hung back until victory and the opportunities for looting were certain. The next day the Goths attacked the city of Adrianople; attempts to scale the walls with ladders were repelled by defenders who dropped lumps of masonry on the enemy below. Joining forces with the Huns, the Goths moved on to Constantinople. Their progress was checked by a unit of Saracens recruited from the Arab tribes that controlled the eastern fringes of the empire from Syria to the Sinai. One of these desert warriors, naked apart from a loincloth, his long hair streaming out behind him, rode into the thick of the advancing troops. With a chilling yell he slit the throat of one of the Goths and, leaning down from his horse, drank the blood that spurted warm from the wound. This sapped the morale of the attackers and, confronted with the strength of Constantinople's walls, they hurriedly withdrew.

The Goths and their Hun allies lacked the skills and resources for siege warfare, yet without capturing cities they could not press home the advantage won at Adrianople or gain access to food stored in granaries. The problems of provisioning the army (and the families that followed behind) could partly be solved by raiding villages and farms, but there is a limit to the number of times the same region can be pillaged. Faced with these shortages, the Greuthungi split off and moved west into Pannonia (modern Slovenia). Given the failure of the Goths to maintain their unity and momentum, some Romans still believed a military solution was possible. That would be the task of Valens' successor as eastern Roman emperor. In January 379 Gratian – who had halted his march east, fearing to engage the Goths after Adrianople – nominated Flavius Theodosius, a general in his early thirties with campaign experience in Africa, Britain and the Balkans. Theodosius' remit was to avenge Valens and crush the Goths and their Hun allies.

In fact, Theodosius managed little more than containment. Despite efforts at conscription and recruitment, the imperial army could not quickly be brought up to strength. Gratian, who defeated the Greuthungi in Pannonia in 380, remained unwilling to commit a large force to a war in the Danube provinces. Both emperors were aware of the risks of being locked into a lengthy conflict. Neither wished to weaken his capacity to respond to any new threat. In dealing with the Goths the options were a continued stalemate across a devastated landscape or a truce. Theodosius chose to negotiate and in October 382 agreed that the Tervingi, Greuthungi and their Hun allies could occupy land immediately south of the Danube. In return they were to contribute troops to the Roman army.

In praising Theodosius' success, the court orator Themistius had to work hard to sidestep the traditional rhetoric of peace through conquest. The agreement with the Goths was still to be seen as a Roman victory: not a victory that had been brought about by sparing he vanquished and warring down the proud, but rather the result of the emperor's overwhelming philanthropy. 'For such are the victories of reason and humanity, not to destroy but rather to improve the lot of those who are responsible for the suffering . . . Was it then better to fill the Danube provinces with the dead or with farmers? To make it full of tombs or of men? To travel through a wilderness or cultivated fields? To count up the number of slain or of those who work the land?'

Themistius' speech was a masterpiece of imperial spin. It was cosy, seductive and knowingly false. The uncomfortable truth could quietly be suppressed: that following the defeat at Adrianople, Valens' death and Theodosius' inability to impose a permanent military solution, the Goths and their Hun allies had finally been allocated land within the empire. To many in the audience – even as they applauded – it must have seemed a biting irony that it was precisely such a settlement that Fritigern had requested six years earlier when the Tervingi had first massed on the banks of the Danube.

Only a small number of Huns entered the empire as Fritigern's allies before the Battle of Adrianople and later accepted Theodosius' offer of land. The majority continued their attacks on Goths north of the Danube. After Fritigern's followers had abandoned the fight, Athanaric withdrew across the Carpathian Mountains into the Banat region (on the Romanian–Serbian border). There he held out for four years before he too fled across the Danube. For the next two decades there is no detailed history of the Huns' advance; Roman writers only recorded its disruptive effects when they threatened the empire's security. In 386 another large group of Greuthungi attempted to break through the northern frontier. Ten years earlier, 80,000 had crossed the Danube and joined the Tervingi outside Marcianople. This time they were deceived by Roman spies. Believing the Romans to be genuine deserters with a grudge against their commander, the Greuthungi leader Odotheus was too trusting in revealing his plans. An advance party set out on a moonless night to cross the Danube and surprise the sleeping Romans – or so they thought. They were met midstream by a well-armed fleet and their crude rafts and dugouts sunk. Those not drowned were quickly killed.

The slaughter of the Greuthungi and the absence of any major incursion in the next decade reflect the steady recovery of the Roman army after Adrianople and its release from six years of grinding warfare with the Goths. The lack of any large-scale raid is also an indication that the Huns were occupied in securing territory north of the Danube rather than attacking the empire. In late 386 the threat of conflict on the eastern frontier was reduced by a power-sharing arrangement that gave the Persians control of part of Armenia. Exploiting peace with Persia and the Goths, Theodosius led the eastern imperial army into Italy to deal with internal revolts: first in 387–8 against Magnus Maximus – who in August 383 had killed Gratian in battle – and then again in 393–4 against Eugenius, defeated at the River Frigidus. The Goths and Huns settled in 382 fought for the emperor in both these campaigns. After his victory over Eugenius, Theodosius never returned to Constantinople. In January 395 he died in the western capital, Milan. The empire was divided between his two sons: the West allotted to the ten-year-old Honorius and the East to the eighteen-year-old Arcadius. Honorius' court was dominated by the general Stilicho, who claimed that on his deathbed Theodosius had named him regent. In the East the ineffectual teenage emperor Arcadius was unable to prevent the rise and fall of a series of power brokers, each claiming to act in his best interests. They were united only in their opposition to Stilicho's ambition to extend his influence from Milan to Constantinople.

Within a few months of Theodosius' death, the Goths rebelled. Their leader Alaric had served as an officer in the Roman army and was aware of resentment amongst his men at their deployment. At the Battle of the River Frigidus the Goths suffered higher casualties than any other units. Many suspected that Theodosius aimed to sap their military strength by using them as front-line troops. Alaric was also able to exploit a growing sense of insecurity. In the harsh winter of 394–5 Hun war bands crossed the frozen Danube and destroyed the villages built by the Goths and their Hun allies. (Clearly there was no bond between these two groups of Huns.) It must have seemed a bitter turn of events that the men who should have been defending their families were 600 miles away in Italy fighting a civil war on behalf of a Roman emperor. Looking at their still-smoking farmsteads, many of the settlers must have wondered whether the imperial government cared about their security. Perhaps it regarded them as no more than a useful buffer: at best, forced to bear the brunt of cross-border incursions; at worst, an expendable group of people who might slow down any full-scale invasion across the Danube.

Fear of further Hun raids pushed the Goths to abandon the land they had occupied since 382. Alaric's forces pillaged the Danube provinces before moving south through mainland Greece to the Peloponnese. Imperial troops under Stilicho failed twice to win a decisive victory, succeeding only in driving the Goths back to the Balkans. The Roman army was unable to operate at maximum effectiveness with legions that only eighteen months earlier had fought each other in the civil war that ended at the River Frigidus. Rivalry between the eastern and western empires was again a crucial factor. In the mid 390s the regime in Constantinople was unwilling to cooperate with Stilicho, fearing that victory against the Goths would make him even more powerful. There were also new threats to the security of Armenia. With increasing pressure on the eastern frontier, Arcadius and his advisers were reluctant to commit to a potentially costly military solution to the problems caused by the Goths. They wished to avoid fighting on two fronts at once.

The challenge in the east came not from the Persians, but from those Huns who had remained north of the Black Sea. In summer 395 raiding parties crossed the Caucasus Mountains, between the Black and Caspian Seas, and moved rapidly through Armenia and into Syria. Further south, in Bethlehem, the Christian monk Jerome wrote as though he too were on the front line. Even in his terror he held fast to his classical education: in the end, the catastrophe of the Hun raids was most powerfully captured in a quotation from Virgil.

> Behold, last year the wolves of the North were let loose upon us from the far-off crags of the Caucasus, and quickly swept through entire provinces. Countless monasteries were captured, innumerable streams that once flowed with water now ran red with human blood . . . Herds of captives were dragged away. Arabia, Lebanon, Palestine and Egypt were seized by fear. 'Not even if I had a hundred tongues and a hundred mouths and a voice of iron could I recite the names of all these disasters.'

Memory of the Huns' attacks was long-lasting. Two centuries later a Christian visionary in Syria warned that the Apocalypse would be heralded by Huns invading from the distant north. Their weapons would be dipped in a magic potion made from foetuses cut from pregnant women roasted alive. They would drink human blood and eat babies. 'They will move faster than the winds, more rapidly than storm clouds and their war cries will be like the roaring of a lion. Terror at their coming will cover the whole earth like the floodwaters in the days of Noah.'

The aim of these Hun raids was plunder, not conquest. As long as the bulk of Roman forces was no further east than the Balkans these attacks could be carried out with impunity. Combined with the failure of Stilicho to defeat the Goths in Greece, the continuing Hun offensive forced the Romans to make peace with Alaric. The agreement brokered by Eutropius, Arcadius' closest adviser, recognised that the Goths had not set out to destroy the empire, but to find a more secure place within it. In 397 Alaric received the rank of general in the Roman army and his followers gold and grain. Negotiations were opened for a more permanent solution, perhaps a new homeland much further away from the frontier than their original settlement under Theodosius. In Milan Stilicho's supporters were outraged. The poet Claudian, his chief propagandist, imagined the return of Alaric as a Roman general administering justice in cities he had only recently besieged as a Gothic rebel: 'this time he comes as a friend . . . and hands down decisions in cases brought by those whose wives he has raped and children murdered'.

Eutropius' agreement allowed Roman troops – now reinforced by Goths – to move east and eject the Huns from Armenia. Victory over 'the wolves of the North' was celebrated in 399 with a parade through Constantinople. An enthusiastic crowd lined the streets to cheer Eutropius as he passed by in triumphal splendour. But success was fleeting. Within a year Arcadius had reversed Eutropius' policies and sent him into exile. After all, as his rivals were quick to point out, once the threat to the eastern frontier had been removed, there was no longer any need to appease Alaric. The shift in attitude was signalled by the termination of the Goths' subsidies and supplies. In early 401 Arcadius also strengthened his diplomatic ties with Uldin, the first Hun leader in Europe to be named by Roman historians. Uldin controlled territory close to the Danube and is unlikely to have had close links with those Huns north of the Black Sea who had attacked Syria and

Armenia. There may have been plans for an alliance, perhaps with the aim of using Uldin's Huns against Alaric's Goths. Certainly it was clear that Arcadius and his advisers were no longer prepared to negotiate. The eastern frontier was quiet and the arrangement with Uldin had secured the Danube. If necessary, the imperial army – now reinforced by Huns – could concentrate on the Goths. These tough tactics worked: by the end of the year Alaric had left the eastern empire and moved west.

The Goths' attempt to enter northern Italy was blocked by Stilicho, and after two hard-fought battles Alaric withdrew to Dalmatia and Pannonia (modern Croatia and Slovenia). Given the apparent impossibility of a conclusive military solution, Stilicho faced a similar problem to Theodosius after Adrianople. The Goths were too strong to be subdued by force and too dangerous to be left unchecked. It was an indication of the seriousness of the threat that the western imperial court abandoned Milan and moved to Ravenna on the Adriatic coast. The new capital was well defended and could only be approached by a narrow causeway across treacherous and stinking salt marshes. (In more peaceful times, the waterlogged ground had made Ravenna famous for its asparagus.)

Like Theodosius and Eutropius before him, Stilicho aimed to neutralise the Goths through negotiation. On offer in 405 was a generalship for Alaric and payments for his followers. Alaric's acceptance allowed Stilicho to concentrate on countering an invasion of northern Italy by another substantial body of Goths. These Goths were not connected to those led by Alaric but had remained north of the Rhine-Danube frontier since the Hun invasions in the 370s. They now sought safety from the disruption caused by the Huns' intrusive presence west of the Black Sea by moving deep into the empire. It must then have seemed to their leader Radagaisus a vicious twist of fate that in seeking to avoid one group of Huns, he should have to face another. The Roman army was strengthened by Hun mercenaries commanded by Uldin who, after Alaric's Goths moved west, had offered his services to Stilicho. In late 406 Radagaisus' army was wiped out. So many of his followers were taken prisoner that the Italian slave market was flooded and the price dropped steeply. Nevertheless, the revenue raised helped pay for the Huns. If well rewarded, they would fight for the empire. Certainly Stilicho felt safest when surrounded by his Hun bodyguard. In the deadly game of court politics he preferred to rely on those whose loyalty he had purchased in advance.

But Stilicho's military success was short-lived: he failed to prevent a much larger movement of people across the Rhine in December 406, the likely result of the continued disruption caused by the Huns' westward advance, which displaced not only Goths but also others including large numbers of Vandals and Alans. (Nothing is known of this group of Alans, nor their reasons for breaking their long-standing alliance with the Huns.) The Rhine crossing was a serious incursion that, according to one fifth-century account, 'ripped France to pieces'. The following year, France and Britain broke away from the empire and proclaimed a new emperor, Constantine III. The official regime in Ravenna was unable to halt the usurper's advance and by the end of 407 Constantine had strengthened the Rhine defences, garrisoned the Alpine passes into Italy and established his own court at Arles. There was little Stilicho could do to restore Honorius' authority. Even with Uldin's Huns, he had insufficient forces either to re-establish imperial rule or to secure the frontier. He was also well aware that his continued willingness to discuss terms with the Goths aroused suspicion. Yet (as Stilicho might have argued) compromise was the only realistic option. His detractors disagreed: Stilicho's lack of success was not to be explained by Roman weakness but by a covert alliance with the ultimate aim of using Alaric's Goths to further his own ambitions. These were wild and unsubstantiated accusations: there is no good evidence that Stilicho had ever concluded a secret pact with Alaric. Rather than accuse him of double-dealing, it is easier to believe that he was no more able to defeat the Goths than Theodosius, and in the end – like Theodosius – he had no choice but to negotiate.

Honorius chose to back Stilicho's critics. The western emperor had always been suspicious of the general, who had once sought to force his regency on the whole empire. Those around Stilicho made their own choices: in August 408 his Hun bodyguards were secretly killed, and a few days later he was arrested and executed. Prudently it was thought worthwhile to maintain cordial relations with at least some Huns. In 409 negotiators agreed on the emperor's behalf that the sons of prominent families at court in Ravenna should be sent beyond the Danube as hostages; in return, later that same year, Honorius called up 10,000 Hun mercenaries. It is not clear whether these troops ever arrived in northern Italy; in the end it is likely that the emperor was unable to pay or supply them properly.

After the death of Stilicho, Alaric again invaded northern Italy and this time marched on Rome. Again he was not bent on destruction, but aimed, in the face of an intransigent imperial government, to compel negotiation. For eighteen months the Goths blockaded the Eternal City and for eighteen months Honorius refused to make any major concessions. Finally, on 24 August 410, frustrated by the military and political deadlock, Alaric's Goths sacked Rome. For three days they looted the city's mansions and seized priceless treasures from its sacred sanctuaries. St Peter's on the Vatican Hill was crammed with terrified citizens seeking refuge. In all the destructive chaos the cathedral was left untouched, yet for many, set against shock at the fall of the city, such public gestures of compassion by a barbarian leader – even if now a Christian – were to be dismissed. 'When the brightest light on the whole earth was snuffed out,' lamented an overwrought Jerome, 'when the Roman empire was decapitated, when – to speak more accurately – the whole world perished in one city, then I was dumb with silence and my sorrow was stirred.'

The sack of Rome was a disaster that could and should have been avoided. It was not the consequence of a surprise attack, nor was it the result of a bloodthirsty horde streaming down the Italian peninsula intent on grabbing gold and violating virgins. Rather, it represented a double failure: the failure of Alaric to force a viable agreement for the permanent settlement of the Goths, and the failure of the Roman government to deal reasonably with a people who had, after all, been permitted to enter the empire. Safe in Ravenna, Honorius sacrificed Rome to preserve his own authority. Safe in Constantinople, Arcadius no doubt congratulated himself on pushing the problem onto his imperial brother. The Goths were not permanently settled for another eight years, and the stalemate that had led to their attack on Rome continued as they moved slowly north into France. There negotiations were opened with Stilicho's successor, the general Flavius Constantius, who finally settled them on land in the Garonne Valley between Toulouse and Bordeaux, forty years and 1,200 miles away from their crossing of the Danube.

The lack of cooperation between the East and the West hampered any earlier solution to the disruption caused by the Goths, as did the shortage of military manpower that after Adrianople arguably made their settlement within the empire a necessary risk. The inability of either imperial government to impose a resolution between Alaric's revolt in 395 and the Goths' settlement in south-western France in 418 starkly exposed the difficulty of attempting to suppress an internal revolt while defending the empire from external enemies. The need to secure the northern and eastern frontiers was a continual drain on resources. It forced the Roman army in both the East and the West to employ mercenaries and placed a critical limit on the number of troops that could prudently be deployed on any one front or against any one threat. Only Theodosius managed to strike a workable balance, and he had negotiated peace with both the Persians and the Goths.

The continued instability along the Rhine-Danube frontier was a direct result of the westward push of the Huns. This was a gradual process. There is no evidence of a solid block of Huns marching west from the Black Sea and systematically propelling the Goths and other peoples into the Roman empire. There is nothing to support what some German scholars, rather splendidly, have called the *Hunnensturm*. The Huns moved into Europe in stages, consolidating their hold on territory disrupted through raiding and the displacement of some of its inhabitants. Their piecemeal progress can be traced by the pressure on the Roman empire's northern frontier: in the 370s and '80s groups of Goths were pushed towards the Danube; in 395 there were Hun raids across the Danube and in Armenia (a sure indication that at least some Huns were still north of the Black Sea); in 401 Uldin controlled territory close to the frontier and was also able to move his men west to fight for Stilicho. The presence of Huns on the middle Danube is also indicated by Honorius' levy of mercenaries in 409. The overall pattern is clear: across forty years from 370 to 410 the focus of Hun activity slowly moved 700 miles, from the Don to the Dniester to the middle Danube; or in modern terms from the Ukraine to Romania and finally west to Hungary.

# 5

## How the West Was Won

By the beginning of the fifth century, the Huns were firmly established on the Great Hungarian Plain in the heart of Europe. The Hungarian Alföld or *puszta* is the most westerly extension of the Central Asian Steppe, separated from it by the Carpathian Mountains. These fertile lands stretch in an arc from eastern Slovakia, through Hungary, northern Serbia and into western Romania. The Great Hungarian Plain is a fragment of steppe marooned in central Europe. It is a landscape of wide horizons shimmering in the summer heat and of endless flat fields; a treeless, grassy expanse broken only by swamps and bright-green algae-rimmed lakes (see plates, picture 3). The open plain offers a stark contrast to the terrain south of the Danube with its narrow valleys and heavily forested mountain slopes. As a home for the Huns the Great Hungarian Plain was self-selecting. West of the Black Sea it is the only area of grassland large enough to support horses on any scale. Located in the middle of Europe it is an ideal base to launch attacks both north and south of the Danube. Yet compared to the vast wildernesses of central Asia, the Hungarian Plain hardly merits the description 'great': it covers an area of about 40,000 square miles, as opposed to the 300,000 of the Kazakh Steppe. These physical limitations are important. Survival in this more constrained European environment forced a social and political revolution amongst the Huns. Failure to adapt would mean defeat or compel a slow and dangerous retreat back to the steppes.

In their initial westward push, the Huns relied on their superior fighting skills and rapid mobility to raid small communities; the unfortified Gothic villages were sitting targets. Yet while the Great Hungarian Plain offered grazing for the Huns' horses, it was simply not extensive enough to sustain the nomadic life they had followed on the steppes. In their new European homeland the Huns could no longer operate, year in year out, as pastoral nomads driving their flocks from winter to summer pasture and supplementing their income by a mixture of trading and opportunistic attacks. Rather, the Great Hungarian Plain offered the Huns a different set of possibilities. In this richer, more densely populated and more productive land they were able to use their military advantage over the local population to establish themselves as an effective and permanent occupying force.

The crucial change in Hun tactics came at the beginning of the fifth century. Instead of leaving shattered villages, slaughtered farmers and burnt-out buildings behind them, it was more profitable to demand regular tribute from prosperous agricultural communities against the threat of reprisals. The Hun empire as it expanded across Europe was successful in systematising the extraction of wealth and manpower. Its main concern was to ensure the maintenance of an army. Provided that recruits and supplies were delivered in full and on time, and suitable land was made available for grazing and breeding horses, the empire's interference in the economic and social arrangements of those it conquered was minimal. It was to the Huns' advantage to exploit rather than wreck Gothic society. The Hun empire in Europe was not an interventionist Roman-style empire relying on the close administrative control of subjugated provinces and peoples. Rather, it was a protection racket on a grand scale.

It is this sense of transformation that is entirely absent from Ammianus Marcellinus' account of the Huns, with its emphasis on many of those elements of their traditional nomadic lifestyle that did not long survive their migration into Europe. Ammianus missed – or at least chose to ignore – the potential of the Huns to establish an empire. He persisted in forcing his description of their customs to conform to conventional literary stereotypes of barbarian outsiders. No contemporary Roman writer was interested in tracing the rise of the Huns beyond the empire's northern frontier or in offering any account of how their society was changed by contact with the Goths. Aside from a few chance remarks, this process of steady consolidation must be reconstructed from archaeological evidence and from consideration of the constraints imposed on the newcomers by the resources available on the Great Hungarian Plain.

★

According to Priscus of Panium, the Hun empire at its height stretched as far as 'the islands in the Ocean', that is as far as the Baltic Sea. This may be correct, although it is impossible to tell whether the scatter of objects from northern Europe associated with the Huns and other steppe peoples is the result of conquest, alliance or trade. The bulk of the archaeological material comes from north of the Black Sea (southern Ukraine and the Crimea) and from the heartland of the Hun empire stretching from western Romania across Hungary and Slovakia to eastern Austria. Finds of flat-mushroom cauldrons are concentrated in this middle Danube region. Here too there are small numbers of burials, datable to the fifth century, of men and women whose skulls show clear signs of artificial flattening. Characteristic items (not all found in graves with individuals displaying cranial deformation) include bone stiffeners for reflex bows, gold diadems and decorative horse trappings.

The diadems are magnificent. The most beautiful was found in the late 1880s in an unrecorded burial site somewhere near the town of Csorna seventy miles east of Budapest. When the grave was opened the diadem was still in place, proudly encircling the skull of its owner. The Csorna diadem consists of a single sheet of gold twelve inches long and two wide, folded around a strip of bronze. Traces of copper oxide on the skull indicate that it was worn without any padding or leather lining. At the centre of the gold band are two smoky-purple carnelians flanked by a row of blood-red garnets and three of similarly shaped red glass (see plates, picture 7). Equally impressive are the splendid decorations for a horse's reins found twenty miles away in 1979 in the sandy soil of the vineyards around the tenth-century Benedictine monastery at Pannonhalma. Twelve strips of gold foil two inches long and three in the shape of a four-leaf clover were found intact. They were attached to leather trappings with small bronze tacks (see plates, picture 8). Certainly no one could doubt the wealth or status of the rider whose shining golden reins glittered so brightly in the sunlight, flashing with every movement of his horse.

Such objects are eye-catching evidence of an intrusive foreign presence in the middle Danube, yet it is important to emphasise that finds of Hun (or perhaps better 'steppe') material are rare. What is most remarkable about the presence of Huns in Europe is the striking lack of archaeological evidence. Only some seventy burials have been identified that, on the basis of their characteristic features, might be thought to belong to Huns. This small number could simply be a reflection of their relatively brief domination of the middle Danube – roughly from 410 to 465, ten years after the death of Attila. Chances of survival play a part too: leading Huns, as Priscus' description of Attila's funeral confirms, were interred beneath great earthen mounds that – despite the brutal precautions taken at the time of burial – acted as prominent markers for tomb robbers.

Of course, the apparent absence of steppe finds in Europe is only puzzling – or only demands an explanation – if Hun burial practices and objects are expected to be different from the settled communities they conquered. Clearly some Huns retained a strong sense of the importance of their traditional customs and habits, taking particular care in the selection of grave goods. But such practices need not have been universal; indeed, they may represent only a minority, who were perhaps regarded as stuffy and old-fashioned by their peers. In other words, the history of the Huns in Europe may reflect a situation common to many migrant communities. Some no doubt insisted on the importance of preserving their distinctive heritage. They clung tenaciously to old ways: they persisted in binding the foreheads of their babies, in stewing their meat in flat-mushroom cauldrons and in wearing gold diadems as a mark of their superior status in this world and the next. Other Huns openly embraced Gothic culture and customs and may not have been buried with any characteristically Hun objects. In death these Huns would be indistinguishable from Goths, a sharp reminder that in dealing with archaeological evidence the absence of artefacts can sometimes be as significant as their presence.

The suggestion that from the early fifth century many Huns began to resemble Goths (at least in their burial practices) is also attractively consistent with the apparent lack of any major disruption to Gothic culture in the same period. Goths still lived in unfortified villages situated along fertile river valleys; they continued to cultivate millet, rye and barley, and raise livestock; they used much the same sorts of glassware and dull, wheel-made grey pottery. There were some changes in the appearance of the wealthiest, most fashion-conscious Goths, who began to wear large semicircular brooches, gold necklaces and belts with big flat buckles. These developments have no certain origin on the steppes. They are more likely to be the result of the intermixing of ideas and styles that followed the displacement and resettlement of peoples within Europe. In other words, changes in Gothic culture may reflect some of the consequences of the disruption caused by the migration of the Huns, but these changes do not draw directly on the heritage of the steppe itself.

The continued vitality of Gothic culture under Hun domination contrasts with conventional modern expectations of empire: that conquerors will impose their culture on the conquered. This is often a painful process, well known – as the imperial adjectives themselves attest – from the histories of Roman Britain, Spanish America or British India. The imposition of Roman, Spanish and British rule shattered local customs and beliefs. Defeated elites were amongst the first to reject traditional ways of life, advertising their willingness to collude with their conquerors by openly embracing their language, culture and habits. This adoption of new ways was actively encouraged by imperial powers keen to maintain and support a local ruling class. In Roman Britain country villas, with their mosaics, wall paintings and central heating, did not house Italians sent out to govern a recently subdued province; rather these new and ostentatiously Roman-looking buildings were the grand residences of a cooperative British-born elite.

Europe under Hun rule was strikingly different. Gothic culture remained largely unchanged, nor is there any clear indication that leading Goths adopted Hun customs. This lack of interaction might be explained by thinking of the Huns and Goths as isolated groups, but this is unsatisfactory. It is difficult to see how the Huns could effectively manage their empire or ensure a regular flow of tribute without establishing a close relationship with the local elite, many of whom, in turn, benefited from association with their new Hun overlords. In this case it is better to assume that the culture of the rulers had no significant impact on the culture of the ruled. In other words, Gothic culture continued largely uninterrupted precisely because it was adopted by many Huns.

The Hun empire is then a significant exception to the usual pattern of imperial domination. Again that reflects the very different circumstances surrounding the conquest of settled communities by nomads. The successful establishment of an empire was in great part due to the Huns' abandonment of many of the customs and practices that had served them well on the steppes but were either redundant or unsustainable in their new homeland. Once in permanent occupation of the Great Hungarian Plain, the Huns transformed themselves into an imperial power whose success relied on the systematic exploitation of existing Gothic society. The Hun empire was, above all, a parasitic state; its success lay in its ability to mimic the culture of those it ruled, to cream off their wealth and to consume the food they produced. A minority of Huns, with their distinctive and recognisable grave goods, persisted in their adherence to the old ways; the majority became more like the settled Goths they had conquered. That shift made the conquerors archaeologically invisible. As Yeh-lü Ch'u-ts'ai, administrative reformer and adviser to Genghis Khan, would shrewdly observe seven centuries later, 'a country can be conquered but not governed from the saddle'. By building an empire, the Huns ceased to be nomads.

Back on the steppes, at least according to Ammianus Marcellinus, the Huns were not 'subject to the direction of a king'; clans of perhaps 500 to 1,000 might group together in time of war under 'the improvised leadership of their chief men'. But as pointed out in Chapter 2, even in peacetime Hun society was much better organised than Ammianus was prepared to allow. However, aside from his sketchy and sometimes misleading remarks, there is little information on the Huns' political organisation. Parallels with other nomads are again worth considering. If the Huns were organised similarly to the Mongols before Genghis Khan, then it is unlikely that all clans had equal influence: some were more powerful, others subordinate, perhaps as a result of military defeat, lack of resources or the need for protection. Collective decisions were probably driven by a few dominant clans, but within that broad framework the decision-making process and its enforcement were loose enough to allow particular clans or clan groups to pursue their own policies. This is consistent with what is known of the westward movement of the Huns into Europe: a general migration, not the tightly regimented advance of a whole people.

It is possible too that clan membership was not fixed. Amongst the Mongols clans most commonly consisted of a number of closely related families, but kinship was not the only way in which a clan might be defined. Mongol custom also recognised the possibility of *anda*, or sworn brotherhood, which allowed clan members to move by being accepted as the equivalent of a blood relative. Key to the establishment of Genghis Khan's power base was the *nöker* system, a less binding form of association in which a member of one clan could declare himself the 'comrade' of a powerful person from another clan. The *nöker* system allowed a charismatic warrior to build up a following; equally that following could quickly dissolve if he failed to live up to his promise. The possibility of ambitious individuals from any clan choosing to offer or withdraw their support permits the rapid rise – and sudden fall – of prominent leaders. It also undercuts the establishment of the more permanent institution of kingship. Allowing loyalties to shift freely works against two of the fundamental assumptions of monarchy: that whatever the circumstances rulers should always be able to rely on their followers, and that authority and allegiance should pass from royal father to princely son.

The rise and fall of Uldin neatly demonstrates the fragile position of Hun leaders. In 401 he dealt directly with Arcadius and in 406 took his followers west to serve as mercenaries in Stilicho's army. Three years later he was back in the east and in late 408 led his men across the Danube deep into Roman territory. Initial offers of a peace settlement were rejected and Uldin demanded a large pay-off before he would agree to withdraw. His threats were expansive: pointing to the sky, he declared that his Hun army could conquer all the lands on which the sun shone. Confronted with such arrogance, Roman negotiators tried a different tactic, opening discussions with Uldin's senior officers. According to the Christian historian Sozomen, writing thirty years later in Constantinople, Uldin's men were moved by the intervention of God to recognise the superiority of 'the Roman form of government, the philanthropy of the emperor and his swiftness and generosity in rewarding the best men'. It may of course have been through a heated debate on political philosophy that Uldin's followers were won over, or, perhaps more likely, it was a result of the solid prospect of the emperor's generosity. Either way, the Roman plan worked; the Huns were bought off and peace concluded. Abandoned by most of his comrades, Uldin only just made it safely back across the Danube. Many of those who decided to stay with him on his desperate dash to the frontier were captured and sold into slavery.

Only as long as they were successful could Hun leaders expect to rely on their followers. This arrangement allowed those Huns important within their clans to support whoever might seem to offer the best prospect of immediate advancement and reward – whether by attacking the Goths or fighting as mercenaries in the pay of a Roman emperor. Such a volatile system was vulnerable to manipulation. Against Uldin in 408 the Romans achieved a double victory: they both purchased peace and undermined a prominent Hun. The latter tactic was repeated four years later when the historian Olympiodorus was sent on an embassy to the Huns on behalf of the eastern court. No coherent account of this mission survives. Olympiodorus' lengthy history covering events from 407 to 425 is preserved in only forty-three fragments, some only a brief paragraph. Worse still, the few lines that deal with his own embassy to the Huns come from a summary of his original text made 400 years later by an unsympathetic scholar in Constantinople, who found Olympiodorus' work 'laid-back and loosely organised with a tendency towards the banal and vulgar – so much so that it is not worthy of being classified as history'.

Olympiodorus left the imperial capital in late 412 or early 413 and sailed in stormy weather around Greece and up the Adriatic Sea, a good indication that the Huns he was to meet were located on the middle Danube. Olympiodorus was accompanied on the voyage by his parakeet. He was very proud of this bird, at least according to the impatient scholar, who also recorded the historian's praise of his pet's abilities, no doubt as further proof of his triviality: 'Olympiodorus also mentions a parakeet he had with him for twenty years. He says there was scarcely any human action it could not imitate. It could dance, sing, call out names and do other things.' Regrettably, the reaction of the Huns to the arrival of this bird-fancying Roman ambassador and his performing parakeet is not known. Perhaps some realised, too late, that it was a colourful front to serious diplomatic business.

The much reduced version of Olympiodorus' history that survives makes it impossible to reconstruct events securely, but it seems that he was involved in the assassination of one prominent Hun, called Donatus, and in buying off the objections of another, called Charaton. Like Olympiodorus' parakeet, Charaton's hostility may have been a decoy to divert suspicion from his own involvement. Perhaps Charaton had invited the Romans and conspired with them to rub out a rival, promising for a price to promote friendly relations with the empire; or perhaps Donatus was eliminated by a competing faction because of his close involvement with the Roman ambassador. More than this it is difficult to say, but it seems likely that Olympiodorus' embassy is another example of Roman exploitation of the unstable nature of Hun leadership. Clearly, whatever the advantages of allowing a talented individual from any clan to acquire a following, there were also drawbacks in fuelling fierce competition that could suddenly flare up in fatal feuds. Ever-changing loyalties encouraged division and internal conflict. Temporary support for one leader might work well in times of war – at least for a short and victorious expedition – but the uncertainty of any continuing obligation made it less suitable for the conduct of a longer campaign or for the management of a settled society.

During the fifty years over which the Huns migrated from the Black Sea to Hungary they had operated as a series of loosely connected clan groups. This arrangement had been sufficient to disrupt and displace those living north of the Danube and for some Hun war bands to take advantage of the Roman army's need for mercenaries. In effect, the Huns both created a persistent security problem for the empire and offered themselves as part of the solution. Yet, as they extended and consolidated their control over new territories and peoples, it was clear that there was a limit to the effectiveness and profitability of continual raids. An unregulated cycle of opportunistic violence was inadequate to meet the demands of a permanent state. If tribute were to be extracted systematically from conquered territory, then it was necessary to establish a more stable form of government. In addition, any expansion of Hun dominance, especially against the Roman empire, required a greater concentration of military effort focused on a single objective, the closer coordination of individual clans and well-planned campaigns. It was not until all clan groups could be united under one leader to whom they owed lasting and unquestioned allegiance that the destructive potential of the Huns could be fully realised. Remarkably, this was substantially achieved in the next thirty years. Key changes mark out the difference in the organisation of Hun society between Uldin and Attila. More widely, they are part of the extraordinary transformation during the first half of the fifth century of a nomadic people who had moved west from the vast wilderness of the steppes to settle permanently in the confines of the Great Hungarian Plain.

PART II

# HUNS AND ROMANS

# 6

## A Tale of Two Cities

In Constantinople in May 408 Arcadius died. The emperor, shrouded in purple, lay in state in the Great Palace. Senior courtiers (in strict order of precedence) filed slowly past, their impassive faces briefly illuminated in the flickering light of the candles that surrounded the golden coffin. The city went into mourning; shops and public buildings were closed. In a solemn procession Arcadius' body was carried from the Great Palace up the hill to the imperial Mausoleum. A huge crowd stood listening to the heavy, rhythmic tread of the dead emperor's guard of honour and to the rising lamentations of the choirs of nuns and priests that followed the cortège. The air was sweet with the purifying smell of incense. At the rear of the funeral procession, in the place of highest honour, was Arcadius' son, the new ruler of the eastern Roman empire, Theodosius II.

Theodosius was then only seven years old. His unchallenged elevation was assisted by Arcadius' foresight: six years earlier he had made his infant son his imperial equal. Following Arcadius' death, there was no succession crisis: Theodosius was already an emperor. For the first years of his sole reign the real business of government was carried out by Anthemius, praetorian prefect of the East. The Prefecture – which had its distant origin in the Praetorian Guard that had once been responsible for the safety of emperors in Rome – had overall responsibility for judicial and financial matters, taxation, army recruitment, public works and administrative affairs in a vast territory that covered most of the eastern empire. After a successful career working his way steadily through the senior posts at court, the Egyptian-born Anthemius had been appointed prefect three years before Arcadius' death. He was one of the emperor's most trusted advisers and well known as a capable consensus politician. In the judgement of one contemporary, the prefect 'was the most resourceful man of his time and held in high regard. He never undertook anything without first taking advice, and on matters of state he sought the opinions of most of his close friends.'

Anthemius not only managed the smooth transfer of imperial power from father to son, he also ensured the confirmation of a non-aggression pact with Persia. In 400 Anthemius had been one of the ambassadors sent to the Persian capital, Ctesiphon, to congratulate Yazdgard I on his accession the year before. In 408 Yazdgard affirmed his intention to maintain cordial relations with the Roman empire and threatened war on any who dared rebel against its new boy-emperor. It was also made known that the Persian king had agreed to act as an executor of Arcadius' will and to look after his young son's interests until he came of age. This might have been true, or it might have been a useful exaggeration of Yazdgard's diplomatic expressions of brotherly affection for Theodosius. Certainly for the prefect and his supporters the apparent intervention in Roman dynastic politics of such a strong ruler was to be welcomed. It helped prevent a repeat of the distrust and disunity that had followed Stilicho's claim to have been named regent by the dying Theodosius I. Fifteen years later, it was to everyone's advantage that Theodosius II's powerful protector should not be at court in Constantinople, but safely distant, over one thousand miles away in Ctesiphon.

The knowledge that the eastern frontier was stable and the Persian king personally friendly allowed more resources to be directed to the defence of the northern frontier and the security of Constantinople. In 412 Theodosius authorised the refitting of the Danube fleet. A carefully worked-out system of repairs, rolling replacements and additions ensured that 225 river patrol craft would be commissioned over seven years. The emperor also approved Anthemius' proposal to build a second line of walls to protect the imperial capital. In 324, as part of his original foundation, Constantine had planned a wall enclosing an area of roughly two and a half square miles. Ninety years later Constantinople had outgrown these defences. The project to construct another set of fortifications was an ambitious one. The aim was to safeguard the whole of the peninsula on which

Constantinople was sited and to allow for the further expansion of the city within that protected zone. Anthemius' scheme nearly doubled the area defended by Constantine by building a new belt of walls just over half a mile beyond the old, running shore to shore from the Golden Horn to the Propontis.

The Theodosian Walls – named in honour of the young emperor who commissioned them – were the most formidable military structure ever built in the Roman empire (see plates, picture 12). The raw statistics are impressive enough. A series of parallel defences 180 feet deep ran for three and a half miles. The inner wall was thirty-six feet high (roughly four storeys) and sixteen feet thick at its base. A strong rubble core was faced with blocks of white limestone set with bands of red brick. The inner wall was punctuated by ninety-six towers, sixty feet high and set at irregular intervals. In front was a raised terrace fifty feet wide. In turn, this dead ground was screened by an outer wall twenty-six feet high and reinforced by ninety towers, off-set from those in the inner wall. Finally, in front of the outer wall, was another broad terrace and a dry moat twenty feet deep and sixty wide. The ongoing maintenance and repair of the newly constructed Theodosian Walls was financed through their partial privatisation. The towers were leased back to those who owned the land on which they were built. In return for these valuable properties – all with stunning city views – tenants were required to pay for their upkeep. In the words of the imperial regulations issued in April 413: 'Thus the splendour of the work and the fortifications of the capital shall be preserved, as well as their use for the benefit of private citizens.'

The Theodosian Walls have been steadily restored over the last decade. Long stretches of the inner wall and many of its towers now stand at near their original height. Little remains of the great moat; it has mostly been filled in. The raised terrace is no longer visible; its stone has long since been carried away. This once vital defensive space is now a green mosaic of suburban allotments: here vines flourish and fruit ripens against the white, sun-warmed limestone. Too few visitors to Istanbul take the time (about half a day) to walk the length of the Theodosian Walls. For those living in Constantinople at the beginning of the fifth century, this solid fortified line represented the power and security of the Roman empire. The walls' protective presence added to the magnificence of the imperial capital. Thanks to its massive defences, no other city in the Mediterranean world was so well shielded from attack. Even if the frontier provinces south of the Danube fell to an invading army, Constantinople would be able to stand firm.

In Ravenna in August 423 the western emperor Honorius died, fifteen years after his elder brother Arcadius. It is probable that Honorius, like his father Theodosius I, suffered from oedema, traditionally known as dropsy, a condition in which the body is unable to regulate the intake and excretion of fluid. Death commonly follows kidney failure or a pulmonary oedema, a heart attack brought on by the pressure of fluid retained in the lungs. Theodosius II, who had carefully prepared for his uncle's death, moved quickly to assert his authority over the West, but his attempt to return to a united Roman empire did not run according to plan. In Ravenna leading courtiers and military officers backed a senior bureaucrat named John. In Constantinople Theodosius had to reckon with the claims of his aunt Galla Placidia and her young son Valentinian.

Galla Placidia was a princess of impeccable imperial pedigree: she was the daughter of Theodosius I and his second wife, Galla, and so half-sister to Honorius and Arcadius. She was accounted a great beauty by many who met her, although flattering convention always insists that princesses are beautiful. More astute observers were struck by her sharp wit, shrewd political judgement and ruthless ambition. At the age of seven Galla Placidia was in Milan when her father died and had remained in the West with its new emperor, Honorius. She had been taken hostage by the Goths during Alaric's siege of Rome. On New Year's Day 417, under pressure from her half-brother, she reluctantly married the general Flavius Constantius who, after the execution of Stilicho in August 408, was Honorius' most trusted commander and responsible for the permanent settlement of the Goths in France.

The marriage between Flavius Constantius and Galla Placidia had clear dynastic implications, particularly since the childless Honorius, in a public display of Christian piety, had declared himself strictly celibate. In late 417 Galla gave birth to a daughter, Justa Grata Honoria, and eighteen months later to a son, Valentinian. In 421 Honorius made Constantius co-emperor and conferred the impressive title of *nobilissimus* ('most noble') on Valentinian, marking out the two-year-old boy as his successor. Theodosius, who regarded himself as Honorius' rightful heir, refused to recognise either Valentinian's title or Constantius' new imperial rank. The stalemate did not last long. Death and exile altered everything. After only seven months of joint rule with Honorius, Constantius died. Two years later, in early 423, his widow and her two young children fled Ravenna to seek safety in Constantinople. Justly or not, Galla Placidia had been accused by Honorius of plotting his downfall. Having carefully designated his successor, Honorius now regretted it. While he was content to be followed by Valentinian he had no intention of being replaced by him.

Galla Placidia received a cool reception at the eastern court. Although offering her protection, Theodosius declined to support Valentinian. Following Honorius' death, he still intended to assert his own claim over the West and make Constantinople – as it had been briefly under his grandfather, Theodosius I – the capital of a unified empire. That was a vain and outdated ambition. In the forty years since Theodosius I had marched into Italy to defeat the usurpers Magnus Maximus and Eugenius, too much had changed: Rome had been sacked by Alaric, the Rhine frontier had been seriously breached, the Goths had found a new homeland in France and the Huns had occupied the Great Hungarian Plain. The West could not be ruled from the other side of the Mediterranean; it was now too unstable and its defences too fragile. Moreover, after Honorius' death, the strong support for the bureaucrat John was a telling indication that influential courtiers in Ravenna would resist any attempt to force them to shift their allegiance 900 miles east to Constantinople.

Confronted with John's rebellion, Theodosius speedily changed his views. He retrospectively recognised the dead Constantius as emperor and Valentinian's status as Honorius' legitimate heir. The connection between the East and the West was to be confirmed by the future marriage of Valentinian to Theodosius' daughter Licinia Eudoxia, then only two years old. In 425 a rapidly assembled force, commanded by Flavius Aspar, was sent to northern Italy. The city of Aquileia on the Adriatic coast, sixty miles east of modern Venice, was captured, and Ravenna fell soon after. Those who saw the advance of the imperial army as confirming the will of God claimed that an angel disguised as a shepherd had shown Aspar a secret pathway across the marshes surrounding the city. Others, more sceptical, thought that the shepherd – well rewarded for his services – had been precisely what he seemed.

This theological dispute was of little consequence to John. Dragged back to Aquileia, the failed usurper was led around the hippodrome on a donkey. The crowd jeered as he was forced to take part in a crude pantomime re-enactment of his downfall. After this humiliation, John's right hand was cut off and he was beheaded. From their seats, shaded by purple hangings trimmed with gold, it may safely be assumed that Galla Placidia and her two children watched the vicious spectacle with pitiless indifference. It was a grim reminder that the risks of court politics were fatally high. The losers, mutilated like criminals, deserved to die in the arena; the winners had earned the privilege to watch their execution from the splendour of the imperial box.

Despite these victory celebrations, the war was not yet over. A few months earlier John had sent a middle-ranking palace official, Flavius Aetius, with a large sum in gold to seek the help of the Huns. Aetius was a good choice: he came from a wealthy and influential family with a distinguished record of administrative and military service. His father, Gaudentius, had governed a province in North Africa before commanding imperial troops in France, where he was killed during a mutiny. Those who favoured Aetius described him in admiring terms.

> He was of average height, manly in appearance with a well-toned body, neither too slight nor too stocky . . . He was never deflected from his goal by those who encouraged him to act improperly. He was at his most patient when wronged. He was always eager to take on work. He was undaunted when facing danger and his ability to endure hunger, thirst and lack of sleep was remarkable. From an early age he seemed aware that he had been marked out by destiny for great power.

In 409, while still a teenager, Aetius had been sent along with other aristocratic hostages as part of Honorius' surety for a levy of 10,000 Hun mercenaries. Beyond the Danube Aetius seems to have been well treated, spending his time in the company of the sons of the Hun elite. He returned an excellent horseman and a deadly accurate bowman. He had also formed a number of genuine friendships with Huns, whom – contrary to Roman prejudices – he found he could both respect and trust. In 425 it was precisely this privileged relationship that John had hoped to turn to his own advantage. The mission was successful. The persuasive combination of Aetius' connections and John's cash raised a sizeable army. Some claimed in panicked exaggeration that 60,000 Huns were marching on Ravenna. But help came too late: the mercenaries entered northern Italy three days after John had been decapitated. Following a costly encounter with Aspar's troops, Aetius abandoned John's cause and instead furthered his own. Galla Placidia had no option but to negotiate; reluctantly, she agreed to pay off the Huns and appoint Aetius commander of imperial forces in France.

When news of John's execution reached Theodosius in Constantinople, he was presiding over chariot races in the hippodrome. Immediately he cancelled the rest of the programme and ordered a service of thanksgiving. A victory procession was hurriedly formed and the chanting of the city's sports fans soon gave way to the singing of hymns in praise of the ever-triumphant Christ. In Ravenna Galla Placidia, while also giving thanks to the divinity, no doubt wished that John's defeat had been followed by the elimination or exile of his supporters. She resented having to promote her enemies to powerful posts. It is unlikely that this was the all-conquering return she had prayed for. In successfully extorting a senior military command, Aetius had exposed the damaging possibility that Hun mercenaries might be used not to defend the empire, but to advance the factional interests of ambitious Roman generals. For the moment, all at court proclaimed themselves loyal to the new boy-emperor Valentinian III and his formidable mother. Yet all must have been uncomfortably aware that had Aetius and his Huns arrived in Italy only a few days earlier, it might be John and his military backers who now ruled in Ravenna.

# War on Three Fronts

In 420, five years before the restoration of Galla Placidia and Valentinian, the fanatical leader of a martyr brigade set fire to a temple in the Persian province of Khuzistan in the south of modern Iraq. This radical extremist expected to be killed on the spot by guards. The aim of his suicide mission was to strike a dramatic blow against Zoroastrianism, the main religion of the Persian empire. Abdaas, a Christian bishop, succeeded in destroying the temple but not in securing his immediate death. Arrested, he was taken before Yazdgard I, who for the last twenty years had been tolerant towards Christianity. Abdaas and his followers changed the Persian king's mind. They rejected his suggestion that as a gesture of reconciliation with other faith communities in Khuzistan they should rebuild the burnt-out temple. Abdaas' refusal convinced Yazdgard that some Christians in his empire had no intention of integrating into Persian society; rather they had taken advantage of his liberal policies to pursue their subversive activities. Reluctantly, he authorised severe counter-measures: Christians were to be rounded up and executed, and their churches demolished. In the face of systematic Persian reprisals some Christians chose to die for their faith; others fled across the frontier to seek refuge in the Roman empire.

Yazdgard's persecution was denounced in Constantinople. When in the following year it was intensified by his son and successor Bahrām V, Theodosius ordered a tough military response. This is an important moment in the history of the Roman empire: it was the first time that an emperor had declared war explicitly to protect Christians. Theodosius' supporters claimed that God was on the Roman side: 100,000 desert Arabs on their way to fight for Persia were reported to have been seized with a divinely inspired terror and thrown themselves into the Euphrates

River. Yet, despite the support of such well-timed miracles and some initial success in the field, Roman forces in northern Mesopotamia failed to achieve any decisive superiority. In 422 negotiations were opened and peace restored. Both sides agreed not to add to the fortifications along the frontier and proclaimed mutual toleration of Christians in Persia and the far fewer Zoroastrians in the Roman empire.

One significant factor in the abandonment of Theodosius' crusade after less than a year was a sudden attack across the Danube. In early 422 the Huns took advantage of Roman troop commitments in Persia and marched south into Thrace (roughly modern Bulgaria). How this offensive was organised is not known, nor is there any record of the name of its leader. The incursion is only reported in one brief entry in a sixth-century chronicle: 'The Huns laid waste Thrace.' The scale of the incursion, clearly more than a cross-border raid, forced the immediate recall of units from Mesopotamia. There were strict strategic limits to Theodosius' religious fervour. Only peace with Persia could ensure that sufficient manpower was available for the defence of the Balkans. A law issued on 3 March 422 formed part of the provisions hurriedly put in place to cope with such large troop movements. The emperor instructed landowners leasing towers in the Theodosian Walls to assist with the provision of emergency accommodation: 'Our most loyal troops returning from active service or setting out to war shall take for their own use the ground floor of each tower in the new walls of this most sacred city.'

The redeployment of troops was sufficient to force an agreement with the Huns, who withdrew on the promise of an annual payment of 350 pounds of gold. In Constantinople the settlements with both the Huns and the Persians were claimed as successes. A statue of the emperor was put up at the Hebdomon, the military parade ground on the shores of the Propontis, just outside the Theodosian Walls. Although the statue has not survived, on its base (the fragments are now in the Istanbul Archaeological Museum) an inscription praised Theodosius as 'everywhere and forever victorious'. That of course was not true, but having failed to defeat either the Persians or the Huns it was shrewder to negotiate peace and then celebrate this as a Roman triumph.

The next crisis that faced Theodosius was unlikely to be resolved so swiftly or simply. It had its origins in the disruption caused by the westward advance of the Huns a generation earlier. In December 406 the Vandals had crossed the Rhine; they had then moved through France and by 409 reached Spain. Twenty years later, having failed to find land on which they could settle safely, they crossed the Strait of Gibraltar. The Vandal push into North Africa was a more serious threat to the integrity of the empire than their presence in Spain. These provinces were amongst the most prosperous in the Mediterranean. The large agricultural estates that ran along the wide coastal strip produced wine, oil, grain and tax revenue in abundance. This was the granary of the Roman world. Carthage, North Africa's main port, was a wealthy city, its great harbour ringed by warehouses and well-equipped dockyards. With a population of 200,000, it was rivalled in size and importance only by Rome, Constantinople, Antioch and Alexandria on the Nile Delta. The Vandal invasion in spring 429 threatened to shatter this imperial world unified around a single sea. The Romans referred to the Mediterranean simply as *mare nostrum* – 'our sea' – and for nearly 500 years the empire had completely encircled its shores. The loss of the North African coast would expose Italy to attack. From Carthage the Vandals could launch an invasion fleet against Rome or Ravenna and even reach Constantinople. The fortifications along the eastern and northern frontiers might provide protection from the Persians and the Huns, but against an attack from Africa they were, quite literally, facing the wrong way.

In the division of the Roman empire in the fourth century, North Africa – apart from Egypt and Libya – had been allocated to the West. Yet in the face of the Vandal invasion Theodosius decided to step in, unwilling to leave the direction of such a critical conflict to the eleven-year-old Valentinian III and his mother. In 431 Flavius Aspar, who had captured Aquileia and Ravenna in 425, was sent with an army to re-inforce troops under Boniface, the western imperial commander. This close military cooperation was in stark contrast to previous frictions. The threat posed by the Vandals was too great to risk disunity. It was hoped that the combined resources of the eastern and western empires might result in a rapid and decisive victory. But the Vandals under their leader Geiseric were not so easily suppressed. Boniface and Aspar were able to halt their advance, but no more. Defeated in battle on open ground in early 432, Roman troops withdrew to Carthage. Two years later it was clear that if the Vandals were to be dislodged, then Theodosius would need to commit additional resources to the African front. For governments determined to go to war in distant lands, justifications for an ongoing commitment can always be found. To pull out after three years of hard fighting was politically unattractive and this time there was little chance of presenting withdrawal as a military triumph. By abandoning North Africa, Theodosius, who had once proclaimed himself 'everywhere and forever victorious', could be seen to be turning his back on the West.

Nor was there any evidence of a significant threat on the northern frontier. Diplomatic relations had been established with the Hun leader Rua. Along with his brother Octar, who died in 430, Rua is the next Hun leader to be named by Roman writers after Uldin, Donatus and Charaton. (Rua or Octar may have been the unnamed Hun leader responsible for the invasion of Thrace in 422.) In early 434, through Eslas, the Huns' ambassador at court in Constantinople, Rua declared his intention to attack a number of tribes north of the Danube. He insisted that any young men who had already fled across the frontier and joined the Roman army should be handed over without delay. Negotiations on a final resolution to these demands were in progress and ambassadors had only recently been dispatched for a further round of talks. Theodosius and his advisers took a carefully calculated risk: on balance they judged the chances of a Hun invasion to be low. Under these circumstances, it was in the empire's best interests to continue the war against Geiseric. The task force would not be recalled for the defence of the Danube provinces. It would remain in Africa and finish the job.

A few months later, in the summer of 434, the Huns attacked. Perhaps negotiations over asylum-seekers finally broke down; perhaps Rua had misled the ambassadors all along, his diplomatic wrangling masking his real intentions; perhaps the change of plan was sheer opportunism once it was clear that Roman troops in Africa would not be redeployed. As the Huns devastated Thrace, moving steadily towards Constantinople, the city's terror-stricken citizens anticipated a long and bloody siege. Their safety would depend on the strength of the Theodosian Walls. It would be the first time that the capital's new defences had been tested in action. At court those criticised for failing to foresee Rua's invasion would have regarded such censure as unjustified. After all, as they perhaps hurried to assure Theodosius, they had reached a reasonable conclusion after a careful consideration of all the available evidence. It is a harsh political truth that some judgements, however correct they may appear at the time, can in hindsight turn out to be completely wrong.

It is equally true that, in the resolution of a crisis, good luck can sometimes be just as important as good judgement. Without warning, the Huns withdrew. The reasons for this abrupt retreat are unclear; the best explanation is the sudden death of Rua. It may be that his successors did not feel confident in establishing their authority while on campaign, and particularly before the walls of the imperial capital. Theodosius believed that the Huns' retreat was an act of God in direct answer to his prayers. In Constantinople it was rumoured that Rua had been incinerated by a providential lightning bolt. His followers were said to have been killed by plague and scorched by fireballs. Proclus, bishop of Constantinople, in a sermon giving thanks for the city's deliverance, was convinced that these events had been foretold in the visions of the Old Testament prophet Ezekiel whose prediction of the defeat of Gog could now be understood to refer to the Huns: 'Thus says the Lord God: "Son of man, set your face toward Gog, of the land of Magog . . . With pestilence and bloodshed I will enter into judgement with him; and I will rain upon him and his hordes, and the many peoples that are with him, torrential rains and hailstones, fire and brimstone."'

The imperial capital had been saved either by chance or the well-directed intervention of the divinity but Theodosius, now parading piety rather than policy, took full credit for the achievement. Two narrow escapes (the rapid reversal of the crusade against Persia and the unexpected death of Rua) had prevented major military disasters. Perhaps the Persian campaign could have been avoided, although as a committed Christian Theodosius had no doubt of his obligation to protect his persecuted fellow believers. The war in Africa was more pressing. To relinquish control to the Vandals without a fight would be to stand aside while the empire was dismembered; the emperor and his advisers had no option but to risk an African campaign, yet to misjudge the situation was to imperil Constantinople itself. To his credit, Theodosius remained willing to accept a compromise that allowed troops to be withdrawn. In 435, the year after Rua's death, a treaty formally ratified by Valentinian – North Africa was part of the western empire – granted the Vandals the land they had already occupied in the province of Numidia. The more fertile territory (roughly modern Tunisia), along with the vital port city of Carthage, remained safe in Roman hands.

Theodosius had no option but to accept these concessions. The need to defend the Danube and the imperial capital against the Huns critically restricted the eastern Roman empire's ability to pursue its wider strategic goals. Improved fortifications, more river patrol craft and the building of the Theodosian Walls reduced, but did not eliminate, the pressure on the northern frontier. These measures helped slow the enemy's advance rather than prevent a full-scale invasion. All the more reason then to celebrate Rua's fiery death. For those who remembered the defeat of Uldin or Olympiodorus' embassy and the murder of Donatus, the sudden withdrawal also held out the possibility that the Hun problem might be solved by opposing clans exhausting themselves in a lengthy civil war. Those, like the bishop of Constantinople, who argued that contemporary events had been predicted by Ezekiel, no doubt drew some cheer from his words: 'Thus says the Lord God: "Behold, I am against you, O Gog . . . I will strike your bow from your left hand, and will make your arrows drop out of your right hand."'

But this was cold comfort. Ezekiel may have foreseen the destruction of Gog, but his vision was of the coming of the Antichrist and the end of the world. Nor could the emperor, for all his religious convictions, be expected to formulate the empire's foreign policy on the basis of a Christian bishop's reading of the Old Testament. Perhaps Gog would eventually be defeated, but analysis of the latest reports indicated that the Huns had regrouped and Rua had been replaced by two of his nephews. Much now depended on their ability to assert their joint authority. And that was difficult to predict, even with the prophetic assistance of Ezekiel. More information was needed by Theodosius and his military advisers before the situation beyond the Danube could be fully understood and its security implications properly assessed. For the moment, the new Hun leaders were no more than two strange and unfamiliar sounding names: Bleda and his younger brother Attila.

# 8

## *Brothers in Arms*

Attila the Hun was no son of the steppes; he was probably born at the beginning of the fifth century somewhere on the Great Hungarian Plain. Attila's father was called Mundiuch, his mother's name is not known. Mundiuch was brother to Octar and Rua, joint leaders of the Huns in the late 420s and '30s. As a member of the most powerful family north of the Danube, Attila had a highly privileged upbringing. Certainly he was not the homeless, half-starved barbarian child of Ammianus Marcellinus' imagination: 'Huns are never sheltered by buildings . . . Not even a hut thatched with reeds can be found among them. Rather they roam freely in the mountains and woods, learning from their earliest childhood to endure freezing cold, hunger and thirst.' Nor, perhaps to Ammianus' disappointment, is Attila ever likely to have worn goatskin leggings or to have been sewn into clothes made from the pelts of wild mice until they fell to pieces bit by bit.

The young Attila spent most of his time in the company of his elder brother Bleda. Together they were taught archery, how to fight with sword and lasso, and how to ride and care for a horse. Both were likely to have been taught to speak, and perhaps to read, Gothic and Latin: Latin for conducting business with the Roman empire, Gothic for controlling conquered territory in central and eastern Europe. Attila and Bleda also learned something of military and diplomatic tactics. They may have been present, somewhere quietly in the background, when Rua and Octar received Roman ambassadors. As young men they took a leading part in Hun raids across the Danube and north of the Great Hungarian Plain. No doubt some high-ranking Huns assumed that one day, like their uncles, Bleda and Attila would rule the Huns together.

This cannot have been certain. After Octar's death Rua resisted any pressure to share power. His own sudden death deep in Roman territory must have been a dangerous moment for his nephews. Perhaps they had the support of those who wished to see joint rule restored; perhaps others were less confident than Rua of the strategic wisdom of advancing on Constantinople and were prepared to follow new commanders brave enough to lead an orderly retreat. Perhaps it was Rua's unexpected death on campaign that really mattered. It allowed Attila and Bleda to secure the loyalty of the army before it returned home. No doubt back on the Great Hungarian Plain there were rival candidates. In seizing power Attila and Bleda are likely to have had blood on their hands. Rua may well have had sons of his own. If so, nothing is known of them. After their father's death, they may not have survived for long.

Both Octar and Rua had strengthened Hun control over territory north of the Danube. Of this process – again due to the disinterest of Roman writers – only a few fragments of information survive. According to Priscus of Panium, prior to the invasion of 434 Rua was concerned to prevent refugees from 'the Amilzuri, Itimari, Tounsoures, Boisci and other tribes living near the Danube' crossing the frontier and joining the Roman army. Nothing is known about these tribes; the best conjecture is that these were some of the steppe peoples settled around the Black Sea swept into Europe by the Huns' westward migration in the fourth century. Now their loyalty could not be guaranteed, and it might be to their advantage to side with the Romans. That was to be prevented by force. Before suddenly changing his plans and marching against the empire, Rua claimed to be considering an agreement with Theodosius that would allow Hun troops to campaign on the northern bank of the Danube without Roman interference.

A few years earlier, in 430, Octar had attempted to push Hun rule further west by attacking the Burgundians, who occupied territory on the Rhine around modern Worms in south-western Germany. The account of this expedition is buried in the story of the Burgundians' conversion to Christianity as told a decade later by the historian Socrates (christened by his parents in honour of the great Greek philosopher who had died 850 years earlier):

There is a nation of barbarians known as Burgundians who live beyond the Rhine . . . The Huns, by repeatedly attacking these people, devastated their territory and often killed large numbers of them. In this crisis the Burgundians decided not to seek any human help, but to entrust themselves to some divinity. As they were clear in their minds that the god of the Romans offered the greatest assistance to those who feared him . . . they went to one of the cities in France and asked the bishop there to baptise them as Christians . . . Then they marched against the Huns, and were not disappointed in their hopes. For when Uptaros, king of the Huns, burst during the night as a result of his over-indulgence, the Burgundians attacked the Huns, who were now leaderless . . . The Burgundians were only 3,000 men, but they destroyed around 10,000 of the enemy. From then on the Burgundians were fervent Christians.

For those who believe in miracles, much may be salvaged from this pious text. The explosive death of Uptaros, painfully rupturing after a night of gluttonous excess, is a delightful moment of divine comedy in a serious tale of the triumph of Christianity. For those less certain of humorous heavenly interventions in the course of history, it is still possible to see in the outline of Socrates' account a memory of the defeat of Octar (here called Uptaros) in his attempt to push the Hun empire as far west as the Rhine.

Rua's need to bring the tribes along the Danube into line and Octar's failed expedition against the Burgundians are reminders that Attila and Bleda inherited an empire established by military force. Nor could its stability be guaranteed. While some peoples fled in the face of the Hun advance, others were capable of putting up a fight. The Hun migration into Europe was no walkover. That said, their superior horsemanship and continual raids, mostly against unprotected farming communities, meant that local resistance was eventually broken. The victory of the Burgundians was an exception, and that was only possible with well-disciplined troops able to take advantage of an unexpected situation.

Octar and Rua's efforts to strengthen the Huns' hold over central Europe were continued by Attila and Bleda. Again, aside from campaigns along the Rhine (discussed in the following chapter), during the first six years of their joint rule (434–40) it is difficult to trace in any detail their part in the expansion of the Hun empire. It was perhaps by the late 430s that it extended, in Priscus' vague description, as far as 'the islands in the Ocean', that is as far north as the Baltic Sea. Alongside the acquisition of new territories, Attila and Bleda also promoted the consolidation of Hun rule. As suggested in Chapter 5, the regular payment of tribute depended on the cooperation of the locally powerful. Some acted out of fear; others out of self-interest. Faced with the alternatives of fleeing into the Roman empire or taking to the hills, they preferred to come to an arrangement with the Huns. Attila and Bleda allowed these collaborators to retain control over their own affairs and welcomed them as friends and companions. For many, the decision to side with the enemy was a pragmatic choice. Not everyone confronted with conquest always joins the resistance.

The extent to which it was possible for local rulers to accumulate considerable wealth is spectacularly revealed by the Pietroasa treasure. This horde was found buried under limestone boulders near the village of Pietroasa in the foothills of the Carpathian Mountains. Amongst the objects now on display in the National Museum of Romanian History in Bucharest are four large brooches, one bowl, two cups, three necklaces, a great circular tray and a tall pitcher (see plates, pictures 15–18). All are solid gold, together weighing over forty pounds. The Pietroasa treasure has a chequered history. The two peasants who discovered it in 1837 divided the twenty-two finds between them by cutting some of them up. The dealer to whom they sold these now badly mutilated objects was interested mainly in their value as bullion. He was responsible for prising out most of the precious stones and for breaking up some of the objects with an axe. By the time the treasure was seized by the authorities it had been severely damaged; only twelve items were recovered. Following repairs, they were put on display in 1842 in the National Museum of Antiquities.

Then one winter night in 1875, during a heavy snowstorm, the treasure was stolen by a young novice priest. The theft was cleverly planned. A small hole was cut in the ceiling of the gallery and an umbrella inserted. The umbrella was then opened and used to catch the plaster as the hole was enlarged. Next, the thief lowered himself on a rope, easily opened the display case and, concealing the contents in an improvised sack made from his underclothes, left the museum quietly by a side door. Attempts to sell pieces to a local jeweller allowed the police to trace the culprit. The golden objects, now bent and flattened, were found jammed inside an upright piano. Repaired for a second time, the treasure remained in Bucharest until 1916 when, to protect it from advancing German troops, it was taken to Russia. It was only returned to Romania by the Soviet government in 1956.

The largest brooch in the Pietroasa treasure is a remarkable piece of workmanship. Its size, ten and a half inches long and six inches wide, suggests that it was worn on the shoulder to pin together the folds of a man's heavy cloak. What survives, battered and twice repaired, is the brooch's framework, made from thick gold plate in the shape of an eagle: the broad body of the bird (with the clasp underneath), its elegantly curved neck, its sharp-eyed stare and cruelly hooked beak. The eagle's tail is suggested by four chains of thin, twisted gold wire that hang down from the bottom of the brooch. Each gold chain terminates in a translucent teardrop of rock crystal. The other stones that once encrusted all the visible surfaces are now sadly missing: the great oval gem in the middle of the eagle's back, a necklace of small stones encircling the throat and for the eyes, most splendid of all, perhaps deep-red garnets glinting with the cold, unblinking gaze of a bird of prey. The man whose cloak was fastened by this magnificent brooch may have hoped that those who saw him parading such finery would also think of him admiringly as possessing noble, aquiline features and perhaps too an eagle-like character: unruffled, ever watchful and deadly accurate in seeking out and destroying his enemies.

The brooch's wearer was probably also the owner of the other precious objects, including the two drinking cups, the tall pitcher and the great circular tray. On the basis of stylistic parallels and method of manufacture, it is likely that the gold tableware, like the eagle-headed brooch, was made somewhere north of the Danube in the first half of the fifth century. The exception is the most beautiful object in the treasure, a shallow bowl just over eleven inches in diameter and three inches deep. At its centre is a statuette of a seated woman about five inches high; around the inside of the bowl runs a vigorous scene of gods and goddesses. Individual deities can be identified: a half-naked Apollo sits holding his lyre, and the goddess Isis (originally Egyptian but worshipped throughout the Mediterranean) stands next to her husband Serapis. The meaning of the scene is unclear, but the quality of the piece is undoubted. Both its design and decoration indicate that it was made by one of the finest goldsmiths in the eastern Roman empire, perhaps working in Antioch or Alexandria.

The owner of the Roman bowl and the rest of the Pietroasa treasure is unknown. The best guess is that these were the proud possessions of a leading Goth. On one of the necklaces there is a short inscription in Gothic. The translation is much disputed – the damage to the fragmentary piece makes a definitive reading impossible – but the words 'sacred' and 'Goth' are clear. Situated on the fertile lower slopes of the Carpathian Mountains, now a prosperous wine-growing region, Pietroasa had always been an important Gothic settlement. It was dominated by a substantial stone fort and farmhouse whose extensive storage facilities suggest that it was the centre of a large estate. It is certainly attractive to think that the Pietroasa treasure might have belonged to a powerful Gothic leader who had found a secure place within the Hun empire. As a mark of his superior status he wore a great eagle-headed brooch and dined in splendour at a table glittering with gold plates and cups. Perhaps this Goth had joined Attila on campaign. That might offer an explanation for the presence of such a valuable bowl. Taken as plunder on some raid across the Roman frontier, it was the share of spoils allotted to a trustworthy subordinate.

That Attila and Bleda allowed such wealth to be distributed to the leaders of subject peoples is one of the keys to the success of their empire. It would be wrong to think of the Huns as grabbing all the gold for themselves. Nor did they seek to dominate the locally powerful by threats and violence alone. Collaboration has its benefits. The wealthy Goth who owned the Pietroasa treasure clearly prospered under Hun rule. Looking back over the violent history of the previous seventy years he must have been pleased that his father or grandfather had refused to join Fritigern. As things turned out, it had proved much more profitable to fight alongside Attila and Bleda than to seek asylum amongst the Romans on the other side of the Danube.

Alongside the regular payment of taxes, the maintenance of an army and the cooperation of local rulers, the promotion of a state-sponsored religion is one of the engines of empire. Theodosius II was committed

to the close coalition between Christianity and Roman rule firmly established by Constantine a century before. It was the emperor's God-given
responsibility to support the Church and all who followed its teachings.
Heretics were to be persecuted and unbelievers made to suffer for
worshipping false gods. In 427, five years after the hurried cancellation
of the crusade in Mesopotamia, Nestorius, the newly appointed
bishop of Constantinople, pointedly reminded Theodosius of his duty
as a Christian monarch: 'Give me the earth undefiled by heretics, and
I will give you heaven. Help me to destroy the heretics, and I will help
you to destroy the Persians.'

To the pious frustration of both Nestorius and Theodosius, the
empire's enemies remained stubbornly faithful to their own religions
– it was only in their desperation to be allowed to cross the Danube
that the Goths had become Christians. Despite the persistent efforts
of missionaries, the Huns had refused to convert. At the beginning of
the fifth century Theotimus, bishop of Tomi on the Black Sea coast,
attempted to inspire conversion by giving the Huns who lived nearby
food and other gifts. Unfortunately this kindly, if not particularly spiritual, tactic backfired. Given his generosity, the Huns assumed that
Theotimus must be a rich man and worth kidnapping for a ransom.
A trap was laid and a meeting arranged with the bishop, who perhaps
thought that he had at last attracted some converts. As Theotimus
approached, one Hun suddenly raised a rope in his right hand and
made to lasso him and drag him away. But the lasso was never thrown.
The Hun remained frozen with his arm outstretched until Theotimus
prayed for him to be released. Despite, or perhaps because of, this
dramatic demonstration of divine power, the Huns who had tried to
seize the bishop remained hostile to Christianity. One afternoon when
riding upcountry Theotimus saw some Huns in the distance. The situation was dangerous. As his servants panicked, the bishop prayed and
the Huns passed by without noticing anything. This was a miraculous escape. Even so, it is a fair indication of the failure of Theotimus'
missionary work that he had to make himself invisible to avoid meeting
the very people he was trying to convert.

The Huns' steadfast refusal to abandon their traditional beliefs was
a direct challenge to a Christian Roman empire. Attila went further.
Against Theodosius' conviction that, as Constantine's imperial
successor, he was especially beloved of Christ, Attila defiantly advanced

his own claim to be favoured by a powerful deity. One day, or so the story recorded by Priscus of Panium goes, a poor herdsman noticed that one of his prize heifers had gone lame. Anxiously he followed the trail of blood left by the animal. It led back to a sword that was almost completely buried in the ground (see plates, picture 20). The herdsman, fearing to keep or sell such a magnificent object, took the sword to Attila, who at once recognised it as sacred to the war god. This sword had disappeared long ago and was thought by many to have been lost forever. Attila was clear about the significance of its extraordinary rediscovery. 'The king rejoiced . . . and, as he aspired to greatness, he supposed that he had been appointed ruler of the whole world, and that through the sword of the war god he was assured supremacy in all armed conflicts.'

For the Huns as for other steppe peoples, swords had great symbolic significance. Of this Priscus was well aware: Herodotus had noted that the Scythians worshipped their war god 'in the form of a sword set up on a platform made from bundles of brushwood'. Hun ceremonial weapons were beautifully made by highly skilled craftsmen. The sword found in 1979 near the monastery at Pannonhalma in Hungary had a scabbard covered in delicately embossed gold foil; its grip was encircled by three decorated gold bands (see plates, picture 19). Attila's striking innovation was to take these traditional beliefs in the importance of the sword and link them to his own claim to rule over the Huns. This was an astute political move. The miracle of the herdsman and the lost sword allowed Attila to assert that he was the one leader whose authority had been confirmed by the direct intervention of the gods. His rise to power was no accident of fate; rather it was part of a divinely ordained plan. Nor is there any reason to think that Attila was any more or less genuine than Constantine or Theodosius in believing that heaven was on his side and had proclaimed the legitimacy of his rule.

How much Bleda cared about all this is uncertain. He may not have felt any need to establish a religious justification for his rule or to contest Theodosius' belief that the Christian Roman empire was uniquely blessed. For the most part, Bleda expected to strengthen the Hun empire by force. No doubt he prided himself on being a man of action. He put his faith in real swords, not sacred ones. Close companions sensed a growing tension between the brothers. In this dangerous game of sibling rivalry those who sided with Attila alleged that on important matters of state Bleda took advice from a Roman captive called Zercon, cruelly delighting in his strange appearance and sniggering at his halting speech. According to Priscus: 'Attila could not stand the sight of Zercon, but Bleda was pleased by him, not only when he was telling jokes, but even when he was not, because of the weird movements of his body as he walked . . . He was rather short, hunchbacked with distorted feet and a nose that, because it was completely flat, was indicated only by the nostrils.'

On one occasion Zercon escaped with some other prisoners of war. Soon recaptured, he was put in chains and brought before Bleda. So terrified he could hardly stammer out a single word, Zercon excused his flight, blaming his master for not finding him a wife. Laughing, Bleda immediately gave him the daughter of a high-ranking Hun. She had been a close companion of one of Bleda's wives but had fallen out of favour following some indiscretion. Attila (it may be assumed) turned away in disgust. Perhaps he felt that this was no way to treat a well-born woman. If guilty of misconduct then she ought to be punished properly, not suddenly married off for Bleda's amusement. For the moment Attila controlled his anger. Always a shrewd strategist, he would continue to rely on his blood ties with Bleda until his own position was secure. Only then would he seek to fulfil the promise of the war god's sacred sword and rule the Hun empire alone.

# 9

## *Fighting for Rome*

Flavius Aetius was the most feared man in the western Roman empire. He owed much of his success to his long-standing association with the Huns. After Honorius' death they had backed his bid to put the bureaucrat John on the throne. When that failed, they had compelled the new regime in Ravenna – the boy-emperor Valentinian III and his mother Galla Placidia – to avoid civil war by paying them off and appointing Aetius to a senior military command. Successive victories enforcing imperial rule in France confirmed his increasingly powerful position. In addition there was always the threat that, if challenged, he might once again persuade the Huns to march on Ravenna in support of his cause.

In the decade before the sudden death of Rua in 434 court politics in the West were dominated by Galla Placidia's attempts to curb Aetius' growing influence. Galla preferred to rely on his main rival, Boniface, commander of imperial forces in North Africa. Boniface had always supported Galla and her son, sending them money when they were forced to flee Ravenna for Constantinople. After Honorius' death, he had refused to join Aetius in supporting John. Given his unstinting loyalty, it was with some sadness and much scepticism that in 427 Galla Placidia faced Aetius' claim that Boniface was planning a revolt. Rather than trust Aetius, she decided to test the truth of his allegations by recalling Boniface from North Africa and giving him an opportunity to clear his name. This was precisely what Aetius had predicted Galla would do. He had already written to Boniface, warning him of a conspiracy to deprive him of his command. To return to Ravenna, Aetius advised, would be to walk into a carefully laid trap. Boniface decided to wait and see whether he would be ordered back to court. When Galla's instruction arrived, Boniface, now believing that there really was a plot against him, refused to comply.

At court Aetius pointed to Boniface's failure to follow a clear imperial directive as certain proof of his intention to revolt. Boniface now had few options. Once he had disobeyed Galla, he doubted he could convince her of his innocence. Reluctantly, he declared North Africa independent of the empire. Ironically, Aetius' false accusation had turned out to be true. For two years troops loyal to Boniface held off reinforcements sent from Italy to suppress the 'rebellion', as Aetius always insisted it should be called. The stalemate was broken in spring 429 by the Vandal invasion. Aetius also blamed this on Boniface. It was, he alleged, all part of the same treasonous pattern of disloyalty: Boniface had concluded a secret pact with Geiseric and they had agreed to divide North Africa between them. It had been Boniface who had connived to help the Vandals cross the Strait of Gibraltar and then deliberately failed to defend Roman territory.

There was no substance to Aetius' slurs. If Boniface had been slow to prevent the Vandal advance, it was due to the need to keep units in reserve to protect himself. No doubt too Geiseric had taken advantage of the Romans' failure to present a united front. Given the seriousness of the Vandal invasion, no one could reasonably object to Galla Placidia seeking to reach an agreement with Boniface, whom she now believed the excusable victim of Aetius' intrigue. All, even Aetius' strongest allies, would recognise the overriding importance of ensuring that North Africa remained Roman. Envoys sent to Carthage easily settled the matter and Boniface was restored to his command. In 431 the army in North Africa was strengthened by the arrival of the task force from the East under Theodosius' trusted general Flavius Aspar.

Aetius, despite the revelation of his dirty dealing, which he strenuously denied, remained in post. He was powerful enough to resist any opposition. With a large part of the western imperial army committed against the Vandals, Galla Placidia was not prepared to risk destabilising Italy or chance the possible intervention of the Huns. As she was all too well aware, no other general could claim such privileged access to military assets outside the empire. In 430 Aetius, as he had done five years earlier, extracted a high price for keeping the peace: he demanded and received supreme command over all Roman troops in the West. For Galla Placidia, this was one humiliation too many. She was after all the daughter, half-sister and mother of emperors. It was intolerable that she should suffer the threats of a man who was prepared to use the empire's enemies for his own ends. She had not struggled to put Valentinian on the throne to have him overshadowed by an upstart general who had once supported a usurper.

Two years later Galla decided on confrontation. In 432 the situation in North Africa was stable – after an initial setback, Roman forces had blocked any further Vandal advance – and, critically, news of Octar's death and the massacre of the Hun army by the Burgundians had reached Ravenna. Galla calculated that, following such a defeat, Aetius would not be able to rely on the support of his friends beyond the Danube. Boniface was recalled from North Africa. This time there was no doubt that he would obey the summons. In Rome, the ancient capital of empire, he was made joint supreme commander in the West. He was also invested with the hallowed title of 'patrician'. A thousand years earlier this hereditary rank had marked out the oldest and most important families in the Roman republic. Now it was a coveted honour conferred only on the most senior courtiers and generals. As joint supreme commander Boniface was Aetius' equal; as a patrician, technically his superior. It was a nicely calibrated insult, deliberately intended to provoke a response.

Aetius, on campaign in France, hurried back to Italy to challenge his newly promoted rival. Suspecting this, Galla had urged Boniface never to travel without a large bodyguard. The clash took place in late 432 outside the town of Rimini, thirty miles down the coast from Ravenna. This was an intensely personal conflict, and in the middle of the battle the two Roman generals faced each other. It was later rumoured that, in anticipation of confronting his rival, Aetius had ordered his lance to be lengthened so that he could attack while remaining out of reach of Boniface's sword. Aetius, it was said, had no intention of offering a fair fight, especially if that meant compromising his chances of killing his opponent. In the struggle Boniface was fatally wounded and Aetius forced to flee. Galla Placidia had given Boniface good advice. His troops had defeated Aetius' men, yet even she had not foreseen that in single combat Aetius might cheat to win.

Now a rebel, stripped of his commission and fearing for his life,

Aetius had only one option left. Travelling in secret he made it by boat to the Croatian coast. Riding mostly at night he did not rest until he had passed the Danube frontier and reached the Great Hungarian Plain. It was nine years since Aetius had visited the Huns. Then he had brought John's gold to back up his promises of victory; this time he could only offer the prospect of plunder. Some of his former supporters, Attila perhaps amongst them, were persuaded of the merits of sending forces west to attack Italy while a large part of the Roman army was engaged in North Africa. Rua remained unconvinced: his concern was with those tribes north of the Danube still resisting Hun domination. No doubt he listened closely to Aetius' account of the Vandal invasion and the extent of Theodosius' military commitment. Indeed it may be that this information was one important factor in Rua's sudden decision the following year to attack the eastern empire. After all, compared to Ravenna, Constantinople was the bigger prize.

Rua offered to help, but it is unlikely that he was prepared to risk more than a small force. Aetius' response was to chance everything on an outrageous gamble. He brilliantly exploited the Huns' terrifying reputation. They had marched against the western Roman empire once before, who was to say they would not do so again? Returning to northern Italy in autumn 433, Aetius dismissed any suggestion that the Huns had been weakened by Octar's defeat. Thousands of Huns, he confidently claimed, would soon follow behind him. When reports of Aetius' triumphal progress reached Ravenna, Galla Placidia feared that she might lose everything. After all, in 425 a real Hun army had missed rescuing John by only seventy-two hours. With large numbers of imperial troops still on active service in North Africa she could not risk calling Aetius' bluff. Galla Placidia knew when to cut her losses: Aetius was reinstated as supreme commander with the title of patrician, taking possession of Boniface's estates and marrying his widow. In return Aetius agreed to halt the Hun advance. His was certainly the easier half of the bargain.

Success in politics is often as much a matter of dare as it is of truth. Real political skill lies in the persuasive presentation of unproven possibilities as though they are facts. Subsequent investigations matter little: they are the dusty business of historians and judicial commissions. Those in power have long since moved on to new concerns. The following year, when Rua suddenly died while advancing on

1.–2. Emperor Valens, medallion from the Şimleu Silvaniei treasure.

3. The Great Hungarian Plain, early-twentieth-century painting.

4. Cauldron from Törtel-Czakóhalom.

5. Cauldron from Uighur
in Ürümqui Museum.

6. Rock drawings from Minusinsk.

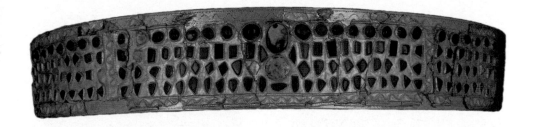

7. Csorna diadem.

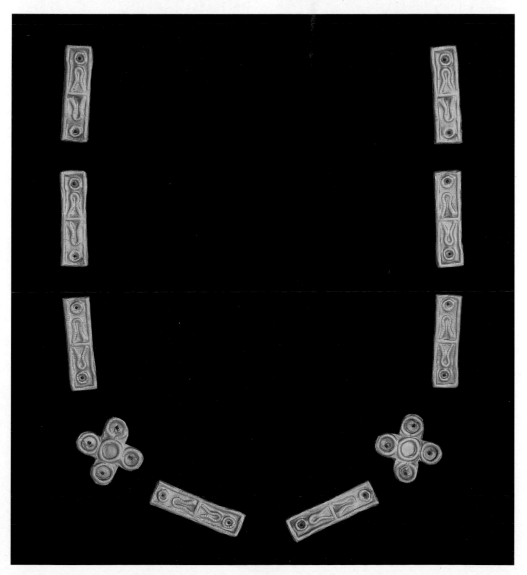

8. Gold harness decoration from Pannonhalma.

9. Emperor Honorius.

10. Galla Placidia.

11. Emperor
Theodosius II.

12. Theodosian Walls.

13.–14. Mevlevihane Gate and inscription commemorating the rebuilding of the walls after the earthquake in 447.

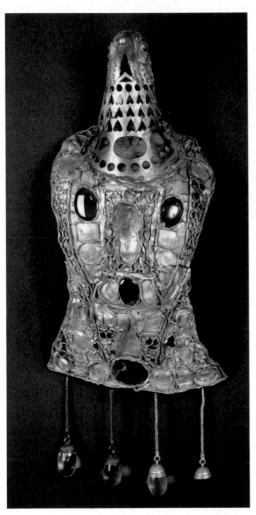

15. Eagle brooch from the Pietroasa treasure.

16. Nineteenth-century restoration of the brooch.

17. Shallow bowl from the Pietroasa treasure.

18. Drinking cup from the Pietroasa treasure.

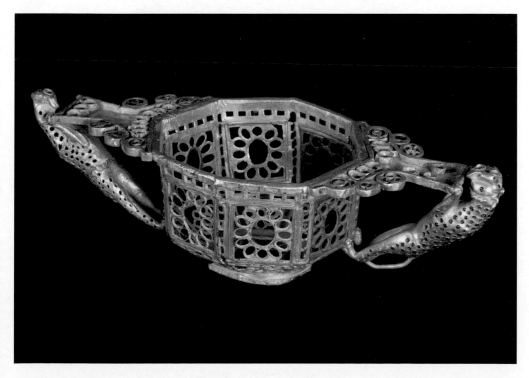

19. Sword from Pannonhalma.

20. *The Warlord's Sword*, nineteenth-century painting.

Constantinople, Galla Placidia may have wondered whether the Huns had ever consented to march their army west to support Aetius. Had they given him victory with only a few horsemen? This was the bitterest of speculations. Perhaps then it occurred to Galla Placidia that, had she held her nerve in the face of Aetius' most audacious falsehood, she might have eliminated him and gained undisputed control of the West for her son.

If not particularly loyal to Valentinian, Aetius believed in a united and coherent western Roman empire. This was still an imperial ideal worth fighting for, although increasingly difficult to defend. Despite his many victories in the last ten years, Roman rule in France was far from secure. The Goths, now settled in the south-west with their capital at Toulouse, were dissatisfied with their landlocked territory and threatened to push through to the Mediterranean. The Burgundians, who had successfully fought off Octar's Huns in 430, remained a dangerous presence on the Rhine, where they had recently seized more land on the Roman side of the river. Lastly, the Bagaudae, a blanket term for a loose alliance of small landholders and their supporters concentrated north of the Loire, refused to recognise the authority of the imperial government. In their rebellious view it was too distant and too weak to protect them or collect their taxes.

Aetius was aware that Roman forces in France were insufficient to deal with all these difficulties. In 435 he again turned to the Huns, hoping that Attila and Bleda might be persuaded to commit troops to a campaign in the West. Perhaps he reckoned that the Hun retreat after the death of Rua might have made the prospect of another expedition against the eastern empire less immediately attractive. No doubt too Aetius felt safer commanding Huns rather than those Roman soldiers who had fought loyally under Boniface in North Africa. The Huns' presence would also silence rumours at court that his much-advertised special relationship was no more than threatening talk. In inviting Attila and Bleda to send troops, Aetius aimed to confound his critics. He would demonstrate that he could still rely on the Huns, and he would use them to support, not undermine, Roman interests in France.

Attila and Bleda, or perhaps mainly Attila, considered Aetius' proposition. The brothers were unwilling to divert significant military

resources away from the immediate aim of consolidating their own
authority. Recognising these concerns, Aetius offered a guarantee that
Roman troops would not contest the extension of Hun control into
part of two frontier provinces, Pannonia and Valeria. In effect, the
western empire conceded a broad belt of land about a hundred miles
wide facing the Danube as it turns sharply upriver from modern
Budapest (at the so-called Great Danube Bend) and runs south for 200
miles before again turning, more gradually, and flowing east through
Serbia. Aetius, with or without Valentinian's approval, was prepared
to sacrifice ultimately indefensible territory along the Danube frontier. This was neither an easy nor, as Aetius' critics were quick to point
out, a particularly patriotic solution to the problem of the Goths and
Bagaudae. Aetius' response was simple: the western empire could
either retain its core possessions in France or protect its less prosperous Danube provinces, but not both.

What clinched the deal was Aetius' offer of a joint offensive against
the Burgundians. For Attila the campaign made good sense. On
balance, rather than deal with the instability that might result from
an aggressive Burgundian kingdom, he could see the benefits of a
clear and defensible western border with the Roman empire. After
all, for the last four centuries the Romans had shown no interest in
holding territory across the Rhine. Attila had also learned much from
studying the difficulties that had dogged Theodosius' campaigns in
Mesopotamia and North Africa. The history of the Roman empire in
the century after Constantine had starkly exposed the dangers of
fighting on two fronts at once. To Attila the benefits of eliminating
the Burgundians and strengthening his alliance with Aetius were clear.
With the Rhine frontier secured, and the western empire relinquishing
its responsibility to defend part of Pannonia and Valeria, he could
again think of crossing the Danube further east and pushing towards
Constantinople.

The alliance of Romans and Huns was an overwhelming success.
In 436 the Burgundians were checked and a truce agreed. The next
year they were wiped out. Roman writers, all too aware that the
Burgundians had only recently converted to Christianity following
their defeat of Octar, were horrified at the inhumanity of the Hun
death squads. The monk Prosper of Aquitaine, who published the

final edition of his *Chronicle* in Rome in the 450s, noted grimly that 'the Huns destroyed the Burgundians root and branch'. In a pitiless act of ethnic cleansing more than 20,000 men, women and children were said to have been butchered. Only the briefest account of this extermination survives. The details must be left to the imagination: terrified families pulled out of hiding, the cruel certainty of death, the corpses of the slain left in heaps to rot. Roman commanders failed to prevent the slaughter. Perhaps they regarded it as a necessary cost of ensuring the preservation of the Roman empire, the bloody price to be paid for a joint expedition with the Huns.

At the same time as the liquidation of the Christian Burgundians, Hun and Roman troops under Litorius, one of Aetius' senior officers, moved west to terrorise the Bagaudae into submission. Pacification followed swiftly as the Bagaudae's leaders were rounded up, perhaps following the selective targeting of a few villages. A laconic notice by one Roman historian offers only the brutal bottom line: 'when some of the leaders of the revolt had been thrown into chains and others killed, the insurrection caused by the Bagaudae was suppressed'. Litorius then turned south to deal with the Goths. As the army marched through the rich countryside of the Auvergne in central France, Hun raiding parties split off from the main column to attack farms and villages. Litorius did nothing to restrain them. Perhaps, like Aetius, he regarded the looting of the estates of even the most loyal of the empire's supporters as part of the unavoidable cost of maintaining Roman rule in France.

Certainly, if challenged, Aetius and Litorius could rightly claim that without the help of the Huns neither the Burgundians nor the Bagaudae would have been defeated, nor could the Goths be brought back into line. In 436, while Hun and Roman forces were fighting the Burgundians, the Goths took the opportunity to attack Narbo (modern Narbonne) eighty miles south-east of Toulouse. Narbonne was a prosperous Mediterranean port at the mouth of the River Aude founded nearly six centuries earlier. It stood at the intersection of two great highways, the via Domitia, which connected Italy to Spain, and the via Aquitania, which ran north-west to the Atlantic coast, following the Aude through Toulouse and Bordeaux. Something of Narbonne's substantial trading wealth is still visible beneath the rue Roger de Lisle in a vast underground warehouse, the only surviving part of one of the large covered markets that once crowded the town centre.

For the Goths, who were aiming to dominate the main access routes between south-west France and the Mediterranean, control of Narbonne was a prime objective. This they hoped to achieve by blockading the town and starving it into submission. It was only the arrival of Litorius' troops in late 437 that broke the siege. The hungry citizens cheered the Hun horsemen, who, according to Prosper of Aquitaine, each carried a sack of grain. The following year both Aetius and Litorius continued to press the Goths. In 439 Litorius, now instructed by Aetius to continue the campaign alone, reached Toulouse. Not all Romans applauded his success. In Marseille, the commercial rival of Narbonne 150 miles along the coast, the monk Salvian doubted God's continuing support for a Roman empire willing to use pagan Huns to subdue Christian Goths. In Salvian's view something was fundamentally wrong when 'the Romans presumed to put their hope in Huns and the Goths dared to trust in God'.

Those committed Christians who shared Salvian's concerns must have been further dismayed when Litorius refused to negotiate with bishops sent by the Goths as peace envoys. Before the walls of Toulouse he permitted the Huns to sacrifice to their gods and agreed to consult their soothsayers. The Huns predicted the outcome of significant events by scapulimancy, a ritual in which the shoulder blades of a sacrificed animal are carefully cleaned and then exposed to fire. It is the pattern of cracks and fissures in the bone caused by the heat that the sooth-sayer interprets. This method of divination was not used by either the Romans or the Goths within the Hun empire; it was a survival of an ancient religious practice from the steppes of central Asia.

The performance of these alien rites must have been an extra-ordinary sight for both the Romans in Litorius' army and the Christian Goths looking down from the battlements. This was the last time in the long history of the Roman empire that one of its generals would consult the old gods on the outcome of a battle. In approving these sacrifices, Litorius may not have intended any polemical purpose; at worst, he may have had to square his own faith with the need to ensure the Huns' continued loyalty. Allowing the Huns freedom of religious expression may have weighed less heavily on Litorius' Christian conscience than having to turn a blind eye to their raiding parties. More intolerant anti-pagan campaigners like Prosper of Aquitaine or Salvian of Marseille allowed no such latitude. Litorius, it was claimed, had ignored the advice of his junior officers and, trusting in Hun soothsayers and the evil demons they had consulted, was determined to attack Toulouse and crush the Goths. For a while the battle hung in the balance. To some it seemed that the Huns might break through and the Goths suffer the cruel fate of the Burgundians. But then some good luck (or perhaps a miracle): Litorius was captured and the battle turned as the Goths steadily advanced. By nightfall the Huns had been routed, and a few days later Litorius was executed. In case his readers had been slow to draw the correct moral conclusion from this clash between patient god-fearing Goths and arrogant Hun-loving Romans, Salvian, quoting from the *Gospel of Luke*, pointedly observed that the truth of the New Testament had been vindicated: 'Everyone who exalts himself will be humbled, and he who humbles himself will be exalted.'

The year before the Huns were humiliated beneath the walls of Toulouse, Theodosius and his advisers had discussed the possibility of a treaty. The timing was right and the arguments persuasive. Since Rua's death four years earlier there had been little activity on the Danube frontier. Attila and Bleda may also have recognised the greater degree of unity between the East and the West. A joint expedition had halted the Vandals and the treaty that followed ensured that Carthage and the richest provinces in North Africa remained part of the empire. In 437, the same year in which both the Burgundians and the Bagaudae were suppressed, Valentinian journeyed to Constantinople to claim the long-promised hand of Theodosius' daughter Licinia Eudoxia. The imperial couple honeymooned at Thessalonica in northern Greece before returning to Ravenna.

Attila, and perhaps too Bleda, could see the benefits of an agreement. A secure border along the Danube would allow them to continue with the consolidation of the Hun empire. It was probably the unwelcome news of the defeat of Litorius that finally convinced them.

Peace would give the Huns a breathing space to recover their military strength. It would allow the brothers to restore their damaged authority by attacking carefully selected targets in northern and eastern Europe, campaigns more likely to end in victory than an expedition across the Danube. A treaty with Theodosius would also mark a significant policy shift away from involvement in the internal politics of the Roman empire. Rua – Attila might now have admitted – had been right to refuse help to Aetius. It would have been wiser for the Hun troops to have returned home after destroying the Burgundians. Hun forces operated best under their own leaders and when pursuing their own objectives; they should never have been at Toulouse fighting someone else's war.

Hun and Roman envoys met in winter 439 at Margum, an important market town at the confluence of the Morava and Danube, forty miles west of modern Belgrade. Theodosius sent Flavius Plinta, one of his senior commanders, and Epigenes, an experienced court official responsible for drafting imperial legislation. The Huns were represented by Attila and Bleda. The summit opened with a dispute over protocol: the Huns refused to dismount from their horses while the Romans declined to stand and look up at them. In the end Plinta reluctantly conceded that all talks should be held on horseback. Already saddle-sore, Epigenes, more accustomed to the comforts of Constantinople, must have felt himself at a painful disadvantage. After some negotiation the parties ratified a four-point peace plan. The Romans were to return all Hun refugees and not offer any assistance to those who crossed the Danube. They were not to enter into an alliance with any people who were enemies of the Huns. Trading rights between the two states were confirmed on an equal basis. The Romans were to make an annual payment of 700 pounds of gold directly to Attila and Bleda.

This was a good deal for both sides. Added to the agreement reached with Aetius in 435 on the extension of Hun rule into territory once part of the western empire, Attila and Bleda had now reduced the threat of hostile military action along a substantial part of the Danube frontier. They had also strengthened their own position by ensuring that they received the payments of gold personally and by demanding the repatriation of asylum-seekers whose loyalties might be suspect. No risks were taken, particularly with those who had been in Roman custody for some time. Their very presence across the frontier was evidence of their hostility to Attila and Bleda and their regime, and there was always the danger that they might agree to lead a rebellion financed by the empire. As soon as they were handed back, two young boys, both blood relations of Attila and Bleda, were impaled. Their execution was a warning to any potential rivals, or to those who might seek to use junior members of the ruling family as the focus for opposition.

For their part, the Romans, in agreeing to the treaty at Margum, had paid a reasonable price for a peace that allowed troops currently committed to the defence of the Balkans to be released (if needed) for deployment elsewhere. It offered a more immediate solution to border control than another expensive investment in recruitment or upgraded fortifications. A secure northern frontier gave the empire the strategic flexibility it needed, especially with the Vandals now occupying part of North Africa. Following the talks with Attila and Bleda at Margum, Theodosius might have been satisfied that – after nearly a century of intermittent conflict – he could at last proclaim with confidence that he had achieved peace on the Danube.

# Shock and Awe

A few weeks after peace broke out on the Danube, war was resumed in North Africa. On 19 October 439 the Vandals, led by Geiseric, seized Carthage in direct violation of the treaty agreed in 435. This was another challenge to the integrity of the empire. As one contemporary noted, it was 585 years since Carthage had been conquered by Rome. That victory was only achieved after nearly a century of fighting. Three long conflicts, known as the Punic Wars, had stretched the Romans to their limits. In the Second Punic War they almost lost to the great Carthaginian general Hannibal, who in 218 BC marched his army of 50,000 men, 9,000 cavalry and thirty-seven elephants out of Spain, across southern France and over the Alps into Italy. Two years later at Cannae Hannibal nearly wiped out the Roman army, killing 50,000 men in a single day's fighting. This was the severest defeat ever inflicted on the Romans. The casualty rate was not matched again until the Battle of Adrianople when, in one sun-baked afternoon, the Goths killed 20,000 troops and the emperor Valens.

The Romans recovered from Cannae. Forcing Hannibal to withdraw from Italy, they went on to crush Carthage seventy years later at the end of the Third Punic War and establish one of the greatest empires in history. It was questionable whether they would ever recover from Adrianople. Since then the Eternal City had been sacked and the West reduced to a rump. In Ravenna the twenty-year-old Valentinian III could not claim to control more than Italy and France, the latter only thanks to Aetius and his Hun allies, and even they had not been able to dislodge the Goths. The loss of Carthage in the same year as Litorius was defeated at Toulouse was a strategic and financial body blow. For six centuries North African grain had helped feed the citizens of Rome. North African tax revenues had made its rulers rich. Now the city of Hannibal and some of the wealthiest provinces in the Mediterranean no longer belonged to the Romans. The empire would have to survive without them or confront Geiseric to get them back.

With the fall of Carthage, the Vandals gained access to one of the best harbours on the African coast. This was a great prize to be exploited. In both the East and the West additional measures were taken to protect major ports against an attack by sea. In late 439 work was begun to improve Constantinople's defences. The sea wall built by Constantine along the Propontis was extended to connect with the Theodosian Walls. In Italy, Valentinian, who spent the winter in Rome, ordered the city's fortifications to be repaired. Citizens were to be organised into a home guard to ensure that all towers, walls and gates were properly manned. As predicted, soon after capturing Carthage a Vandal armada set sail for Sicily. In an imperial edict issued on 24 June 440, Valentinian declared: 'Geiseric, the enemy of our empire, is reported to have issued forth from the port of Carthage with a large fleet whose swift transit and capacity for opportunistic marauding is to be feared along all coastlines . . . as it is by no means certain, particularly given the advantages of navigation during the summer, how far enemy ships may be able to sail.'

In Constantinople Theodosius was ready to go to war. The case for military action was clear. The invasion of Sicily might be the beginning of a wider Vandal offensive that could further weaken Roman control of the Mediterranean. If Geiseric chose to advance east along the African coast, his army could split Egypt off from the empire. The great commercial harbour of Alexandria might be blockaded, disrupting the shipments of grain on which Constantinople depended. The dangers of sending a task force were obvious, but it could plausibly be argued that the policies pursued over the last twenty years had brought a new stability to the Danube provinces. The Huns had not crossed the frontier since Rua's incursion in 434. That attack had followed lengthy, but inconclusive, talks conducted through envoys. By contrast, the recently ratified treaty had been negotiated with Attila and Bleda in person, and confirmed by the immediate handover of high-ranking refugees and the promised annual payment of 700 pounds of gold.

The general Flavius Aspar is likely to have disagreed. He had fought Geiseric in North Africa in the early 430s and a decade earlier defeated the usurper John in Ravenna. He was aware of the Huns' frightening ability to muster large numbers of men quickly and to move them rapidly across great distances. On this view, as long as the Vandals did not march into Libya and then Egypt, a campaign in North Africa was not worth the risk. There was no guarantee that Attila and Bleda could be trusted to respect their treaty obligations, any more than Geiseric had respected his. The Huns had crossed the Danube in 422 when the empire's troops were fighting in Mesopotamia and again in 434 when they were in North Africa. History, Aspar may tartly have observed, can have an unpleasant habit of repeating itself. The emperor was unconvinced. In his opinion those who argued against war had too hastily dismissed the treaty with Attila and Bleda. Nor had they grasped fully the pressing need to counter Geiseric. The safety of Constantinople and the security of its food supply demanded that Carthage be returned to Roman rule. Theodosius was not prepared to wait and see if Egypt was threatened. The expedition against the Vandals would go ahead and Aspar – who had failed in North Africa before – would not be in command.

The army did not set sail from Constantinople until spring 441, the year's delay an indication of the lengthy and careful preparation insisted on by Theodosius. This was not a high-spirited adventure by a reckless ruler in search of military glory. Success depended on two critical factors: the state of the northern frontier and the speed at which the Vandals could be defeated. Theodosius believed that his treaty with Attila and Bleda would hold. That was a crucial calculation: units released from Danube defence made up the bulk of the task force. By deploying these experienced legionaries, it was hoped that any Vandal resistance could be quickly overcome. As the emperor reviewed the fleet, safely moored in the harbour built by his grandfather Theodosius I, he was increasingly confident of victory. In the bright spring sunshine all looked full of promise. Led by three capable generals – Flavius Ariobindus, Ansila and Germanus – it would not be long before the army landed in Sicily and then advanced on Carthage. If the reconquest of North Africa went as planned, the troops would be back home in Constantinople by Christmas.

As soon as Attila and Bleda received reliable intelligence that the Roman fleet had left for Sicily, they opened their Danube offensive.

Given the recent heavy losses at Toulouse, the brothers had been reluctant to cross the border while the Roman army was at full strength. Under those circumstances a treaty had suited their interests. The transfer of units to the North African expeditionary force altered the balance of advantage. The Huns' first objective was Constantia across the river from Margum, where barely two years earlier Roman ambassadors had settled the terms of the peace. Then both sides had agreed to facilitate cross-border commerce. Constántia, one of the few remaining Roman forts on the north bank of the Danube, was officially designated a secure trading post. On a crowded market day the Huns struck without warning, easily taking the town in a carefully coordinated attack on its Roman garrison.

Theodosius refused to believe that Attila intended all-out war; rather it was now a matter of skilful negotiation, of understanding the Huns' grievances and moving quickly to reach an acceptable settlement. With a nice sense of irony, the emperor appointed Flavius Aspar as his envoy. Aspar's instructions were to arrange a truce and to investigate the reasons for the Huns' apparent breach of the peace accord. Arriving at the frontier, Aspar found to his discomfort that Attila regarded the treaty as void. In his view it had already been broken by the Roman authorities at Margum. The accusations were striking. The town's bishop was alleged to have crossed the Danube at night to steal valuables from Hun tombs. Even more seriously, this Christian treasure hunter was said to have desecrated burials belonging to members of Attila and Bleda's own family. (If the *strava*, as in Attila's case, had included the slaughter of servants involved in the funeral rites, this had apparently not been sufficient to conceal the location of these rich graves.) Attila demanded that the tomb-raiding bishop of Margum be handed over, along with other refugees who, it was claimed, had been offered protection, contrary to the terms of the treaty.

The facts behind these allegations are impossible to establish and it may not have been much easier for Aspar at the time. Given the Huns' open hostility to Christianity, it might be thought just too suspiciously neat that they should accuse a bishop of violating their dead. No doubt Aspar was shown evidence of looting (soil disturbed, coffins damaged and bones displaced), but there was no proof linking the bishop, or any other resident of Margum, with these crimes. Nor could Aspar be sure that these were really the tombs of Attila and

Bleda's relatives, or that they had ever contained any precious grave goods worth taking. That said, the Huns might be telling the truth. The issue of refugees was also unclear. The terms of the treaty ratified in 439 had been vague. Against the Huns' claim that the authorities at Margum had been at fault in failing to hand over fugitives, it might have been suggested that the treaty fell short of imposing any formal obligation on the Romans to round up and regularly repatriate asylum-seekers. After all, they had only undertaken 'not to offer assistance' to those crossing the Danube. While clever argument on the precise meaning of the treaty's wording might win admiring applause in Constantinople, such sophistry stood little chance of impressing the Huns on the frontier.

In the end Aspar had little diplomatic room to manoeuvre. If he admitted the charges and authorised the extradition of the bishop or any refugees, he would in effect concede that the Romans had breached the treaty and, in turn, that the Huns' attack on Constantia had been justified. On the other hand, a flat denial could result in a dangerous deadlock. Aspar is most likely to have attempted a middle course: questioning the nature and relevance of the Huns' allegations, but also welcoming negotiation on issues of mutual concern. Perhaps he suggested that there were some misunderstandings that could benefit from further amicable discussion. If Theodosius was right in believing that Attila did not want war, this approach would at least offer the opportunity for a fresh round of meetings and the possibility of agreement.

Attila did not stay to talk. For him, Aspar's failure to hand over the bishop of Margum and the refugees was the confirmation he needed that the treaty was no longer in force. Over the next nine months (from summer 441 to spring 442) the Huns attacked, captured and destroyed almost all the major cities on the middle Danube and south-east along the Morava River Valley. Roman writers, preferring not to dwell in any detail on the collapse of imperial authority along the frontier, offer only the names of the places besieged and sacked: Sirmium (modern Sremska Mitrovica), Singidunum (Belgrade), Margum (Dubrovica), Viminacium (Kostolac), Naissus (Niš), Serdica (Sofia). Of the hundreds of unfortified settlements that must also have been plundered and set on fire there is no record, not even a name. The many who risked death protecting their families and livelihoods have no memorial to their courage. The cowardly, the craven and the terror-stricken are also unknown. The arrival of a Hun raiding party at farmstead after farmstead is a story of repetitive brutality and suffering. At first a smudge on the horizon; gradually through the dust the horses and their riders take shape, then the sickening realisation that this is not help but destruction; the harsh shouts of anonymous men blankly uniform in their helmets and armour, the cruel flash of swords and the hot flow of blood. There is nothing new about the horrors of war; they do not shock until a brief list of cities destroyed becomes – at least in our imagination – a roll-call of thousands of individuals raped, enslaved or killed.

At Margum the citizens debated how best to face the Huns. Once Attila had rejected negotiation, Aspar left the city. To any who might have complained that he was deserting his post, he could point out that he did not wish to give the Huns a valuable hostage and that in any event a general is no use without an army. As an imperial envoy it was his duty to carry the news back to Constantinople. With Aspar gone, some wondered whether it might be worth trying to reach an agreement with Attila. As a gesture of goodwill they could hand over the bishop. The less pious perhaps suggested that God would be certain to approve: if the bishop was guilty then justice would be done; if he was innocent then he would undoubtedly embrace martyrdom at the hands of the Huns in return for saving his fellow Christians.

The bishop did not wait to find out whether his congregation would turn into a lynch mob. Slipping quietly out of the city and across the river, he offered to betray the town to the Huns in return for guarantees of protection. Attila accepted and no doubt smiled as he swore a binding oath on his sword, calling on the war god to preside over his pact with a Christian. That night, mindful of his own pledge invoking the saints, the bishop of Margum kept his word. He convinced those manning the town's defences that he was returning with urgent information from an undercover reconnaissance mission. (As he perhaps pointed out, his very presence before the walls demonstrated that he had not gone over to the Huns.) His story was believed: after all, he was still a bishop. He then seems to have urged a surprise attack against Attila and his men. He may have claimed that the Huns were preparing to cross the Danube and could be caught at their most vulnerable while landing. The inevitable followed: the ambush by Attila's troops who lay concealed by the riverbank, the slaughter of the remaining defenders and Margum's destruction.

Not every city fell through treachery. Part of the success of Attila's Danube campaign lay in his army's skill at siege warfare. Seventy years earlier the inability to take Roman strongholds, and to seize the treasure and grain stored there, had hampered the Goths' offensive after Adrianople. Attila ensured that the Huns had mastered siege technology and were able to attack and capture fortified cities using textbook Roman military tactics. It is likely that these were learned from prisoners of war, some, like the bishop of Margum, willing to strike a bargain to ensure their survival. It was this new expertise that made Attila's Huns a much more formidable enemy than any that had previously penetrated the Danube cordon. The Romans could no longer depend on well-defended cities to act as islands of security in a hostile countryside, protecting supplies, people and wealth.

In attacking Naissus the Huns first crossed the river that protected part of the walls and then brought up tall cranes mounted on wheels. Shielded by light willow screens covered with rawhide, men positioned high up on the arm of each crane were able to fire arrows directly over the battlements. Once a stretch of walls had been cleared of defenders, the cranes were replaced by battering rams. Priscus of Panium, who described the siege in detail, was particularly impressed by the rams' size and effectiveness. 'The ram is a very large machine. A beam with a sharp metal point is suspended on chains hung loosely from a V-shaped timber frame . . . With short ropes attached to the rear of the ram, men vigorously swing the beam away from the target and then release it, so that as a result of the force the section of wall opposite the ram is completely demolished.'

Naissus was wiped off the map. Its population was killed, dispersed or captured and sold as slaves. The city would not be rebuilt for another century. Seven years after Attila's attack Priscus found it deserted save for a handful of monks whose unceasing prayers rose thinly above the desolation. His travelling companions took some time to find a clean place to pitch camp. The ground towards the river, where the battering rams had smashed through, was strewn with the bleached bones of the slain. Looking back at the shattered walls, it was difficult to believe that only 150 years ago Naissus had been the birthplace of the emperor Constantine, who had cherished and beautified his hometown. All that had been brutally obliterated by Attila and his Huns. Now the ruins sheltered only religious fanatics who looked forward with joyous expectation to the end of the world. For these Christian holy men, the burnt-out shell of a once great imperial city must have seemed a fitting place to wait patiently for the Apocalypse.

In the golden throne room of the Great Palace in Constantinople Theodosius sat in sullen silence. Each day messengers brought news of the Huns' steady progress. Unable to assemble an army large enough to oppose them in the field, the emperor had little option but to hope that Attila's insistence on taking each city in turn would slow his advance. Under the circumstances, there was only one possible course of action: peace would have to be concluded swiftly with Geiseric and the task force recalled. Roman troops had been in Sicily for the best part of a year and had not yet attempted to capture Carthage. Aware of the deteriorating situation on the Danube frontier, their commanders had been understandably reluctant to commit to what they knew might be a long and difficult war against the Vandals.

Geiseric did not overplay his advantage. He was all too aware that if the northern frontier was stabilised there could be another attempt at reconquest. It was in the Vandals' long-term interests to compromise and allow themselves time to consolidate their hold over the territory they had seized. The partitioning of North Africa, first sanctioned under the treaty of 435, was renegotiated. The most fertile part (an area slightly larger than modern Tunisia) with Carthage as its capital was formally recognised as Vandal territory. The rest of the African coast (roughly Algeria and Morocco), including some of Numidia originally ceded in 435, was retained as part of the western Roman empire. To avoid giving any pressing cause for war, Geiseric also agreed to pay an annual sum to Valentinian's government, reducing the immediate consequences of the loss of African tax revenue.

The fleet returned to Constantinople in spring 442, too late to prevent the fall of Naissus. Attila, by then as far forward as Serdica, decided not to chance any direct conflict with the newly reinforced Roman army. The Huns marched in good order through a devastated provincial landscape back to the Great Hungarian Plain. This had been a substantial victory. The destruction of the main cities in the central sector of the Danube had punched a hole in the empire's frontier defences. The capture of Naissus and raids east of Serdica had opened the way to Constantinople. Attila used the loot brought back from the Danube provinces to his advantage. Booty and captives were distributed to reward and reinforce the loyalty of leading Huns and their supporters. The golden bowl from the Pietroasa treasure, with its delicately modelled scenes of gods and goddesses, may have been snatched from a grand house in Sirmium, Singidunum or Naissus. It may have been taken by a Goth fighting alongside the Huns, or it may have been a generous gift from Attila, part of a carefully calculated distribution of spoils deliberately intended to tighten his personal control over the Hun empire.

Of Attila's steady strengthening of his own authority, Roman writers – focused on the wreckage that followed the Huns' attacks – have almost nothing to say. At some point during the three years after the campaign Attila decided to challenge Bleda. This may have been a long and bitter struggle. Bleda may also have secured his own position by giving lavish presents of Roman gold to comrades and relatives. Many may have felt that, as the elder brother, he had every right to demand an equal share of empire. On the other hand, Bleda could have been unaware that Attila had any intention of ruling alone. Perhaps Bleda – boorish, violent, vulgar – never noticed a thing. Or perhaps Bleda – hearty, hospitable, open-handed – laughingly dismissed the idea that his kid brother was capable of such treachery. Or perhaps Bleda – shrewd, nasty, cunning – fought viciously like a trapped animal to hold on to power.

Regrettably these rivalries cannot be reconstructed. In the years immediately following the Huns' invasion the Romans had only the haziest idea of events on the Great Hungarian Plain. That is reflected in the terse notices in the histories of the mid-440s that do no more than register a scatter of matters outside the empire. It is as though all that remained of a newspaper were a few torn headlines. The detailed stories are lost, the particular circumstances and precise chain of events open to endless speculation. Only one thing is sure: in the brief words of the most reliable Roman account, in 445, three years after Hun troops had returned home from their Danube offensive, 'Bleda, king of the Huns, was assassinated as a result of the plots of his brother Attila.'

# Barbarians at the Gates

Even modern monarchs who claim to dislike the pomp and circumstance of state occasions (and make it known that they would prefer to ride a bicycle) rarely walk barefoot though the main streets of their capital cities. Roman emperors, regarded by many of their subjects as closer to heaven than earth, understood the importance of ceremonial displays of power. In front of their admiring subjects they appeared in all the scintillating magnificence of their imperial office: heavy purple robes, bejewelled diadem, pearl earrings and gem-encrusted shoes. If they left the protected confines of the Great Palace, they rode in a golden carriage pulled by a pair of snow-white mules. Above them dragon-shaped standards (made from imported Chinese silk) fluttered in the breeze; on either side marched a double line of troops in scarlet uniforms, their burnished shields and gilded parade armour flashing in the sun. Crowds greeted the procession with cheers and applause. Young men scrabbled across rooftops or rushed ahead in the hope of getting a better view. Screened by his bodyguard, the emperor sat rigid and unmoved with his gaze firmly fixed ahead. He did not wave or smile. Amidst such shimmering splendour he was transfigured. To awestruck onlookers the emperor seemed more like a statue than a man; no longer an individual, he now appeared as a glittering icon of imperial power.

On 26 January 447 Theodosius II refused to wear jewels or a diadem. He dismissed his golden carriage and bodyguard and set out into the city dressed only in a simple white robe. The emperor walked barefoot, his feet bleeding and his forehead glistening with sweat, the seven long miles along the hard marble-paved streets of Constantinople from the Great Palace to the military parade ground at the Hebdomon beyond the Theodosian Walls. He was followed by high-ranking dignitaries and a great crowd of citizens. At the Hebdomon they all chanted the *Trisagion*, the invocation (still in daily use in the Eastern Orthodox Church) that a decade earlier was said to have been revealed by angels: 'Holy God, Holy Mighty One, Holy Immortal One, have mercy upon us.'

The normally prosperous and self-confident residents of the imperial capital, who assumed as a matter of course that God was on their side, were in penitent and prayerful mood. In the dark hours of the early morning of 26 January a severe earthquake had shaken the city. Educated people in the fifth century knew how earthquakes happened (that had been worked out 800 years earlier by the Greek philosopher Aristotle): they were the result of the sudden movement of vast bodies of air in huge voids deep underground. For many Christians Aristotle might have explained what caused the earth to shake, but not what caused the air to move in the first place. These tremors, it was believed, were in accordance with the will of God who sought to turn sinners to repentance. An earthquake was a warning from heaven – not a notion that would have appealed to Aristotle. The sight of a barefoot emperor walking painfully through the city was an indication of how seriously God's purpose was to be taken.

On the way to the Hebdomon the scale of the destruction was clearly visible. The recently completed sea wall along the shores of the Propontis was severely damaged. Great stretches of the Theodosian Walls were now heaps of rubble: fifty-seven towers had collapsed. The city lay wide open to any invading army. That alone was sufficient reason for an emperor to cast off his royal robes and join his people in prayer. This was a spectacular act of public penance that might ensure divine protection for the city, yet only Theodosius and his closest advisers appreciated how desperate the situation was. They looked at the defenceless capital in the terrifying knowledge that, shortly before the earthquake shattered the Theodosian Walls, the northern frontier had been breached. According to the latest military intelligence, Attila and his Huns had already begun a new Danube offensive. 'Holy God, Holy Mighty One, Holy Immortal One, have mercy upon us.'

Towards the end of 446, a few months prior to the earthquake, Attila had sent diplomatic letters to the imperial court again insisting that any asylum-seekers who had crossed the Danube be handed over. He also demanded the back-payment of the 700 pounds of gold a year that had been agreed in 439 at Margum. (Perhaps only one or two instalments had been received before war broke out in 441.) Theodosius refused to hand over either the money or the refugees. He proposed instead to send ambassadors and begin talks on these disputed issues. The emperor knew the risks involved: five years earlier Flavius Aspar's offer to discuss the night-time activities of the bishop of Margum and the aid allegedly given to those escaping across the frontier had been brushed aside with an immediately hostile response.

This time Theodosius was confident of containing any Hun attack. The legions protecting the Danube provinces were now back to strength and the frontier defences had recently been reviewed. In September 443 senior officers had been instructed to ensure that those under their command were properly trained and fully paid. The emperor, seeking to encourage the permanent settlement of land near the border, confirmed that rank-and-file soldiers were permitted to own farms along the Danube free of all rents and taxes. An annual audit of troop strength and condition reports on both river patrol craft and army camps were now to be submitted to officials at the imperial court every January. Theodosius was robust in setting out the benefits he hoped would flow from these reforms. 'For we believe that if military affairs are organised exactly as we have decreed, then in whatever territory an enemy might be tempted to invade, a victory that is advantageous to us (according to the will of God) will be proclaimed – even before any battle.'

Undaunted by such grand claims, Attila rejected outright Theodosius' suggestion of negotiation. The Huns opened their offensive by taking Roman forts along the frontier, including Ratiaria the headquarters of the Danube fleet. This was a more rapid and damaging attack than had been expected. With the Huns only sixty miles northeast of Naissus (or at least its blackened ruins), Theodosius may still have been prepared to chance war, or he may now have preferred to offer concessions in return for peace. Whatever the emperor's plans, they were wrecked by the earthquake in January 447. The priority was now the security of the imperial capital. The pious chants of its citizens and their barefoot ruler might move the divinity to support the Roman cause and protect the city. As some of the emperor's advisers quietly observed, it would now take a miracle to repair the Theodosian Walls before Attila reached Constantinople.

Although never doubting the power of prayer, the praetorian prefect of the East, Flavius Constantinus, had no intention of waiting for God to come to Constantinople's rescue. He speedily organised gangs of skilled artisans and labourers to work on the walls. These were joined by members of the Blues and the Greens, the two main sporting associations in the city whose fanatical followers were more accustomed to cheering on their teams in the chariot races held in the hippodrome. Like modern football or baseball clubs, the Blues and the Greens were both well managed. They each had a professional staff of highly trained charioteers involved in talent-spotting, coaching, selection and the running of the games. More visible were the fans, who at the races sat together in designated rows. The most dedicated had identical haircuts and wore green (or blue) tunics with huge, baggy sleeves that billowed out like flags whenever they waved their arms to urge on their favourites.

Successful charioteers were celebrities in Constantinople. Statues were erected in their honour and their lavish lifestyles admired and imitated. In the hippodrome the entry of these superstars might be greeted with as much applause as the appearance of the emperor; after all, it was the races that the crowd had come to see. Excited supporters shouted in praise of their heroes and their athletic prowess – both on and off the racetrack – and insulted their opponents. The rhythmic barracking of the cheer squads and their obscene verbal sparring were all part of the excitement. They added to the thrill of watching charioteers expertly manoeuvre their horses along the narrow straights and around the dangerously tight turns at either end of the course. Sometimes the intense competition between the Blues and the Greens spilled out into the city. Residents of Constantinople regularly blamed fires, street fights and vandalism on hooligans leaving the hippodrome.

It was then all the more remarkable that the praetorian prefect was able to marshal these rowdy sports fans. Unsurprisingly, the Blues refused to cooperate with the Greens. That too the prefect turned to his advantage, allocating the rival clubs different sections of the broken defences and encouraging them to compete against each other. They worked without break for sixty days; during the night masons cut and laid stones by torchlight. For all involved, this was a deadly serious race: not between pampered charioteers and their sleekly groomed horses, but between terrified Romans and advancing Huns. The Romans were victorious – but only just. The Theodosian Walls were repaired in time to discourage Attila from attacking the imperial capital.

The memorial to this extraordinary feat by an exhausted populace is still visible. Before reaching the impenetrable confusion of Istanbul's vast and dusty bus station, one of the city's main thoroughfares, Millet Caddesi, cuts its way through the Theodosian Walls. Just to the south is the Mevlevihane Gate. Yeni Mevlevihane Kapısı (as it is called in Turkish) belongs to an older and less hurried world. It is just wide enough for a donkey, or for a swiftly skilful moped rider who knows that the passage through the walls – as an extra defensive measure – sharply narrows. To the left of the gateway in the outer wall is a greyish marble slab cemented securely into the stonework precisely where Flavius Constantinus ordered it fixed more than 1,500 years ago (see plates, pictures 13–14). On the slab a laconic inscription in Latin is still clearly legible:

THEODOSII IVSSIS GEMINO NEC MENSE PERACTO
CONSTANTINVS OVANS HAEC MOENIA FIRMA LOCAVIT
TAM CITO TAM STABILEM PALLAS VIX CONDERET ARCEM

'By Theodosius' command, Constantinus triumphantly built these strong walls in less than two months. Pallas could hardly have built such a secure citadel in so short a time.'

This was a proud boast. In the scale and speed of the undertaking, the restored Theodosian Walls surpassed any fortifications that might have been raised by Pallas Athene, the divine protectress of cities and patron of Athens. (Athens' natural citadel, the great limestone rock of the Acropolis, was still dominated by Athene's wondrously beautiful temple. The Parthenon, built 900 years earlier, was now a church dedicated to the Virgin Mary.) Constantinus had every reason to be satisfied with his achievements. He had seen off his critics – as always there were some who regarded the whole scheme as ill-advised – and accomplished more than those who had prayed for some heaven-sent deliverance. By rebuilding Constantinople's defences, the prefect had outdone even a Greek goddess. By completing the project in only sixty days, he had actually made a miracle happen.

*

Despite the damage caused by the earthquake in January 447, Attila was not prepared to jeopardise the success of his offensive with a sudden push to Constantinople. Two obstacles lay between the frontier and the capital. Firstly, Attila was reluctant to leave any well-defended cities in Roman hands. At the end of the campaign, or if a rapid retreat were needed, these might compromise the safe return of his troops to the Danube. Secondly, and more importantly, Attila must have been aware that, although he had broken through the frontier defences, as he marched towards Constantinople he would face a Roman army that had not been depleted by the need to oppose either the Persians or the Vandals. Rather than rush to the capital, it was more prudent for the Hun army to advance steadily and then meet – or choose to avoid – any serious opposition.

So, after taking Ratiaria, the Huns moved to attack the major cities and forts that stood between them and Constantinople. As in 441–2, Roman historians, as if too shocked to offer more than the briefest account of the Huns' success in 'plundering no less than seventy cities', again record only a few of the places destroyed: Philippopolis (Plovdiv), Arcadiopolis (Lüleburgaz in Turkey, one hundred miles north-west of Istanbul), Calliopolis (Gelibolu in the north of the Gallipoli Peninsula), Sestus (Eceabat to the south near Çanakkale) and Athyras (Büyükçekmece on the northern shore of the Sea of Marmara). The last place on the list is a striking indication of how close the Huns came to Constantinople. The fort of Athyras was less than twenty miles from the Theodosian Walls.

Attila's inexorable progress was also time-consuming. Philippopolis was protected by substantial walls and, like Naissus in 441–2, could only be taken by siege. The Huns also had to deal with more effective resistance the closer they came to Constantinople. Two cities managed to beat off the attackers: the well-fortified Adrianople (Edirne), near the site of the great battle between Romans and Goths, and Heraclea (Mamara Ereğli), sixty miles along the seashore from Constantinople. These slight successes might also have been connected with the activity of the Roman army, which was now directed by three veterans: Flavius Aspar, who must have been relieved to abandon diplomacy for armed response, Flavius Ariobindus, one of the leaders of the expedition against the Vandals in 441, and Arnegisclus, who commanded imperial troops in Thrace.

The army was divided between these three generals in order to cover all possible land routes to the capital. Their defensive strategy failed to halt the Hun advance, but it did slow it down. While Roman troops were never victorious in the field, they may have been able to harry the Hun marching column and compel it to move more cautiously. The capture of Callipolis and Sestus on the Gallipoli Peninsula is evidence of further deliberate diversion. Although some Roman units were defeated, their Gallipoli campaign across difficult and broken terrain did deflect Attila from the imperial capital. The cost of such tactics was high: soldiers and cities were repeatedly sacrificed to save Constantinople. Nor were Aspar and his fellow generals prepared to stake all on one decisive encounter. They elected instead to sustain severe and demoralising losses over two long and weary months to win the time needed for the rebuilding of the capital's defences. Only when that had been completed would Constantinople again be safe.

Attila and the Huns never saw the Theodosian Walls. Their assault on the Roman empire had been too successful to risk attacking the best-defended city in the Mediterranean world. The outbreak of disease in the capital and its surroundings added to Attila's unwillingness to attempt what was certain to be a long siege. He recognised the problem of provisioning a stationary army in a region already ruined by invasion and earthquake. The Huns now swung away from Constantinople and moved north to Marcianople. Like other cities obliterated in the 440s, it would not be rebuilt for another century. The need for supplies dictated that the Huns return to the Great Hungarian Plain avoiding land that had already been pillaged. About 150 miles to the west of Marcianople near the Utus River Roman forces under Arnegisclus blocked the Huns' homeward march. Only with Constantinople secure was a Roman commander prepared to deploy a substantial number of troops in such an aggressive action. During a long and exhausting engagement both armies suffered heavy casualties. Arnegisclus' horse was killed beneath him. Trapped in the middle of the fray he fought on bravely until his death. In the end the Huns gained the upper hand, but Arnegisclus – in a final bid for glory – almost managed to register the only Roman victory of the whole campaign.

Despite Arnegisclus' heroic last stand, Attila's second Danube offensive was a devastating success. He had smashed through the empire's frontier defences and brought his army within twenty miles of Constantinople. According to the sixth-century historian Marcellinus, the Huns had 'attacked and pillaged forts and cities, lacerating almost all the territory surrounding the capital'. Again Attila had skilfully exploited Roman weaknesses: in 441 the transfer of troops to deal with the Vandals in North Africa and now in 447 the disruption following a serious earthquake. Perhaps Aspar and his colleagues should have taken on the Huns in a set-piece battle, but there was always the possibility of another Adrianople. If in February or March 447 the Roman army had been wiped out in an afternoon's fighting, Constantinople would have fallen soon after and the eastern Roman empire come to an abrupt and bloody end. Even so, the narrow defeat of Arnegisclus on the banks of the Utus showed what might have been achieved. It also demonstrated that Attila was right to be wary of the Roman army. There was always the chance that he might lose.

In 447 the Huns had not embarked on an unstoppable craze of slaughter and destruction. Careful strategic thinking on Attila's part prevented a dash for Constantinople. That would have provoked a dangerous confrontation with Roman forces in the Balkans and forced – no matter what the strategic risk – the emergency recall of crack troops from the eastern frontier. Nor was Attila prepared to expend the time and resources a siege demanded. The Huns could find themselves trapped before the Theodosian Walls, short of food, threatened by disease and too far from the safety of the Danube. Without a fleet, they could not impose an effective blockade. The decision not to attack Constantinople ensured they returned to the Great Hungarian Plain with their plunder and captives. Certainly with its defences repaired – even with the Huns' new skills in siege warfare – the empire's capital was too formidable a target. History confirms Attila's judgement. The Theodosian Walls shielded the city for another 800 years: they withstood the Avars in 626, the Arabs in the 670s, Krum the Bulgar in 813, the Russians in 860 and the First Crusade in 1097. They were scaled by the Venetians in their attack during the Fourth Crusade in 1204. The Theodosian Walls were finally breached in 1453 by Mehmet the Conqueror, whose Ottoman army had one explosive advantage that Attila would have envied: gunpowder.

# I2

# The Price of Peace

After the defeat of Arnegisclus, Theodosius sent the senior general Flavius Anatolius to negotiate peace with Attila. For most of the last fifteen years Anatolius had been responsible for the security of the eastern frontier. He may also have been accompanied by Nomus, master of the offices, one of the most powerful officials at court, whose duties included the oversight of all imperial business and the regulation of access to the emperor. Attila was impressed by such high-ranking envoys. He indicated that he was prepared to discuss terms and withdraw from Roman territory. Central to his demands, as on every occasion in the previous decade, was the prompt return of refugees and continued annual payments of gold.

Given the success of Attila's attack, the Roman negotiators were in no position to object. They agreed to the extradition of any Huns sheltering in the empire and settled on a payment of 2,100 pounds of gold a year with an additional 6,000 to cover arrears. This lump sum may also have included a tariff per head to ransom prisoners of war. It was a substantial increase on previous payments, set at 350 pounds of gold annually in 422 and raised to 700 under the treaty agreed at Margum in 439. Anatolius and Nomus also conceded that the Danube would no longer mark the extent of Roman imperial rule. Attila demanded the evacuation of territory extending from Singidunum (modern Belgrade in Serbia) 300 miles east along the river to Novae (Svishtov in Bulgaria) and at its maximum extent five days journey wide. This depopulated buffer zone protected the Huns from a surprise attack and deprived the Romans of the natural defensive advantages of the Danube. In some places the border was pushed back up to 120 miles. The ruins of Naissus were now right on the frontier.

For many contemporaries the peace settlement was an outright humiliation. Priscus of Panium was clear in his condemnation of Theodosius' cowardice.

> Because of the overwhelming terror that gripped their generals, the Romans were compelled to accept cheerfully every injunction, no matter how harsh, in their eagerness for peace . . . Even senators contributed a fixed amount of gold. . . . They paid only with difficulty . . . so that men who had once been wealthy were putting up for sale their wives' jewellery and their furniture. This was the disaster that happened to the Romans after the war, and the result was that many killed themselves either by starvation or by hanging. The imperial treasuries were also emptied.

Priscus is correct in emphasising the size of the agreed annual payout to Attila: 2,100 pounds of gold is equivalent to 151,200 solidi (there are 72 solidi, or gold pieces, to a pound). Even one solidus was no small amount. A single working person could live for several months on such a sum. Upon enlistment an army recruit in the fourth century received six solidi to cover his uniform, equipment and other initial expenses. Personal documents, wills, leases and bills of sale surviving from the sixth-century village of Nessana (in the south of modern Israel) show that on the provincial market one solidus purchased a donkey, two solidi a colt, three a slave girl, five a camel and six a slave boy. Set against this scatter of figures, 151,200 solidi was a vast sum, but did it, as Priscus claims, threaten the financial integrity of the imperial government?

Regrettably there is insufficient evidence to allow any detailed reconstruction of state revenue and expenditure in the Roman empire. Only the roughest of estimates is possible. In 445 a law issued by Valentinian III, after the partitioning of Africa with the Vandals, estimated the annual revenue from Numidia at 78,400 solidi, or just under 1,100 pounds of gold. On a crude calculation, reckoning Numidia as an average province – some, such as the Egyptian provinces, were much more prosperous; others, such as the war-damaged Danube provinces, significantly less so – the annual tax-take from the sixty provinces that made up the eastern Roman empire was 66,000 pounds of gold. In other words, the annual payment to Attila was somewhere around three per cent of revenue. That is still a large sum, but even with the addition of a heavy burden of arrears, it is unlikely to have emptied the imperial treasury or resulted in any lasting financial instability. Indeed in 457, ten years after the peace settlement with the Huns, Theodosius' successor Marcian was said to have left a surplus of 100,000 pounds of gold.

Nor is it likely, if the funds to pay Attila were clawed back through increased taxation, that this would have bankrupted senators, amongst the richest men in the empire. In Rome, where old aristocratic families had accumulated property over generations, middle-ranking senatorial households are reported to have enjoyed an annual income of 1,000–1,500 pounds of gold, the few super-rich considerably more, perhaps as much as 4,000. In other words, an annual payment of 2,100 pounds of gold to Attila put him on a par with the wealthiest families in the Roman empire. It was by any measure a huge sum, but – despite Priscus' exaggerated claims – it is most unlikely to have resulted in a tax hike that forced senators to dispose of their furniture and their wives' jewellery, and then go out and hang themselves.

If the lurid detail of Priscus' objections to the treaty of 447 is open to serious question, the general thrust of his criticism is clear: Theodosius was an ineffectual ruler unable to cope with the problems that confronted him. Rather than fight his enemies he pursued a supine policy of appeasement. For Priscus, war was the most effective way for a dynamic superpower to defend its interests. To avoid battle and instead to purchase peace undermined the self-confident superiority of the Roman empire. As with many morally forthright views, these arguments are superficially attractive, but ultimately incorrect. Above all, they misunderstand the complex international situation faced by Theodosius in the first half of the fifth century. The risks were high and the losses, especially in the Danube provinces, punishingly heavy. Even so, over three decades the eastern Roman empire managed to contain not only the Huns, but also the Vandals and an ever-present Persian threat. Securing a thousand miles of frontier from Armenia through Syria to the Sinai was a continual strain on resources. Roman historians focus on major wars, and tend to ignore the frequent fire-fights and low-grade incursions along the often ill-defined edges of empire. Yet from a military point of view to deal effectively with these incidents required a significant commitment of manpower stationed in forts and garrison towns.

Given these constraints, Theodosius' master plan was fundamentally sound. He resisted calls to transfer more troops to the northern
frontier or to chance them in a major strike against the Huns. No
doubt too financial considerations played a crucial part in the formulation of policy. To mount an effective military operation across the
Danube would have been hugely expensive. In 468, eleven years after
the emperor Marcian's death, his successor, Leo, sent a task force in
yet another attempt to dislodge the Vandals from North Africa. The
bill for the campaign was estimated at just over 100,000 pounds of
gold – and it ultimately failed. At 2,100 pounds per year the price paid
by Theodosius to secure peace was high, but modest compared to the
cost of war.

The result of these careful calculations was a grim strategy of
containment. As a matter of cold realism, unless or until the imperial
capital was directly threatened, it made both military and financial
sense to allow the Huns to plunder the Danube provinces. The alternatives were either to risk Roman forces in an offensive that might
end disastrously in a second Adrianople or – by refusing to send reinforcements to other areas of conflict – to offer a weak response to
potentially more damaging threats. It was precisely this problem that
had confronted Theodosius in 421–2 in attacking Persia, in 431–4 in
dealing with the first phase of the Vandal invasion, and again in 441–2
when Geiseric seized Carthage. Hence too the importance of the
Theodosian Walls and the crisis following their collapse. It was the
sheer strength of Constantinople's defences that allowed the legions
to be deployed elsewhere. In an emergency, no matter how severe the
situation south of the Danube, there would always be time to recall
the army or send reinforcements from the eastern front to protect
the imperial capital.

But what amounted to a strategic willingness to sacrifice Roman
territory was never likely, as Priscus' complaints underline, to be a
popular policy. For the local population whose cities and farms were
wiped out, the empire's response to Hun aggression was inadequate
and inept. It seemed that the army had not put up much of a fight
and the three generals – Flavius Aspar, Flavius Ariobindus and
Arnegisclus – had been reluctant to chance a major pitched battle.
Only when it was clear that the Huns were on their way back to the
Great Hungarian Plain did Roman troops go on the offensive, and

then not entirely successfully. The hard-fought encounter at the Utus River cost Arnegisclus his life.

Aspar and Ariobindus also paid for their caution: by the end of 447 neither was still in post. It is easy to see why Theodosius decided to let these generals go. Above all, he was not prepared to admit publicly the cruel consequences of his frontier defence policies. Removing Aspar and Ariobindus from their commands was an immediate and pragmatic response to the devastation of the Danube provinces. It deftly shifted responsibility away from the emperor – but it was also unjust. Like Priscus' accusations of cowardice, it refused to recognise that Aspar and Ariobindus' prudent tactics had prevented any major confrontation and ensured the safety of Constantinople while the Theodosian Walls were hurriedly rebuilt. To attempt more would have been to risk too much. Yet in politics the well-judged avoidance of defeat is not always enough. Aspar and Ariobindus' achievement fell far short of a decisive victory. For their failure they were unfairly forced to take the blame.

The carefully considered deployment of military assets, even if at times unpopular, or the construction of massive defences for the imperial capital were not the only keys to the preservation of empire. As Theodosius and his advisers recognised, well-targeted payments of gold were just as important. (For governments in need of a policy fig leaf to justify the transfer of large sums to often hostile regimes, these funds may more diplomatically be termed 'subsidies' or 'development aid'.) At first sight, the Romans seem to have derived little obvious benefit from these payouts – they did not prevent the Hun invasions in 434 and 441. Yet it is unlikely that anyone at court in Constantinople ever thought that peace could simply be purchased. Rather, these subsidies had more diffuse aims. On a day-to-day basis, they helped to promote cross-border exchange. Some of the money paid over to the Huns filtered back across the Danube to the benefit of Roman merchants. Continued small-scale commercial contact also permitted the unobtrusive transfer of information. Business trips abroad still remain one of the most plausible covers for espionage.

The transfer of cash across the border also offered a covert means of supporting dissident groups or individuals. Roman gold might be used to fund a coup, replacing Attila with a more cooperative leadership. In many ways this was an attractive option. It certainly carried less risk than regime change by armed intervention. By itself war is a crude and unpredictable weapon. In the unlikely event that sufficient manpower could ever be found to launch a major Roman campaign across the Danube, Attila and his close comrades might be removed after heavy fighting, but that could then trigger the collapse of a defeated Hun empire. The resulting instability and civil unrest could pose a serious security threat to the northern frontier and even to Constantinople. To counter the dissolution of the Hun empire would require an additional and costly long-term investment of military, administrative and financial resources impossible without critically restricting the Roman empire's ability to react to the threats posed by Persia and the Vandals.

Sending in the troops is always a risky and expensive option. There was a real chance that if a large Roman force had ever been sent against the Huns, it would only have succeeded in making a bad situation worse. Against the warmongering of critics like Priscus, Theodosius' skilfully balanced foreign policy again made good sense. He attempted to ensure the integrity of the northern frontier and the safety of the imperial capital while recognising the advantages of maintaining a stable, if hostile, state beyond the Danube. Resource rich, the eastern Roman empire purchased the opportunities it needed to allow its armies to deal with serious security threats elsewhere. Given the limited options available, Theodosius was right: Attila was more cheaply and effectively bought off than fought off.

For his part, while still demanding Roman subsidies, Attila moved to minimise their negative (as he saw it) consequences. He was particularly concerned to prevent the formation of any opposition encouraged or financed from across the Danube. In 439 at Margum, he insisted that all payments be made to him or his brother Bleda personally. He closely monitored Hun dealings with Romans, repeatedly demanding the deportation of asylum-seekers. After 447 some exiles refused to be repatriated. According to Priscus, many were executed by the Romans – unwilling to give Attila any grounds for breaking the peace treaty – 'among them were some members of the Hun royal family who had refused to accept orders from Attila'. More widely, Attila also moved to regulate trans-Danube commerce, dictating the location of trading posts. Markets were only to be held at specific sites: the fort of Constantia on the left bank of the Danube opposite Margum was designated in 439, the devastated city of Naissus in 447.

Despite these tough counter-measures, Attila recognised the benefits of being paid to keep the peace. (Theodosius would have been in much greater difficulty if he had faced a more conventional enemy who fought to conquer and hold territory.) Alongside his undoubted skill as a general and his claim to the divine favour of the war god, it was Attila's lavish reward of loyal supporters that guaranteed his own continued dominance. He depended on the steady flow of Roman gold across the Danube to underwrite his position at the apex of Hun society. Hence the seemingly endless round of sudden raids, lengthy diplomatic negotiations and substantial payments that dominated the relationship between Huns and Romans in the first half of the fifth century. To the booty seized in war, Attila added an annual subsidy. It was to his advantage that the Huns should remain parasitic on their much wealthier imperial neighbour. While ruthlessly exploiting its weaknesses, it was not in Attila's long-term interests to hasten the decline and fall of the eastern Roman empire. He had too much to lose.

# PART III

# DINNER WITH ATTILA

# 13

## Mission Impossible

Five hundred years after Attila's attacks and the hurried rebuilding of the Theodosian Walls, Constantinople was still the capital of the eastern Roman empire (or Byzantium, to give it its Greek name). By the tenth century the empire was no longer a superpower – it was no more than a local state surrounded on all sides by enemies who over the next hundred years would reduce its territory even further. In defiance of political reality, the magnificently titled emperor Constantine VII Porphyrogenitus ('born in the purple') persisted in calling himself 'lord of the whole Earth'. In fact, Constantine controlled only the western half of Turkey, the Balkans and the southern part of Italy. This was an imperial rump, a mere excuse for an empire. North Africa, Egypt, Sicily, Palestine and Syria had been lost to invading Arabs. In 732 an Arab army had even reached Poitiers in western France. Much of the Mediterranean world formerly part of Christendom was now securely under Islamic rule.

Embattled emperors in Constantinople held fast to their Roman heritage. If they could no longer match ancient glories, they could ensure they were not forgotten. Constantine Porphyrogenitus commissioned a series of summaries of a vast amount of information taken from classical texts. Only a fraction of this project is preserved, including a manual on court protocol, a practical guide to the conduct of foreign policy and a descriptive survey of the empire's provinces. For those who found libraries daunting places where (in the emperor's words) 'the vast quantity of material induces fear and dismay', Constantine ordered a compilation of extracts taken from historical works. In selecting suitable passages he instructed his editors 'to break up that great mass of scholarship which is so ponderous and dull that just thinking about it is exhausting'. In its place Constantine's anthology claimed to offer 'an overview . . . of all the most valuable lessons from history'. Even so readers were still confronted with fifty-three large volumes, each one dealing with a key theme: victories, letter-writing, public speaking, brave deeds, hunting, conspiracies. From this enormous undertaking only a handful of items remain. By chance these precious relics have escaped the loss or destruction of most of the literature and history written in the ancient world. One of Constantine's scrapbooks collected reports of embassies sent by the Romans and received from their allies and enemies. It is in this scissors-and-paste form that the most important ancient work on Attila and the Huns survives.

Sandwiched between often-tedious accounts of endless diplomatic negotiations are the remnants of Priscus of Panium's *History of Attila*. Published at intervals between the mid-450s and early 480s, it dealt chiefly with contemporary events in the eastern Roman empire, focusing on the conflict with the Huns in the late 440s. Priscus' *History* was dismembered by Constantine's research assistants, who reduced its eight books to thirty-five fragments. A few long extracts offer a reasonably coherent account of a Roman embassy that met with Attila in summer 449 at his main residence on the Great Hungarian Plain. Priscus' report of this encounter attracted the attention of the tenth-century editors and their fascination is easy to understand. This is not a second-hand narrative put together after long hours in a research library. (It is the melancholy fate of most historians to write about events rather than to shape them.) Priscus was actually there. He offers his readers the only surviving eyewitness description of Attila and his court. No other history gets so close to the Huns. No other account makes it so tantalisingly possible for us to imagine what it might have been like to be there too. What follows – with thanks to Constantine Porphyrogenitus and his editorial team – is Priscus' story.

Priscus was born around 420 in the town of Panium on the northern shore of the Propontis, eighty miles down the coast from Constantinople. Like most people in the eastern Mediterranean his first language was Greek; only a small minority knew Latin. Those engaged in official matters – bureaucrats, petitioners, litigants, lawyers, judges, courtiers, emperors – spoke Greek to each other, but almost all the written business of administration and the courts was conducted in Latin. After all, this was still the Roman empire.

Like many ambitious Greek-speakers from well-off families, Priscus was taught Latin at school. This was language learning the hard way: the endless chanting of grammar and vocabulary, and the humiliation of corporal punishment that followed any hesitation or mistake. Most of the school day was spent studying the classics. The well educated could recite long passages of poetry by heart. Amongst their favourites were tragic speeches from Euripides (one of the great Athenian dramatists of the fifth century BC) and the quarrel between Achilles and Agamemnon that opens Homer's *Iliad*. Hard as it is for us to believe, spotting and swapping quotations from long-dead authors was regarded by many privileged Romans as one of the most enjoyable forms of polite dinner-party entertainment.

Priscus got out of Panium as soon as he could. From a provincial town where nothing much ever happened he moved to Constantinople, where he continued his education in philosophy and rhetoric, the art of elegant and persuasive speaking and writing. As a student in the crowded wine bars of the capital, Priscus no doubt spent a great deal of time debating politics. How should the Hun threat be managed? Should the empire stand and fight, or was it a shrewder and longer-sighted strategy to pay Attila off? After completing his studies, Priscus decided to stay on in the city as a private tutor. It was perhaps through such a connection that, sometime in the early 440s, he met a young army officer called Maximinus. Maximinus was Constantinople born and bred, and his wealthy relations might have been willing to help an up-and-coming teacher of rhetoric. This was precisely the kind of highbrow cultural activity that a prominent household with connections to the imperial court could be expected to support. Maximinus' parents probably encouraged the friendship. They may have regarded conversation with Priscus as a useful counterbalance to the time their son now spent away on tours of duty. It is unlikely that many dinners in the officers' mess ended with a round of witty quotations from Homer or Euripides.

In their mid-twenties, Priscus and Maximinus experienced the fear that the Huns could inspire. After the collapse of the Theodosian Walls, Maximinus may have been involved in the campaign to delay Attila's progress towards Constantinople. Meanwhile Priscus and his pupils probably cheered on the Greens and the Blues as they worked day and night to repair the earthquake damage. Both Priscus and Maximinus must also have shared the relief and joined in the celebrations when the Huns, skirting the imperial capital, turned north and marched back towards the Danube. The peace negotiated by Anatolius and Nomus in late 447 was to be welcomed, even if Priscus would have preferred it to follow a crushing demonstration of Roman military superiority rather than an ongoing commitment to pay an annual subsidy to one of the empire's most destructive enemies.

In spring 449 a high-ranking Hun arrived in Constantinople. Edeco was a close companion of Attila and one of his bodyguards. He was accompanied by Orestes, a Roman who had been born and raised near the Sava River (on the border of modern Croatia and Serbia). Orestes' family estates fell within the territory along the Danube surrendered in 435 by Aetius in return for Attila and Bleda's support in France. Marooned outside the empire, Orestes had coped with the imposition of Hun rule as well as he could. Perhaps in return for being allowed to keep his lands, he had offered his services to Attila as a confidential private secretary. His knowledge of Latin would be useful in furthering the Huns' diplomatic efforts in Ravenna and Constantinople.

At the Great Palace lengthy ceremonial was set aside as Edeco was ushered into the throne room. Orestes was instructed to wait. In the capital no one paid any attention to just another moderately well-off Roman from the provinces. Edeco was awestruck by the magnificence of the court. Some may have hoped that it would leave a definite and lasting impression of imperial power; others, more cynical, may have thought that the sight of so much wealth would only encourage the Huns to think again of attacking Constantinople. In the golden halls of the Great Palace the battle-hardened Hun in his fur-lined cloak, leather jerkin and trousers must have looked out of place. Perhaps some of the courtiers in their beautifully patterned silken robes sneered as he passed. Official etiquette specifically prohibited the wearing of trousers in the emperor's presence. This was the uniform of a barbarian, not of someone who dared offer Theodosius II a letter and who clearly expected to talk terms.

But emperors do not negotiate – at least not in person. This was a formal meeting. As he approached the throne Edeco prostrated himself: face down to the floor, eyes lowered, body tensed. Then, easing himself forward until his head was level with Theodosius' gem-encrusted shoes, he kissed the hem of the emperor's purple robe. Once Edeco had 'adored the purple', as this ceremony was known, he retreated and stood at a respectful distance. At this point it became clear that he did not know a word of either Greek or Latin. Silently one of the emperor's chief advisers came forward. Like Nomus before him, Flavius Martialis held the powerful court post of master of the offices. No petition was answered, no edict signed, no ambassador admitted, no honours conferred without him knowing about it.

Martialis signalled one of his subordinates to approach. Vigilas was an unimpressive sight, even in court dress. He is best pictured as a nervous man, perhaps always pulling at his robe and offering exaggerated compliments to all he met. Like many unused to the brittle world of high politics, he misunderstood the purpose of flattery. Of course the powerful expect to be flattered, but they also expect the distinctions of rank to be observed. Vigilas' mistake was to flatter everybody and in many people's eyes that made him untrustworthy. Yet for the moment (after the emperor himself) Vigilas was the most important person in the throne room. Aside from Orestes, politely detained on Martialis' orders, he was the only Roman in the Great Palace who spoke Hunnic. How he had learned it was unclear. Most assumed the Huns had captured him as a boy on one of their raids across the Danube and that later he had managed to escape. Vigilas had exploited his only skill, offering his services as an interpreter to the eastern Roman government, most recently translating for Anatolius and Nomus at the peace talks in 447.

Attila's letter was read out by another of Martialis' bureaucratic underlings. It had probably been written by Orestes in his impeccable Latin. In formal exchanges Attila was determined to present himself as Theodosius' equal. In this letter he insisted that the emperor honour his recent undertakings. Despite sending at least four embassies to the imperial court in the last year – including one led by Edeco himself – he alleged that not all of the Hun refugees had been handed over. Nor, he complained, had the Romans withdrawn to the agreed frontier, five days journey south of the Danube. Parts of the buffer zone were still being farmed and the cross-border trading post at Naissus was not yet operational. Edeco expanded on these grievances. Standing

defiantly in the middle of the Great Palace, the Hun envoy was an
unsettling reminder of how close the Roman empire had come to
disaster in the last ten years. As Vigilas' translation made clear, Attila
insisted that high-ranking ambassadors should be sent to explain why
the treaty provisions had not yet been fully implemented. Unless
these matters were speedily resolved, the Huns might not keep the
peace. Theodosius made no response to these belligerent threats. He
did not move. This was a good diplomatic ploy; it both avoided
confrontation and helped to maintain the fiction that the godlike
ruler of the Roman world was closer to heaven than earth. The real
negotiations took place elsewhere. Leaving Orestes waiting, Edeco
was escorted through the palace to another splendid suite of rooms.
Here he was greeted by Chrysaphius, the commander of the imperial
bodyguard.

Edeco had never dealt with a eunuch before. There were none at
Attila's court and in the great cities of the empire they were rarely
seen outside the wealthiest households. At first meeting, many found
their appearance disturbing. Most eunuchs were tall and gangling with
broad hips and prominent breasts. They seemed to sweat continu-
ously. From a distance their smooth skins had a shiny gloss like a
young girl's; close up, under layers of artfully applied cosmetics, their
wrinkled faces were like an old woman's. Eunuchs' crumpled features,
in the words of one of their most spiteful detractors, 'are like raisins
and their bodies deformed, half male and half female'. Flourishing in
the secret world of the Great Palace, gliding through the shadows of
its cool marble colonnades, moving silently down its long dark corri-
dors, eunuchs lived, it was said, 'like bats in a cave'.

For all their strangeness – the cruel physiological consequence of
castration before puberty – eunuchs were capable of acquiring great
power. Many emperors preferred to trust advisers who could not be
swayed by their own family interests. Eunuchs do not have wives or
sons to think about; they depend for their position on the emperor
alone. Proximity to the throne guaranteed their influence. Eunuchs
could make or break an ambitious aristocrat. A quiet word might
ensure the emperor's favour; malicious gossip result in exile. It was
rumoured that Theodosius was too easily swayed by eunuchs, who
had looked after him since childhood. Certainly they were convenient
scapegoats. Loyal Romans rarely criticised a living emperor openly,

rather they blamed unpopular policies on the jealousies and misinfor-
mation of those closest to him. Eunuchs were with the emperor while
he ate, dressed and bathed. At night they were locked into his bedroom
and slept across the doors. In these private moments, it was suspected,
Theodosius was most vulnerable to their malign insinuations. It was
widely believed that things would be different if the emperor only
knew what really went on behind his back in the seclusion of the
Great Palace.

Chrysaphius was one of Theodosius' closest confidants; his meeting
with the Hun envoy could not have taken place without the emperor's
knowledge. Away from the stiff formalities of the throne room, it was
now time to talk business. Slaves brought dainty pastries soaked in
honey and cool sweet wine in delicate silver cups. Three distinct voices
were clearly audible: Chrysaphius' fluting high-pitched tones were an
ever-present reminder that he was a eunuch; Edeco's guttural Hunnic
that he was an enemy of the Romans; Vigilas' wheedling translations
that he was in this for whatever he could get. Vigilas again emphasised how much Edeco was impressed by the opulence of the Great
Palace. Chrysaphius' small talk was probably all about chariot racing.
He was a dedicated fan and generous backer of the Greens. In Priscus'
account: 'Vigilas – translating – said that Edeco admired the palace
and regarded those who had such wealth as fortunate. Chrysaphius
remarked that Edeco could also possess riches and rooms with golden
ceilings if he were to set the interests of the Huns aside and work
instead for the Romans.'

Chrysaphius then asked Edeco how well he knew Attila. Edeco
assured him that he was part of his inner circle. Feigning a professional interest as commander of the emperor's bodyguard, Chrysaphius
pressed him for more details. How was Attila's retinue organised? How
were his guards selected? What was the process of security clearance?
Edeco replied that only the most trusted of Attila's friends were armed
in his presence. A group of high-ranking men shared the responsibilities of a bodyguard according to a duty roster and each knew in
advance when it was his turn to protect Attila. Satisfied, Chrysaphius
changed the subject. Looking up at the great gilded ceiling, the eunuch
slowly closed his eyes and mused again on the advantages of wealth
and how it might most easily be acquired. Vigilas made sure that
nothing was lost in translation.

That evening Edeco and Vigilas were entertained alone in the eunuch's private residence while Orestes was dispatched elsewhere on some pointless diplomatic errand.

> With Vigilas translating, they shook hands and exchanged oaths. The eunuch swore not to say anything to Edeco's detriment, but only to his great advantage. Edeco swore he would not reveal what was said to him even if he did not take it any further. Chrysaphius then said to Edeco that if he agreed to journey into Hun territory, kill Attila and return to the Romans, he would enjoy a life of happiness and the greatest wealth. Edeco promised he would undertake the mission.

And so the deal was done. The details were worked out over dinner. The most pressing issue was how to secure the cooperation of Attila's bodyguard. Edeco reckoned that fifty pounds of gold would be sufficient to persuade them to join his cause. As a gesture of goodwill Chrysaphius ordered the money to be fetched immediately, but Edeco advised he could not safely carry such a quantity of bullion back across the Danube. Attila was always suspicious of gifts received by Huns while on embassies to the Romans. Instead it was agreed that Vigilas should accompany Edeco on his return journey to Attila's court. Through Vigilas, Edeco would then send instructions on how the gold was to be delivered.

Chrysaphius was all too aware of both the risks and advantages of his scheme. If it failed, it might provoke revenge attacks. If it succeeded, then Attila might be replaced by a ruler more sympathetic to the Romans and the northern frontier would again be secure. From within the Great Palace the shrewd strategies of a eunuch would have removed one of the empire's greatest threats. In the war against Attila there was no need of armies or a costly offensive. Astute diplomacy and well-directed bribery offered a better chance of achieving regime change. These pleasant thoughts in mind, Chrysaphius made his way to the most heavily guarded part of the palace, where he discussed his plans with Theodosius. For those who have only seen an emperor in his throne room, or riding in a procession or walking barefoot through the streets of the capital, it is difficult to envisage such a scene. How does the ruler of the Roman world behave in private? Chrysaphius perhaps interrupted a conversation about horses or hunting dogs or about some new entertainment in the hippodrome, or perhaps the pious emperor was at prayer.

Theodosius said very little. A plan to murder a hostile foreign leader presented him with no moral difficulty. In his view an ethical foreign policy was one that best advanced the interests of the Roman empire. Even so, the emperor had no wish to be associated openly with Chrysaphius' conspiracy until it had achieved its objective. Nor did he request to be kept informed of progress. It was important to minimise the consequences of failure. If ever confronted by Attila's ambassadors, Theodosius would of course deny all knowledge of a plot. Sometimes an emperor does not want to know what really goes on behind his back. Then, if things do not work out, he can always blame the eunuchs.

Theodosius also consulted the master of the offices, Flavius Martialis. He may have needed convincing that the project was worth backing. Surely Edeco had been won over too easily and too cheaply? Martialis suggested that Vigilas' presence would seem more plausible if he were associated with an official Roman embassy. As an interpreter he would have perfect cover. But this was not a simple matter. Attila had insisted that he would only negotiate with an ambassador of the highest rank and, given the circumstances, no prominent courtier would be prepared to take the risk. Of course the Huns would offer the usual diplomatic immunities that went with an embassy, but in the long trek to the Great Hungarian Plain there were too many opportunities for a fatal accident. Martialis advised sending a young man, someone not too far advanced in his career who would find an appointment as the emperor's envoy impossible to refuse. The difficulties and dangers involved argued for a military man, rather than a desk-bound bureaucrat.

The ambassador would carry a letter from Theodosius rejecting Attila's suggestion that Roman non-compliance with the provisions of the treaty threatened to undermine peace and hinting that it was the Huns' actions which called into question the agreed withdrawal south of the Danube. According to Priscus: 'Then it was written, "Anyone jeopardising the treaty is not justified in taking possession of Roman territory," and, "In addition to those handed over so far, I am sending you seventeen refugees, and there are no others." These quotations are from the emperor's letter.'

The repatriation of seventeen more refugees was a clear gesture of conciliation and also a tacit admission that there was some foundation to Attila's complaint that the empire was still harbouring renegade Huns. The letter would also make it clear that its bearer came from a distinguished family and was amongst Theodosius' closest confidants. To avoid any pre-emptive objection to his status, the ambassador would be given strict instructions to insist on speaking to Attila in person and not to submit the letter in advance of a meeting. Chrysaphius suggested that a copy should secretly be shown to Edeco, so that he would have no reason to question the emperor's motives in sending an embassy.

Once these details had been settled, Martialis carefully scanned the army lists to identify a suitable candidate for the post of ambassador. After some discreet inquiries, he recommended Maximinus. This was a good choice: an ambitious young man with a promising record and eager to serve the best interests of the empire. Maximinus was no doubt delighted – his merits had at last been noticed by the powerful in Constantinople. In the dark-purple ink exclusively reserved for imperial use, the emperor had signed his formal letters of accreditation as an imperial envoy. Nothing at all was said of Chrysaphius' plot to assassinate Attila. Maximinus could be forgiven for thinking that his mission to the Huns was the beginning of what promised to be a brilliant diplomatic career.

# Close Encounters

Maximinus left Constantinople in early summer 449. Travelling in the official party with him were Attila's envoy Edeco and his secretary Orestes, and the interpreter Vigilas. They were also joined by Rusticius, a businessman who had his own private dealings with another of Attila's secretaries. He was a welcome addition as he had personal contacts with those close to Attila and was fluent in Hunnic. Maximinus perhaps thought this might prove useful if Vigilas turned out to be unreliable. Certainly it must have been a relief not to have to depend solely on Vigilas' translations. Priscus also joined the mission. 'Maximinus by his entreaties persuaded me to accompany him on this embassy.' It was not uncommon for those skilled in rhetoric to be part of an ambassador's staff. Maximinus' competence was on the battlefield rather than around the negotiating table. In his new role he may have felt the need for a mind more attuned to the advantages and pitfalls of subtle argumentation. He also seems to have been confident that his embassy would mark a significant moment in the Roman empire's relationship with the Huns. Perhaps he was eager that his achievements should be properly recorded. Priscus could be relied upon to submit a well-judged report to the master of the offices, presenting Maximinus as a key player. If the emperor approved, then Priscus could write a more literary account of his best friend's diplomatic achievements.

Priscus had probably already published some of his set-piece lectures. Aside from friendship, what may have convinced him to accept Maximinus' offer was the opportunity to collect first-hand data on the Huns. No other writer had ever had access to such information. The majority of Priscus' Greek-speaking contemporaries still based their views on Herodotus' account of *nomades*. Writing in Latin in the early 390s Ammianus Marcellinus had made some advances in understanding the Huns, but he was not as reliable as was sometimes claimed. Priscus intended to go much further: aside from its literary merits (and Priscus prided himself on his stylish prose) his new account of the world beyond the Danube would be based on his own research in the field. That alone might be enough to make his *History of Attila* – only a working title at this early stage – a best-seller in Constantinople.

Thirteen days after leaving the capital the travellers passed through Adrianople before reaching the burnt-out shell of Serdica (modern Sofia in Bulgaria). The 300-mile journey along the well-built road was a stark reminder of the damage caused by the Huns two years earlier. Between Adrianople and Serdica were only ruins. Edeco was perhaps diplomatic enough not to boast of Attila's victories, or at least Rusticius and Vigilas were diplomatic enough not to translate. At Serdica Maximinus decided to host a barbecue. Camp was pitched at a distance from the devastated city, now sheltering only a few shepherds who approached warily at the sight of Huns and Romans travelling together. Was this a sign of lasting peace on the northern frontier or a prelude to the surrender of even more of the empire's territory? Maximinus saw no reason to explain his mission. It was enough that these peasants acknowledged his status as an imperial ambassador and were prepared to sell him some of their sheep. Since leaving Constantinople, Maximinus and Edeco had communicated only when necessary. They had eaten apart, each with his own companions. Now Huns and Romans were sitting together around the embers of a campfire in that convivial mood which commonly follows an excellent dinner in the open air. Priscus took advantage of the occasion to study the Huns. There was much to be learned. Perhaps he was careful to note how Edeco preferred his steak. The standard view that Huns ate their meat half-raw, or concealed it under their saddles, clearly required revision.

All seemed to be going well. As the wine, diluted with water in the traditional Roman manner, circulated freely, Maximinus proposed the emperor's health and continued good fortune. Edeco immediately interjected with his own toast to Attila. All had raised their cups when Vigilas was heard to comment 'that it was not right to compare a god and a man, meaning by a man, Attila and by a god, Theodosius'. Edeco was understandably offended. To the Huns, Attila's claim to be especially favoured by the war god seemed as credible as Theodosius' belief in his closeness to Christ. After all, as Edeco might have said, had he really been spoiling for an argument, what better proof of Attila's divinely inspired destiny than the shattered walls of Serdica silhouetted behind them against a clear night sky? The evening turned sour. Maximinus hurriedly apologised. Perhaps it was obvious that Vigilas had drunk too much or that his remark was nothing more than a bad joke. Priscus attempted to move things on, his friendly conversation preventing Edeco's immediate withdrawal. What had seemed a successful meeting now stuttered to an unsatisfactory close. As the Huns prepared to return to their tents, Maximinus offered Edeco and Orestes rich presents of silk and pearls. Edeco seemed pleased but said nothing. The whole incident, as Priscus realised much later, had been carefully stage-managed. The contrived public clash between Edeco and Vigilas had been intended to draw any suspicion away from their private arrangement. But not everyone was convinced that all was quite what it seemed. Before leaving, Orestes drew Maximinus aside.

> He said that Maximinus was a wise and a very good man not to have acted in the same insulting manner as those at court, for they had invited Edeco to dinner on his own and had honoured him with gifts. This remark meant nothing either to Maximinus or to me since we had no idea of what had happened, and so we asked Orestes repeatedly how and on what occasion he had been excluded and Edeco honoured. But he withdrew without replying.

The following morning Maximinus is likely to have expressed his disappointment to Vigilas. He probably took the view that sensitive diplomatic behaviour could reasonably be expected from an experienced interpreter. Perhaps Maximinus was content to draw a line under the incident if Vigilas could assure him that there would be no further lapses. Vigilas apologised. The faked disagreement with Edeco had served its purpose. Maximinus then asked him to explain Orestes' remarks. Was it true that Edeco had been entertained on his own in the Great Palace and given gifts? This was Vigilas' first hint that Edeco's companions suspected that their embassy to Constantinople might have been compromised. In reply, Vigilas carefully avoided the specifics of what he suggested were no more than petulant comments. In his view it would hardly be surprising if the difference between the status of Orestes and Edeco had been reflected in their reception at the imperial court 'since Orestes was a servant and private secretary to Attila, while Edeco, distinguished in war and a Hun, was by far his superior'.

Nothing more was said on the subject. Confused and wary, all involved preferred to remain quiet. A few days later, while trying to find a place to pitch camp outside Naissus, the Romans were faced with a cheerless memorial to their failure to defend the Danube provinces. Near the walls – smashed by battering rams seven years earlier – the riverbank was still littered with the bones of the slain. That night it seemed best that Huns and Romans should eat apart. Leaving Naissus they entered the buffer zone stipulated by Attila as part of the peace settlement of 447. For five days they journeyed through territory that had once been part of the Roman empire. In a mostly deserted landscape the wreckage of farm buildings and villages was another bitter reminder of past prosperity. Perhaps here Priscus felt, even more strongly than at the time of the peace nego-tiations, that Theodosius and his generals should have put up a fight. Surely after more than four centuries of Roman rule there could be no excuse for the deliberate abandonment of empire?

At last the travellers reached the Danube, probably somewhere near the ruins of Margum. Priscus is vague on directions and travel times. He clearly found the route difficult and disorienting. He disliked the twisting paths through the dark and overgrown woods. Sometimes, at least as far as he could judge by the sun, he seemed to be travelling west, and then, as the narrow track corkscrewed again, back towards the east. Ferried across the Danube in dugouts hollowed from single tree trunks Priscus must have felt that he had left civilisation far behind. Constantinople was now more than three weeks away. It was a relief when messengers arrived instructing them to attend a meeting with Attila the following day. Maximinus remained optimistic about the prospects for the embassy. After all, despite Orestes' cryptic complaints, he still knew nothing about Chrysaphius' assassination plot. To demonstrate that, even beyond the frontier, Roman hospitality was undiminished, Maximinus invited Attila's messengers to dine. Priscus is clear that the guests were well entertained. Regrettably he gives no account of any after-dinner toasts. Perhaps this time Maximinus, practising his diplomatic skills, decided they should quietly be omitted.

From the moment the delegation arrived, things went badly. Roman tents pitched on a grassy rise had to be moved as the Huns were insistent that no foreigner could be allowed to overlook Attila's camp. Edeco and Orestes soon returned from their own audience with Attila. They were now accompanied by Scottas, reputed to be one of his most valued advisers. (In 447 he had been sent to Constantinople to collect the 6,000 pounds of gold that had been agreed as the down payment for peace.) Scottas asked Maximinus what he hoped to achieve by his embassy. Maximinus' reply was courteously evasive. He regarded the enquiry as abrupt in tone and hostile in intent, but Scottas persisted, demanding a straight response to a direct question. Maximinus, closely following the instructions he had received in Constantinople, made it clear that he had been ordered to deliver the emperor's letter to Attila in person. Repeating his question, Scottas emphasised that he asked it at Attila's specific request. 'Surely,' he remarked, 'you did not think that I would come to you just to interfere on my own account?' Maximinus stuck to the rule of international law, calmly if rather pompously observing, 'It is not the convention for ambassadors to discuss the reasons for their mission with third parties before they have even met those to whom they have been sent.' This, he noted, was a practice well known to the Huns, and it had always been followed when they had sent ambassadors to Constantinople. 'We deserve to be treated in an equal fashion, otherwise we will not divulge the purpose of our embassy.'

Scottas departed, his question still unanswered. Perhaps Maximinus was pleased with the result of this first encounter. He had made his position clear and was confident that he would soon speak to Attila. A little while later Scottas returned and, to Maximinus' embarrassment, summarised – without pause or apology – the contents of the emperor's letter. He then requested that the Romans leave Hun territory immediately unless they had any other matters to discuss. Priscus and Maximinus were at a loss: 'we were unable to understand how decisions that the emperor had made in secret had come to be known'. Perhaps at this point they should have realised that something was wrong. Yet, to be fair, there was no reason why they should have suspected Vigilas, who was unlikely to have had access to such sensitive state documents, or have associated this incident with Orestes' baffling remarks at Serdica ten days earlier. The security breach, they might well have reasoned, was most likely to have occurred in the imperial capital. The culprit was perhaps to be found amongst the officials working for Flavius Martialis. Such a surmise would of course be only half right. The letter had been shown to Edeco in Constantinople – but by Chrysaphius. Of course at the time Chrysaphius was not to know that Edeco would later double-cross him and share its contents with Attila.

Back beyond the Danube, Maximinus and Priscus were not the only ones to have misunderstood the situation. Vigilas too failed to realise that Edeco had already betrayed him. He may have told Orestes about the plot on the way to Serdica, or he may have waited to tell Attila and Scottas. Priscus was never able to establish the truth. 'For Edeco had either made his promise to Chrysaphius falsely, or he was afraid that Orestes might tell Attila what he had said to us after dinner at Serdica and blame him for speaking on his own to the emperor and the eunuch.' Certainly Vigilas assumed that everything was still running to plan. He had not been surprised that Scottas could quote from Theodosius' letter. Edeco had been shown it precisely so that, if questioned about any private meetings in the Great Palace, he could claim that they were aimed at obtaining this confidential information. What dismayed Vigilas was Maximinus' reaction. He stood his ground, insisting on a meeting with Attila and refusing to confirm or deny Scottas' account of the emperor's letter.

As Priscus later realised, it was of vital importance to Vigilas that the embassy go ahead, so that he and Edeco 'might have a pretext to discuss the plot against Attila and decide how to transport the gold that Edeco had said he needed for distribution to those under his command'. Hence Vigilas' frustration at Maximinus' intransigence. In Vigilas' view, it would have been better to fabricate some new topic for negotiation in order to secure an audience with Attila. Maximinus – who repudiated such falsehoods as beneath a Roman ambassador – could now see no way forward. He lay on the grass despondently. Perhaps he was watching the clouds go by and thinking how he would explain the failure of his mission when he returned to Constantinople.

Priscus, as he is proud to record, saved the day. With Rusticius as interpreter he made his own approach to Scottas. It lacked subtlety (greater sophistication might perhaps have been expected from an experienced teacher of rhetoric): Scottas was offered gifts and asked to intercede with Attila. Priscus picks up his own story: 'I said to Scottas that we had learned that his views carried weight with Attila, but what we had heard about him would not seem credible unless we had a demonstration of his power.' Priscus was pleased with his tactics since Scottas, apparently all too eager to prove his influence, 'immediately mounted his horse and galloped away to Attila's tent'. Perhaps, if just for a fleeting moment, Priscus thought that dealing with the Huns was not so difficult after all. It had seemed childishly simple to play on Scottas' pride and get him to appeal to Attila to change his mind. But it was Priscus who had been fooled. It must already have occurred to Attila that if Maximinus knew his embassy had been compromised, then his insistence on an audience was an act of near suicidal recklessness. Given Maximinus' actions and those of his patronising friend, it made more sense to assume that they still knew nothing about Chrysaphius' conspiracy. If so, this was a situation that could be turned to the Huns' advantage. Scottas was instructed to return to the Romans and invite them to Attila's tent.

The audience was a diplomatic disaster. Attila was surrounded by heavily armed guards. This was a reasonable precaution: after all, there was still a chance that Maximinus had been aware of Chrysaphius' conspiracy all along and was now prepared to risk his own life to strike a blow for the Roman empire. (Somehow it seemed unlikely that the professorial Priscus would turn out to be a heroic man of action.) Entering the tent, Maximinus and Priscus found Attila seated on a wooden chair. Maximinus presented Theodosius' letter with the flourish of a traditional Roman salutation, 'The emperor prays that you and those dear to you are well.' Attila replied that he wished the Romans precisely the same as he understood they now wished him. This cutting remark was completely lost on Maximinus. Only much later when he learned of Chrysaphius' plot did he understand its biting irony.

Priscus observed everything carefully. This was his first sight of a man who for many personified terror and destruction. He may have been expecting a barbarian monstrosity, a kind of nightmarish combination of Homer's one-eyed, man-eating Cyclops and the crude

animal-like disfigurement typical of Herodotus' *nomades*. But outside
the comfortingly simple worlds of the ancient moralist or the modern
action movie – where the goodies are generally handsome and the
baddies conveniently unattractive – the powerful whom we dislike
or fear do not always oblige by being loathsome or depraved. In
Priscus' eyewitness view, Attila the Hun 'was short with a broad chest
and a large head; his eyes were small, his beard sparse and flecked
with grey; his nose was flattish and his complexion dark'. Perhaps to
Priscus' surprise, there was nothing at all in Attila's appearance that
was immediately frightening.

Nor did Attila find the Romans who stood uneasily before him
particularly impressive. Ignoring Maximinus and Priscus, he turned to
Vigilas reminding him that it had been agreed at the peace talks two
years earlier that no Roman embassies would be sent until all Hun
refugees had been returned. Vigilas assured Attila that there were no
more on Roman territory. Priscus continues: 'Attila became angrier
and grossly insulted him, shouting that, had he not known that it
would violate the rights of ambassadors, he would impale him and
leave him as carrion for the birds to punish him for the shameless
effrontery of his claims.' He instructed his secretaries to read out the
names of those he alleged were still being sheltered by the Romans.
Furious, he ordered Vigilas back to Constantinople, where he was to
demand that Theodosius hand over any remaining refugees. He was
then to return and report the emperor's response. To add weight to
Vigilas' mission, he would be accompanied by Eslas, one of the most
experienced Hun ambassadors, who, fifteen years earlier, had negotiated with Theodosius on Rua's behalf. Maximinus and Priscus were
to remain behind so that in due course they could receive a formal
reply to the emperor's letter. Meanwhile they were specifically directed
not to attempt to ransom Roman prisoners of war or purchase any
slaves or horses. The money they had brought with them from
Constantinople could only be used to buy food.

Debriefing back at camp, Maximinus was at a loss to understand
Attila's anger. Priscus rather lamely suggested that he might have been
insulted by the report of Vigilas' objection to the toasts at Serdica.
Vigilas could only comment that at the peace talks in 447 Attila had
been reasonable throughout. Vigilas' puzzlement at Attila's fury was
genuine; he was still convinced the conspiracy was a secret. 'For he

did not think, as he confessed to us later, that either what had happened at Serdica or the details of the plot had been reported to Attila.' That belief was strengthened by the arrival of Edeco. Taking Vigilas aside, he assured him that all was now in place and that on his return from Constantinople he should bring the gold to pay off Attila's bodyguard. Questioned by Maximinus about this conversation, Vigilas offered only a barefaced lie. He said Edeco had reported that Attila was angry because all the refugees had not been returned and – this a low blow – because it was obvious that he had not been sent an ambassador of any great experience or standing.

The Romans had been outwitted. Maximinus was still unaware of the plot. Despite the leaking of Theodosius' letter he was determined to continue with the embassy. His best friend Priscus readily agreed. After all, he was under the smug impression that it had been his resourceful intervention with Scottas that had secured the interview with Attila. Vigilas still believed that Edeco intended to carry out the mission as arranged with Chrysaphius. From the Huns' point of view things looked very different. Edeco had confessed everything he knew. Scottas' deliberately loutish questioning had been successful in confirming that Maximinus and Priscus knew nothing. Still unaware of Chrysaphius' schemes, the Roman envoys were willing to remain as guests of the Huns. Most importantly, Vigilas had taken the bait. He had been given a plausible reason for returning to Constantinople and had promised Edeco that he would bring back fifty pounds of gold. If he were then to be searched, Vigilas would have difficulty in explaining away such a large sum. With the ban on ransoming prisoners or purchasing slaves or horses, it was a great deal more than was necessary to buy food. This was a risk he was prepared to take. Only later did Priscus realise that this was part of Attila's trap 'so that Vigilas should be caught easily and incriminate himself as he would have no excuse for bringing the gold'. Vigilas had been cleverly set up. As far as Attila was concerned, the great game had now begun.

# 15

## Eating with the Enemy

The next ten days were the most miserable part of the entire journey. There were no further meetings with Attila. Instead, as instructed by their Hun guides, Maximinus and Priscus made their way to his main residence on the north-western part of the Great Hungarian Plain. They probably travelled roughly parallel to the course of the Danube as it runs north for 200 miles to the Great Danube Bend. In contrast to his precision within the empire, once beyond its frontiers Priscus' confused geography makes it difficult to map his route or locate Attila's residence with any certainty. To Priscus the landscape seemed a featureless expanse of open plain, broken only by marshes and rivers whose names he could barely pronounce. In this unfamiliar world without roads or cities – or even their ruins – he found it impossible to tell exactly where he was.

The going was tough. Rivers were crossed, as on the Danube, in large dugouts or in marshy areas on light rafts. As Maximinus and Priscus had by now used up most of the provisions they had brought with them, they obtained supplies from the villages through which they passed. 'We were provided with plenty of food, millet instead of wheat and instead of wine . . . a drink made from barley.' Eager not to seem ungracious, Priscus can be imagined smilingly eating the local produce, chewing his way through the hard bread made from hand-ground millet and trying the beer. The strong and sometimes sour ale made from malted barley was not a Hun import, but the continuation of a long Roman tradition of brewing. Beer was a frontier drink. Perhaps Priscus, as he hesitantly sipped a huge mug, hoped that no one would notice that, like most educated people in the Roman empire, he would have preferred a small white wine – mixed with water and sweetened with honey.

Without doubt, for Priscus the lowest point of the journey was the collapse of his tent in the middle of the night. During a storm it had been caught in a violent gust of wind that also blew his baggage into a nearby creek. At such moments Priscus encountered more of life beyond the frontier than he wished. With their campsite flooded, Priscus and Maximinus pressed on through the heavy rain to find shelter. In a nearby village they were looked after by an aristocratic woman. Drenched and shivering as he was, Priscus admired her poise and dignified authority. She had once been, as he learned in conversation, one of Bleda's wives. The following day, after they had recovered their baggage and dried it in the sunshine, Priscus and Maximinus presented her with gifts including three silver bowls, dates and Indian pepper. From his close observation of their eating habits, Priscus already knew that spices and dried fruits were greatly prized as delicacies amongst the Huns.

These handsome offerings were also an apology in case such an evidently important woman had been offended. As part of her generous hospitality she had offered her Roman guests Hun women as partners for the night. It was a difficult situation, particularly, as Priscus was informed, such a courtesy was only extended to the highest-ranking Huns. Although they regarded the women as 'good-lookers' (to translate Priscus' praise precisely), the Romans had politely declined. With what reluctance Priscus does not reveal. Perhaps he and Maximinus preferred their own or each other's company; if they were married, perhaps they remembered their wives. Exhausted after the storm they may not have been ready for a difficult cultural exchange that they would have to manage without the help of an interpreter. At all events, this was one first-hand experience of the Huns that Priscus decided to forgo. Perhaps he felt that sleeping with the enemy was taking the demands of fieldwork too far. Certainly, nothing like this had ever happened to him in a library.

Priscus was impressed by his first sight of Attila's residence. The palace complex was sited on high ground in the middle of a large village. The main hall was a substantial wooden-framed building with walls of carefully planed planks tightly fitted together. The whole structure rested on circular stone piles. The surrounding compound was screened by a tall wooden fence with towers at intervals along it. Some distance away, near the entrance to the village, Priscus noted a second cluster of buildings, similar in construction to Attila's, but not as imposing. This was the principal residence of Attila's closest comrade and adviser Onegesius, the brother of Scottas. Standing outside Onegesius' compound, Priscus and Maximinus had a good view of the crowd gathered to greet Attila. As he rode towards the village, young women rushed out to meet him. They lined up in groups of seven, while above their heads others held long white linen cloths. This was a carefully choreographed ceremony. Flanking the processional route under fluttering canopies, these women welcomed Attila with songs. Then Onegesius' wife presented him with food on a great silver platter and a cup of wine. It was later explained to Priscus that the offering and acceptance of food and drink was considered a great honour and a public affirmation of loyalty and friendship. There could be no doubting the significance that Attila placed on his relationship with Onegesius.

That evening Priscus and Maximinus were guests of Onegesius' wife and the most important members of his family. Onegesius himself was not at dinner as he had been summoned to a meeting with Attila. One urgent item for discussion was how to deal with the Romans, who clearly expected an audience. To make their point they had made it known they would pitch their tents near the palace. This was a situation that required careful handling, especially since – as Onegesius was now made aware – it was certain that Maximinus and Priscus still knew nothing of the murder plot. It is likely that Onegesius advised that the Roman ambassador's status should be respected. If Maximinus were well treated it would greatly strengthen Attila's position when he finally had proof of Chrysaphius' conspiracy; and that of course would have to wait until Vigilas had returned from Constantinople with fifty pounds of gold.

For his part, Maximinus, reviewing his initial experience with Attila and his companions, decided to do more than repeatedly insist on a face-to-face meeting. He also needed the help of influential intermediaries. Priscus was probably quick to emphasise his achievement in persuading Scottas to intercede on their behalf. He was only too willing to try a second time. He had the advantage of being able to make informal approaches to leading Huns, while Maximinus was constrained by his position and his instructions that he should only

discuss official business with Attila himself. To his considerable satisfaction, Priscus was once again successful. Early the following morning,
shortly after receiving the gifts that Priscus delivered in person to his
compound, Onegesius made his way across the village to the Romans'
camp.

Rather than risk discussion on any substantive issue, Maximinus
preferred to rely on smooth talking. He observed that this was an
unparalleled opportunity for Onegesius to make his mark in history
and he could win lasting fame if he were willing to travel to
Constantinople and settle the disputes between Theodosius and Attila.
He would not only benefit as a statesman serving the interests of his
own nation, he would also gain personally '"since you and your children would always be friends of the emperor and his family"'. In reply,
Onegesius enquired, with just the slightest suggestion of sarcasm,
what he would have to do to merit Theodosius' lasting friendship.
Maximinus delivered another volley of platitudes. By leading a Hun
embassy Onegesius would earn the thanks of the Roman emperor.
He would easily dispose of any remaining disagreements by '"examining their causes and resolving them under the terms of the peace
accord"'.

Onegesius had heard enough. He made it clear that even if he
were to consent to act as an ambassador he would do no more than
repeat whatever he had been instructed to say by Attila. '"Or do the
Romans think that they can be so persistently persuasive that I would
betray my lord, or would disregard my upbringing as a Hun, my
wives and children, or would ever think that slavery with Attila could
not be better than wealth with the Romans?"' These were well-chosen
words and made more melodramatic in Priscus' later write-up of the
scene. As far as Onegesius was concerned, to protect his own position he needed to emphasise his reluctance to negotiate with
Theodosius. The risks of expressing even the slightest interest in such
a mission were too great. After Edeco's entrapment, Attila would be
wary of any prominent Hun who journeyed to Constantinople. Edeco
had confessed all, but it must have occurred to Attila that someone
cleverer and better paid might have kept his bargain with Chrysaphius.
Aside from the matter of a Hun embassy – on which he had been
unambiguously clear – Onegesius expressed himself willing to assist
the Romans in their dealings with Attila. He suggested that he might

discuss the issues involved with Priscus, rather than continue formal meetings with Maximinus. It was not to Onegesius' advantage to be in frequent private contact with the Roman ambassador.

The next day Priscus continued his efforts to secure the goodwill of those close to Attila. He entered the palace compound unchallenged – by now he was well known to the guards – and made his way to the residence of one of Attila's most important wives. Erecan impressed Priscus; she was clearly a woman of sophistication and style. On being admitted to her presence he found her reclining gracefully on a cushioned couch. She was surrounded by attendants and supervising a group of servant girls embroidering fine linen. The complex designs, which Priscus only glimpsed, probably incorporated many differently shaped and coloured beads. Embroidery beads have been found in fifth-century female graves in eastern Europe and southern Russia. The meticulous report of a rescue dig carried out during 1991–3 near the centre of Belgrade (ancient Singidunum) catalogued 764 beads from twenty-two graves dating from after the city's sack by the Huns in 441–2. The overwhelming majority were of glass, mainly blue, violet, red and yellow, with a small number made from amber and coral. One tomb located within the old Roman fort contained 231 beads, two in amber and the rest in glass, mostly green and red, with a few larger examples in midnight blue with swirls of white. It is attractive to imagine that when Priscus first saw Erecan relaxing on her couch in her comfortable apartment she too was wearing a linen dress prettily decorated with coloured glass beads. Perhaps these caught the light and shimmered as she rose slowly to greet her Roman guest.

Priscus does not recount any conversation he had with Erecan. He may have preferred a private visit without an interpreter. However, all seems to have gone well. Perhaps Priscus bowed graciously in what he hoped was a pleasing, but not too deferential, manner. Perhaps Erecan smiled encouragingly in return and indicated her pleasure at the presents Priscus had brought. In his account of the meeting – as with Onegesius early the previous morning – Priscus passes quickly over these gifts providing no description, not even a brief list. It may be that, given his strong objections to the annual subsidies paid by Theodosius' government, he was unwilling to call attention to his own part in adding to the total of Roman gold handed over to the Huns.

Priscus is likely to have presented Erecan with choice examples of the most costly jewellery from Constantinople. These pieces may have been similar to some of those discovered in 1797 and 1889 in two locations in the village of Şimleu Silvaniei in western Romania. (As Şimleu Silvaniei, then known as Szilágysomlyó, was part of the Austro-Hungarian empire the finds were split between the Kunsthistorisches Museum in Vienna and the National Museum in Budapest.) The seventy-four items, all in gold, many inlaid with precious stones – coins, shoulder brooches, pendants, rings, necklaces and bowls – were not hidden by Huns. Because the various objects seem to have been accumulated over 150 years from the beginning of the fourth century (there are coins minted under Constantine) through to the mid-fifth century, it seems more likely that the two Şimleu Silvaniei hordes were part of a dynastic treasure belonging to a local ruler who now answered to Attila but whose ancestors had been independent before the expansion of the Hun empire. The fourth-century coins (some surviving only as copies made by skilled Gothic craftsmen) reflect close contacts across the Danube and the efforts of Roman emperors from Constantine onwards to win the support of the powerful beyond the frontier (see plates, pictures 1–2). Some of the late-fourth- and early-fifth-century jewellery was perhaps valuable loot taken in the destructive raids of the 430s or 440s and later distributed to loyal followers. Some pieces may originally have been Roman diplomatic gifts to prominent Huns.

The Şimleu Silvaniei treasure gives some idea of the jewellery that might have been worn by high-ranking women north of the Danube. One piece is outstanding and, judging from its quality, was made by a skilled goldsmith in Constantinople. Thirty small loops, set at regular intervals, are attached to a heavy twisted chain seventy inches long (see plates, picture 25). Hanging from these loops are fifty-one miniature objects, mostly workman's tools. The whole looks just like a modern charm bracelet, but, at twenty-five ounces of twenty-two-carat gold, executed on a much grander and more ostentatious scale. The 'charms', each about an inch long, are delicately modelled. There is no need to search for any deep meaning in this delightfully amusing collection: a blacksmith's hammer and anvil, shears and a ladder, a chisel and pliers, a billhook and secateurs, an axe and a cudgel, five stylised vine leaves, a curved handsaw and rasp, a sword, a shield and a naked man in a fishing boat holding the rudder with both hands. How this chain was worn is not known: perhaps round the waist with a double drop at the front or, as it is long enough, over the shoulders crossing both chest and back. In either arrangement it would have been conspicuously elegant. It is attractive to imagine that Priscus, on behalf of the emperor, may have given Erecan something similar, or certainly no less chic. Wealthy women north of the Danube had expensive tastes. They wanted jewellery that equalled the finest worn at court in Constantinople. Any successful gift from a Roman embassy would need to satisfy their high expectations.

Whatever his reservations about handing out presents to leading Huns, Priscus must have been pleased with the results. Onegesius was willing to move matters forward by opening discussion on the possibility of a further round of talks. Repeating one of Attila's demands, Onegesius indicated that any new Roman embassy should be led by an eminent courtier. Priscus reported this to Maximinus. Together they discussed the best reply, deciding to trade on Onegesius' own reluctance to act as an ambassador. Priscus returned with the message that if Onegesius would not go to Constantinople, then Theodosius would appoint his own envoys and send them to the Huns. Immediately following this exchange of carefully formulated statements, Maximinus was granted an interview with Attila. As Priscus was not admitted, there is no detailed description of this encounter, although he does record that it was only a brief meeting. Maximinus was handed the names of those whom Attila said he would regard as acceptable ambassadors, a list that included Anatolius and Nomus, who had negotiated the peace settlement in 447. Revealing an increasing grasp of the subtleties of negotiation, Maximinus replied that Attila was misguided in seeking to nominate particular individuals. To do so would only lead Theodosius to suspect that they were no longer fully committed to the advancement of Roman interests. Attila refused to continue the diplomatic sparring; he simply declared that if his wishes were not respected, then he would resort to war.

Despite his abrupt dismissal and Attila's curt statement, Maximinus was confident that he had made progress. He was sure that an understanding could be reached. Even if Theodosius were to send Anatolius and Nomus, it could always be made clear that this was his own considered choice and not the result of Attila's demands. For the moment, what mattered was to keep the channels of communication open. Maximinus was pleased when shortly afterwards he received an invitation to dine that evening with Attila. Priscus was also to attend as an honoured guest. Maximinus was glad that he had stood his ground and not responded to threats of military action. In his view, the dinner invitation was a positive sign that he was not far away from a diplomatic breakthrough.

When Maximinus and Priscus arrived at the main hall in the middle of the palace compound they were directed to stand at the threshold, where they were given a cup of wine before being shown to their places. For Priscus, this was the beginning of an experience that more than justified the hardships of his journey beyond the Danube. At last he could observe at first hand some of the customs and habits of the most powerful of the Huns, and from a privileged position as one of Attila's guests. But the accuracy of fieldwork is only as good as the memory of the researcher. Sometimes Priscus is unclear in his descriptions, sometimes inconsistent. To be fair, the surviving text, as well as being cut down has in places been carelessly summarised by Constantine Porphyrogenitus' editorial team, but it is also clear that at times Priscus was struggling to recall the details of the evening.

One thing Priscus could not remember with any certainty was the seating plan. Attila was in the middle of the hall on a couch and to his right, in the place of highest honour, sat Onegesius. Down one side of the hall were seated high-ranking Huns, including two of Attila's sons. Or perhaps the elder – Priscus wasn't sure – was on the same couch as his father. The chairs to the left of Attila were occupied by other Hun notables, one of whom, Berich, was able to speak some Latin. A little further along sat Maximinus and Priscus. As a Roman ambassador at a state banquet Maximinus might reasonably have expected to be much nearer to Attila and his senior advisers.

Priscus was also confused in his account of the rituals at the start of the evening. Attila was handed a wooden cup of wine by one of the attendants. He then took the cup and offered it to his guests in strict order of precedence. Each guest stood up then sipped the wine or drank the whole cup – Priscus could not remember which – and gave it back to the attendant. When, in turn, the guest honoured by Attila had sat down, all the other guests raised their silver cups and drank together. After these greetings, tables were set up – again in order of precedence, beginning with Attila. There followed a lavish and well-prepared feast. The food was served on silver dishes and the wine offered to guests in gold and silver cups. After the first course, all rose and drank a full cup of wine to Attila's health. Next an equally splendid second course was served. Then all again stood and drained another full cup in a further salute to Attila. Perhaps Maximinus privately thought that the repeated toasting was a none too subtle response to Vigilas' own refusal in Serdica to honour Attila along with Theodosius. Needless to say, at Attila's feast no one proposed the health of the Roman emperor.

Priscus never forgot the scene. As darkness fell, the jewels worn by the Huns flashed in the flickering light of the pinewood torches that illuminated the hall. The second horde from Şimleu Silvaniei contained a beautiful shoulder brooch for fastening a heavy cloak (see plates, picture 24). Its oval-shaped body consists of a perfectly cleaved dark-purple onyx stone three inches in diameter. The cross-piece is set with pale-grey rock crystals and red garnets. (At the *strava* described in the Prologue this brooch is imagined as part of Attila's funeral regalia.) The superb quality of the piece indicates, as with the long charm chain, that it was made by a specialist jeweller within the Roman empire. Brooches similar in design were worn by emperors. A large silver plate, now in Madrid, is engraved with an idealised portrait of Theodosius I enthroned in all his glittering majesty. The emperor wears a cloak held in place on his right shoulder by a great oval brooch (see plates, picture 26).

These imperial fashions were reproduced in workshops beyond the frontier. An oval brooch from the Pietroasa treasure is set with garnets and rock crystals under a perforated gold plate. This piece is less ambitious in its method of manufacture and uses poorer-quality stones than Roman originals but follows the same design. The Şimleu Silvaniei horde also includes eight rectangular brooches likely to have been based closely on Roman models. For Priscus and Maximinus all this must have come as something of a shock. Far beyond the Danube, they cannot have expected to find a hall full of Huns wearing jewellery that would not have looked out of place on the wealthiest courtiers in the Great Palace at Constantinople.

After dinner, two bards came and stood in front of Attila. Priscus continues with one of the most striking of his recollections: 'They sang songs that they had composed, telling of Attila's victories and his deeds of valour in war. The guests at the feast gazed at them: some were delighted by the poetry, some were stirred by their memories of the wars and others were moved to tears.' Then the after-dinner amusements. First a madman whose unintelligible ravings provoked much laughter. (In this regard it must be emphasised that the Huns were not exceptional in their unsympathetic enjoyment of mental illness. The Romans were no more enlightened. Indeed, even in eighteenth-century London a visit to an insane asylum was regarded as a diverting afternoon's entertainment.) Next Zercon, the strange, stunted, stuttering favourite of Attila's dead elder brother Bleda. Once, on a whim, Bleda had given him the daughter of a high-ranking Hun in marriage. After Bleda's murder Attila had sent Zercon to France as a somewhat ambiguous gift to Aetius. He had made his way back to demand the return of his wife. 'He came forward and by his appearance, his clothes, his voice and by the words he spoke, which were all muddled up (for he scrambled Latin, Hunnic and Gothic), he put everyone in a good mood and caused them to laugh uncontrollably.'

Everyone, that is, except Attila. Although seated some distance away from the Hun leader, Priscus had observed him carefully from the moment the evening began. He noted with interest that amidst all the splendour of the feast, the silver tableware and fine food, Attila was served separately. For the first course he had eaten only meat from a wooden plate and drunk wine from a wooden mug. His clothes were plain and did not gleam with gold or jewels. He remained aloof from the laughter that greeted Zercon. Only once did Priscus see Attila's attitude soften – when he was standing next to Ernac, his youngest son. He had drawn Ernac close and looked at him affectionately, 'gazing at him with gentle eyes'. Noticing that Priscus was watching the two intently while everyone else was enjoying Zercon's antics, Berich quietly explained (in Latin) that a soothsayer had once told Attila that the future of his empire depended on Ernac alone.

Wide-eyed Priscus treasured such moments. It was for these that he had agreed to accompany Maximinus on his embassy. By contrast, Maximinus had had enough. He knew when his status as an ambassador had not been properly respected. Perhaps his frustration showed.

After all he had put up with a low-ranking position at dinner. Seated on an uncomfortable chair some distance away from Attila and Onegesius, he had not been able to exchange a word with them all evening. In a long and boring ritual he had been compelled to welcome every guest with a drink. He had toasted Attila's health three times and, worst of all, he had been forced to listen to interminable and tuneless Hun songs in praise of their victories in war. Maximinus could see little point in staying if all that remained was to laugh at Zercon's incoherent ramblings. Priscus was probably reluctant to go, although he may have recognised that he had already drunk too much and that this might blur his memory of some of the details of the evening. Yet there was a great deal more to be learned about the Huns and their leader. No doubt Maximinus insisted that his friend accompany him back to their tents. Indeed, if Maximinus had not made it absolutely clear that it was now time to leave, Priscus might have stayed up all night drinking with the Huns and staring at Attila.

# What the Historian Saw

The next morning Priscus' mind was still full of vivid images of the feast. As he tried to make sense of his experiences and put them into some order that might be useful when he later came to writing his history, it became increasingly clear how misleading it was to describe the Huns as 'barbarians' – as if that label explained anything. Certainly, for Priscus some aspects of Hun society remained unappealing. He was unlikely, for example, ever to approve of polygamy. For Priscus, one wife was enough. Monogamy was an ancient practice that Christianity had sanctified as morally correct. Nor, no matter how broad-minded he thought himself, could Priscus consider as anything other than backward a people whose elite shunned cities. Only the ignorant would turn away from the delights of urban living: the sunlit squares cooled by fountains, the hippodromes, the baths, the libraries, the theatres, the cathedrals and the sophisticated societies that built and enjoyed them. Equally, although not a deeply committed Christian, Priscus, like most of his contemporaries, was uneasy when confronted by others' unshakeable belief in gods whose existence he refused to recognise except perhaps as evil demons and enemies of the true faith.

Like many classical historians – the intellectual heirs of Herodotus – Priscus could have listed the differences between the Christian Roman empire and these devil-worshipping lands. Their inhabitants could again have appeared grotesque, threatening and primitive. For the educated in Constantinople – most without the inconvenience of ever having met a Hun – that might seem a plausible way of imposing order on a mass of miscellaneous and second-hand information about faraway peoples and places. Ten days journey beyond the Danube had exposed the poverty of that approach. Priscus was determined that his account would be emphatically different. His *History of Attila* would

offer readers something more challenging than another description of
Hun society as the Roman world turned upside down.

One of the most remarkable things Priscus noticed when he first
entered the village that clustered around Attila's palace was a stone-
built bathhouse adjacent to Onegesius' compound. Its construction,
Priscus learned, had posed severe problems, as the surrounding plain
provided neither timber nor stone. The dressed blocks had been
obtained by dismantling a building in a burnt-out Roman town or on
some abandoned great estate. The architect was a Roman prisoner of
war captured at Sirmium, probably when the city had been destroyed
in the campaign of 441–2. 'The architect had hoped to gain his freedom
as a reward for his ingenuity. But he was disappointed . . . for he was
made a bath attendant and waited on Onegesius and his companions
whenever they bathed.'

Onegesius' building was a long way from any of the huge public
baths that were amongst the most prominent structures in Roman
town centres. The more important the city – or at least the greater
its pretensions – the bigger the baths. These luxurious complexes,
sometimes including shopping malls, performing arts centres, lecture
halls, libraries and museums, were visible expressions of prosperity
and civic pride. Wealthy Romans reproduced miniature versions in
their private houses. Some features were standard: a changing room
(*apodyterium*), an unheated room (*frigidarium*) with a cold-water basin,
a warm room (*tepidarium*) and a hot room (*caladarium*) with a plunge
pool. Top-of-the-range bath suites might also include a sauna (*sudato-
rium* literally, 'sweat room'). The heat was provided by a wood-fired
furnace. Hot air circulated through a hypocaust, a space under the
tiled floors, which were raised two or three feet and supported on
narrow brick pillars.

In Sirmium, part of a bath building was excavated in 1961 in a
hurried two-week rescue dig ahead of the construction of a new hotel.
The floor of the *caladarium* was raised on brick pillars two feet high.
At one end was a semicircular plunge pool lined with waterproof
white concrete. Directly behind, with separate access from outside
the building, was a furnace, securely identified by a thick layer of charcoal. There is a strong possibility that this bath suite was associated
with a large mansion whose foundations were discovered nearby.
Acquainted with the layout of private baths in his hometown, the

captive architect from Sirmium may have designed something similar for Onegesius. Priscus was right to be amazed at the result. On a treeless and stoneless plain the construction and operation of even a modestly sized bathhouse were expensive undertakings. The very presence of such a building was an ostentatious proclamation by a leading Hun of his willingness to adopt a key Roman custom. Certainly it was more difficult to think of Onegesius and his companions as incomprehensibly barbaric if one could picture them vying to see who could stand the heat longest in the *caladarium* or splashing about in the plunge pool before bracing themselves for the invigorating shock of the cold water in the *frigidarium*. Perhaps Priscus wondered whether Onegesius ever invited Attila to bathe.

Onegesius' bathhouse was an identifiable fragment of Roman civilisation north of the Danube. It was a solid point of contact between two very different cultures. In introducing the Huns, Priscus was determined to offer his readership a description of a society that, at least in part, they could understand. He set out to challenge earlier versions of the Huns that had presented them as impenetrably foreign. Against Ammianus Marcellinus' claim that they were a people 'without permanent settlements or homes' who 'like refugees . . . are continually on the move with their wagons in which they live', Priscus set his detailed description of Onegesius and Attila's compounds. These were no temporary squatters' camps, an unsightly collection of sheepskin tents with wagons drawn up nearby. Rather they created an impression of order and permanence. The design of Attila's palace followed architectural principles that any Roman would appreciate. It was well laid out and cleverly sited. Its superior status was made clear by its elevated position on a natural rise and by the towers set into its wooden circuit wall.

Priscus' encounter with Erecan directly contradicted Ammianus' statement that the Huns' 'horrid clothes' were woven for them 'in their wagons by their wives'. When Priscus had met her, Erecan was supervising embroidery on the finest linens. It is also clear from the comfortable decoration of her apartments that she was not accustomed to live in the back of a wagon. Nor is there the slightest suggestion in Priscus that there was anything unusual about the Huns' eating habits. He offers no corroboration of Ammianus' assertion that 'they have no need of fire or pleasant-tasting foods, but eat the roots of uncultivated plants and the half-raw flesh of all sorts of animals'.

Priscus reports no bizarre culinary practices. If some Huns preferred beer to wine, then they were no more uncouth than many Romans who lived near the Danube frontier. High-ranking Huns clearly demanded that their meat should be cooked and had a liking, in common with upper-class Romans, for spices and exotic dried fruits.

Of course in all this Priscus is acutely sensitive to matters of scale. Attila's residence might be well planned and permanent, but it does not stand comparison with the splendour of the Great Palace in Constantinople. One private bathhouse does not make for urban civil-isation. A few dates, some Indian pepper and a well-done steak do not constitute *haute cuisine*. The Huns could never compete with the wealth and magnificence of Roman imperial culture. Yet, rather than following previous writers in underscoring the obvious contrasts between Huns and Romans, Priscus aimed to direct his readers' attention to a signifi-cant set of cultural coincidences – architecture, bathing habits, clothes and food. After all, it doesn't take much to spot the differences, but it takes an open-minded and observant enquirer to isolate those precious moments when two worlds, if only briefly, can be seen to touch.

It is precisely this pattern of explanation that shapes Priscus' account of his evening with Attila. There are many ways in which the feast fell far short of what might be expected at a grand Roman dinner party. The setting was a long wooden hall decorated with tapestries and dimly lit by pine torches. It was not a purpose-built room embel-lished with the finest marbles and mosaics and brightly illuminated by oil lamps. An account of a lunch held in the 460s at a stately home near Nîmes in southern France records that the guests were first received in the library, where some admired the host's extensive collec-tion of manuscripts, some amused themselves with board games while others held a serious theological debate. When all had been made welcome, the party moved through to lunch. In the houses of the wealthy the dining room was usually square with spacious alcoves on three sides. Each alcove held a semicircular couch on which the guests reclined. Only peasants sat on chairs. Each couch comfortably accom-modated up to nine guests lying alongside each other (like the spokes of a wheel) facing low portable D-shaped tables on which the food was served. The seating plan directly reflected status, with the more important guests placed on the right-hand side of the couches. Dinner-party conversation was meant to be erudite and amusing, although no doubt not every guest managed to achieve such an exacting ideal. After the meal, dancing, music or actors might provide further entertainment and provoke yet more edifying discussion.

The contrast with the arrangements for Attila's feast was plain: from the telltale use of chairs rather than couches through to some of the after-dinner performances. There could be nothing further from the cultured trading of well-chosen quotations from classical literature than Zercon's pleading for the return of his wife in a meaningless jumble of languages. Yet rather than scoff at the Huns' failure to live up to Roman standards, Priscus offered some thoughtful parallels with more familiar conventions. Attila's feast may have lacked the sophistication of a Roman dinner party, but it had its own complex etiquette. Attila's guests may not have been greeted in a well-appointed reception room, but they were individually honoured in an elaborate and courteous ceremony of welcome. They may (except for Attila himself) have sat upright on chairs, but the seating plan was carefully worked out – and cleverly calculated to offend the Roman ambassador. The food was well prepared and beautifully presented on silver platters. The Huns drank wine out of gold and silver vessels, not beer out of earthenware mugs. The entertainment not only included Zercon, but also a moving recital of Hun songs and poetry. Overall, the emphasis of the evening was on order and decorum. On this showing, the Huns could not simply be dismissed as a boorish bunch of *nomades*.

To be sure, Priscus did not doubt the merits of Roman civilisation, but he was concerned to stress that its superiority could not be taken for granted. One morning while he was waiting outside Attila's compound he was approached by a man wearing Hun clothes. Priscus was surprised to be addressed in Greek. 'I returned the greeting and enquired who he was and where he came from . . . In reply he asked why I was so eager to know. I said the fact that he spoke Greek was the reason for my curiosity.' Priscus learned that the man was a wealthy trader from the frontier town of Viminacium sacked in the Hun offensive of 441–2. Taken captive, he had been allocated to Onegesius as part of his share of the spoils from the campaign. He had then fought for the Huns and had bought his freedom by giving his booty to his master. Now he had a Hun wife and children, and boasted that 'as part of Onegesius' household, he had a better life than he had enjoyed previously'.

The trader went on to offer a critique of Roman rule. The encounter, as reported by Priscus, is less of a conversation and more like an exercise set by a tutor of rhetoric. Even so, the staged debate again allows Priscus – here through the mouthpiece of a renegade Roman – to question some of the assumed differences between the two empires. The trader pointed to the Huns' skill in warfare. He pitied the citizens of the Roman empire, who, untrained in the use of weapons, '"are put in even more danger by the cowardice of their generals who are unable to conduct a war properly"'. In addition, he alleged, they suffered high taxes and a poor system of justice in which the rich paid to secure an acquittal. '"If the wrongdoer is rich, he does not pay the penalty for his offence, but if he is poor, and does not know how to deal with the matter, he suffers the penalty laid down by law."'

Priscus replied in detail. From the start it is obvious that in this exchange he will have the upper hand – after all, this is his story. For the most part, Priscus' emphasis is on the ideals of the Roman empire, rather than the everyday realities of its operation.

> 'Those who founded the Roman state,' I said, 'were wise and good . . .
> They laid down that those involved in farming and the cultivation of the
> land should provide for themselves and through taxation for those fighting
> on their behalf . . . The founders appointed others to have as their concern
> those who had been wronged, others to take charge of the cases of those
> who, because of their incapacity, were unable to represent themselves
> and others to sit in judgement so the law might be upheld.'

And so on for some time. (Priscus gave himself even more space in his original text. There are some obvious cuts by Constantine Porphyrogenitus' impatient editors.) Worn down by Priscus' rhetoric, or perhaps wishing that he had never started the argument, the trader finally agreed that '"the laws were fair and the Roman state was good"'. But Priscus' victory was not clear-cut. The trader was allowed the last word: 'Weeping he said . . . those in charge were wrecking the state by not having the same thought for it as those in the past.' Priscus offered no response. Unlike previous criticisms, it was not countered by a long-winded rebuttal. Priscus' uncharacteristic silence leaves open the possibility that, on this matter at least, he might have agreed.

*

In presenting Attila to his readers, Priscus pursued these themes even further. In his account of Attila's appearance he turned his back on the long-standing tradition of describing *nomades* as more bestial than human. Attila did not look like a Roman, yet he was not so hideously ugly that, like Ammianus Marcellinus' Huns, he might be mistaken for a 'two-legged beast or for one of those images crudely hewn from tree stumps that can be seen on the parapets of bridges'. Nor did Priscus attribute to Attila any of the depravity or irrational behaviour normally associated with the enemies of Rome either in civil wars or external conflicts, and, since Constantine, with non-Christians. Images of madness and immorality are commonplace in the histories of the fourth and fifth centuries. Indeed after a while these seemingly inexhaustible catalogues of tyrants' personal failings dull through constant repetition. In 389 in a speech delivered in Rome before Theodosius I to celebrate the defeat of the usurper Magnus Maximus, the orator, claiming to have witnessed these events himself, abandoned any subtlety in order to drive his point home.

> We were the first to bear the brunt of the raging beast and his savagery was satisfied only with the blood of the innocent . . . As drinking aggravates thirst in the sick, as flames are not dampened, but gain strength by the addition of kindling, so riches amassed through the impoverishment of the public excite the greed of the ravenous-minded . . . in pandering to his gullet and belly . . . he spends freely and carelessly. With an equal ease he accumulates and squanders . . . To Maximus all ways of earning praise seemed fatuous. Rejecting that model of virtue that is innate even in the worst of men, he defined his greatest happiness in terms of acquiring possessions and doing harm.

This bravura tirade continues for another twelve printed pages, or – since this is a speech – for at least another half an hour.

Priscus deliberately avoids these litanies of lurid claims and, given the tone and content of the surviving fragments of his *History*, there is no reason to think that a lengthy section of abuse has been edited out. The notable absence of any sustained personal attack on Attila's character will have caught the attention of his readers. Some, knowing Priscus to be an accomplished rhetorician, might well have been looking forward to a virtuoso display of vituperation. It is highly unlikely that anyone actually expected Priscus to praise Attila. Yet in his account of the feast Priscus made a point of emphasising Attila's moderation, frugality and restraint: he wore no jewels; he did not find Zercon amusing; during dinner he was served only simple food and used a wooden plate and mug. 'For us there were lavishly prepared dishes presented on silver platters, for Attila there was nothing more than meat on a wooden plate. He showed himself moderate in other ways as well. For while gold and silver cups were handed to the men at the feast, his mug was of wood.'

The educated knew how to read such signs. For nearly five centuries, ever since the first Roman emperor Augustus, behaviour at banquets had been one of the moral measures of a ruler. Gluttony and excessive feasting were indications of a dangerously capricious monarch unfit to govern. It was at dinner that the most hated emperors of the first century had revealed their true natures. It was the disorderly seating at a sumptuous banquet that for many confirmed their suspicions of Caligula's incest with his sisters. According to his biographer Suetonius, Nero held feasts that 'lasted from noon to midnight, with frequent breaks for plunging into a warm pool or in the summertime into snow-cooled water'. It was over dinner that Nero was first seduced by his mother Agrippina. By contrast, the best Roman emperors were restrained and moderate. Augustus sometimes ate nothing or only a little plain food. Again according to Suetonius, 'He was a frugal eater . . . and usually had simple fare. He was especially fond of coarse bread, whitebait, hand-made soft cheese and green figs.' For Eusebius, it was Constantine who, as the first Christian emperor, was the most virtuous ruler the empire had ever had. His dinners too were marked by moderation. A state banquet held in 326 to celebrate the twentieth anniversary of his rule was so restrained and orderly, and there were so many bishops as guests, that any onlooker 'might have thought that he had imagined a vision of the kingdom of Christ'.

It is against this rich backdrop of moralising about the dining habits of Roman emperors that Priscus' readers would have placed his account of Attila. It is the absence of drunkenness, gluttony and excess that would have been most striking. His behaviour displayed a degree of moderation and restraint that could favourably be compared with the best of emperors. Remarkably too, Priscus revealed Attila to be a subtle and effective diplomat able to outwit the most powerful courtiers in Constantinople. The irony of Chrysaphius' plot is that it might have succeeded if Attila had been the stupidly cruel barbarian that the eunuch clearly assumed him to be. Priscus was prepared to take these comparisons even further, suggesting that in some respects Attila achieved a higher standard of kingly virtue than Theodosius. In his criticism of the emperor's policy of subsidising the Huns, Priscus implies that this is precisely the kind of cowardly action that might be expected from a ruler who squandered money on 'absurd spectacles, unreasonable displays of liberality, pleasures and recklessly extravagant banquets that no right-thinking person would countenance even in prosperous times'. The pointed contrast between Theodosius and Attila is too sharp to miss. On this view, Attila the Hun was a successful leader, not because he violated Roman moral codes or stood defiantly outside them, but because he fulfilled them. Judged by Roman standards, Attila was in some ways a more praiseworthy monarch than Theodosius. In Priscus' opinion it was precisely Attila's frugality, moderation and shrewdness as a ruler – rather than any uncontrolled savagery – that made him truly frightening.

In daring to reach these thought-provoking conclusions, Priscus' *History of Attila* is exceptional. It is rare in fourth- or fifth-century Roman literature to find an author willing to attempt some kind of balanced account of those who lived beyond the frontiers. Of course in offering a less prejudiced picture of the Huns, Priscus was not intending to downplay the brutality of their Danube offensives. He did not seek to excuse Attila; rather he aimed to show that the conflicts between Romans and Huns were more complex than clashes between good and evil, civilisation and barbarism, virtue and tyranny. Black-and-white explanations of events, however attractive they may at first seem, are always likely to be wrong. This approach may not have been popular with all of his readers. For many Romans it was comfortable to think of the Huns as uncultured, uncivilised and irredeemably foreign, and their leaders as treacherous, immoral and wildly unstable. Priscus' *History* offered a more sophisticated description of the world beyond the Danube, and a deliberately more disturbing one. After all, it is always reassuring to think of our enemies as godless barbarians. It is troubling to learn that they might be more like us than we would ever care to admit.

# Truth and Dare

From the moment he crossed the Danube, Maximinus had been trapped in a pointless series of exchanges intended by Attila to give the impression that he knew nothing of the arrangements that had been made between Chrysaphius, Edeco and Vigilas for the delivery of fifty pounds of gold. Attila hoped that Chrysaphius would be convinced to proceed as planned. There was no reason for Priscus to be suspicious either of the pretext for Vigilas' return to Constantinople or of the Huns' continued courteous treatment of the Roman envoys. At the time, Maximinus, still ignorant of the plot to assassinate Attila, was acutely aware both of his lack of progress and of his inability to understand the cause. Summer had nearly passed and he had been away from Constantinople for over a month. Rather than attempt another fruitless round of discussions, Maximinus decided that it was time to return home.

Attila offered no objection to Maximinus' departure. By now Vigilas should have arrived at the imperial court and there was nothing further to be gained by detaining the Roman ambassador more than another five days, sufficient to ensure that Vigilas had met privately with Chrysaphius. Meanwhile, there was every reason for Attila and Onegesius to keep up their show of tactful civility. On the same day he announced he was leaving, Maximinus at last received a formal reply to the letter from Theodosius he had handed to Attila at their first meeting. The reply was drafted by Onegesius in consultation with Attila's closest advisers and one of his Latin-speaking private secretaries. Nothing of its content is known. Any further references have not survived the cuts made by Constantine Porphyrogenitus' editors. There may have been little for Priscus to report. With Vigilas soon to leave Constantinople, Onegesius may have advised against any strongly worded response. Perhaps he recommended that Attila's letter to Theodosius – like so many other diplomatic communiqués – should simply substitute courtesy for content. Tough talking could wait until Vigilas had been stopped and searched, and confessed his part in Chrysaphius' conspiracy.

The round of dinner parties continued. Erecan invited Priscus and Maximinus to the house of her steward Adamis, who managed all her property. Priscus briefly records another excellent meal with (in his admiring phrase) an impressive 'spread of eatables'. The Romans were again welcomed with an elaborate drinking ritual. All the Huns stood up and in turn offered a full cup of wine to their guests; they then embraced and kissed them and took back the cup. The next night Priscus and Maximinus dined again with Attila. The feast took the same form as before. No doubt the food was as fine and the gold and silver tableware as impressive. There was one significant difference: the Romans were seated nearer to Attila. Maximinus certainly welcomed this. He may have thought that it offered one last opportunity to resolve matters of mutual interest.

But Maximinus was again wrong-footed. Avoiding any reference to issues discussed in their previous meetings, Attila began a lengthy account of an alleged wrong suffered by Constantius, one of his confidential private secretaries. Constantius originally came from Italy and was fluent in Latin. He had been sent by Aetius to serve on Attila's personal staff. Attila claimed that, while on an embassy to the imperial court, Constantius had struck a bargain with Theodosius offering to promote peace with the Huns in return for the emperor agreeing to arrange his marriage to a wealthy and well-connected woman in Constantinople. The undertaking had never been fulfilled and the bride nominated by Theodosius had been seized – under what circumstances it was not clear – by the powerful general Flavius Zeno, responsible for the security of the empire's eastern frontier. She had then been married off to one of his senior officers. Attila demanded that Constantius should have his promised wife or be given another of similar standing. He instructed Maximinus to inform Theodosius of Zeno's intervention. Attila was sure that the emperor would act immediately to rectify the situation, 'for it is not like a ruler to lie'. Of course, if Theodosius was not strong enough on his own to control the actions of his subordinates then he, Attila, was always ready to offer an alliance to enable the emperor to assert his full imperial authority.

Attila's allegations and his extraordinary offer to help Theodosius discipline a senior general tested Maximinus' diplomatic abilities to the limit. At times he must have wondered whether the interpreter had made a mistake. Certainly, Attila's mocking remarks were intended to discomfit his guest. After all, how should one respond when the leader of the Huns presents himself as a loyal ally of the Roman emperor? It was hardly a suggestion to be taken seriously, and yet to laugh might be insulting, or perhaps Attila meant it as a joke and not to laugh would be equally offensive. Maximinus may now have appreciated the advantages of being seated too far away from Attila to engage in conversation. As Priscus had found at the first feast, it had been better – and much safer – just to stare.

Maximinus is best imagined as sitting with a fixed expression that he hoped was suitably ambiguous and listening attentively as Attila's tale of Constantius' disappointments unfolded. Perhaps too Attila should be thought of as having enjoyed the situation, taking the opportunity to point out some of Theodosius' weaknesses to a Roman ambassador who listened dutifully with his face set in a kind of rigid half-smile. To be sure, it was not the first time the emperor had been accused of being unable to curb his powerful courtiers. In such situations eunuchs were usually the first to be suspected. But, as Maximinus might later have remarked, it is one thing to hear that said quietly at a private dinner party in Constantinople, quite another when it is a matter for ridicule at a feast hosted by one of the empire's most dangerous enemies.

After this final, disagreeable encounter, Maximinus was glad to leave. As a parting gesture of goodwill Attila ordered each of his closest companions to present him with a horse. Such generosity was again clearly intended to embarrass Maximinus who selected only a few and returned the rest of the horses, explaining that his own modesty and dislike of lavish display prevented him from accepting such costly gifts. He hoped that the Huns would understand his natural restraint. In the virtuous game of competitive moderation Maximinus was determined not to be outdone by Attila.

On their homeward journey Priscus and Maximinus were accompanied by Berich, the Latin-speaking Hun who had sat near them at

Attila's first feast. Then he had been helpful in explaining Hun etiquette and talking to Priscus about Attila. For the next few days Berich's good humour continued, and the Romans enjoyed riding, eating and conversing with him – 'we thought him gracious and affable'. But after crossing the Danube his demeanour changed abruptly. From then on he was hostile, 'treating us as though we were the enemy'. He rudely took back the horse he had given to Maximinus, refused to speak and took his meals alone. Challenged to explain this sudden shift in attitude, Berich would only say that he had heard – precisely how was unclear – that Maximinus had blamed the Romans' recent defeats on the failings of the generals Aspar and Ariobindus, who had both been relieved of their commands after the Hun offensive in 447. Berich rejected Maximinus' explanation outright: to claim that Aspar and Ariobindus had been incompetent was an insult to the military prowess of the Huns and the strategic brilliance of Attila.

Berich's exaggerated objection to Maximinus' remarks was only part of the problem. Like Onegesius before him, Berich feared that any report of an amicable association between him and the Romans, particularly once they were inside the empire, might be regarded by Attila as evidence of treachery. He may have felt himself especially vulnerable to such accusations as he spoke Latin. Any courtier wishing to entrap him would not even need an interpreter. Maximinus and Priscus, entirely unaware of these concerns, could only puzzle at Berich's behaviour. Given his previous friendliness, his offensive rejection of everything Roman was strange and his excuses plainly inadequate. It must have seemed an unexpected irony that the closer Berich came to Constantinople the more he chose to act like a stereotypical barbarian.

As they neared the capital, Priscus and Maximinus passed Eslas and Vigilas, who were starting out on their long journey back to the Great Hungarian Plain. This time Vigilas was travelling with his son. The meeting with Chrysaphius had gone as Attila had hoped. The eunuch had found no reason to think that the assassination plot had been compromised and Vigilas was given the fifty pounds of gold for delivery to Edeco. Nor can anything that Priscus and Maximinus had to say about their time at Attila's court have aroused Vigilas' suspicions. For the most part they had been courteously treated and no attempt had been made to prevent them from returning to Constantinople. Confident in the success of his mission and that Edeco had kept his side of the bargain, Vigilas continued on his way. His journey was uneventful. It was not until its final day that he walked straight into the trap carefully prepared for him. As he approached the village surrounding Attila's palace, he was arrested and searched. The fifty pounds of gold concealed in leather bags in his luggage was confiscated.

Brought before Attila, Vigilas was asked to explain why he was carrying so much money. His reply was predictable: some of the gold was to purchase food for himself and his servants as well as fodder for the horses and pack animals; the rest had been given to him by those in the empire who were eager that he should ransom their relatives still held captive by the Huns. Attila's response was curt and to the point: "'You will not evade justice by your clever talk. Your excuses will not be good enough for you to escape punishment. The amount of money you have is more than enough to purchase provisions for yourself, your horses and pack animals, and to ransom prisoners of war, the very thing I banned you from doing when you came before me with Maximinus.'"

When Attila threatened to kill his son, Vigilas confessed everything, implicating Chrysaphius, Martialis and Theodosius and confirming Edeco and Orestes' earlier reports of a conspiracy. Perhaps at that moment Vigilas expected to be executed. Unmoved by his tears, Attila dismissed his desperate pleas for mercy. But Vigilas, yet again, had failed to read the situation correctly. He was in no danger of death. Instead Attila imprisoned him and ordered his son to return to Constantinople. In the Great Palace he was to insist on a meeting with Chrysaphius and on receiving a further fifty pounds of gold, the ransom Attila now demanded for his father.

Along with Vigilas' son, Attila sent two ambassadors, Orestes and Eslas. This was a nicely ambiguous choice. Chrysaphius would wonder how much each of them had known, and for how long. The Hun envoys were given specific instructions for the conduct of their audience with Theodosius. One of the leather bags in which Vigilas had hidden the gold was to be hung around Orestes' neck. The bag was to be shown to both the emperor and Chrysaphius, who were to be asked directly if they recognised it. The envoys were to demand that the eunuch should be sent across the Danube to explain his actions face-to-face with Attila. Eslas was then to observe that Theodosius was as nobly born as the Hun leader (itself a startling comparison), but while Attila had maintained his honour as a ruler, the emperor by his involvement in the assassination plot had reduced himself to the status of a slave. The claim was obviously exaggerated, and yet like Attila's earlier jibe that Theodosius was unable to control his most powerful courtiers, it could not entirely be dismissed. Priscus hoped that it would again compel his readers to confront some difficult questions. At stake was the conventional and uncompromising contrast between virtuous Roman emperor and evil barbarian tyrant. Any who doubted the moral force of Attila's challenge to Theodosius only had to imagine Orestes standing silently in the glittering throne room of the Great Palace with an empty leather bag slung around his neck.

# 18

# End Game

In cutting down Priscus' *History of Attila*, Constantine Porphyrogenitus' editorial team had no sense of how to finish a good story. It is not at all to their credit that one of the passages they chose to discard was Priscus' account of the arrival of the Hun envoys in Constantinople in autumn 449. It is not known whether Orestes and Eslas ever played out their dramatic scene with the empty leather bag before the impassively enthroned Theodosius and his court. Sadly it seems more likely that they never made it very far into the Great Palace. Perhaps, instead of confronting the emperor, they were seen by the master of the offices, Flavius Martialis, and their concerns dealt with in an entirely businesslike way. Nor is there any record of Maximinus or Priscus' immediate reaction to the news that their embassy to Attila had been a dangerous blind. Priscus' anger can be assumed from the hatred for Chrysaphius that seeps through the surviving text of the *History of Attila* and was condensed by one of its later readers, the seventh-century monk and historian John of Antioch.

> Theodosius, who ruled after his father Arcadius, was unwarlike and lived a life of cowardice. He obtained peace by money and not by arms. Everything he did was under the supervision of eunuchs, and these eunuchs brought matters to such a ridiculous state that, in brief, they distracted Theodosius – just like children are distracted with playthings – and prevented him from achieving anything worth recording . . . in particular Chrysaphius possessed the power of an emperor.

For Priscus, there was nothing praiseworthy in the way Theodosius or Chrysaphius had conducted themselves. Their attempt at regime change through assassination was as defective as their continued payment of subsidies and that, in turn, was the result of a shameful failure by the emperor and his generals to defend the Danube provinces. In Priscus' view, his own advocacy of military action was not inconsistent with his revisionist portrayal of the Huns or with his claim that Attila possessed virtues traditionally associated with good Roman emperors. Priscus' time with the Huns had not made him any less patriotic; he had not 'gone native'. The Huns were still the enemy, and if an enemy is to be defeated then it must first be understood. (It is a mistake to think that greater comprehension necessarily leads to greater sympathy or closer cooperation. Effective warfare also depends on accurate intelligence.) A direct comparison with Attila further emphasised Theodosius' deficiencies. For Priscus, the merits of the Hun leader – as judged by Roman standards – were not an argument for a more friendly relationship. On the contrary, they suggested that Attila could be overcome by a properly virtuous Roman emperor.

Not all of Priscus' brash polemic against Theodosius and his advisers is persuasive. There were sound reasons for the military tactics adopted in 447. Given the security situation on three frontiers it made good sense to pay subsidies rather than risk a major offensive that might result in the dangerous fragmentation of the Hun empire. No doubt, with a better understanding of Attila and the Huns, these strategies could have been more effectively pursued. Yet Priscus shows no interest in exploring these possibilities. He is not prepared to concede that Theodosius' Danube policy could ever have produced positive results. Such conclusions are limited and unsatisfactory. They are a reminder that Priscus' strength as a historian lies in his description of the Huns, which is often perceptive and provocative, and not in his discussion of Roman foreign relations, which, tightly focused on a single frontier, is often hostile and blinkered. This he can be forgiven: after all, in attacking Theodosius and Chrysaphius, Priscus was understandably settling a score with those who were prepared to risk his life by using him as a front for an assassination attempt.

However loudly Priscus voiced his views on his return from the Danube, no one seems to have been listening, and of course he is very unlikely to have criticised Theodosius openly or to have offered his own favourable account of Attila's personal qualities. If Priscus expected Chrysaphius' position to be weakened by allegations that he had secretly masterminded a failed attempt to murder Attila, then he must have been disappointed. In Constantinople the news was greeted with well-practised disbelief. Theodosius is likely to have made it clear that he had no knowledge whatsoever of any conspiracy. For many at court the explanation was clear: the whole story had been fabricated to embarrass the emperor and his advisers. Any claims to the contrary could be dismissed. After all, the Huns were still holding Vigilas captive. In the face of Attila's accusations it was Chrysaphius' counter-claims that were believed. A disgusted Priscus bitterly concedes that the eunuch continued to enjoy 'universal goodwill and support'.

Denial was followed by cover-up. In early 450 the senior courtiers Anatolius and Nomus – the latter described by Priscus as a staunch supporter of Chrysaphius – were sent to discuss terms with Attila. (The same duo had successfully negotiated peace after the Hun invasion in 447). The ambassadors' tactics were simple: 'At first Attila negotiated arrogantly, but he was overwhelmed by the number of gifts and pacified by their conciliatory statements.' Chrysaphius had ensured that Anatolius and Nomus had more than enough gold to buy off Attila and ransom Vigilas. There were to be no loose ends. Even Attila's complaint on behalf of his secretary Constantius was dealt with. The sorry tale of abduction and frustrated matrimony as told to Maximinus was probably false, but the Roman ambassadors preferred to provide a solution rather than provoke any further argument. Constantius was offered another bride of equivalent wealth and status to the one he claimed had originally been promised by Theodosius. In return for these concessions, Attila affirmed his commitment to peace – with of course the continued payment of subsidies. Perhaps to the surprise of the ambassadors, he was also willing to agree a package of measures aimed at reducing diplomatic friction between the Huns and the eastern empire. Large numbers of prisoners of war were released and without ransom; demands for the return of asylum-seekers were dropped; all claims over Roman territory five days journey south of the Danube were withdrawn; and no further reference was made to the alleged conspiracy or the extradition of Chrysaphius.

Chrysaphius might reasonably have congratulated himself on surviving the crisis. Attila had been placated and Anatolius and Nomus had secured peace on the northern frontier; Vigilas would not dare to return to Constantinople; Priscus had gone back to teaching rhetoric;

and Maximinus had rejoined his regiment. At that time too it must have seemed to Priscus unlikely that his *History of Attila* would ever be published. He could not risk revealing Chrysaphius' involvement in the conspiracy to assassinate Attila or implicate the emperor. Maximinus would never agree to that. It would end their friendship and jeopardise their careers. As long as Theodosius was on the throne and the eunuch in power the truth was better suppressed. It might instead be wiser to publish another collection of lectures on rhetoric. For the moment working on a set of model orations seemed a safer prospect than writing history.

Within six months all that had changed. On 26 July 450 Theodosius, then in his late forties, suffered a serious spinal injury in a riding accident. He was carried back to the Great Palace and died in extreme pain two days later. Following long-established precedent, the new emperor, Marcian, rid himself of many of his predecessor's confidential advisers. It was rare for prominent eunuchs to survive such purges. Their loyalty was always suspect and their removal a clear sign of the independence of the new regime. Eunuchs such as Chrysaphius simply knew too much and after Theodosius' death there was no one to argue against his execution.

With Chrysaphius eliminated, Vigilas returned to Constantinople. Priscus was eager to meet the one man he knew was key to understanding the plot that had dogged Maximinus' mission. It was from Vigilas that Priscus finally learned the details of the meeting in the Great Palace between Edeco and Chrysaphius. Vigilas also explained Orestes' cryptic remarks at Serdica, as well as Scottas' rudeness and then sudden willingness to arrange an audience with Attila. For his own part, Vigilas admitted to having been taken in by Attila's anger over asylum-seekers (he had not seen that it was a pretext to get him to return to Constantinople) and by Edeco's assurances that he could bribe Attila's bodyguard. No doubt it was with grim amazement that Priscus realised that Attila must have known about the conspiracy right from the start. It was also clear that Vigilas' information would transform Priscus' *History*. Alongside his radically new assessment of the society and customs of the Huns he planned to place a full account of Maximinus' embassy and of Chrysaphius' failed conspiracy. Thanks to Vigilas' eyewitness evidence, Theodosius and his advisers could now be exposed as outright liars.

Whatever his enthusiasm to get on with writing it, Priscus' *History* was again delayed. Marcian seems to have accepted that the embassy to Attila had been compromised from the start and Maximinus had conducted himself as well as could be expected. He was again dispatched on diplomatic missions and invited Priscus to accompany him. In late 450 they journeyed together to Rome; a year later they set out from Constantinople, travelling first to Damascus, then overland to Alexandria and down the Nile. Maximinus was responsible for negotiating with tribes threatening the security of southern Egypt. Late the following year, soon after a peace treaty was ratified at Philae (just upriver from modern Aswan), Maximinus became seriously ill. He never recovered. In 453 Priscus returned alone to Constantinople, determined to commemorate his friend by completing his account of their experiences four years earlier at the court of Attila.

Priscus' *History of Attila* – the first part written in the mid-450s – met with immediate critical acclaim. Like most ancient books it reached the majority of its contemporary audience through public readings, often given by the author himself. It was thought by its admirers to be 'very learned' and 'elegantly written'. It soon became the most authoritative and widely quoted account of relations between the Roman empire and the Huns. It launched Priscus on a successful literary career. He continued his project of writing contemporary history, publishing his work at intervals over the next twenty-five years. In addition, Priscus edited collections of his correspondence and lectures. None of these has survived. No doubt they too were learned and elegantly written, but they are unlikely ever to have been as popular as his historical writing.

Aside from the critics' praise, which like any author he is sure to have enjoyed, Priscus hoped that his *History* was a fitting memorial to his best friend. He had attempted to show Maximinus as a loyal and honourable Roman, a trustworthy and straightforward soldier prepared to carry out his duty even in the most adverse circumstances. Regrettably it is not known what Vigilas thought of Priscus' version of events. Given his importance in supplying so much crucial material, he might have wished for a more sympathetic portrayal. Too often he appeared as either deceitful or foolish. On the other hand, if it were not for Priscus' *History of Attila*, no one would ever have heard of Vigilas the interpreter.

Of course that is what Chrysaphius had intended. It may safely be reckoned that the palace archives contained no record of any private meeting with Edeco or any payments to Vigilas. Chrysaphius had always assumed that were his schemes ever to be compromised, Attila could be relied on to do the rest. An embarrassing failure in Roman foreign policy would disappear without trace. Once Edeco had confessed, Priscus, Maximinus and Vigilas should have been butchered by a hot-blooded Hun seeking a swift revenge. If all had turned out as Chrysaphius expected, and Attila had behaved like a barbarian tyrant, then Priscus would never have survived to write his *History*. The truth should have been buried with him somewhere beyond the Danube.

PART IV

# THE FAILURE OF EMPIRE

# Hearts and Minds

In summer 442 the once-beautiful daughter of the Gothic ruler Theodoric returned to her father. Her ears clipped and her nose slit, she would never again be seen in public. No historian even recorded her name. This vicious punishment had been carried out on the orders of Geiseric, leader of the Vandals, whose teenage son Huneric had married Theodoric's daughter only a short while before. Geiseric accused her of involvement in a plot to poison him and had sent her back – disgraced and disfigured – to her father's court at Toulouse. This painful story is offered by the sixth-century historian Jordanes in his *Origin and Acts of the Goths* as an explanation for the hatred between Geiseric and Theodoric. It is a sharp reminder that those peoples who now occupied territory within the empire cannot be assumed to have been natural allies. They fought amongst themselves as frequently as they fought together against the Romans.

The deterioration in relations between the Goths and Vandals was connected to Geiseric's attempts to strengthen his own ties with the western Roman empire. In late 442 he announced Huneric's engagement to Valentinian III's daughter Eudocia. At the time she was just three years old. There was nothing unusual in this arrangement. Twenty years earlier Eudocia's mother, Licinia Eudoxia (the daughter of Theodosius II), had been promised to Valentinian. Then Eudoxia had been a two year-old and her future husband five. Huneric was only free to make such a politically astute match once his first wife had been banished. The suspicious asserted her role in the conspiracy to remove Geiseric; the sceptical may have thought the timing rather too convenient. Geiseric himself had no regrets: if the mutilation of Theodoric's daughter had antagonised the Goths, it had been a price worth paying to clear the way for a dynastic connection between the Vandal ruling house and the Roman imperial family. For Jordanes, Geiseric's brutal international diplomacy was an indication of his strength of character, which in other circumstances might have been admirable, and his determination to secure the permanence of Vandal rule in North Africa. 'Geiseric was of medium height and limped as a result of a fall while out riding. He thought deeply, said little and despised luxury. He had a violent temper, was single-mindedly acquisitive and remarkably far-sighted. He was prepared to sow the seeds of discord and incite hatred in order to stir up others.'

In promoting the special relationship between Carthage and Ravenna, Geiseric aimed to erase his past as an enemy of the Roman empire and hoped to dissuade Theodosius and Valentinian from any further attempt at reconquest. Under the treaty agreed after the withdrawal of Roman troops from Sicily, Geiseric undertook to compensate the western imperial government for the loss of African tax revenue. Not all leading Vandals approved of these pro-Roman policies. The finalisation of the peace settlement was followed by a major revolt. Internal opposition was brutally stamped out. Prosper of Aquitaine commented acidly in his *Chronicle* that Geiseric's suspicions meant that through torture and execution he 'lost more men as a result of his own insecurity than if he had been defeated in war'. For Valentinian, the rebellion underlined the importance of keeping Geiseric in power. It was clear that if he were to fall, he might be replaced by a regime openly hostile to the empire.

It was also in Geiseric's interests to prevent an alliance between Valentinian and Theodoric. As long as the main threat to imperial rule came from the Goths, even the most warlike of advisers in Ravenna would be reluctant to argue for a campaign in Africa. With this in mind, Geiseric made diplomatic contact with Attila, sending gifts and encouraging him to attack the Goths. Chaos in France would be to North Africa's advantage. The Romans would be compelled to fight Goths or Huns, rather than Vandals. The success of Geiseric's scheme depended on Flavius Aetius. Sometime in the 440s Aetius persuaded, or forced, Valentinian to confer the honorary rank of general on Attila. This does not mean that Attila ever commanded any Roman legions; at most, he received the substantial salary that went with the post. But as an honorary general Attila could formally be recognised as part of the imperial military establishment. However strange it must have seemed, Aetius could now claim Attila as his colleague. As comrades in arms they exchanged gifts. Attila made a present of Zercon, the Roman prisoner of war whose bizarre appearance and curious antics had once so amused Bleda. Aetius sent Attila the educated Italian Constantius to act as his private secretary. (This is the Constantius whose frustrated marriage plans were the subject of Attila's lengthy protest to Maximinus.)

For Aetius, public affirmation of his friendship with Attila was a useful insurance policy. Anyone who challenged him would need to risk the possibility of Hun intervention. Whether troops would be sent was always open to question – in 435, despite Aetius' bravado, the Huns had never turned up. Even so, it was certain that no other Roman general could threaten to draw on military resources from outside the empire. Importantly too, should Attila decide to advance west on his own initiative, no other Roman general could hope to turn a Hun offensive to his own advantage. Attila may have viewed his relationship with Aetius differently: a temporary convergence of mutual interest rather than a lasting friendship. The gift of Zercon was not without its ambiguity as it was well known that Attila loathed him. Aetius was perhaps not entirely sure what to make of his present. It was unflattering to think that Attila had chosen to rid himself of Zercon because he thought that his murdered brother's favourite would better suit Aetius' tastes.

Of greater concern was Attila's unwillingness to support – at least consistently – imperial interests in France. In 437, after the massacre of the Burgundians, Roman and Hun troops under Litorius had suppressed the Bagaudae. Despite the ferocity of the campaign, Aetius had to deal with another rebellion a decade later. This was no peasants' revolt. At its core was a coalition of landowners – locals and those who had moved north to escape the permanent settlement of the Goths around Toulouse. Some of these economic migrants had managed to hang on to at least part of their wealth. The Bagaudae were concerned about their security and doubted whether allegiance to the empire offered any lasting guarantee of protection. Given this uncertainty, they preferred to rely on their own initiative and resources; but while they could offer some limited opposition to Roman rule, they could never muster sufficient manpower to defend themselves against any serious military threat. The Bagaudae could never withstand the Huns.

That same thought had occurred to those coordinating the unrest. In 448, after Aetius had crushed the latest uprising, a prominent member of the Bagaudae is reported to have fled to the Huns. This appeal for asylum should not be taken as any indication that Attila might have considered marching into France in support of a loose alliance of those disaffected with Roman rule. That said, as long as there was even a distant possibility of a Hun campaign in the West, it made good sense for the Bagaudae to establish direct contact with Attila. They could only benefit from a weakening of Aetius' much-advertised relationship with the Huns. No doubt too Attila welcomed the opportunity to demonstrate his independence. In sheltering a rebel leader hunted by Aetius, he made it clear that the Huns could not always be trusted to side with the empire.

How far Attila and Aetius had drifted apart was evident to Priscus in summer 449. As he and Maximinus approached the village that surrounded Attila's palace, they met another group of Roman ambassadors acting on behalf of Aetius and Valentinian. One of the purposes of this embassy was to resolve a long-running dispute. Eight years earlier, in the Danube offensive of 441–2, the Huns had sacked Sirmium. Before the siege, the city's bishop had given some golden bowls to one of Attila's secretaries, Constantius. (This is not the same man as the educated Italian sent by Aetius to serve on Attila's staff.) Constantius promised that, should the city fall to the Huns, then the bowls would be sold and the funds used to ransom prisoners. With Sirmium in flames and the bishop dead, he saw no reason to keep his word. Two years later, while on business in Rome he pawned the bowls and received a good sum from the banker Silvanus. On his return to Attila's service, Constantius was suspected of dishonesty and executed. Meanwhile, as the pledge had not been redeemed, Silvanus disposed of the bowls. As they had once belonged to the cathedral in Sirmium, he sold them on to priests. He did not think it proper that they should be melted down or used as part of a grand dinner service. But as far as Attila was concerned the bowls were his property – legitimate spoils of war from a conquered Roman city. Hun ambassadors sent to Aetius and Valentinian insisted that Silvanus be handed over for receiving stolen goods. It was alleged that he and Constantius had been part of a scheme to defraud Attila by converting the bowls to cash through a series of transactions they had intended could not be traced.

Valentinian and Aetius refused Attila's request. In their view Silvanus had acted in good faith. However, they were prepared to compromise. If, in Priscus' words, 'Attila would not withdraw his demand for the bowls, they would send gold as compensation for them, but they would not extradite Silvanus, since they would not hand over a man who had done nothing wrong.' How this stalemate was eventually resolved is not recorded. If Priscus knew, his account has not survived the cuts of Constantine Porphyrogenitus' editors. In this case, the particular terms of any settlement may not have been that important – except, of course, to Silvanus. Like the convoluted complaint about the (Italian) Constantius' marriage, which took up so much of Maximinus' time, what mattered was not the detail of the dispute, but the pretext it gave for Attila to take offence. These were not intended to be issues that could be resolved quickly or reasonably; rather they were barometers of Attila's willingness to cooperate with the Roman empire.

Given the right conditions, Attila was always ready to negotiate. Anatolius and Nomus had found him attentive and reasonable. They had made good progress in 447 and again in 450, when he had agreed to substantial concessions to ease tensions along the Danube frontier. By contrast, in summer 449, with delegations from both the East and the West camped outside his palace gates, Attila avoided serious discussion by arguing over specific claims. Maximinus, his mission already undercut by Chrysaphius' conspiracy, made little progress in the face of Attila's insistence that he would only negotiate on issues of real importance with ambassadors of the highest rank. In the case of the western embassy, the deliberate miring of the talks in the trivial and time-consuming matter of Silvanus and the golden bowls was a sure indication of the fragility of Attila's relationship with Aetius.

That something more serious was at stake is suggested by a conversation Priscus reports with Romulus, one of the western envoys, while they were both waiting for Onegesius to return from a meeting with Attila. Then Romulus had expressed the view that the Huns' next campaign would take them further east: '"Attila is aiming at more than he has at present and to expand his empire further he wishes to attack the Persians."' Romulus pointed out that Attila already knew what route he would take. Fifty years earlier, in 395, a Hun army had crossed the Caucasus Mountains between the Black and Caspian Seas. Some units had terrorised the Roman empire, moving through Armenia and Cappadocia before being defeated by Eutropius; others had followed the Tigris River as far as Ctesiphon. In Romulus' depressing assessment, if the Huns decided to march east, the Persians '"would be subdued and forced to pay tribute, as Attila has an armed force that no nation can resist"'.

In his prediction that the Huns were looking ahead to an eastern campaign, Romulus may have been offering an accurate account of Attila's intentions. Even so, it should be noted that Attila made no reference to any such plans in his discussions with Maximinus, nor the following year with Anatolius and Nomus, nor – as far as is known – at any other time. Rather than a Hun invasion of Persia being part of Attila's grand strategy, it is equally plausible that it was part of Romulus' brief to suggest it to him. Carefully devised by Aetius, the presentation of such an apparently attractive proposition may have been the main objective of the western embassy. If so, it was a purpose only half shared with Priscus. Knowing that his comments would be passed on to Theodosius and his advisers, Romulus would not want it known in Constantinople that the government in Ravenna had encouraged Attila eastwards. In talking to Priscus it would be more prudent to shift the blame and suggest the idea was entirely Attila's own.

For Aetius, frustrated in the late 440s in his attempts to secure any credible assurance of assistance from the Huns, the advantages of dissuading Attila from intervening in a politically divided West are self-evident. The consequences of a Hun offensive were difficult to assess and there was no guarantee, despite Geiseric's prompting, that the Huns would confine their attack to the Goths. Nor was there any certainty (as in their Balkan campaigns) that they would return to the Great Hungarian Plain, and no knowing how they might seek to exploit their new links with the Bagaudae. If the Huns could not be relied upon to march west in support of the empire, then it made good sense to push them even further east. The suggestion of a Persian campaign was a daring attempt by an increasingly insecure Aetius to divert Attila's attention away from France. It was a final bid to make the Huns someone else's problem.

# The Bride of Attila

Despite the best efforts of Aetius' envoys, Attila was not deflected from disruptive interference in the West. He had been successful in creating a deliberate sense of doubt about his intentions. Would he, as Geiseric advocated, attack the Goths or would he support dissident groups such as the Bagaudae? Would he respect his long-standing friendship with Aetius? Would Valentinian's grant of an honorary generalship be sufficient to ensure some lingering loyalty to the empire or would Attila choose to fight alone, seizing any opportunities that might arise from the chaos of a Hun invasion? Whatever his ultimate strategy, Attila's plans were altered in early spring 450 following the unexpected arrival on the Great Hungarian Plain of the eunuch Hyacinthus. The eunuch, who had travelled in secret from Ravenna, was a curious choice for a diplomatic mission. Roman ambassadors were normally high-ranking administrators like Nomus or senior military officers like Anatolius and Romulus. It must have been extraordinary to see Hyacinthus in his flowing silks standing before Attila; even more so to hear his shrill, high-pitched voice as he announced that he came not from the emperor Valentinian, but from his older sister, the imperial princess Justa Grata Honoria.

A few months earlier Honoria, then in her early thirties, had been forcibly engaged to the Italian aristocrat Flavius Bassus Herculanus. Valentinian's choice was carefully made. He was all too aware of his sister's ambitions: like their mother Galla Placidia she too wished to be the wife and mother of emperors. For Valentinian, determined that his sister's marriage should not undermine his own position, Herculanus was a safe option: a respectable, middle-aged landowner unwilling to lose his life or his estates in a bid for imperial power. Herculanus could be relied upon to keep Honoria in style in one of his magnificent country houses. She would appear only infrequently at court.

But no matter how uncompromising Valentinian's insistence on marriage, Honoria had no intention of being paired off with Herculanus. Her daring reply to her brother's increasingly brutal behaviour (as she saw it) was to send one of the few people she could trust across the Danube. Honoria's proposition was simple: in return for a substantial down payment in gold, and with more promised to follow, she hoped to convince Attila to intervene on her behalf. As a token of good faith, and so that Hyacinthus' astonishing message might be believed, she also sent Attila a signet ring. No doubt Attila discussed Honoria's proposal with his senior advisers. The cautious must have wondered whether this was a trap to entice Attila to Ravenna. On the other hand, if Honoria's predicament was genuine, it offered an unparalleled opportunity to put pressure on Valentinian. Attila's response was a brilliant piece of brinkmanship. Hyacinthus was instructed to return to Ravenna and assure the princess that her marriage with Herculanus would not take place. On one condition: Justa Grata Honoria, daughter of Galla Placidia and sister of the western Roman emperor Valentinian III, was to become the next wife of Attila the Hun.

In seeking the Huns' assistance, Honoria had not acted rashly or foolishly. Nor is it likely, as Jordanes later claimed, that she was driven by a secret passion for Attila. Jordanes tended to explain actions he disapproved of as stemming from uncontrollable desires, especially in women. (At such moments it is worth remembering that Jordanes was a monk as well as a historian.) In fact, Honoria's bid to involve Attila in a family quarrel was a well-calculated attempt to strengthen her own dynastic position. Her situation had always been difficult. From her brother's point of view, she represented both a threat and an opportunity: a threat because of her ambition to ensure that her husband and children would be contenders for imperial power; an opportunity since the prospect of marriage with a princess might help to secure an alliance beneficial to the empire.

Honoria objected to being treated as a bargaining chip in her brother's schemes. Above all, she resented her confinement within the palace at Ravenna. Strict supervision of her movements was imposed from 429, when she turned twelve, the minimum age under

Roman law at which a girl could be married. For Valentinian, the diplomatic value of his sister demanded that she remain a virgin until her wedding night. Honoria was also made an unwilling participant in their mother's renewal of her Christian faith. Sometime in the late 430s Galla Placidia, then nearly fifty, decided on a life of prayer, fasting and chastity. For her, two marriages, two dead husbands (one an emperor) and two adult children (one an emperor) were enough.

Galla Placidia had spent two of the most difficult years of her life under Theodosius' protection in Constantinople. In early 423 she fled Ravenna and her half-brother Honorius' accusations of treason. At Theodosius' court she first met Aelia Pulcheria, the emperor's older sister. In 413 Pulcheria, then aged fourteen, had sidestepped marriage by taking a public vow of virginity and had persuaded her younger sisters Arcadia and Marina to join her. Pulcheria's influence at court rested not on her prospects as a wife and mother, but on her displays of piety and generous encouragement of holy causes. In the admiring description of the contemporary Christian historian Sozomen, the three saintly sisters were reported 'to care greatly about the clergy and churches; they are open-handed to strangers in need and to the poor. These sisters generally take their walks together, and pass their days and nights in each other's company, singing the praises of God . . . Although princesses, born and brought up in palaces, they avoid pleasure and idleness, regarding them as unsuitable for those who have dedicated themselves to virginity.' As long as Pulcheria occupied apartments in the Great Palace, she insisted on the imperial household observing early-morning prayers and fasting on Wednesdays and Fridays. She was an unstinting supporter of Christian orthodoxy and skilled at arguing subtle points of doctrine. In the evenings she enjoyed reading religious tracts and discussing edifying passages from scripture.

During her later years at Ravenna Galla Placidia, following Aelia Pulcheria's example, founded churches and monasteries. Like Pulcheria too, Galla had an almost magnetic fascination for Christian holy men. In 446 one of the most charismatic, Germanus, bishop of Auxerre (eighty miles south-east of Paris), visited Ravenna seeking to soften imperial hostility towards the Bagaudae. Over the previous twenty-five years Germanus had built up a formidable reputation as an ascetic, faith healer and wonder worker. He hoped to avoid the crowds of well-wishers by entering Ravenna after dark, but Galla ordered its citizens to maintain an all-night vigil. On his arrival, she sent him a huge silver dish with a choice selection of beautifully prepared dainties – all vegetarian, out of respect for the bishop's strict diet. Germanus gave the food to his servants and ordered the dish to be sold and the money distributed to Ravenna's poor. In return he sent Galla a loaf of barley bread on a small wooden platter. She proclaimed herself delighted. That may have surprised Germanus: perhaps in offering such an ostentatiously humble gift he had hoped to disturb Galla's apparently untroubled reconciliation of her piety with her wealth and imperial rank. If that had been Germanus' intention, he failed. Galla Placidia, always an astute politician, knew how to deal with such competitive displays of holiness. She had the barley bread preserved – it was later said miraculously to cure the sick – and the wooden platter mounted in a magnificent frame of solid gold.

It is unlikely that Honoria enjoyed such carefully calibrated exercises in public religiosity. She objected to being forced to share what she regarded as Galla's dreary daily round of compulsory devotion. Honoria blamed her gilded confinement on her brother, but she also recognised that she was responsible for making a bad situation even worse. As a teenager she had been closely watched. There were persistent rumours that she had succeeded in smuggling a handsome youth past the palace guards. In fact, she had been much cleverer. Her lover was Eugenius, her own steward of estates, who had every reason to visit the palace frequently on legitimate business. It should also be supposed that in this instance Honoria had allowed passion to outstrip ambition – Eugenius was hardly likely to be the father of emperors – or else, and to her subsequent regret, the seventeen-year-old princess had been seduced by one of her senior staff.

The affair was exposed when Honoria could no longer hide her pregnancy. On Valentinian's orders Eugenius was immediately arrested and executed; Honoria was hurriedly shipped off to Constantinople, where she was taken in by Pulcheria and her sisters. The choice of such righteous company was no doubt deliberate. Honoria must have found the unwavering disapproval of the three imperial virgins difficult to bear. She was probably housed in the seclusion of their palace outside the Theodosian Walls near the Hebdomon. Here she gave birth. Despite her misery and suffering, it is unlikely that she received much sympathy. Honoria never saw her child. No historian recorded its name or its fate. The baby was probably quietly disposed of by Pulcheria; for all her piety, she knew precisely what dynastic politics required. As soon as Honoria was well enough to travel, she was returned to Ravenna under heavy guard. There her position was completely compromised. Now the mother of an illegitimate child she was no longer the sought-after bride whose marriage might seal an alliance for the benefit of the empire. Honoria had also missed her opportunity – as Valentinian no doubt acidly observed – to follow Pulcheria's example and declare herself a lifelong virgin.

The problem of what to do with Honoria resurfaced with the approach of Eudocia's marriage to Huneric. It was probably intended that the ceremony would take place in 451 when Eudocia turned twelve. Valentinian was determined that nothing should overshadow his daughter's wedding. He aimed to have his troublesome sister married off and out of Ravenna. Hence his obstinate demand that she should accept Herculanus. Honoria objected that her future husband was unremarkable, unambitious and unattractive. Despite his name, she complained, Herculanus was no Hercules. Faced with her implacable brother, who insisted that the marriage should go ahead, Honoria appealed to Attila. What she had not predicted was his reply. It is unlikely, despite Jordanes' insinuations, that Honoria had ever imagined herself as one of Attila's wives. It is difficult to envisage her living contentedly amidst the rolling grasslands of the Great Hungarian Plain or joining Erecan supervising embroidery in her comfortable wooden hall. Nor, for all her dislike of Galla's devotions, was Honoria ready to marry a non-Christian.

When news of Honoria's dealings with the Huns reached Ravenna, Valentinian was furious. Tortured before his execution, Hyacinthus confessed the details of her message to Attila. A short while later (in summer 450, a month or so before his fatal riding accident) Theodosius also learned of Attila's claim that Honoria had agreed to become his wife. Pulcheria was probably not surprised; she remembered Honoria from her enforced visit to Constantinople. Even then – Pulcheria may be pictured primly remarking – she was a headstrong and sinful woman. In Theodosius' view, if protecting Honoria meant giving the Huns a pretext for war, then she was expendable. Valentinian agreed. He ordered his sister to pack her bags and make ready to join her new husband beyond the Danube.

Honoria had never thought that it would come to this. Perhaps she begged to join a holy order and live out the rest of her life in cloistered chastity, or even to marry Herculanus. Nothing moved Valentinian; he no longer believed any of Honoria's promises. As far as he was concerned, her appeal to Attila had been a betrayal of the imperial family. This was too much for Galla Placidia. The bitter quarrel between her two children had now gone too far. She had not raised Valentinian to the imperial purple so that he could humiliate his sister. She also regarded her daughter's disgrace as poor diplomacy. There was a risk that Attila might regard Honoria's expulsion from Ravenna as welcome evidence that the empire would seek to avoid conflict at all costs. If Attila took Honoria's punishment as a sign of weakness, then Valentinian might risk encouraging the very attack he was attempting to avoid. Appeasement, as Galla might shrewdly have remarked to her son, does not always guarantee peace – sometimes it can hasten war.

In the end Valentinian relented. He could stand up to his sister, but not to his mother. Honoria was handed over to Galla's care on condition that she married Herculanus and lived in the decent obscurity of the Italian countryside. It was one of Galla's last interventions on behalf of her children before her death in Rome in November 450. Two years later Valentinian conferred the high honorary office of consul on Herculanus. By then it is to be hoped that Honoria had reconciled herself to a tedious existence with her ever-patient husband. She may even have come to appreciate the advantages of an entirely uneventful marriage.

# *Taking Sides*

Attila refused to give up his claim to Honoria. As far as he was concerned the gift of her signet ring and her plea for help were evidence of her willingness to assent to marriage. She had only been prevented from following her desires by the bullying of her oppressive brother and the religious scruples of her interfering mother. In her heart – Attila claimed – Honoria still wished to be the wife of the leader of the Huns. It was to appeal on behalf of this princess in distress that an embassy was sent to Ravenna in autumn 450 to announce Attila's engagement. The ambassadors also declared that Honoria, as the emperor's sister, should be recognised as joint ruler of the western Roman empire. These demands were intended to be impossible for Valentinian to accept. No doubt Attila was well aware that Honoria was now married to Herculanus. Equally there is no good reason to think that he was ignorant of the basic constitutional constraints governing imperial succession: a woman could not rule the Roman empire. Certainly there had always been powerful women at court, particularly the wives, sisters and mothers of emperors, but none of these had ever formally held imperial authority. Priscus, whose history of the early 450s survives in nine heavily edited fragments, briefly notes Valentinian's replies: 'the western Romans responded that Honoria could not come to Attila in marriage as she had been given to another man', and they affirmed what was well known, 'that the right to rule the Roman empire was not granted to females, but to males'. At the same time as these exchanges with Valentinian in Ravenna, Hun envoys arrived at the Great Palace in Constantinople. This embassy was also deliberately confrontational, its aim to challenge the new eastern Roman emperor Marcian.

Few could have predicted Marcian's sudden rise to power. For a

short while after Theodosius' riding accident in late July 450, a vicious
contest must have seemed likely. There had been no obvious successors: Theodosius' sisters were dedicated virgins; one daughter, Flaccilla,
had died in childhood twenty years earlier; the other, Licinia Eudoxia,
was the wife of Valentinian III. In good health in his late forties,
Theodosius had not yet thought of sharing power. Strictly speaking,
in the absence of any direct male heirs or an imperial colleague,
Valentinian, as the surviving emperor, became ruler of both the West
and the East, just as Theodosius had done briefly in 423 on the death of
his uncle Honorius. But whatever Valentinian's ambitions, the threat
of a Hun attack meant that it was impossible for his dream of reuniting
the Roman empire to be translated into political reality.

In Constantinople a powerful coalition of interests had moved
swiftly to prevent a succession crisis. They agreed to ignore
Valentinian's claim and endorse Marcian, a retired junior military
officer in his late fifties. He was, according to one brief and unenthu-
siastic account written a century later, 'a tall man with lank grey hair
and swollen feet'. It was precisely Marcian's lack of distinction that
made him such an attractive prospect. Like many compromise candidates he enjoyed a wide range of support. His backers each believed
that they could influence their man, or at least would not be threatened by his elevation. Amongst Marcian's strongest promoters were
the senior generals Flavius Aspar and Flavius Zeno. For fifteen years
Marcian had served on Aspar's personal staff and had been with him
during the early 430s in the first campaign against the Vandals. For
Aspar, unfairly stripped of his command by Theodosius in 447,
supporting Marcian offered a way back to an influential position at
court. To anyone who would listen, Aspar also claimed – whatever
his differences with Theodosius – that he knew what the dead emperor
would have wanted. In Aspar's own version of the imperial deathbed
scene, the injured Theodosius had turned to Marcian and whispered,
'It is clear that you must rule the empire after me.'

Whatever Theodosius' wishes might have been, Zeno's backing had
been crucial. As commander of imperial troops on the eastern frontier he had the military clout to make or break a new emperor. In the
late 440s Theodosius had become increasingly uncertain of Zeno's
trustworthiness. He had apparently been responsible for thwarting the
marriage deal struck between the emperor and Attila's secretary (the

Italian) Constantius, although it is not clear how far Attila's story should be believed. Even so, Attila's suggestion to Maximinus that Zeno might be amongst those senior figures who could threaten the emperor revealed yet again his close knowledge of court politics. At the beginning of 450 Theodosius became convinced that Zeno was preparing to revolt. A few months before his unexpected death the emperor began covert preparations for a pre-emptive strike against military bases and units he suspected of disloyalty. Theodosius' fatal fall prevented what might have developed into a serious civil war. In agreeing to Marcian's elevation, Zeno seized the opportunity to dominate imperial policymaking without having to fight.

The key player in Marcian's rapid rise to power had been the fifty-one-year-old virgin princess Pulcheria. She acted to prevent the eclipse of the Theodosian dynasty and with it the overshadowing of her own influence, agreeing to advance Marcian's cause by marrying him. On 25 August 450, shortly before their wedding, they appeared before troops at the Hebdomon. Screened by a wall of interlocking shields, Pulcheria presented Marcian with a diadem and a purple robe. This was the first time in the history of the Roman empire that the imperial insignia had been conferred by a woman. Not all accounts agree – for some Pulcheria's role was perhaps too embarrassing to record. (In the future, in the absence of a senior emperor the coronation would be performed by the bishop of Constantinople.) To the sound of cheers and the ringing clash of arms, the soldiers slowly raised their legionary standards in honour of the new emperor. Marcian, now swathed in purple, was greeted by a crowd chanting carefully rehearsed acclamations: 'You conquer, you are pious, you are blessed! God has given you, God will protect you! Worshipping Christ you are always victorious! God will keep watch over the Christian empire!' Marcian agreed not to consummate his union with Pulcheria – there was to be no honeymoon and no marriage bed – a gold coin struck by the imperial mint in Constantinople to celebrate their wedding showed the happy couple shaking hands. Between them stood Christ, the wary guardian of Pulcheria's perpetual chastity (see plates, picture 27). As always, there were doubters: high society gossips sniggered that Pulcheria had at last succumbed to her passions, and all the more violently having been suddenly released thirty-seven years after her public vow of virginity.

The Hun delegation that arrived in the imperial capital shortly after Marcian was proclaimed emperor was intended to test the commitment of the new imperial regime to the peace settlement renegotiated by Anatolius and Nomus eight months earlier. The ambassadors had only one demand: they bluntly requested that 'the tribute agreed by Theodosius' should be handed over. They were met with a robust reply. As reported by Priscus, 'The eastern Romans said that they would not undertake to pay the tribute agreed by Theodosius and that if Attila remained at peace they would give him gifts, but if he threatened war they would bring against him men and equipment no less powerful than his own.' Marcian's response was not, as is often assumed, a reckless or negligent repudiation of Theodosius' Danube policy. It was not a refusal to pay. Rather what was at stake was the diplomatic language that characterised the relationship between the Roman and Hun empires. No matter how contentious the policy of purchasing peace on the northern frontier had been, Theodosius had never accepted that the subsidies paid to the Huns could be described as 'tribute'. The Roman emperor was not subservient to Attila. The funds disbursed annually from the imperial treasury were 'gifts' to a foreign ruler who held the rank of honorary general in the western imperial army.

So, in the face of Attila's demands, Marcian rejected any payment of tribute, but he did offer to continue sending gifts. His claim to be prepared to match force with force was not a petulant declaration of war, rather it was the first shot in what he assumed would be a new round of talks. It was timely, not ill-advised, to press the point. The concessions that Attila had been prepared to offer at the beginning of the year could now be seen as necessary measures intended to ensure stability on the Danube frontier ahead of a fresh Hun offensive in the West. If, as his growing interest in Honoria would seem to indicate, Attila was now set on campaigning in France or Italy, then he might be open to further negotiation. After all, like Roman emperors, he would wish to avoid fighting on two fronts at once.

Marcian's response, with its firm emphasis on correct diplomatic terminology, was of no consequence. Attila had already decided to go to war. From that point of view, the sending of simultaneous embassies to Ravenna and Constantinople in autumn 450 had been a success. The envoys' provocative propositions had been predictably rebuffed. It was impossible for Honoria to marry twice or to share in imperial rule. No Roman emperor could ever countenance the payment of tribute to the Huns. By forcing Valentinian and Marcian to dismiss his demands, Attila had secured pretexts for war. According to Priscus, it only remained to be decided whether the Hun army should march east or west: 'Attila was in two minds and entirely uncertain whom he should attack first, but it seemed best to him to prioritise the greater war and move against the West. There he would be fighting not only against the Romans but also the Goths . . . against the Romans to win Honoria and her wealth, and against the Goths to earn Geiseric's gratitude.'

At the beginning of the following year, as Attila prepared for the campaign, he continued to send embassies to the West. In January or February 451 a Hun envoy in Ravenna repeated his demand: Honoria's right to a share in imperial power should be recognised by Valentinian, who was to hand over half of the western empire to her without delay. The envoy also claimed that Honoria had been betrothed to Attila before she had been forced to marry Herculanus. The proof was her signet ring. Hyacinthus had given it to Attila and the Hun ambassador now presented it to Valentinian. No doubt the emperor recognised the ring as his sister's, although of course he refused to accept that it could ever have been a token of matrimony. Perhaps too, as war now seemed unavoidable, he regretted that he had not sent Honoria across the Danube. Whatever his private feelings, Valentinian had no alternative but to reject the envoy's arguments. He is not likely to have been any more persuaded by a second embassy that assured him that, in going to war, Attila's objective was to attack the Goths in France and 'as his disagreement was with Theodoric . . . not in any way to breach his friendly relations with the empire'. The ambassador heading a third delegation, dispatched as the Hun army was on the march, did not bother with any diplomatic courtesies. He simply informed Valentinian: 'Through me, Attila – my lord and your lord – has instructed you to prepare the palace for him.'

This series of embassies had a serious point. Attila had nothing to lose by sending contradictory indications of his intentions; anything that caused even the slightest hesitation in Ravenna was to the Huns' advantage. In Jordanes' judgement, 'Beneath his great savagery Attila was a subtle man, and fought with diplomacy before he went to war.' Most importantly, Attila aimed to delay, and if possible prevent, an alliance between the Goths and the Romans. From that point of view it was vital to emphasise the danger faced by Valentinian personally. Hence Attila's reiterated claims to be married to Honoria and his threat to occupy the imperial palace. The chance of a Hun offensive in northern Italy might make Valentinian reluctant to send reinforcements to France. Rather than risk troops in aggressively engaging an enemy north-west of the Alps, he might instead prefer to guard the mountain passes. Then, if the Goths were defeated, the Huns could be prevented from marching on Ravenna.

Aetius argued against any Roman retreat from France. Leaving Theodoric's Goths to fight alone was not worth the risk. If they were defeated, then the empire would still have to deal with the Huns. Attila's campaign would not be confined to a surgical strike on the Goths; large areas of France still loyal to the empire would also be devastated. Even if the Huns withdrew, it would still require a major military operation to restore imperial authority across a countryside wrecked by Attila's offensive. There was of course a chance that the Goths might defeat the Huns. This too, Aetius argued, would mean the end of Roman rule in France. Theodoric would certainly move to enlarge his territory. Controlling the Goths would be much easier if the Romans fought with them against the Huns. Some agreement might be reached while Roman troops were still on the ground. However things turned out, Valentinian could not simply stand aside. In Aetius' view, it was not in the Romans' interest to see either Attila or Theodoric victorious. Nor was there much time left. By late March 451 the Hun army was already on the move. If an alliance was to be made with the Goths, then the offer needed to be sent at once. Valentinian reluctantly agreed. In truth, he had no choice. Whatever his view of the likely outcome of a Hun invasion, he must also have been aware that Aetius could act on his own initiative. This was the most dangerous scenario of all. Aetius might join with the Goths, or even the Huns, and turn against the empire. Valentinian's reign had begun twenty-five years earlier with Aetius leading a Hun army into northern Italy. He had no intention of it ending the same way.

The offer of an alliance with Theodoric was one of Valentinian's most significant policy decisions: it forced him to recognise the permanence of the Gothic state. He was compelled, as he had been in his dealings with Geiseric, to concede that he no longer controlled territory once securely part of the empire. The Goths were invited to fight alongside the Romans against a growing barbarian menace.

> *The emperor Valentinian to Theodoric, king of the Goths.*
> Bravest of nations, we are well advised to unite against this universal despot who wishes to enslave the whole earth. Attila requires no reason for battle, but thinks whatever he does is justified. The measure of his ambition is his strength; his arrogance is boundless; despising both law and religion he shows himself hostile even to the natural order of things. He deserves everyone's hatred since he is undoubtedly the common enemy of all . . . Can you permit such arrogance to go unpunished? Since you are a military power, face your own troubles by joining together with us.

Something fundamental had changed. Valentinian's message to Theodoric was phrased in the language of international diplomacy between heads of state on equal terms, not a superior condescending to issue orders to an ill-disciplined subordinate. The defence of France now depended as much on Gothic goodwill as it did on Roman military might. For Valentinian, to appeal to Theodoric for help as a valued friend and ally must have seemed almost a defeat in itself. Only fear of Attila and Aetius could together have overcome his imperial pride.

# 22

## The Fog of War

Meanwhile in Belgium, Servatius, bishop of Tongeren (near Maastricht, about fifty miles east of modern Brussels), returned from a pilgrimage to Italy. A few months earlier, despite all-night vigils, fasting and tears, he had not received a satisfactory response to his appeal to the Almighty that the Huns should be prevented from marching against the Roman empire. Dissatisfied, Servatius decided to take his cause to Rome and seek an authoritative answer from the shrine of St Peter. After many days of fasting, he was finally granted a vision of the, somewhat unsympathetic, apostle:

> 'Why do you, most holy of men, disturb me? Behold! It has been un-alterably decided in the counsels of the Lord that the Huns should invade France and that it should be devastated as if by a severe storm. Now follow these instructions: travel swiftly, put your house in good order, prepare your tomb and make ready your burial shroud! Behold! Your spirit will have left your body so that your eyes will not see the evil deeds of the Huns in France. Thus the Lord our God has spoken.'

Servatius did as he had been ordered. He travelled quickly home to Tongeren and made the necessary arrangements for his death. Weeping, he informed his faithful fellow citizens that they would not see him again. He remained unmoved by their pleas: 'Do not abandon us, holy father; do not forget us, holy shepherd.' Turning his back on his congregation, Servatius journeyed eighty miles north to Utrecht, where a short time later he died of a fever. Through unquestioning obedience to his divine instructions, St Servatius ensured that by abandoning Tongeren he had saved it from the Huns, who passed one hundred miles to the south.

Not all cities were as blessed as Tongeren. Metz, ninety miles west of the Rhine frontier, was completely destroyed save for a chapel dedicated to Stephen, the first Christian martyr. This confirmed the vision of one devout Christian in the city, who before the Hun attack had seen Stephen in heated conversation with the apostles Peter and Paul. These senior saints had turned down the martyr's request that Metz should be saved: 'For the sin of its people has increased, and the noise of their wickedness ascends to the presence of God; therefore this city shall be consumed with fire.' As a concession, they agreed that Stephen's chapel should be spared. At Reims, ninety miles west of Metz, the looting and slaughter were only interrupted by its bishop, Nicasius. Along with his virgin sister he was killed while reading from the Bible before the doors of the city's cathedral. While reciting Psalm 119, at the beginning of the twenty-fifth verse, *adhaesit pavimento anima mea* – 'my soul clings to the dust' – Nicasius was decapitated. As his head rolled down the cathedral's steps it was heard to complete the line, *vivifica me, Domine, secundum verbum tuum* – 'give me life, Lord, according to your word'. St Nicasius' talking head was sufficient to frighten the Huns into quitting the city (see plates, picture 31).

Not all saints had to die for their cause. At Lutetia (now Paris) the young virgin Genovesa (or Geneviève) begged the population not to abandon the town. Through prayer and fasting its safety could be assured. The women were convinced and persuaded the men not to leave. Their faith in the virgin was affirmed when the town escaped the Huns. Only the mean-spirited would doubt Geneviève's achievement. Lutetia, it might be pointed out, was some distance away from Attila's route into central France. It was not a great prize like Metz or Reims; by the mid-fifth century it was a run-down settlement concentrated on a flood-prone island in the middle of the River Seine – the modern Île de la Cité, now dominated by the cathedral of Notre Dame. For all her holiness, St Geneviève cannot be said to have deflected Attila from one of his main objectives. The Huns were not marching on Paris.

By contrast, Lupus, bishop of Troyes (seventy miles due south of Reims), had to deal with the Huns as they prepared to attack his city. After prayer and fasting he went out to face Attila himself. 'Who are you?' asked Lupus fearlessly. Attila, in an apparently learned biblical reference, countered, 'I am Attila, the whip of God.' The penitent bishop's reply was heavy with his own sense of shame at his failure to prevent his fellow citizens from sinning: 'And I am Lupus, the destroyer of God's flock, and I have need of the whip of God.' St Lupus' humility was sufficient to save the city. The gates were opened to admit the Huns, 'but they were blinded by heaven and they passed straight through, in one gate and out by another, neither seeing nor harming anyone' (see plates, picture 30).

In all these dramatic tales of steadfast holiness Attila is absorbed into an entirely Christian world. He is, as he boasts to Lupus, *flagellum dei*, 'the whip of God' – the phrase most frequently associated with Attila in medieval and Renaissance literature. For many Christians – both contemporaries and those who later celebrated these triumphant moments in saints' lives – the Huns' invasion had been ordained by God as a punishment for the erring cities of central France. Writing in the seventh century the Spanish philosopher and theologian Isidore of Seville argued that Attila's attacks were part of God's plan for the correction of Christendom. The Huns were the 'rod of divine anger' – *virga furoris dei* – sent to scourge the unrepentant and 'force them to turn away from the desires and errors of the age'. Long ago the Old Testament prophet Isaiah had threatened the sinful Israelites with the righteous fury of the Lord: 'when the overwhelming whip passes through, you will be trampled down by it'. For many committed Christians, events in the fifth century continued to follow the ancient pattern laid down in the Bible. History was divinely inspired. The decisions of the Almighty might be revealed to those holy few who could withstand the harsh regimen of fasting, prayer and all-night vigils. But, as Servatius' encounter with the apostle Peter suggests, these are matters of faith best left to hungry bishops and chastising saints. Such visionary truths are not the business of historians.

By mid-June 451 the Hun army had advanced as far as Orléans, about 250 miles west of the Rhine. The city may have been besieged. As with Metz, Reims and Troyes, the account of Attila's attack is part of a later, explicitly Christian tradition. At Orléans it was the intercession of its bishop, Anianus, that was said to have saved the city. He visited Aetius at Arles, over 300 miles south, not far from the Mediterranean coast, and insisted that the Roman and Gothic troops march north immediately. On the day when Anianus knew his prayers would be answered he sent his congregation up to the ramparts: 'Look out from the city walls and see if God's mercy has yet come to our rescue.' Nothing was visible and, as in all good stories, the faithful had to repeat their actions, with ample time to doubt the holy power of their bishop. As the dull thud of the Hun battering rams threatened to splinter the city's gates, Anianus exhorted the sceptics, 'If you pray with conviction, God comes with speed.' Only on the third climb from the cathedral to the walls did the sharp-eyed see a dust cloud on the horizon. St Anianus confidently proclaimed, 'It is the help of the Lord.'

The dust cloud was the Romans and Goths on the move, and it may be that the arrival of the allies saved Orléans from destruction. Jordanes reports a different version, with no dramatic siege, no persistent bishop and no timely dust cloud. After marching north, the Goths and Romans arrived at Orléans well ahead of the Huns and constructed an extensive network of ditches and earth barriers to protect the approaches to the city. When Attila arrived, 'he was so discouraged by this turn of events and uncertain of his troops that he was afraid to begin any conflict'. The Huns withdrew to the east, retreating a hundred miles across territory they had already pillaged. The allied forces probably shadowed them.

No account survives of the few days at the end of June 451 between the encounter at Orléans and the afternoon when the two armies faced each other. On one side stood the Romans under Aetius, together with the Goths under Theodoric and Thorismud, the eldest of his six sons. They were reinforced by units from the Burgundians and the Bagaudae. Both these groups had an ambiguous relationship with the empire. In 437 the Huns in alliance with Aetius had butchered 20,000 Burgundians. Six years later the survivors, with Aetius' support, had been settled on Roman territory west of Geneva. The Bagaudae had also been ruthlessly suppressed, in 437 by the Huns and again in 448 by Aetius. Then one of the rebel leaders had sought refuge with Attila. Nothing had come of this contact; bitter memories of their violent destruction in 437 may have made many Bagaudae wary of risking an alliance with the Huns. They must have had similar reservations about Aetius. Perhaps in finally choosing sides it mattered to the Bagaudae, despite their deep distrust of imperial rule, that they should still be seen as Romans.

Fighting alongside the Huns were troops drawn from, in Jordanes' phrase, 'the countless peoples and various nations that Attila had brought under his control'. Most important were Goths, the descendants of those who, seventy-five years earlier, had remained north of the Danube. Some had moved into parts of the former Roman provinces of Pannonia and Valeria. (In the mid-430s Aetius had agreed not to dispute Hun control over this territory in return for Attila and Bleda's help in France.) The Goths in this frontier region were led by Valamer, Thiudimer and Vidimer. These three brothers were especially favoured by Attila, who treated them as close comrades and valued advisers. Valamer was said by Jordanes to be 'steadfast in keeping secrets, subtle in speech and skilled in deception'. The prominent presence of the brothers is a reminder that the conflict in central France was not just about Huns and Romans or the rancorous end to a lifelong friendship between Aetius and Attila; it was also about the divisions that separated two groups of Goths with sharply opposing histories.

According to Jordanes, the two armies clashed on the Catalaunian Plains. This is not a specific location but part of the Champagne region in northern France, a rough triangle bounded by Reims, Châlons-en-Champagne (known until 1998 as Châlons-sur-Marne) and Troyes. Jordanes also offers as an alternative name for the battlefield *locus Mauriacus*, which has often been identified with the similar sounding Méry-sur-Seine, a small town about twenty miles north-west of Troyes. Sometimes correspondences between ancient and modern place names can be helpful (as in Londinium to London), sometimes not (as in Lutetia to Paris). Without other evidence it is impossible to tell if the apparent connection between *Mauriacus* and Méry is meaningful or just a misleading coincidence. In the end, despite the understandable pride of local historians, all that can be said with certainty is that the 'Battle of the Catalaunian Plains' took place somewhere amidst the green fields and gently rolling hills of Champagne.

The battle began in the early afternoon. The first struggle was for possession of a ridge at the top of a steep slope. To follow Jordanes' account: 'Hun forces seized the right side, the Romans, Goths and their allies the left, and then the fight began to occupy the crest.' The Roman advance was led by Aetius supported by Goths under Theodoric and his son Thorismud. 'Attila sent his men to take the top of the rise, but was beaten to it by Thorismud and Aetius whose troops, in their attempts to reach the crest, gained the higher ground

21. *Feast of Attila*, nineteenth-century fresco: Priscus and Maximinus seated front right.

22. *Entry of King Etzel (Attila) with Kriemhild into Vienna*, early-twentieth-century painting.

23. The Danube at Budapest, nineteenth-century painting.

24. Onyx brooch from the Şimleu Silvaniei treasure.

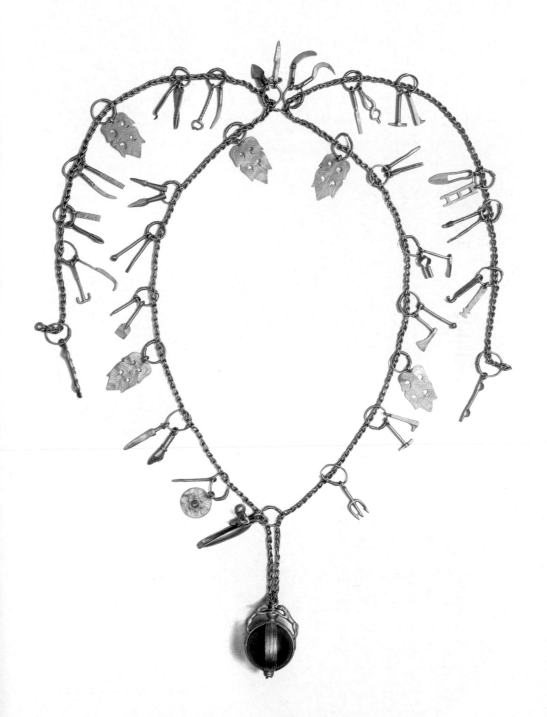

25. Gold chain from the Şimleu Silvaniei treasure.

26. Emperor with shoulder brooch:
Missorium of Theodosius I.

27. The Emperor Marcian,
Christ and Pulcheria: gold coin
celebrating their marriage.

28. Justa Grata Honoria.

29. Emperor Valentinian III.

30. St Lupus confronts Attila at the gates of Troyes.

31. Martyrdom
of St Nicasius.

32. Emperor
triumphing
over barbarians:
'Barberini Ivory'.

33. Jonah and the whale: mosaic from Aquileia.

34. Pope Leo I confronts Attila: fresco by Raphael.

35. Kaiser Wilhelm II addresses German troops at Bremerhaven.

and, with the advantage of their position on the ridge, were able easily
to dislodge the Huns as they came up.' As the Hun army was pushed
back down the slope, Attila rallied his troops with a speech. What
might seem to modern tastes a rather strange interruption to the
action would have been expected by Jordanes' readers. This was an
important literary fiction. There are usually speeches in accounts of
battles by great classical authors. Certainly no one would have assumed
that Jordanes had access to Attila's actual words, or that Attila had
stopped fighting to deliver an oration. It was up to the historian to
imagine what ought to have been said. Meanwhile the narrative was
put on hold – just long enough to allow time for Attila to speak.

'Huns, here you stand after victories over many nations and after
conquering the world . . . For what is war to you but a way of life?
What is more satisfying for a brave man than to seek revenge with his
own hand? Nature imposes on us this heavy duty: to glut our souls
with vengeance. Let us attack the enemy keenly, for those who press
on with the battle are always bolder . . . Let the wounded claim in
recompense the death of his opponent; let those who are unharmed
glory in the slaughter of the enemy . . . I shall throw the first spear at
the foe. If any man can stand unmoved while Attila fights, then he
must already be dead.'

Inspired by Attila's speech – only about a sixth of the text is quoted
above – the Huns engaged the enemy even more fiercely. That, at
least, is Jordanes' explanation. Whatever the cause, they surged dangerously across the flat ground in front of the ridge. 'Hand to hand they
fought, and the battle was fierce, convulsed, dreadful, unrelenting –
like none ever recorded in times past.' A stream running through the
middle of the battlefield gushed red, flooded with gore. In the midst
of this bloody chaos, Theodoric was killed. Some reported that while
urging on his troops he had been thrown from his horse and trampled to death. Jordanes preferred the more grimly symbolic alternative: that he had been transfixed by a spear thrown by a leading Goth
loyal to the Huns. Fighting ceased only at nightfall. In the confusion
Thorismud strayed into the Hun lines. He was rescued by his own
men, but not before he had been pulled from his horse and attacked.
Aetius, stumbling directionless in the dark, failed to find the Roman

camp and spent the night sheltering with his Gothic allies. The following morning, as the summer mist burned slowly off the plain, the shattered corpses of the slain were visible piled high across the battlefield. Both sides had suffered significant losses. Most frightening for Aetius and Thorismud was the stillness. The Huns had withdrawn behind the protective screen of their wagons, silently waiting to see what Attila would decide.

'Attila was like a lion brought low by hunting spears that paces back and forth in front of his den and dares not spring but does not cease to terrify those around him by his roaring.' In the middle of the Hun laager Attila ordered saddles to be piled high. Here he proclaimed that, if need be, he would fight to the death. Attila the Hun would never be taken alive, but throw himself onto a funeral pyre of burning saddles 'so that the overlord of so many peoples should not be taken by his enemies'. For all of Attila's destructive hostility towards the Roman empire, the Hun leader's courage demands admiration. For Jordanes, there is no doubt that Attila was the most valiant warrior on the Catalaunian Plains. The contrast with Aetius is clear. Jordanes offers no dramatic scene in which his courage is on display. Attila is the only commander to be given a rousing speech. Theodoric, without saying a word, is killed by an enemy spear; Attila roars majestically like a lion at bay while Thorismud and Aetius, dazed and disoriented after the battle, cannot even find the way back to their own camps.

Despite Attila's challenges, Aetius and Thorismud decided against further fighting. Instead they resolved to starve the Huns and their allies into surrender by blockading their camp. Theodoric's body was recovered from the battlefield and buried nearby. Thorismud led the mourners, publicly asserting his own position as the new leader of the Goths in France. Only in death is Theodoric finally praised by Jordanes: 'The Goths honoured him with songs and carried him away in full view of the Huns . . . Tears were shed – but only those fitting for brave men. For this was death, but the Huns can testify that it was a glorious one.'

The morning of the next day, the second after the battle, Hun scouts reported that Thorismud's Goths had broken camp and were marching swiftly south. This was one of the oldest tricks in ancient warfare. (It had once fooled the Trojans: leaving the wooden horse

behind, the Greek army had sailed out of sight just over the horizon.)
Attila suspected that the Goths' manoeuvre was a ploy to draw him
out into open ground. The Huns stayed alert but under strict orders
not to break cover. After a tense delay, scouts reported that the Romans
were also preparing to leave. Again it is likely that the Huns remained
behind their wagons until they had confirmation that both Thorismud
and Aetius' troops were well clear of the battlefield and moving in
different directions. There was now no time to be wasted. Attila gave
the order to march east with all speed back to the Rhine. He aimed
to reach the safety of his own territory as quickly as possible.

For Jordanes, the sudden withdrawal of the allied forces from the
Catalaunian Plains was a disgrace. Bristling with monkish disapproval
he observed tartly that 'human frailty' too often prevents leaders from
seizing 'the opportunity to perform great deeds'. In this instance, the
frailty was Thorismud's, and his weakness was to listen to Aetius, who
had raised doubts about the security of his position as Theodoric's
heir. Aetius advised Thorismud to return to Toulouse and prevent any
of his five younger brothers from seizing power. He warned that delay
might mean fighting a difficult civil war. 'Thorismud – motivated by
what he perceived to be his own interests – accepted Aetius' advice
without grasping its ambiguity.' Many historians have followed
Jordanes' suggestion that Aetius deliberately misled Thorismud, his
duplicity the result of his long-standing friendship with Attila. Aetius
deliberately threw the Battle of the Catalaunian Plains – the Huns, so
the argument goes, could easily have been wiped out on the first day
– and then engineered a plausible excuse to get rid of the Goths. The
seventh-century Burgundian chronicler Fredegar claimed that Aetius
had played a clever double game. The night after the battle he went
secretly to Attila's camp. There he expressed his regret that he had
not joined with the Huns to defeat the Goths. He also warned Attila
that Gothic reinforcements would arrive the following day. In return
for 10,000 solidi (140 pounds of gold) he agreed to convince Thorismud
to withdraw. Aetius then went to Thorismud's camp to warn him that
Hun reinforcements would soon arrive. In return for a further 10,000
solidi he agreed to persuade Attila to retreat and advised Thorismud
to return without delay to Toulouse.

Much less scandalous than these elaborate conspiracy theories is
the possibility that Aetius actually gave Thorismud good advice or

that Thorismud reached the same conclusion on his own. Certainly
he was right to be concerned about the succession. In 453, only two
years after the Catalaunian Plains, he was assassinated in the palace at
Toulouse by two of his brothers; the elder, Theodoric (named after
his father), immediately took his place. Of course it might be argued
that Thorismud would have been in a stronger position had he waited
to return in triumph after defeating Attila. Yet victory was by no means
assured, and it was certain that Attila would never surrender. On the
first afternoon of the battle the two armies were fairly evenly matched.
There were large numbers of Goths on both sides and the Huns'
tactics – the flights of arrows, the cavalry charges, the lassos and the
sword fighting at close quarters – cannot have come as any surprise
to either Aetius or Theodoric. Aetius had spent his teenage years
beyond the Danube and the Huns had fought alongside Romans and
against Theodoric's Goths in France only twelve years earlier. What
made the difference was Aetius and Thorismud's early success in taking
the ridge that dominated the battlefield. If hostilities resumed, there
was no certainty that the Goths and Romans would hold the high
ground. Whatever the outcome, losses on both sides would again be
heavy. As with most battles in the ancient world casualties are not
easy to quantify. Jordanes offers the impossible figure of 165,000 dead
in one afternoon. Prosper of Aquitaine is more honest in admitting
that 'the number of the slain could not be calculated'. On balance,
both Aetius and Thorismud may have decided that it was more important to preserve the combat strength of their troops. Thorismud did
not wish to arrive in Toulouse with an exhausted and depleted army
that could not enforce his authority as the new leader of the Goths.

Undoubtedly the withdrawal of the allied forces from the Catalaunian
Plains was to Aetius' advantage. According to Jordanes, 'He feared that
if the Huns were annihilated by the Goths, then the Roman empire
would be overwhelmed.' Aetius had always suspected that victory would
prompt a renewed attempt by the Goths to expand their territory. At
least he now commanded a Roman army in France that could counter
their ambitions. Most importantly, Aetius also recognised the dangers
of wiping out Attila and his loyal supporters. Confronting the problem
of regime change had been part of Theodosius' strategic thinking in
the 440s. Even if sufficient manpower had been available, there were
strong arguments against a campaign north of the Danube. Attila might

well be eliminated, but without his leadership the Hun empire could dissolve into civil war. For Theodosius an effective military response to the Huns was never a possibility; for Aetius it was a real option. Despite the difficulties, he could choose to hold his position on the Catalaunian Plains. If Roman troops managed to seize an early advantage on the battlefield, Attila might be forced to fight to the death or order the pyramid of saddles to be set alight.

This is a risk analysis that has no need of conspiracy theories. Despite the undoubted glory of destroying Attila and the Huns, Aetius was aware that victory might mean little more than the replacement of one threat with another. If Attila's empire collapsed, then in the violent competition for control that followed, there might again be pressure from the displaced and the defeated to move across the frontier. Aetius doubted that he had sufficient military manpower both to prevent a mass movement of refugees into the Roman empire and to deal with the Goths 350 miles away in south-west France. The Battle of the Catalaunian Plains had been sufficiently damaging to force an immediate Hun withdrawal. There was nothing to be gained, and too much to be lost, by risking another engagement. It is to Aetius' credit that he grasped a key paradox: the preservation of Roman rule in France depended on the survival of Attila the Hun. The flaw in Aetius' strategic thinking was the security of Italy.

# The Last Retreat

The experienced general, Apollonius, was widely regarded as one of the bravest men in the eastern Roman empire. In late 451, less than six months after the Battle of the Catalaunian Plains, he was sent across the Danube by Marcian to open negotiations with Attila, who had renewed his demands for the payment of 'tribute'. Apollonius took with him only the customary diplomatic gifts. Like Maximinus and Priscus in 449, he probably carried silks, spices, pearls, fashionable jewellery and some gold. For Attila this was not enough. Through one of his close advisers, perhaps Onegesius, he made it clear that as the Roman envoy had not come with any tribute, there would be no meeting and no talks. Instead Apollonius was instructed to hand over all the gifts he had brought. If he refused, then his safety in Hun territory could no longer be guaranteed.

Apollonius' response was uncompromising, and his supporters insisted that he would have been no less forthright in front of Attila himself. He tersely remarked, 'It is not right for the Huns to demand what they can receive as gifts or take as spoils.' Perhaps Onegesius grasped this (almost) pithy one-liner. In his *History* Priscus offers a helpful explanation: 'Apollonius meant by this that if the Huns welcomed him as an ambassador, then what he had brought would be given to them as gifts, but if they killed him, then what he had brought would be taken from him as spoils.' Priscus does not report Attila's response, only noting that Apollonius travelled back to Constantinople without achieving anything. Nor is there any further mention of the gifts. If Apollonius left them behind, then this was perhaps best forgotten. Priscus did not want to tarnish a glowing tale of Roman courage (almost) in the face of Attila the Hun.

Relations between Attila and the eastern Roman empire had steadily

deteriorated in the two years since the diplomatic row over the payment
of 'tribute'. Whatever Marcian's initial intentions, once it was certain
that the Huns were marching west, he decided to stop the transfer of
Roman gold across the Danube. But there is no indication that he
took any military advantage of Attila's offensive 1,400 miles away in
France. Not until August and September 451 was there any increase
in activity along the northern frontier. Details of the Roman opera-
tions are sketchy and known only from the official minutes of a conference of 500 bishops from across the eastern empire. This Church
council met at Chalcedon, directly opposite Constantinople on the
eastern shore of the Bosphorus. The meeting was delayed until
October to allow the emperor to take command of troops in the
Balkans. In September Marcian wrote to a preliminary gathering of
the bishops at Nicaea in north-western Turkey asking them to pray
'that our enemies may yield to us, that peace may be secured
throughout the world and that the Roman state may continue untroubled'. It is not known how extensive the campaign was or how great
the threat; even the identity of the enemies is unclear. This lack of
detail may not be accidental. Perhaps, while repelling some small-scale
raids, Marcian took the opportunity for a show of strength on the
Roman side of the frontier. No doubt the bishops would have celebrated loud and long if the emperor had led a successful expedition
across the Danube.

Despite these provocative gestures, it is unlikely that Marcian was
spoiling for war. For all Apollonius' tough talk, the purpose of his
embassy had been to open negotiations on the contested issue of subsidies. The campaign along the Danube had been safely undertaken in
the knowledge that, only a few weeks earlier, Attila's army had been
forced out of France. Above all, Marcian still had to take into account
the same strategic constraints that had limited Theodosius' response
to the Huns in the 430s and '40s: the Vandal occupation of North
Africa and the security of the eastern frontier. It is equally unlikely
that Attila was prepared to risk another major conflict. His army had
sustained substantial losses in France. Previous Hun attacks across the
Danube had been carefully timed to take advantage of competing
Roman military commitments – or, in 447, the earthquake that had
so severely damaged Constantinople. Importantly too, the Huns had
now lost the psychological advantage that had once made them seem

such terrifying enemies. On the Catalaunian Plains Aetius and Theodoric had demonstrated that the Huns could be defeated. Whatever Attila's plans, there was no reason to call off his diplomatic offensive. He continued, as his abrasive treatment of Apollonius demonstrated, to insist that the eastern empire should keep to the terms of the peace settlement negotiated by Anatolius and Nomus in early 450. Well-advertised hostility towards Marcian also had a wider purpose. As Jordanes remarked of Attila's tactics, 'shrewd and cunning, he threatened in one direction and moved his troops in another'.

In spring 452, nine months after the Catalaunian Plains, seasoned Hun-watchers at court in Ravenna and Constantinople agreed that there was no immediate threat. Attila was unlikely to march against Marcian or attempt another strike against Aetius in France. The real danger would come the following year after the Huns had recovered from their losses. Until then their army would probably remain on the Great Hungarian Plain while the Goths and other contingents were stood down. This strategic assessment was only half right. Although unwilling to chance another major engagement with Roman forces, Attila was, according to one contemporary observer, 'furious about the unexpected disaster he had suffered in France'. He was determined not to react as if he had been defeated. The Hun army was mobilised in summer 452 and, as correctly predicted by Roman military analysts, made no move either towards France or the Balkans. Instead, in a lightning strike, it marched unopposed 350 miles southwest through Hungary, Slovenia and straight into Italy. Attila had at last made good his threat that he would come to claim Honoria as his bride.

Attila had carefully considered the risks. He is likely to have calculated that by invading Italy he would not have to take on the combined forces of the Romans and the Goths. Valentinian may have been coerced into an alliance the previous year to preserve imperial interests in France, but it was another, and much more dangerous, step to invite Thorismud to send an army to Italy. There was the strong possibility too that, even if Valentinian was desperate enough to seek help, Thorismud, still fearing the ambition of his younger brothers, would refuse to leave France. Aetius might also be unwilling to march back over the Alps, aware that the return of Roman units would allow the Goths to expand their territory unopposed. Some even doubted the strength of Aetius' commitment to Italy. According to Prosper of Aquitaine, after he had failed to block Attila's advance, Aetius was then suspected of planning a complete withdrawal, including the evacuation of Valentinian and the imperial court. In Prosper's hostile view, Aetius only agreed to even a limited deployment of troops in Italy 'out of a sense of shame'.

Attila's first objective was the wealthy and well-defended city of Aquileia. Situated at the head of the Adriatic, it was a vital trading link between central Europe and the Mediterranean. Aquileia's harbour has long since silted up, but the docks – now marooned inland – are well preserved. Here merchant ships loaded their cargoes in front of a long row of stone-built warehouses. Here it is possible to imagine the noise: the creaking of wooden cranes, the rattle of crates stacked on the quayside and the swearing of stevedores hard-worked in the summer heat. The town is still dominated by its magnificent basilica. This great church has the largest early-Christian mosaic floor in Europe: about 12,000 square feet in all, an area not far short of four tennis courts. The most beautiful of the mosaics were laid at the beginning of the fourth century, around the time Constantine became the first Roman emperor to convert to Christianity. One large panel shows the story of Jonah and the whale, a good choice for a port city (see plates, picture 33). Even so, the craftsmen who designed the floor had clearly never seen a whale. A long snake-like creature with a surprised expression looking more like some sort of seagoing dragon disgorges a naked Jonah feet first, while his companions on a very Roman-looking boat drag him aboard. Nearby, in another boat – and entirely ignoring Jonah's difficulties – naked cupids play at being fishermen.

At first sight these two images are difficult to reconcile. To our eyes, playful putti enjoying an afternoon's fishing seem to have no place next to a serious story from the Old Testament. For contemporaries, the conjunction of these scenes was reassuring. It confirmed the fragile alliance between their classical heritage and their new faith. Like witty quotations from Homer, Euripides or Virgil exchanged at smart dinner parties, the well educated in the Roman empire celebrated the possibilities of connecting a non-Christian past with a Christian present. It was important that Old Testament figures and laughing cupids could occupy the same space and be seen as part of the same world. Christianity in the Roman empire attracted converts because it was more than a religion for just the poor or underprivileged. It had room for the socially superior along with their intellectual pretensions and their wealth. Leading members of the Christian community in Aquileia who donated money for the building of the basilica were publicly commemorated. Their portraits were carefully worked into the mosaics on the floor. Their smug, complacent stares still challenge the inquisitive gaze of modern tourists. Nor were these self-satisfied Christians embarrassed to advertise their benefactions. The precise extent of their generosity is still plainly visible. A matter-of-fact inscription, again worked into the floor, records that 'as a gift to God' the wealthy Januarius was responsible for financing '880 square feet' of mosaic. In Aquileia there were no anonymous donors.

It was this prosperous and devout world, as in so many other cities across the empire, that was wrecked by Attila and the Huns. Aquileia did not fall as quickly as some of the fortified cities south of the Danube. The prolonged siege was an unwelcome delay for an army that relied on speed for its success and on plunder for its supplies. According to the sixth-century historian Procopius, Attila was considering bypassing the city when his attention was caught by an abandoned stork's nest on one of its towers. Attila observed that the stork had recently flown off with its young. Procopius, clearly no bird-watcher, explains: 'the fledglings, as they were not yet quite ready to fly, sometimes shared their parent's flight, and at times rode on his back'. Attila took this remarkable sight as a favourable omen. If the stork and its family were fleeing Aquileia, it must be a sign of forthcoming destruction. 'Look at the birds, they can see the future and are leaving the city because it will perish, abandoning its defences because they will be destroyed by the danger that now threatens . . . for birds can foresee events, and out of fear of what is to come they change their behaviour.'

Attila – or at least the stork – was right. The Huns resumed their attack and the walls were soon undermined. The tower that the stork had deserted was said to have been the first to collapse. The Huns gutted Aquileia, massacring the inhabitants and setting the city ablaze. Paradoxically, the scale of the devastation ensured the town's preservation as a modern archaeological site. The floor of the basilica is still scarred by scorch marks. Here, as the whole building collapsed, burning roof timbers covered the mosaics in a protective layer of ash. Long-held local tradition holds that those who survived abandoned the ruins and settled sixty miles along the coast on the shores of a sheltered lagoon. It may then be one of the curious accidents of history that by destroying Aquileia Attila the Hun was responsible for the founding of Venice.

Leaving Aquileia behind, the Huns advanced west along the edge of the Po Valley, sacking Pavia and then Milan. The loss of life in these cities may not have been so severe. There is some indication that Aetius had already implemented a policy of systematic withdrawal towards the Alps and, ultimately, the safety of France. This can be seen as a prudent defensive strategy rather than proof of Prosper's damning claim that Aetius wished to abandon Italy. If the evidence of an anonymous sermon preserved amongst the works of Maximus, the fifth-century bishop of Turin, is reliable, the Hun army pillaged Milan – 'what once seemed to be ours was despoiled by looting or was destroyed by the sword and consumed by fire' – but many of its citizens had already left, easily outdistancing the Huns, who now moved slowly, their wagons heavy with booty.

Milan was a great prize. It had been the capital of the western Roman empire from 340 to 402, until Alaric's invasion had forced Honorius to move to Ravenna. Although much more compact than either Rome or Constantinople, Milan was still a splendid imperial city with an imposing palace, a hippodrome, a monumental bath complex and grand colonnades, one extending a mile beyond its main gate. The city's prosperity was evident in the mansions of the powerful, its piety – or so its citizens claimed – in the beauty of its churches. Some of these, like S. Lorenzo and S. Nazaro, survive imprisoned within later medieval and Renaissance rebuildings. Nothing of the imperial palace remains. It was somewhere in its golden halls that high-ranking Huns gathered after securing the city. It is regrettable that Priscus' account of this evening with Attila is lost. Only one incident can be recovered. A few lines that probably come from the *History of Attila* are included in the entry under 'Milan' in the *Souda* (a bulky and often unreliable tenth-century encyclopedia whose compilation had perhaps been inspired by Constantine Porphyrogenitus' vast editorial projects). 'When Attila saw a painting of Roman emperors sitting on golden thrones and Huns lying dead at their feet, he sought out an artist and ordered him to paint Attila upon a throne and the Roman emperors with sacks on their shoulders pouring out gold at his feet.'

Priscus' readers would have immediately recognised the image. Tribute-bearing barbarians were part of the standard representation of Roman victory. The magnificently carved Barberini Ivory (now in the Louvre) shows a sixth-century emperor fully armed and on horseback (see plates, picture 32). Above, in celestial clouds and surrounded by angels, a serene Christ offers an approving blessing; below, the leaders of vanquished peoples, some bent almost double, stagger under the weight of their offered wealth. It was this striking image of imperial power that Attila instructed the painter in Milan to reverse. It is difficult to believe that, in the full text of his *History*, Priscus would have let such an extraordinary moment pass without comment. Even in his own imagination Attila the Hun wished to look like a triumphant Roman emperor.

While the Huns advanced across northern Italy, Valentinian remained in Rome. This was neither an act of cowardice nor a grand dramatic gesture – a Roman emperor choosing the ancient capital to make a last stand in defence of a shattered empire. Valentinian's actions made good sense and may have been carefully coordinated with Aetius' steady westward withdrawal. The same strategy had been used 700 years earlier after the Roman army had been wiped out at the Battle of Cannae by the Carthaginians under Hannibal. Following the advice of Fabius Maximus – admiringly named Cunctator, 'the Delayer' – the Romans had avoided pitched battles. Instead, they burned their crops and retreated to fortified cities. Slowly starved by this scorched-earth policy, Hannibal's army abandoned the campaign. Valentinian may have had a similar idea. Under the late-summer sun he hoped to drive a hungry enemy into retreat. Only the boldest, or most pedantic, of his courtiers would have dared to remind the emperor that it had taken fifteen years to force Hannibal out of Italy.

Attila was aware of the risks of striking south. For the moment the Hun army stayed north of the Apennines and by late summer 452 had moved eighty miles south-east of Milan to Mantua. Just outside the city, near the River Mincio, Attila received ambassadors sent by Valentinian from Rome. The delegation was headed by the pope, Leo I. This is one of the great encounters in history. Regrettably no eyewitness report survives. Constantine Porphyrogenitus' editors failed to include this embassy in their collection of excerpts from Priscus' *History*. Prosper of Aquitaine's brief account reminded his Christian readers that the pope 'trusted in the help of God, whom he knew never neglects the labours of the devout'. Faced with the sternness of Leo's gaze and the magnificence of his gold-embroidered pontifical robes, Attila fell silent. Later tradition added to the scene a mysterious old man, perhaps St Peter himself, who protected Leo and threatened Attila with a drawn sword. The confrontation is most dramatically imagined in one of the brilliant frescoes painted by Raphael between 1512 and 1514 for the papal apartments in the Vatican (see plates, picture 34). Leo, followed by two cardinals, rides a snow-white mule. Pope Leo X, who carefully supervised Raphael's designs, ensured that his own aristocratic profile provided the model for his predecessor. Attila's ash-coloured charger is caught just in the moment before it rears in fear at the sudden appearance of both St Peter and St Paul, who hover menacingly above the pope's head brandishing swords. Thanks to Leo's intervention, the city of Rome – which with a miraculous disregard for Italian geography fills the background of Raphael's fresco – will not be sacked by barbarians for a second time in fifty years.

There are other explanations for Attila's willingness to withdraw from northern Italy. It is not unreasonable to speculate that Valentinian had supplied the embassy with gifts and gold to be presented to Attila, perhaps in belated recognition of his claim to Honoria. If he would not hand over his sister, Valentinian might still have been prepared to offer a dowry. It is also likely that the Huns were already facing difficulties in provisioning their army. The previous year, harvests had failed in many parts of Italy and the crops were little better in 452. In addition, in some rural districts a malarial plague had broken out. By now too news had probably reached Attila of Marcian's renewed offensive, this time across the Danube frontier: the first and only occasion that Roman forces fought Huns outside the empire. The operation was far from a full-scale invasion, but Marcian's limited success exposed the dangers Attila faced in moving the Hun army west without a firm guarantee of security along the Danube.

Attila's Italian campaign cannot be regarded as a failure either because the Huns did not reach Rome or because they finally negotiated a withdrawal. As they had done at the conclusion of their two offensives in the Danube provinces in the 440s, they returned to the Great Hungarian Plain with their wagons piled high with plunder. For Valentinian, the invasion of Italy had been a stark demonstration of his own political and military weakness. In 451 he had been forced to recognise that the Goths could never be dislodged from France; in 452 it was evident that the Roman army was unable to protect Italy. Attila's brief and bloody intervention had decisively shifted the balance of power in the West. It was clear that the Roman imperial government could now neither control nor defend the empire.

Many in Constantinople must have wondered if Marcian's daring dash across the Danube had been worth it. It had helped to force the Huns to quit Italy, but it might also provoke Attila into attacking the East. As he had done for each of the last three years, Attila continued to issue threats. In late 452 he sent another embassy to inform Marcian that he was planning a campaign the following year that would 'devastate the provinces because the promises made by the previous emperor, Theodosius, have not been kept'. This time 'the fate of his enemies would be even crueller than usual'.

At the beginning of 453 Attila decided to take another wife (how many he had is unknown). His new bride, Ildico, was said by Roman writers to be a woman of outstanding beauty. After the wedding Attila feasted late into the night. The next morning he did not appear. When his anxious bodyguard finally broke down the doors of the bridal chamber, they found Ildico weeping hysterically over her husband's lifeless body. There was no wound and it seemed that Attila had haemorrhaged through the nose during the night. While he lay on his bed in a stupor blood had drained into his throat and he had choked in his sleep. Some suspected Ildico of murder; others believed that the death was just what it appeared, an extraordinary accident. For the abstemious monk Jordanes, judgemental to the very end, Attila's inglorious demise was a warning against the dangers of binge drinking: 'Thus did drunkenness put a disgraceful end to a famous war leader.'

The news travelled quickly to Constantinople. At court all waited to see how Marcian would react. The emperor was equal to the moment, calmly informing his advisers that he already knew of Attila's death. Two nights earlier he had been unable to sleep and his troubled thoughts had turned to the defence of the Danube provinces. Then he became aware of an angel standing beside his bed. This heavenly messenger silently showed the emperor a broken bow. God, as the pious Pulcheria was no doubt quick to point out, had at last

answered the prayers of the Roman empire. There is no account of
Valentinian's reaction in Ravenna. Amidst all the rejoicing that followed,
the emperor must have been aware of the extraordinary twist of fate
that decreed Attila had not been slain in battle or flung himself on a
burning heap of saddles. Aetius was later to allege, in a strange reprise
of Chrysaphius' assassination plot, that he had bribed the commander
of Attila's bodyguard to commit the murder, but it is doubtful whether
anyone believed him. Whatever the truth, no Roman could claim the
credit for Attila's death. He had died after feasting with his fellow
Huns in their new homeland on the Great Hungarian Plain. It must
then have been with a curious mix of emotions that Valentinian
reported the news of this fatal marriage night to his sister Honoria.
The bare facts probably sufficed: Attila the Hun, one of the most
feared enemies in the history of the Roman empire, had collapsed
drunk in bed and died of a nosebleed.

# 24

## *Endings*

Aetius' fears were proved right: after Attila's death the Hun empire fell apart. Three of his sons – Ellac, Dengizich and the youngest, Ernac – fought among themselves, their rivalry disrupting the careful balance of oppression and reward so skilfully maintained by their father. The immediate result was the break-up of the army as those once loyal to Attila now chose one of his sons. Jordanes was quick to point out the political and moral lessons: 'A struggle for overall control broke out among Attila's heirs – for the minds of young men are often inflamed by an ambition for power. Each was driven by a rash desire to rule and together they destroyed their father's empire.'

Disunity amongst the Huns was exploited by their subjects. Subsequent cooperation between the brothers came too late to prevent a major revolt. The crucial battle was fought in 454 on the banks of the Nedao, an unidentified river probably somewhere in modern Slovenia. The Huns were overwhelmed by a new confederation of peoples once part of their empire. Ellac was slain and the victors claimed 30,000 Hun casualties. These severe losses came less than two years after Attila's death. For Jordanes this was a satisfyingly swift reversal of fortune. 'And so the Huns were halted – a people to whom it was once thought the whole world would yield. So destructive a thing is division that the Huns who were so terrifying when their strength was united, were now brought down separately.'

After their defeat at the Nedao, Dengizich and Ernac marched south to threaten Goths settled along the middle Danube and in the former Roman provinces of Pannonia and Valeria. Again according to Jordanes, these Goths successfully fought off the Huns, 'who came at them as though they were seeking to recapture runaway slaves'. A decade later troops under Dengizich were turned back as they attempted to re-establish control along the Danube west of the ruined Roman city of Singidunum. The Goths' leaders – the brothers Valamer, Thiudimer and Vidimer – had considerable experience of Hun battle tactics. At the Catalaunian Plains they had been close comrades of Attila.

Not everyone fought to regain their independence. Further east along the Danube, outside territory controlled by the three brothers, some Goths took the opportunity to cross into the Roman empire. Throughout the 450s and '60s a number of separate groups, in all about 50,000 men, women and children, were resettled in Thrace (roughly modern Bulgaria) on condition they recognised the authority of the emperor and supplied recruits for the army. Some of the problems of a century earlier were avoided. There were no mass movements of refugees and no internment camps; fertile farmland was quickly found, and the Goths' leaders secured high-ranking posts in the army and at court. The eastern imperial government at last seemed committed to establishing an effective cordon of migrant settlements between Constantinople and the northern frontier.

Instability along the Danube intensified with Dengizich and Ernac's attempts to reassert Hun dominance. In 468, ahead of a major campaign, they sent ambassadors to Constantinople to offer a peace treaty and the establishment of a frontier trading post. The emperor Leo, who had taken the throne after Marcian's death in 457, dismissed the embassy without seriously considering its proposals. Dengizich and Ernac disagreed over their response. Ernac argued that his limited military strength was already fully engaged in protecting the greatly reduced Hun territories north of the Danube; he could not risk war on another front. After this warning, no historian ever mentions Ernac again. Twenty years earlier at dinner Priscus had witnessed the affection shown by Attila towards his youngest son: 'he drew him close . . . and gazed at him with gentle eyes'. At the time Berich explained that a soothsayer had predicted the survival of Attila's empire would depend on Ernac alone. Certainly he had failed to live up to his promise.

Dengizich, despising his brother as a coward, decided to lead his own troops against the Roman empire. He sent another embassy to the Great Palace to demand both land and money. Leo offered to allow the Huns into Thrace on the same conditions as the Goths: in exchange for resettlement they should recognise the authority of the emperor. Dengizich refused and crossed the Danube. The Huns were quickly overwhelmed by Roman forces under Anagast the son of Arnegisclus who at the Utus River had come closer than any of Theodosius' generals to defeating Attila. Dengizich's body was pulled from the rout and his severed head paraded through the streets of the imperial capital. Stuck on the end of a long wooden pole, it was displayed above the Xylokerkos (the modern Belgrad Kapısı), one of the gates in the Theodosian Walls restored after the earthquake in 447. Then Constantinople had been threatened with destruction by Attila; those who remembered the dangerous days when the city was without its defences now came to jeer at the rotting head of his son.

With the defeat of Dengizich the Roman empire was finally freed from the threat of the Huns, who had now been forced back as far east as the Black Sea, where only a century before they had first appeared in Europe. But this did not restore order along the Danube. The Goths under Valamer, Thiudimer and Vidimer had to defend themselves against the expansionary ambitions of other peoples previously held in check by the Huns. Effective resistance was hindered by Valamer's death in battle and the growing rivalry between his two brothers. According to Jordanes, the Goths also suffered shortages of both food and clothing. Faced with these new pressures, those loyal to Vidimer elected to march west, first into Italy and then to join the Goths in France, while in 473, Thiudimer – carefully assessing the risks of defending Pannonia alone – decided to take his followers across the frontier and into the eastern Roman empire.

The imperial government in Constantinople was unable to concentrate enough military force to deal conclusively with this sudden movement of 50,000 people. Attempts to encourage those Goths already settled in Thrace to block the advance of the newcomers failed; peace was only assured through the payment of subsidies and the provision of land for both groups together. In 484 their joint leader Theodoric, son of Thiudimir, was appointed to a consulship. That high honour is an indication that the eastern empire was prepared to attempt some degree of reconciliation. This time there was to be no Adrianople. Instead the objective was to contain the Goths and prevent them from establishing a secure state on the model of Alaric's successors in France or the Vandals in North Africa. Sheltered behind the walls of Constantinople, the imperial army was sufficiently threatening to ensure a military and diplomatic deadlock.

Rather than fight for land in the Balkans, in 488 Theodoric marched his Goths west into Italy. The pattern was familiar: in the 390s Alaric had also been pushed west. Twice in one hundred years the East was unable to eliminate Goths but coerced them into moving on. Similarly, in securing peace with Attila on the Danube in the 440s, Theodosius had been well aware that the likely consequence would be to increase Hun pressure on the Rhine. In the end, the continued ability of the eastern empire to shunt its military problems west was a vindication of Constantine's decision 160 years earlier to abandon Rome and establish his new capital on the Bosphorus. Not only was the East wealthier, but the division of the empire meant that after Valens, the imperial government in Constantinople was ultimately prepared to put its own interests first. Repeated – and unsuccessful – attempts to dislodge the Vandals from North Africa were not matched by any similar commitment to the security of Roman rule in France or Italy. In the fifth century the East ensured its survival by sacrificing the West. The tough truth is that one of the chief reasons for the fall of the Roman empire in the West was the success of the Roman empire in the East.

The western Roman empire, as Aetius clearly saw, had fewer options. The balancing strategy between Romans, Goths and Huns in France, which had led to the decision at the Catalaunian Plains to let Attila go, was wrecked within a year by the invasion of Italy. This exposed the limits of any alliance with the Goths and the difficulty of establishing even a workable arrangement to coordinate the defence of just a handful of Roman provinces. Aetius' failure to defeat the Huns – either in France or northern Italy – undermined his own position. Ironically too, the death of Attila removed any possibility, no matter how remote, that Aetius might again be able to rely on the Huns to fight on his behalf.

In 454 Aetius fell victim to a group of Italian courtiers led by the wealthy landowner Petronius Maximus. They were convinced that Aetius had little interest in defending Rome or Ravenna and claimed that under pressure he would even have been prepared to surrender Italy to save France. Valentinian seems to have been persuaded that

Aetius was aiming at imperial power. Some blamed the emperor's
suspicions on his closest advisers. It was said that the eunuch Heraclius
had convinced him that Aetius planned to have him killed. Valentinian's
violent reaction to the allegation must have surprised even Petronius
and his supporters. John of Antioch, drawing on his reading of Priscus'
*History*, offers the fullest account of Aetius' last visit to the imperial
palace in Rome.

> As Aetius was explaining the imperial budget and calculating the
> revenues raised through taxation, Valentinian suddenly leapt from the
> throne with a yell, shouting that he could no longer be insulted by
> such disloyalty. The emperor claimed that Aetius wished to deprive
> him of his power by blaming the empire's troubles on him . . .
> Valentinian drew his sword from its scabbard and along with Heraclius
> – who had come prepared with a cleaver concealed under his cloak –
> rushed at him. Together they continued to hit Aetius about the head
> until they had killed him.

Attila had never been so foolish. The murder of his brother Bleda
secured him sole rule; the murder of Aetius lost Valentinian an empire.
In response to the emperor's claim that he had been wise to remove
a potential usurper, one courtier remarked boldly that he had
succeeded only in harming himself: 'the one thing I understand
perfectly is that you have behaved like a man who cuts off his right
hand with his left'. Valentinian did not survive long. Six months later,
while out riding with only a small retinue, he was ambushed and,
along with Heraclius, killed by two former members of Aetius' bodyguard. It was rumoured that the assassins had been bribed by Petronius
Maximus. Certainly he was quick to take advantage of Valentinian's
death: the next day he seized the imperial throne and shortly afterwards compelled the emperor's widow Eudoxia to marry him.

The bloody elimination of Aetius was a self-indulgent moment of
dynastic politics that Valentinian could ill afford. His own murder shortly
afterwards marks the beginning of the final phase of Roman rule in
western Europe. Without Aetius and Valentinian there was no longer
any chance of maintaining the empire intact. Nor would this arrangement have been to the advantage of the Goths in France: unless their
own security was directly threatened, it was in their interests to see the

Roman empire fall. They offered no assistance when Attila invaded Italy in 452. Three years later they refused to send help when a Vandal fleet attacked Rome. Petronius, whose reign lasted only seventy-seven days, was killed in panic by his own troops and his corpse dumped in the Tiber. The next morning the Vandals sacked the city. The disruption in Italy caused by the removal of Aetius and Valentinian allowed Geiseric to achieve what Attila had only hoped for. Again Pope Leo intervened, persuading the Vandals to refrain from setting the city on fire and slaughtering its citizens. Instead, for two weeks Geiseric's troops systematically stripped the old imperial capital of its accumulated riches. Tradition has it that the Jewish holy treasures from the Temple in Jerusalem (the great seven-branched candlestick, silver trumpets and the scrolls of the law), which four centuries earlier had been paraded in triumph through the streets of Rome, were now carried off to North Africa. For Geiseric the greatest prize was Valentinian's daughter Eudocia. Dragged back to Carthage she was made to honour her childhood engagement and forcibly married to Geiseric's son Huneric.

The western Roman empire collapsed fitfully over the next twenty years. The disintegration of a superstate develops its own momentum as the powerful – those able to command troops and resources – become less willing to risk them in distant campaigns. The death of Aetius, the fragmentation of the Hun empire and the renewed Vandal threat to Italy allowed the Goths to expand without encountering any serious opposition. In the late 450s they invaded and took most of eastern and southern Spain; in France, Narbonne was brought under Gothic control in 462 and Arles and Marseille in 476. Twenty years after the Catalaunian Plains the Gothic kingdom in the west extended from the Loire Valley to the Strait of Gibraltar. Any advance further northward was blocked by the Franks. Originally concentrated east of the Rhine and subject to the Huns, the Franks had moved across the old Roman frontier after Attila's death. There was no army to stand in their way. Like Theodoric's Goths in the Balkans, the Franks may have been pushed into the empire by expansionary pressure from other peoples in northern Europe now freed from Hun rule. It had been precisely such instability that Aetius had warned against. The tightening of the Franks' hold over territory once part of the Roman empire was followed by aggressive moves south. In 507, under their king Clovis, they defeated the Goths and sacked Toulouse. The Goths retreated across the Pyrenees to Spain leaving Clovis and his successors – the Merovingian dynasty – to rule a new kingdom in France.

The history of Italy in the second half of the fifth century is also marked by the erosion of long-standing political and economic ties with the rest of the Mediterranean. Initially isolation was strongly resisted as the combined military resources of the eastern and western empires were directed against the Vandals. That made good strategic and economic sense. For the East the Vandals still posed a threat to the security of Egypt. For the West there was a better prospect of reestablishing Roman rule in North Africa than in northern Europe. War in France brought with it the risk that one enemy would simply be replaced by another. If the Goths were defeated, then the Roman army would face the Franks. Yet the Vandals were too firmly entrenched in Africa to be dislodged without a long and bloody campaign. Both Roman attempts were utter failures. In 460 newly refitted troop transports were captured even before they had crossed the Mediterranean. In 468 initial progress on land was forfeited when the Roman fleet anchored off Carthage was destroyed by Vandal fireships. After these defeats Italian politics turned in on themselves. A series of short-lived rulers attempted, and failed, to secure the support of powerful generals. In 476 the last Roman emperor was deposed in a bloodless coup. Romulus Augustulus, his name a pathetic recollection of Rome's legendary founder and its first emperor, was pensioned off and permitted to live in retirement on a comfortable country estate. It was a measure of Romulus' unimportance that he was not even thought worthy of assassination. The Roman emperor was now an irrelevance. At the very end, the western empire did not fall; it was simply declared redundant.

Odoacer, Romulus' replacement, might reasonably be called the first king of Italy. With strong military backing his rule lasted over a decade, but he could not withstand the invasion of the Goths in the late 480s. These were the same Goths who had been pushed into Roman territory following the collapse of the Hun empire. Unable to establish themselves securely in the Balkans, in 488 they had moved west under Theodoric. In March 493 Odoacer ended a three-year siege of Ravenna by agreeing to share power. Ten days after surrendering he was killed at a banquet by Theodoric, who remarked, after he had skilfully sliced his rival in half in full view of his guests, that Odoacer 'did not seem to have any bones in his body'. Over the next thirty years, as he steadily consolidated his rule, Theodoric provided security and prosperity for the local population and encouraged their integration with the invading Goths. His achievement was to manage the transformation of Italy from the centre of a fractured Roman empire into a successful and independent Gothic kingdom.

Throughout these dramatic shifts in political control there are clear signs of an accommodation between Roman landowners and these new centres of authority. In the early 460s Sidonius Apollinaris, who owned estates in central France, praised the virtues of the Gothic king Theodoric II. (This is the Theodoric who had taken the throne in Toulouse in 453 after murdering his brother Thorismud.) Sidonius was eager to point out the extent to which Theodoric conformed to traditional Roman ideals of good kingship. 'The judgement of God and the designs of nature have together endowed him with the most pleasing combination of qualities.' He is impressive in appearance, prompt and fair-minded in the administration of justice, modest in demeanour and careful to restrain his temper. He allocates the proper amount of time to his work, his devotions, his leisure and his sleep. After lunch and a brief rest, he enjoys playing board games. All is summed up by Theodoric's dinner parties. Reclining comfortably on couches, his guests are served fine food and wine, but in elegant moderation. 'When you join him at dinner . . . there is no great tarnished heap of old, discoloured silver set down by exhausted servants on sagging tables. The weight here is in the conversation, for nothing is said on these occasions unless it is serious.' This was a Gothic king with whom a Roman aristocrat could do business. Here was a ruler who understood perfectly the courtesies of courtly life. Sidonius sometimes found it politic to lose an afternoon game of backgammon. 'On such occasions, if I have a request to make, I am happy to be beaten, for I allow my pieces to be taken in order to win my cause.' No doubt too at times Theodoric chose to play along.

Throughout his description of Theodoric II, Sidonius turns his back on classical images of the barbarian. There is nothing outlandish in Theodoric's appearance; he is not deficient in morality or self-discipline; he is not irrational or lawless in his behaviour. The firm distinction between Romans and barbarians so well exploited by Ammianus Marcellinus 150 years earlier had lost much of its force. Its sharp distinctions had already been doubted by Priscus in his *History of Attila*. Sidonius, Priscus' contemporary, deliberately blurred

any categorisation of the differences between Romans and those barbarians now permanently settled within the empire. The Goths could no
longer be thought of as outsiders. They were to be allowed to merge
into a world that could still be portrayed in very Roman terms.

This deliberate emphasis on continuity was not a denial of reality
in the face of a collapsing imperial state; rather it was an attempt to
make sense of that transition in traditional ways. The educated elite
in the West was remarkably successful in waging these cultural wars.
It was a significant victory that their new rulers, even if not as perfect
as Sidonius claimed, were prepared to accept Roman forms of rule.
Amongst the Franks, Roman law was enforced and well-educated aristocrats continued to write first-rate Latin poetry. In Ravenna, after his
defeat of Odoacer, Theodoric followed Roman protocols in his administration. His imposing palaces mirrored the magnificent architecture
of Constantinople. As a Christian ruler, Theodoric continued to assert
the special relationship between his kingdom and its heavenly model.
In the golden mosaics of the churches in Ravenna Theodoric appeared
opposite Christ, both shining in majesty like Roman emperors. These
continuities eased some of the consequences of the decline of the
western Roman empire. They helped to ensure that many wealthy
families in Italy and France prominent under the emperor Valentinian
continued to exercise influence with his kingly successors. But the
attractive sheen of Roman-ness that makes the courts of Clovis in
France and Theodoric at Ravenna so seemingly familiar should not
mask the sheer scale of political change in the fifth century. It is a
striking register of the dissolution of Roman authority that within
ninety years of Alaric's half-hearted sack of Rome, the western empire
had fragmented into separate kingdoms and the Eternal City had been
properly pillaged by the Vandals.

Of course Attila cannot be held responsible for all this. He cannot
in any straightforward way be blamed for the fall of the Roman empire
in the West. Nor could he have foreseen it. That said, it could not
have happened without him and without his unexpected death.
Without the threat of the Huns' intervention Galla Placidia might
have eliminated Aetius in the early 430s. Without the Hun offensives
in the 430s and 440s it might have been possible for the empire to have
defeated the Vandals before they consolidated their hold on North
Africa. Without Attila's western campaign Valentinian would never

have been forced into an alliance with the Goths in France and Aetius would never have let both the Goths and the Huns go at the Catalaunian Plains. Without the sudden appearance of the Huns in the 370s Fritigern's Tervingi would never have been propelled across the Danube. Without the collapse of the Hun empire less than a century later the Franks would not have moved across the Rhine and Theodoric's Goths would not have been pushed into the Balkans in the 470s and west into Italy a decade later. And so on.

In any attempt to understand the past, the 'what ifs' can always be endlessly multiplied. What is certain is that the Huns' sudden attacks on France and Italy in the early 450s hastened the end of the western Roman empire. In deciding to invade France rather than campaign across the Danube, Attila forced Valentinian to recognise the Goths settled around Toulouse as partners in an alliance against the Huns. This was a risky venture brilliantly managed by Aetius, who drove the Huns back across the Rhine without significantly weakening Attila's hold over his own empire. That fragile equilibrium lasted less than a year. The reasons for the Huns' invasion of Italy are unclear: an opportunistic raid while the bulk of the Roman army was in France, a quickly executed revenge for the Catalaunian Plains or a dramatic attempt to seize Honoria. The consequences were to expose the difficulty of maintaining imperial authority in France while ensuring the security of Italy. It was that problem which fatally divided Aetius and Valentinian. After their deaths the western Roman empire never recovered its balance. Its rulers were unable to prevent the expansion of the Goths or the invasion of the Franks now released from Hun domination. They failed to reconquer North Africa, protect Rome from Vandal raids or defend Italy against Odoacer or Theodoric's Goths. The Huns' intervention in France, and then swiftly afterwards in Italy, was the catalyst that set this complex chain of events in motion. The Roman empire in the West disappeared within a generation of Attila's death. The new kingdoms that seized control marked a significant shift in the pattern of European power. In the end a Mediterranean empire that had lasted for five centuries was finally replaced by separate states. A grand imperial narrative fractured into a set of divergent national histories. After Attila, the Hun empire left no trace, while the fragments of the western Roman empire – now shattered into France, Spain and Italy – formed the foundation of a recognisably medieval Europe.

# EPILOGUE

# *Reputations*

On 27 July 1900, at the naval dockyard in the North Sea port of Bremerhaven, Kaiser Wilhelm II addressed German troops who were to be sent to China to help the British suppress the 'Boxer Rebellion' (see plates, picture 35). This nationalist uprising had broken out in protest at the occupation of Chinese territory by the colonial powers. Europeans in Peking were besieged and the German ambassador had been assassinated. The kaiser was determined to send an uncompromising message to the rest of the world.

> You must know, my men, that you are about to meet a crafty, well-armed, cruel foe. Meet him and beat him; give him no quarter; take no prisoners. Kill him when he falls into your hands. Even as, a thousand years ago, the Huns under King Attila made such a name for themselves as still resounds in fable and legend, so may the name of Germans resound through Chinese history a thousand years from now, so that no Chinaman, no matter whether his eyes be slit or not, will dare to look a German in the face.

There is a self-evident irony that one of the most powerful equations between Germans and Huns should have been made by the kaiser himself. The German chancellor, Prince Bernhard von Bülow, was appalled. He later described the kaiser's outburst as 'the worst speech of the period and perhaps the most harmful that Wilhelm II ever made'. Von Bülow did his best to suppress the text, circulating a censored copy to the press. His efforts were in vain: a reporter out of sight on a roof overlooking the dockyard took down the speech in shorthand and telegraphed a translation to major newspapers in Britain and the United States.

At Bremerhaven the kaiser had not so much fabricated a new German Attila as misjudged his audience. He had been inexcusably unaware that his speech would attract international attention. He had thought of himself as speaking only to his fellow countrymen. It is significant that on this occasion Wilhelm chose to refer to Attila by his German name King Etzel. Etzel is the wise king of the *Nibelungenlied*, a medieval romance that brought together a series of much older courtly tales, which – again refashioned – formed the basis of Richard Wagner's cycle of operas, *Der Ring des Nibelungen*. One tale in the *Nibelungenlied* tells of Siegfried's widow, Kriemhild, and her marriage to Etzel, king of the Huns (see plates, picture 22). Etzel is a courteous and civilised monarch who celebrates the marriage with festivities lasting seventeen days. On the eighteenth Hagen, Siegfried's murderer, arrives with sixty men. Etzel welcomes them, but Hagen has not come to enjoy his hospitality but to take Seigfried's sword back from Kriemhild. Without warning, Hagen's warriors attack the wedding guests. 'Etzel's men strongly defended themselves, but the visitors moved through the king's hall from one end to the other, slashing with their bright swords.'

Even amidst the bloodshed Etzel remains calm. Finally Kriemhild attacks Hagen with Siegfried's sword. Hagen is decapitated, but not before he has fatally stabbed Kriemhild. They fall together: 'There lay the bodies of all who were doomed to die. The noble lady was cut to pieces; Etzel began to weep and greatly lamented both his kinsmen and his vassals.' In this tale Etzel/Attila is the victim rather than the perpetrator of seemingly senseless violence, and it is his court that is wrecked. While it is true that this tale offers a different view of Attila and the Huns, even so – as von Bülow might have pointed out to the kaiser – it still has slaughter as its centrepiece. It is difficult to think that this story might successfully support Wilhelm's vision of Etzel/Attila as the saviour of European civilisation.

Certainly the English-speaking world would have rejected King Etzel out of hand. Most well-educated people in the late nineteenth century formed their view of Attila from the famous character sketch offered a century earlier by Edward Gibbon in his *The History of the Decline and Fall of the Roman Empire*. For Gibbon, Attila was one of the causes of that fall. He had wantonly smashed Roman civilisation wherever he had found it: 'The haughty step and demeanour of the king of the Huns expressed the consciousness of his superiority above the rest of mankind.' The Huns themselves – 'the Scythian shepherds' in Gibbon's contemptuous phrase – were 'uniformly actuated by a savage and destructive spirit'. This was not a heroic story – Attila was not a noble savage uncorrupted by civilisation. Rather, in Gibbon's view, the Huns had thrown themselves mercilessly against an empire that was already rotten at the core. Theodosius II was one of a succession of rulers who 'had abandoned the church to bishops, the state to eunuchs, and the provinces to the Barbarians'. Valentinian III was 'feeble and dissolute', 'without reason or courage'. These 'incapable princes' no longer cared to maintain civic virtue or military discipline. Gibbon concluded that even the early elimination of Attila would not have saved the Roman empire. 'If all the Barbarian conquerors had been annihilated in the same hour, their total destruction would not have restored the empire of the West.' For Gibbon, Attila was a warning from history. States that failed to secure freedom and liberty for their citizens would inevitably decline and fall.

Victorian morality found Gibbon's homilies on degeneracy and the perils of prosperity very much to its taste. The destructive power of Attila the Hun served as a permanent reminder that civilisation would always have to be defended and the great imperial powers would need to be on their guard. For Victorian readers, Gibbon's analysis was matched by that of Thomas Hodgkin. Hodgkin is now unread, but in the 1880s his eight-volume history *Italy and her Invaders* was widely regarded as offering a more balanced account of the end of the Roman empire than *Decline and Fall*. The second volume, published in 1880, dealt at length with Attila. Compared to Gibbon, one of the most striking differences in Hodgkin's account is its strong emphasis on the Mongolian origin of the Huns. Victorian ethnography insisted on a close link between many of the peoples who had invaded Europe since the collapse of the Roman empire. Hodgkin argued strongly for a racial connection between the Tartars under Genghis Khan and Tamberlane, the Huns, the Bulgars, the Magyars and the Ottoman Turks. The Huns were another example of 'a multitude of dull barbarians, mighty in destruction, powerless in construction, who have done nothing for the cause of civilisation or human progress, and who, even where they have adopted some of the varnish of modern customs, have remained essentially and incurably barbarous to the present day'.

Looking back to the beginning of the nineteenth century, Hodgkin reflected on the near-destruction of Europe by Napoleon. Here was a latter-day Attila, although not, as Hodgkin was all too predictably eager to point out, from a racial point of view. There were vast 'differences between the uncultured intellect of the Tartar chieftain, and the highly-developed brain of the great Italian-Frenchman who played with battalions as with chessmen'. But in his aim to destroy Europe, in his 'insatiable pride, in the arrogance which beat down the holders of ancient thrones . . . in the wonderful ascendancy over men . . . in all these points no one so well as Napoleon explains to us the character and career of Attila'. England had survived Napoleon and established a worldwide empire. One of the main purposes of Hodgkin's historical project was to ask, 'Will England fall as Rome fell?' He returned a qualified answer, arguing that a balance of power between the Old and New Worlds would prevent any one state being consumed by 'an overweening arrogance which is unendurable by God and Man'. He also believed that a strong Anglican Church would ensure a high standard of morality in public life. But the fall of Rome and the destructive success of the Huns offered a salutary lesson. Hodgkin advocated democracy as the best defence against despotism. He was particularly concerned that contemporary politicians might abuse the prosperity of the nations they governed. 'Will the great Democracies of the Twentieth Century resist the temptation to use political power as a means of material self-enrichment?' Success itself might mark the beginning of a new cycle of decline and fall. A wealthy and complacent populace would allow the construction of 'palaces in which British or American despots . . . will guide mighty empires to ruin, amidst the acclamations of flatterers'. And, like the Roman empire, these modern superstates would fall easy prey to some new Attila.

Attila and the Huns have remained powerful symbols of the threats that face European civilisation and might again cause its fall. For Gibbon, Attila exploited the Roman empire's failure to maintain the integrity of its political institutions. For Hodgkin, he represented the dangerous forces of oriental barbarism ranged against a virtuous and democratic Christendom. The sense that there might be a fundamental and irreconcilable antagonism between the nomadic Huns and the settled peoples of Europe was deep-rooted. It is a basic pattern that has been repeated again and again. For British soldiers in World War I, the Germans were the Hun – an identification ironically authorised by the kaiser himself. In 1914 Rudyard Kipling captured the national mood.

> For all we have and are,
> For all our children's fate,
> Stand up and take the war,
> The Hun is at the gate!
> Our world has passed away,
> In wantonness o'erthrown.
> There is nothing left to-day
> But steel and fire and stone!

Again the theme was the preservation of civilisation against the barbarous destruction of 'a crazed and driven foe'. The sentiment was both inspiring and uncompromising. Thomas Hodgkin would have approved. Edward Gibbon, who was more wary of such unrestrained patriotism, would have been slower to applaud.

> There is but one task for all —
> One life for each to give.
> Who stands if Freedom fall?
> Who dies if England live?

More recent versions of Attila have offered variations on this theme. In 1954 the Hollywood epic *Sign of the Pagan*, with Jack Palance in its title role, returned to the orientalist fears of the nineteenth century. This was a film that would have appealed to Senator McCarthy. Attila, conceived as a cross between Ming the Merciless and Mao Zedong, galloped with Mongol-style hordes across central Asia to attack a decadent Roman empire. This was an unambiguous warning of the grim consequences of moral weakness. Middle America must not make the same mistakes as the Romans; to do so was to risk decline and fall. The Huns were to be both feared and despised. They had no regard for private property, for the sanctity of the family, for Christian values or for personal cleanliness. These were signs of an anti-American barbarity. Attila's advance on Europe was one Long March against civilisation. The Huns were clearly proto-communists on horseback.

*

There are many Attilas. He can be viewed through the powerful lens of First World War propaganda, through the distasteful conclusions of Victorian historical racism, through the communist scare of 1950s America, through the romantic stories of the *Nibelungenlied* or through Gibbon's *Decline and Fall* and his memorable tableau of Scythian shepherds smashing a once-great European civilisation. In truth, Attila does not merit any of these reputations. He is not always what we expect, or perhaps not always what we would like him to be. Attila was not part of a yellow peril; he was not on a single-minded mission to destroy the Roman empire; he was not a prototype for medieval chivalry; he was not a forerunner of either Napoleon or Mao Zedong.

To reject these images of Attila is not for a moment to downplay the impact of the Huns on the Roman empire. They crossed the Danube in 408, 422, 434, 441–2 and again in 447; in 450–1 they invaded France and in 452 northern Italy. No other enemy faced by the Romans had ever breached the frontiers of both the eastern and western empires in the short space of a decade. In both East and West the Huns burned undefended farms and villages to the ground and sacked a long list of cities, some strongly fortified: Sirmium, Singidunum, Margum, Viminacium, Naissus, Serdica, Ratiaria, Philippopolis, Arcadiopolis, Marcianople, Metz, Reims, Aquileia, Pavia and Milan. The brutality of these attacks should not be doubted. A terror-stricken population faced, in the monk Jerome's striking phrase, 'the wolves of the North'. Even for the most sympathetic, it is difficult not to be desensitised by the dull repetition of stories of the Huns' ruthlessness. Not every incident has the memorable force of the extermination of 20,000 Burgundians or Priscus' grim account of the bleached bones of the slain strewn along the riverbank outside the broken walls of Naissus. To echo Jerome, himself echoing Virgil: 'Not even if I had a hundred tongues and a hundred mouths and a voice of iron could I recite the names of all these disasters.'

If the Huns' cruelty is not to be diminished, it must be put in context. The Huns were not the only threat faced by the Roman empire in the fifth century, and not the only enemy to sack its cities. Italy was pillaged by Goths and Vandals, France by Goths, Burgundians and Bagaudae, the Balkans by Goths and North Africa by Vandals. These too were bloody and disruptive incursions, and unlike the Huns, who withdrew beyond the frontier after each campaign, the Goths and Vandals fought to establish themselves on Roman territory. Moreover, in direct encounters with the Roman army the Hun record is not particularly impressive. Against Arnegisclus at the Utus River, they sustained heavy casualties. The Battle of the Catalaunian Plains was at best a stalemate. By contrast, Geiseric and his Vandals seized North Africa by force and repulsed a series of Roman expeditions. At Adrianople Fritigern and the Goths wiped out 20,000 legionaries in one afternoon. Attila registered no such achievement. His strategic brilliance lay not in fighting the Romans but in seeking to avoid any large-scale confrontation.

Arguably too, the dislocation associated with the disintegration of the empire in the West is eclipsed by the sheer brutality that had accompanied its formation. The most violent force in the ancient Mediterranean world was the Roman empire. In the annexation of France five centuries before Attila, Julius Caesar's troops had massacred one million people in battle and reprisals, and enslaved a further million. In human and economic terms, Caesar's imperial achievement was not to be equalled in the scale of its destruction until the Spanish invasion of the Americas. A consistent policy of merciless oppression is one of the keys to the Roman empire's success. In AD 60 the Iceni in south-eastern Britain revolted. Roman counter-attacks swiftly imposed control. Tens of thousands of Britons were killed in battle; Roman casualties numbered barely 400. In an early example of ethnic cleansing, the Roman army continued to target the Iceni until all opposition was eliminated. Boudica, one of the Iceni leaders, took her own life. Her attempt to expel the Romans from Britain had been a miserable and costly failure.

Of course such cruelty had a point. It was repeatedly presented as a necessary and unavoidable part of Rome's fulfilment of its divinely sanctioned mission to conquer the independent peoples of Europe, North Africa and the Middle East.

> Roman, remember through your empire to rule
> Earth's peoples – for your arts are to be these:
> To pacify, to impose the rule of law,
> To spare the vanquished and war down the proud.

On this view, the pain and suffering of subjugation was a fair price to pay for the peace and prosperity that came with empire. By contrast, for their actions the Huns seemingly offered no moral or religious justification, however thin or unconvincing. They neither sought to find a new homeland on Roman territory nor to glorify themselves as heroic freedom fighters warring down a harsh imperial regime. The Huns appear more brutal precisely because they had no known motive for their raids beyond the acquisition of booty and captives. Or at least because not a single line of Hun poetry survives to contradict that powerful image presented by their Roman enemies.

Alongside Attila's reputation for ruthless destruction should be set his success as an empire-builder. No coherent story can be told of the consolidation of Hun dominance over peoples from the Urals to the Rhine; there are only occasional fragments which hint at the scale of this enterprise and its possible justification: the discovery of the Pannonhalma, Pietroasa and Şimleu Silvaniei treasures, the presence on the Catalaunian Plains of troops from (to quote Jordanes) 'the countless peoples and various nations that Attila had brought under his control', the prominence of the Gothic leaders Valamer, Thiudimer and Vidimer, and Attila's claims to have been favoured by the war god. The Hun empire did not survive Attila's sudden death. It quickly broke apart when fought over by his sons. Even so, and if only fleetingly, Attila achieved the social and economic transformation of the Huns on the Great Hungarian Plain. By systematically exploiting a network of tributary states, they became the dominant power in northern Europe. This remarkable achievement has received very little attention – perhaps because it does not fit comfortably with conventional images of either Attila or the Huns.

But it was celebrated in Renaissance Hungary, whose rulers and their historians sought to create a national history for an emerging state by reaching back beyond the Magyar conquests of the ninth and tenth centuries to imagine the foundation of Hungary by the Huns. Attila's new champion was the Hungarian king Matthias Corvinus, who in the fifteenth century annexed large parts of Austria, Slovakia and Poland, establishing his capital in Vienna. Corvinus claimed Attila as his ancestor. In this version of the past, most fully set out in János Thuróczi's *Chronica de gestis Hungarorum* (published in 1488), Attila – like Corvinus – was a skilful general and an enlightened monarch. Both enjoyed sophisticated philosophical debate. Corvinus was pleased to be known as 'a second Attila'. In this king's successes, enthused Thuróczi, 'fate revives the ancient glory of the Huns that shone in brilliance during the time of Attila'.

Attila had to wait a millennium before he was first portrayed as a European nation-builder rather than a destructive outsider. By contrast, the transformation of the Goths took less than a century. In the 370s and again after Alaric's sack of Rome in 410 Roman writers had regarded the Goths as the ultimate barbarian menace, yet in the 460s Sidonius Apollinaris offered a strikingly different picture of the civilised courtesies at the court of Theodoric II. Whatever the history of their hard-fought opposition to the empire, the Goths had converted to Christianity, settled permanently in France and now received the enthusiastic praises of Roman aristocrats eager to reach an accommodation with their new rulers. In the end the Romans had sided with the Goths who could no longer be seen simply as barbarian outsiders. The Huns had none of these advantages. Perhaps if the pattern of alliances established by Aetius in the 430s – when Huns fought alongside Romans against Goths – had been successfully maintained, then the Huns might have been treated differently by Roman writers. Instead, in electing to attack both the eastern and western empires, Attila confirmed his reputation as a pitiless savage whose malevolent presence in a Christian world could only be explained by God's righteous anger against the sinful cities of the Roman empire. Attila stood condemned as both nomad and devil. 'The Huns will move faster than the winds, more rapidly than storm clouds and their war cries will be like the roaring of a lion. Terror at their coming will cover the whole earth like the floodwaters in the days of Noah.'

These exaggerated images, either of ruthless barbarity or enlightened nationalism, are a stark reminder of the problems surrounding any final assessment of Attila and the Huns. Any satisfactory judgement is unlikely to be so clear-cut. Hence the importance of Priscus of Panium. In summer 449 Priscus set off to meet a bloodthirsty barbarian hell-bent on wrecking the Roman empire. The reality, as he discovered, was disturbingly different. The Huns could not easily be dismissed as *nomades* who had nothing in common with the elegance of classical culture. Attila turned out to be surprisingly civilised and a dangerously shrewd player of international politics. His attacks on Roman cities were not pointless acts of destruction.

They were part of a careful strategy to force an already overcommitted empire to pay for protection rather than fight. In Priscus' story it was Theodosius II and his advisers – prepared to use diplomatic immunity as a cover for a poorly planned assassination plot – who appeared morally questionable.

Of course Priscus never doubted Attila's hostility towards the Roman empire. His intention was neither to excuse nor justify. Rather, by exploring the complexities of that conflict, his *History of Attila* aimed to move its readers beyond crude stereotypes of Huns and Romans. Priscus opens the door on a different understanding of the Roman empire in the fourth and fifth centuries. This book has enthusiastically followed his lead. As Priscus would be amongst the first to affirm, history should continually seek to challenge our assumptions. It should prompt us to look differently at the world and make us less self-assured about our own ideals and beliefs. What makes great empires endure or collapse? How do governments defend their actions? What causes the break-up of a leviathan superstate? When is it right to go to war, or purchase peace or pay off an enemy? What justifies the label 'barbarian' or constitutes a convincing claim to 'civilisation'? These are issues of enduring importance. They are not abstract questions best left to the ivory-tower discussions of graduate seminars in classics; rather they involve intensely personal dramas which demand that we confront the motives and the reputations of those who seek to preserve empires and of those who aim to bring about their destruction. It is always perilous to suppose that the past is over and done with or that it can ever safely be disconnected from the pressing concerns of the present. At the end of a history of Attila and the Huns we should gently be encouraged to think about more than the decline and fall of the Roman empire.

# Chronology, AD 375–455

| | |
|---|---|
| 410 | Alaric's Goths sack Rome (24 August) |
| 412 | construction of Theodosian Walls in Constantinople |
| 413 | Olympiodorus' embassy to Charaton and Donatus |
| 418 | Goths settled by Constantius in south-western France |
| 418–451 | Theodoric rules Goths in France |
| 420 | Abdaas burns Zoroastrian temple in Khuzistan |
| 421 | **Constantius** (western Roman co-emperor with Honorius) |
| 421–422 | Theodosius' failed crusade in Mesopotamia |
| 422 | Hun attack on Thrace |
| 423 | Galla Placidia flees to Constantinople with her children |
| 425 | Western usurper John defeated in Ravenna; Hun army under Aetius arrives too late |
| 425–455 | **Valentinian III** (western Roman emperor) |
| 427 | alleged conspiracy of Boniface |
| 429 | Vandal invasion of North Africa |
| 430 | death of Octar on campaign against Burgundians |
| 432 | Boniface promoted and made patrician; killed by Aetius at Rimini |
| 433 | Aetius claims that a Hun army is marching on Italy |
| 434 | Hun attack on Thrace and sudden death of Rua; Honoria sent to Constantinople in disgrace |
| 434–440 | Attila and Bleda joint rulers of Huns |
| 435 | treaty with Geiseric and Vandals in North Africa; agreement between Aetius and Huns; surrender of parts of Pannonia and Valeria |
| 437 | Huns and Romans wipe out Burgundians and suppress Bagaudae |
| 439 | Romans and Huns defeated by Goths at Toulouse; Attila agrees treaty of Margum with eastern empire; Geiseric takes Carthage (19 October) |
| 441 | Roman expeditionary force sails to Sicily; Attila and Bleda open Balkan offensive |
| 442 | expeditionary force recalled; Huns withdraw; new treaty with Geiseric who returns Theodoric's mutilated daughter to Toulouse; engagement of Huneric and Eudocia |
| 445 | Bleda murdered |
| 445–453 | Attila sole ruler of Huns |

| | |
|---|---|
| 446 | Hun ambassadors in Constantinople demand enforcement of treaty of Margum |
| 447 | earthquake in Constantinople (26 January); Theodosian Walls rebuilt by Constantinus; Attila's major and most destructive Balkan offensive; narrow defeat of Arnegisclus at Utus River; peace negotiated by Anatolius and Nomus |
| 448 | Aetius suppresses Bagaudae in France |
| 449 | Priscus, Maximinus and Romulus (western ambassador) at the court of Attila |
| 450 | further negotiations by Anatolius and Nomus; appeal of Honoria to Attila; death of Theodosius (28 July); death of Galla Placidia (November) |
| 450–457 | **Marcian** (eastern Roman emperor) |
| 451 | Attila's offensive in France, ends with Battle of the Catalaunian Plains (June); Apollonius' failed embassy; Marcian commands troops in the Balkans (September); Priscus and Maximinus travel from Constantinople to Alexandria |
| 451–453 | Thorismud rules Goths in France |
| 452 | Attila's offensive in Italy; Marcian leads only Roman attack across Danube; death of Maximinus in Egypt |
| 453 | death and *strava* of Attila |
| 453–466 | Theodoric II rules Goths in France |
| 454 | defeat of Huns at the battle of the River Nedao; murder of Aetius in Rome |
| 455 | murder of Valentinian; murder of Petronius Maximus; Vandals sack Rome (June) |

# Illustrations

9.          Framed gold medallion of Honorius, minted in Ravenna, probably early 420s (*Département des Monnaies, Médailles et Antiques, Bibliothèque Nationale de France, Paris*).

10.         Framed gold medallion of Galla Placidia, minted in Ravenna 425–30 (*Département des Monnaies, Médailles et Antiques, Bibliothèque Nationale de France; The Art Archive/Jan Vinchon Numismatist, Paris/Gianni Dagli Orti*).

11.         Emperor Theodosius II, marble bust (10 inches high), probably carved in Constantinople, 430–40. The lower half of the nose is restored, and the irises and diadem have been drilled for inserts in coloured stone. This is the only known bust of the emperor (*The Art Archive/Musée du Louvre/Gianni Dagli Orti*).

12.         The Theodosian Walls (*Chris Hellier/Corbis*).

13.–14.     Mevlevihane Gate and inscription of the praetorian prefect Flavius Constantinus commemorating the rebuilding of the walls after the earthquake in 447 (*author's collection*).

15.         Eagle brooch from the Pietroasa treasure (*National Museum of Romanian History, Bucharest*).

16.         Nineteenth-century restoration of the eagle brooch, from Richard Soden Smith, *The Treasure of Petrossa*, London, 1869, 18.Plate 8 (*reproduced by kind permission of the Syndics of Cambridge University Library*).

17.         Shallow bowl from the Pietroasa treasure (*National Museum of Romanian History, Bucharest*).

18.         Drinking cup from the Pietroasa treasure (*National Museum of Romanian History, Bucharest*).

19.         Sword from Pannonhalma (*Xantos János Museum, Györ, Hungary/Tanai Csaba Taca*).

20.         *The Warlord's Sword* (1890), painting by Béla Iványi Grünwald (1867–1940) (*Hungarian National Gallery, Budapest*).

21.         *Feast of Attila* (1870), fresco by Mór Than (1828–99), painted as part of a cycle of scenes from Hungarian history for the Grand Staircase in the Hungarian National Museum. Priscus and Maximinus are seated front right. Priscus is shown bearded and holding a copy of his *History*, and Maximinus wears Roman military uniform. The young Ernac is next to Attila. It is clear from the details of the scene that Mór Than

and his advisers were neither accurate nor attentive readers of Priscus' account of Attila's feast (*Hungarian National Gallery, Budapest*).

22. *Entry of King Etzel (Attila) with Kriemhild into Vienna* (1909–10), painting by Albin Egger-Lienz (1868–1926) as a design for the banqueting rooms of the Rathaus in Vienna. The scene is imagined from *Nibelungenlied* Aventiure 22 (*Tiroler Landesmuseum Ferdinandeum, Innsbruck/akg-images*).

23. *View of Pest and Buda*, 1870s, Hungarian School (*Nicolas M. Salgo Collection, USA/Bridgeman Art Library*).

24. Onyx brooch from the Şimleu Silvaniei treasure (*Hungarian National Museum, Budapest*).

25. Gold chain from the Şimleu Silvaniei treasure (*Kunsthistorisches Museum, Vienna*).

26. Missorium of Theodosius I, detail, emperor with shoulder brooch; silver plate commemorating the tenth anniversary of Theodosius' reign in 388 (*Real Academia de la Historia, Madrid/Werner Forman/Corbis*).

27. Gold coin (solidus) depicting the emperor Marcian, Pulcheria and Christ, minted in Constantinople in 450 to celebrate their marriage. Marcian standing on the left clasps hands with the smaller Pulcheria on the right; in the middle Christ places each hand on the shoulder of the other two (*Hunterian Museum and Art Gallery, University of Glasgow*).

28. Gold coin (solidus) of Justa Grata Honoria, minted in Ravenna 430–45: Honoria wears a diadem and necklace and has a cross on her shoulder; she is blessed by the hand of God above (*Glenn Woods*).

29. Gold coin (solidus) of Valentinian III, minted in Rome: the emperor is shown triumphing over his enemies in the form of a human-headed serpent (*Bibliothèque Nationale de France, Paris/Bridgeman Art Library*).

30. St Lupus (Loup) confronts Attila at the gates of Troyes, early sixteenth century, Limoges; enamelled panel by Nardon Pénicaud from the reliquary of St Loup (*Treasury, Troyes Cathedral/Photo Monsallier, Troyes*).

31. Martyrdom of St Nicasius, thirteenth century, north portal of Reims Cathedral (*AISA*).

32.        Emperor triumphing over barbarians: 'Barberini Ivory' (13½
           x 11½ inches), sixth century, Constantinople (*Musée du Louvre/
           Giraudon/Bridgeman Art Library*).
33.        Jonah and the whale, early fourth century, floor mosaic from
           the Basilica Patriarcale, Aquileia (*akg-images/Cameraphoto*).
34.        *The Meeting of Leo the Great and Attila*, fresco by Raphael
           (*Vatican Museum and Galleries, Vatican City/Bridgeman Art
           Library*).
35.        Kaiser Wilhelm II addresses German troops at Bremerhaven,
           27 July 1900 (*akg-images*).

# Notes and Further Reading

The last serious, full-length historical study of Attila and the Huns in English was published sixty years ago: Edward Thompson, *The Huns*, Oxford, 1948, revised with an afterword by Peter Heather in 1996. In January 1969 the great Austrian scholar Otto Maenchen-Helfen handed in a manuscript to the University of California Press just a few days before his death. Much of the work was not yet in its final form; under the exemplary editorial supervision of Max Knight all that was publishable was included in Maenchen-Helfen, *The World of the Huns: Studies in their History and Culture*, 1973. Aside from Maenchen-Helfen, the most important recent contributions to Hun archaeology are István Bóna, *Das Hunnenreich*, Budapest, 1991, which offers a comprehensive overview of the material, but is confusingly, and frequently irritatingly, arranged, and the thorough and meticulously detailed study by Bodo Anke, *Studien zur Reiternomadischen Kultur des 4. bis 5. Jahrhunderts*, 2 vols, Weissbach, 1998. Four shorter discussions are also useful introductions: Michael Whitby in Averil Cameron, Bryan Ward-Perkins and Michael Whitby, eds, *The Cambridge Ancient History, Volume XIV, Late Antiquity: Empire and Successors, A.D. 425–600*, Cambridge, 2000, 704–12; Hugh Kennedy, *Mongols, Huns and Vikings*, London, 2002, 22–55; Herwig Wolfram, *The Roman Empire and Its Germanic Peoples*, University of California Press, Berkeley, 1997, 123–44 and Denis Sinor, 'The Hun period', in Sinor, ed., *The Cambridge History of Early Inner Asia*, Cambridge, 1990, 177–205. Two exhibitions on the Huns – at the Musée de Normandie in Caen, June–October 1990, and the Historischen Museum der Pfalz in Speyer, June 2007–January 2008 – have resulted in valuable catalogues: Jean-Yves Marin, ed., *Attila, les influences danubiennes dans l'ouest de l'Europe au V^e siècle*, Caen, 1990, and *Attila und die Hunnen*, Stuttgart, 2007.

Full and detailed coverage of the third to fifth centuries AD (a period conventionally known as 'late Antiquity' or 'the later Roman empire') is provided by *The Cambridge Ancient History* (= *CAH*): Alan Bowman, Averil Cameron and Peter Garnsey, eds, *Volume XII, The Crisis of Empire, A.D. 193–337*, 2nd edn,

Cambridge, 2005; Averil Cameron and Peter Garnsey, eds, *Volume XIII, The Late Empire, A.D. 337–425*, Cambridge, 1998, and *Volume XIV, Late Antiquity*. Three older works remain indispensable: Ernst Stein, *Histoire du Bas-Empire: De l'État Romain à l'État Byzantin (284–476)*, 2 vols, Paris, 1959 (the first volume originally published in German in 1928); Émilienne Demougeot, *La formation de l'Europe et les invasions barbares de l'avènement de Dioclétien au début du VIᵉ Siècle*, 2 vols, Paris, 1979 and A.H.M. Jones, *The Later Roman Empire 284–602: A Social, Economic, and Administrative Survey*, 3 vols, Oxford, 1964. For a comprehensive collection of the evidence for the biographies and career patterns of all known fifth-century civil and military post-holders, professionals (doctors, poets, rhetors) and their families see John Martindale, *The Prosopography of the later Roman Empire, Volume II, A.D. 395–527*, Cambridge, 1980. This is one of the most impressive examples of fundamental scholarship undertaken in the last generation.

All translations from Greek and Latin texts are my own. At the end of these notes there is a consolidated list of the most frequently cited late-antique authors with a guide to modern translations.

## 1 *First Contact*

Ammianus 31.3–9 is the most important account of events from the advent of the Huns west of the Black Sea to the revolt of the Goths under Fritigern. The most helpful modern discussions are Noel Lenski, *Failure of Empire: Valens and the Roman State in the Fourth Century A.D.*, U. of California Press, Berkeley, 2002, 320–34; Peter Heather, *Goths and Romans 332–489*, Oxford, 1991, 122–47, reworked in *The Goths*, Oxford, 1996, 97–104 and 130–4, and *The Fall of the Roman Empire: A New History*, London, 2005, 151–3 and 158–67; Herwig Wolfram, *History of the Goths*, U. of California Press, Berkeley, 1988, 64–75 and 117–24; Michael Kulikowski, *Rome's Gothic Wars*, Cambridge, 2007, 123–37 and Maenchen-Helfen, *Huns* 26–8. Valens' insistence that the Tervingi convert to Christianity is reported in Socrates 7.33.4 with Heather, *Goths and Romans* 127–8; but see Noel Lenski, 'The Gothic Civil War and the Date of the Gothic Conversion', *Greek, Roman and Byzantine Studies* 36 (1995) 51–87 and *Failure of Empire* 320–1 and 347–8 suggesting that Fritigern may have converted in response to Valens' earlier support of his insurgency against Athanaric. Peter Heather defends Lupicinus (with deepening sympathy) in *Goths and Romans* 133, *Goths* 131 and *Fall* 165–6. The transformation of the Roman empire from Augustus to Constantine is beautifully evoked in Peter Brown, *The Making of Late Antiquity*, Harvard, 1978. For innovative studies of the problems faced at the frontiers of empire, see Dick Whittaker, *Frontiers of the Roman Empire: A Social and Economic Study*, Johns Hopkins UP, Baltimore, 1994, and Benjamin Isaac, *The Limits of Empire:*

*The Roman Army in the East*, 2nd edn, Oxford, 1992. Christopher Kelly, *Ruling the later Roman Empire*, Harvard, 2004 explores the transformation in the way the Mediterranean world was governed and the impact and extent of imperial power. The division of the empire and its causes are thoughtfully considered by Émilienne Demougeot, *De l'unité à la division de l'Empire romain, 395–410: essai sur le gouvernement impérial*, Paris, 1951; on the administrative and legal aspects, see Malcolm Errington, *Roman Imperial Policy from Julian to Theodosius*, U. of North Carolina Press, Chapel Hill, 2006, 79–110. The first Christian emperor, Constantine (ruled 306–37) is a pivotal figure. Averil Cameron, *CAH* XII 90–109 and Noel Lenski, ed., *The Cambridge Companion to the Age of Constantine*, Cambridge, 2006 offer excellent introductions; for a more detailed consideration of his political and religious aims, Raymond van Dam, *The Roman Revolution of Constantine*, Cambridge, 2007. The best description of Constantinople in English is Richard Krautheimer, *Three Christian Capitals: Topography and Politics*, U. of California Press, Berkeley, 1983, 41–67. Key to understanding the city are Gilbert Dagron, *Naissance d'une capitale: Constantinople et ses institutions de 330 à 451*, 2nd edn, Paris, 1984, and Raymond Janin, *Constantinople byzantine: développement urbain et répertoire topographique*, 2nd edn, Paris, 1964. In Istanbul the commemorative porphyry column that marked the centre of Constantine's forum still stands (not far from the Grand Bazaar); the pleasant park, known as At Meydanı, next to the Sultan Ahmet (or Blue) Mosque marks out the area of the hippodrome. The remains of the Milion are visible, now marooned in the middle of a traffic island at the northern end of At Mydanı, just beyond the ugly cast-iron fountain presented by Kaiser Wilhelm II to Sultan Abdül Hamit II. The main narrative for the lead-up to Adrianople and the battle itself is Ammianus 31.11–13; see too Socrates 4.38 (jeering in the hippodrome at 4.38.4); Zosimus 4.21–24.2 (body on the road at 4.21.2–3). The most considered account of Adrianople, its causes and consequences, is Lenski, *Failure of Empire* 334–67, usefully read alongside Heather, *Fall* 167–81; Kulikowski, *Rome's Gothic Wars* 137–43 and Wolfram, *Goths* 117–31. Themistius' dark remark is from *Oration* 16.206d. For the imperial Mausoleum in Constantinople, see the remarkable description in Eusebius, *Life of Constantine* 4.58–60 and Cyril Mango, 'Constantine's Mausoleum and the Translation of Relics', *Byzantinische Zeitschrift* 83 (1990) 51–62 at 54–8 (= *Studies on Constantinople*, Variorum reprints 394, Aldershot, 1993, no. V). The highest hill in Istanbul is now dominated by the Fatih Mosque. Nothing remains of the Mausoleum.

## 2 A Backward Steppe

Ammianus 31.2.1–12 for his description of the Huns with important discussions in John Matthews, *The Roman Empire of Ammianus*, London, 1989, 332–42 and Thomas Wiedemann, 'Between Men and Beasts: Barbarians in Ammianus Marcellinus', in I.S. Moxon, John Smart and Tony Woodman, eds, *Past Perspectives: Studies in Greek and Roman Historical Writing*, Cambridge, 1986, 189–201. Classical views of 'the barbarian' are treated comprehensively by Yves Dauge, *Le barbare: recherches sur la conception romaine de la barbarie et de la civilisation*, Brussels, 1981, 330–52 (on Ammianus), 413–66 (on barbarian character traits), 604–9 (on comparisons to animals) and 620–34 (on barbarian social structures). For thoughtful approaches to the material, see Peter Heather, 'The barbarian in late antiquity: image, reality, and transformation', in Richard Miles, ed., *Constructing Identities in Late Antiquity*, London, 1999, 234–58, and Brent Shaw, '"Eaters of Flesh, Drinkers of Milk": the ancient Mediterranean ideology of the pastoral nomad', *Ancient Society* 13/14 (1982–3) 5–31 (= *Rulers, Nomads, and Christians in Roman North Africa*, Variorum reprints 497, Aldershot, 1995, no. VI). For the Roman imperial mission, Virgil, *Aeneid* 6.851–3; for barbarians dragged by the hair, Annalina Caló Levi, *Barbarians on Roman Imperial Coins and Sculpture*, New York, 1952, 25–6; for triumphant gaming boards, Max Ihm, 'Römische Spieltafeln', in *Bonner Studien: Aufsätze aus der Altertumswissenschaft Reinhard Kekulé*, Berlin, 1890, 223–39, quoting 238 no. 49. Themistius' deliberately divisive characterisation of the Goths is from *Oration* 10.133; on the peace settlement between Valens and Athanaric in 369, see Lenski, *Failure of Empire* 132–7; Ammianus 31.4.9 for the volcanic image of the Tervingi. François Hartog, *The Mirror of Herodotus: The Representation of the Other in the Writing of History*, U. of California Press, Berkeley, 1988 (French revised edn, Paris, 2001), Part I, and Paul Cartledge, *The Greeks: A Portrait of Self and Others*, 2nd edn, Oxford, 2002, 51–77 are both brilliant explorations of Herodotus' Greek-centred world view. Herodotus, *Histories* 4.46–7, 59–82 and 110–17 describes the Scythians; 4.16–36 and 100–9 the strange peoples who live on the steppes beyond. Homer, *Odyssey* 9 narrates the Greeks' confrontation with Polyphemus. Hun customs and social organisation, especially as presented by Roman historians, are best understood within the wider physical and economic constraints imposed by life on the Eurasian steppes: see the essays in Wolfgang Weissleder, ed., *The Nomadic Alternative: Modes and Models of Interaction in the African-Asian Deserts and Steppes*, The Hague, 1978; Antal Bartha, 'The Typology of Nomadic Empires', in *Popoli delle Steppe: Unni, Avari, Ungari*, Settimane di studio del Centro italiano di studi sull'alto Medioevo 35, 2 vols, Spoleto, 1988, I 151–79, and the impressively wide-ranging comparative study by Anatoly Khazanov, *Nomads and the Outside World*, 2nd edn, U. of Wisconsin Press, Madison, 1994 (first published in Russian in 1983). The archaeological evidence for cranial deformation is carefully surveyed in Anke, *Reiternomadischen Kultur* I, 124–36 and Luc Buchet, 'La déformation crânienne en Gaule et dans les régions limitrophes pendant le haut Moyen Age son origine – sa valeur historique', *Archéologie médiévale*

18 (1988) 55–71. The 'practical' aspects of what is here presented as a process of beautification are attractively illustrated by Maria Teschler-Nicola and Philipp Mitteröcher, 'Von künstlicher Kopfformung', in *Attila und die Hunnen* 270–81. The incidence of cranial deformation in Europe in the fourth and fifth centuries offers solid evidence of the intrusion of a steppe practice. Its association with the Huns is more problematic. Joachim Werner, *Beiträge zur Archäologie des Attila-Reiches*, Munich, 1956, 5–18 was over-hasty in arguing that it was an index of the Huns' steady advance from the Black Sea to France. There are four main complications. Firstly, it is clear that cranial deformation is widespread amongst steppe nomads; it may well have been practised by the Huns, but certainly not exclusively. Secondly, cranial deformation was already established north of the Black Sea in the first and second centuries, well before the westward migration of the Huns. It is known, for example, amongst the Alans who came into violent contact with the Huns in the fourth century and in the 360s fought as their allies against the Goths (Ammianus 31.3.1). Cranial deformation in Europe may then be an indication of the intrusive presence of Alans as plausibly as Huns or (most likely) indistinguishably both. Thirdly, it is not clear how common cranial deformation was amongst the Huns. If it was intended to mark out an elite group or was viewed as beautiful, then Attila, his wives, relatives and advisers might be thought to be likely candidates. The eyewitness description of Attila and his high-ranking retinue by the Roman historian Priscus of Panium never mentions anything as striking as cranial deformation (Chapter 14, 134). Fourthly, the practice continued in Europe well beyond the fifth century and the dissolution of the Hun empire, an indication that – if it ever had been – it was now unlikely to be a trait that had any direct associations with Hun culture or conquest. The Mongol prohibition on the washing of clothes is cited in Paul Ratchnevsky, *Genghis Khan: His Life and Legacy*, Oxford, 1991, 193. The observations on raw meat by Hans Schiltberger are from his own account of his travels, Valentin Langmantel, ed., *Hans Schiltbergers Reisebuch*, Tübingen, 1885, Chapter 37 (trans. J. Buchan Telfer, *The Bondage and Travels of Johann Schiltberger, a native of Bavaria, in Europe, Asia, and Africa, 1396–1427*, London, 1879, 48). Hun cauldrons are discussed in Chapter 3, 31–2. Khazanov, *Nomads and the Outside World* 15–84 provides a fascinating account of the pastoral economy of nomads and the limitations imposed by the ecology of the Eurasian steppes. For a detailed discussion of the Hun horse, see Maenchen-Helfen, *Huns* 203–14; Vegetius' description is from his *Handbook on Equine Medicine* (*Mulomedicina* 2.Prologue and 3.6.5, ed. Ernest Lommatzsch, Leipzig, 1903). The information on Hun bows in Maenchen-Helfen, *Huns* 221–32 is expanded and updated in Anke, *Reiternomadischen Kultur* I 55–65. The effectiveness of the Egyptian composite bow is discussed by Wallace McLeod, 'The Range of the Ancient Bow', *Phoenix* 19 (1965) 1–14

and *Composite Bows from the Tomb of Tutankhamun*, Oxford, 1970, 37. Taibugha's remarks on bow manufacture are quoted from his *Essential Archery for Beginners* translated in John Latham and William Paterson, *Saracen Archery: An English Version and Exposition of a Mameluke Work on Archery*, London, 1970, 8. On Hun battle tactics, see the useful observations in Thompson, *Huns* 58–60 with Ammianus 31.2.9 on the use of the lasso. The problem faced by nomads disposing of a surplus in an undiversified economy is part of wider pattern of regular contact between nomads and settled communities elaborated in Khazanov, *Nomads and the Outside World* 202–12.

## 3 The Yellow Peril

Ammianus 31.2.1 for his speculation on the origin of the Huns. For excellent introductions to the Xiongnu, see Ying-shih Yü, 'The Hsiung-nu', in Sinor, ed., *Cambridge History of Early Inner Asia*, 118–49 and 'Han Foreign Relations', in Denis Twitchett and Michael Loewe, eds, *The Cambridge History of China, Volume I, The Ch'in and Han Empires, 221 B.C. – A.D. 220*, Cambridge, 1986, 377–462 at 383–421. The arguments in favour of a connection between Huns and Xiongnu were efficiently summarised and effectively rebutted by Otto Maenchen-Helfen, 'Huns and Hsiung-nu', *Byzantion* 17 (1944–5) 222–43, quoting 243 on the Ordos bronzes, and *Huns* 367–75; see too the level-headed conclusions of Ursula Brosseder, 'Zur Archäologie der Xiongnu', in *Attila und die Hunnen* 62–73 on the difficulty of finding specific links between the two. The data on Hun cauldrons is summarised in Anke, *Reiternomadischen Kultur* I 48–55, adding to the surveys in Maenchen-Helfen, *Huns* 306–18 and Bóna, *Hunnenreich* 240–2 and 275 (for Törtel-Czakóhalom). The rock drawings from Minusinsk were published by M.A. Dévlet in *Sovetskaia Arkheologiia* 3 (1965) 124–42 at 128–9, figs 3–6. The hypothesis that a series of typological changes in cauldron design might offer a convincing connection between Huns and Xiongnu (an idea touched on by Maenchen-Helfen, *Huns* 337) has been restated by Miklós Érdy, 'An Overview of the Xiongnu Type Cauldron Finds of Eurasia in three media, with Historical Observations', in Bruno Genito, ed., *The Archaeology of the Steppes: Methods and Strategies*, Naples, 1994, 379–438 and 'Hun and Xiong-nu Type Cauldron Finds throughout Eurasia', *Eurasian Studies Yearbook* 67 (1995) 5–94. At 45–6 Érdy accepted that the dating of the Ürümqi cauldron by the Uighur Museum was problematic; his revised date (on stylistic grounds) now places it in the mid-second century AD: in other words, and unsurprisingly, precisely at the time the Xiongnu, now defeated by the Han, were supposedly on their westward trek to Europe. But it is clear, as Alexander Koch, 'Ein hunnischer Kessel aus Westchina', *Archäologisches Korrespondenzblatt* 27 (1997) 631–43 points out, that stylistically the closest parallels are with the mushroom-handled cauldrons in Russia and eastern Europe (for example, Törtel-Czakóhalom) dating from the first half of the fifth century. The Ürümqi cauldron might then be an example of a continuing pattern of contact across the Eurasian steppes, see Koch, 'Hunnisches in Xinjiang? Überlegungen zum europäisch-asiatischen Kulturaustausch an der Wende zum Mittelalter', in *Attila und die Hunnen* 134–45. The excavations at Tsaraam 7 were published by Sergei Minjaev and L. Sacharovskaja in *Peterburgskii arkheologicheskii vestnik* 9 (2002) 86–118; for Derestuy, see Sergei Minjaev, 'Archéologie des Xiongnu en Russie: nouvelles découvertes et quelques problèmes', *Arts asiatiques* 51 (1996) 5–12; for Ivolga, Antonina Davydova, 'The Ivolga Gorodishche (A monument of the Hiungnu culture in the Trans-Baikal region)', *Acta Archaeologica Academiae Scientiarum Hungaricae* 20 (1968) 209–45 and *Ivolginskii arkheologicheskii kompleks II: Ivolginskii mogil'nik (The Ivolga Archaeological Complex II: The Ivolga Cemetery)*, St Petersburg, 1996. Herodotus describes Scythian royal burial practices in *Histories* 4.71–2. The *strava* is described in Jordanes, *Getica* 255–8, explicitly citing Priscus for the information; for the description of Attila, see Chapter 14, 134.

## 4 Romans and Barbarians

The history of the Goths from Adrianople to their settlement in France in 418 is reviewed in Wolfram, *Goths* 117–71; Demougeot, *La formation de l'Europe* I 143–78 and II 450–72; Stein, *Bas-Empire* I 191–267; Heather, *Goths and Romans* 147–224 reworked in *Goths* 135–51, *CAH* XIII 507–15 and *Fall* 182–250; Alan Cameron, *Claudian: Poetry and Propaganda at the Court of Honorius*, Oxford, 1970, 63–188 and Alan Cameron and Jacqueline Long, *Barbarians and Politics at the Court of Arcadius*, U. of California Press, Berkeley, 1993, 301–36. The best account of the political impact of Stilicho and Alaric on the court at Ravenna is John Matthews, *Western Aristocracies and Imperial Court*, A.D. 364–425, Oxford, 1975, 253–306. Maenchen-Helfen, *Huns* 29 doubts the Huns' involvement at the Battle of Adrianople. Ammianus 31.15.2–15 for the failed attack on the city of Adrianople and 31.16.3–7 for the bloody defence of Constantinople. Themistius' artful misrepresentation of Theodosius' peace settlement in 382 is *Oration* 16.211a–b. Odotheus' failed attempt to cross the Rhine is reported in Zosimus 4.35.1 and 4.38–9. The Hun raids across the Danube in 395 are mentioned in Philostorgius 11.8 with Wolfram, *Goths* 139–40 and Demougeot, *La formation de l'Europe* I 389–90. Peter Heather, *Goths and Romans* 201 and *CAH XIII* 502 (following Maenchen-Helfen, *Huns* 53) doubts these raids took place: Philostorgius was only making a general point, not referring to a specific incident, and it is unlikely that the Huns would have been able to cross the Danube and the Caucasus in the same year. But if the Huns in the late fourth century were not a solid mass moving slowly west under a unified leadership then it is possible to envisage war bands moving independently east and west, particularly if the main concentration of Huns was still north of the Black Sea. For the Huns' eastern campaign, see Maenchen-Helfen, *Huns* 51–9; Eutropius' military successes are sneered at by Claudian, *Against Eutropius* I 234–86 (ed. John Hall, Leipzig, 1985, trans. Maurice Platnauer, Loeb Classical Library, Harvard, 1922); see Cameron, *Claudian* 125. Jerome's lament in *Letter* 60.16 quoting *Aeneid* 6.625–7 (ed. Isidore Hilberg, Vienna, 1910, trans. Frederick Wright, Loeb Classical Library, Harvard, 1933). The late-seventh-century apocalyptic sermon, attributed to the fourth-century poet and preacher Ephrem, survives in Syriac, the language of Christians in Syria and northern Mesopotamia: Edmund Beck, ed., *Des Heiligen Ephraem des Syrers: Sermones III*, Corpus Scriptorum Christianorum Orientalium, Scriptores Syri 138/9, *Sermon* 5.281–8. Uldin's activities in the east are reported in Zosimus 5.22.1–3; his alliance with Stilicho and the defeat of Radagaisus in Zosimus 5.26.3–5, Marcellinus 406.2–3, *Chron. Gall. 452* 50–2 and Jordanes, *Rom.* 321; the Rhine crossing of the Vandals and Alans in Prosper 1230; the devastation in France in *Chron. Gall. 452* 55 and 63. None of these brief ancient accounts offers any indication of the motivation of Radagaisus' Goths or the Vandals and Alans in entering the empire. It is important to emphasise that both are more than invading armies; they were accompanied by large numbers of women and children – at a rough estimate, the Vandals and Alans may have totalled 100,000 people. These are entire societies on the move. The suggestion that the Rhine crossings can be linked to the disruption caused by the westward advance of the Huns has been most fully argued by Peter Heather, 'The Huns and the End of the Roman Empire in Western Europe', *English Historical Review* 110 (1995) 4–41 at 11–19. Walter Goffart, *Barbarian Tides: The Migration Age and the Later Roman Empire*, U. of Pennsylvania Press, Philadelphia, 2006, 73–118 especially 75–8 makes the minimalist case: because the Huns are not mentioned by any ancient author they cannot fairly be regarded as a factor. I am not persuaded. Goffart offers two alternative motives: the failure of the Roman empire to maintain its frontier defences and the success of Alaric's Goths. The first is more a consequence than a cause of the Rhine crossings. In any case, weak defences might explain an invasion force (such as the Huns in the 440s), but the movement of people is a more substantial event. The Goths might have looked successful in the decade after Adrianople, but shunted from East to West in 401 and held to a stalemate by Stilicho, it is not clear that Alaric's experience would have seemed worthy of imitation. The reasons suggested by Goffart were certainly important, but to my mind they are not sufficient to explain the highly risky movement of large numbers across the Rhine frontier. The

Vandals were successful (Chapter 7, 65–9), but Radagaisus and his followers, in part thanks to Uldin's Huns, were wiped out. Jerome's lament on the fall of Rome is from the preface to his commentary on the Old Testament prophet Ezekiel; the biblical quotation is Psalm 39.2 (ed. François Glorie, Corpus Christianorum 75, Turnhout, 1974). For the Goths in France, see Thomas Burns, 'The settlement of 418', in John Drinkwater and Hugh Elton, eds, *Fifth-Century Gaul: A Crisis of Identity?*, Cambridge, 1992, 53–63 and Michael Kulikowski, 'The Visigothic Settlement in Aquitania: The Imperial Perspective', in Ralph Mathisen and Danuta Shanzer, eds, *Society and Culture in Late Antique Gaul: Revisiting the Sources*, Ashgate, Aldershot, 2001, 26–38. The defensive advantages of Ravenna are surveyed in Neil Christie and Sheila Gibson, 'The City Walls of Ravenna', *Papers of the British School at Rome 56* (1988) 156–97. For the cultivation of asparagus, see Pliny, *Natural History* 19.54.

## 5 How the West Was Won

The political transformation of Hun society on the Great Hungarian Plain is thoughtfully discussed in Thompson, *Huns* 177–95; Demougeot, *La formation de l'Europe* II 530–3; Peter Heather, *Goths* 109–10 and *CAH* XIII 506–7 reprised in *Fall* 326–9, and from a defiantly Marxist standpoint by János Harmatta, 'The Dissolution of the Hun Empire I', *Acta Archaeologica Academiae Scientiarum Hungaricae* 2 (1952) 277–304 at 288–96. The economic constraints (and advantages) of the Great Hungarian Plain and its limited grazing capacity are explored in Rudi Lindner, 'Nomadism, Horses and Huns', *Past and Present* 92 (1981) 3–19 and Denis Sinor, 'Horse and Pasture in Inner Asian History', *Oriens extremus* 19 (1972) 171–83 (= *Inner Asia and its Contacts with Medieval Europe*, Variorum Reprints 57, London, 1977, no. II). For 'steppe' diadems, see Anke, *Reiternomadischen Kultur* I 31–41; Bóna, *Hunnenreich* 147–9 and Ilona Kovrig, 'Das Diadem von Csorna', *Folia Archaeologica* 36 (1985) 107–45. The finds from Pannonhalma are described in detail by Peter Tomka, 'Der Hunnische Fürstenfund von Pannonhalma', *Acta Archaeologica Academiae Scientiarum Hungaricae* 38 (1986) 423–88. On the archaeological difficulty of locating the Huns, see Bóna, *Hunnenriech* 134–9 and the, at times rather optimistic, discussions in Michel Kazanski, 'Les Goths et les Huns: à propos des relations entre les barbares sédentaires et les nomades', *Archéologie médiévale* 22 (1992) 191–221 and Mark Ščukin, Michel Kazanski and Oleg Sharov, *Des les Goths aux Huns: le nord de la mer noire au Bas-Empire et à l'epoque des grandes migrations*, Oxford, 2006, 105–97. The clearest introductions to the complexities of Gothic archaeology are Michel Kazanski, *Les Goths (Iᵉʳ–VIIᵉ après J.-C.)*, Paris, 1991, especially 66–87;

Heather, *Goths* 18–25 and 68–93; and Kulikowski, *Rome's Gothic Wars* 60–70. *Anda* and the *nöker* system are explained by David Morgan, *The Mongols*, 2nd edn, Oxford, 2007, 34–5. Uldin's failed attack on the eastern empire in 408 is reported in Sozomen 9.5. Roger Blockley, *The Fragmentary Classicising Historians of the Later Roman Empire*, 2 vols, Leeds, 1981–3, I 27–47 and John Matthews, 'Olympiodorus of Thebes and the History of the West (A.D. 407–425)', *J. of Roman Studies* 60 (1970) 79–97 (= *Political Life and Culture in late Roman Society*, Variorum reprints 217, London, 1983, no. III) both offer sympathetic appreciations of Olympiodorus and his project. His history survives only in the precis of the ninth-century Byzantine bishop and bibliophile Photius. Given Photius' low estimate of Olympiodorus' intellectual merits it is not clear why he bothered to summarise the text; see Photius, *Bibliotheca* 80 (ed. René Henry, Paris, 1959, trans. Nigel Wilson, London, 1994). Olympiodorus 19 for the eight-line note on his embassy to the Huns, with Maenchen-Helfen, *Huns* 73–4. Olympiodorus 35 for the praise of his performing parakeet. The bird was perhaps *Psittacula eupatria* (the Alexandrine parakeet) or *Psittacula cyanocephala* (the plum-headed parakeet), both brought back to the Mediterranean from India by Alexander the Great.

## 6 A Tale of Two Cities

Arcadius' death is noted briefly in Marcellinus 408.3, Theophanes 5901, Socrates 6.23.7 and Sozomen 9.1.1. There is no mention of his funeral. In imagining the ceremonies, I have drawn on two accounts: the funeral of Constantine in 337 as reported in Eusebius, *Life of Constantine* 4.66 and 70–1, Socrates 1.40.1–2 and Sozomen 2.34.5–6; and the funeral of Justinian in 565 as celebrated by the poet Corippus writing in honour of the new emperor Justin II (*In laudem Iustini Augusti Minoris* 3.1–61, ed. and trans. Averil Cameron, London, 1976) with the helpful discussion in Sabine MacCormack, *Art and Ceremony in Late Antiquity*, U. of California Press, Berkeley, 1981, 116–21 and 150–8. For Anthemius' career, see Martindale, *Prosopography* 93–5; he is praised by Socrates 7.1.3. The involvement of Yazdgard in securing the succession is reported (amongst other competing versions) in Procopius, *Persian Wars* 1.2.1–10 and Theophanes 5900. I follow Roger Blockley, *East Roman Foreign Policy: Formation and Conduct from Diocletian to Anastasius*, Leeds, 1992, 48–52 in understanding it as part of a series of diplomatic exchanges between Constantinople and Ctesiphon initiated by Arcadius – who, according to Procopius, made his last request of Yazdgard from his deathbed. Geoffrey Greatrex and Jonathan Bardill, 'Antiochus the *Praepositus*: A Persian Eunuch at the Court of Theodosius II', *Dumbarton Oaks Papers* 50

(1996) 171–97 at 172–80 suggest that, given the inconsistencies in the various accounts, it is plausible that the request might have been made as early as January 402, when the nine-month-old Theodosius was formally made co-emperor. *Theodosian Code* 7.17.1 preserves the authorisation for the refitting of the Danube fleet. The most important survey of the Theodosian Walls remains Bruno Meyer-Plath and Alfons Schneider, *Die Landmauer von Konstantinopel*, Berlin, 1943, usefully supplemented by Janin, *Constantinople byzantine* 265–83. It is unlikely that the moat could be flooded, although some sections were designed to catch and retain rainwater. The leaseback arrangement is set out in *Theodosian Code* 15.1.51. The best guide for walking the walls is Jane Taylor, *Imperial Istanbul: A Traveller's Guide*, revised edn, London, 1998, 27–38. Honorius' death is recorded in Olympiodorus 39.1 and Philostorgius 12.13. Stewart Oost, *Galla Placidia Augusta: A Biographical Essay*, Chicago, 1968 provides a detailed and well-judged account of its important subject; see 142–68 (marriage to Constantius) and 169–93 (exile and restoration). Events in Constantinople and Ravenna are related in Olympiodorus 33, 38, 39 and 43, Socrates 7.23–4 (for the shepherd), Hydatius 73–5, Prosper 1280–9, Procopius, *Vandal Wars* 3.3.8–9 and Philostorgius 12.12–14. Aetius' support of John is discussed in detail by Giuseppe Zecchini, *Aezio: L'ultima difesa dell'occidente romano*, Rome, 1983, 125–40 and Timo Stickler, *Aëtius: Gestaltungsspielräume eines Heermeisters im ausgehenden Weströmischen Reich*, Munich, 2002, 25–35. His mission to the Huns and late arrival in Italy is reported in Philostorgius 12.14, Prosper 1288 and Gregory of Tours 2.8, quoting the now lost fifth-century historian Renatus Frigeridus (see Martindale, *Prosopography* 485–6). Gregory's information on Aetius' family and his early life as well as the description of his appearance and character are all based on Renatus. Aetius was born sometime around 390, see Martindale, *Prosopography* 21 and Zecchini, *Aezio* 116. For Gaudentius' career, see Martindale, *Prosopography* 493–4; his death is noted in *Chron. Gall. 452* 100. The dating of Aetius' time with the Huns is uncertain. According to Renatus, Aetius also spent three years as a hostage with Alaric. I follow the careful discussion in Zecchini, *Aezio* 120–4 arguing that Aetius is most likely to have spent 405–7 with the Goths and to have been sent to the Huns at some point between 409 and 416. Honorius' levy of Hun mercenaries in summer 409 seems to offer a suitable context for the sending of hostages. How long Aetius spent beyond the Danube is unknown.

## 7 *War on Three Fronts*

Abdaas' incendiary activities are related in Theophanes 5906 and Theodoret 5.39.1–5. The Persian War of 421–2 is discussed in detail in Blockley, *Foreign*

*Policy* 56–8; Omert Schrier, 'Syriac Evidence for the Roman–Persian War of 421–422', *Greek, Roman and Byzantine Studies* 33 (1992) 75–86; Kenneth Holum, 'Pulcheria's Crusade A.D. 421–22 and the Ideology of Imperial Victory', *Greek, Roman and Byzantine Studies* 18 (1977) 153–72 and *Theodosian Empresses: Women and Imperial Dominion in Late Antiquity*, U. of California Press, Berkeley, 1982, 102–11 and 121–3. The requisition order for the towers in the Theodosian Walls is at *Theodosian Code* 7.8.13. Robert Demangel, *Contribution à la topographie de l'Hebdomon*, Paris, 1945, 33–40 includes a detailed study of the remains of Theodosius' victory column and its inscription. The laconic notice on the Hun incursion is quoted from Marcellinus 422.3. The sequence and dating of the Hun attacks on the eastern Roman empire in the 420s and 430s are uncertain. I follow the elegant solution to a number of difficult problems proposed by Constantin Zuckerman, 'L'empire d'Orient et les Huns: notes sur Priscus', *Travaux et Mémoires byzantines* 12 (1994) 159–82 at 159–63. Zuckerman clearly distinguishes three episodes: 422, 434 (Rua's death) and 439 (peace talks at Margum, Chapter 9, 88–9). For a radically different reconstruction, see Brian Croke, 'Evidence for the Hun Invasion of Thrace in A.D. 422', *Greek, Roman and Byzantine Studies* 18 (1977) 347–67 (= *Christian Chronicles and Byzantine History, 5th–6th Centuries*, Variorum reprints 386, Aldershot, 1992, no. XII). I agree with Croke, 351–2 that the previous treaty provisions mentioned in Priscus 2, including the payment of 350 pounds of gold, relate to the peace settlement in 422. Given the circumstances of the Hun withdrawal after Rua's unexpected death in 434 it seems unlikely that there were any formal negotiations at that point, and not until Margum in 439. The order of events for the 420s and 430s presented in this chapter and following leads to a different understanding of the relationship between Huns and Romans – and the strategic connections with North Africa and France – to that advanced, for example, in Thompson, *Huns* 69–86, Maenchen-Helfen, *Huns* 76–94 and Bóna, *Hunnenreich* 46–56. For the Vandal push into North Africa see the discussions in Walter Pohl, 'The Vandals: Fragments of a Narrative', in Andrew Merrills, ed., *Vandals, Romans and Berbers: New Perspectives on Late Antique North Africa*, Aldershot, 2004, 31–47 at 38–41; Stein, *Bas-Empire* I 319–21 and Christian Courtois, *Les Vandales et l'Afrique*, Paris, 1955, 155–71. The Hun invasion of 434 is reported in *Chron. Gall. 452* 112, Theodoret 5.37.4 and Socrates 7.43, citing Proclus' sermon on *Ezekiel* 38–9.


## 8 Brothers in Arms

The accession of Attila and Bleda following Rua's death is noted in Jordanes, *Getica* 180. The expansion of the Hun empire under Rua and Bleda is helpfully discussed in Maenchen-Helfen, *Huns* 81–5. The tribes pressured by Rua are listed in Priscus 2; Jordanes, *Getica* 126 associates them with the Huns' earlier westward progress from the steppes. Octar's defeat by the Burgundians is piously reported in Socrates 7.30. The extent of the Hun empire under Attila and Bleda is discussed in Thompson, *Huns* 83–5 with doubts in Maenchen-Helfen, *Huns* 125–6. The archaeological evidence, which may suggest transcontinental trading contacts rather than conquest, is surveyed in Jan Bemman, 'Hinweise auf Kontakte zwischen dem hunnischen Herrschaftsbereich in Südosteuropa und dem Norden', in *Attila und die Hunnen* 176–83. The Pietroasa treasure is now on display in the National Museum of Romanian History in Bucharest. The objects were described in detail in a magnificent three-volume work by the Romanian historian and politician Alexandru Odobescu, *Le trésor de Pétrossa, historique, description: étude sur l'orfèverie antique*, Paris, 1889–1900 (reprinted as *Opere IV: Tezaurul de la Pietroasa*, Bucharest, 1976, 44–735). Odobescu III 15–26 argued that the treasure had been buried by the Tervingi leader Athanaric sometime before his death in 381. Recent studies have suggested that on stylistic grounds the treasure dates to the fifth century and was probably buried sometime around 450, perhaps as a response to the break-up of the Hun empire (Chapter 24, 210–12), see Radu Harhoiu, *The Fifth-Century* A.D. *Treasure from Pietroasa, Romania, in the light of recent research*, Oxford, 1977, especially 7–18 (descriptions) and 31–5 (historical context). Ecaterina Dunăreanu-Vulpe, *Le trésor de Pietroasa*, Bucharest, 1967 is useful for its descriptions (15–44) and especially for the account of the modern history of the treasure (7–13) following Odobescu, *Le trésor* I 1–68. The patera (shallow bowl) and its iconography are treated in detail by Madeleine von Heland, *The Golden Bowl from Pietroasa*, Stockholm, 1973, identifying (at 71–4) Antioch as a possible place of manufacture and Gerda Schwarz, 'Der Götterfries auf der spätantiken Goldschale von Pietroasa', *Jahrbuch für Antike und Christentum* 35 (1992) 168–84 proposing Alexandria. The treasure has been extensively restored. The great eagle brooch, when recovered from the dealer Anastase Vérussi, was in at least two pieces with its precious stones removed. Major restoration was carried out in Paris before the treasure was displayed at the Universal Exhibition of 1867; before then, Odobescu, *Le trésor* I 41 specifically notes that the head and body were separate. Immediately after the Paris exhibition the treasure was put on public view for six months at the South Kensington (now Victoria and Albert) Museum in London. The Arundel Society for Promoting the Knowledge of Art commissioned a portfolio of photographs of the objects 'for the use of Schools of Art and Amateurs': Richard Soden Smith, *The Treasure of Petrossa*, London, 1869. The photograph of the eagle brooch shows three significant differences from its current state: the head is turned slightly to the left (it now looks straight ahead); there is no 'collar' extending from the last row of heart-shaped perforations on the neck to the breast; and there are two (not four) rock-crystal pendants hanging from the tail (see plates, pictures 15–16). These changes were made following damage to the brooch in the robbery of December 1875. The treasure was shown January–March 1971 in the British Museum's special exhibition *Treasures from Romania* (catalogue nos 354–64). Following that exhibition, David Brown, 'The brooches in the Pietroasa treasure', *Antiquity* 46 (1972) 111–16 suggested that in the repairs carried out during the nineteenth century the eagle brooch had been incorrectly restored. If the brooch was worn on the shoulder, as seems likely given its size, the curve of the body and the pendants at both ends, then, as currently positioned, the eagle's head is arguably the wrong way round – its beak points straight up in the air rather than out across the wearer's shoulder. Harhoiu 18 accepts that the brooch is to be worn on the shoulder, registers Brown's suggestion but offers no comment. The restoration has not been altered. For the site of Pietroasa, see Gheorghe Diaconu, 'L'ensemble archéologique de Pietroasele', *Dacia* 21 (1977) 199–220 at 199–206. Maenchen-Helfen, *Huns* 267–96 offers a fascinating, and unapologetically speculative, discussion of Hun religion. Thompson, *Huns* 42–5 and Maenchen-Helfen, *Huns* 260–7 for the Huns' hostile attitude to Christianity. Nestorius' challenge to Theodosius is quoted in Socrates 7.29.5; the story of the invisible bishop of Tomi is told in Sozomen 7.26.6–8. The finding of the war god's sword is recounted in Jordanes, *Getica* 183, explicitly citing Priscus as the source. For literary parallels, see Herodotus, *Histories* 4.62 and Ammianus 31.2.23. The sword from Pannonhalma is described in Tomka, 'Der Hunnische Fürstenfund', 433–43 and Bóna, *Hunnenreich* 279. The story of Zercon survives in the tenth-century encyclopedia the *Souda Z* 29 (ed. Ada Adler, Leipzig, 1928–38). The information most probably derives from Priscus, see Blockley, *Fragmentary Classicising Historians* I 118.

## 9 Fighting for Rome

The story of Aetius' plot to discredit Boniface is related in Procopius, *Vandal Wars* 3.3.14–30, followed by Theophanes 5931. There are other versions (Prosper 1294 does not mention Aetius), but no sure way of selecting between them. Rather than attempt a compromise – which might of course turn out to be the least accurate version – I have followed Procopius. For discussion see John O'Flynn, *Generalissimos of the Western Roman Empire*, U. of Alberta Press, Edmonton, 1983, 77–81; Martindale, *Prosopography* 23; Oost, *Galla Placidia* 220–4; Heather, *CAH* XIV 5–6; Zecchini, *Aezio* 146–50 and Stickler, *Aëtius* 44–8. Galla's attempts to exploit the rivalry between Aetius and Boniface are noted in Hydatius 89 and *Chron. Gall. 452* 109, with Oost, *Galla Placidia* 227–35;

Zecchini, *Aezio* 159–65; Stickler, *Aëtius* 54–8 and Martindale, *Prosopography* 22–4 and 239–40. The allegation that Aetius lengthened his lance before the battle at Rimini is made in Marcellinus 432.3. Both Prosper 1310 and *Chron. Gall. 452* 112 note Aetius' appeal to Rua and his offer of help. The number of Hun troops that accompanied Aetius back to Italy is unknown. There is no record that any battle was ever fought. I follow the suggestion in Oost, *Galla Placidia* 234 and Maenchen-Helfen, *Huns* 87 that what really mattered was Aetius' threat of an invasion. There is no clear-cut solution to the problem of when part of Pannonia and Valeria were ceded to the Huns. I follow the carefully argued conclusion of Maenchen-Helfen, *Huns* 87–90 (applauded by Stickler, *Aëtius* 108) that the deal was not made with Rua, but Attila (for a recent opposing view, see Zecchini, *Aezio* 161–3). Priscus 11.1, who reports the exchange with the Huns without naming either Rua or Attila, affirms that it was the result 'of a treaty concluded with Aetius'. I suggest that such an arrangement makes good sense in the context of Aetius' success in persuading Attila and Bleda to support Roman interests in France. There is no straightforward account of the campaigns of the Romans and their Hun allies in the 430s, only a series of scattered and often frustratingly brief notices in the chronicles. The most important are: Hydatius 102, *Chron. Gall. 452* 118 and Prosper 1322 on the Burgundians; *Chron. Gall. 452* 117 and 119 on the Bagaudae (see Chapter 19, 173–4); Hydatius 108 and Prosper 1324 and 1335 on Litorius before Narbonne and Toulouse. The most useful modern discussions are Stein, *Bas-Empire* I 322–4; Maenchen-Helfen, *Huns* 95–107; Thompson, *Huns* 72–9; Heather, *CAH* XIV 8–10; Wolfram, *Goths* 175–6 and Zecchini, *Aezio* 212–22. The ritual of scapulimancy is described in Jordanes, *Getica* 196 and discussed in Maenchen-Helfen, *Huns* 269–70. The warnings of Salvian of Marseille are taken from his polemical social critique *On the Governance of God* (*de Gubernatione Dei* 7.39, ed. Georges Lagarrigue, Paris, 1975, trans. Jeremiah O'Sullivan, Washington, 1947), quoting the *Gospel of Luke* 14.11.

## 10 Shock and Awe

The fall of Carthage is lamented in Prosper 1339; see, Stein, *Bas-Empire* I 324–5. *Chron. Pasch.* 439 with Dagron, *Naissance d'une capitale* 270 and Janin, *Constantinople byzantine* 294 for the extension of the sea walls in Constantinople; the regulations for the improved defence of Rome issued in March 440 are set out in an imperial law collected in the *New Laws of Valentinian* (Valentinian III, *Novellae* 5.2–4; ed. Theodor Mommsen and Paul Meyer, Berlin, 1905, trans. Clyde Pharr, *The Theodosian Code and Novels and the Sirmondian Constitutions*, Princeton, 1952, 515–50); the announcement of the sailing of the Vandal fleet is *Novellae* 9. Theodosius' armada and the expedition to Sicily are noted in Prosper 1344 and Theophanes 5941–2. As with Aetius' campaigns in France in the 430s, there is no surviving narrative history of the Huns' attacks on the eastern empire in the 440s; the sequence of events must be jigsawed together from the notices in the chronicles and the fragmentary text of Priscus (Chapter 13, 117–18). I have followed the chronology suggested in Zuckerman, 'L'empire Orient' 164–8, building on Maenchen-Helfen, *Huns* 112–16; Blockley, *Fragmentary Classicising Historians* I 168–9 n. 48 (but see *Foreign Policy* 62); Brian Croke, 'Anatolius and Nomus: Envoys to Attila', *Byzantinoslavica* 42 (1981) 159–70 at 159–63 (= *Christian Chronicles* no. XIII) and 'The Context and Date of Priscus Fragment 6', *Classical Philology* 78 (1983) 297–308 (= *Christian Chronicles* no. XIV). There are four propositions on which this reconstruction rests. First, that Priscus 9.3, which deals with Anatolius and Nomus' negotiations with Attila, should be dated to 447 and not 443; second, that there were no peace negotiations in either 442 or 443; third, that the first Hun invasion should be dated to 441–2; and fourth, that Theophanes 5942 telescopes into his summary of 449 events that occurred across the previous eight years. For examples of alternative readings, see William Bayless, 'The Treaty with the Huns of 443', *American J. of Philology* 97 (1976) 176–9 and Croke, 'Anatolius and Nomus' 164–70 arguing for an embassy led by Nomus in 442. None of the standard, and in other respects extremely helpful, accounts of the Hun invasion of 440s take fully into account the revisions consolidated in Zuckerman; see for example Demougeot, *La formation de l'Europe* II 534–40; Thompson, *Huns* 86–95; Bóna, *Hunnenreich* 61–72; Stephen Williams and Gerard Friell, *The Rome that did not Fall: The Survival of the East in the Fifth Century*, London, 1999, 63–81 and Heather, *Fall* 300–12; but *CAH* XIV 41 (Doug Lee) and 704 (Michael Whitby). As with the campaigns in France in the 430s, any shift in the basic sequence of events has an impact on understandings of the broader pattern of strategic, political and diplomatic considerations confronting both Romans and Huns. The most important ancient account is Priscus 2 (location of Constantia), 6.1 (attack on Constantia and tomb-raiding bishop of Margum), 6.2 (siege of Naissus) and 11.2 (the later visit to Naissus, Chapter 14, 130). Priscus does not name the Roman envoy at Margum in 441. I have speculated that it might have been Aspar on the basis of the brief notice in Marcellinus 441.1 that indicates he commanded troops in the Balkans in that year; see Martindale, *Prosopography* 166 and Maenchen-Helfen, *Huns* 116. I understand the one-year peace of 441–2 mentioned in Marcellinus to refer to the eastern frontier and not to Aspar's campaign. The suggestion that it refers to both (Brian Croke, *The Chronicle of Marcellinus*, The Australian Association for Byzantine Studies, Sydney, 1995, 85; Blockley, *Foreign Policy* 61–2 and Martindale, *Prosopography* 84–5 and 166) stretches an already ambiguous text too far. Priscus' description of the siege of Naissus is another fine example of the problematic representation of events by a self-consciously literary author eager to demonstrate his knowledge of the classics. Edward Thompson, 'Priscus of Panium, Fragment 1b', *Classical Quarterly* 39 (1945) 92–4 doubts the historical value of Priscus' account of the siege; in Priscus' defence, Roger Blockley, 'Dexippus and Priscus and the Thucydidean account of the Seige of Plataea', *Phoenix* 26 (1972) 18–27 and Barry Baldwin, 'Priscus of Panium', *Byzantion* 50 (1980) 18–61 at 53–6. The Huns' ability to take cities by siege is usefully discussed in Hugh Elton, *Warfare in Roman Europe, AD 350–425*, Oxford, 1996, 82–6. Only the main cities attacked are listed: Priscus 6.1 records Margum and Viminacium, 6.2 Naissus; Marcellinus 441.3 Singidunum and Naissus (thus establishing a context and date for Priscus 6.2). Following Maenchen-Helfen, *Huns* 116 and Thompson, *Huns* 89 the sacking of Sirmium, noted in Priscus 11.2 (Chapter 19, 174), can reasonably be added as it lies at the head of the same marching route along the Sava River and through the Morava River Valley. Marcellinus 442.2 reports that the Huns reached as far as Thrace; hence, as it also lies on the same route, I have followed Thompson, *Huns* 92 and included Serdica mentioned in Priscus 11.2 (Chapter 14, 128). For the cruel impact of war on urban and rural communities, see the excellent discussion in Doug Lee, *War in Late Antiquity: A Social History*, Oxford, 2007, 133–41. The murder of Bleda is reported in Marcellinus 445.1; see too Jordanes, *Getica* 181, Prosper 1353 and *Chron. Gall. 452* 131.

## 11 Barbarians at the Gates

For the magnificence of an imperial procession, see Christopher Kelly, *CAH* XIV 141–3 and Michael McCormick, *Eternal Victory: Triumphal Rulership in late Antiquity, Byzantium and the early medieval West*, Cambridge, 1986, 84–111. The earthquake in 447 is reported in Marcellinus 447.1 (fifty-seven towers destroyed), Malalas 14.22 and *Chron. Pasch.* 450. Theophanes 5930 explains the origin of the *Trisagion*. I follow the understanding of these sometimes contradictory versions as worked out in an elegant essay by Brian Croke, 'Two Byzantine Earthquakes and their Liturgical Commemoration', *Byzantion* 51 (1981) 122–47 (= *Christian Chronicles* no. IX). Aristotle's understanding of earthquakes is set out in his *Meteorology* (*Meteorologica* 2.7–8, trans. Jonathan Barnes, ed., 2 vols, Princeton, 1984, I 591–6). The sporting and political activities of the circus factions are discussed by Dagron, *Naissance d'une capitale* 348–64 and in detail by Alan Cameron, *Circus Factions: Blues and Greens at Rome and Byzantium*, Oxford, 1976. Constantinus' achievement is noted by Marcellinus 447.3; the commemorative inscription is recorded in Janin, *Constantinople byzantine* 278 and Meyer-Plath and Schneider, *Die Landmauer* 133 no. 35. The

notices in the chronicles for the invasion of 447 are disappointingly brief:
Marcellinus 447.2 and 4–5 (no cities listed); *Chron. Gall.* 452 132 (no less than
seventy cities, but none named) and Theophanes 5942 (compressing the Hun
invasions of the 440s into a single entry). I have aimed to make the best of
the ten cities and forts listed in Theophanes, who notes that these are just
a selection from 'very many others'. I have excepted Naissus and Constantia
as belonging to the campaign of 441–2. The remainder – Ratiaria (also
mentioned in Priscus 9), Philippopolis, Arcadiopolis, Calliopolis, Sestus,
Athyras, Adrianople and Heraclea – make coherent strategic sense in terms
of an advance on Constantinople and the Roman army's attempts to impede
it. For the walls of Adrianople, see Ammianus 31.15 (Chapter 4, 36); for
Philippopolis, Ammianus 26.10.4. The Balkan landscape and its numerous
fortified settlements are surveyed in a fascinating study by Ventzislav Dinchev,
'The Fortresses of Thrace and Dacia in the early Byzantine Period', in Andrew
Poulter, ed., *The Transition to late Antiquity: On the Danube and Beyond* (=
*Proceedings of the British Academy* 141), Oxford, 2007, 479–546.

## 12 *The Price of Peace*

The terms of the peace negotiated by Anatolius are outlined in Priscus 9.3
and 11.1 (the evacuation of territory) along with the harsh criticism of
Theodosius and the impact of his policy of appeasement. Zuckerman,
'L'empire d'Orient' 168 suggests that the lump sum quoted by Priscus may
have included the cost of ransoming POWs. The master of the offices,
Nomus, may have been part of the delegation. This is no more than an infer-
ence. Croke, 'Anatolius and Nomus' 166–7 makes the attractive suggestion
that those senior courtiers declared acceptable as envoys by Attila in 449
(Priscus 13.1, Chapter 15, 142) were already known to him from previous
embassies. Attila's list included Nomus who certainly joined Anatolius in
negotiations with Attila in 450 (Priscus 15.3, Chapter 18, 164); this was perhaps
a reprise of their partnership three years earlier. For attempts to estimate
the purchasing power of the solidus, see the examples collected in Jones,
*The Later Roman Empire*, I 445–8 and Evelyne Patlagean, *Pauvreté économique
et pauvreté sociale à Byzance 4ᵉ–7ᵉ siècles*, Paris, 1977, 341–421. The costs for a
fourth-century recruit are set out in *Theodosian Code* 7.13.7.2; the prices from
Nessana in Caspar Kraemer, *Excavations at Nessana III: Non-Literary Papyri*,
Princeton, 1958, no. 89. There are insufficient hard data to reconstruct the
revenue of the Roman empire with any certainty; using these fragile figures,
I offer no more than a sighting shot following Jones, *Later Roman Empire* I
462–5; Michael Hendy, *Studies in the Byzantine Monetary Economy c. 300–1450*,
Cambridge, 1985, 157–60 and 164–78; and Elton, *Warfare in Roman Europe*

119–20. If anything, the figure of 66,000 pounds of gold is likely to be low; Jones (at I 463) estimated the annual revenue from Egypt, the empire's wealthiest province, at 20,000 pounds. The taxation settlement in Numidia is set out in Valentinian III, *Novellae* 13. Senatorial wealth is helpfully estimated in Jones, *Later Roman Empire* II 554–7 and 782–4; the figures quoted are from Olympiodorus 41.2. For the costs of war see Elton, *Warfare in Roman Europe* 120–7 and Lee, *War in Late Antiquity* 105–6. Generally positive assessments of Theodosius' foreign policy are offered by Edward Thompson, 'The foreign policies of Theodosius II and Marcian', *Hermathena* 76 (1950) 58–75 and *Huns* 211–24; Blockley, *Foreign Policy* 59–67 and Lee, *CAH* XIV 39–42. The use of subsidies in Roman diplomacy is helpfully discussed in C.D. Gordon, 'Subsidies in Roman Imperial Defence', *Phoenix* 3 (1949) 60–9; Roger Blockley, 'Subsidies and Diplomacy: Rome and Persia in late Antiquity', *Phoenix* 39 (1985) 62–74; Hendy, *Byzantine Monetary Economy* 257–64 and especially in the level-headed analysis of Lee, *War in Late Antiquity* 119–22. Zuckerman, 'L'empire d'Orient' 169–72 suggests that Theodosius relieved both Aspar and Ariobindus of their posts in 447. Priscus 6.1 reports the designation of trading posts at Constantia, across the river from Margum, and 11.1 at Naissus. Priscus 9.3 notes the execution of Hun exiles by the Romans.

## 13 Mission Impossible

For Constantine VII Porphyrogenitus' editorial projects, see Arnold Toynbee, *Constantine Porphyrogenitus and his World*, London, 1973, 575–82; Paul Lemerle, *Le premier humanisme byzantin: notes et remarques sur enseignment et culture à Byzance des origins au 10ᵉ siècle*, Paris, 1971, 274–88 and Carl de Boor, 'Die Excerptensammlungen des Konstantin Porphyrogennetos', *Hermes* 19 (1884) 123–48. The selection of excerpts on embassies is edited by de Boor, *Excerpta de Legationibus*, Berlin, 1903. Together with three further anthologies collecting examples of virtues and vices (*de Virtutibus et Vitiis*), wise remarks (*de Sententiis*) and conspiracies (*de Insidiis*), roughly 3 per cent of Constantine's original project has survived. The most important discussion of Priscus of Panium is Blockley, *Fragmentary Classicising Historians* I 48–70; see too Baldwin, 'Priscus of Panium'; Thompson, *Huns* 12–16; Warren Treadgold, *The Early Byzantine Historians*, Macmillan, Basingstoke, 2007, 96–102 and Martindale, *Prosopography* 906. On the exact title of Priscus' history, its publication date and contents, see Baldwin, 'Priscus' 25–9 and Blockley, *Fragmentary Classicising Historians* I 49–52. For sophisticated and sympathetic accounts of the Roman education system, see Raffaella Cribiore, *Gymnastics of the Mind: Greek Education in Hellenistic and Roman Egypt*, Princeton, 2001, and Teresa Morgan, *Literate Education in the Hellenistic and Roman Worlds*, Cambridge, 1995, with a discussion at 105–16 on the popularity of Homer and Euripides. On Maximinus' career, see usefully Martindale, *Prosopography* 743. From Priscus' description (especially 20), I have presented Maximinus as a well-connected army officer; there is no persuasive reason to follow Thompson, *Huns* 113 or Baldwin, 'Priscus' 21 and conflate this military Maximinus with any of the legally trained Maximini known to have worked in the 430s on the compilation of the *Theodosian Code*. The account of Edeco's experiences in Constantinople is based on Priscus 11.1; the previous four Hun embassies are noted at 10. The intricate formalities of court etiquette and their ideological importance are discussed by Christopher Kelly, *CAH* XIII 139–50 and *Ruling the later Roman Empire* 19–26, and Michael McCormick, *CAH* XIV 156–60; trousers and garments made from animal skins are prohibited in *Theodosian Code* 14.10. For the ceremony of 'adoring the purple' (*adoratio purpurae*), see *Theodosian Code* 8.7.8, 9 and 16; W.T. Avery, 'The *Adoratio Purpurae* and the Importance of the Imperial Purple in the Fourth Century of the Christian Era', *Memoirs of the American Academy in Rome* 17 (1940) 66–80. For eunuchs at the Roman imperial court, the splendid essay by Keith Hopkins has not been bettered, *Conquerors and Slaves*, Cambridge, 1978, 172–96; see too Jacqueline Long, *Claudian's 'In Eutropium', or How, When, and Why to Slander a Eunuch*, U. of North Carolina Press, Chapel Hill, 1996, 107–46 and Shaun Tougher, *The Eunuch in Byzantine History and Society*, London, 2008.

## 14 *Close Encounters*

The most important treatment of Priscus' journey beyond the Danube by any modern scholar is Thompson, *Huns* 108–36. Priscus' narrative is retold in Wolfram, *Germanic Peoples* 130–6 and Heather, *Fall* 313–24. The carelessness of Constantine's editorial team means that Priscus' now-fragmentary text is not always coherent; sometimes the narrative stumbles and the links between incidents are difficult to explain. In the reconstruction offered in this chapter, I have assumed that the dispute between Vigilas and Edeco at Serdica was staged. The alternative might be, as suggested by Thompson, *Huns* 114, sheer tactlessness on Vigilas' part, perhaps the result of drunkenness. I have given Vigilas more credit. Nor is it clear (as assumed by Thompson, *Huns* 115) that Edeco had already revealed the details of the assassination plot to Orestes. Orestes' remark to Priscus and Maximinus could equally well be the result of a well-judged suspicion. In the surviving text Priscus never explains or speculates on how Attila came to know the contents of Theodosius' letter before it had been handed over by Maximinus. It seems consistent with the careful preparations made in Constantinople to imagine that the letter was shown to Edeco before he left, not least to give him a plausible justification for his private meetings with Chrysaphius. The narrative in this chapter is based on Priscus 11.2 with the exception of the description of Attila from Jordanes, *Getica* 182. Jordanes specifically notes (at 178) that this information comes from Priscus. Priscus' route after Naissus is difficult to follow; however at 11.1 he clearly states that Naissus is five days journey from the Danube frontier. Thompson, *Huns* 116 and Robert Browning, 'Where was Attila's Camp?', *J. of Hellenic Studies* 73 (1953) 143–5 (= *Studies on Byzantine History, Literature and Education*, Variorum reprints 59, London, 1977, no. II) both only allow a day's journey from Naissus to the frontier. On the basis of Priscus' journey time, I assume he travelled north-west from Naissus, remaining for five days within territory once part of the Roman empire, and crossing the Danube near Margum or Viminacium; see too Blockley, *Fragmentary Classicising Historians* II 382 n. 29.

## 15 Eating with the Enemy

The narrative is based on Priscus 11.2 and 13. Scottas' embassy to Constantinople in 447 is noted at 9.3. Priscus' vague geography makes it impossible to locate Attila's main residence; detailed discussions in Blockley, *Fragmentary Classicising Historians* II 384 n. 43 and Thompson, *Huns* 276–7. For a careful review of Priscus' descriptions of Attila's compound and the surrounding village, Edward Thompson, 'The Camp of Attila', *J. of Hellenic Studies* 65 (1945) 112–15. For Priscus' confusion about the seating plan and the ceremonies at Attila's feast, see Blockley, *Fragmentary Classicising Historians* II 387–8 nn. 78–80. The evidence for the brewing of barley beer in the northern provinces of the Roman empire is surveyed in Max Nelson, *The Barbarian's Beverage: A History of Beer in Ancient Europe*, London, 2005, 1–3, 41–4 and 55–63. The beads found in the graves at Singidunum are catalogued, illustrated and described in superb detail in Vujadin Ivaniševič, Michel Kazanski and Anna Mastykova, *Les nécropoles de Viminacium à l'époque des grandes migrations*, Paris, 2006, 51–117. The excavation of the graves is reported in Vujadin Ivaniševič and Michel Kazanski, 'La nécropole de l'époque des grandes migrations à Singidunum', in Marko Popović, ed., *Singidunum* 3, Belgrade, 2002, 101–57. The Şimleu Silvaniei treasure is presented in a magnificently illustrated catalogue published by the Kunsthistorisches Museum in Vienna for an exhibition in 1999: Wilfried Seipel, ed., *Barbarenschmuck und Römergold: der Schatz von Szilágysomlyó*. For the fourth-century material as evidence of high-level contacts across the Danube, see Radu Harhoiu, 'Die Medaillone aus dem Schatzfund von Şimleul Silvaniei', *Dacia* 37 (1993) 221–36 and Lenski, *Failure of Empire* 347–8. For the dating of the concealment of the finds see the discussion in the exhibition catalogue by Attila Kiss, 'Historische Auswertung',

163–8, substantially revising his earlier views in 'Der Zeitpunkt der Verbergung der Schatzfunde I und II von Szilágysomlyó', *Acta Antiqua Academiae Scientiarum Hungaricae* 30 (1982–4) 401–16. Kiss now argues for a date in the 440s, as a response by a local ruler to the expansion of the Hun empire, but as the latest objects in the treasure cannot be dated on stylistic grounds with any more precision than to the mid-fifth century, it is equally plausible – as has been suggested for the Pietroasa treasure – that the Şimleu Silvaniei treasure was buried in the 450s during the Hun empire's collapse (see Chapter 24, 210–12). If so, then some of the magnificent items manufactured in the Roman empire in the fifth century might represent the profitable results of cooperation with the Huns. The large silver plate (29 inches in diameter) known as the Missorium of Theodosius is discussed in MacCormack, *Art and Ceremony* 214–21 and described in detail in Martín Almagro-Gorbea, ed., *El disco de Teodosio*, Madrid, 2000.


## 16 *What the Historian Saw*

Onegesius' bath building is described at Priscus 11.2. For a comprehensive introduction to Roman baths and bathing culture, see Fikret Yegül, *Baths and Bathing in Classical Antiquity*, New York, 1992, 30–47 and 314–49. The excavation of the private bath building in Sirmium is briefly reported in Noël Duval and Vladislav Popović, *Sirmium VII: Horrea et thermes aux abords du rempart sud*, Rome, 1977, 75–8. For excellent surveys of Roman dining practices in the fourth and fifth centuries, see Jeremy Rossiter, 'Convivium and Villa in Late Antiquity', and Katherine Dunbabin 'Triclinium and Stibadium', in William Slater, ed., *Dining in a Classical Context*, U. of Michigan Press, Ann Arbor, 1991, 121–48 and 199–214. For an elegant exploration of the dining habits of the Roman elite, see Matthew Roller, *Dining Posture in Ancient Rome: Bodies, Values, and Status*, Princeton, 2006, with discussion at 84–95 on sitting and standing at dinner as expressions of inferior social status. The use of chairs was common in cheap restaurants and pubs, see Tönnes Kleberg, *Hôtels, restaurants et cabarets dans l'antiquité romaine: études historiques et philologiques*, Uppsala, 1957, 114–15. The grand luncheon at the villa of Tonantius Ferreolus is described in Sidonius, *Letters* 2.9. Priscus relates his meeting with the renegade Roman trader at 11.2; the staged nature of the debate and its philosophical and literary pretensions are noted in Blockley, *Fragmentary Classicising Historians* I 55–9 and Baldwin, 'Priscus' 40–1. In his account of the feast, Priscus uses a rare word, *kissybion*, for Attila's wooden cup. Some readers may have recognised its origin: it was used by Homer, *Odyssey* 9.346, for the Cyclops' drinking cup. Priscus delighted in such knowing literary games. His deliberate use of Homeric vocabulary recalled one of the powerful evocations of *nomades* in classical literature. It reminded readers of the stereotype that this description of Attila was intended to undercut. The virtues that well-educated Romans expected their emperors to exemplify included moderation, clemency, frugality, accessibility, self-control and a willingness to uphold the rule of law; a tendency to tyranny (or barbarity) was indicated by telltale vices such as cruelty, self-indulgence, capriciousness, unpredictability and excess; see Andrew Wallace-Hadrill, 'The Emperor and his Virtues', *Historia* 30 (1981) 298–323 and Christopher Kelly, *CAH* XIII 145–50. One of the best guides to contemporary attitudes is the *Panegyrici Latini*, a collection of twelve speeches given before (always virtuous) emperors, often celebrating their victories over (always vicious) usurpers; for an excellent introduction and translation, Ted Nixon and Barbara Rodgers, *In Praise of Later Roman Emperors: the Panegyrici Latini*, U. of California Press, Berkeley, 1994. The vilification of Magnus Maximus is quoted from *Pan. Lat.* 2.25–8. For first-rate discussions of dining habits as an index of morality, see Justin Goddard, 'The Tyrant at Table', in Jaś Elsner and Jamie Masters, eds, *Reflections of Nero: Culture, History and Representation*, London, 1994, 67–82, and Emily Gowers, *The Loaded Table: Representations of Food in Roman Literature*, Oxford, 1993, 1–49.

## 17 Truth and Dare

The narrative follows Priscus 14–15.2. Attila was right to single out Flavius Zeno as a potential threat to Theodosius; see Chapter 21, 184–5 with Thompson, *Huns* 133–4 and Zuckerman, 'L'empire orient' 172–3.

## 18 End Game

The surviving text of Priscus jumps straight from Attila's instructions to Orestes and Eslas (15.2) to an account of Anatolius and Nomus' embassy (15.3–4). I have filled some of the gap with a passage from John of Antioch. The evidence for the close relationship between John and Priscus is set out in Blockley, *The Fragmentary Classicising Historians* I 114 and Umberto Roberto, *Ioannis Antiocheni Fragmenta ex Historia chronica*, Berlin, 2005, CXLIV–VI. Like Priscus' *History*, much of the surviving text of John is preserved in Constantine's *Excerpta* (see the important discussion in Treadgold, *Byzantine Historians* 311–29). John's remarks on Theodosius and the baleful influence of Chrysaphius were included in the collection on virtues and vices (ed. Theodor Büttner-Wobst, Berlin, 1906, *Excerpta de Virtutibus et Vitiis* 72 = Priscus 3 = ed. Roberto, John of Antioch 291). Priscus does not indicate when he was able to interview Vigilas; but at 11.2 (quoted 134–5) he mentions that sometime later he and Maximinus learned the truth from Vigilas about the assassination plot. I have placed that meeting in Constantinople after Chrysaphius' execution when Vigilas might have felt it safe to return. Priscus mentions his further missions with Maximinus and his death at 20.3 and 27; the complex chronology of these events is discussed in Zuckerman, 'L'empire orient' 176–9. Priscus' other works (none survive) are mentioned in the brief entry on the historian in the *Souda* Π 2301. Praise for Priscus' *History* is quoted from Evagrius *Ecclesiastical History* 1.27 (ed. Joseph Bidez and Léon Parmentier, London, 1898; trans. Michael Whitby, Liverpool, 2000) and *Chron. Pasch.* 450.

## 19 Hearts and Minds

Jordanes, *Getica* 184 for the cruel story of Theodoric's daughter and Geiseric's gifts to Attila; for the rebellion, Prosper 1348. For the dating of Huneric and Eudocia's engagement, see Frank Clover, 'Flavius Merobaudes: A Translation and Historical Commentary', *Transactions of the American Philosophical Society* 61 (1971) 1–78 at 23–4; for its implications, Oost, *Galla Placidia* 260–4. Jordanes, *Getica* 168 for his uncompromising assessment of Geiseric. Attila's honorary rank is noted by Priscus 11.2 (as part of his account of his conversation with the envoys from Valentinian and Aetius); see Martindale, *Prosopography* 182–3. Priscus 13.3 for Attila's gift of Zercon and 11.2 for Aetius' gift of Constantius. As Stickler, *Aëtius* 110–14 advises, the 'friendship' between Attila and Aetius should again be seen firmly within a diplomatic context. The Bagaudae have long been favourites of historians seeking to find evidence of class struggle in the ancient world, or at least the uprising of an exploited peasantry against the oppressions of imperial rule. The classic account is by Edward Thompson, 'Peasant Revolts in late Roman Gaul and Spain', *Past & Present* 2 (1952) 11–23 (= Moses Finley, ed., *Studies in Ancient Society*, London, 1974, 304–20). By contrast, recent studies have stressed the involvement of local landowners and the well educated. Eupraxius, the Bagaudae leader who sought asylum with Attila, was a doctor: *Chron. Gall.* 452 133. The best-argued response to Thompson is Raymond van Dam, *Leadership and Community in Late Antique Gaul*, U. of California Press, Berkeley, 1985, 25–56. The role of displaced landowners is explored in John Drinkwater, 'The Bacaudae of fifth-century Gaul', in Drinkwater and Elton, eds, *Fifth-Century Gaul*, 208–17. Priscus 11.2 reports his meeting with Romulus, the story of Constantius and the silver bowls, and Romulus' claims that Attila was thinking of a Persian expedition.

## 20 The Bride of Attila

The core of the narrative is preserved in a fragment of John of Antioch included in Constantine's collection of extracts on conspiracies and based on John's reading of Priscus (ed. Carl de Boor, Berlin, 1905, *Excerpta de Insidiis* 84 = Priscus 17 = John of Antioch 292). Jordanes, *Getica* 224 briefly notes his disapproval of Honoria's passions. Marcellinus 434 dates Honoria's affair with Eugenius to that year and combines it with her appeal to Attila. John also combines these incidents but places them in 449. I follow the arguments of Croke, *Marcellinus* 80–1 for separating the two events and dating the liaison with Eugenius to 434. For an alternative reconstruction (disregarding Marcellinus), see Martindale, *Prosopography* 416 and 568–9; Oost, *Galla Placidia* 282–4 and J.B. Bury, 'Justa Grata Honoria', *J. of Roman Studies* 9 (1919) 1–13. Honoria's story is curtly dismissed by Maenchen-Helfen, *Huns* 130 as having 'all the earmarks of Byzantine court gossip'. For the minimum legal age for marriage, see Susan Treggiari, *Roman Marriage: Iusti Coniuges from the time of Cicero to the time of Ulpian*, Oxford, 1991, 39–42. Galla's time in Constantinople in the mid-420s is discussed in Chapter 6, 61. The saintliness of Pulcheria and her sisters is described in Theophanes 5901 and Sozomen 9.3.1–2; their vow of virginity and Pulcheria's outstanding intellectual ability at 9.1.5; for the strict regime of holiness in the Great Palace, Socrates 7.22.1–5 with Holum, *Theodosian Empresses* 91–3 and 143–6. Jordanes, *Rom.* 328 records the confinement of Honoria in the sisters' palace in Constantinople; for its location near the Hebdomon, see Janin, *Constantinople byzantine* 139–40 and Demangel, *L'Hebdomon* 43–7. Only Marcellinus 434 reports that Honoria was pregnant. For Galla Placidia's piety, Oost, *Galla Placidia* 264–78; her encounter with Germanus is related in the saint's life written around 480 by Constantius of Lyon (*Vita Germani* 35, ed. René Borius, Paris, 1965; trans. Frederick Hoare, *The Western Fathers*, London, 1954, 283–320). For Herculanus' consulship in 452, see Martindale, *Prosopography* 544–5. The date of Honoria's death is unrecorded; Oost, *Galla Placidia* 285 argues for sometime before 455.

## 21 Taking Sides

Priscus 20.1 recounts the diplomatic confrontation between Attila and Valentinian over Honoria. My understanding of the complex set of political alliances behind Marcian's sudden advancement follows Zuckerman, 'L'empire orient' 169–76 in making Aspar and Zeno the prime movers, but acting in close concert with Pulcheria, see Holum, *Theodosian Empresses* 206–9 and Jones, *Later Roman Empire* I 218. Richard Burgess deprives Pulcheria of any leading role in determining the succession: 'The accession of Marcian in the light of Chalcedonian apologetic and Monophysite polemic', *Byzantinische Zeitschrift* 86/7 (1993–4) 47–68 at 61–8. Aspar's claim of Theodosius' approval for Marcian is reported in John Malalas 14.27 and *Chron. Pasch.* 450. The emperor's planned military strike against Zeno is noted by John of Antioch 292 = Priscus 16 = *de Insidiis* 84. The unflattering description of Marcian is quoted from John Malalas 14.28. On his marriage and coronation, the brief notices in the chronicles disagree: *Chron. Pasch.* 450 (no detail), Theophanes 5942 (proclaimed by Pulcheria), John Malalas 14.28 (crowned by the Senate). Pulcheria's role in the coronation is strenuously defended by Wilhelm Ensslin, 'Zur Frage nach der ersten Kaiserkrönung durch den Patriarchen und zur Bedeutung dieses Aktes im Wahlzeremoniell', *Byzantinische Zeitschrift* 42 (1943–9) 101–15, 369–72 and denied with equal vigour by Burgess, 'The accession' 65–7. The details of the ceremony are not known; I have followed the description of the coronation of Leo I seven years later in February 457. These were included in Constantine Porphyrogenitus' handbook on imperial ceremonial (*de Ceremoniis* 410–12 (1.91), ed. Johann Reiske, Bonn, 1829); see too the helpful discussion in MacCormack, *Art and Ceremony* 242–5. Thompson, 'Foreign Policy' 69–72 and *Huns* 147–8 views Marcian's 'blunt refusal of the tribute' as a 'display of audacity' that 'brought the East Romans to the edge of the abyss'. By contrast, Robert Hohlfelder, 'Marcian's Gamble: A Reassessment of Eastern Imperial Policy toward Attila AD 450–453', *American J. of Ancient History* 9 (1984) 54–69 at 60 suggests that Marcian's response was an 'opening move' in a more complex strategy. Hohlfelder's view is strengthened if Priscus can be assumed to be reflecting the precise diplomatic language central to the Roman agreement with the Huns. The three embassies sent by Attila to Valentinian in late 450/early 451 are reported in Priscus 20.3 (Honoria's signet ring), Jordanes, *Getica* 185 (disagreement with Theodoric) and *Chron. Pasch.* 450 (demand to prepare the palace). Jordanes, *Getica* 186 notes Attila's diplomatic skill. Valentinian's communiqué to Theodoric is quoted from *Getica* 187–8.

## 22 *The Fog of War*

The most helpful introductions to the complex web of miracle stories associated with the Hun invasion of France are Jean-Yves Marin, 'La campagne des Gaules dans l'hagiographie', in *Attila, les influences danubiennes*, 135–9 and Émilienne Demougeot, 'Attila et les Gaules', *Mémoires de la Société d'Agriculture, Commerce, Sciences et Arts du département de la Marne* 73 (1958) 7–42 at 25–34 (= *L'Empire romain et les barbares d'Occident (IV*ᵉ*–VII*ᵉ *siècle): Scripta Varia*, 2nd edn,

Paris, 1988, 215–50 at 233–42). The accounts of Servatius of Tongeren and the destruction of Metz follow Gregory of Tours 1.5–6. Nicasius' defiant Bible reading is related by the tenth-century historian Flodoard of Reims in his *History of the Church at Reims* (*Historia Remensis Ecclesiae* 1.6, ed. Johann Heller and Georg Waitz, *Monumenta Germaniae Historica, Scriptores* XIII, Hannover, 1881, 405–599). By contrast with this much later account, the *Life of St Geneviève* probably dates back to the early sixth century; see Martin Heinzelmann and Joseph-Claude Poulin, *Les vies anciennes de sainte Geneviève de Paris: études critiques*, Paris, 1986. The story of Geneviève rallying the people of Paris is from *Vita Genovesae* 12 (ed. Bruno Krusch, *Monumenta Germaniae Historica, Scriptores rerum Merovingicarum* III, Hannover, 1896, 204–38). The tradition of Lupus' confrontation with Attila (and the phrase *flagellum dei*) is by far the latest of all these miracle stories: it is part of the *Life of Germanus of Auxerre* as told in the thirteenth-century *Legenda Aurea* by Jacobus de Voragine, one of the most popular books in the Middle Ages. An English translation was published by William Caxton in 1483; for a modern version, see, William Ryan, *Jacobus de Voragine, The Golden Legend: Readings on the Saints*, 2 vols, Princeton, 1993 with the *Life of Germanus* at II 27–30. Isidore of Seville's understanding of the Huns' role as agents of God's anger is set out in his *History of the Goths, Vandals and Sueves* (*Historia Gothorum Wandalorum Sueborum* 29, ed. Theodor Mommsen, *Monumenta Germaniae Historica, Auctores Antiquissimi* XI, Berlin, 1894, 241–303; trans. Guido Donini and Gordon Ford, 2nd edn, Leiden, 1970). The biblical reference is to the *flagellum iundans* (the 'overwhelming whip') of *Isaiah* 28.15 and 18. For the contrasting versions of the Hun attack on Orléans, see Jordanes, *Getica* 194–5 and Gregory of Tours 1.7. Aside from brief notices in the chronicles, the only detailed account of the clash on the Catalaunian Plains is Jordanes, *Getica* 197–218 (with praise of the Gothic brothers at 199–200, Attila's speech at 202–6 and Aetius' advice to Thorismud at 215–17). Ulf Täckholm, 'Aetius and the Battle on the Catalaunian Fields', *Opuscula Romana* 7 (1969) 259–76 offers a meticulous reconstruction of events. The substantial local literature and speculation on the precise location of the battlefield on the Catalaunian Plains is sympathetically reviewed by Demougeot, 'Attila et les Gaules' 34–7 and summarily rejected by Maenchen-Helfen, *Huns* 131. Suspicions of Aetius' motives are insinuated by Jordanes, *Getica* 216–17 and less subtly elaborated by medieval writers such as Fredegar, *Chronicle* 2.53 (ed. Bruno Krusch, *Monumenta Germaniae Historica, Scriptores rerum Merovingicarum* II, Hannover, 1888, 1–168). A distrust of Aetius still lies behind many modern accounts. Recent reassessments are more sympathetic; for example, Stickler, *Aëtius* 143–4; Täckholm, 'Aetius and the Battle' 268–71; Williams and Friell, *The Rome that did not Fall* 87–8; Heather, *Fall* 339 and particularly Zecchini, *Aezio* 273, suggesting that it was Thorismud's decision to leave for Toulouse that compromised the safety of Aetius' remaining troops.

Thorismud's assassination in 453 is reported in Jordanes, *Getica* 228, Hydatius 148 and Prosper 1371.

## 23 *The Last Retreat*

Apollonius' adventures across the Danube are recounted in Priscus 23.3. Marcian's three letters to the bishops at Nicaea were included in the official record of the Council of Chalcedon, ed. Eduard Schwartz, *Acta Consiliorum Oecumenicorum* II.3, Berlin, 1935, 20–1 (*Letter* 32) and II.1 (Berlin, 1933) 28–30 (*Letters* 14 and 16), translated with an excellent introduction by Richard Price and Michael Gaddis, 3 vols, Liverpool, 2007, I 107–10, nos 12, 14 and 15. Jordanes' assessment of Attila's tactics at *Getica* 225; Attila's fury at his defeat in France reported in *Chron. Gall.* 452 141. The Christian community in Aquileia is thoughtfully illuminated in a superb study by Claire Sotinel, *Identité civique et christianisme: Aquilée du IIIᵉ au VIᵉ siècle*, Rome, 2005. Giovanni Brusin and Paolo Zovatto, *Monumenti paleocristiani di Aquileia e di Grado*, Udine, 1957, 20–140 offer a fascinating and detailed description of the mosaics in the basilica. The siege of Aquileia and the flight of the stork is reported in Jordanes, *Getica* 219–21 and Procopius, *Vandal Wars* 3.4.30–5; the story may derive from Priscus, see Blockley, *Fragmentary Classicising Historians* I 115. The fortified landscape threatened by the Huns is surveyed by Neil Christie, 'From the Danube to the Po: the defence of Pannonia and Italy in the Fourth and Fifth Centuries AD', in Poulter, ed., *The Transition to late Antiquity* 547–78. For the short sermon associated with Maximinus of Turin, see *Patrologia Latina* LVII, 469–72 and Maenchen-Helfen, *Huns* 138–9. Little remains of fourth- and fifth-century Milan apart from its churches, the best introduction is Krautheimer, *Three Christian Capitals* 68–92. The few, uninspiring archaeological traces of what may be the imperial palace are surveyed in the exhibition catalogue *Milano capitale dell'impero romano, 286–402 d.C.*, Milan, 1990, 99–100 and 201. The immense, and at times frustratingly idiosyncratic, editorial project that resulted in the *Souda* is outlined in Lemerle, *Le premier humanisme* 297–300. The entry on Milan is at M 405; its possible connection with Priscus' account is explored by Blockley, *Fragmentary Classicising Historians* I 118. The Barberini Ivory is described in detail in Richard Delbrueck, *Die Consulardiptychen und verwandte Denkmäler*, 2 vols, Berlin, 1929, I 188–96 no. 48 and usefully discussed in MacCormack, *Art and Ceremony* 71–2. The meeting between Leo and Attila is piously reported in Prosper 1367; the saintly detail of the old man appears in the *Roman History* of the eighth-century monk Paul the Deacon (*Historia Romana* 14.12, ed. Amedeo Crivellucci, Rome, 1914). Raphael's 'L'incontro di Leone Magno e Attila' is one of the frescos in the Stanza di Eliodoro originally commissioned by Pope Julius II, but completed – with suitable alterations in the design – under his successor Leo X. Raphael's shrewd diplomatic and artistic manoeuvring between these two powerful patrons is explored in Jörg Traeger, 'Die Begegnung Leos des Grossen mit Attila: Planungsphasen und Bedeutungsgenese', in Christoph Frommel and Matthias Winne, eds, *Raffaello a Roma: il convegno del 1983*, Rome, 1986, 97–116. For the plague in Italy, see Hydatius 146 with Maenchen-Helfen, *Huns* 139–40. Marcian's military activity across the Danube is mentioned in a confused notice in Hydatius 146 explained by Zecchini, *Aezio* 277 n. 65 and Richard Burgess, 'A New Reading for Hydatius *Chronicle* 177 and the Defeat of the Huns in Italy', *Phoenix* 42 (1988) 357–63 at 360–2. Attila's threatening embassy to Marcian in 452 is reported in Jordanes, *Getica* 225. For Attila's death, *Getica* 254, information Jordanes explicitly notes is derived from Priscus, Theophanes 5946 (an accident), Marcellinus 454.1 (Ildico or an accident) and Malalas 14.10 (accident or Ildico or the result of Aetius' bribery). For Marcian's angelic visitation, see Jordanes, *Getica* 255, again explicitly attributed to Priscus.

## 24 Endings

The most important discussions of the collapse of the Hun empire are Thompson, *Huns* 167–75 and Maenchen-Helfen, *Huns* 144–68. Jordanes, *Getica* 259–63 briefly comments on the rivalry between the sons of Attila and the Battle of the River Nedao; the subsequent clashes between the Huns and the Goths are noted at 268–9 and 272–3. The consolidation of Gothic control over Pannonia under Valamer, Thuidimer and Vidimer is explored by Heather, *Goths and Romans* 242–6 and Wolfram, *Goths* 258–68. Heather 251–63 also discusses the settlement of Goths in Thrace. Priscus 46 reports Leo's response to Dengizich and Ernac's embassy and at 48.1 Dengizich's demands the following year. For Dengizich's defeat and decapitation, see Marcellinus 468 and *Chron. Pasch.* 468. For the identification of the Xylokerkos, see Janin, *Constantinople Byzantine* 274 and 440–1, and Dagron, *Naissance d'une capitale* 305. By far the best discussion of the movement of the Goths, conventionally known as the Ostrogoths or 'eastern Goths', into the eastern empire in the 470s and their consolidation under Theodoric is Heather, *Goths and Romans* 264–308, condensed in *Goths* 154–65 and 216–18. The assassination of Aetius in September 454 is reported in John of Antioch 293.1 = *de Insidiis* 85 = Priscus 30.1, Hydatius 152, Prosper 1373, Marcellinus 454.2 and Theophanes 5946. The unnamed courtier's acid quip (surely never said to Valentinian's face) is quoted in Procopius, *Vandal Wars* 3.4.28. For the Vandal sack of Rome, see Procopius, *Vandal Wars* 3.5.1–6, Prosper 1375 (emphasising Leo's role) and Theophanes 5947 (the treasures from Jerusalem). For excellent studies of the transition from imperial to local rule in France, see Wolfram, *Goths* 181–246; Jill Harries, *Sidonius Apollinaris and the Fall of Rome, AD 407–485*, Oxford, 1994; Ian Wood, *The Merovingian Kingdoms, 450–751*, London, 1994 and *CAH* XIV 506–24; and Edward James, *The Franks*, Oxford, 1988. The best account of the Vandal kingdom in North Africa remains Courtois, *Les Vandales* Parts II and III, and see too Averil Cameron, *CAH* XIV 553–9. For the failed expeditions against Geiseric, see Hydatius 195, Procopius, *Vandal Wars* 3.6 and Theophanes 5961 = Priscus 53. The collapse of imperial rule in Italy and the rise of Theodoric is thoughtfully discussed in Stein, *Bas-Empire* I 365–99; Heather, 'The Huns and the End of the Roman Empire' 29–41 and *CAH* XIV 18–30; O'Flynn, *Generalissimos* 104–49; Penny MacGeorge, *Late Roman Warlords*, Oxford, 2002, 165–293; Mark Humphries, *CAH* XIV 525–51; John Moorhead, *Theodoric in Italy*, Oxford, 1992 and Patrick Amory, *People and Identity in Ostrogothic Italy, 489–554*, Cambridge, 1997. Theodoric's comment after murdering Odoacer is reported in John of Antioch 307 = *de Insidiis* 99. Sidonius, *Letters* 1.2 for his description of a day in the courtly life of Theodoric II, with Marc Reydellet, *La royauté dans la littérature latine de Sidoine Apollinaire à Isidore de Séville*, Rome, 1981, 69–80 and Harries, *Sidonius* 127–9 for the date. For Theodoric's Roman-ness and local aristocratic responses to his regime in Ravenna, see Moorhead, *Theodoric* 39–51 and Sam Barnish, 'Transformation and survival in the western senatorial aristocracy, c. A.D. 400–700', *Papers of the British School at Rome* 56 (1988) 120–55. More generally, Julia Smith, *Europe after Rome, 500–1000: A New Cultural History*, Oxford, 2005 and Peter Brown, *The Rise of Western Christendom: Triumph and Diversity, A.D. 200–1000*, 2nd edn, Oxford, 2003 both offer brilliant and humane expositions of the cultural and religious transformation of classical antiquity in the formation of medieval Europe. For a broad perspective on the complexities of this transition, see the sophisticated and wide-ranging discussion in Chris Wickham, *Framing the Middle Ages: Europe and the Mediterranean, 400–800*, Oxford, 2005. For a superb introduction to Byzantium, see Averil Cameron, *The Byzantines*, Oxford, 2006.

## Epilogue: Reputations

For useful guides to the afterlife of Attila, see Franz Bäuml and Marianna Birnbaum, *Attila: The Man and his Image*, Budapest, 1993; *Attila, les influences danubiennes* 143–201; and Herbert Pahl, 'Attila und die Hunnen im Spiegel von Kunst und Literatur', in *Attila und die Hunnen* 368–73. The circumstances of Wilhelm II's speech are usefully set out in Robert Massie, *Dreadnought: Britain, Germany and the Coming of the Great War*, London, 1991, 282–3; Thomas Kohut, *Wilhelm II and the Germans: A Study in Leadership*, Oxford, 1991, 143–8; and in the detailed study by Bernd Sösemann, 'Die sog. Hunnenrede Wilhelms II: Textkritische und interpretatorische Bemerkungen zur Ansprache des Kaisers vom 27. Juli 1900 in Bremerhaven', *Historische Zeitschrift* 222 (1976) 342–58 (with the full text of the speech at 349–50). The transformation of Attila into good King Etzel is thoughtfully discussed in Jennifer Williams, *Etzel der rîche*, Berne, 1981, 177–98; Ursula Schulze, 'Der weinende König und sein Verschwinden im Dunkel des Vergessens: König Etzel im Nibelungenlied und in der Klage', in *Attila und die Hunnen* 336–45 and Teresa Pàroli, 'Attila nelle letterature germaniche antiche', in *Popoli delle Steppe* II 559–619 at 600–13. The fight in King Etzel's hall is told in *Nibelungenlied* Aventiure 33 (ed. Ursula Schulze, Düsseldorf, 2005, trans. Arthur Hatto, Penguin Classics, revised 1969). Edward Gibbon's matchless account of Attila and the Huns occupies most of Chapters 34–5 of *The History of the Decline and Fall of the Roman Empire*, vol. III, London, 1781. Thomas Hodgkin's version, freighted with Victorian morality, in *Italy and her Invaders, Volume 2, The Hunnish and Vandal Invasion*, Oxford, 1880 (reprinted, London, 1996), Book I, Chapters 1–4 (comparison of Attila with Napoleon at 80–1; the dangers faced by twentieth-century democracy at 612–13). Matthias Corvinus' re-presentation of Attila as a Hungarian nation-builder is explored in Marianna Birnbaum, 'Attila's Renaissance in the Fifteenth and Sixteen Centuries', in *Attila: The Man and his Image* 99–105 and *The Orb and the Pen: Janus Pannonius, Matthias Corvinus and the Buda Court*, Budapest, 1996, 121–9. Corvinus' new image was (unsurprisingly) easily turned against him by his Italian critics, see Birnbaum, 'Attila's Renaissance' 84–6 and the fascinating discussion by Lajos Elekes, 'La politica estera di re Mattia e gli Stati italiani nella seconda metà del secolo XV', in Tibor Klaniczay, ed., *Rapporti veneto-ungheresi all'epoca del Rinascimento*, Budapest, 1975, 243–55. *Sign of the Pagan* was directed by Douglas Sirk for Universal Pictures. According to the film's studio publicity: 'Against the ravaging hordes of Attila stood a warrior's might and a people's faith. Against his ruthless pagan lusts the power of a woman's love.' In this epic revision of Roman history, the mighty warrior is the future emperor Marcian (Jeff Chandler) and his bride (the ballerina Ludmilla Tchérina) is Pulcheria. This is, of course, a passionate love match, and once Attila is defeated the couple go on to rescue the West from a feckless Valentinian and reunite the Roman empire.

## Ancient Texts

I have included editions of ancient texts. I hope this helps to resolve any confusion in the numbering of sections/paragraphs that sometimes, and tediously, varies between modern editions and translations.

### AMMIANUS MARCELLINUS

Ammianus Marcellinus, the most important Latin historian of the fourth century; the surviving part of his *Res Gestae* deals with the period 354–78; ed. Wolfgang Seyfarth, Leipzig, 1978, trans. John Rolfe, Loeb Classical Library, 3 vols, Harvard, 1935–9; Walter Hamilton, Penguin Classics, 1986.

### CHRON. GALL. 452

*Chronica Gallica ad annum CCCCLII* = *The Gallic Chronicle of 452*; an anonymous Latin chronicle written in France around the year 452; ed. Theodor Mommsen, *Monumenta Germaniae Historica, Auctores Antiquissimi* IX, Berlin, 1892, 615–66; Richard Burgess, 'The Gallic Chronicle of 452: A New Critical Edition with a Brief Introduction', in Ralph Mathisen and Danuta Shanzer, eds, *Society and Culture in Late Antique Gaul: Revisiting the Sources*, Ashgate, Aldershot, 2001, 52–84, trans. Alexander Murray, *From Roman to Merovingian Gaul: A Reader*, Broadview, Peterborough, Ontario, 2000, 76–85.

### CHRON. PASCH.

*Chronicon Paschale* = *Easter Chronicle*; an anonymous Greek chronicle written in Constantinople in the early seventh century; ed. Ludwig Dindorf, Bonn, 1832, trans. Michael and Mary Whitby, Liverpool, 1989.

### EUSEBIUS

Bishop of Caesarea, contemporary and self-appointed biographer of the emperor Constantine. *Life of Constantine*, ed., Friedhelm Winkelmann, 2nd edn, Berlin, 1991, trans. Averil Cameron and Stuart Hall, Oxford, 1999.

### GREGORY OF TOURS

Sixth-century historian, bishop and saint; *History of the Franks*, ed. Bruno Krusch and Wilhelm Levison, *Monumenta Germaniae Historica, Scriptores rerum*

*Merovingicarum* I, 2nd edn, Hannover, 1951, trans. Ormonde Dalton, Oxford, 1927 and Lewis Thorpe, Penguin Classics, 1974.

## HYDATIUS

Spanish bishop, his *Chronicle* completed around 470 concentrates on events in France and Spain; ed. and trans. Richard Burgess, Oxford, 1993, trans. Murray, *Roman to Merovingian Gaul*, 85–98.

## JORDANES

*Getica* = *de origine actibusque Getarum* = *The Origins and Deeds of the Goths*; written around 550 in Constantinople. The most important early history of the Goths; ed. Theodor Mommsen, *Monumenta Germaniae Historica, Auctores Antiquissimi* V, Berlin, 1882, 53–200, trans. Charles Mierow, 2nd edn, Princeton, 1915.
*Rom.* = *Romana* = *de origine actibusque gentis Romanorum* = *The Origins and Deeds of the Roman People*; a brief summary of all of Roman history; ed. Theodor Mommsen, *Monumenta Germaniae Historica, Auctores Antiquissimi* V, Berlin, 1882, 1–52.

## MALALAS

John Malalas, an imperial bureaucrat from Antioch in Syria, completed his *General History* around 565; a world history in eighteen books, the last five concentrate on the East after Constantine; ed. Hans Thurn, Berlin, 2000, trans. Elizabeth and Michael Jeffreys and Roger Scott, Australian Association for Byzantine Studies, Melbourne, 1986.

## MARCELLINUS

Count Marcellinus (no relation of Ammianus), an army officer from the Balkans who wrote his *Chronicle* in Latin covering the period 379–534 for readers in the East; ed. Theodor Mommsen, *Monumenta Germaniae Historica, Auctores Antiquissimi* XI, Berlin, 1894, 37–108, trans. Brian Croke, Australian Association for Byzantine Studies, Sydney, 1995.

## OLYMPIODORUS

Early-fifth-century historian, diplomat and bird fancier; part of his *History* survives in the summary by the ninth-century bibliophile Photius, ed. and trans. Roger Blockley, *The Fragmentary Classicising Historians of the Later Roman Empire*, 2 vols, Leeds, 1981–3, II 151–220.

### PHILOSTORGIUS

Church historian, writing in the early fifth century and unlike Socrates, Sozomen and Theodoret from an heretical viewpoint. As a result his work survives only in fragments. *Ecclesiastical History*, ed. Joseph Bidez and Friedhelm Winkelmann, 3rd edn, Berlin, 1981, trans. Philip Amidon, Society of Biblical Literature, 2007.

### PRISCUS

Most important historian of Attila and the Huns; ed. and trans. Roger Blockley, *The Fragmentary Classicising Historians of the Later Roman Empire*, 2 vols, Leeds, 1981–3, II 221–400.

### PROCOPIUS

Most important Greek historian of the sixth century, especially of the emperor Justinian. *The Wars*, Books 1 and 2 = *The Persian Wars*; *The Wars*, Books 3 and 4 = *The Vandal Wars*; ed. Jakob Haury, Leipzig, 1962, trans. Henry Dewing, Loeb Classical Library, Harvard, 1914–16.

### PROSPER

Prosper of Aquitaine, a French monk at the papal court in Rome; his *Chronicle* covers 379–455; ed. Theodor Mommsen, *Monumenta Germaniae Historica, Auctores Antiquissimi* IX, Berlin, 1892, 341–499, trans. Murray, *Roman to Merovingian Gaul*, 62–76.

### SIDONIUS

Sidonius Apollinaris, fifth-century French aristocrat, poet, politician and bishop; his *Letters* ed. and trans. William Anderson, Loeb Classical Library, Harvard, 1936–65.

### SOCRATES

Church historian, lived in Constantinople 380–440. *Ecclesiastical History*, ed. Günther Hansen, Berlin, 1995, trans. Andrew Zenos, *A Select Library of*

*Nicene and Post-Nicene Fathers of the Christian Church*, 2nd series II, Oxford, 1891.

## SOZOMEN

Church historian, lawyer in Constantinople in the fifth century. *Ecclesiastical History*, ed. Joseph Bidez, 2nd edn, Berlin, 1995, trans. Chester Hartranft, *A Select Library of Nicene and Post-Nicene Fathers of the Christian Church*, 2nd series II, Oxford, 1891.

## THEODOSIAN CODE

Collection of imperial laws complied and edited on the orders of Theodosius II; contains 2,500 imperial rulings issued since 312, ordered by topic; ed. Theodor Mommsen, Paul Krüger and Paul Meyer, Berlin, 1904, trans. Clyde Pharr, Princeton, 1952.

## THEOPHANES

Theophanes the Confessor, monk from a wealthy family; *Chronicle* written in the early ninth century covering the period 284–813; ed. Carl de Boor, Leipzig, 1883, trans. Cyril Mango and Roger Scott, Oxford, 1997.

## THEMISTIUS

Fourth-century court orator. *Orations*, ed. Heinrich Schenkl, Glanville Downey and Albert Norman, 3 vols, Leipzig, 1965–74, trans. Peter Heather and John Matthews, *The Goths in the Fourth Century*, Liverpool, 1991 (*Orations* 8 and 10), Peter Heather and David Moncur, Liverpool, 2001 (*Orations* 1, 3, 5, 6, 14–17, 34).

## THEODORET

Church historian, bishop of Cyrrhus in Syria in the fifth century. *Ecclesiastical History*, ed. Léon Parmentier and Günther Hansen, 3rd edn, Berlin, 1998, trans. Blomfield Jackson, *A Select Library of Nicene and Post-Nicene Fathers of the Christian Church*, 2nd series III, Oxford, 1892.

## ZOSIMUS

*New History* written in Greek at turn of the fourth century; valuable perspective on contemporary events from an ardent anti-Christian; ed. François Paschoud, Paris, 1971–89, trans. Ronald Ridley, Australian Association for Byzantine Studies, Sydney, 1984.

# Index